# of love & life

SPECIAL COLLECTION

ISBN 978-0-276-44667-2

www.readersdigest.co.uk

Published in the United Kingdom by Vivat Direct Limited (t/a Reader's Digest),
157 Edgware Road, London W2 2HR

and in Canada
www.rd.ca

The Reader's Digest Association (Canada) ULC, 1100 René-Lévesque Blvd. West, Montréal,
Québec, H3B 5H5 Canada

# of love & life

SPECIAL COLLECTION

Four novels selected and condensed
by Reader's Digest

Reader's Digest

The Reader's Digest Association Inc., London, Montreal

For over ten years, we at Reader's Digest have been publishing our Of Love & Life series and over this time have brought a wealth of the very best fiction writing to our readers. In this Special Collection we have included four of the best, most popular, entertaining and yet very different novels from the last decade, by four of today's best-selling authors. These novels will transport you to exotic locations and a fascinating period of history, will make you laugh and make you cry, and will ultimately give you hours of pure reading pleasure.
We hope that you enjoy this Special Collection.

CONTENTS

NIGHTS OF RAIN AND STARS

MAEVE BINCHY

In a Greek taverna high in the hills above the little village of Aghia Anna, four strangers meet: Fiona, a young Irish nurse; Thomas, a Californian academic; Elsa, a glamorous German television presenter; and David, a shy young English boy. Drawn together by the horror of a tragedy that unfolds in front of their eyes, their dependence upon one another grows—with surprising results.

CHAPTER ONE

ANDREAS THOUGHT HE SAW the fire down in the bay before anyone else did. He peered and shook his head in disbelief. This sort of thing didn't happen. Not here in Aghia Anna, not to the *Olga*, the little red and white boat that took visitors out to the bay. Not to Manos, foolish head-strong Manos whom he had known since he was a boy. This was some kind of dream, some trick of the light. That could not be smoke and flames coming from the *Olga*.

Perhaps he was not feeling well.

Some of the older people in the village said that they imagined things. If the day was hot, if there had been too much *raki* the night before. But he had gone to bed early. There had been no *raki* or dancing or singing in his hillside restaurant.

Andreas put his hand up to shade his eyes and, at the same time, a cloud passed overhead. It wasn't as clear as it had been before. He must indeed have been mistaken. But now he must pull himself together. He had a restaurant to run. He continued fixing the red and green plastic-covered cloths with little clips to the long wooden tables on the terrace outside his taverna. He had laboriously written the menu on the black-board. He often wondered why he did it . . . it was the same food every day. But the visitors liked it; and he would put 'Welcome' in six languages. They liked that too.

The food was not special. Nothing they could not have got in two dozen other little Greek tavernas. There was *souvlaki*, the lamb kebabs. Well, goat kebabs really, but the visitors liked to think they were lamb. And there was *moussaka*, warm and glutinous in its big pie dish. There were the big bowls of salad, white squares of salty feta cheese and lush red tomatoes. There were the racks of *barbouni*, red mullet, waiting to be grilled, the swordfish steaks. There were the big steel trays of desserts in the fridge, *katai* and *baklava*, made from nuts, honey and pastry. The chilled cabinets of retsina and local wines. People came from all over the world and loved what Andreas, and dozens like him, could provide.

He always recognised the nationality of any visitor to Aghia Anna and could greet them in a few words of their own language. The English didn't like it if you offered them a *Speisencarte* instead of the menu, the Canadians did not want you to assume they were from the United States. Italians did not like to be greeted with a *Bonjour* and his own fellow countrymen wanted to be thought of as important people from Athens rather than tourists. Andreas had learned to look carefully before he spoke.

And as he looked down the path he saw the first customers of the day arriving.

His mind went on to automatic pilot.

A tall man, wearing those shorts that only Americans wore, shorts that did nothing for the bottom or the legs. He was on his own and stopped to look at the fire through binoculars.

A beautiful girl, possibly German, tall and tanned, with hair streaked by the sun or a very expensive hairdresser. She stood in silence, staring in disbelief at the scarlet and orange flames licking over the boat.

A boy in his twenties, small and anxious-looking with glasses that he kept taking off and wiping. He stood open-mouthed in horror, looking at the boat in the bay below.

A couple, also in their twenties, exhausted after the walk up the hill; they might be Scottish or Irish—Andreas couldn't quite make out the accents. The boy had a sort of swagger about him, the girl had red hair and a freckled nose.

In their turn, they each saw an old man, slightly stooped, with grey-white hair and bushy eyebrows.

'That's the boat we were on yesterday.' The red-haired girl had her hand over her mouth in shock. 'Oh my God, it could have been us.'

'Well, it isn't, so what's the point in saying that?' her companion said firmly.

And then, there was the sound of an explosion from down in the bay and, for the first time, Andreas realised that it was true. There *was* a fire. Not just a trick of the light. The others had seen it too. He began to tremble and hold on to the back of a chair to support himself.

'I must telephone my brother Yorghis, he is in the police station . . .

maybe they don't know about the fire. Maybe they cannot see it from down there.'

The tall American spoke gently. 'They see it. Look, there are lifeboats already on the way.'

'I can't believe it,' the young girl said. 'Yesterday he was teaching us to dance on that very boat, *Olga*, he called it, after his grandmother.'

'Manos—that's his boat, isn't it?' asked the boy with the glasses. 'I was on his boat, too.'

'Yes, that is Manos,' said Andreas gravely. *That fool Manos with too many people on the vessel as usual, trying to make kebabs with some outdated gas cylinder.* But none of the people of the village would ever say any of this. Manos had a family here. They would all be gathered now, down by the harbour.

'Do you know him?' asked the tall American with the binoculars.

'Yes, indeed, we all know everyone here.' Andreas wiped his eyes with a table napkin.

They stood as if transfixed, watching the distant boats arriving and trying to douse the flames, the bodies struggling in the water hoping to be picked up by the smaller craft. They were at a loss for words, too far away to go and help, but still they couldn't stop looking at the tragedy.

Andreas felt a hand on his arm. It was the blonde German girl. 'It's worse for you—this is your place,' she said. 'Why don't you sit down?'

He felt tears come to his eyes. She was right. It *was* his place. He knew the families who would be standing waiting at the harbour.

Her face was kind but she was practical too. 'Why don't you sit down? Please do,' she said gently.

It was the spur he needed. 'I'm Andreas,' he said. 'You're right, this is my place, and I will offer you all a Metaxa brandy for the shock and we will say a prayer for the people in the bay.'

'Is there nothing, *nothing* that we can do?' asked the English boy with the glasses.

'It took us about three hours to get up this far. By the time we got back I guess we'd only be in the way,' said the tall American. 'I'm Thomas, by the way.'

'I'm Elsa,' said the German girl, 'and I'll get the glasses.'

They stood with tiny glasses of the fiery liquid in their hands and raised a strange toast in the sunshine.

Fiona, the Irish girl, said, 'May their souls and all the souls of the faithful departed rest in peace.'

Her boyfriend seemed to wince at the expression.

'Well, why not, Shane?' she asked him defensively. 'It's a blessing.'

'Go in peace,' said Thomas to the wreckage.

'*Lehaim*,' said David, the English boy with the glasses. 'It means "To life",' he explained.

'*Ruhet in Frieden*,' said Elsa with tears in her eyes.

'*O Theos n'anapafsi tin psyhi tou*,' said Andreas, bowing his head in grief as he looked down on the worst tragedy Aghia Anna had known.

They didn't order lunch, Andreas just served them. He brought them a salad with goat's cheese, a plate of lamb and stuffed tomatoes, and afterwards a bowl of fruit. They spoke about themselves and where they had been. They were all in it for the long haul—several months at least.

Thomas, the American, was travelling and writing articles for a magazine. He had a year off, a proper sabbatical from his university in California. Teachers of every kind needed a chance to go out and talk to people of other countries, he said. He looked a little far away as he spoke, Andreas thought, as if he were missing something back home.

It was different with Elsa, the German girl. She seemed to miss nothing she had left behind and had enough money saved to finance a year's travel. She had been on the road for three weeks.

Fiona, the Irish girl, was more uncertain. She looked at her moody boyfriend for confirmation as she spoke of how they wanted to see the world and find somewhere to settle where people wouldn't judge them or try to change them. He just shrugged as though it was all very boring.

David spoke of his wish to see the world while he was still young enough. There was nothing sadder than an old man who found what he was looking for decades too late.

But even as they talked and told each other a little of their lives in Düsseldorf, Dublin, California and Manchester, Andreas noted that they said nothing of the families they had left behind.

He told them of life here in Aghia Anna and how the place was rich today, compared to his childhood when a living was earned in the olive groves or minding goats on the hills. He spoke of brothers long gone to America, and his own son who had left this restaurant after an argument nine years ago.

'And what did you argue about?' asked Fiona.

'Oh, he wanted a nightclub here and I didn't—the usual thing about age and youth, about change and not changing.' Andreas shrugged sadly. 'If I had known how lonely it would be to have my only son in Chicago, far across the world and never writing to me . . . then, I would have had the nightclub.'

'And what about your wife?' Fiona asked. 'Did she not beg you to get him back and open the club?'

'She had died. Nobody left to make peace between us.'

The afternoon shadows grew longer. Andreas served them coffees and none of them seemed to want to leave. A sunny day had turned into death and disaster. Through the binoculars they saw bodies on stretchers and crowds gathering, people pushing to see if their loved ones were alive. Up here on the hill, even though they knew nothing of each other, brought together like this they talked as if they were old friends.

They were still talking as the first stars came into the sky. Now, down in the harbour they could see the lights of flashing cameras and of television teams recording the tragedy to tell to the world. It hadn't taken long for news of the disaster to get to the media.

'I suppose they have to do it,' said David with resignation. 'But it seems so ghoulish, monstrous, preying on people's lives in a tragedy.'

'It is monstrous, believe me, I work in it. Or worked, anyway,' Elsa said, unexpectedly.

'A journalist?' David asked with interest.

'I worked on a television current affairs show. There's somebody like me now, at my desk in the studio, asking questions at long distance of someone down there in the harbour: how many bodies have been recovered, how did it happen, are there any Germans among the dead? I'm glad to be no part of it now.'

'And yet people do have to know about famines and wars—otherwise how can we stop them?' Thomas pointed out.

'We'll never stop them,' Shane said. 'There's big money in this kind of thing.'

Shane was different from the others, Andreas thought. Dismissive, restless, anxious to be somewhere else.

'Not everyone is interested in money,' David said mildly.

Fiona looked up sharply as if she had been down this road before, defending Shane for his views. 'What Shane means is that that's the system—it's not the God in his life nor in mine. I certainly wouldn't be a nurse if it was money I was looking for.'

'A nurse?' Elsa said.

'Yes, I was wondering, would I be any use down there, but I don't suppose—'

'For God's sake, Fiona, get real. What could you do?' Shane protested. 'Tell them in Greek to keep calm? Foreign nurses aren't in high demand at a time of crisis.' There was a sneer on his face.

Fiona flushed darkly.

Thomas was looking through his binoculars again. 'I don't think you'd even be able to get near to the wounded if you were there,' he said reassuringly. He passed her the glasses and with trembling hands she looked down at the distant harbour and the people jostling each other.

'Yes, you're right,' Fiona said in a small voice.

'It must be wonderful being a nurse, I guess it means that you're never afraid,' Thomas said, trying to make Fiona feel better. 'What a great career. My mother is a nurse and she works long hours but doesn't get paid enough.'

'Did she work while you were a kid?'

'Still does. She put my brother and me through college and we got careers out of all that.'

'What career did you get out of college?' David asked. 'I have a degree in business studies but it never got me anything I wanted to do.'

Thomas spoke slowly. 'I teach nineteenth-century literature at a university.' He shrugged as if it weren't a big deal.

'What do you do, Shane?' Elsa asked.

'Why?' He looked back at her directly.

'Don't know. It's just that the rest of us said. I suppose I didn't want you to be left out.' Elsa had a beautiful smile.

He relaxed. 'Sure, well, I do a bit of this and a bit of that.'

Just then, Andreas spoke very slowly. 'I think you should all call and tell them back at home that you are alive. As Elsa says, this will be on the television news tonight. They will all see, they may know you are here in Aghia Anna, they will think that you might be on the boat of Manos.' He looked around him. Five young people from different families, different homes, different countries.

'Well, my mobile phone doesn't work here,' Elsa said cheerfully. 'I did try a couple of days ago and I thought, so much the better, now it's a real escape.'

'It's the wrong time of day in California,' Thomas said.

'I'd get the answering machine, they'll be out again at some business function,' David said.

'It would only be another earful of "Dear, dear, look what happens when you leave your nice, safe job and go gallivanting round the world,"' said Fiona.

Shane said nothing at all. The notion of phoning home had just never occurred to him.

Andreas stood up at the table and addressed them. 'Believe me, when I hear there has been a shooting in Chicago or a flood or any disaster, I wonder to myself, could my Adoni be caught up in it? It would be so good if he were to ring . . .'

'You see, Andreas, you're the kind of father who *does* care. Some fathers don't,' David explained.

'Every parent cares, they just have different ways of showing it.'

'And, of course, some of us have no parents,' Elsa said in a light voice. 'Like me, a father long disappeared, a mother who died young.'

'But there must be someone in Germany who loves you, Elsa,' Andreas said, and then thought perhaps he had gone too far. 'I tell you, my telephone is there in the bar. Now I will open a bottle of wine to celebrate that we were here tonight, with all our hopes and dreams still left to us as we sit in another night of stars.'

He went inside and could hear them talking out on the terrace.

'I think he really *does* want us to use his phone,' Fiona said.

'Well, you just said what you'd be letting yourself in for,' Shane objected.

'Perhaps it's making too much of it all,' Elsa wondered.

They looked down again at the scene below. And there was no argument, this time.

'I'll call first,' said Thomas.

Andreas stood polishing glasses and listening to their calls. They were a strange little group gathered today in his taverna. None of them seemed at ease with the people they phoned. It was as if they were all running away from something. Each of them sounded like someone escaping from a bad situation.

Thomas's voice was clipped. 'I *know* he's at day camp, Shirley. I just thought . . . no, it doesn't matter . . . believe me, I had no agenda . . . please, I am not trying to make trouble. All right, Shirley, think what you like. No, I haven't made any plans yet.'

David sounded apprehensive. 'Oh, Dad, you're at home. Yes, well, of course you should be. It's just that I wanted to tell you about this accident . . . no, I wasn't hurt . . . No, I wasn't on the boat.' A long silence. 'Right, Dad, give my love to Mum, won't you . . . no, tell her there's nothing definite about when I'm coming back.'

Fiona's conversation was hardly about the boat tragedy at all. 'I can't give you a date yet, Mam, we've been through this a million times. Where he goes, I go, Mam, and you must make your own plans for that—it would be much better that way.'

Elsa's conversation was a mystery. Andreas spoke German, and he understood perfectly. She left two messages on answering machines.

The first was warm: 'Hannah, it's Elsa. I am in this glorious place in Greece called Aghia Anna and there was a terrible accident today. People died in a boat tragedy. But in case you wondered was I involved in it, I wanted to tell you I'm one of the lucky ones . . . Oh, Hannah, I do miss you and your kind shoulder to weep on. You're such a friend— I don't deserve you. I'll get in touch soon, I promise.'

Then she made a second call and this time her voice was ice cold. 'I wasn't killed on that boat. But you know that there are times I would not mind if I had been. I only called you because I imagine the studio is hoping that I was either burned in that pleasure-boat fire or that I am standing on the harbour waiting to give an eye-witness account. But I am miles away from it, and even more miles away from you, and that's all I care about, believe me.'

And Andreas saw the tears on Elsa's face as she replaced the receiver.

None of them wanted to leave his place, Andreas realised. They felt safe here on his terrace, far from the tragedy unfolding below. And far from their own unhappy lives back home. He left their wine on the table and sat in the shadows with his worry beads moving from hand to hand while they talked. As the night came, and more wine was poured, they were no longer secretive about their home lives.

Poor Fiona was the most eager of all.

'I shouldn't have called, Shane, it just gave them another chance to tell me what a mess I am making of my life, and how they can't get their silver wedding plans organised until they know where I am going to be. I told my mother straight out that I hadn't a notion of where we'd be in five months' time, and she starts to cry. She's actually *crying* about a party, and here we are with all those people down at the harbour who really *do* have something to cry about.'

'Told you.' Shane inhaled. He and Fiona were smoking a joint.

Thomas spoke up. 'I had no luck, either. Bill, my little boy, was out at day camp. My ex-wife, Shirley, was less than pleased by the call. Still, at least the boy won't look at the news and worry about me.'

'How would he know that you were even in this area?' Shane obviously thought the phone calls home were a waste of time for everyone.

'Shirley is meant to put my telephone numbers up on the bulletin board in the kitchen.'

'But has your son called?'

'No.'

'Then she doesn't, does she?' Shane had it all figured out.

'I guess not, and I don't imagine she'll call my mother either.' Thomas's face was set in hard lines. 'I wish I had thought of calling Mom instead. But I wanted to hear Bill's voice . . .'

Finally David spoke quietly. 'When I called, I was getting ready to leave a message on the answering machine—but they were at home and it was my father . . . And he said . . . he said that if nothing had happened to me, what was I ringing about?'

'He didn't really mean that, you know,' Thomas said, soothingly.

David shook his head. 'But he *did* mean it, and I could hear my mother calling out from the sitting room, "Ask him about the award, Harold, is he coming home for that?"'

'Award?' the others asked.

'It's a pat on the back for having made so much money, like the Queen's Award for Industry. There's going to be a big reception. Nothing else on earth matters to them except this.'

'Is there anyone else at home who could go to the ceremony in your place?' Elsa asked.

'That's the problem. That's the whole problem,' David replied sadly.

'You're an only child then?' Elsa said.

'It's *your* life, do what you want to,' Shane shrugged. He couldn't see what the problem was.

'It might just be a way of saying, "Come home", mightn't it?' Elsa suggested softly.

'Everything's a way of saying, "Come home", but "Come home and get a good job and help your father in his business", and that is not what I am going to do.' David took off his glasses and wiped them.

Elsa had said nothing about herself. She sat looking far out to sea over the olive groves at the coastline of the little islands where all those people had thought they would be spending a sunny holiday afternoon. She felt everyone looking at her, waiting for her to talk about the phone call *she* had made.

'Oh, what response did I get? Well, I called two friends, got two answering machines, and they'll both think I'm mad, but what the hell?' Elsa gave a little laugh. There was no hint that she had left a vague, cheery message on one machine and tense, almost hate-filled words on the other.

From the shadows Andreas looked at her. The beautiful Elsa, who had left her job in television to find peace in the Greek Islands, had certainly not found it yet, he told himself.

The phone rang and Andreas started. It might be his brother Yorghis, calling from the police station.

But it wasn't Yorghis, it was a man speaking German. He said his name was Dieter and he was looking for Elsa.

'She is not here,' Andreas said.

'She can't have left,' the man said, 'she only called me ten minutes ago. I have traced the number she called from . . . where is she staying, please?'

'I have no idea, Herr Dieter, no idea at all.'

'And who was she with?'

'A group of people—I think they leave this village tomorrow.

Sincerest regrets at not being able to help you, Herr Dieter.' He hung up, and turned to find Elsa standing looking at him. She had come in from the terrace when she heard him speaking German on the phone.

'Why did you do that, Andreas?' Her voice was steady.

'I thought it was what you would want me to do, but if I was wrong—'

'You were not wrong. You were absolutely right. Thank you. Usually I am strong but tonight I could not have had that conversation.'

'I know,' he said gently. 'There are times when it's best not to have to say anything at all.'

The phone rang again. This time it was his brother Yorghis.

Twenty-four people dead.

Twenty from abroad and four from Aghia Anna: not only Manos but also his eight-year-old nephew who had proudly gone out for the day to help his uncle. And the two local boys who had worked on the boat.

'It's a dark time for you, Andreas,' Elsa said, her voice full of concern.

'These are not bright days for you either,' he answered.

They sat there, each thinking their own thoughts. It was as if they had always known each other. They would talk when there was something to say. Elsa spoke eventually.

'Andreas?' She looked outside; the others were talking together.

'Yes?'

'Will you do one more thing for me?'

'If I can, yes, of course.'

'Write to Adoni. Ask him to come home to Aghia Anna. Tell him that your village has lost three young men and a boy, that you all need to see the face of someone who left, someone who *can* come back.'

He shook his head. 'No, my friend Elsa, it would not work. Why do you want to change the lives of people you don't know?'

She threw back her head and laughed. 'Oh, Andreas, if you knew me in my real life, that's what I do all the time, I'm a crusading journalist— that's what the television station calls me. I'm always trying to keep families together, get children off drugs, get integrity into sports . . . It's my nature to change the lives of people I don't know.'

'And does it ever work?' he asked.

'Sometimes. It works enough times for me to want to keep at it.'

'But you've left?'

'Not because of the work.'

He looked at the telephone.

She nodded. 'Yes, you're right, it's because of Dieter. It's a long story.'

'No need to tell me your business, Elsa,' he said.

'You are my friend, I want to tell you.'

But they heard the others approaching.

Thomas was the spokesman. 'We must let you sleep, Andreas, tomorrow will be a long day,' he said.

'We think we should go back down the hill, back to where we are staying,' David began.

'My brother Yorghis is sending a truck up this way for you soon. I told him I had friends who would need a lift; it's a long way.'

'And can we pay you now for our meal—our long day and night with you?' Thomas asked.

'As I told Yorghis, you are friends, and friends do not pay for their food,' he said with dignity.

They looked at him: old and slightly bent, poor, working hard in a restaurant where they had been the only customers all day.

Elsa spoke slowly. 'What do you say that we make a collection for the family of Manos and his little nephew and the others who died today? There will undoubtedly be a fund for them. We can gather what we think our food and drink here would have cost, and then get an envelope and write on it, "From the friends of Andreas".'

Fiona had an envelope in her shoulder bag. She took it out and without a word they poured their euros onto a plate. The sound of the police truck was heard coming up the hill.

'You write the message for the people, Elsa,' Fiona suggested.

And Elsa did with a steady hand.

'I wish I could write in the Greek language,' she said to Andreas, and looked at him as if they shared a secret.

'It's fine—your generosity, all of you, is very fine in any language,' he said, sounding choked. 'I was never good at writing any sort of letter.'

'It's just the first words that are the hardest, Andreas,' she persisted.

'I would begin "*Adoni mou*,"' he said haltingly.

'Now you're halfway there,' Elsa said, and held him to her for a quick moment before they climbed into the truck to go back down the hill to the little town.

None of them slept well that night. They all tossed and turned, the starlight too bright somehow and seeping into their bedrooms.

Elsa stood on the tiny balcony of her apartment hotel and looked out at the dark sea. She was staying at the Studio Apartments, run by a young Greek man who had learned the property business in Florida and had returned with the idea of having six little self-contained units here. Simply furnished, with Greek rugs on the wooden floors and colourful Greek pottery on the shelves. No one balcony overlooked the others. He charged a lot by Aghia Anna standards but his apartments were always full.

Elsa knew she wouldn't sleep for hours. There was no point in going to bed. She brought a chair out onto the tiny balcony and sat with her elbows on the small, wrought-iron balustrade, looking at the patterns the moonlight was making on the water.

David's little room was too hot and stuffy. It had been fine up to now but tonight was different. The people in the house were wailing too loudly for anyone to sleep. Their son had died on Manos's boat today.

When David had walked into the house and discovered the family and friends comforting each other he had been stricken. He had shaken hands awkwardly and fumbled for the words to express what could not be said. They spoke little English, and they looked at him wild-eyed. They hardly noticed when he came downstairs again to walk in the night air. Their grief was too great.

David wondered what would have happened if he had died on the boat. It could so easily have been. He had just chosen one day for a tour rather than another. Would there have been wailing like this in his home? Would his father have rocked forward and back in misery? Or would he have said grimly that the boy had chosen his life and he had to live with that choice and die by it.

Suddenly David felt very anxious as he walked around the sorrowing town. He thought he might go to a small taverna where people were still sitting, talking. He might even meet some of the people he had spent all that time with. He could speak to Fiona about Ireland, a place he had always wanted to go to. He could ask her about nursing, and if it really was as rewarding as people said. Did you get a glow of pleasure as patients got better?

Or he could ask Thomas about his writing: what kind of thing he wrote, why he was going to be away from his university for so long, how often he got to see his little boy. David loved to listen to people's stories. It was why he was so useless in his father's investment-broking business. Clients needed him to tell them what to spend and how. David was much more interested in asking about their houses as homes rather than investments, when what they really wanted to talk about was a quick turnover.

As he walked he saw Elsa on her balcony but didn't call out to her. She was so calm and in control, the last thing she needed was a bumbling fool like him in the middle of the night.

Thomas had booked himself for two weeks into a little apartment over a craft shop. It was owned by an eccentric woman called Vonni. In her late forties or so, she always dressed in a different floral skirt and a black shirt. She looked like someone you would have to give money to for her next meal, Thomas thought, but in fact she owned this splendid luxury apartment which she let out to visitors. It was expensively furnished and had some valuable little figurines and pictures.

Vonni was Irish originally, he gathered, though she didn't want to talk about herself. She was a perfect landlady in that she left him alone. She offered to take his clothes to a local laundry and she left an occasional basket of grapes or a bowl of olives on his doorstep.

'Where do you live while I stay here?' he had asked at the start.

'I sleep in an outhouse,' she had replied.

Thomas was unsure if she was joking or was in fact somewhat simple in the head. And he asked her no more—he was happy in Vonni's place, where there was a phone in case Bill wanted to call him. He had felt that a cellphone would be intrusive on his travels, and anyway people were always complaining that they couldn't get a signal in remote places. And what did it matter how many euros he spent on an apartment with a telephone? He had nothing else to spend his professor's salary on, and even his poetry was beginning to earn him money.

A prestigious magazine had paid for him to go abroad and write travel articles, in his own style from wherever he wanted. It had been the perfect assignment when he'd realised that he needed to get away. He had wanted to write about Aghia Anna, but the world's press would be arriving tomorrow and Aghia Anna would already be notorious.

Once he had thought it would be easy to go on living in the same town as his ex-wife, seeing his son Bill as often as possible, keeping a civilised and non-combative relationship with Shirley. But now things were different.

Shirley's new boyfriend was Andy, a car salesman she had met at the gym. When Shirley announced that she was getting married to Andy it changed everything. She had explained that she had found a real and permanent love.

Thomas had been surprised to find how much he had resented it. Andy wasn't a *bad* guy, it was just that he'd moved too easily into the house that Thomas had bought for himself, Shirley and Bill.

'Because it's all so much *easier*,' Shirley had explained.

Bill had said that Andy was OK, and that's just what he was: OK. But he was a bit of a jock and not into reading, not into holding a book with Bill at night and saying, 'Come on, you choose what to read and we'll read it together.'

And, to be fair, Andy had sensed the awkwardness of it all. He had suggested that Thomas visit Bill between five and seven when he, Andy, was in the gym.

It had been reasonable, sensible, sensitive even, but that had annoyed Thomas even more. As if he were being tidied away to a place that didn't impinge on their lives. Every time he visited he had come to hate the house more, with the jars of vitamins and health supplements all over the kitchen and bathrooms, the magazines about health and fitness on the coffee tables.

When the chance to get away came, Thomas was sure he was right in taking it. He could keep in touch with his boy by phone, by letter, by email. He had convinced himself it was better for everyone. And for the first few weeks it had worked well. He didn't wake up angry any more, nor drive himself crazy thinking about his son's new household. The break had been a good thing.

But the events of today had changed everything. All those people dead, a village plunged into mourning. He could hear the sounds of their crying floating up to him over the harbour. There was no way he could sleep, and his thoughts kept buzzing round like angry insects.

Fiona too was awake in their room in a cramped little house outside town. It belonged to a thin anxious woman called Eleni, who had three little boys. There didn't seem to be any sign of a husband. Fiona and Shane had found the place by knocking at various doors and offering a small handful of euros in return for overnight accommodation.

Now Shane lay sprawled in the chair asleep, the only one who had managed to get a night's rest. Fiona couldn't sleep because Shane had said, out of the blue, that they should move on next day.

She had been startled.

They had both thought Aghia Anna the kind of place where they might stay a while. But now Shane had changed his mind.

'No, we can't stay. It's going to be a creepy place after all this,' he had said. 'We'll get a boat to Athens tomorrow.'

'But Athens is a big city . . . it will be so hot,' she had protested.

Then Shane said that he had a fellow to see, someone there he just had to meet.

Nothing at all had been mentioned about this fellow when they had set off a month ago, but Fiona knew from experience that it was not wise to upset Shane over something so trivial. It was just that she had wanted to go to the funeral for Manos, the handsome, sexy Greek who had pinched her bottom and said she was *orea*, which meant wonderful, *beautiful*. He was a silly guy, but good-tempered and cheerful, he thought all ladies were *orea*, he drank wine from the bottle and he danced Zorba-like dances for them. But there had been no harm in him, he didn't deserve to die with his little nephew and his work-mates and all those tourists who had been having such a great time.

And Fiona would have liked to see the people she'd met today again. The old man, Andreas, had been so gentle, so generous. Thomas, the college professor, was a wise, good person, and she might even have encouraged David to be more outgoing.

And as for Elsa . . . Fiona had never admired anyone so much, for knowing exactly what to say and when to say it. No wedding ring, and yet she must be about twenty-eight. Fiona wondered who she had telephoned in Germany.

Shane was still asleep in the chair.

Fiona wished that he had not brought out the pot in front of Andreas and the others today, and that he had been a bit nicer to them all. He could be so prickly and difficult. But then he had lived a confused life with no love in it. Not until he had met Fiona, that was. And she alone knew how to reach the real Shane.

The room was very hot and pokey. She wished they could have stayed somewhere a little better. Then Shane might not want them to move on so quickly tomorrow.

During the night, as the stars shone down on the bay, Andreas wrote a letter. He wrote several versions and decided that the last one was the best. By morning he was ready to post the first and only letter he had written in nine years to his son in Chicago.

When the sun came up he got on his putt-putt bike and made the journey to the town.

When the sun came up on Aghia Anna, the phone rang in the tasteful apartment over the craft shop.

It was Thomas's son Bill calling him.

'Dad, you OK?'

'I'm great, son, just fine. Your momma gave you my number?'

'It's on the board, Dad. It's just Mom says it's always the middle of the night out there. Andy said I should try anyhow.'

'Say thanks to Andy.'

'I will. He got out a map of the world to show me roughly where you are, when we saw the fire on television. It must have been scary.'

'Well, it was sad,' Thomas said.

'It's a long way away, where you are, Dad.'

Thomas yearned to be beside his boy. It was a real ache. But he had to remain cheerful. 'Nowhere's a long way away these days, Bill, the phone is always there. Listen to you! You could be in the next room.'

'Yeah, I know,' the boy agreed. 'I called Gran to tell her you were OK and she said you are to take care.'

'I will, Bill, believe me, I'll take care.'

'I've got to go now. Bye, Dad.'

He was gone but the sun had come up on Aghia Anna and the day was beautiful. His son had called.

Outside the town, when the sun came up, Fiona went to the bathroom and suddenly realised that her period was six days late.

Down by the harbour, when the sun came up, Elsa passed by the church, which had become a temporary morgue. As she rounded a corner, she saw with horror that among the crowds arriving from Athens was a German television crew from her own network setting up shots of the still-smouldering wreck that had been towed into the harbour.

She knew the cameraman and the sound man. And they would know her if they saw her. And then Dieter would know where she was and would be here in a matter of hours.

She backed carefully into a little café and looked around wildly. Some old men were playing a form of backgammon—no help there. Then at a table she saw David, the kind English boy.

'David,' she hissed.

He was overjoyed to see her.

'David, can you go and get a taxi and bring it here for me? I can't go outside. There are people out there I just don't want to see. Can you do that for me, *please* . . .'

He seemed alarmed that she was so different from yesterday.

'Where will I tell the taxi you're going?' he asked.

'Where were *you* thinking of going today?' she asked, desperately.

'There's a place about fifty kilometres away, a little temple and an artists' colony. I was going to get a bus there.'

'We'll take the taxi there,' she said firmly.

'No, Elsa, we'll go out and get on a bus, a taxi would cost a fortune, believe me,' David argued.

'And I *have* a fortune, believe me,' she said, showing him a wad of notes. 'Please, David, just act now, this minute. I haven't committed a crime or anything, but I am in trouble. I'm begging you. If you don't help me now then honestly I don't know what I'll do.' She spoke from the heart, not acting.

'There's a line of taxis in the square. I'll be back,' said David.

Fiona had quite a long time to wait until Shane woke up. He lay there in the chair with his mouth open, his hair damp and stuck to his forehead. He looked so vulnerable when he was asleep. She longed to stroke his face but she didn't want to wake him.

Downstairs she could hear Eleni calling to her three little sons. Neighbours kept calling in, obviously telling the story over and over to each other, shocked by the tragedy.

She wouldn't disturb these people by going down, not until Shane woke, until he was ready to go.

When he did wake he was not in good humour.

'Why did you let me sleep in the chair?' he asked, rubbing his neck. 'I'm as stiff as a bloody board.'

'Let's go and have a swim—that will make you feel better,' she tried to encourage him.

'Easy for you—you've been in the bed all night,' he grumbled.

This was not the time to tell him that she had been awake most of the night, and it was certainly not the time to tell him that she could be pregnant. That must wait.

'Will we pack before breakfast?' she asked.

'Pack?' he said, puzzled.

Perhaps he had forgotten the whole idea.

'Don't mind me, I don't know where I am half the time,' Fiona said with a laugh.

'You can say that again . . . Here, I'm going to bed for a bit and you could go and get us a couple of coffees.'

She walked along the beach back towards the town, her bare feet kicking the warm sand at the edge of the sea. She could not believe this was happening. Fiona Ryan, the most sensible of her whole family, the most reliable nurse on the whole ward, had thrown up her job to go off with Shane, the man they had all warned her against.

And she might now very possibly be pregnant.

It wasn't just her mother who had rejected Shane as the other half of her life, it was all her friends, including Barbara, her best pal since they had been six years of age. And her sisters. But what did they know?

And, anyway, love was never meant to be uncomplicated. Think of any of the great love stories and you realised that. Love had nothing to do with meeting a nice *suitable* person, who had a good job, who wanted a long engagement and to save a deposit on a house.

That wasn't love, that was compromise.

She thought about the possible pregnancy and her heart lurched. There had been a couple of times, fairly recently, when they had not been careful. She felt her flat stomach. Was it possible that a child was growing there, someone who would be half Shane and half her? It was too exciting to imagine.

In front of her on the beach she saw the strange baggy shorts and over-long T-shirt of Thomas, the nice American. He recognised her and called out, 'You look happy!'

'I am.' She didn't tell him the way her mind was filling up with wild and wonderful plans for living here in Aghia Anna and bringing up a child with these people, Shane working on the fishing boats or in the restaurants, she helping the local doctor, maybe even as midwife. These were all dreams that would be discussed later when Shane had his coffee. She would tell him then.

'My son called me from the States. We had a great conversation.' Thomas couldn't help sharing his news.

'I'm so very glad. You know I *thought* he might call you back last night—I felt it when you were telling us about him.'

'Let me buy you a coffee to celebrate,' Thomas said, and they walked together along to a small taverna near the beach. They sat down at a table and ordered coffee, and found that they could talk as easily as they had yesterday.

'We were meant to be going to Athens today, but I think Shane's too tired,' Fiona said, when they'd sat there for some time. 'In some ways I'm actually rather glad he's too tired. I like this place. I want to stay on.'

'So do I. I'm going to walk up in those hills, and I want to stay for the funeral.'

She looked at him with interest. 'So do I, and it's not just ghoulish wanting to see it all first hand, I wanted to be part of it.'

'Wanted? Does that mean you'll not stay?'

'Well, we don't know what day it will be and, as I said, Shane wants to go to Athens.'

'But surely if *you* want to . . .' His voice trailed away.

Fiona saw the look on his face. The same look that eventually came over everyone's face when they met Shane. She stood up.

'Thanks for the coffee. I'll go now. If you see the others, David and Elsa . . .'

'I'll say that you and Shane had to go to Athens and you said good-bye,' he said gently. 'I saw them heading out of town in a taxi together this morning. But it's a tiny place. I'll see them again.'

He watched her go and buy some warm bread and a little pot of local honey to take back to that selfish young man and he sighed. A professor, a poet, a writer—and he didn't understand the smallest thing about life and love.

Elsa bent down in the taxi and hid her head under a scarf until they had left the town. Only then did she straighten up. Her face looked strained and anxious.

'Why don't I tell you what I know about this place we are going to?' David offered.

'Thank you. That would be perfect.' She lay back and closed her eyes while his words rolled over her. It was the site of a minor temple that had had some excavation, but the money had dried up so it had been left in a semi-exposed state. There were those who said it was well worth a tour.

And an artist's colony had started there years ago, which was still going strong. Even today, silversmiths and potters came from all over the world. The artists brought their wares to town to sell.

David looked at her from time to time as he spoke. Her face was relaxing. Obviously, she didn't want to tell him what she was frightened of, so he wouldn't ask. Better to go on burbling on about this place they were visiting.

Shane felt a lot better after the coffee, bread and honey. He said that they would have one last day in this crazy place and leave for Athens the following day. It was no big deal. He wondered where they would find a place with some action.

'I don't think there'll be much action today or tonight—the whole town is full of press and officials. The funeral is tomorrow,' Fiona said. She longed to ask if they could leave after the funeral. But she could let that question wait a while. 'There's a lovely little place I saw out on a point—they catch fish and grill them straight from the sea, will we go there?'

He shrugged. Why not? The wine was probably cheaper there than in the fancy places by the harbour anyway.

'We should go now before it gets too hot,' she said, and they walked down the shabby stairs and through the crowded kitchen. She longed to stop and sit there with the family, but she knew that Shane was anxious for his first cold beer of the day. It would soon be noon and it was very hot. They should go to the taverna by the sea straight away.

The day was indeed becoming very hot.

Thomas decided against going up into the hills. He should have left much earlier in the morning for that kind of trip. He looked into the craft shop. Vonni had not opened for business and was asleep in her chair. Suppose she really slept in the henhouse? She could easily sleep in the empty bedroom in the apartment—but he knew better than to ask her.

The shops were closed but he decided to walk along the coast to a simple place on a point that he'd seen a few days back. There had been a wonderful smell of grilling fish when he had passed it then, and it would be just the spot to sit and look out to sea and think. There had been some raggedy umbrellas there that would protect him from the sun, and a cool breeze coming in from the sea. Just the place to go.

Elsa and David's taxi arrived in the old square in the centre of Kalatriada. They stepped out and Elsa paid the driver. Then they stood and looked around. The place had certainly not been discovered by developers. Half the buildings around the square seemed to be tiny restaurants or cafés, and there was a selection of pottery shops. The sea was far below, down a narrow track.

'I'm sure you want to go and find your temple,' Elsa said to David. 'This is a good safe place you brought me, I can hide here.'

'I'm in no great rush to see the temple,' David said. 'I can sit with you for a while.'

'Well, after all those turns and corners, I must say I would love a coffee,' Elsa smiled. 'But truly this is a fine place to come to. You really are my hero.'

'Oh, hero, you say!' David laughed at the idea. 'Not my usual role.'

'Now don't try to tell me that you're normally cast as a villain.' Elsa was cheerful again.

'No, nothing as dashing. The buffoon more often,' he admitted.

'I don't believe it for a moment,' Elsa said.

'That's because you haven't seen me in my real life. I've let my father down in everything, Elsa. Honestly, if he had been given any other kind of son it would have worked. A ready-made business, a position of honour in the community. A lovely home—but it all choked me and made me feel trapped. No wonder he despises me.'

'Shall we sit here, do you think?' Elsa indicated the nearest café and sat down.

The waiter came and spread a piece of waxed paper on another table.

David ordered two *metrios*, the medium-sweet coffees. They soon arrived and the two sipped them companionably.

'I didn't *know* my father, David, but I had many, many arguments with my mother.'

'You see, that's probably more healthy. In my case there aren't any real arguments at all, it's all sighs and shrugs,' David said.

'If you had the time all over again what would you do?' Elsa asked.

'The same, mess it up I imagine.'

'That's so defeatist. You're young. Your parents are alive, for you there is time.' She put down her cup. 'Now, come on. Finish your coffee and we'll go and investigate Kalatriada. And then at lunch I'll tell you my problems and you can give *me* advice.'

Andreas sat with his brother in the police station. Yorghis's desk was piled high with reports about the accident. His phone had been ringing constantly. Now there was a lull.

'I wrote to Adoni today,' Andreas said slowly.

'Good, good,' Yorghis said after a little time.

'I didn't say sorry or anything.'

'No, of course not,' Yorghis agreed.

'Because I'm *not* sorry. You know that.'

'I know, I know.' Yorghis did not need to enquire why his brother had written to the long-estranged son in Chicago. He knew why.

It was because the death of Manos and all the people on the boat had shown them how very short life was. That was all.

Thomas passed the television crews and photographers in the square beside the harbour. It was a job like any other, he supposed, but they did seem somehow like a swarm of insects. They didn't gather where people were having a good time and getting on with life, only where there had been a disaster.

He thought about Elsa, that golden handsome German girl. She had been fairly dismissive of her own role in it all. He wondered where she had been going today in the taxi. Perhaps she knew these German television crews who were gathered around the harbour. Greece was a popular destination for Germans, and it was said that two German visitors had lost their lives on Manos's boat. But even though he looked, she was nowhere to be seen. Perhaps she had not come back from her taxi ride. He walked on to the restaurant on the point.

David and Elsa walked around the ruins of the temple. They were the only visitors. An elderly guide asked them for half a euro and gave them an ill-written and near incomprehensible account of what the temple had once been.

'There could be a fortune made from writing a proper leaflet in German,' Elsa said.

'Or even in English,' David laughed as they wandered back to the square.

'Let's see about this great lunch I'm going to take you to,' she said.

'I'm easy, Elsa . . . look, the waiter where we were before is waving at us, I'm happy to go back there if you are.'

'Of course I am—but then I wanted something more grand because I have to ask another favour of you.'

'You don't have to pay me with an expensive lunch, and I don't suppose Kalatriada has a posh restaurant.'

Their waiter was delighted to see them. 'I knew you come back, lady,' he said, beaming all over his face. He brought a dish of olives and little bits of cheese, he indicated the kitchens where, proudly, he opened up each dish so that they could choose what they would like to eat.

They sat companionably and talked as if they were old friends, wondering what it would have been like to have grown up in a small village like this instead of in big cities. It was only when they were sipping the dark sweet coffee that Elsa said, 'I'll tell you what this is all about now.'

'You don't have to.'

'No, I have to tell you, because I want us to stay here until tomorrow when the funeral in Aghia Anna is over.'

David's mouth opened. '*Stay here?*'

'I can't go back to the town, David, my television crew is there, people will recognise me, they'll tell Dieter, our boss back home, and he'll come and find me. I couldn't bear that.'

'Why?'

'Because I love him so much.'

'So that's bad—if the man you love comes to find you?'

'If it were only as simple as that,' she said, and she took his two hands and held them to her face. He felt the tears splash down over his fingers and onto the table.

'I understand that of course we have to stay here in Kalatriada tonight,' said David, who felt that he was indeed becoming more like a hero as every hour passed.

It was early. Fiona and Shane were the only people in the restaurant. The waiter left them alone with their fish and some wine by the dark blue sea and white sand. Shane had already drunk two beers and a glass of retsina very quickly. Fiona watched him, waiting for the right time to tell him her news. Finally, when she could wait no longer, she put her hand on his arm and told him that she was six days overdue. She said that since she had been twelve years old she had never been one day late and she felt sure that it really did mean she was pregnant. She looked hopefully into his face.

She saw disbelief written all over it.

He drank another glass of wine before he spoke. 'I can't take this in,' he said. 'We took precautions.'

'Well, we didn't . . . all of the time. If you remember—'

'How could you be so stupid?' he asked

'Well, it wasn't only me.' She was hurt.

'God, Fiona, you really have a way of spoiling everything and wrecking everyone's life,' he said.

'But we *did* want children, we said, you said . . .' Fiona began to cry.

'One day, I said, not now. You're such a fool . . . not now that we're only a month out on the trip.'

'I thought we might stay here, you know, in this place, and we could bring up the baby here.'

'It's not a baby, it's a six-day-overdue period.'

'But it could be a baby, *our* baby.' She struggled to speak through her tears. 'You could get a job in a restaurant maybe, and I could work too . . .'

He stood up and leaned across the table to shout at her. She could hardly hear the things he was saying, so hurtful and cruel were they all. She was a whore, like all women. Scheming and plotting to get him tied down with a brood of children and make him work as a *waiter*. A waiter in a godforsaken place like this.

She must get rid of the baby and never think of coming up with this kind of fairy story again. Never. She was a stupid, brainless fool.

She must have argued with him, none of it was clear, but then she felt the stinging blow on her face with such a shock that she had begun to reel back as he was coming at her again with his fist clenched.

The ground was coming up at her, she felt sick, she was shaking all over. Then she heard the running and shouting behind her and two waiters held Shane back and Thomas, who had arrived from nowhere, was pulling her away, guiding her to a chair.

She closed her eyes as he dabbed her face with cold water.

'You're all right, Fiona,' he said as he stroked her hair. 'Believe me, you're all right now.'

CHAPTER TWO

THE RESTAURANT GAVE THOMAS the number of the police station. Fiona heard Shane laugh when he heard that the call was going to be made.

'Waste of time, Thomas, she's not going to press charges.' He reached for another glass of wine.

The two waiters looked at Thomas as if for advice. Should they let Shane drink or should they restrain him?

But Thomas just nodded slightly. The more drunk Shane became, the worse the impression he would make when the police turned up.

He went into a back room to make the call to the police. He introduced himself to Yorghis, the brother of Andreas, on the phone, who immediately knew who he was.

'You were one of the generous people who gave such a donation to the family of Manos.'

'It was really your brother who did that, he didn't charge us for the meal.'

'Andreas said you were friends.'

'And we are proud to be his friends, but, sir, we have a problem . . .' Thomas explained it all to Yorghis who understood the situation instantly. There was remarkably little red tape. Then Thomas quietly asked the waiters to take Shane into a back room and lock him in. Shane didn't even put up a struggle.

'Leave him some wine, I'll pay,' he said to the waiters, and went to sit down beside Fiona, whose tear-stained face showed someone still in shock.

'It will be fine,' he said, stroking her hand.

'It will never be fine,' she said with a terrible finality. 'We survive, you know, that's why we're all here roaming the earth instead of being extinct.'

And then he didn't say any more while they waited for the police van to arrive. Her face looked sad and empty, but Thomas knew that he was some kind of strength and company for her just by being there.

When Yorghis arrived he told Shane that an assault had been seen by three independent witnesses, that he would be locked up in the police station for twenty-four hours.

'But she didn't mind.' Shane's voice was slurred now and nervous. 'Ask her. I love her, we're together, we might even be going to have a baby—right, Fiona? Tell them.'

She still had her eyes closed.

'That's not important,' Yorghis explained. 'The complaint has not been made by this lady, what she says is irrelevant.' Then he handcuffed Shane and helped him into the police van.

The van had driven off in the sun just as people started to arrive for their lunch. The waiters were relieved. Order had been restored and trade had not been interrupted.

Fiona had said nothing during the whole time but now she started to cry. 'I wish I had a friend, Thomas,' she said.

'I'm your friend.'

'Yes, I know, but I meant a woman friend like Barbara back home, she'd tell me what to do.'

'Do you want to call her? I have a telephone in my apartment,' he suggested.

'It's not the same now. Too many times she offered to help and I didn't listen.'

'I know, you'd have to start too far back.' He was sympathetic.

'I *could* talk to Elsa, but we don't know where she is,' Fiona said sadly, wiping her eyes with a napkin.

'We could find out where she is. I saw her getting into a taxi this morning with David. I don't know where they were going. But why don't we have something to eat to build you up a little? When you are strong enough to walk we'll go and ask the taxi drivers. They won't have forgotten someone like Elsa. She's very warm and sympathetic . . . she's just the person to talk to.'

He was right. They all remembered the German blonde and the small man with glasses. The driver who had taken them to Kalatriada said it had been a wonderful fare.

'Let's go there,' Thomas said, and offered the startled taxi driver his second great fare of the day.

It was certainly a twisty road up through the hills. Once they got to the small town of Kalatriada it was easy to find Elsa and David. The place was not very much more than a big square ringed with cafés and craft shops. Elsa's blonde hair was hard to miss as she bent over some pottery plates in a little shop. There was hardly any need for explanations. It was obviously not a coincidence.

Elsa panicked. 'Is anyone looking for me?' she asked urgently.

Thomas went straight to the point. 'In a way, Elsa. We were hoping that you and Fiona could have a talk. She's been a bit upset, you see.'

'I can see that,' David said, looking at the livid red mark on Fiona's cheek.

'Next one would have broken her nose,' Thomas said grimly.

'Well, certainly we'll have a talk.' Elsa had her hand on Fiona's arm. 'Sorry for immediately thinking it was about me but I have a few problems, which is why David and I are staying here tonight.'

'Staying here?' Fiona and Thomas spoke together, amazed.

'Sure, it's a nice place, isn't it, and there's a lovely little hotel over there on the other side of the square. We have two rooms. Fiona can share with me and you men can share a room. Is that suitable, do you think?' Elsa's confident smile was back, and they all agreed that it was very suitable indeed.

Irini, the woman who ran the little hotel, seemed to show no surprise at the ill-assorted group of people with no luggage who had turned up so unexpectedly. She looked tired and bent as she got them towels and a little cake of soap. Her smiles warm but weary, she appeared to do all the cleaning and cooking while three men sat playing a board game in the corner; not one of them helped her.

'A lot of work to be done by the women's movement here in this house, I think,' Elsa whispered to Fiona as they went upstairs to claim their room, leaving Thomas and David downstairs.

'You could probably start with me, Elsa,' Fiona said humbly. 'You don't need to look much further than at me to see a victim.'

Elsa's face was full of sympathy. 'Sleep for a little,' she urged. 'Everything is better after a couple of hours' sleep.'

'I want to tell you about him, and why he does what he does,' Fiona began.

'No, you don't,' Elsa said. 'You want to hear me say you're perfectly right to go back to him and that he didn't mean it.'

Fiona's eyes opened wide.

'Maybe I *will* say that but not now, Fiona. Rest now. We'll talk later. There's all the time in the world. I'll sit here and look at the mountains.'

To her amazement Fiona felt her eyelids become heavy and soon she was breathing deeply.

Elsa sat in the little cane chair and watched the shadows come down over the valley. There was rain tonight, covering the blanket of stars.

They could not eat out of doors, too much rain, Irini said, but they could sit inside and see the square in Kalatriada. And with the background of old men clicking dice and counters from the backgammon game in the corner, they sat down at a table with a blue and yellow checked cloth and began to eat the kebabs and salad that Irini proudly produced for them.

'*Orea,*' David said. '*Poli poli kala!*'

Irini's tired face smiled a big toothless smile. She might only be forty, Elsa thought, less even. It was no life here for her, but she was surrounded by the people she knew and liked, and now four guests were praising the simple food and saying it was beautiful. One of those men at the backgammon tables might be her husband, another her father. There were children's clothes flapping on the line. She probably had a family, little children who knew everyone in the village.

Elsa sighed. Once she would have urged Fiona to look hard at Shane and realise that he would never love her and was probably incapable of loving anyone. She would have said that Fiona should consider all aspects of carrying Shane's child to term. But nowadays Elsa was not at all certain about what was the right thing for anyone to do.

She realised that she had been daydreaming and dragged herself back to the conversation at the table. She had come away to clear her mind, not to sit confused and brooding. She must pay attention and not allow herself to drift off like this again.

Thomas was talking about his landlady. 'Vonni's a real character. She's been here for years, apparently. She never talks about herself, but she speaks Greek like a native. She knows this place Kalatriada well. She comes every few weeks to buy pottery to sell in her craft shop.'

'She's from Ireland, Andreas told me yesterday,' Fiona said. 'I was thinking about her . . . you know, if she could stay here, maybe I could.' Her small pale face looked very sad.

'Did she come here with anyone, do you think?' Elsa wanted to inject some reality back into the discussion before Fiona started living in some fantasy world where she and Shane might raise a family here in the purple Greek mountains.

Thomas didn't know. He told them that although Vonni was so open and friendly you didn't ask her questions. 'But, I think she's fairly pushed for a living. She teaches English, and she sleeps in a sort of shed out back so that she can rent her apartment.'

'How old is she?' Elsa asked.

'Fifty to sixty,' David said.

'Forty to fifty,' Thomas said at the same time. They all laughed.

'Well, so much for dressing up to please men,' Elsa said with a wry smile.

'No, Vonni doesn't dress up, she wears a T-shirt and a coloured skirt and open sandals. I don't expect she's ever worn make-up.' Thomas was thoughtful. 'It's oddly restful, somehow.'

'Do you fancy her then, this restful woman of uncertain age?' Elsa teased him.

'No, not remotely, but she does interest me. I called her before dinner tonight in case she saw no lights in her place and wondered whether I'd disappeared on her.'

'That was thoughtful of you,' Fiona said. It wasn't the kind of thing Shane would have done.

'I told her that I thought we would all probably go back tomorrow for the funeral. I checked that we wouldn't be in the way. She said we should take the bus from the square; one leaves every two hours. Is that OK with everyone?'

'It's fine with me,' David said.

'Yes, and I can go to the police station and talk to Shane,' Fiona said eagerly. 'He will be so sorry and upset by now.'

Elsa was the only one who hadn't spoken.

'Elsa?' Thomas spoke gently.

'I might just stay on here for a couple of days. I could join you all later.' It seemed to need an explanation. She hesitated and then decided to speak. 'It's a little bit awkward, you see. I'm trying to avoid someone and I would prefer to hide out until he has gone away. It would be stupid to meet up with him again in a tiny place like Aghia Anna.'

'And you are certain he's there?' Thomas asked gently.

'Well, this is just his sort of story. No one does human interest better than he does.'

'We could all keep him away from you.' David was busy living up to his heroic role.

'We could tell Yorghis, you know, Andreas's brother, if this man tried to stalk you or harass you.' Thomas was reassuring.

Elsa looked from one to the other. 'No, it's not that. I'm not afraid of him, I'm afraid of myself. Afraid that I might go back to him and then all this—all the business of coming here—would have been such a waste of time.' Her lip was trembling. Elsa the cool, confident Elsa.

They were perplexed.

'I'd stay with you, Elsa,' Fiona began. 'Only I have to go to the police station and check about Shane.'

'You don't *have* to, Fiona, you just want to,' Elsa said.

'Well, I love him, *you* must understand that.' Fiona was stung by this remark. 'Seriously, Elsa. You have to be in love with this fellow otherwise you wouldn't be so afraid of meeting him.'

Thomas intervened. It was getting too serious between the women.

'We've all had a long day . . . suppose we meet here for breakfast at eight. We could get the nine o'clock bus . . . those of us who want to go. Is that OK?' He had a gentle voice, but from years of teaching students he had an air of authority.

They realised he was right, and started to move off.

'Just a moment,' Elsa said. 'I'm very sorry, Fiona, I was rude to you. You have every right to go and see the man you love. And I apologise for putting my own selfish affairs before other people's tragedy. Of course I'll come to the funeral with you and I would be delighted to have the protection of kind friends like you.' She looked from one to the other, her eyes over-bright, as if the smile was hiding a lot of tears.

In the holding cell at the back of the police station, Shane sat with his head in his hands. He needed a cold beer very badly but he was highly unlikely to get one from that ignorant Greek policeman, the brother of the tiresome Andreas up in the taverna.

Where *was* Fiona? He would have thought that she would be here by now. He could send her down to the fish bar at the harbour to get him three cold cans. Of course he would have to do the *sorry, sorry* bit, explaining that he had been so upset by the way she had sprung things on him, he couldn't help his reaction.

He banged the plate which had held hard bread against the door.

Yorghis pulled back the shutter and peered in. 'Yes?'

'My girlfriend, I'm sure she's been to see me. Have you kept her away from me? You can't get away with this, you know.'

Yorghis shrugged. 'Nobody came.'

'I don't believe you.'

'Nobody came.' Yorghis began to move away.

'Look—I'm sorry, I didn't mean I didn't believe you exactly, it's just that, you see, we are very close and—'

'It didn't look as if you were very close yesterday,' Yorghis said.

'No, you don't understand, we have a very passionate relationship, naturally it explodes from time to time.'

'*Endaxi*,' Yorghis said.

'What does that mean?'

'It means right, or OK, or whatever you say.' Yorghis moved off. 'I heard she left Aghia Anna yesterday,' Yorghis called over his shoulder.

'I don't believe you!' Shane shouted.

'Believe what you like, I was told she took a taxi and left the place.'

Shane sat there in disbelief. It couldn't be true. Fiona would never leave without him.

'**K**alimera sas, Yorghis, you look worried.' Vonni stopped to lean on the wall of the police station.

'Well, we have all these crowds of cameramen trampling on everyone for the funeral, the station is full of accident investigators, I have eleven different reports still to compile and I have this young pup in a cell. I don't know what to do with him.'

'The boy who hit the Irish girl?' Vonni asked. Nothing happened that she didn't know about.

'Yes. I wish he were hundreds of miles from here.'

'Well, export him so.'

'What?'

'That's what we used to do in Ireland years ago: if some tearaway was causing trouble the judge or the guards would say that if he was on the mailboat to England that night no further action would be taken.'

Yorghis smiled in disbelief.

'No, it's true, terrible thing to do to England, but we thought, well, England is bigger, it can cope.'

'I see.'

'Suppose you put him on the eleven o'clock boat to Athens. Seriously, Yorghis, he'd be out of here before the funeral starts. It would be an ease to everyone.'

'And indeed Athens is big enough to cope with him.' Yorghis stroked his face thoughtfully.

Vonni's lined, tanned face broke into its wide smile. 'True, Yorghis, Athens is well big enough,' she agreed.

'You can't order me off the island,' Shane said.

'Take it or leave it. We have no time to deal with you now. Locked up here until next week then a prosecution—maybe jail. That's on the one hand. On the other, you get a free trip to Athens. You choose. You have ten minutes.'

'What about my things?' Shane asked.

'One of my boys will drive you past Eleni's house. You can pack your rucksack and be on the boat at ten thirty.'

'I'm not ready to go yet.'

'Suit yourself,' said Yorghis, turning to leave the cell.

'No—wait a minute, come back. I think I'll go.'

Yorghis ushered him out to the police van. Shane got in sulkily.

'Bloody strange way of running a country,' he said.

Back in Eleni's house he noticed that Fiona's things were still there in the room.

'I thought you said she had gone away.'

Eleni explained in Greek that the girl would be back that day. The young policeman knew better than to translate. His boss wanted this violent boy aboard the 11 a.m. ferry and out of his jurisdiction. No point in delaying things because that foolish girl was coming back.

The bus from Kalatriada wound its way through the little hill villages as it headed slowly towards Aghia Anna.

Old women in black got on and off, saluting everyone: some of them carried vegetables, which they might be going to sell at a market; one woman had two hens. A young man played the bouzouki, but the four passengers returning for the funeral were all lost in their own thoughts and concerns about the day that lay ahead of them.

Elsa wondered what were the odds against Dieter turning up in this tiny village where she had run to flee from him.

Fiona hoped that Shane would feel much calmer now. Perhaps she could persuade that nice old man Andreas to put in a word for him; maybe they would let him out for the funeral.

Thomas worked out how he could ask Vonni to sleep in the spare bedroom of her own apartment rather than in that terrible shed.

David looked out at the families of children who waved at the passing bus. He wished he could have had brothers and sisters who would have shared the load. If he had a brother who had trained as an accountant, a sister who had read law and another brother who had gone into Dad's business when he was sixteen and learned it from the ground up—then he, David, would have been properly free to go and learn about pottery somewhere like Kalatriada.

He sighed as he looked out at the hills covered in olive groves. Instead of that, here he was, tortured with guilt. Last night Fiona had touched on Catholic guilt. She didn't even begin to know what Jewish guilt was like!

Vonni gave English lessons to the children in the big room behind her craft shop. She suggested that she would teach them a verse of an English hymn which they could sing at the funeral. It might be a small consolation to the English-speaking relatives who had been arriving on every boat for the past thirty-six hours, coming to the scene of the tragedy. She might even find something in German too.

Everyone thought it was a good idea.

And it would distract the children, take them away from weeping households for a while. The families were grateful to Vonni as they had been for years and years since first she had come to Aghia Anna as a young girl. She had grown older with them all, spoke their language, taught their children, shared the good times and bad. A lot of them could not even remember why she had come here in the first place.

As Thomas went up the whitewashed steps to the apartment above the shop and let himself in, he heard the voices of little children singing: '*The Lord's my shepherd, I'll not want . . .*'

It had been a long time since he had been in church. Possibly at his father's funeral. That was the last time he had heard it sung. He paused, stricken, in the sunshine.

Andreas and his brother Yorghis, together with a young policeman, stood beside the ferry.

'Is there anything you would like to do before you leave?' Andreas asked.

'Like what? Like congratulate you on your legendary Greek hospitality for example?' Shane sneered.

'Like write a letter to your girlfriend.' Andreas was curt. 'She might like to know that you are safe and well, and free . . . and that you'll contact her when you are settled.'

'I don't have any paper or a pen,' Shane said.

'I do.' Andreas offered both. 'A few short words perhaps?'

'Oh, for God's sake.' Shane turned away.

They blew the whistle to show the boat was about to leave. The young policeman escorted Shane on deck and came back to Andreas and Yorghis.

'It's better he doesn't write to her,' he said to the older men.

'In the long term certainly,' Andreas agreed. 'But in the short term it will break her poor little heart.'

David and Fiona walked with Elsa back to her apartment.

'Look, nobody around,' David said. It was true. The streets that had thronged with press and bureaucrats were quiet now.

'I wish I could stay longer, I just have to check Shane is all right,' Fiona apologised, as she went up the hill towards the police station. From down in the harbour they all heard the hooting of the 11 a.m. ferry as it left for Athens. At midday another boat would arrive carrying even more people coming to the funeral.

'Would you like me to stay with you here, Elsa?' David asked.

'Just for five minutes so that I don't run away again,' she laughed.

'You won't do that.' He patted her hand.

'I hope not, David. Tell me, did you ever in your life love anyone obsessively, foolishly?'

'No. I never loved anyone at all,' he said.

'I'm sure that's not so.'

'I'm afraid it is, and it's not something to be proud of at twenty-eight.' He was apologetic.

'You're exactly the same age as I am!' she exclaimed in surprise.

'You put your years to better use than I did,' he said.

'No, you wouldn't say that if you knew. I'd prefer never to have loved.' She reached out and stroked his cheek. 'You're a dear gentle person, and I'm so happy to have you here. Shall we make ourselves a little lunch together? We could eat on the balcony and see without being seen. Would you hate that?'

'Of course not, I'd love it,' said David.

'**H**ello, I wonder if I could speak to the police chief, please.'

Yorghis stood up wearily.

Fiona stood there in a little blue cotton dress with a white wool shoulder bag. Her hair falling over her face didn't hide the bruise. She looked frail and unable to cope with the hand that life had dealt her.

'Come in, *Kyria*, sit down,' he said, offering her a chair.

'You see, my friend stayed here with you last night,' she began, as if Yorghis ran some up-market bed and breakfast instead of a jail.

Yorghis spread out his hands in front of him. She looked so anxious to see this boy, so forgiving of what he had done. How did young pigs like that get good women to love them?

'He has gone to Athens,' Yorghis said baldly.

'No, he can't have, not without me, it's not possible.'

'On the eleven o'clock ferry.'

'Did he not leave me a note? Tell me where I should meet him? I must go on the next boat, I must go to him,' she said. She was weeping now. 'I have to be with him . . .'

'There will be no more boats leaving today, because of the funeral. Please, please be calm. It's better that he left.'

'No, no, how could it be better?'

'Because otherwise he would be in jail, locked up. At least he is free.'

'Oh, why did I go away? I'll never forgive myself . . .'

Yorghis patted her shoulder awkwardly as she sobbed. Over her shoulder, down at the foot of the hill, he saw Vonni passing by with her little troupe of children and it gave him an idea.

'Andreas tells me you are a nurse?' he said. 'Do you see Vonni down there, she's looking after the children during the funeral, I know she'd love you to give her a hand.'

'I'm not sure I could help anyone just now . . .' Fiona began.

'That's often when we help best,' Yorghis said.

Thomas went to Elsa's apartment, as he had promised, and was surprised to hear voices inside. Perhaps she had met her friend after all. He knocked on the door and was confused when David opened it.

'It's only Thomas,' David called out. It wasn't much of a welcome.

'Well, I *did* tell Elsa that I'd walk with her to the church,' Thomas said huffily.

'I'm so sorry, Thomas, it's just we thought . . . we were afraid that . . .'

Elsa came out to join them. She was wearing a smart cream linen dress with a navy jacket.

'Thomas, I asked David to answer the door for me because I still think that Dieter will come calling. Forgive me.'

'What's to forgive?' Thomas was putting on his tie at the little mirror in the hall.

'I should have gone home for a tie too.' David was worried.

'No, you look fine, David,' Thomas said, and they set out together following the crowds to the little church. People stood on both sides of the street winding up from the harbour.

Then a hush came over the crowd and they stood in silence at the approach of the funeral party. Lines of men and women walked behind the coffins in a little procession.

At the back walked the English and German families who had come so unexpectedly to this Greek village to mourn their loved ones.

There was room in the little church for only a tenth of the people gathered to mourn. Crackling speakers relayed the service to the people outside and, unexpectedly, in the middle of the Greek prayers and music, came the sound of children singing 'The Lord is My Shepherd', then a verse from a German hymn.

When the congregation came out of the church and prepared to walk the short journey up to the graveyard, Elsa spotted Fiona. She was with Vonni and the children, all of whom had armfuls of wild flowers.

'Another day, another surprise,' Thomas said. 'Who would have thought she would have got her act together.'

'It's probably to take her mind off Shane,' Elsa decided.

Yorghis made an announcement. The families would like to go alone to the burial service in the graveyard. They thanked people for coming to the church, but now they wanted to be alone. They had asked the café owners and restaurants to open again and for life to carry on. They were sure everyone would understand.

'I don't really want to be alone just now,' Elsa appealed.

'I could treat you to a glass of retsina and a little plate of *kalamari* and olives down at the harbour. Look, they're all putting out chairs,' Thomas said.

'I think Elsa would feel happier out of the public eye,' David said.

'Sure, I forgot. Listen, I have some nice cold retsina in my place, you know, over the craft shop. Is that an OK plan?'

'Very OK,' Elsa smiled. 'I'll just go home and get a scarf for the evening breeze and then I'll get some olives in Yanni's on the way back and see you at your place.' She seemed happy with what had been arranged.

Thomas was soon tidying up his sitting room and getting out glasses. The two men chatted easily for a while as they set out paper napkins and little plates.

Eventually David said what they were both thinking. 'Elsa is a very long time getting the olives, isn't she?'

There was a long pause.

'I suppose she met him,' Thomas said.

'And went off with him,' David said.

Elsa saw Dieter as soon as she came out of Yanni's delicatessen. He was at the end of the street, talking to Claus, the chief cameraman, and looking at his watch. She moved back into the doorway of Yanni's shop but not quickly enough.

Dieter had seen her.

She could see him running towards her.

'Elsa! Elsa!' he called, pushing past the people in the narrow street. His face was flushed and his eyes were bright. She had forgotten how handsome he was, like Robert Redford in his early years.

There was no escape: he was beside her.

'Dieter?' she said uncertainly.

'Darling Elsa, what are you *doing* here, what did you mean by running away?' He stood with his hands on her shoulders, admiring her and drinking her in.

She said nothing, just looked into his very blue eyes.

'Claus heard you were here. Someone from one of the other networks saw you yesterday, but I didn't believe them. Oh, my dearest lovely Elsa—how very, very good to have found you.'

She shook her head. 'You haven't found me, you've just met me by chance. Now I must go.'

She saw Claus move back discreetly: he wanted no part of this lovers' quarrel.

'Elsa, don't be ridiculous—you leave your job, you leave me, no explanation for either . . . you think there is nothing to discuss?' He called out to the cameraman, 'Claus, I'm going to stay the night here, you go back with the others and I'll call you tomorrow.'

'Don't stay for me, Dieter, I beg you. And if you try to force me or threaten me, I swear I'll get the police.'

'Threaten you, Elsa?' He was astounded at the idea. 'As if I would! I *love* you, Elsa. Is it so demanding and mad that I ask you to tell me why you left me?'

'I wrote to you,' she said.

'Twelve lines,' he said, reaching into his jacket. 'I carry it everywhere, I know it by heart, I am always hoping one day I will read it and it will make sense.' He looked so confused she felt herself softening.

'It's all there,' she said.

'Nothing is there, Elsa. I'll go away, leave you alone, I swear, if you tell me. Just tell me why you threw away two years like that. You owe me that much.'

She was silent. Perhaps she did owe him more than a twelve-line letter.

'Where are you staying? Let me come to your place,' he asked quickly, seeing her hesitation.

'Not my place, no. Are you at the Anna Beach?' It was the one vaguely touristy, comfortable place. She would have expected him to be there.

'Yes, exactly,' he agreed.

'Right, I'll go there with you, we can talk in the conservatory.'

He seemed to expel a sigh of relief. 'Thank you,' he said.

'First I have to leave a message.'

He produced his mobile phone.

'No, I don't know the number.' She went into the delicatessen and gave the olives back to Yanni. There was some discussion and it was agreed. Yanni's little brother would take the bag of olives and a note to the apartment over Vonni's craft shop. She scribbled something on a piece of card.

'You didn't even write twelve lines to this guy—I suppose I should be flattered,' Dieter said.

She smiled at him. 'No, it's not a guy, it's two guys actually.'

'You were so helpful today, Fiona. The parents said to thank you very much.'

'It was nothing, I love children.' Her voice was sad.

'You will have your own one day.'

'I don't know, Vonni, I really don't. Did you have children?'

'One,' Vonni said. 'A son, but it wasn't what you'd call straightforward.' Her tone meant that the subject was closed. She was prepared to talk, but not about her son.

'Vonni, I could be pregnant now,' Fiona said in a rush. 'And . . . well, it's not what you'd call straightforward either.'

'And the young man who has gone to Athens—does he know?'

'Sort of, I told him badly, you see.'

'You shouldn't be on your own now,' Vonni said.

'I'll go to Elsa's place,' Fiona said. But there was no reply there.

The people in David's house said he had not come home, so Vonni escorted her to the apartment above the craft shop.

'I'll wait here until I see you have someone to be with,' she said, and stood in the street as Fiona went up the steps to the apartment.

Vonni saw Thomas open the door and welcome Fiona in, then she went back to the harbour.

At the Anna Beach most of the journalists were at the checkout desk. Another job was over, another disaster recorded, and now they were heading off to the next one.

Dieter and Elsa went over to the big rattan chairs and low tables of the conservatory. Below them the dark blue sea lapped innocently against the rocks.

Dieter ordered coffee for two.

'Sorry.' Elsa called the waiter back. 'He is having coffee, I'm not. He ordered for me by mistake. I would like an *ouzo* and water, please.'

'Please don't be difficult,' Dieter begged her.

'Difficult? Choosing what I want to drink?' she asked, perplexed.

'No, you know, scoring points,' he said.

'Oh, I'm way beyond that now. Anyway, Dieter, you wanted to talk, so here I am. Talk to me.'

'No, I wanted *you* to talk, I wanted you to tell me why you disappeared, ran out on everything . . . to hide in a backwater like this.'

'I'm not hiding,' Elsa said indignantly. 'I resigned from my work formally; I am here under my own name; when you asked me to come and meet you I came. So where's the secrecy bit? And why do you call it a backwater? Look over at that desk—half the world's media is here . . . plenty of action I'd say.'

'I hate it when you're flippant, Elsa, it's an act, and it doesn't suit you.'

The waiter arrived. Elsa poured some water into the aniseed drink and watched it go cloudy. Then she drained it in one gulp.

'That was fast!' He was startled and amused as he began to sip his coffee.

'Well, why don't you finish yours too—then we can go to your room?'

'*What?*' he looked at her in astonishment.

'Your room,' she repeated as if he were a little deaf. 'You said talk, but you don't mean talk, do you? You mean screw.'

He looked at her. 'Elsa, there's no need to be crude about it all. That's not what we had.'

'Sorry, I thought that's just what we had every night you came to my apartment, and lunchtime too, when it could be managed.'

'Elsa, I love you, you love me, why on earth are you reducing it all to such coarse words?'

'So you don't want me to go to bed with you?' She looked at him innocently.

'You know I do.'

'Well, finish your coffee and get your key,' she said.

David didn't want to go back to the house where he was staying. The family were wiped out with grief over their dead son and he felt in the way. Fiona didn't want to walk all the way out to Eleni's house to sleep there alone in the knowledge that Shane had left her.

'Why don't you both stay here?' Thomas suggested suddenly. 'Fiona can have that room at the back, David can have the sofa bed.' He looked at their faces, both of them very grateful and relieved.

The Hotel Anna Beach had little bungalows facing the sea. Dieter opened his bungalow door with his key and stood back to let Elsa go in first. She didn't sit down but stood looking at the pictures on the walls, big blown-up photographs of the coast.

'This is not what I had expected,' he said.

'But we have agreed that it's what you'd like,' she smiled.

'That's not a real smile, Elsa,' he began.

'You taught me to smile for television. Teeth and eyes, you said. Teeth and eyes. I remember it well.'

'Please, my love, you *are* my love. Please don't be brittle.'

'No, indeed. And let's not waste time either.' Elsa had already taken off her navy jacket. Now she drew the cream linen dress over her head and laid it neatly on the back of the chair.

He was still very unsure.

She removed her lace bra and pants and placed them on top of her dress, then finally she stepped out of her smart navy sandals.

'You are so beautiful, and to think I believed I'd never see you again.' He looked at her in open admiration.

'Not you, Dieter. You get everything you want.' She put her arms around his neck and kissed him. And suddenly it was as if they had never been apart.

In the apartment over the craft shop, Fiona had gone to bed in the small white room that Vonni had furnished with a turquoise bedspread and a bright blue chair. The little white chest of drawers had a blue-framed mirror and some shells and pottery on top. It was cool and welcoming.

Fiona was weary and sad. It had been a nightmare of a day, and further nightmares were ahead. She didn't think she would sleep. Too much had happened and the future was too frightening. She gave a little sob. It was such a tragedy that people misunderstood Shane and brought out the worst in him.

She lay on the bed with its blue cover and cried herself to sleep.

In the room next door Thomas and David heard the sounds of weeping through the wall.

'She's crying over that bastard!' David whispered in amazement.

'I know, it's beyond comprehension,' Thomas whispered back.

And they sat there and waited until the sobs had died down. Then they smiled at each other in relief.

'Do you know what we're like?' David said. 'We're like the parents of a toddler who won't go to sleep.'

Thomas sighed. 'Yes, there was always that moment of not wanting to leave the room until you were *sure* he was asleep, and then just when you crept to the door he'd call you back. They were great days really.' He looked sad, thinking about his son.

David thought hard about what to say. He so often got it wrong.

'It's hard to understand women, isn't it?' he said eventually.

Thomas looked at him thoughtfully. 'It sure is, David, the exact same thought was going through my mind. Fiona crying over that drunken brute who would have beaten her senseless, Elsa going off with the man she had run a thousand miles to escape, my wife who used to tell me she loved poetry and literature and art living with a bonehead who has some exercise machine in every room of my house.' He sounded very bitter.

David looked at him, stricken. It had not been a good thing to say after all.

Dieter stroked Elsa's face.

'I must have been mad to think I had lost you,' he said.

She said nothing.

'It will all be fine again,' he said.

Still no reply.

'You could not love me like that and not mean it?' he said, just a little anxiously now.

Elsa lay there saying nothing.

'Speak to me, tell me that you'll come back with me and it will all be fine again . . .'

She still said nothing at all.

'Please, Elsa . . . please?'

She got up slowly from the bed and put on the big white fluffy robe that was hanging on the bathroom door, then sat down in the big bamboo chair looking at him.

'You'll come home with me, Elsa?'

'No, of course I won't. This is goodbye. You know this and I know this, so let's not be foolish, Dieter.'

'Goodbye?'

'Yes, goodbye. You are going home, I am going to go to . . . well, somewhere. I haven't decided exactly where yet.'

'This is insane, we were meant for each other. You know it, I know it. Everyone knows it.'

'No. Everyone does *not* know. A few people at work know and say nothing, because they take their lead from you. And, because you do not want us to go public, we have lived a secret life for two years. So less of the *everyone knows we are meant for each other* line.'

He looked at her, startled. 'We went into it, eyes open. Both of us,' he said.

'And I'm walking out of it, eyes open,' Elsa said calmly.

'So what are we talking about then?' He was genuinely bewildered. 'What do you want? Tell me. If you're holding a gun to my head and saying we must be married, then all right. If that's what it takes, all right, that's what we'll do.'

'I've heard of better proposals,' she said with a smile.

'Stop playing the fool. If it's the only way I can have you with me, I'll marry you. Be *proud* to marry you,' he added as an afterthought.

'No, thank you, Dieter. I don't want to marry you.'

'So what *do* you want?' he cried, in near despair.

'I want to get over you, to forget you, to make you no longer any part of my life.'

'You took an odd way to show all that.' He looked down at the bed she had so recently left.

Elsa shrugged. 'I told you. I no longer trust you, I don't admire you or respect you any more. Sex has nothing to do with those things. Sex is just sex, a short amount of pleasure, excitement. You told me that yourself, if you remember.'

'I do remember, but it was in totally different circumstances. We were talking about a meaningless drunken encounter at a film festival with some silly girl whose name I can't even remember.'

'Birgit. And she remembers you.'

'Only well enough to tell you and upset you over something that couldn't have mattered less.'

'I know, I realise that.'

'So tell me, Elsa, if you realise this, what in God's name is all this drama about? Why did you leave?'

'I wrote it in my letter.'

'You did *not* write it, you wrote some rubbish about responsibilities and lines having to be drawn.' His handsome face was working with emotion and his thick hair was tousled.

'Birgit told me about Monika,' Elsa said.

'Monika? Monika? But she was ages before I met you. We agreed that the past was past. Didn't we?'

'Yes.'

'So why bring her up? I swear I never saw her since I met you. Not even once.'

'I know.'

'So explain to me. I beg you. If you know I haven't seen or thought of Monika in years . . . what is this about?'

'You haven't seen or thought of your daughter either.'

'Ah,' Dieter said. 'Birgit really went to work, didn't she?'

Elsa said nothing.

'It was never meant to happen. I told Monika I wasn't ready to be a parent, to settle down. She knew that from the very start.' He was beginning to bluster now.

'How old is she, Dieter?' Elsa's voice was level.

He was genuinely confused. 'Monika?'

'Gerda. Your daughter.'

'I don't know . . . about eight or nine, I suppose. But all that has nothing to do with us, Elsa.'

'You fathered a child. That has got something to do with you.'

'No, it has not. That was not my fault. Monika was in charge of contraception. I have nothing to do with her child. We both began again.'

'But Gerda began with no father.'

'Stop calling her by her name, you don't know her.'

'You should have told me.'

'No. If I had that would have been wrong too. You would have said I was always hanging around a child from a previous relationship. Be fair, Elsa, you would not have liked that either.'

'I'd have liked it a hell of a lot more than a father who opted out and left a child hoping and wondering. It's my own story all over again. My father left home and I spent years waiting and hoping that he would write or call or come to see me.'

'It was different in your case: your father *had* lived at home with you. In my case I had nothing to do with Monika's child. There were no expectations.'

Elsa gave him a long look, then stood up.

'What do you want me to do?' he asked eventually.

'Nothing, Dieter.'

'You'd come back to me if I made some kind of link to this totally strange child?'

'No, I will not come back to you ever.'

'But all this . . .' Again he looked at the bed where they had made love. 'Did it mean nothing to you?'

'You know it did. It meant goodbye,' she said. She put on her dress and her sandals, slipped her underwear into her bag, and walked to the door.

'You *can't* do this!' he cried.

'Goodbye, Dieter,' she said and walked through the manicured little rock gardens of the Anna Beach towards the gate.

From his bungalow Dieter called after her. 'Don't go, Elsa, please don't go. I love you so much. Don't leave me . . .' But she walked on.

CHAPTER THREE

THOMAS HAD GONE OUT for hot fresh bread and figs for their breakfast. He made a large pot of coffee and rattled the cups.

Fiona emerged pale and tired-looking, but with a grateful smile. David came eagerly to the breakfast table.

'He spoils us, Fiona. Weren't we lucky to find a benefactor?'

'Oh, I know.' Fiona too was fervent. 'I feel much, much stronger today, I'm full of plans now, so I am.'

Thomas smiled at her. 'Tell us your plans,' he said.

'I'm going up to the station to see the chief of police. I'll ask him to help me find Shane. We were only in Athens for twenty-four hours on the way here, but he loved Syntagma Square. Perhaps Yorghis might know some policemen there who could give Shane a message. Then I'll go back to Eleni's and change my clothes—I've been wearing this dress for days—then I'm going to find Vonni and ask her does she need any help with the children.' Her eyes were bright and enthusiastic.

David too seemed to be energised. 'I'm going to walk up to that taverna and see Andreas again.'

'Later on, when they're all awake in California, I shall call my son,' said Thomas. 'But first I'm going to find Vonni. I'm going to *insist* that from now on she stays in her own bedroom. I'm getting antsy just having her living in that place in the yard.'

'*Antsy?*' Fiona asked.

'I know, it's a great word, isn't it. Means something irritates you, gives you ants in your pants.'

'Shane will love that,' Fiona said happily.

Elsa was in her apartment. She knew that she would not sleep so she sat on her balcony and watched the dawn come up in Aghia Anna. Then she went in, had a long shower and washed her hair. She put on a fresh yellow cotton dress and sat down on the balcony again to watch the ferry getting ready to leave.

He would leave on the 8 a.m. for Athens. She was utterly certain of this. Dieter knew that she wasn't coming with him, so why wait for the 11 a.m.? He wasn't a person to hang about.

And then she saw him, his hair tousled, wearing an open-necked shirt, and gripping that leather bag she had seen so often. His eyes were raking the crowds around as if he were going to see her in their number. He saw nothing, but he knew her well enough to assume that she was watching. He put down his bag and raised both his arms in the air.

'I love you, Elsa!' he called out. 'Wherever you are I will always love you.'

Some of the young men near him clapped him on the back approvingly. Declaring love was good.

Elsa sat like stone as the little ferry sailed across the sea to Piraeus, the harbour of Athens. The tears dropped slowly down her face and splashed into her coffee and onto her lap.

'David, my friend, welcome, welcome.' Andreas was delighted to see him.

David wished that he could have a father like this, a man whose face lit up when he approached, not a man whose features had set in discontent and disappointment over his only son for as long as David could remember. Andreas and David talked easily about the sad funeral and how Aghia Anna would never be the same again.

'Did you know Manos well?' David asked.

'Yes, we all know each other here, there are no secrets. We know everyone's history. Manos used to come to play with Adoni and little Stavros when he was a child. They made a swing on that tree over there. He used to come up here to escape from his family—there were eight of them. Adoni was an only child so we were happy to have friends come up here to play with him.' Andreas nodded several times. 'Now, come, David. Share a lunch with me. We won't see many visitors here today.'

David looked at the open cabinets of food the old man had prepared and he felt a lump in his throat. To have got all this ready and then for nobody to arrive . . .

'I never tried that big pasta dish,' he began.

'David, if you don't mind, I can freeze that one. I only make it this morning. Could I persuade you to have the *moussaka* or the *calamari*?'

'I'd prefer the *moussaka*. I only said the pasta because I didn't want all your hard work to go to waste,' David said.

'What a kind person you are. Sit here in the sunshine and I will get the glasses and plates . . .'

And David sat wondering what that foolish young man was doing in Chicago when he could be here.

Eleni welcomed Fiona back. It was a shock to see all Shane's things gone, his crumpled shirts and jeans, his canvas bag, his tin of tobacco and whatever else it might contain. Fiona had hoped desperately that he might have left a note for her with Eleni, but it hadn't happened. She felt very dizzy suddenly. Perhaps it was the stuffy room or the realisation that Shane really had gone out of her life. She felt as if she might faint, but she steeled herself in front of the kindly Eleni, whose face was sympathetic and pitying.

Then she felt a hot, wet sensation on her thighs.

It must be sweat. It was such a hot day.

But as she looked down at her sandals she knew what it was.

And Eleni knew too, as she saw the blood. The Greek woman helped her to a chair. 'Ela, ela, ela,' she said and ran for towels.

'Eleni, could you find Vonni for me, please. Vonni . . . you know?'

'Xero, yes, Vonni,' Eleni said, and shouted down to the children.

Fiona closed her eyes. Vonni would be here soon and would know what to do.

Vonni was sitting opposite Thomas in her apartment over the craft shop.

'I've told you before, I'm telling you again, you are paying me an enormous number of euros so that this is your place. Because of you I am a rich woman, so I will not take your pity and sleep in your house.'

'Have you no concept of friendship, Vonni?' he asked. 'I am asking you, as my friend: sleep in that little room you decorated so beautifully. Sleep there, not where chickens are crapping all over you.'

Vonni pealed with laughter. 'Oh, Thomas, you are so Californian, so hygienic, there are no chickens crapping on me. A couple of hens . . .'

Just at that moment, they heard children shouting something urgently up the staircase.

'I must go,' she said, standing up.

He reached out and grabbed her wrist. 'Vonni, you are not going anywhere unless you agree to what I offer. Do you hear me?'

'I hear, I agree,' she said to his surprise.

'Good, well then, OK, you can go.'

'Come with me if you like, you can help, get us a taxi from the square.' To his even greater surprise she snatched some towels from his bathroom and ran down the steps to talk in Greek to two little boys.

'What's happening?' he asked as he ran after her.

'What's happening is . . . that Fiona is losing the baby of that little shit who beat her up.'

Thomas ran for a taxi and Vonni bundled Eleni's two little sons into the back seat, congratulating them for having found her. A taxi ride was a rare treat and they were beaming with pleasure.

When they arrived at Eleni's house, they asked the taxi to wait in case they might need him. Thomas stayed downstairs watching the little boys play and make occasional journeys to stroke the car in which they had travelled. Vonni had gone upstairs and he could hear the women's voices as they spoke in English and Greek. From what he could make out, Fiona would be all right.

Then Vonni came down and reassured him.

'She's going to be fine, she's lost some blood but she's a nurse after all and she's a sensible little thing about everything except that fool. She thinks he'll be upset when he hears. God protect us!'

'Is she all right staying here?'

'I don't think so. They don't speak English in any real sense . . . what I was thinking—' Vonni began.

'Was that she might come and stay with us,' Thomas interrupted.

'No, not that at all. I was going to suggest she spent a couple of days with Elsa, the German girl.'

Thomas shook his head. 'I think Elsa's a bit tied up with her own affairs just now, better if she comes to us,' he said.

'You might find she's not tied up any more,' Vonni said. 'I hear her German friend left on the eight a.m. ferry.'

'I imagine she must be very upset then.' Thomas was pessimistic.

'No, I think it was her doing, but we needn't necessarily say that we know all this?' Vonni suggested.

'I expect you know where she lives?' Thomas said, smiling.

'I know the apartment building, but perhaps you could take the taxi that's outside and ask her?'

'Would I be the right person?' He was doubtful.

'Nobody better. I'll wait here until you come back.'

Eleni's little boys had never known such a day.

A trip in a taxi, people coming and going, sheets and towels being pinned on the line in great numbers to wave in the sunshine. The tall American man with the funny trousers had brought them a big watermelon to share when he came back the second time. They went behind the house and ate it all, then planted the seeds in the earth.

The American man, who was waiting near the taxi, watched them with a pleased expression on his face. Then the woman who had been sick came down with Vonni and their mother and the smart woman in a yellow dress who looked like a film star.

The sick woman's bag had been packed for her, so she must be leaving for good. She kept talking about money and their mother kept shaking her head. Eventually the man with the mad trousers, who must be a millionaire, travelling all day in a taxi, insisted their mother take some notes and then they were all gone.

Except Vonni, who sat down to have coffee with their mother.

'I'll only stay a couple of days until I get myself together,' Fiona promised.

'I'll be glad of your company,' Elsa assured her as she took out Fiona's clothes from the canvas bag, shook them and hung them up. 'There's an iron here, we can get all domestic later on.'

Fiona looked at Elsa's cream linen dress and navy jacket drying on hangers out on the balcony.

'Aren't you disciplined, Elsa, that's what you were wearing at the funeral yesterday, and look, you have it all laundered already.'

'I'll never wear either of them again but I wanted to give them away to someone, so I washed them first.' Elsa spoke calmly. 'Try it on later, and if it fits you, Fiona, and suits you, then you are more than welcome to it.'

Fiona lay back against the pillow and closed her eyes. It was all too much to take in.

Elsa pulled the curtains to darken the room. 'I'm going to sit and read. It's too hot outside so I'll be here in the room with you.'

'Will you be able to read in the dark?' Fiona asked.

'Sure. There's a nice beam of light coming in here.' She settled in a chair by the window.

'Did you meet him, Elsa?' Fiona asked.

'Yes. Yes, I did.'

'And are you glad you did?'

'Well, it was just to say goodbye, really. It had to be said, it wasn't easy, but it's finished now.'

'Dead easy to say, but not to do.' Fiona's voice sounded sleepy. Soon she was asleep, breathing regularly. Elsa looked at her as she slept. She must be about twenty-three or twenty-four, but she looked even younger. Hadn't it all been a great mercy?

Thomas had worked out when best to call his son, Bill. It would be when the boy was having breakfast. He dialled the number, wondering what the chances were that he would get straight through to his son.

As it happened, it was Andy who answered the phone.

'Well, hi, Thomas. Good of you to call the other night. One helluva scene that must have been.'

'Yeah, it was very tragic.' Thomas felt his voice becoming clipped and curt. The man was insufferable, calling a catastrophe that had ripped the soul out of a small village 'one helluva scene'. 'Is Bill around?'

'He's helping his mother do the dishes,' Andy said, as if that's all there was to it.

'Sure, and could you perhaps tell him he might dry his hands and come talk to his father phoning from the other side of the world?'

'I'll see if he's through.' Andy was genial about it. In the distance Thomas was aware that Vonni was watching him from the kitchen door. It didn't help his mood.

'Hi, Dad.' Bill always sounded delighted to hear him.

'How are things, son. Good?'

'Yeah, fine.'

'So what are you going to do today? It's only morning there, isn't it?'

'Yes, well, we'll be going to the shopping mall first. I'm getting new sneakers and then Andy is going to take me for a run to try them out.'

'Sounds great,' said Thomas, in a voice that sounded sepulchral across the thousands of miles between them. 'I miss you, son.'

'Yeah, Dad, and I miss you too. A lot. But it *was* you who went away,' the child answered.

'Who told you that? Was it your mother? Andy? Listen to me, Bill. We discussed this endlessly; better for me to go and give you space together as a family—'

'No, Dad. She doesn't say that,' Bill interrupted. 'And Andy doesn't either. I just said I missed you and that I was still here and you were the one that was gone.'

'I'm sorry, Bill. We're all upset here. So many people died. Please forgive me. I'll call again soon.'

Vonni came towards him with a brandy.

'You made a right dog's dinner out of that,' she said.

'You don't understand what it is to have a son,' he said to her, willing the tears away from his eyes.

'Why the hell do you assume I don't have a son?' she asked him, her eyes blazing.

'You do?' He was astonished.

'Yes, so you don't have a monopoly on being a parent.'

'And where is he? Why isn't he with you?'

'Because like you I made a mess of things.'

Yorghis drove up to the taverna. Someone had given him a big leg of lamb. He thought maybe Andreas could cook it for his customers. Andreas explained, sadly, that nobody but David had come to the taverna today and it didn't look likely that anyone would come tonight.

But then Andreas had an idea. Why didn't they cook it at the police station, give all those men who had worked so hard at the funeral a real dinner?

They would ask David and his friends to join them, and Vonni. Andreas scraped up all the salads into a big bowl. He was pleased and excited at the thought of cooking for people rather than sitting in his empty taverna.

'It's not very comfortable, of course, in the police station,' Yorghis said doubtfully. 'Not very welcoming.'

'We'll get those long red cushions. We can put them on benches.' Andreas would not let the idea die. 'David, run up to Adoni's room and get them, will you?'

David looked at him in surprise. Adoni had been gone for years in Chicago yet he still had his own room in this house?

'At the top of the stairs on the left,' Yorghis advised him and David hastened up the narrow steps.

The room had pictures of Panathinaikos, the Athens football team, and posters of a Greek dance troupe; it had images of the Panayia, the Virgin Mary. He was a man of varied tastes, the missing Adoni.

His bed was made as if he were coming back that night, with a bright red rug folded at the end. On the window seats were long red cushions.

David looked out of the window. The afternoon sun shone down on the hills, over the olive groves to the blue bay of Aghia Anna. What could that boy be looking at in Chicago, Illinois, that would be one-tenth as beautiful as this? He grabbed them and went down to help them pack Yorghis's van.

'This will cheer us all up, brother Yorghis,' Andreas said with a happy smile.

They called first on Thomas and left David there. Thomas sounded pleased at the prospect of the feast and said he would go out to get some wine. Vonni said she'd check out the situation with Elsa and Fiona. She explained briefly to David what had happened to Fiona.

'That's terrible,' David said. 'But maybe it might be all for—'

'Don't even go there, David. You might think it, I might think it, but Fiona most definitely does *not* think it. I thought I'd warn you.'

'Very wise,' David agreed. 'I always say the wrong thing anyway. But what of Elsa? I thought that she had gone off with her German friend?'

'I know,' Vonni said. 'But to be honest, I wouldn't go there either!'

The young policemen were delighted with the great smells of cooking meat, basted with garlic and oregano. It had been an exhausting and draining time. It was good to relax with their boss, his brother, Vonni and the four tourists. One of the girls looked like a beauty queen, the other very washed out, as if she had been ill.

The two men were very different: one tall and lanky in ludicrous baggy Bermuda shorts with pockets, the other small and serious with spectacles.

Andreas carved proudly and the moonlight made patterns on the sea as the clouds raced across the sky.

'It seems so long since we were in Kalatriada,' Fiona said.

'When the night was full of rain beating against the roof and the walls. It was only two nights ago,' Elsa said. 'And so much has happened since.' She reached out and held Fiona's hand as a gesture of solidarity.

Down near the harbour they saw a group of young men gather in front of the little house that belonged to Maria and Manos. And soon they saw other people leave the cafés and restaurants to join them.

'What's happening?' Thomas asked, anxious in case anything was wrong.

Yorghis was peering down. 'I can't tell. One of you boys go down and see is everything all right.' He pointed at one of the policemen.

Vonni spoke gently. 'It's no problem. Some of the young men said they would like to dance tonight in honour of Manos and his friends, outside his house, in memory of how he used to dance *Syrtaki*.'

'There isn't usually dancing after a funeral here,' Yorghis said.

'This isn't a usual funeral,' Vonni said quietly.

And as they watched, twelve men with black trousers and white shirts lined up, arms on each other's shoulders. The bouzouki players played a few chords and then they began. Bending, swooping, leaping in the night, as Manos and his friends had done until just a few short days ago.

Maria and her children sat on chairs outside their little house. When all this was a long-distant memory, perhaps the children would recall the night that Aghia Anna had come out to dance for their father. The crowd grew ever bigger and they could see people wiping tears from their eyes.

Then the crowd began to clap in time to the music and dancing, every single person joining in. From their verandah at the police station, the group watched too. All of them were wordless, watching the scene. It was so different to anything they had ever seen before.

Elsa passed a paper table napkin to Fiona who was crying openly.

'What a wonderful thing to do,' Fiona said when she could speak. 'I'll never forget this night. And those same stars are shining on Athens and on all our homes everywhere.'

CHAPTER FOUR

IN FIONA'S HOME they were talking about her as they did almost every evening. Her mother was looking at the pictures of Aghia Anna in the *Evening Herald*.

'Imagine Fiona being in that very place!' she said in surprise.

'Imagine!' her husband grunted.

'But, Sean, it *was* good of her to ring in case we'd be worried about her. At least she thought that we might be concerned.'

'Why would we be concerned? We didn't know where the hell she was except joined at the hip to that lout.' Fiona's father found very few silver linings in the whole situation, very little cause to see the bright side. He picked up the remote control and turned on the television deliberately to end the conversation.

His wife went over to the set and turned it off.

'Maureen! Why did you do that? I wanted to watch that.'

'No, you didn't want to watch anything, you just didn't want to talk about Fiona. But she's your child as much as mine.'

'She's not a child, according to you . . . she's a woman of twenty-four. She is entitled to make her own decisions, that's what you said.'

'Sean, I said that we were only going to alienate her by attacking Shane, that she was old enough to know the choices she was making. I didn't say that any of them were right.'

'Huh,' he said.

'I want you to listen to me. I invited Barbara around tonight to talk to her about everything. They've been friends for fifteen years and she's as upset as we are.'

'She is not. She's just as bad as Fiona. If a drug-crazed drunken loser like Shane turned up for her, she'd be off too. They're all the same.'

'This is *not* the way we must talk, we must try to keep a lifeline open to Fiona, tell her that we are here when she wants us.'

'I'm not sure that I am here if she wants us. She said some very hurtful things to you as well as to me, remember?'

'That's because we said things to her about Shane that she thought were hurtful.' Maureen struggled to be fair. 'We can't help who we fall in love with, Sean.'

'Yes, we can. We don't all go out looking for lunatics like Fiona did.'
He was unbending.

The doorbell rang.

'That's Barbara. Be nice, be reasonable please, Sean, she may be our
only link with Fiona; our only hope.'

In David's house in the smart suburbs of Manchester they had been
looking at the televised events in Aghia Anna.

'It must have been a terrible thing to see,' David's mother said.

'It must indeed have been terrible if he telephoned us,' his father
agreed.

'He has been away for six weeks, Harold, we have had ten letters
from him. He does keep in touch.'

'Some of them were only picture postcards,' David's father said.

They sat in silence for a while.

'Miriam, should I have been different, please tell me?' He looked at
her begging for the truth.

She reached for his hand and stroked it. 'You have been a wonderful
husband, a wonderful father,' she said.

'So why is our son out in this one-horse town in Greece if I was so
wonderful? Should I have said something like *be* an artist, *be* a poet, *be*
whatever you want to be? Should I? Is this what was needed? Tell me!'

'I don't think so, he always knew you wanted him to run the company, he knew that since his bar mitzvah.'

'So why was that such a crime? I built up this business for my father.
He came to England with nothing. I worked day and night to try to
show him that his suffering had all been worth while. I try to hand over
to my only son a thriving business, that's so bad?'

'I know, Harold, I know all this.' She was trying to soothe him.

'If you understand it, why can't he?'

'Let me tell him, Harold, please let me tell him.'

'No, a thousand times no. I will not have his pity. If I can't have his
company, I will not settle for his pity.'

Shirley and Bill came back from the shopping mall. Andy had gone up
to the university to motivate some of the students training for a
marathon.

Bill helped his mother to unpack the shopping and stack it away.

'You're a great kid,' she said unexpectedly.

'Am I?'

'Sure you are. I've never loved anyone on earth more than I love you.'

'Aw, come on, Mom . . .' He was embarrassed.

'No, I mean it. Truly I do. There's something truly earth-shaking about the love you have for your child, it's unconditional.'

'What's that?'

'It means that there are no ifs and buts. You are this special kind of person, nothing can get in the way of it.'

'And would Dad feel the same about me as you do?'

'Totally the same. Your dad and I didn't see eye to eye about a few things, Bill, you know that, but we both thought and do think you were the best thing that ever happened to us. We just want the best for you.'

'Does Dad still love you, Mom?'

'No, honey, he still respects me and likes me I think, but love, no. We just share our love for you.'

Bill thought about it for a while. 'So why doesn't he act like that?' he asked.

'I think he does,' Shirley said, surprised.

'I don't think he does,' Bill said. 'I think he wants me to miss him and be sorry he's not here. But *he's* the one who went away. I didn't. I stayed right here.'

Birgit saw Claus coming into the newsroom.

'You're back from Greece!' she said, delighted.

'Hi, Birgit.' Claus, the chief cameraman, had no illusions that Birgit was happy to see him. If he were back, then Dieter would be back too. That was what interested her.

Claus sighed. Dieter didn't even try, and the women just fell over themselves for him. He waited until Birgit asked about Dieter. He assumed it would be thirty seconds. He was wrong: it was even sooner.

'Dieter back too?' she asked casually.

'No, he stayed on for a bit. He met an old friend out there. Amazing coincidence.'

'An old friend? Some guy he knew in the press corps?'

'No, it was some woman who used to work here, actually. He met Elsa.'

Birgit was a hard woman. It was a pleasing moment to see her face.

'But it's all over between them,' Birgit said.

'I wouldn't hold your breath, Birgit,' Claus said, and moved on.

Adoni looked at the newspaper pictures of the village where he had grown up. He saw the face of his friend Manos, whom he had known all his life. There was a picture of Maria too. Adoni had danced at their wedding.

How extraordinary that newspapers all over America would have pictures and stories of his home town. But he wouldn't tell anyone here in Chicago. The people here in the greengrocer's where he worked knew little about him and his background. If he told them then they would have to know why he didn't stay in touch. They would learn about his fight with his father, the years of silence. They would never understand. These people that he worked with just lived for family, their fathers were in and out of their houses all the time.

Of course he could call his father to offer sympathy over what had happened to Aghia Anna. But then his father would take this as some sign of weakness, a giving in, an admission that Adoni had been in the wrong. His father knew where he was. If he wanted to say something then let him say it.

Shane didn't know how to use the Métro in Athens. When they had been here before Fiona had worked it out. He knew that he wanted to go to the Exarchia area, because he had heard on the ferry that it was full of ouzo shops and tavernas. He still had plenty of grass in his bag, he could sell it there. Then he would sit down, work out what he would do. He was free now, free as a bird. Nobody would be coming at him with cracked notions that he should be a waiter in some backwater. Fiona must have been soft in the head to suggest it.

In the end, of course, like everyone else she had let him down. But then Shane had learned to expect that of people. And she wasn't really pregnant. He knew that. If she had been she wouldn't have gone off and left him when he was in the police station. She could well be on her way home to her awful family in Dublin.

He worked out that he needed the Métro stop called Omonia. God, they had really ridiculous names here, and writing that nobody could read as well.

'Come in, Barbara.' Fiona's mother ushered her in.

'You're out late.' Fiona's father didn't sound very welcoming.

'You know how it is, Mr Ryan, eight a.m. to eight p.m. and we're an hour from the hospital.' Barbara threw herself into an armchair as she had done for years in this house, her red hair tousled, her face tired after a long day's work

'Will you have tea, Barbara, or something stronger?'

'Oh, I could murder a gin, Mrs Ryan, specially if we are going to talk about Shane,' Barbara said apologetically.

'Sean?'

'Well, if we're going to have to talk about him then I need an anaesthetic, too,' he said.

'I was wondering if we could write to Fiona and say that we sort of misunderstood the situation.' Fiona's mother served the gin and tonics and sat down looking from one to the other.

Her husband glowered at her. 'I think we understood the situation only too well. Our daughter is infatuated with a bog-ignorant criminal. What else is there to understand?'

'But it hasn't worked, our saying that. Fiona's hundreds of miles away. And I miss her, Sean, every moment of the day.'

'I agree with Mr Ryan, actually,' Barbara said. 'We didn't misunderstand anything. Shane is a real bastard because he manipulates her, he makes things seem to be her fault, not his. He plays the victim card.'

'What I find the hardest is that they say they *love* each other.' Maureen Ryan's face was troubled.

'Shane's never loved anyone but himself. He'll only stay with Fiona for as long as it suits him, and then she'll be alone, miles away with no friends and humiliated. She won't want to come back to us. She'll know that we'll all be thinking, I told you so, even if we manage not to say it.'

'You miss her as much as we do.' Fiona's father sounded surprised.

'Of course I do, I miss her at work every day and I miss going out with her in the evening. I think of a dozen things to tell her and then remember she's gone . . . I was wondering if we could try to build some kind of a bridge?'

'What kind of bridge?' Sean Ryan didn't hold out much hope.

'Well, could you write her a letter sort of implying that we all know now she and Shane will be together in the long run? And I could do the same, like asking would she and Shane be home for your silver wedding or Christmas, something like that?'

'But we can't assume that she's going to be with him for ever, Barbara. What kind of message are we giving the other children if they think we accept Shane as part of their sister's life?'

'Listen, Mrs Ryan, he *is* part of her life. They've gone off to live together, for God's sake. But deep down I've a feeling it's not going to last that long, and if we pretend that we think it's normal then we stop being part of the Bad Cruel World that's beating up on Poor Misunderstood Shane.' Barbara looked from one to the other. 'Believe me, I don't like it either. And I don't like sitting here talking about my friend Fiona behind her back. But I think that we've got to do something or else we'll have lost her entirely.'

The letter was pushed through the door and fell to the floor. Miriam Fine went to see who could possibly be delivering something by hand at this time of night.

It was a big thick envelope addressed to them both. She brought it in to her husband and they opened it together.

It was the confirmation that Harold Fine had won the coveted Businessman of the Year award and details of the ceremony. It would be presented in November at the Town Hall before an invited audience. They hoped that he would ask a group of family and friends to join them for drinks first with the mayor and dinner later.

'Oh, Harold, I'm so pleased for you, to see it there in black and white,' she said, tears in her eyes. 'David will be so proud and pleased. We'll tell him the actual invitation has arrived. I know he will come home for it all,' Miriam said.

'Let's not be too confident, Miriam. From where David stands, a Businessman of the Year would be the worst thing he could encounter.'

Hannah, a secretary in the television centre, had overheard the conversation between Claus and Birgit. She could hardly credit it. Elsa had gone so far away to leave what had been the love of her life and this catastrophe had brought them together.

'Claus, excuse me, can I have a word?'

'Of course!' Everyone liked Hannah, a bright, helpful, confident young woman. She had been Elsa's friend.

'I just wanted to ask is Elsa coming back?' Hannah asked. She too spent no time beating about the bush.

'I wish I could tell you what has happened, but truthfully I don't know,' Claus said. 'Dieter told us to go home ahead of him. So of course we did. But she looked different. She wasn't the same Elsa that we know. She was changed, somehow, as if she had made up her mind.'

'I see.' Hannah was doubtful.

'I know you probably think that men are hopeless about reading the signs, but, believe me, even you would have found it difficult to know what was happening.'

Adoni decided he would telephone his father. It would be evening in Greece, his father would be at the taverna. It would be busy so his father would not be able to talk for long, which was just as well. Adoni would say that he was very sorry about the tragedy and that he sent his sympathies. They would not talk about what had passed between them.

He could hear the telephone ringing.

It rang and rang and there was no reply. He must have dialled the wrong number. He dialled again. But in the empty taverna the phone rang and nobody answered.

Adoni hung up. In many ways it was probably all for the best.

Shane found exactly the place he was looking for. This was his clientele. It was just the kind of place he would have gone if he had been looking to score. It didn't matter that he didn't know the language. There was an international language over this sort of thing. He spoke to a guy who was some kind of thicko, who understood nothing, then to another who shrugged at him. The third man looked more promising.

'How much?' the man asked. He was small, with quick dark eyes.

'How much do you want?' Shane asked.

'Well, how much do you have?' the man wanted to know.

'Enough,' said Shane.

At that moment there was the flash of a Polaroid camera and then another. Right in his face.

'What the hell—?' Shane began. Then he felt a hand on his collar.

The face of the man with the quick dark eyes was an inch from Shane's face. 'Listen to me good. We have two pictures of you, one in this bar, one we will show to the police. If they see you trying to deal again it will be very, very bad for you.'

'You *said* you wanted to buy.' Shane choked the words out somehow.

'This is my father's bar, my family runs this place. I would go very far from here very quickly. That is my uncle holding you. He is expecting you to apologise and leave. In twenty seconds from now.'

'I don't know how to apologise in Greek.'

'*Signomi* will do.'

'*Signomi!*' Shane cried over his shoulder to the older man who was holding him. Then the grip was released and Shane staggered out of the door into the warm Athens night.

CHAPTER FIVE

THOMAS WOKE with a slight headache. It didn't take him long to remember why. The red wine they had drunk last night at the police station had not been allowed to age for any respectable time. Yorghis said it could well have been made last month.

Still, a couple of cups of good coffee would cure that. Maybe he would go out and get fresh oranges and hot crusty rolls for breakfast. Possibly Vonni would have a hangover too.

But when he got up, he saw the door to the spare bedroom was open. The bed was neatly made. No sign of any personal possessions around the place. She was truly using it only as a bed for the night. He wondered where she was now.

She was such a self-sufficient little figure, hair braided around her head, suntanned lined face with its broad smile, that made it impossible to know what age she was. Hard to learn from anyone how long she had been in Aghia Anna. And she told little or nothing about herself, so you would be a long time guessing.

Thomas yawned and went into the kitchen. She had beaten him to it. There were four large oranges on the table and, wrapped in a little check cloth to keep them warm, some fresh bread rolls. Thomas sighed with pleasure and sat down to his breakfast.

Fiona was still asleep, so Elsa left her a note.

> *Gone down to the harbour. Didn't want to wake you. Why don't you come and meet me at noon. Bring a swimsuit if you feel like it and we can have something in that nice place with the blue and white tablecloths. I can't remember its name. I'd like that. Love, Elsa*

She walked through the narrow streets looking at the people washing the pavements in front of their shops, or laying out their wares. In the cafés and restaurants they were laboriously writing their menus on big blackboards. There wasn't the same carefree, cheerful way as before the accident. But at least they were getting on with it. Like Elsa herself.

She was able now to nod and smile at people she passed, saying, 'Kalimera,' here and there. But she had never felt so isolated. No family, no love, no job, and since she had left Germany . . . no home.

Somebody in a shabby van hooted at her. Elsa put up her hand to shield her eyes from the sun and see who it was.

It was Vonni with a load of children.

'We're going for a swim on a really fantastic beach you might not know. Would you like to come?'

'Great, I said I'd meet Fiona at noon in the harbour but I'd be back by then, right? Elsa was glad that she had her bathing suit and straw hat in her basket. She was now prepared to go anywhere.

Vonni nodded at her in agreement. 'Oh, we'll be back by then. I can't expose children to the midday sun.' She said something in Greek to the five- and six-year-olds in the back of the van and they all smiled at her and chorused, 'Yassu, Elsa!'

Elsa felt a sudden lump in her throat as if, in a small way, she did belong somewhere. Just for a while.

David had hired a bicycle and was cycling five miles to where the family he was staying with had told him there was a wonderful beach. He puffed up the hills and sailed down the slopes on the other side. The countryside was so beautiful. Why would anyone want to live in a crowded city?

But when he arrived at the beach, to his disappointment he saw a parked van. And then he saw Elsa and that strange older woman, Vonni, already down by the sea with eight or nine children.

David lay on a grassy mound and watched them all. Elsa was so beautiful in her elegant turquoise swimsuit, her short blonde hair reflecting the sun; she had a light suntan and moved gracefully in and out of the sea, playing with the children.

Vonni, small and swarthy, her hair in plaits over her head, wore a functional black swimming costume that would not have been in fashion twenty years back. She too ran in and out of the little waves calling and encouraging the youngsters to join her, and helping the more timid ones by holding a hand under the chin.

David longed to join them but he felt he would be intruding. Just at that moment, Elsa saw him.

'*Ela, ela*, David, come and swim, it is total magic!'

Awkwardly he went to join them. He had his swimming trunks on under his shorts. He took off his glasses and left them on top of his neatly folded clothes.

He greeted the children. '*Yassas, ime Anglos.*'

'As if they ever thought you were anything but English!' Vonni said, teasing him.

'I suppose so,' David said ruefully.

One of the children splashed him with a handful of water. 'Very good, *poli kala*,' he said.

'I hope you have six children, David, you'll be a wonderful father,' Vonni said unexpectedly.

Fiona woke up and read the note. Wasn't life so odd that she should meet by accident such a kind and generous person? Elsa was almost as good a friend to her as Barbara had been. Shane would be so glad when she told him. She washed her hair and used Elsa's hairdryer. She didn't look too bad. Pale, a bit wishy-washy but nothing that would frighten the birds off the trees, as her father used to say.

Fiona thought about her father. He had been such a loving, marvellous man until she had brought Shane home. She wished in many ways that she could be there for her parents' silver wedding party.

But that was her father's mistake.

He had been so definite about Shane. No time must be spent thinking about it now. She must get on with her life until Shane sent for her. She would dress as well as she could and then walk slowly down to the harbour. She would show her best face.

They left David sitting on the beach learning his ten phrases for the day, then Vonni let the children off in the square and dropped Elsa off from her van at the harbour shortly after 11 a.m.

'Thank you for your company,' Vonni said.

'Why do people in Aghia Anna hand over their children to you, Vonni?' Elsa asked.

'I don't know. They've seen me here for many years now and believe I am fairly reliable, I suppose.' Vonni was not at all certain.

'How many years, Vonni?'

'I came here over thirty years ago.'

'What?' Elsa said in shock.

'You asked me. I told you.' Vonni looked impassive.

'Indeed. Forgive me. I am sure you do not want people to intrude.'

'As it happens, I don't mind people asking reasonable questions. I came to Aghia Anna to be with the man I loved.'

'And were you with him?'

'Yes and no. I'll tell you another time.' Vonni revved up the van and drove away.

'Thomas!'

He looked up at her from where he sat on an wooden box looking out of the mouth of the harbour to sea where the wind was lifting the waves.

'Good to see you, Elsa. Would you like a nice easy chair?' He pulled over another box for her. 'Your hair is damp, were you swimming?'

'Yes, there's a truly beautiful beach in a little lagoon about five miles away. Up that coast,' she pointed.

'Don't tell me you've walked ten miles today!' He was disconcerted.

'No, shamefully, Vonni drove me both ways. We met David there. He's the fit one, he has actually hired a bicycle. Am I imagining it, Thomas, or is the sea much more attractive here than anywhere else?'

'It sure beats my part of California anyway, very flat where we are. Nice sunsets, but no surf, no changing colours like this.'

'No wonder people get inspired by the place. I mean, I know it's meant to be a reflection of the sky, but don't tell me that water isn't dark blue.'

'"Roll on, thou deep and dark blue Ocean—roll!"' Thomas quoted.

To his astonishment Elsa continued, '"Ten thousand fleets sweep over thee in vain; Man marks the earth with ruin—his control stops with the shore . . ."'

He looked at her open-mouthed. 'You can quote English poetry. How dare you be so well educated!'

Elsa laughed, pleased at the praise. 'We had an English teacher at school who loved Byron. If you had picked another poet I wouldn't have done so well!'

'But I mean it. I couldn't quote you one line of German poetry. What am I talking about? I can't even speak a word of the German language.'

'Yes, you can, you said *Wunderbar* and *Prosit* last night,' she consoled him.

'I think I said *Prosit* a little too often last night as it happens . . . oh, I've remembered another German word. *Reisefieber*.'

Elsa pealed with laughter. 'What a marvellous word to know . . . how on earth do you know that?'

'It means "journey fever", doesn't it? Being in a panic at airports and railway stations?'

'That's exactly what it means, Thomas. Imagine you knowing that!'

They sat companionably together as if they had known each other all their lives.

Vonni drove the van back to Maria's house, where Maria was sitting at the kitchen table in front of an empty coffee cup. 'It's getting harder, not easier,' she said. 'I thought that was Manos coming back in his van.'

'Of course it's getting harder. It's sinking in and that's what hurts so much.'

Vonni hung up the keys on a hook on the wall and then produced a pot of hot coffee and some flaky *baklava*. Then she sat down at the table. 'The dancing was beautiful last night. He would have loved it,' she said.

'I know.' Maria was weeping again. 'And last night I felt strong and as if his spirit was still here. That feeling has gone today.'

'Well, it might come back when I tell you my plan,' Vonni said, passing her a piece of kitchen paper.

'Plan?'

'Yes, I'm going to teach you to drive.'

Maria actually managed a watery smile. 'Drive? Me drive? Vonni, stop joking. Manos wouldn't even let me hold the keys of the van.'

'But he would want you to drive now, I know he would.'

'No, Vonni, he wouldn't, he'd think I'd kill myself and everyone in Aghia Anna.'

'Well, we'll have to prove him wrong then,' Vonni said. 'Because you'll have to drive for your new job.'

'Job?'

'Oh, yes, you're going to help me in the shop, aren't you? And a lot of your work will involve driving to places like Kalatriada and collecting stuff. Save me trekking for miles on buses.'

'But you can drive there in Manos's van, Vonni.'

'No, I can't. Manos would hate that, he saved long and hard for that van, he wouldn't want you just handing it away. No, he'd be so proud of you if you used it for your work.'

And, magically, Maria smiled again. A real smile this time. It was as if she saw his spirit back in the house again.

'Right, Manos, this is going to amaze you,' she said.

David came across them during the driving lesson up on a big patch of waste ground at the top of the town.

'*Siga, siga,*' Vonni was screaming as the van jerked and shuddered.

'What does *siga* mean? I've often heard it,' David asked, interested.

'Well, you never heard it said with such fervour as this time.' Vonni had got out of the van, mopped her brow and taken some deep breaths. Maria sat gripping the steering wheel as if her hands had been glued to it.

'It means "slow down", but the lady doesn't get the concept.'

'That's Manos's, isn't it?' David peered at the woman still clutching the wheel. 'Does she need to drive?'

'I thought so this morning, now I'm not so sure. But of course I had to open my big mouth and suggest it.' Vonni sighed.

'I taught my mother to drive when no one else could,' David said slowly. 'Perhaps I could give it a go?'

'How did you do it?' Vonni said, with hope beginning to show in her eyes.

'I was very patient. I never raised my voice once and I spent hours on the clutch,' he said.

'Would you, David? Oh, please, would you?'

'Sure. If it would help. You'll have to tell me the words for brake and accelerator and gears, though.'

He wrote them down in his notebook and went over to the van. Maria looked at him doubtfully as he sat in beside her.

'*Kalimera,*' he said formally and shook hands. He turned back to Vonni. 'How do you say, "Let's go"?' he asked her.

'*Pame*, but don't say it yet or she'll drive you into that wall.'

'*Pame*, Maria,' David said gently and with a lurch they moved forward.

Vonni looked on, amazed. She watched as he taught Maria to stop the van. He really did have a gift.

'Drive her home when you've finished, will you?' Vonni said. 'I'll cycle down on your bike and leave it for you at Maria's house.'

Before he could answer she had swung her leg over the man's bicycle and was heading off down to the town.

Fiona sat at a table outside the little café and was surprised to see Vonni streaking by on a bike. Vonni saw her and did a wheelie turn to come back.

'All on your own?' she asked.

'I'm meeting Elsa here at midday.'

'Oh, yes, Elsa did tell me. She helped me take the children for a swim.'

'Did she?' Fiona sounded envious.

'Yes, and David came by on his bicycle. He lent it to me and I'm just leaving it at Maria's house for him. David's taking his life in his hands and teaching Maria to drive.'

'Lord, everyone's really settling in.' Fiona was wistful.

Vonni leaned David's bike against one of the empty tables. 'I'll sit with you until Elsa arrives,' she said.

Fiona was pleased. 'Will you have an ouzo?' she asked.

'No, just a *metrios*, please,' Vonni said.

They sat there peacefully, watching the life of the harbour going on around them. That was an interesting thing about Vonni, Fiona observed. She had a great sense of stillness. She knew that you don't need to talk all the time. It was very restful.

'Vonni?'

'Yes?'

'I was wondering . . . could I get some kind of a job here in Aghia Anna? I could learn Greek. I could help Dr Leros. What do you think?'

'Why do you want to stay here?' Vonni's voice was gentle.

'It's beautiful here and I want to be sort of settled when Shane comes back for me.'

Vonni said nothing at all.

'You think he might not come back, don't you?' Fiona cried. 'But you don't know him like I do.'

'True.'

'Believe me, Vonni, he has never in his whole life had anyone who understood him until he met me. We love each other, we went away to be together for ever. Why wouldn't he come back?'

Vonni swallowed and looked away.

'No, please, tell me. I'm sorry I shouted at you, Vonni, I just get so upset when people come out against Shane. I keep thinking that this is going to go on for ever until we're an old, old couple. Perhaps you know something I don't.'

She looked so anxious. She had her hand on Vonni's weather-beaten arm, her eyes were wide, wanting to know more.

Vonni took a deep breath. She had been responsible for Shane going to Athens. She had advised the police chief Yorghis to ship him away from Aghia Anna. She did therefore owe Fiona some explanation.

'No, I don't think I know anything that you don't,' she said slowly. 'But I was going to suggest that Shane might not expect you to stay on here, you know, without him. If he does contact you . . .'

'He will, of course he will. One day he'll get off one of those ferries and I want to be here and settled when he does.'

'It's not realistic, Fiona, this is a holiday place. Not a place to settle down in.'

'You did,' Fiona said simply.

'It was different then, and I came here to live with a man from Aghia Anna.'

'You did?'

'I did indeed, years and years ago. There were hardly any tourists here then. I was considered very unusual, a slut of course. In those days people here, as well as at home, got engaged and then married.'

Vonni looked out to sea remembering it all.

'So then you know it's possible to leave Ireland and come to a beautiful place like this and be happy?' Fiona was trying desperately to find similarities between them.

'In a way,' Vonni said.

'And what happened to the . . . er . . . man . . . from Aghia Anna?' Fiona felt daring to ask such a direct question.

Vonni looked her straight in the eye. 'Stavros? I don't know really,' she said and closed the conversation.

Vonni said she had a hundred things to do and she wanted to thank God above that one of them was not giving Maria a driving lesson.

'Are you all right here on your own?' she asked Fiona.

'I'm fine, and thank you so much for being so kind,' Fiona said politely.

She was glad that the older woman was leaving. She should not have asked Vonni what had happened to her man. She saw Elsa coming towards her and waved.

'I'll leave you in good hands then,' Vonni said.

Elsa sat down and told Fiona about the morning on the beach.

They ordered a salad and talked easily about life on this island. Just as they were finishing they saw an old van come sputtering past them. It was being driven somewhat erratically by Maria, and David was in the passenger seat.

'**V**onni?'

'Come in, Yorghis, sit down.'

'You have nice things here.' The policeman looked around the craft shop.

'Some of it is nice, yes. Thank you again for your hospitality last night, Yorghis.'

'It's not a time to be alone . . . We got a call from Athens, Vonni. That boy we exported, the Irishman . . .'

'Oh, yes?' So he *had* called after all. Fiona had been right. Vonni didn't know whether to be pleased or disappointed. 'What did he say?'

'*He* said nothing. We got a call from a police station in Athens. He had been taken in for dealing in a bar. They found my card on him and wondered what I knew.'

'And what *did* you know, Yorghis?' she asked.

'Nothing as yet. I wasn't there to take his call. I wanted to discuss it with you. She's such a nice little girl.'

'I know. So nice she'd probably get on the next ferry and go to Stand by Her Man.'

'That's what I thought,' Yorghis said. 'I think I'll just tell them that we had a bit of girlfriend battering and drunkenness here. I don't think I'll say anything specific about Fiona, do you?'

'I think you're right. And we might not say anything *to* Fiona either. Do you agree?'

'Is that playing God, do you think?' Yorghis wondered.

'Even if it is, let's do it. Maybe the Almighty needs a hand now and then,' said Vonni.

The sun was setting and there was a gold-red light over the harbour. Thomas saw that Vonni was still working in her craft shop. He thought about going in to invite her to come up for an evening drink with him. But he remembered how much she liked to be left alone. She had only agreed to sleep in the spare bedroom after a lot of reassurance that they would not intrude on each other's lives.

He wanted to call Bill. It had been left so awkwardly hanging in the air last time. He still felt stung by Vonni overhearing him and saying that he had made such a mess of it all.

Thomas climbed the stairs to the apartment and sat down at the table to make a list of things he wanted to tell Bill. Like that he'd had dinner in a police station, like the men who danced after the funeral. Like the Germans learn English poetry even though we don't know any of theirs.

He looked at the headings. What dull, odd things he had picked. A child would not be interested in these things. He sat with his head in his hands, thinking how pathetic he was not to be able to find something to say to the boy that he loved with all his heart.

When Vonni went upstairs much later that night, she found Thomas sitting in the dark. 'Holy St Joseph, you put the heart across me,' she said.

'Hi, Vonni.' He was very down.

'Did you ring your son and annoy him again?' she asked.

'No, I sat here for hours wondering what to say and I couldn't think of anything so I didn't call him,' he confessed.

'Probably wiser in the long run,' Vonni said approvingly.

'What kind of a horse's ass does that make me, not able to find things to say to a nine-year-old?' he asked.

'I'd say it makes you like every father and son in the world, unable to communicate.' She wasn't as unsympathetic as the words might have sounded.

'He's not my son,' Thomas said flatly.

'What do you mean?'

'What I say. Nearly ten years ago when Shirley and I were trying for a baby I went for a medical. Childhood mumps had made me sterile apparently. I walked around all day wondering how to tell Shirley. But when I got home *she* had something to tell me. Wasn't it wonderful— she was pregnant.'

'Did you tell her?'

'No. I needed time to think. I had no idea that she was playing away. Not a clue. And because I didn't speak then I couldn't later. But I love him as much as if he *were* mine. It wasn't Andy, he only turned up years later. Andy thinks Bill's my son.'

'Did you raise it during the divorce?'

'What, and lose any chance of access to Bill?'

'Of course.' She nodded.

'He's a wonderful boy, Vonni.'

'I'm sure he is. I'm very sure he is.'

There was a long silence.

'Go back to him, Thomas. It's breaking your heart to be so far away.'

'I can't. We all agreed it was for the best this way.'

'Agreements can be changed, plans can be rewritten,' Vonni said.

'I'd be worse back there than here. Suppose I had to look at that fool every day, posturing, pretending to be his father.'

'You are his father in every way that counts.' Vonni looked at the floor as she spoke.

'I wish I could believe that,' he said.

'You should believe it, Thomas.' She spoke with quiet certainty as if she knew what she was talking about. His eyes met hers and suddenly it was crystal-clear to Thomas that Vonni really did know what she was talking about.

Vonni and David were sitting drinking coffee at the café with the blue and yellow checked tablecloths. Maria would be out shortly to have her driving lesson.

'She says you are a very good man and you don't shout at her,' Vonni said approvingly to David. 'I told her that you taught your mother to drive. She said your mother was fortunate to have such a son.'

'Well, my mother certainly doesn't think so. She sides with my father over everything: I am so lucky, most men would love to have a business they could walk into.'

'And can you not tell her that you love them both but not the work?'

'I've tried and tried, but it ends in recriminations and arguments every single time.'

'When you go back you'll find that they have softened,' she began.

'I'm not going back,' he said.

'You can't run away, stay here for ever.'

'You did,' David said simply.

'I'm weary of telling people that those were different times.' Vonni sighed.

'I'm taking Maria up some of those mountain roads today.' David changed the subject. 'I thought we'd go up to see Andreas.'

'You like him, don't you?' Vonni observed.

'Who wouldn't like him? He's so kind and gentle. He doesn't pressurise people into doing what they don't want to do.'

'He's set in his ways, of course,' Vonni said.

'But good ways,' David said. 'His son must be a real fool, not to come back from Chicago and help him.'

Vonni stood looking at David quizzically, her head on one side.

'What is it?' he asked eventually.

'You *know* what it is, David. Couldn't someone say exactly the same about you? You have a father and, in your case, a mother too, who miss you and wonder what *you* are doing miles and miles away.'

'It's different,' David said mutinously. 'My father's just never wrong. No one could live with him.'

'Adoni found the very same thing in his father. Andreas wouldn't get lights on the taverna roof, he wouldn't have live bouzouki music in the evening. Adoni could change nothing. Andreas was always right.'

'I don't see him like that,' David said a little coldly.

'No? Well, people are not always courteous to their own sons.' She looked thoughtful.

'You have a son, Vonni?'

'Yes. Stavros, like his father.'

'And are you courteous and polite to him?' David asked.

'I don't see him, to be either courteous or discourteous to. But in the days when I did see him I was going through a period when I was polite to nobody, least of all to him.' She straightened up and looked purposeful again. 'Right. I'm taking those children with me so that you can take their mother up the Wall of Death or wherever you want to go with her.'

The bookshop had a small section of poetry, including a book of Goethe's work, German on one side and English on the page opposite. Thomas bought it and went to sit on a bench outside. He studied the book until he found something appropriate. Then he took out his notebook and wrote it down.

> Kennst du das Land, wo die Zitronen blühn,
> Im dunkeln Laub die Gold-Orangen glühn?

He wrote the translation beside it.

> Do you know the land where the lemon-trees blossom,
> Where the golden oranges glow in the dark foliage?

He would learn it by heart and quote it to Elsa. She must not be allowed to think he did not know German writers.

He was just beginning to copy the next bit, when he saw a shadow fall on the page. It was Elsa looking over his shoulder to see what he was reading. Then she moved back and spoke the lines to him.

> 'Kennst du es wohl? Dahin! Dahin
> Möcht ich mit dir, o mein Geliebter, ziehn.'

'All right, I give in,' he said. 'I haven't read the translation. What does that bit mean?'

'It means . . . let me see . . . "Do you know it perhaps? It is there, there that I would like to go with you, my beloved."'

And as she said it they looked at each other, slightly embarrassed.

'Did Goethe come to Greece? Is this the land where the lemon-trees blossom?' Thomas asked, steering the conversation into safer waters.

'It was the Mediterranean certainly, but I think it was mainly Italy he travelled in. He was mad about Italy. Of course he could have come to

Greece as well. This is where I show my ignorance.' Elsa look apologetic.

'What about mine? Until today I've never read a word he wrote in any language,' Thomas confessed.

'And why are you reading it now?'

'To impress you,' he said simply.

'You don't have to, I'm impressed already,' Elsa said.

Andreas got a phone call from Ireland.

'Is that a taverna in Aghia Anna?' the voice asked.

'Yes, it is. Can I help you?'

'Fiona Ryan called her family from your taverna on the day of your terrible tragedy.'

'Yes, yes, I remember. This is Andreas. This is my taverna.'

'I'm Fiona's best friend at home. Barbara. Fiona gave your number in case she got cut off so I rang because . . . well, I was wondering . . . are they still in Aghia Anna?'

'Yes, is there any problem?'

'Fiona's all right, is she?'

Andreas paused. All right? The girl looked wretched. But even though his instinct was to tell this woman Barbara all that had happened, he knew it wasn't his story to tell.

'They all seem to like it here,' he said lamely.

'All? You mean she's been able to make friends with Shane in tow? Usually people avoid them like the plague.'

'Nice people. German, American, English,' he said to reassure her.

'Well, that is a surprise. Listen, Andreas. Is there anywhere I could send her an email or a fax, do you think?'

'Certainly.' He gave her the email address of the police station.

Yorghis was driving around Aghia Anna. He knew he would see Fiona or one of her friends somewhere along the way. He saw her with a straw basket buying vegetables.

'Oh, Yorghis, just the man I need. What's the Greek for watermelon?'

'*Karpouzi*,' he said.

'Good! *Karpouzi, karpouzi*,' she said happily.

'I have a letter for you,' Yorghis said.

'Shane! I just *knew* he would get in touch.' Her face was radiant.

'No, it's from your friend Barbara in Ireland.' He handed over the printed-out email.

She barely looked at it, she was so disappointed. She just put it in her basket. When she had finished her shopping, she sat down at a café and pulled out the email.

You must wonder how Sherlock Holmes Barbara tracked you down, but it was easy: your mother had the number you phoned from, and Andreas told me his brother ran the cop shop. He said you and Shane had nice friends from all over the world. That's great news.

Oh, I do miss you in the hospital, Fiona. Any news on when you and Shane are coming back? It's just that if it were going to be at the end of the summer there are some really great flats coming on the market. You and Shane could easily get one of them, it would only be a ten-minute walk to the hospital.

In fact, I was telling your mam and dad about them, I said that was probably the kind of place the two of you would want to live when you came back. They didn't even flicker an eyelid. Remember when they wouldn't hear his name mentioned? You've certainly laid down the ground rules OK.

They were very pleased you called about that awful tragedy. It must have been terrible.

Anyway, you have my email address now, do tell me how you both like Greece. I always wanted to go there but never got any further than Spain!

Love to you both, Barbara

Fiona sat there stunned.

Barbara sending her love to Shane? Her mother and father accepting the fact that she was going to live with Shane for ever? The world was tilting slightly.

She read the email again and went back to Elsa's apartment to make soup and a fruit salad.

Elsa stopped by Vonni's shop and invited her to join them for supper.

'No, thank you, Elsa, very kind of you, but I have to work. Every week I go to a group of blind people who make rugs. I choose the colours of the wool for them. Then I try to sell the rugs.' She shrugged. 'I had to give something back and I realised that the blind could weave with the best.'

'What do you mean, you had to give something back?' Elsa asked.

'This place was good to me. I was nothing but a nuisance for years, howling and frightening their children. They put up with me until I recovered.'

'I can't believe this . . . *you* howling and frightening people?'

'Oh, I did, believe me. My husband betrayed me, you see. He saw beautiful Magda, and he forgot everything we had. He was entranced by her. Stavros moved out of our house and into hers. He would not come home to me. I did a lot of stupid things—that's when the people here were so tolerant and good. I had a little boy and they helped me look after him while I worked up in the petrol station. I'll never forget that . . . I was the foreigner and they would have been tempted to side with him rather than me.'

'What kind of stupid things did you do?' Elsa wanted to know.

'Another time possibly.' The shutters came down in Vonni's face.

'It's just that *I've* done some very stupid things recently. It's comforting to know others did and survived,' Elsa said.

'Is this the man who was staying in the Anna Beach?'

'You know everything!' Elsa exclaimed. 'Yes, it is. And I still love him so much, that's the problem.'

'Why is it a problem?'

'Well, it's complicated. His name is Dieter, he runs the television station where I work . . . used to work. He taught me everything and I became a sort of star there, presenting the big news programme at night. And anyway we fell in love, got together, whatever you'd call it, and have been together for over two years.'

'You live together?' Vonni asked.

'No, it's not as simple as that.'

'Is he married to someone else?'

'No, it's not that. It's just awkward in the Network if people know. People would think I only got my job because I was living with him.'

'Sure.' Vonni was clipped. 'So what are you doing here then?'

'I discovered that he has a child by a woman he knew years back.'

'So?'

'He has a child that he has never acknowledged, he's no part of her life. You don't think that's bad?'

'I think it happens all over the world every day. People survive.'

'It happened to me,' Elsa said. 'My father walked away, didn't give a damn.'

'And look at you! Didn't *you* survive, Elsa? In the end we all have to rely on ourselves. We are not tied to our children, nor they to us. Happy Families is a game people play with cards, it's not reality.'

'I don't know what has made you so bitter and cynical but I'm glad I don't feel like that,' Elsa said.

'You want Dieter to play Saturday Father to some child he probably never intended should exist.'

'But she *does* exist and that's exactly what he should do.'

'That's not why you are leaving him,' Vonni said. 'You're leaving him because you thought that he would eventually admit that he needed you as part of his life. You are such a beautiful young woman, you are accustomed to getting your own way. If you truly loved him you could put this child out of your mind. But no, you can't be sure that he loves you. That's why you are seizing on this episode of his life. You are making it the excuse, aren't you?'

Elsa felt her eyes stinging at the injustice of the attack. 'You're so wrong, he *does* love me. And I have such a huge hole in my heart without him. I've decided that I'm going back to Germany as soon as I can.'

Vonni leaned forward. 'Don't go back there, keep going, leave him be. He's never going to love you the way you want to be loved.'

Elsa stood up, not trusting herself to speak. She wanted to get back to her own apartment.

You're very quiet, Elsa,' Fiona said. 'Don't you like that lovely healthy soup I made you?'

'It's very good. I'm sorry, I just don't feel too cheerful tonight. I had a row with Vonni of all stupid things,' she said. 'I told her about me and Dieter and she wants me to stay away from him.'

Elsa had mentioned nothing to Fiona about her situation up to now.

'But you still love him, don't you?'

'Oh yes, most definitely, and he feels the same,' Elsa said.

'Well, there's no question about it then.' Fiona was matter-of-fact and businesslike about it. 'You have to go back to him.'

They had all agreed to meet at the harbour café after dinner and the four of them talked about their day.

'Do any of you get the feeling that we are just marking time here— that we should be doing something else?' Thomas asked at last.

'I'm happy here. I like it,' David said.

'And I do too,' Fiona agreed. 'Anyway, I have to stay here until Shane gets back.'

'I'll probably go back to Germany next week,' Elsa said. 'I'm just thinking it through. What about you, Thomas?'

'Well, Vonni thinks I should go back to California to see my son.'

'Vonni's busy dispatching us all home! Once Maria can drive that van, Vonni wants me out too, back to make peace with my parents and work with my father.' David sounded gloomy.

'She doesn't think Shane is coming back and she says there are no jobs here,' said Fiona sadly. 'She says I'd be better to go back to Dublin.'

'She's more of a policeman than Yorghis is. She says I should end my relationship with a man who doesn't really love me,' Elsa said, giggling.

'She never put it like that?' David said.

'Almost precisely like that—anyway, I'm different to the rest of you. She wants me to keep on the move and *not* to go home.'

They pooled what they knew about Vonni: she came from the west of Ireland over thirty years ago because she loved a man called Stavros. Somehow she managed to buy him a petrol station, where Vonni worked night and day. She had one son, Stavros, who she didn't see now. Stavros senior had left the island, possibly with Vonni's young son. Vonni had gone through a troubled time but the people of Aghia Anna had looked after her and she felt she owed them in return.

'What kind of a troubled time?' Fiona wondered. 'Maybe she had a breakdown when Stavros left?'

'I think she was an alcoholic,' David said softly.

The others were startled. That quiet, capable, together woman a slave to drink? Impossible.

'Why do you say that?' Elsa asked.

'Well, have you noticed she never drinks any wine or ouzo?'

They looked at him with respect. Only the gentle, sensitive David had noticed what was now so obvious to the rest of them.

CHAPTER SIX

'VONNI, COME UPSTAIRS for a *portokalatha* when you're through, OK?'

'So you've finally noticed I only drink soft drinks,' she laughed at Thomas.

'I didn't, David did. He's the one who notices things. Anyway, what you drink isn't important—I want your advice.'

'I'll be up in ten minutes,' she said. He noticed she was wearing a clean, fresh, yellow blouse with little embroidered roses on it. She must keep her clothes in the craft shop.

'That's pretty,' he indicated the stitching. 'Did you do that?'

'No, it was done by someone else. It's thirty years old.'

'Really? Who did it?'

'It doesn't matter now, Thomas, but she could sew like an angel.'

Thomas swallowed. He had been too intrusive. 'I guess I ask too many questions, Vonni, forgive me. You don't have to talk about it.'

'Well, I do, really. You four are all anxious to know about me . . . I hear that you have been asking everyone in Aghia Anna about me.' She smiled at him innocently.

Thomas looked at the floor. 'I suppose we wanted to know what your husband was like, and what happened to him,' Thomas said uneasily.

'Very hard questions to answer, both of them. His name was Stavros, he was very dark, with brown, almost black eyes, and long black hair.

His father was the barber here. He used to say he was ashamed of his wild and woolly son, but the moment I saw him I knew I never wanted any other man.'

'And where did you see him? Here in Aghia Anna?' Thomas asked.

'No, I met Stavros in Ardeevin, a small village in the west of Ireland in the spring of 1966. He came to work in a garage on the main street. We had never seen anything quite so exotic. He was learning English, he said, and the motor trade, and seeing the world . . .' Vonni sighed at the memory. 'We didn't think Ardeevin was the right place to start seeing the world. What about Paris? London? Even Dublin? But he said he liked it, it reminded him of his home town, Aghia Anna.

'I was still at school, in my last year. My family hoped I would become a primary teacher, but I was so much in love with Stavros I had stopped going to school, abandoned studying. My only purpose each day was to sneak into the back of Ardeevin Motors. I didn't care about anything but being with him.

'But Jimmy Keane, who ran the garage, began to think Stavros wasn't concentrating fully on his work and started making sounds that he was going to sack him. I could neither eat nor sleep with the worry of it all. What would I *do* if Stavros had to move on? Then the most marvellous event occurred in Ireland that summer. There was a bank strike!' Her eyes shone at the memory.

Thomas was enthralled. 'The banks went on strike? Never!'

'Oh, they did,' she said happily. 'And what happened then was nothing short of a miracle,' Vonni said. 'Supermarkets would have a lot of cash and no banks to lodge it in, so they cashed these "cheques" for people they knew. The big town ten miles away had a supermarket where I was known, because the manager was my mother's cousin. So I cashed a cheque for two and a half thousand pounds. And that day Jimmy Keane said he'd have to let Stavros go.' Vonni began to pace the room. 'Stavros told me he would miss me, that I was his true love and that one day we would meet again. He said he would go back to Aghia Anna, open up a petrol station and send for me to come and join him. And I asked what was wrong with going right now? That I had the funds to set him up. I told him that it was my savings.'

'Tell me he was pleased.'

'Oh, he was, but my parents weren't. I told them that day that I was seventeen and a half, in six months I could marry without their permission anyway. What were they going to do? Lock me up?'

'So you wore them down?'

'No. But I told them I was leaving that very night, and we did, on the seven thirty bus.'

'And the money?'

'Ah, yes, the money. We were well in Aghia Anna by the time the bank strike ended. We'd had a wonderful journey, travelling through Switzerland and Italy. I was never so happy in my life.'

'And you arrived here?'

'And it wasn't so great. There was this girl, you see, very pregnant with Stavros's child. She thought he had come back to marry her. She was Christina, the sister of Andreas and Yorghis. When she discovered he had *not* come back for her, she tried to kill herself. But she killed the child she was carrying, not herself. It was a terrible time.'

'What happened to Christina?'

'She went to the hospital on the hill, on the Kalatriada road. I went to see her every week. She didn't speak to me for forty-five weeks, then one day she did. Soon afterwards she met and married a good man. She has children and grandchildren. They live on the other side of the island. I see her often.'

'And what happened to you, Vonni? You married Stavros?'

'In a civil ceremony in Athens. No one thought it was a real wedding— not my family back in Ardeevin, not his family here in Aghia Anna. I learned to speak Greek, I bought the petrol station. I learned how to change wheels, pump up tyres.'

She had begun to sound tired and weary.

'And in 1970 our son Stavros was born. By this time, people were used to me. We had a christening at the church, and even Stavros's father relaxed and sang songs. No word from Ireland, of course. I wrote and told them they had a grandson. No reply at all. I think the money had been the final straw. I was always going to pay it back. And I did.'

David opened the letter. It was the first time his mother had written to him. He read unbelievingly of his parents' pride and delight in the actual invitation to this award his father had won. They had sent him a photocopy but described how the wording was embossed on the card.

David knew those awards; businessmen patted each other on the back every year. It was a reward for nothing except making money. No philanthropy, no research, no generosity to charity was being praised. No, it was the huge god *profit* that was being worshipped here.

His mother wrote on and on—about seating in the Town Hall, what they would all wear, that there would be a table plan. She wondered how soon he would come home for it.

He would calm himself and write a courteous letter explaining why he would not be there. A letter was wiser than a phone call. No danger of anyone losing their temper.

Fiona went to the Anna Beach Hotel and sent an email to her friend Barbara in Dublin.

> It was good to hear from you, Barb, I'm so glad we chose this place. The accident was terrible, but the people are full of courage. Shane's gone to Athens for a few days on work. I'll write again when I know our plans.
> Love, Fiona

'**T**here is a fax for your friend the German woman,' the man at the reception desk said as Fiona was leaving the Anna Beach.

Fiona marvelled at how everyone knew who they all were.

'I'll take it back to the villa,' she said.

She was becoming very familiar with Aghia Anna by now, even knew little short cuts from one side to the other. She laid the piece of paper on the table in front of Elsa.

'I'd have read it but it's in German,' Fiona said.

'Yes.'

'Aren't you going to read it?' Fiona asked.

'I know what it says,' Elsa said.

'That's pretty psychic of you,' Fiona said in surprise.

'It's telling me to pull myself together and come back to where I belong, which is in bed with him two nights a week, and no more gestures of independence.'

'Maybe it's not that,' Fiona encouraged her.

'All right—I'll translate . . .' She picked up the paper. 'It's fairly short anyway. "Darling Elsa, Come back to me and we will move together into an apartment openly. We will even be married, if that's what you want. I will write letters and send gifts to that child, if it makes you feel better. We were intended for each other, you know that and I know that. What is the point in playing games? Fax me yes, soonest. Love until the world ends, Dieter."'

In Chicago, Adoni took the letter with the Greek stamp to the men's room and sat down to read his father's spidery handwriting.

'*Adoni mou*,' it began and told simply of the pleasure boat that had burned in full sight of the town with rescuers unable to get to it in time.

'It makes everything else that has happened seem very unimportant,' his father wrote. 'Arguments about the taverna are so small compared to life and death. It would give me great pleasure, my son, if you were to come back to Aghia Anna and see me before my death. I assure you that I would not speak to you in that tone of voice that I used when you were here. Your room is always there if you come for a visit, and of course bring anyone you like. I hope there is somebody to bring.'

And Adoni took out a big blue handkerchief to wipe his eyes. And then he cried again because there was nobody to bring.

There was no bail for Shane in Athens, so he was brought back to the cells after the initial hearing.

'I'm allowed to make a phone call!' he shouted. 'You're meant to be in the bloody European Union. One of the reasons we let you in was so as you'd pay some attention to human rights.'

They passed the phone to him without comment.

He dialled the police station in Aghia Anna. He wished he could remember that old guy's name. But what the hell.

'I'm phoning from a police station in Athens,' he began. 'I'm trying to get in touch with Fiona Ryan.'

'We told you before, she is not here,' Yorghis lied smoothly.

'She *must* be there, she's expecting my child, she'll have to get the bail money . . .' He sounded frightened.

'As I say, I'm sorry we can't help you,' Yorghis said and hung up.

Shane begged for a second call. The policemen shrugged.

'Barbara! They took a hell of a time to find you, it's Shane.'

'I was on the wards, Shane, it's called work,' she said.

'Very droll. Listen, has Fiona gone back to Dublin?'

'What? Have you two split up?' She couldn't keep the pleasure out of her voice.

'No, don't be ridiculous, I had to go to Athens . . .'

'For work?' Barbara suggested drily.

'Sort of—and those half-wits in Aghia Anna say she's left there so it's been a breakdown in communications, you might say.'

'Oh dear, Shane, I'm so sorry. How can I help you exactly?' Barbara purred. She had not heard better news since the day her friend Fiona had taken up with Shane.

'You paid the supermarket back?' Thomas said.

'It took some time—like nearly thirty years,' Vonni admitted. 'But they got every penny.'

'And do you keep in touch with your family?'

'They used to send a cold little note every Christmas, proving to themselves they are big-hearted, capable of *forgiveness*. I wrote long letters, sent them pictures of little Stavros. And then things changed.'

'Changed? They came round?'

'No, I meant *I* changed. I went mad, you see.'

'No, Vonni. This I can't see.'

She looked tired. 'I haven't talked about myself so much for ages. I'm a bit weary. You can tell the others what I told you, Thomas. I don't want them bothering people here for my story.'

He looked embarrassed. 'They don't need to know. None of us needs to know anything about your business.'

'I'll tell the rest another time . . . you know, like "New readers start here . . ."' She had a wonderfully infectious smile.

Thomas told them the story next day down by the harbour. They had got into the habit of turning up at the place with the blue and yellow checked tablecloths around noon.

David reported on the latest driving lesson, Elsa and Fiona said nothing about their messages from home but told how they had spent the morning helping an old man to paint some wooden chairs, and Thomas told them Vonni's story.

'She did want you to know. It's as if she were going to take it up with one of the three of you.'

They wondered about a country where the banks went on strike. 'I remember my father talking about it. He said that the country ran perfectly well without them. There were a few loose cannons like Vonni who went off with small fortunes, but not many,' Fiona said.

'I wonder who she'll tell the next episode to,' Elsa said.

It turned out to be David. Later that afternoon.

Thomas and Elsa had gone for a walk down the coast; Fiona had gone to ask Yorghis had there been any news from Athens. David sat on the harbour wall with his Greek phrase book. Vonni came to join him and helped him with some pronunciation.

Then David told Vonni about the invitation to his father's award back home. He handed her his mother's letter to read as well. To his surprise she had tears in her eyes.

'You'll go back, of course?' she said.

'No, I can't. Six months later it would be something else. I'd never escape, I'd be sucked back in. You never went back to Ireland, did you?'

'No, but I wanted to, a thousand times. But I was never welcome, so I didn't go. Anyway, I went mad and that sort of changed everything.' She spoke as casually as if she was saying that she'd gone somewhere on the bus instead of out of her mind.

'It wasn't *really* mad, was it?' David asked.

'Oh, I think so. It was because of Magda. She had a terrible husband, very violent, always imagining that Magda was flirting. She was a gentle woman with a beautiful smile. Sometimes she had bruises or a cut but she would say she was clumsy or had fallen. Then one day I went to the café to collect a tablecloth, and she was sitting there, the blood dripping down onto the white material. I ran for old Dr Leros, the father of Dr Leros who is here now. He patched her up and he said that this could not go on, we needed a strong man, someone like Stavros, to do something. Stavros and two of his friends held Magda's husband down on the floor of the café and told him what would happen to him if there was another incident.'

'And did her husband take them seriously?'

'Very seriously, apparently, and Magda stopped being "clumsy", as she called it. That was when people realised that she was very beautiful,' Vonni explained in a small sad voice.

'Did you suspect that Stavros was . . . well . . . interested in her?' David asked gently.

'No, not at all. I was the last to know, the very last person in Aghia Anna, but it finally dawned on me.'

'How?'

'Well, not the best way really. Little Stavros was with me at the petrol station—he was four then, going on five. He asked why Magda was always so tired. She always had to go to bed when she came to our house, and Papa always had to go and sit with her. I felt so dizzy and faint. Magda and Stavros? In our house? In my bed?'

'So what did you do?'

'I closed the petrol pumps and went home early the next day. Little Stavros was playing at a neighbour's house. I opened the door quietly and I heard them laughing. I opened the bedroom door and stood and looked at them. She was beautiful with her long dark curls and her olive skin. I caught a reflection of myself in the mirror. I knew I had lost. Of course he would want her not me.'

David listened, chilled by her intensity.

'I walked away. Out of the door of our bedroom, out of our house, up to the top of the town and into a little bar. I ordered *raki*, the very rough spirit they have, and I drank until I fell on the ground.

'They carried me home, I remember nothing of it. I woke up next day in our bed. There was no sign of Stavros. I remembered her there in the bed and I got up to be very sick. There was no sign of little Stavros either. I went to the bar where I had been the previous day, apologised for my behaviour, and asked them what had been the reception when they took me home.

'Magda had taken my child, *my* child, to his grandfather the barber. Stavros had just pointed them to the bedroom and left. They couldn't help me further. I had brandy this time, good Metaxa brandy to get me over the shock. Four days and nights of drinking, then I realised they had taken my child away from me. I heard like in a dream that Magda's husband had gone away on a fishing boat to another island. And then I remember waking up in the hospital on the Kalatriada road. Christina came to see me. "Pretend to be calm, pretend to be better, then they'll let you out," she said. So that's what I did. I pretended.'

'It worked?' David asked.

'For a bit. Stavros would not speak to me, wouldn't tell me what he'd done with my son, and I knew I must not raise my voice again or I would be back in that hospital where they locked every door behind them.'

'And Stavros?'

'Was living with Magda. I bought a bottle here, a bottle there, and drank until I passed out. I don't know how long it went on.

'Then Christina came and helped me pull myself together. And I went to see Stavros. He said I could stay in the house. That our son was living in Athens with his aunt and that I would never see the child again. He explained that soon he would sell the garage, *his* garage, and that he and Magda would settle somewhere new, collect little Stavros, and build a life for him.

'And suddenly I realised that I would be here alone, without my son, without my love, without my garage. Unable to go home, owing two thousand pounds . . . How was I going to find that money now?'

'But in fairness, Stavros knew about the debt, surely he must have said he'd help you?' David was shocked.

'No, he never knew about it. I never told him. He thought it was my savings,' Vonni said.

Then she moved away, and left David sitting on the harbour wall.

'**D**o you know what I don't understand,' Fiona said the same day as the four friends were putting together the jigsaw pieces of Vonni's story.

'Why she didn't get a lawyer?' Thomas suggested.

'She was in no position to do that. Stolen money in her background, he *did* give her the house, and she didn't really know their ways here,' Elsa said.

'No, wait. I don't understand why Andreas said that little Stavros came up to the taverna on the hill to play with his son Adoni and climb trees. He couldn't have done that at four.'

'Maybe Stavros and Magda stayed for a while longer, even a good time longer, and brought Stavros back here,' David suggested. 'That would have been even harder for Vonni to bear.'

'Well, she'll tell one of us, she promised that she would,' Thomas said.

'You're an easy person to talk to, David. I would not be at all surprised if she came back to you,' Elsa said to him with her wonderful smile.

Vonni came back to David sooner than he had expected.

'I have to deliver some potting clay and moulds to the hospital, for their rehab classes. Will you come with me, David? You see, I just hate going there on my own. I keep thinking that they'll lock the door behind me as they did before.'

'But you weren't there very long, were you?' David said. 'Didn't Christina get you out by telling you to pretend?'

'Oh, yes, that was the first time. But I went back. I was there for years on and off really,' Vonni said casually. 'Will we go and pick up Maria's van now and head off?'

'We will, we will.' David smiled.

'Are you imitating my accent, young fellow?'

'Imitate you, Vonni? I wouldn't dare!' he said.

'There's a very nice part of the garden, I'll show you,' she said when the goods had been handed over. And they sat together looking down from one of the many hills that surrounded Aghia Anna, as she picked up her story as if there had been no interruption.

'Once I knew I had lost everything I didn't see any point in pretending. I sold things out of the house, *his* house I always considered it, and bought drink. So I was back in here and out like a yo-yo. Stavros explained to everyone that I was an unfit mother. I saw little Stavros once a week on a Saturday for three hours. There was always someone else there, Stavros's father sometimes or his sister, or Andreas. The visits were not a success. I used to cry, you see, cry over all I had lost. And I would clutch at little Stavros and tell him how much I loved him. He was terrified of me. Andreas used to drive him up the hill to his place, to the swing on the tree, to cheer him up after he had to deal with me, then I would get bladdered with drink to get over it. It went on for years. He was twelve when they took him away.'

'They?'

'Stavros and Magda. Oddly, it was when they were gone that I decided there was still a life to be lived. So I got sober. But it was too late. My son was gone. No point in my trying to find out where. The boy's grandfather, the old barber, was kind to me, but he wouldn't tell me. I wrote to him, young Stavros—letters on his birthday through his grandfather and later through his aunts—every year.'

'And no answer ever?' David asked.

'No answer, ever.'

'Does Andreas not know where your son is? He's such a kind man, he'd understand. His own selfish son won't come back to him from Chicago. Andreas knows what it feels like.'

'David, listen to me. Andreas doesn't know where Stavros is. And there are two sides to everything. I was a pig of a mother when young Stavros was growing up, so how does he know I am mellow and easy-going now?'

'Someone might tell him,' David said.

Vonni brushed it away. 'Listen to me, David, in a similar way, Andreas knew everything about running a taverna when Adoni was growing up, how does Adoni know that his father is lonely and sad, and wants him to come home?'

'As I said, Vonni, someone could tell him. They are *so* foolish, these young men, Adoni in Chicago and Stavros wherever he is. Why they can't see sense and come back to you both is beyond me,' David said.

'There are probably people in England who wonder the same about you,' Vonni suggested. 'In that letter from your mother, she's *begging* you to come home.'

'Where does she say that?'

'In every line. I'm certain your father's ill. He may be dying.'

'Vonni!'

'I mean it, David,' she said.

Elsa had written nothing back to Dieter. She still needed time to think about it. There was no doubt that he had meant what he said. If Dieter said he would marry her then he was prepared to do that. Up to now he had genuinely believed that their lives could run easily together and that there was nothing about the situation that needed to be altered. Now it was up to Elsa to tell him when she would be back home and he would be there, waiting for her.

So what was holding her back?

Elsa walked on her own up one of the windy roads away from Aghia Anna. She had not been this way before, and since she would be leaving soon, she wanted to imprint the whole place on her mind.

No smart restaurants, traditional tavernas or craft shops on this road. Small poor dwellings, sometimes, with a goat or two outside, children playing among the hens and chickens.

Elsa stopped and looked at them. She was smiling at their antics when Vonni came out of a house.

'Heavens, Vonni, you're everywhere!' Elsa exclaimed.

'I could say the same about all of you! I never move but I fall over one of you,' Vonni said with spirit.

'Where does this road lead? I just came up this way to explore.'

'It doesn't really lead anywhere—just more of the same—but I have to deliver something a bit further on. Come and walk with me, I could do with the company.' Suddenly, she looked downhearted.

'Is something wrong?' Elsa asked.

'That house I was in just now, the young woman is pregnant. The father was one of those who drowned on Manos's boat. She doesn't want the child. It's just such a mess. I've been there for an hour saying we'll all help her to look after the baby. But will she listen? No.'

'That's an unusual position for you to be in, Vonni. People not listening to you,' Elsa teased her.

'Why do you say that?'

'Well, we all listen and take notice of everything you say. We spent hours talking to David about your theory that his father might be ill.'

'Not *might* be ill, *is* ill,' Vonni said. 'And what did David decide?'

'He thinks it's all a trap, a way to get him home, and then it will be harder for him to get away again. But you've succeeded—he's going to call his home today.'

'Good,' Vonni nodded her approval. She stopped at a small ill-kept building. 'I'm going into this house—come with me. I have to give Nikolas some magic medicine.'

'You make magic medicines too?' Elsa gasped.

'No, it's an antibiotic cream actually, but Nikolas doesn't trust modern medicine so Dr Leros and I have this little ruse.'

Elsa watched as Vonni moved around the old man's simple house, picking up things here, arranging them there, talking away effortlessly in Greek; and then she produced the magic ointment from her woollen shoulder bag and applied it solemnly to the sore on his leg.

When they left, the old man smiled at them both.

Elsa and Vonni continued to walk companionably down the windy road and Vonni pointed out landmarks as they passed.

'You love it here, don't you?' Elsa said.

'I was lucky to find this place. I'd never live anywhere else.'

'I'll be sorry to leave, I really will,' Elsa said.

'You are leaving? Going back to Germany?' Vonni did not sound best pleased.

'Yes, I have to move on,' Elsa said.

'Move back, more like, move back to what you ran away from.'

Elsa was angry. 'That's not true. Dieter wants to marry me. It will all be out in the open now.' Her eyes flashed.

'And the reason you ran away in the first place . . . that was all about forcing him to propose, was it? I thought you said you felt guilty because he had abandoned his daughter and thought it didn't matter. Has all this disgust with him vanished?'

'We only have one life, Vonni. We have to put out our hands and take what we want.'

'No matter who we take it from? Oh, Elsa, just listen to yourself speaking. I told you before that you were too used to getting your own way. And I mean it.' Vonni sighed. 'But you're not going to take any notice of what I say. You are going to do what you want to. Forget I spoke.'

They walked on in awkward silence until they reached the town.

'**S**hirley?'

'Yes, Thomas?'

'Is Andy there?'

'You don't really want to talk to Andy?'

'No, I was just hoping that I might be able to talk to my son without Andy-the-athlete breathing down his neck.'

'Are you picking a fight, Thomas?'

'No, of course I'm not. I just want to talk to my kid. OK?'

'Well, hold on, I'll get him for you.' He could almost hear her shrug. 'Hi, Dad.'

'Bill, tell me about your day,' he said and half listened as the boy went on about a track and field event for families at the university. He and Andy had won a three-legged race.

'Father-Son race, was it called?' Thomas asked bitterly.

'No, Dad, they don't call them that now—you know so many families have sort of re-formed themselves.'

'Re-formed themselves?' Thomas gasped.

'Well, that's what our teacher calls it, it's got to do with so many people being divorced and everything.'

It wasn't such a bad word, but it didn't begin to hint at the whole story.

'Sure, so what do they call it?'

'A Senior-Junior race.'

'Great. Well, I got you a wonderful book today, there's a bookshop here in this tiny place. It's stories from Greek myths but written for the modern day. I've been reading it myself all afternoon. Do you know any Greek stories?'

'Is the one about the kids who flew off to find the Golden Fleece a Greek story?'

'Sure it is, tell me a bit about it,' Thomas said, pleased.

'It was about this brother and sister and they rode on the back of a sheep . . .'

'Did you read it at school?'

'Yes, Dad, we have a new history teacher and she keeps making us read stories.'

'That's great, Bill.'

'It'll be great when I have a brother or sister next year.'

His heart felt like a lump of lead. Shirley was pregnant again. She and Andy were starting a family and she had said nothing.

'That's *great* news,' he heard himself say through gritted teeth.

'Andy's painting a nursery for the baby. I told him how you made one for me and put in bookshelves even before I was born.'

And Thomas felt the tears in his eyes as he waded in with his two big feet and broke the whole mood.

'Well, I guess Andy will be busy putting up shelves for trainers and trophies and sports gear for the poor little kid. To hell with books this time round.'

He heard Bill gasp.

'That's not fair, Dad.'

'Life's not fair, Bill,' said Thomas, and hung up.

'Tell me about it,' Vonni said when she saw Thomas's face a couple of hours later. 'You messed it up again with that kid, didn't you?'

'Shirley is pregnant,' Thomas said, bleakly. He didn't move from the chair where he had sat since the phone conversation with Bill.

'Your son will need you all the more now if his mother is pregnant. But no, you have to be noble and distant and break that child's heart by giving him space he doesn't want. I get impatient with people like you, Thomas. I know I am a different generation, my son is your age, but I have never indulged in self-pity like you do. Especially since the solution is in your own hands. You love this child, nobody but yourself is putting any distance between you and him.'

'You don't understand, I'm on sabbatical leave.'

'They're not going to get out the FBI if you go back to your home town to see your own son.'

'Would that it were so simple,' he sighed.

Fiona was talking to Mr Leftides, the manager at the Anna Beach Hotel, about a job.

'I could mind the guests' children for you, take them off their parents' hands. I'm a qualified nurse.'

'You don't speak any Greek,' the manager objected.

'No, but most of the visitors here are English-speaking, I mean even the Swedes and Germans all speak English.'

She saw Vonni across the foyer, stacking the shelves of the hotel's tiny craft shop.

'Vonni will speak for me,' Fiona said. 'She'll tell you that I can be relied on. Vonni!' she called out. 'Can you tell Mr Leftides that I'd be a good person to work here?'

'As what?' Vonni sounded curt.

'I'm going to need somewhere to live when Elsa goes back. I was asking Mr Leftides if I could work here in exchange for board and lodging and a little money.' Fiona looked pleadingly at the older woman.

'Why do you need a job? Aren't you going home?' Vonni was terse.

'No, you know I can't leave here until Shane comes back.'

'Shane is not coming back.'

'That's not true. Of course he's coming back. Please tell Mr Leftides that I'm reliable.'

'You're not reliable, Fiona, you are deluding yourself that this boy is coming back to you!'

Mr Leftides, who had been looking from one to the other as if he were at a tennis match, decided he had had enough. He shrugged and walked away.

'*Why* did you do that, Vonni?' There were tears of annoyance in Fiona's eyes.

'You are being ridiculous, Fiona. Everyone was sorry for you and kind when you had the miscarriage and all that upset. But surely by now you must know there's no future for you here, waiting foolishly for a man who will never return. Go back to Dublin and take up your life.'

'You're so cruel and cold—I thought you were a friend,' Fiona said in a shaky voice.

'I'm the best friend you ever had, if you had the intelligence to see it.'

'**V**onni? You want a Morning Glory?' Andreas often looked into the craft shop and treated her to a little metal dish with three colours of ice cream across the road in Yanni's delicatessen.

'No, I'd prefer a bottle of vodka with a lot of ice,' she said.

Andreas was startled. Vonni never joked about her drinking, and did not refer to her alcoholic past.

'Is there a problem?' he asked.

'Yes, there is. I've fought with every one of those foreign kids. Every single one of them.'

'I thought you liked them. They're very attached to you.' Andreas was surprised.

'I don't know what it is, Andreas. Everything they say annoys me.'

'That's unlike you. You are always keeping the peace, smoothing things down.'

'Not these days, I'm not, Andreas. I feel like stirring everything up. I suppose it was the boat and all the unnecessary waste of life. It makes everything seem pointless.' She was pacing around her little shop.

'There's a lot of sense in your life,' he said.

'Is there? Today I can't see any. I think I'm a foolish woman, perched here in this place until I die. I used to feel this years back, and then I would hit the *raki* until I was senseless. Don't let me go down that road again, Andreas, my good friend.'

He laid his hand on hers. 'Of course I won't. You've fought so hard to get out of that pit you fell into, nobody is going to let you fall in again. Come with me now and help me make *dolmadhes*. I can't bend the old fingers to stuff the vine leaves and stitch them up. Please close your shop and come up to the taverna with me. As a favour, will you?'

'And of course you'll have plenty of coffee and ice cream to distract me and keep me away from the demon drink?' She gave him a weak smile.

'Certainly. That was my very plan,' he said, and they went out of the door together.

They sat and discussed Vonni at midday by the harbour.

'I can understand her attacking *me*, because, to be honest, a lot of people have a problem with Shane,' Fiona said. 'But the rest of you? I don't get it.'

'Well, it's easy to see where she's coming from with me,' Elsa said. 'I'm a tramp who has somehow blackmailed a poor innocent guy into proposing to her.'

'And did he?' Thomas asked.

'Yes, but it's much more complex than that. Why has Vonni turned on you?' Elsa changed the subject.

Thomas rubbed his chin thoughtfully. 'I truthfully don't know what annoyed her so much about my situation, but she went on about how I had a choice over my son, and she didn't. I felt tempted to say that at least I didn't lose my senses in a vat of alcohol like she did. But I didn't want to offend her. I just wanted her to agree that I was trying to be responsible and do the right thing.'

David tried to stand up for Vonni. 'You can see why she envies you though. If she had been allowed anywhere near her son she'd have been there. She knows it's her own fault—that's what makes her so enraged.'

'You're very forgiving, David, since she lit into you unmercifully as well,' Fiona said.

'Yes, but she got that all wrong. You see, she doesn't know what kind of people my parents are, she doesn't begin to understand. I've read my mother's letter over and over and there's nothing in it to suggest that my father isn't well . . .'

'But, David, why did she get angry with you exactly?' Elsa asked.

'Because I was saying what a good man Andreas was and how selfish his son was not to come back and help him. She said I was exactly the same as Adoni, staying away instead of helping my father. But, of course, it's a totally different thing.' He looked round the table and thought he saw a look on all their faces that suggested it might not be so different after all.

Vonni sewed up the vine leaves neatly around their little packages of rice and pine nuts. She was very quiet.

Andreas looked at her from under his big bushy eyebrows. Vonni was right to be concerned. She had the same sense of unease and restlessness that had led her to those frightening drinking bouts all those years ago.

He wondered if he should contact his sister Christina. She and Vonni had been good friends and a huge mutual support. But then, he would do nothing without consulting Vonni.

Her face was lined as always, but today she had a deeply worried look. She frowned and gnawed at her lip.

They worked on the open-air terrace looking down over the town. Twice she got up and went into his kitchen for no reason. He watched her without appearing to do so. Once she reached up to where bottles of brandy and olive oil stood on a line on the shelf. She was breathing fast as if she had run in a race.

'What can I do for you, Vonni? Tell me,' he begged.

'I've done nothing of any use in my life, Andreas. What can anyone do for me? Ever?'

'You've been a good friend to my sister, to me, to all the people in Aghia Anna. That's worth while, isn't it?'

'Not particularly. I'm not looking for pity, I hate that in a person, it's just that I actually can't see any point in the past, the present or the future.' Her voice was flat.

'Well, then, you'd better open the brandy,' Andreas said. 'It's on the shelf in the kitchen. You've been looking at it all morning. Take it down, drink it, then none of us will have to worry about *when* you're going to do it, it will be done.'

'Why are you saying this?'

'Because it's one way to go. You can throw away the work and discipline and denial of years in an hour or so. Because it will bring this oblivion you want.'

'I don't *want* to,' she said piteously.

'No, I know that. But if you see nothing in the past, the present or the future, then I suppose you have to.'

'And do you see any point in anything?' she asked.

'Some days it's harder than others,' Andreas said. 'You have good friends everywhere, Vonni.'

'No, I end up driving them away.'

'Who are you thinking about?'

'That foolish little Fiona, for one. I told her that her boyfriend won't come back. But then, I know where he is. She doesn't know.'

'You did it for the best,' he soothed her.

'I must tell her where he is,' Vonni said suddenly.

'I wonder if that's wise?'

'May I use your telephone, Andreas?'

'Please . . .'

He heard her dial the number and then speak to Fiona. 'I called to say I had no right to shout at you today. To say that I'm sorry. Very sorry.'

Andreas moved away to give her privacy. He knew how very hard it was for Vonni to admit that she was wrong.

In Elsa's villa, Fiona looked at the telephone in her hand, mystified. Whatever she had expected it wasn't this. She was at a loss to know what to say.

'That's OK, Vonni,' she said awkwardly.

'No, it's not OK, as it happens. The reason he didn't get in touch is because he's in jail in Athens.'

'Shane in jail! Oh my God, what for?'

'Something to do with drugs.'

'No wonder I haven't heard from him. Poor Shane—and would they not let him get in touch and tell me?'

'He did try to get in touch eventually, but only so that you'd get him bail, and we said—'

'But of course I'll get him bail. Why did nobody tell me?'

'Because Yorghis and I thought you'd be better without him,' Vonni said lamely.

Fiona was outraged. 'How dare you, Vonni! How dare you meddle in my life? Now he thinks I haven't bothered to get in touch with him.'

'I'll take you to him,' Vonni said. 'I owe it to you. I'll go with you on the eight o'clock ferry to Athens in the morning, take you to the jail, find out what's happening.'

'Why are you doing this?' Fiona was suspicious.

'I suppose I realised that it is your life,' said Vonni. 'I'll see you at the harbour tomorrow morning.' Then she came back and sat down with Andreas.

'Did that work?' he asked.

'I don't know, tomorrow will tell. But I feel stronger somehow.'

'I think we have to keep struggling on, Vonni. Manos and those who died on the boat didn't get a chance to, so I'm going to keep going until the end.'

CHAPTER SEVEN

'MOTHER? I GOT your letter. About the award.'

'Oh, David!' The delight in her voice was hard to take. 'I just knew that you'd call. I knew it. You're such a good boy to phone so quickly.'

'Well, you see, I'm not certain yet what's happening . . .' He did not want to be railroaded into dates of return, times of flights. Already he felt the familiar heavy weight that their pressure always created.

His mother was still talking excitedly. 'Your father will be so pleased when he hears you called. It will make his day. He'll be back in about an hour.'

'He's not in the office on a Saturday surely?'

'No, no, just . . . um . . . out . . .'

David was surprised. His father did not go to synagogue every week, only at the High Holidays. Saturdays were always spent at home. He felt suddenly cold. 'Is Father ill?' he asked suddenly.

'What makes you think that?' He could hear the fear in her voice.

'I don't know, Mother. I sort of got the idea that he might have an illness and that neither of you were telling me.'

'You got that feeling . . . far away in Greece?' She spoke in wonder.

'Sort of.' He shuffled. 'But is it true, Mother?'

He felt that time was standing still as he waited for her to answer. It could only have been seconds but it felt like an age.

'Your father has cancer of the colon, David, they can't operate. They've given him six months.'

There was a silence on the line as he caught his breath.

'Does he know, Mother? Has he been told?'

'Yes, that's what they do these days. They tell people. He's very calm. He has a lot of medication.'

David gave a gulping sound, as if he were trying to stifle a sob. 'Why didn't you tell me?'

'You know your father. He is such a proud man. He didn't want you coming back just out of pity.'

'I see,' David said miserably.

'But imagine you sensing from all that distance away, David. It's uncanny, but then you always were so sensitive.'

David had rarely felt so ashamed in his life.

Thomas called his mother.

'Don't call me from so far away, son, wasting all the money on me.'

'It's OK, Mom. I get my full salary, I told you. Plenty to live on like a millionaire out here, and to pay support for Bill.'

'And to send me treats too. You're a good boy, I love those magazines you send me every month. I've been blessed with you and your brother.'

'It's not easy being a parent, is it, Mom?'

'I didn't find it too bad, but then my spouse went and died on me rather than take up with someone else like yours did.'

'It takes two to break up a marriage, Mom. It wasn't all Shirley's fault.'

'No, but when are you finding yourself a partner?'

'One day, I assure you, and you'll be one of the first to know. Mom, I called to ask you about Bill. Do you talk to him at all?'

'You know I do, son, I call him every Sunday. He misses you like hell, Thomas.' She paused. 'He told me you didn't feel good about the baby.'

'I was meant to dance with joy, I suppose,' Thomas said bitterly.

'He said he thought you would love it, like Andy loves him.'

'He thought I'd love the new baby?' Thomas was astounded.

'He's a child, Thomas. He's just nine years of age, his father has left him, left America. He was clutching at straws. He thought that maybe you would come back if there was a baby for you to be stepfather to.'

'What do you think I should do?'

'I don't know. Be near him, not thousands of miles away, I guess.'

'You think that would sort it?'

'Well, at least Bill wouldn't think you had abandoned him.'

Fiona woke very early and saw the dawn come up over Aghia Anna. She was still furious with Vonni and Yorghis for having lied to her. How dare they tell her that Shane had not been in touch? He *had* tried to contact her and these old busybodies had interfered. They said his motive was only to get her to raise the bail money. Well, of course he had to get bail first to get out, to get on with life.

She was not relishing the thought of the ferry trip with Vonni as a companion. She wished too that she hadn't told it all to Elsa last night. Elsa had been less than supportive.

Fiona wished mightily that she could turn the clock back. Why had she asked Elsa to help her raise the money? To lend her a thousand euros, just for a few days until Barbara could send it to her from Dublin.

'Lend you money to get him out to finish off your face?' Elsa had scoffed.

'That was different,' Fiona began. 'He was in shock, I told him the news all wrong, you see.'

Elsa had lifted Fiona's hair. 'The bruises are still there,' she had said softly. 'Nobody on earth, Fiona, is going to lend you money to get that guy out of a place where he should be kept permanently.'

When Vonni and Fiona met at the harbour, Vonni had already bought the tickets. The ferry pulled out of the harbour and Fiona looked back at Aghia Anna. So much had happened since she first came here.

Vonni had gone downstairs to where they were serving coffee and drinks and had returned with coffee and two sticky-looking cakes.

'*Loukoumadhes*,' she explained. 'They're honey fritters with cinnamon. They'll give you energy for the day.'

Fiona looked at her gratefully. The woman was making every attempt at an apology. Fiona knew she must be gracious.

'You have been kindness itself,' she said, patting Vonni's hand.

To her surprise she saw tears in Vonni's eyes. And they sat companionably and ate their honey cakes.

'Are you looking forward to seeing Shane?' Vonni asked.

'I can't wait, I hope he won't be angry that it took me so long.'

'I'll explain, I'll tell him it wasn't your fault.'

'Thank you, Vonni . . . it's just . . . you know . . .' Fiona was twisting her hands awkwardly.

'Tell me,' Vonni encouraged her.

'Well, you've met Shane. He can say things that sound much more aggressive than he intends. I wouldn't want you to think . . .'

'Don't worry, Fiona, I won't think anything,' said Vonni through gritted teeth.

'Elsa! I'm delighted to see you,' Thomas called. 'I was going to rent a rowing boat and go out for a couple of hours, would you trust me enough to come with me?'

'I'd love it. Shall we go now?'

'Sure. David's not coming to the café, his father is ill, Vonni was right about that anyway. He's going to arrange a ticket home.'

'Poor David.' Elsa was sympathetic. 'And Fiona's gone to Athens with Vonni. She left this morning.'

'So we're on our own,' Thomas said.

'I'd love a farewell boat journey, I'll help with the rowing if you like.'

'No, lie back and enjoy it. A farewell journey? You *are* going back to Germany then?'

'Oh, yes. I don't know exactly what day, but I am going.'

'Is Dieter very pleased?'

'He doesn't know yet,' she said simply.

Thomas was surprised. 'Why haven't you told him?' he asked.

'I don't know. There are a few things I haven't sorted out in my mind,' Elsa said.

'I see,' said Thomas, in the voice of one who didn't.

'And when will *you* go back, Thomas?'

'It depends on whether I really believe Bill wants me there.'

'Of course he does. That's obvious,' Elsa said.

'How is it so obvious to you?' he wondered.

'Because *my* father left us when I was young. I would have given anything to have had a phone call saying that he was on the way home to live near our street and I could see him every day. That would have been the best thing that could have happened. But it never did.'

Thomas looked at her, astounded. She made it seem so simple, so easy. He put his arm round her shoulder and headed down to where they hired out the brightly coloured boats.

In the crowded harbour of Piraeus, Fiona followed, lugging her heavy bag, as Vonni led the way to the *Ilektrikos* and bought the tickets.

'Do you know, I'm a bit afraid of seeing him again,' Fiona said, as they got on the train for Athens.

'But he loves you. He'll be delighted to see you, won't he?' Vonni asked doubtfully.

'Yes, yes, of course. It's just that we don't know how much the bail will be, and I'm not sure how I'm going to get it when we *do* know. It's not the kind of thing that they're going to help me with from Dublin. I might have to tell them back home that it's for something else.'

Vonni said nothing.

Yorghis had phoned ahead to let the police in Athens know that Vonni and Fiona were on their way. He had given a short thumbnail sketch of who they were and when they would arrive.

Dimitri, the young policeman who had taken the call, only told Shane ten minutes before the visit that Fiona was on her way.

'Has she got the money?' he asked.

'What money?' Dimitri asked.

'The money you bloodsuckers want!' Shane shouted.

'Do you want a clean shirt to wear?' Dimitri was impassive.

'No, I don't want a clean bloody shirt. I want her to see things as they are.'

'They'll be here very shortly.' The policeman was curt.

'They?'

'She has another woman from Aghia Anna with her.'

'Another lame duck. That's just typical of Fiona. She takes her time getting here and then she drags someone else in on the act.'

As he closed and locked the door, Dimitri reflected on the nature of love. They often said that girls liked a whiff of danger. That old policeman in Aghia Anna had said that the young woman who was coming to see Shane was a nurse, a gentle soul, an attractive girl . . .

A short while later, Dimitri returned to the cell and opened the door. 'Your friends are here,' he said tersely.

'Shane!' Fiona cried.

'You took your time.'

'I didn't know where you were until yesterday,' she said, moving towards him.

'Huh,' Shane said, not responding to her arms held out to him.

'I was responsible for all that, I did not pass on the fact that you had been in touch,' Vonni said.

'Who the hell are you?' Shane asked.

'I'm Vonni, from Ireland originally, but I've lived in Aghia Anna for over thirty years. I came with Fiona to help her find you here.'

'OK, thank you. Can you piss off now and leave me with my girl-friend?' he asked with darkened brow.

'Up to you, Fiona,' Vonni said pleasantly.

'Not up to her actually. Up to me,' Shane said.

'Perhaps you could wait for me . . . outside, Vonni?' Fiona begged.

'I'll be there when you need me, Fiona,' Vonni said and left.

Fiona moved towards Shane to kiss him, but he didn't seem to be interested.

'Did you bring the money?' he asked.

'Sorry?'

'The money, to get me out!' he said.

'But, Shane, I don't *have* any money. You know that.'

'Don't tell me you've turned up here with nothing to say,' he said.

'I have plenty to say, Shane . . .'

'Say it then.'

Fiona wondered why he was not reaching out to hold her, but she knew she must keep talking.

'Well, the good news is that I heard from Barbara. There are lovely apartments very near the hospital and we could easily get one and go back to Dublin. But the sad news is that we lost our baby. It was awful but it happened. Dr Leros said that as soon as we want to try again—'

'*What?*'

'I know you're upset, Shane, I was too, desperately, but Dr Leros—'

'Fiona, shut up talking rubbish about Dr this and Dr that. Do you have the money or do you not?'

'Of course I don't have the money.' He still hadn't embraced her or talked about their dead baby. 'Shane, aren't you sad about the baby?'

'Shut up and tell me where on God's earth we're going to find the *money!*' he said.

'We'll ask them, Vonni and I will, how much it is they want and then I'll try to raise it—but that's not the most important thing, Shane.'

'So what's the most important thing?' he asked.

'Well, that I've found you and that I love you for ever. So why don't you kiss me?' she asked.

'Oh God, Fiona, will you shut up about love and think who might get us the money,' he said.

'If we are able to borrow it, then we'll both have to get jobs to pay it back,' she said anxiously.

'*You* get a job if you want to, as soon as I'm out of here I have people to meet, contacts to make. I'll have plenty of money then. I'll hang around Athens for a bit and then I might move up to Istanbul.'

She looked at him levelly. 'And am I to go with you?'

He shrugged. 'If you want. But you're not to nag me about settling down and getting jobs. We left Ireland to get away from all that shit.'

'No, we left Ireland because we loved each other and everybody kept putting difficulties in our way.'

'Whatever,' Shane said.

Fiona knew that tone of voice. It was his switch-off voice. He used it when talking to people who bored him rigid. She began to understand now that she bored Shane and that he had never loved her.

It was staggering and almost impossible to take in, but she knew she was right. All her hopes and dreams had been for nothing. He would never have tried to get in touch if he hadn't wanted the money for bail.

'You don't love me,' she said in a shaky voice.

'Oh Lord God above, how often do I have to play the record? I *said* you could come with me if you wanted to.'

There was a wooden chair in the corner. Fiona sat down and buried her head in her hands.

'No, Fiona, not now. This is not the time to go all weepy and emotional on me. Leave it off, will you . . .'

She looked up at him, her hair was back from her face. Despite the make-up, the bruising was still very visible.

He stared at her. 'What happened to your face?' he asked.

'You did it, Shane. In the restaurant out on the point.'

He began to bluster. 'I did *not*,' he said.

Fiona was calm. 'It's not important any more.'

She stood up as if to leave.

'Where are you going? We have to work this out.'

'No, Shane, *you* have to work it out.'

'Stop threatening me.'

'I'm not threatening you. I've seen you and now I'm leaving.'

She knocked on the door and Dimitri opened it for her. There was a smile on his face.

This drove Shane into a frenzy. He leaped towards Fiona and caught her by the hair.

'You are *not* coming in here playing games with me!' he roared.

But Dimitri was more speedy than anyone would have thought. He had his arm across Shane's throat, forcing his chin upwards. Shane was no match for him and was forced to let go of Fiona.

She stood at the door for a moment, watching, then moved out into the corridor and walked to the front office.

Vonni was sitting there with a senior policeman. 'They're talking about two thousand euros,' she began.

'Let them talk about it.' Fiona's head was high and her eyes were bright. 'He's not getting it from me.'

CHAPTER EIGHT

THOMAS ROWED THE LITTLE BOAT back to the harbour. It seemed like coming home.

They looked up towards the hills and pointed to the places they knew. That was the hospital in the Kalatriada road. And that was the road up to Andreas's taverna. And there, finally, was the harbour and the café with the blue and yellow checked tablecloths.

It was as if the escapism were over.

Thomas and Elsa had returned the little boat.

'It was good, your voyage?' the old man asked.

'Very good voyage,' Elsa said with a smile.

They walked up the harbour road towards the town.

'I wonder if we'll forget this place eventually,' Thomas said.

At exactly the same moment, Elsa said, 'Imagine all this busy world going on without us!'

They laughed at thinking almost the same thought, and as they were passing a café, Thomas indicated that they should sit down.

'Why not?' Elsa was pleased. 'By this day next week there'll be very little chance of dropping into a café.'

'Ah, you speak for yourself,' Thomas said. 'I'll still be here dropping into cafés, rowing boats, reading in the sunshine.'

'No, you'll be on your way back to California,' she said with a great sense of being right about it.

'Elsa! You're as bad as Vonni.' He was puzzled at her certainty.

'I'll send you a postcard. You'll be there to get it,' she laughed.

Andreas came over to their table.

'May I join you? I have some good news to share.'

'Adoni?' Elsa gasped with excitement.

Andreas shook his head. 'No, not as good as that, alas, but still good. The little Fiona has turned her back on Shane, she has walked out on him. She and Vonni are on the last ferry, they will be back by sunset.'

'How do you know?' Thomas asked.

'One of the police telephoned Yorghis with the news. She did not even try to raise his bail—just left.' Andreas spread out his hands at the mystery of it all. 'But it is all very much for the best,' he said. 'And David is coming up to dinner in my taverna tonight to say goodbye. He is leaving Aghia Anna tomorrow afternoon. I wanted to ask you to join us.'

Thomas asked, 'And will Vonni and Fiona join the dinner too?'

'I hope so, yes.' Andreas's smile was warm.

Thomas spoke quickly. 'You are so kind, Andreas, but alas Elsa and I have to meet someone tonight for dinner. What a pity.'

Elsa picked it up quickly. 'Yes, that's such bad timing,' she said. 'Can you tell David we'll see him at the harbour at midday?'

Andreas understood.

He understood more than they realised. Of course, it was very last-minute, he reassured them. But he could read signs as well as anyone. These two wanted to be alone. He left them courteously.

'Amazing to be so centred, so rooted in a place like he is,' Thomas said admiringly, watching the old man leave.

'Why did you say that, about us having dinner?' Elsa asked.

Thomas was silent for a moment. 'I don't really know, Elsa, but I knew you didn't want another run-in with Vonni, and as it happens I share your view. I also didn't want to hear one word tonight about Shane. And . . . and . . .'

'And what?'

'And I'll miss you when you go. I wanted some more time together before you left. Just the two of us.'

David was helping Andreas in the kitchen. 'I'll miss all this so much,' he said.

'Perhaps you could cook for your father? I tell you how to make a good *moussaka*. Do you have *melitzanes* in England?'

'Aubergines? Yes, we do.'

'Then I'll show you. It will please him to see you cook for him.'

'Do you think so?' David was doubtful.

'I don't *think* so, I *know* so,' said Andreas.

Yorghis telephoned from the harbour. He had waylaid Fiona and Vonni and they would be at the taverna in fifteen minutes.

'Yorghis says that Fiona is in great form,' Andreas said.

'She must have got that fool out of jail then,' David said glumly.

'No, on the contrary, I was about to tell you. She turned her back on him. Left him there.'

'For the moment. She'll go back for him.'

'I think not, but I suggest that we let her tell us herself. Do you agree?'

'Oh, yes, that's always my policy,' David said. 'And is she speaking to Vonni still?'

'The best of friends, apparently, according to Yorghis.'

David laughed. 'Aren't you a wonderful pair of old gossips!'

'If you can't gossip with your own brother, I ask you, then who is there to gossip with?'

'Would you like to go to the Anna Beach?' Thomas suggested to Elsa.

'No, it's too . . . I don't know . . . too full of chrome and opulence. Besides, it doesn't have good memories for me. What about that little place out on the point where the waves break?'

Thomas didn't want to go there. 'It reminds me too much of the day that savage hit Fiona.'

'But now she has left him,' Elsa soothed. 'So where should we go? It can't be too public, we did say we were meeting someone . . .'

'Why don't we get some kebabs and wine and go back to my place?' Thomas suggested.

'Sure, that's great. I'll leave a note for Fiona saying I'll be back later and then let's go and buy supper.'

There was a definite change in Fiona, they could all sense it. She held her shoulders back, she smiled more readily.

There were three tables of customers at the taverna, all of them English-speaking. Fiona translated the menu and advised them all to start with *dolmadhes*, which, she explained, were little fat packets of stuffed vine leaves. She suggested the house wine, which was inexpensive and good. Soon she had them so well organised that little Rina, the girl who helped in the kitchen, could serve them.

That meant that Andreas could sit down with his party and look at the lights going on down in the heart of Aghia Anna.

'A pity Thomas and Elsa couldn't join us,' David said.

'Oh, well,' Andreas shrugged. 'And you, Fiona, you are very good with people, you look after them well, would you like to work here?' he said unexpectedly.

Fiona laid her hand on his. 'If you had asked me this last night or even early this morning I would have cried with gratitude. But now, now I say thank you from my heart, but I will not be able to come and work here.'

'It is too far up from the town?' Andreas asked.

'No, Andreas, not too far. It's just that I'm going home. Back to Dublin.'

She looked around the table at their astonished faces.

Thomas and Elsa finished their meal and sat on the balcony looking out over the rooftops.

'You have a nicer view from your place,' Thomas said.

'You can still see the stars from here, that's all that matters,' Elsa said.

'"What is the stars, Joxer?"' Thomas quoted in a heavy Irish accent.

'Will you say that I am showing off if I say I know where that's from?'

'Go on, tell me, shame me, put me down!' he laughed.

'It's by Sean O'Casey,' she said.

'Top of the class, Elsa. Another devoted teacher?'

'No, Dieter and I went to London, on a secret trip, and we saw it there. It was brilliant.'

'Are you looking forward to being back with him again?' Thomas asked.

'There's a problem,' she said.

'Isn't there always?' he sympathised.

'I suppose so. This problem is an unusual one: although he has promised that there will be no more deception and hiding and sneaking away from people, he never owned up to something else. Like the fact that he and another woman had a child.'

'Since you and he were together?' Thomas asked.

'No, years before, but the point is that he never acknowledged that little girl.'

'Is that what you ran away from?'

'I did not run away, I left my job and went to see the world. But I did think less well of him. Anyone who has a child, either deliberately or accidentally, must be there for that child.'

'And he didn't agree?'

'No, and somehow I was revolted by it. I felt I could never trust him again. I felt ashamed of loving him. I told him all this.'

'And so what has changed? What makes you think that it's right to go back to him now?'

'Meeting him here, knowing he loves me and will do anything for me.' She looked at him, hoping he understood.

Thomas nodded. 'Yes, I would have believed him, too. If you love someone you'll pretend anything to keep that person. I did, I know.'

'What did you pretend?' she asked gently.

'I pretended that I believed Bill was my son. I loved Shirley so much then that I couldn't face her with the absolute proof that he couldn't be.'

'He's not your son?' Elsa was astonished.

Thomas told the story simply and without emotion. The tests that had proved him to be sterile, the joyful announcement of Shirley's pregnancy, and the totally unexpected bonus that when Bill arrived Thomas discovered that he adored the boy.

'Do you still love Shirley?'

'No, I don't hate her either. She irritates me, and now she and Andy are having a child together and that irritates me too. The fact that they *can* for one thing, and for another that Bill is so excited about . . . his new brother or sister.'

'Did you ever think Shirley was having an affair?'

'No, not remotely. But let's put it this way: the very existence of Bill meant that Shirley was not exactly the faithful type. I guess I thought it was just one fling.'

'It probably was,' Elsa said.

'Yes, I think so. But for whatever reason we found less and less to say to each other. And then we got divorced.' He looked gloomy.

'And did you find anyone else?'

'No, I guess I didn't really look. I cared so much about Bill, you see. And I was really very surprised when she brought Andy to meet me so that they could tell me their plans. Shirley said she wanted us to be up-front about everything.' He was scornful.

'Well, what was wrong with that?' Elsa asked.

'Oh, there had been months of secrets and pretence there! People in love can be so smug.'

Elsa was silent. She was thinking hard, working something out.

'Sorry for droning on,' Thomas said.

'No, not at all, you've just clarified something for me.'

'I have?'

'Yes. If Dieter is to be any kind of a worthwhile human being, he must accept the fact that he has a daughter, and recognise her.'

'Even if it means losing you?' Thomas asked.

'He wouldn't lose me over it, if he could genuinely believe that this girl needs a father. The problem is that he might just put on some kind of an act. He thinks that what I want is a diamond ring, respectability, commitment.'

'He doesn't know you very well then, if you have been with him for over two years and he doesn't understand your values.'

'You think I should give him up, don't you?'

'What I think doesn't matter.'

'It matters to me.'

'All right, then. I think you should be with someone who does understand you . . . as well as the other thing.'

'What other thing?' she laughed.

'You know what I mean—sex, love, attraction. All of those are very fine but if you held out for the understanding as well, then you'd be very happy.'

'And where would I find all that in one package, Thomas?' Elsa asked.

'Ah, if I knew the answer to that I'd run the world,' he said, raising his wineglass to her. 'But I suppose I could tell you that we can and do get over loving people and I hope you might contemplate getting over Dieter.'

'Why? You know that Dieter is the love of my life.' She was confused.

'You asked me what I thought, I told you.' Thomas spoke simply.

'But I can't think why you would want me to give him up, get over him . . .'

'Because then I could comfort you.'

She looked at him open-mouthed. 'Thomas, this cannot be true!' she gasped. 'You and I are mates, friends. You don't fancy me, it's only the wine and the stars.'

'You never thought of me in that way at all?' he asked, his head on one side.

'I did think that it would be very easy to love a gentle, thoughtful person like you, rather than a restless, urgent man like Dieter. But then I've often wished idly for things that didn't happen. Couldn't happen.'

'All right, then I think you should go back to him tomorrow. Why hang around?' he said.

'You give up pretty easily,' she said flirtatiously.

'Come on, Elsa. Everything I say is wrong. I did you the courtesy of considering what you said. You are not doing that.'

'I'm only playing with you,' she said.

'Don't,' said Thomas.

She was contrite. 'I'm only playing games because I don't know what else to do. I know what you should do. It's so obvious and easy. And what everyone else—Dieter, David, Fiona, Andreas, Vonni—all of you should do. It's just my own decision that isn't clear.'

'What should Vonni do?' Thomas asked with interest.

'She should get Andreas and Yorghis to find her son and tell him what kind of person she is now. Young Stavros would come home if they told him.'

Thomas smiled at her. 'Elsa the Crusader,' he said affectionately, and patted her hand.

In the taverna they talked about Fiona's journey home and when she should leave.

'Perhaps you could come on the last ferry with me tomorrow,' David said. 'We would be company for each other, and you might even fly to London with me.'

'That's not a bad idea, it would make it less hard to say goodbye.'

'For a while,' Vonni said. 'You'll come back again. You've both got friends here.'

'Tomorrow I'll go and say goodbye to Eleni and thank her for everything and call on Dr Leros as well,' Fiona said.

'I'll give Maria a last driving lesson and tell her that Vonni will take over now. Is that right, Vonni?'

'Has she *any* coordination these days?' Vonni asked.

'Much improved,' David soothed. 'And she's great if you can manage not to shout at her but to build up her confidence.'

'Aren't we all great when people don't shout at us and build up our confidence,' Vonni grumbled.

'Have you told them in Ireland that you are going back?' Andreas asked Fiona.

'Not yet. I'll call from the Anna Beach tomorrow.'

'Go in and use my phone,' he said, as he had said all that time ago on the day that Manos had perished with his boat.

'Just a quick call, then, to my friend Barbara. Thank you so much, Andreas.' And Fiona ran into the kitchen.

'Isn't it unusual that you young people don't have mobile phones?' Yorghis wondered.

'Yes, it is odd. Not one of the four of us has one that works here,' David said.

'It's not unusual at all,' Vonni said. 'You have all been running away. Why would you want a phone so that you could be tracked down?'

'**B**arbara?'

'God Almighty, it's Fiona!'

'Barbara, I'm coming home!'

'Well, that's great news! When will the pair of you be back?'

'Not the pair of us. Just me.'

There was a silence at the other end.

'Shane is staying there?' Barbara said eventually.

'In a manner of speaking, yes.'

'Well, that's a pity,' Barbara said neutrally.

'Don't be such a hypocrite, Barbara, you're delighted.'

'That's not fair—why should I be delighted that my friend is upset?'

'I'm not upset, Barbara—could you and I share a flat, do you think?'

'Of course we could. I'll start looking right away.'

'Great, and . . . Barbara, could you sort of tell my ma and da?'

'Sure . . . what exactly will I tell them?'

'That I'm coming home,' Fiona said, surprised that there should be any question about it.

'Yes, but you know the way people of that generation always want to ask questions . . .' Barbara began.

'Oh, head them off at the pass,' Fiona said casually.

Thomas walked Elsa back to her villa and kissed her on the cheek.

'*Schlaf gut*,' he said.

'You're learning German just to impress me?' She smiled at him.

'No, I think I'd have to do much more than say, "Sleep well", to impress you, Elsa,' he said ruefully.

'Like what?' she asked.

'I'd have to be restless and urgent. I could try but it might take a long time.'

'You're better the way you are, believe me, Thomas. See you midday tomorrow at the harbour.'

Fiona was in Elsa's villa already packing her suitcase.

'Before you say anything, I want to apologise, I was completely out of order with you, trying to borrow money and everything,' Fiona said.

'It doesn't matter a bit, anyway I was very short and harsh with you, I am the one to be sorry.'

'It doesn't matter now. I'm over Shane. I'm going back to Dublin. I suddenly looked at him and saw what the future would be like with him, and that it wasn't worth it. I suppose you'll say or think anyway that it can't have been real love if it vanished so quickly.'

'No, it was real love all right,' Elsa consoled her. 'But as you say it has ended, and that will make life easier for you.'

'I didn't give him up to have an easy life,' Fiona explained. 'I just suddenly saw him in a different light, like you all saw him in, I suppose. And then it was quite easy to walk away. I'm sorry of course that he wasn't the person I thought he was. But it's not like your situation, Elsa.'

'Why do you say that?'

'Well, Shane only tolerated my attaching myself to him. In your case, Dieter writes begging you to come back to him, promising to change for you. That's real love.'

Elsa ignored this. 'What was it that finally made you choose to walk away from Shane?' she asked quietly.

'I think there was a kind of indifference in his tone. He didn't care.'

'I know what you mean.' Elsa nodded slowly.

'You can't know! Your guy is down on his knees beseeching you to come back to him. That's utterly different.'

'Something you said there about a tone of voice seemed fairly relevant to me. I'm going out on the balcony to look at the sea, do you want to join me?'

'No, Elsa, I'm exhausted. I've been to Athens and back in one day, changed the whole direction of my life. I'm going to have to go to sleep.'

Elsa sat for a long time looking out at the moonlight on the sea, then she went back into the sitting room. She took some paper and began to write a letter which she would fax the next day.

My dear Hannah,

You have been such a good unselfish friend. Asking nothing and always ready to listen. It was, as it turned out, a very good decision for me to come here. And it was even better that I met Dieter again as now I can make a decision based on the facts, not on some fantasy world. I'm still not sure what I am going to do. But a few more days on this peaceful island will make it all clear to me. I heard two things tonight, one from an American man who told me that we can get over people. He just said it casually, like you can get over whooping cough. I don't know if he's right. Then an Irish girl said to me that I was lucky because Dieter had promised to change for me. And I have been wondering why we should want to change people. Either love them as they are or move on.

It's late at night and I am writing this by moonlight. I've been thinking in a way I never did before about my life with Dieter. And then I thought of

you, Hannah, and your happy marriage to Johann. On the day you married
five years ago, you said there was nothing about him you would change.
I envy you that, my dear, dear friend.
Love, Elsa

CHAPTER NINE

MIRIAM FINE HAD PREPARED David's room for him, bought a new lilac-coloured duvet cover and laid out dark purple towels.

'They look nice and manly, somehow. I hope he'll like them,' she said.

'Don't fuss over him, Miriam, he hates fuss,' David's father said.

'You tell me not to fuss? What will you do the moment he comes in the door? You'll start talking to him about responsibility. If there is anything guaranteed to fuss him, it's that!'

'No, I won't talk about responsibility. At least he's seen sense and decided to give up these mad ideas.'

'He's coming home because you're ill, Harold. He worked that out for himself, you saw the letter I sent. I never mentioned it. Not once.'

'I don't want his sympathy, I will not have his pity.' The man's eyes filled with tears.

'But you might want his love, Harold.'

Fiona's father turned the key in the lock. It had been a long tiring day in the office. He had been tempted to go and have three pints in his local pub, but realised that Maureen would have his supper ready. It wasn't worth the hassle.

As soon as he opened the door she ran to meet him.

'Sean, you just won't believe this! Fiona's coming home. This week!' Maureen Ryan was overjoyed.

'How do you know?'

'Barbara rang when you were out.'

'Could that lout not draw his dole money out there?' Sean grumbled.

'No, wait till you hear. She dropped him. She's coming home alone!'

Sean put down his briefcase and his evening paper and sat down. 'She's really coming back?'

'Tomorrow or the day after. She phoned Barbara and asked her to tell us. She's looking for her old job back and she wants to live in a flat with Barbara.'

'Well, that's all right, isn't it?'

'I think it's all for the very best, Sean,' said Fiona's mother with tears in her eyes.

Bill dialled the number of Thomas's apartment in Greece but there was only an answering machine. He left a message.

'Dad, Andy is driving us to Arizona to see the Grand Canyon. We're going to cross the Sierra Nevada and we're going to meet Gran there. She's going with her book club. Andy says I can call you when we get there so that Gran and I can both say hello.'

Then Andy took over the phone.

'Thomas, just in case you don't get this message before we leave and you want to call Bill, this is the number of my cellphone. I'll try to show things properly to your boy; we have the atlas out now looking at the journey. But I guess there'll be a lot I miss out. Maybe he could go again with you some time when you get back.'

'That's if he *ever* comes back,' Bill said before Andy had hung up.

Because Andy had not yet hung up when Bill said this, it was there on the message when Thomas came back from walking Elsa home and listened to his answering machine.

He sat up for a long time wondering about the world. He saw the torchlight moving around in the henhouse and knew that Vonni would not come to sleep in the guest room tonight. He thought of the strange tortured life she had lived among these people in Aghia Anna. He thought of the beautiful, bright Elsa going back to that selfish German who only looked on her as a trophy. He thought of the simple decent Andy, the man who he had always demonised.

Who was only doing his best.

He thought of his Bill, who believed he might never come home. He sat there thinking until the stars faded from the sky and the early light came up over the hills.

They met for a last lunch at the restaurant with the checked tablecloths.

'I'll miss you all. I don't have many friends back home,' David said.

'Me neither, but I'd be very surprised if you were without friends for long,' Thomas said. 'And don't forget, you'll make a whole new circle through your driving lessons!'

'It's easy here, but a bit different in England,' David said. 'I don't think I'll set up my own school.'

'Do you have a lot of friends back in Germany, Elsa?' Fiona asked.

'No, hardly any, a lot of acquaintances but only one good friend. She's called Hannah.' She spoke regretfully.

Fiona announced that she was going on the train with David to help smooth over the homecoming for him. 'Will you be here for much longer, Thomas?' she asked.

'No, I don't think so. I think I'll go back to California fairly soon,' Thomas said. His eyes had a faraway look. They didn't want to ask him any more. It was clearly a decision not fully made.

'And when are you going back to Germany, Elsa?' David asked gently.

'I'm not going back,' she said simply. 'I don't know where I'll go, but I'm not going back to Dieter.'

'When did you decide this?' Thomas leaned forward and looked at her very intensely.

'Last night, on my balcony, looking out at the sea. I wrote to Dieter. I posted the letter this morning on the way to meet you all. He should get it in four or five days. So now I have time to make up my mind about what I am to do.' She smiled a slow warm smile at Thomas.

You're not going to go down to the café to say goodbye to them, Vonni?' Andreas asked as he called into the craft shop.

'No, I annoyed them all enough while they were here. I'll let them go in peace,' she said, not looking up.

'You are a difficult woman, Vonni, prickly like a thorn bush. Both David and Fiona said last night how grateful they are to you.' Andreas shook his head, mystified.

'Yes, they did; they were very polite. And by the way, the urge to drink seems to have passed over like a summer cloud. No, it's the other two, Thomas and Elsa, who I really upset. But you and I have heard plenty of advice, Andreas, and did we ever take it? The answer is no.'

'And what would you have changed if you could have your life all over again?' he asked. This was unfamiliar territory for Andreas. Normally he left things as they were, without question or analysis.

'I should have fought Stavros for the petrol station. The people here are fair, they would have known I had bought it for him. I could have raised my son. But, no, I thought the solution was somewhere at the bottom of a *raki* bottle. So it didn't happen.' She looked around her despondently.

'You haven't asked me what I would have changed,' he said.

'I suppose you'd have managed to keep Adoni here. Am I right?'

'Yes, of course I should have done that.' His eyes were sad. 'And I also should have asked you to marry me twenty-five years ago.'

She looked at him, astounded. 'Andreas! You don't mean that. We never even remotely loved each other.'

'I didn't love my wife either, not in any real sense, that is. Not like people read about and sing about. We got on all right and we were company for each other. You and I could have been fine companions.'

'We *are* fine companions, Andreas,' she said. 'It would never have worked out. Believe me. You did the right thing there. You see, I loved Stavros exactly the way you read about, sing about and dream about. I could never have settled for any other kind of love.'

She said it in a matter-of-fact way that brought normality back to their conversation.

'So it was for the best,' Andreas said.

'Definitely. And listen to me, Andreas. Adoni will come back to see you. I know it.'

He shook his big head. 'No, it's only a wish, a fairy tale.'

But Vonni's faith was unshaken. 'He needs time, Andreas. Chicago is a long way away. He'll need to get his head round it. But he'll be here.'

'Thank you, Vonni. You are indeed a good companion,' Andreas said, and blew his nose very loudly.

They agreed to meet at the ferry half an hour before departure and then all headed off from the café in their different directions.

Fiona and David went to say their goodbyes, but when they arrived at the craft shop Vonni was not at home.

'She'll come to wave us off,' David said.

'She's very sad these days, she's lost her sparkle somehow,' Fiona said.

'Maybe she's envious with you going back to Ireland . . . something she was never able to do,' David speculated.

'Yes, but she says herself it turned out all right, her love affair, for quite a time, and she did have a son to show for it.'

'Wouldn't it be wonderful if he came back? If he met Adoni somewhere out in Chicago and they decided to go back and swing again on the old tree up at the taverna,' David said.

Fiona pealed with laughter. 'Ah, David, and they say the Irish are the sentimental ones believing in fairy tales.'

Vonni wasn't in her henhouse, nor in her craft shop nor at the police station.

Elsa decided she would go out on the road to the old man who didn't believe in modern medicine. She might find her there. The sun was high in the sky and she wore her white cotton sun-hat against the heat. The road was dusty. Children came from the tumbledown buildings and waved at her. Elsa wished she had brought some candy, *karameles*, they called it.

She remembered the old man's house and gathered together some sentences in halting Greek to say she was looking for his friend Vonni. But they weren't necessary. Vonni was there, sitting by the old man's bed, holding his hand. She didn't look remotely surprised to see Elsa.

'He's dying,' Vonni said in a matter-of-fact tone.

'Should I go and get the doctor?' Elsa was practical.

'No, he wouldn't let a doctor cross the door, but I'll tell him that you are a herbalist and he'll take what you bring him.'

'You can't do that, Vonni.' Elsa was shocked.

'You'd prefer he died in pain?'

'No, but we can't play games with someone's life.'

'He has about six or seven hours more of life, if that. If you want to help go to Dr Leros. Tell him the situation here, ask him for morphine.'

'But won't I need—'

'You won't need anything. Call into my shop and get a pottery bowl as well. Go quickly now.'

As Vonni had predicted, there was indeed no problem getting the drugs. On her way back up the dusty road, an old van came along. Elsa stopped it and the driver took her back to the old man's house.

'That was very speedy,' Vonni said approvingly, and then she ground up some of the morphine tablets, mixing them with honey in her pottery bowl, and spooned the mixture into the old man's mouth.

The old man mumbled something.

'What did he say?'

'He actually said that the herbalist is very beautiful,' Vonni said wryly.

'I wish he hadn't said that.' Elsa sounded sad.

'Come on, these are the last things he's going to look at—your face and mine. Isn't it good he has yours to concentrate on?'

'Vonni, *please*.' She had tears in her eyes.

'If you want to help, keep smiling at him, Elsa. Think of him as if he were your father, put love and warmth in your eyes.'

Elsa felt that this wasn't the time to remind Vonni that she hardly remembered the father who had abandoned her. Instead she looked at this poor old Greek man and thought of him and his life that was ending with an Irishwoman and a German woman at his deathbed, giving him a very large dose of morphine.

Fiona and David waved until the ferry had turned along the coast and they were out of sight of their friends on the quay.

'I feel desperately lonely,' Fiona said.

'Me too. I could have lived there happily for ever,' David said.

'Could we? Or are we just fooling ourselves, do you think?' Fiona wondered.

'It's different for you, Fiona. You love your job, you have friends, your family aren't going to suffocate you.'

'I'm not sure how they're going to react. I'm the eldest of the family, I didn't show much example to my sisters by running off with a lunatic.'

'But at least you have sisters. I'm the only one. I bear the whole brunt of it. And my father is dying. I shall have to look at him every day and tell him I'll be proud to work in his company.'

'Maybe it won't be as bad as you think.' Fiona was hopeful.

'Yes, it will. You're very good to come and help me break the ice.'

'Will they think I'm your girlfriend, a frightening Catholic coming to destroy your tradition?'

'They already do,' he said gloomily.

'Well, it'll cheer them up enormously when I hare off to Ireland next day,' Fiona said cheerfully. 'They'll be so relieved they'll gather you to their bosoms.'

'We were never slow on the bosom gathering—that's part of the problem,' David said.

And for some reason they both found this incredibly funny.

Elsa and Thomas watched until the ferry was out of sight. Then they walked slowly back up to the town.

'Where were you this afternoon?' he asked. 'I was looking for you, I thought we could take off together in the little boat again.'

'Tomorrow would be lovely,' she said. 'That's if you're free.'

'I'm free.'

'Let's make the most of what time we have left,' Elsa said. 'By renting a boat tomorrow, having a picnic; another day taking the bus to Kalatriada. I'd love to see that place again when I'm not so stressed.'

'That's settled then,' he said. And they both smiled conspiratorially.

To change the subject, he asked, 'You didn't tell me what you were doing all afternoon.'

'I was in a small cluttered house with Vonni, watching an old man die. An old man with no family, no relations, only Vonni and me. I never saw anyone die before.'

'Oh, poor Elsa.' He leaned towards her and stroked her hair.

'Not poor Elsa. I am young, I have my life ahead; he was old and lonely and frightened. Poor old Nikolas. Poor old man.'

'You were kind to him. You did what you could.'

Elsa pulled away from him. 'Oh, Thomas, if you could have seen

Vonni. She was wonderful. She fed him honey on a spoon and made me hold his hand. She was like a sort of angel.'

They walked together back to her place.

'Tomorrow we'll take out a little boat again and go to sea,' he said and, as she turned to leave, she gave him a big hug.

'**A**ndy, is this an OK time to call?'

'Sure, Thomas, for me it's fine, but I'm afraid Bill and his mother have gone exploring.'

'Exploring?'

'I mean shopping really, they call it exploring. Could you call in thirty minutes, or make it forty-five? You know what shopping can turn into, I don't want you to waste your nickel just talking to me.'

'I'm happy to talk to you, Andy. I want to ask you something.'

'Sure, Thomas, ask what you want.' He could hear the slightly wary note in Andy's voice.

'I was wondering, if I came back, like a bit sooner than anyone thought, do you think that would be a good thing?'

'Came back? Sorry, Thomas, I'm not entirely with you. You mean came back here to town?'

'Yes, that's what I meant.' Thomas felt cold. The guy was going to say that it would be a bad idea. He knew it.

'But you leased your apartment for a year, didn't you?'

'Yeah, but I thought I'd get a place, a bigger place, with a yard for Bill to play in.'

'You're going to try to take Bill back?' Andy's voice was choked.

'Not back to live, of course not, just a place he could visit.' Thomas tried not to sound impatient.

'Oh, I see.'

God, Andy was slow. It took for ever for an idea to sink in and another age for him to answer.

'So what do you think? Do you think it would be something Bill would like . . . to have me down the street from him? You're the guy on the spot, Andy. Tell me. I just want to do what's best.'

Across thousands of miles, Thomas could almost hear the slow smile crossing Andy's handsome, empty features.

'Thomas, that boy would love it, it would be like Santa Claus and all his birthdays coming together!'

There was no doubting the utter sincerity of the man. Thomas could hardly stumble out the words. 'I won't tell him just yet, if that's OK with you. I'd like to set it up and give him a definite date before I begin talking to him about it. Does that make sense to you, Andy?'

'Sure it does, I'll say nothing until we hear from you.'

'Thanks for understanding,' Thomas mumbled.

'Understanding? That a man should want to be near his own flesh and blood? What's to understand?'

Thomas hung up. Everyone believed that Bill was his flesh and blood. Everyone except Shirley. And indeed for all he knew she might believe it too. After all, he had never told her about the doctor's report. It had been too late to tell her. She might well not know.

Vonni settled herself down in the shed that Thomas called her henhouse. She had seen him talking on the telephone. And earlier she had seen him holding Elsa's hand. They had so much ahead of them. She sighed. It would be wonderful to have years and years ahead. Time to go places, to learn new things. To fall in love again. She wondered what they would do. She wondered about Fiona and David taking a late plane tonight to London from Athens. Would their homecomings be stormy, awkward or emotional? She hoped they would let her know.

She tried to imagine her own son, Stavros, who would never come back and who, as a boy, had once sent a message to say that she had stolen his childhood and he never wanted to see her again. In all her confessions and recitals of her story she had never told any of them that. It was too hurtful to say, even to think about.

CHAPTER TEN

ELSA HAD THE PICNIC ready when Thomas came by to pick her up next morning. It was in a basket with a cloth tucked in to cover the food.

'I was wondering . . .' Thomas began.

'What were you wondering, dear Thomas?'

'Don't mock me, I'm a frail poor creature!' he begged.

'I wasn't mocking you, I swear.'

'I was wondering if we might row up the coast to Kalatriada . . . and stay there. For the night. That's what I was wondering.'

'I think you should wonder no more, it's a great idea.' She began to go back into the villa.

'Where are you going?' he asked anxiously.

'To get a toothbrush, an extra pair of panties, a clean blouse. OK?'

'Very OK.' He had been expecting some kind of resistance.

Elsa was out in thirty seconds. 'Will the man with the little boats let us take one away for so long?' she asked.

'I've been down there to check . . . well, in case you said yes . . . and he said it would be fine.' Thomas looked slightly embarrassed.

'Go on, Thomas, what did he really say?' She laughed affectionately.

'He kept talking about you as . . . my *sizighos* . . . it's a partner or a spouse or something, I'm afraid.'

'Well, all right, *sizighos*, let's hit the high seas!' Elsa said cheerfully.

They took a boat and rowed out of the harbour. The sea was calm and they went up the coast identifying places they knew as they passed. Halfway to Kalatriada they found a wooden platform about a hundred yards from shore. The kind of place that people might swim out to.

Thomas tied their little boat to one of the posts. It was ideal for their picnic and Elsa climbed out of the boat and laid the cloth out between them. She spread the taramasalata and hummous on the pitta bread, arranged the figs and watermelon on a plate. Then she poured a glass of wine from a bottle and held it out to him.

'You know, you really are quite dazzlingly beautiful,' he said.

'Thank you, but it's not important,' she said in a matter-of-fact voice.

'All right, it's not *that* important, but it's true,' he said and spoke of it no more.

Kalatriada didn't have a real harbour, so they tied up to a jetty and walked up the steep road to the little village.

Irini remembered them from the last visit. She took their hands in hers and greeted them warmly. She seemed to think it in no way unusual that this happy, handsome couple asked for two rooms.

'We have only one room free, but it has two beds—one for each person,' she said.

'I think we could survive that, don't you, Elsa?'

'Certainly,' she agreed.

Did he say anything about this girl he's bringing with him?' Harold Fine asked for the third time.

'No, but I don't think it's a romance,' David's mother said.

'He's never brought a girl home before, Miriam,' Harold Fine said.

'I know but I still don't think so. She's only staying one night, Harold.'

'That's what they say now,' David's father said darkly.

'**A**nd what in the name of God is she stopping off in Manchester for?' Sean Ryan asked Barbara.

'There wasn't much time to explain but apparently it's someone she met whose father is dying and so Fiona is going to spend a night with the family to ease the situation,' Barbara said.

'Another lame duck,' Fiona's father grumbled.

'Just Fiona being kind,' Barbara said.

'Look where being kind got her before,' he muttered.

'But that's all over now, Mr Ryan.' Barbara sometimes felt that life was all about being relentlessly cheerful both on and off the wards. 'Her plane lands at four, she'll be here before six.'

'I wonder, Barbara, if you were free could you ever . . .' Fiona's mother began.

'Like, be here when she arrives . . .' Fiona's father finished for her.

'To ease the situation?' Barbara asked.

'To stop me saying the wrong thing,' Sean Ryan said bluntly.

'Sure, I'll ask them to let me change my shift,' Barbara said.

It was their second night in Kalatriada and, unlike the time that they had been here with David and Fiona, it was a clear starry night.

Irini set a little table for Thomas and Elsa out in the open air where they could see the square. She had put little sprays of bougainvillaea in a white china vase as a decoration on their table.

As they came to the end of their meal, Thomas took Elsa's hand. 'I feel very happy here. Calm, as if the storms have died down.'

'I feel the same,' Elsa said.

'Which of course is ridiculous,' Thomas said. 'The storms haven't really gone away at all. They'll have to be dealt with sooner or later.'

'But maybe we feel we can deal with them now,' Elsa suggested.

'How do you mean?'

'Well, you are going back to Bill—the only question is when? And I'm not going back to Germany, so the only question is where?'

'We'll waste no time on regrets, though, will we?' Thomas said.

'No, regrets are useless. Destructive even.'

'Would you like coffee?' he asked.

'Maybe . . . I'm a little nervous actually, Thomas,' she admitted.

'So am I, but I don't think coffee ever calmed anyone. Shall we go, do you think?' She held his hand as they walked up the wooden stairs.

Irini smiled at them and seemed to understand that this was an important night.

In the bedroom, Thomas went towards Elsa, held her to him and kissed her neck gently. She gave a little shiver.

He drew away. 'Was that gross or something?' he asked, irresolute.

'No, it was exciting and lovely. Come here,' she said.

And first she stroked his face and then she kissed him. Her hands went up and down his back and gently he opened her blouse.

'Elsa, I don't know . . . I hope . . .' he began.

'I don't know either, and also I hope,' she murmured. 'Please love me, Thomas. Love me in this beautiful island and let's not think about anything beyond tonight . . .'

David sat and talked to his father along the lines that he and Fiona had rehearsed. Nothing about his illness but a lot about the office and the upcoming award.

'I didn't think you'd care about that kind of thing,' Harold Fine said.

'But they are honouring you, Father. Why should I not care and be very proud?'

His father nodded and smiled. 'Well, I'll tell you frankly, son, it wouldn't have been the same if you weren't here to take part in it.'

In the next room, Fiona talked to David's mother.

'Mrs Fine, you are very kind to put me up for the night. I so appreciate it.'

'Well, of course, any friend of David's is most welcome.'

'He told me all about your lovely home but he didn't do it justice, it's gorgeous.'

Miriam Fine was pleased and confused in equal measure.

'And you live in Dublin, David tells me?'

'Yes, I've been away for many weeks now. I'm so looking forward to seeing them all again.' Fiona's smile never faltered.

'And it was a nice place, this island you were all visiting?'

'Oh, it was lovely, Mrs Fine. They were very kind people.'

'And what exactly were you doing there?'

'Having a career break,' Fiona said blithely.

'And you're a nurse in Dublin?' Miriam Fine was beginning to breathe more easily. This was not a girl with designs on her only son.

'I spent six months on an oncology ward before I went away. They can do so much to help people nowadays, Mrs Fine, you'd be amazed.'

And to her amazement Miriam Fine found herself sitting down and talking to this girl with an Irish accent who was extraordinarily helpful on many different levels. She could not have asked for a better visitor.

At the desk of the Anna Beach Hotel they held several faxes for Elsa. They were increasingly urgent, asking her to pick up her email.

The desk clerk spotted Vonni in the foyer craft shop.

'I wonder could you advise me about these messages? The German woman hasn't come in for a while . . .'

Vonni looked at them with interest. 'I can't read German—what do they say?'

'Some man in Germany saying she can't play games like this, can't leave him. That sort of thing.'

'I see.' Vonni was pleased.

'Do you think we should fax him back saying she isn't around?' the clerk asked, anxious that the hotel should not be blamed for inefficiency.

'No, I'd leave it. If he calls, of course, you could say that you heard she has gone away for a few days.'

Dublin

My dear Vonni,

I swore to you that I'd write when I was home for twenty-four hours. So here goes. The journey was fine, a plane full of tourists, holidaymakers. David and I felt very superior because we knew the real Greece, not just beaches and discos. We took the train up to David's place. His family have this huge house full of antiques and valuable ornaments. His mother is very innocent and fussy. Mr Fine looks badly, he only has a few months to live. He was quite frightened, but he was able to talk to me about palliative care. He didn't really know what they did and didn't want to ask. David and I cried at Manchester Airport—people thought that we were lovers saying goodbye!

Barbara was at home when I got there, to take the edge off things. Dad was walking on eggshells trying not to say anything that would offend; Mam was like some kind of TV commercial about gravy and home cooking. You'd think I'd been in some gulag or other rather than on an island full of wonderful smells and tastes. I still yearn for the smell of the roast lamb and pine nuts up in Andreas's.

Do give him my love, I'll write when I start my job and when Barbara and I get our new flat.

I can never thank you enough, Vonni, especially for that day in Athens. I have a hope, a dream that you find your husband and son again. You deserve to.

Love, Fiona

Manchester

Dear Vonni,

Oh, I miss you and Aghia Anna every hour of every day. How good it would be to wake up to that bright sky and spend a day without care until the stars came out. I suppose there are stars here, it's been overcast so I don't seem to see them.

My father looks awful. Fiona was wonderful with him, by the way. Talking to him as if she had known him all her life and telling him how great the drugs were to take the edges off pain. Even my mother loved her and was quite sorry to realise that we actually were just friends. We cried at the airport when she left.

Am I glad I came back? Well, put simply, I had to come back. I feel weak at the thought that I might not have done so if it hadn't been for you. The days are dreary, and I will soon be starting work in the office. I have to concentrate because my father wants to talk about it each evening. The man who was running the show naturally hates me, and is very resentful. He keeps wanting to know when I start. I so want to tell him how I feel about it all. But of course I can't. The award is next week.

I dreamed the other night that your son came back. Right into the harbour in a boat with an outboard engine. It could happen, couldn't it?

Love, David

'**W**hen should we go back to the real world?' Elsa asked after days spent wandering around the hills and coves of Kalatriada.

'Do you mean back to Aghia Anna or points further west?'

'I suppose Aghia Anna as a base camp,' Elsa said.

They had been living a strange life here, totally disconnected from the real world. They had gone shopping in the markets and bought cheese for their lunches on the hills. Because they hadn't really packed for such an extended visit, they bought a couple of extra garments at stalls on market day. Thomas looked splendid in a colourful Greek shirt and Elsa had bought him a pair of elegant cream-coloured trousers in a desperate attempt to get him to abandon the three-quarter-length shorts with all the pockets.

'*Orea*,' Irini said when she saw him dressed up.

'Yes, indeed, he is beautiful,' Elsa agreed.

'I miss my other trousers,' Thomas grumbled.

'You're the only one who does—they're terrible!'

'Oh, Elsa, indulge me, let me wear them. Please,' he begged.

'Hey, this will never do. Wear what you like,' Elsa laughed at him.

'Shall we row back to Aghia Anna tomorrow?' he suggested.

'Yes, it's not as if it were goodbye, we can still be together there,' Elsa consoled herself.

'Of course we can, we're in no hurry to go anywhere,' Thomas agreed.

The following evening, Elsa sat in the Anna Beach with her big organiser diary beside her. For the first time in months she was looking up media contacts back in Germany.

The desk clerk brought her a sheaf of faxes. The last one said that Dieter would be coming out in two weeks' time to find her.

Elsa calmly ripped all the faxes in half and threw them into the wastepaper basket. Then she went to the business centre, where she could log on to her email, and there she began to work.

Her first email was to Dieter:

I have written a long letter explaining why I am not coming back. Come out to Greece if you like, Dieter, but I will be gone. It will be a wasted journey. Elsa

'**A**ndy, am I disturbing you? It's Thomas.'

'No way. We're down in Sedona today, another canyon, it's real pretty here, Thomas.'

Thomas could hear Bill calling out excitedly.

'Is that Dad? Can I talk to him?'

'Sure, Bill, he called to talk to you. Take the phone and go off to have a real good chat with him.'

'Dad? Is it really you?'

'Nobody else, Bill, just me.'

'What have you been doing, Dad?'

'I went to a little village, a tiny little place, real old-fashioned. One day I'll take you there.'

'Was it lonely for you in this little village all by yourself?' Bill asked.

'Um, no, not lonely . . .'

'So you don't miss us or anything?' the boy asked, sounding very disappointed.

'Oh, I do, Bill, I miss you every single day. And do you know what I'm going to do about it? I'm going to come back there in ten days' time and we'll have a great time.'

'Dad, that's *fantastic*! How long are you coming back for?'

'For good,' he said.

And as he heard the boy who would always be his son shouting out, 'Mom, Andy, Dad's coming home. In ten days' time and he's going to stay for ever,' Thomas felt the tears falling down his face.

'**V**onni, do you know what I want to talk to you about?' Takis the lawyer asked her, as he led her into his office.

'Is it something about Stavros?' she asked hesitantly.

'No, not at all,' he said, taken aback. 'It's about Nikolas Yannilakis. As you know, Nikolas died last week. Vonni, he left you everything.'

'But he didn't have anything to leave!' Vonni said, wide-eyed.

'He had enough. He came in here six months ago and made a proper will. Left it all to you. His little house, his furniture, his savings . . .'

'Well, imagine him thinking of doing that!' Vonni was stunned. 'I suppose we should give the house to his neighbours, they have a lot of children and could do with more space. I could clear it out for them.'

'You haven't asked about his savings,' Takis said gravely.

'Sure, poor Nikolas didn't have any savings to speak of,' Vonni said.

'He left you over a hundred thousand euros,' Takis said.

Vonni looked at him in amazement and sank into a chair. 'That can't be, Takis. The man had nothing, he lived in a hovel . . . where on earth did he get that amount of money?'

'Family apparently.'

'But why didn't he use it to give himself some comfort?'

'Oh, Vonni, I don't know. But Nikolas didn't touch the money, so now it's all yours. And rightly so. You looked after him in a way no one else could have done.'

She sat very still in shocked silence.

Takis wasn't used to Vonni being like this.

'Of course, you don't have to make any decisions yet. I'll arrange all the transfers when you've had time to think about things and feel like giving me instructions.'

'I feel like doing it now, Takis, if that's all right.'

'Certainly.' He sat down opposite her and pulled a pad of paper towards him.

'I don't intend to touch any of that money. Just leave it where it is. I will, as I said, give the little house to the family next door, but I would like them to think it came directly from Nikolas. And I want to make a will . . .'

'Very sensible, Vonni,' Takis said in a low voice. He didn't think it was sensible at all, but it wasn't his business.

'And I would like to leave everything, my craft shop, my apartment, and this legacy from Nikolas, to my son Stavros.'

'I beg your pardon?'

'You heard me.'

'But you haven't seen him in years. He never came back to you despite all your pleas.'

'Are you going to make this will for me, Takis, or do I have to go and find another lawyer?'

It was two days before Thomas would leave for Athens.

'I want you to come up to Andreas's tonight for dinner,' Elsa said. 'We have a lot to talk about. I'll see that we have a quiet table,' she promised.

She wore a simple white cotton dress that night and had a flower clipped in her hair.

'You look lovely and so dressed up. I'm so pleased I wore my smart new Kalatriada trousers,' he said when he saw her.

'I got this dress today to impress you and I have a taxi to take us to the restaurant. How about that for style?'

They went up the winding road to Andreas's taverna, watching the usual starry sky unfold out over the sea.

They had indeed been given a little table for two right at the edge of the terrace with an uninterrupted view.

Little Rina served them. Andreas was indoors. Yorghis, Vonni and Dr Leros were in there with him too. They would talk to them later, when it was time for the second coffee.

'I need to talk to you about my looking for a job,' Elsa said.

'Yes.'

'Why didn't you ask?'

'Because I was afraid you would be offered a big position back in Germany. And, to be honest, I was afraid you might meet Dieter again and . . . and . . .'

'I got a job, Thomas.'

'Where?' he asked in a very shaky voice.

'I'm almost afraid to tell you.'

'Then it *is* Germany,' he said with a defeated face.

'No. based in Los Angeles, but roaming up and down the west coast. A weekly column for a big magazine, interviews, politics, features. Whatever I can come up with really.' She looked at him anxiously.

'Where?' he asked, dumbfounded.

'California,' she said nervously. 'Is it too much of an assumption? Too soon? I mean I just couldn't bear to lose you . . . but if you think . . .'

A slow smile began to broaden across his face.

'Oh, Elsa, darling . . .' he began.   z

'I don't have to live with you or anything, I don't want to crowd you out . . . you see, I know that we haven't been together long, but now I couldn't exist without you . . .'

Thomas stood up and went to her side of the table, he pulled her to her feet and kissed her. Someone took a photograph of them but they didn't care, they stood locked in each other's arms as if they were never going to be able to draw apart. Then of course the group in the kitchen came out to join them, and many toasts were drunk. To the couple.

'That man who took your picture, he was German,' said Vonni. 'He recognised you, Elsa, from the television. He asked who Thomas was. I explained you were a high-powered American academic, Thomas, and that you were Elsa's fiancé.'

'*What?*' Thomas and Elsa spoke at the same time.

'Well, I wouldn't have told them anything, Thomas, if you had been wearing those terrible shorts with all the pockets. But once I saw you in a decent pair of trousers, then I thought it doesn't matter for Elsa if some fan sells the picture to a German newspaper!'

They talked on easily as always, looking down on the harbour way below. The last ferry had come in an hour ago but Andreas's taverna hadn't expected any guests coming from that sailing. It was too late and too far to walk. So they were surprised when they saw someone toiling up the winding path.

It was a man of about thirty. He had a pack on his back and carried a suitcase in each hand.

'There's a dedicated diner,' said Elsa admiringly.

'Maybe he's heard of Vonni's stuffed vine leaves,' said Thomas with a smile. He loved Vonni for calling him Elsa's fiancé even though he was bewildered that everyone hated his lovely shorts with the pockets.

'It's late for anyone to come up here,' Dr Leros said, mystified.

'Unless they really intended to,' said Yorghis in an odd sort of voice, peering at the gateway.

Vonni had stood up to look at the man hesitating at the entrance.

'Andreas!' she said in a choked voice. 'Andreas, my friend, it *is*, it really is!'

Elsa and Thomas looked from one to the other without any idea what was happening. Andreas had stood up and was staggering towards the gate with his arms out.

'Adoni . . .' he cried. '*Adoni mou!* You came back. *Adoni ghie mou.* My son, you came back to see me.'

'I came back to stay, Father, if you'll have me?'

The men embraced in a grasp that looked as if it would never end.

Then Yorghis moved forward, and Vonni and Dr Leros. And they were a little group talking excitedly in Greek and embracing.

Thomas and Elsa held hands very tight.

'We'll never forget this night,' Thomas said.

Elsa said, 'Was I too forward, too pushy? Tell me, Thomas?'

Before he could answer, Andreas and his son came over.

'Adoni, this is the wonderful young woman who told me that I should write to you, when I wondered if you would care. She said everybody loves a letter . . .'

Adoni was tall and handsome. He had a shock of black hair which would one day go grey-white like his father's, but not for a long time and then possibly here in Aghia Anna. Elsa, who could summon words at will on television in front of millions of viewers, was without words. Instead she stood up and hugged Adoni tight as if they were old friends.

'Aren't you just beautiful,' Adoni said admiringly to the blonde girl in the white dress.

'Elsa and Thomas are together,' Andreas said hastily, lest there should be any misunderstanding.

Adoni shook Thomas by the hand. 'You are a very lucky man,' he said with great sincerity.

Thomas agreed. 'I am a very lucky man.' And then he stood up to address the group of friends. He looked straight at Elsa.

'I want to tell you all that Elsa will be leaving with me. We will be going to California together.'

'Yet another reason to celebrate tonight,' Andreas cried out, tears in his eyes.

Thomas and Elsa kissed again, and then they sat with his arm around her shoulders as they watched the homecoming unfold.

Andreas, Yorghis and little Rina ran to get food and wine for the prodigal son.

Vonni sat beside Adoni, her eyes sparkling, flanked on either side by her friends Andreas and Yorghis.

'One night Stavros will come into that harbour,' Andreas said.

'And it will be a night like this,' Yorghis encouraged.

'Yes, yes, I'm sure,' Vonni said, eyes bright, face hopeful.

They knew she was putting on a cheerful manner. At the same time they each stretched out a hand to hold hers. Now her smile was genuine.

'Of course he will come back one day,' she said as she gripped their hands. 'We only have to look at tonight to know that miracles happen. And there is no point in going on if you don't believe that.'

Dr Leros came out of the kitchen excitedly.

'There are two bouzouki players out there, they want to play to welcome you home, Adoni,' he begged.

'I'd love that,' he laughed.

And as the music rang out into the night and the people in the restaurant began to clap to the beat, Adoni stood up and went into the centre of the terrace.

And in front of everyone he began to dance. Adoni danced in front of forty people, some of them customers who knew nothing of what was happening, some like Thomas and Elsa who knew part of the story, and some like his father, his uncle, the doctor and Vonni who knew everything.

His arms high in the air, he swooped and bent and danced, overjoyed to be back where he belonged.

And a little light rain came down but nobody cared.

It didn't get in the way of the stars.

Maeve Binchy

Maeve Binchy was born in Dalkey, Ireland and attended University College, Dublin. 'My mother hoped I would meet a nice doctor or barrister or accountant who would marry me and take me to live in what is now called Fashionable Dublin Four. But I was a bit loud to make a nice professional wife, and anyway, I was too keen on spending my holidays in far flung places to meet any of these people. The future leaders of society did not holiday on the decks of cheap boats, or work in kibbutzim in Israel or mind children as camp counsellors in the United States. My mother abandoned this hope on my behalf and got great value out of my escapades in foreign parts. I wrote marvellous long rambling letters home from these trips, editing out the bits they didn't need to know, bits about falling in love with highly unsuitable foreigners. In fact my parents were so impressed with these eager letters from abroad they got them typed and sent them to a newspaper and that's how I became a writer.' Maeve also met and married writer Gordon Snell, with whom she is still blissfully happy, and who 'believed I could do anything'. So she tried her hand at fiction and, as she says modestly, 'that took off fine,' and for over twenty-seven years Maeve has been writing memorable novels, selling over forty million copies of her books worldwide.

A few years ago, Maeve Binchy decided to turn her back on the 'hurly-burly' of a best-selling author's life, much to the distress of her fans across the world. But Maeve says she found herself quite unable to resist the impulse to write. 'In my mind I never really retired from writing, I just retired from promoting books, which is quite different. My health has not been great and I just do not have the energy for book tours. Now I just write at home at my own pace and it works very well.' That's pure understatement. *Quentins*, her first novel after temporary retirement, shot straight into the best-seller lists, and since writing *Nights of Rain and Stars*, Maeve has also written *Whitethorn Woods*, *Heart and Soul* and *Minding Frankie*.

Nights of Rain and Stars explores the lives and emotions of a group of young tourists who arrive in a small coastal village in Greece. 'I used to love going to Greece when I was a young teacher, and then later I went back there with my husband Gordon. I'm fairly familiar with the country so it wasn't a strange location for me. And people are the same all over the world. They love, hope and dream; they do foolish things, then heroic things. They are unselfish and they are thoughtless; they laugh and they weep in every land. So I don't think it matters if I make them German, American, Irish or English like the four young people in my book—they feel the same as we all do.'

By the same token, then, maybe there is something of Maeve herself in the central character of Vonni, a generous-hearted Irish woman who has spent her adult life in the Greek village of Aghia Anna. 'Yes, there is a lot of me in Vonni. But I'm not a tiny elfin person like she is, and I am not a recovering alcoholic. Also, I am not a mother, and nor did I have a tragic relationship with a husband . . . but on the other hand I did cash a cheque in the 1966 bank strike in Ireland, and I know I am very bossy and think I can run everyone else's lives for them. So we are alike in many ways!'

Also from Maeve Binchy:

Fiction:
Light a Penny Candle, Echoes, The Lilac Bus, Firefly Summer, Silver Wedding, Circle of Friends, The Copper Beech, The Glass Lake, Evening Class, Tara Road, Scarlet Feather, Quentins, Nights of Rain and Stars, Whitethorn Woods, Heart and Soul, Minding Frankie.

Non-Fiction:
Aches & Pains, The Maeve Binchy Writer's Club.

Short Stories:
Victoria Line, Central Line, Dublin 4, This Year It Will Be Different, The Return Journey.

Plays:
Deeply Regretted By.

Novella:
Star Sullivan.

The
Undomestic
Goddess

Sophie Kinsella

My name is Samantha Sweeting.
I am twenty-nine years old and about to
be made a partner at Carter Spink, one
of the biggest law firms in London.
OK, there are a few drawbacks—
I spend all my waking hours
at work, have no home life and have
never had time to learn
to cook or sew on a button.
But then, who needs to be
a domestic goddess?

One

WOULD YOU CONSIDER **yourself stressed?**

No. I'm not stressed.

I'm . . . busy. Plenty of people are busy. It's the way the world is. I have a high-powered job, my career is important to me and I enjoy it.

OK. So sometimes I do feel a bit tense. Kind of pressured. But I'm a lawyer in the City, for God's sake. What do you expect?

On average, how many hours do you spend in the office every day?

~~14~~

~~12~~

~~8~~

It depends.

Do you exercise regularly?

~~I regularly go swimming~~

~~I occasionally go swim~~

I am intending to begin a regular regime of swimming. When I have time.

Do you drink 8 glasses of water a day?

~~Yes~~

~~Someti~~

No.

I put down my pen and clear my throat. Across the room, Maya looks up from where she's rearranging all her little pots of wax and nail varnish. Maya is my beauty therapist for the day.

'Everything all right with the questionnaire?' she says in her soft voice.

'Are all these questions absolutely necessary?' I say politely.

'We like to have as much information as possible to assess your beauty and health needs,' she says in soothing yet implacable tones.

I glance at my watch. Nine forty-five. I don't have time for this. But it's my birthday treat and I promised Aunt Patsy.

To be more accurate, it's *last* year's birthday treat. In the card that came with the 'Ultimate De-stress Experience' voucher she wrote *Make Some Time For Yourself, Samantha!!!*

Which I did fully intend to do. But we had a couple of busy patches at work and somehow a year went by without my finding a spare moment. I'm a lawyer with Carter Spink, and just at the moment things are pretty hectic. It's a blip. It'll get better. I just have to get through the next couple of weeks.

Anyway, then Aunt Patsy sent me *this* year's birthday card—and I suddenly realised the voucher was about to expire. So here I am, on my twenty-ninth birthday. Sitting on a couch in a white towelling robe and surreal paper knickers. With a half-day window. Max.

Do you smoke?

No.

Do you drink alcohol?

Yes.

Do you eat regular home-cooked meals?

I look up, a bit defensive. What does that have to do with anything? What makes home-cooked meals superior?

I eat a nutritious, varied diet, I write at last.

Which is absolutely true. Everyone knows the Chinese live longer than we do—so what could be more healthy than to eat their food?

'I'm done,' I announce, and hand the pages back to Maya, who starts reading through my answers. Her finger is travelling down the paper at a snail's pace. Like we've got all the time in the world. Which she may well have. But I have to be back in the office by one.

'I've read your answers carefully.' Maya gives me a thoughtful look. 'And you're obviously quite a stressed-out woman.'

What? Where does she get that from? I specifically put on the form, I am *not* stressed out.

'No, I'm not.' I give her a relaxed, see-how-unstressed-I-am smile.

Maya looks unconvinced. 'Your job is obviously very pressured.'

'I thrive under pressure,' I explain. Which is true. I've known that about myself ever since . . .

Well, ever since my mother told me, when I was about eight. *You thrive under pressure, Samantha.* Our whole family thrives under pressure. It's like our family motto or something.

I love my job. I love the satisfaction of spotting the loophole in a contract. I love the adrenaline rush of closing a deal. I love the thrill of negotiation, and arguing, and making the best point in the room.

I suppose, occasionally, I do feel as though someone's piling heavy weights on me and I have to keep holding them up, no matter how exhausted I am. But then everyone probably feels like that. It's normal.

'Well.' Maya gets up. She presses a button set in the wall and gentle panpipes music fills the air. 'All I can say is, you've come to the right place, Samantha. Our aim here is to de-stress, revitalise and detoxify.'

'Lovely,' I say, only half listening. I've just remembered, I never got back to David Elldridge about that Ukrainian oil contract.

'The aim of the Green Tree Centre is to provide a haven of tranquillity, away from all your day-to-day worries.' Maya presses another button in the wall and the light dims to a muted glow. 'Before we start,' she says softly, 'do you have any questions?'

'Actually, I do.' I lean forward. 'Could I send a quick email?'

'Samantha, Samantha . . .' Maya shakes her head. 'You're here to relax. Not to send emails. It's an obsession! An addiction!'

That's ridiculous. I'm not *obsessed*. I check my emails about once every . . . thirty seconds, maybe. A lot can change in thirty seconds.

'This is why we ask that you leave all electronic equipment in the safe. No mobile phones are permitted. No little computers.' Maya spreads her arms. 'This is a retreat. An escape from the world.'

'Right.' I nod meekly.

Now is probably not the time to reveal that I have a BlackBerry hidden in my paper knickers. I did see the rule about no electronic equipment. And I did surrender my Dictaphone. But three hours without a BlackBerry? I mean, what if there was an emergency?

'So, let's begin.' Maya smiles. 'Lie down on the couch, under a towel.'

She turns away discreetly and, a little awkwardly, I arrange myself on the couch, trying to avoid squashing my precious BlackBerry.

'I'm going to begin with a relaxing foot rub,' says Maya, and I feel her smoothing some kind of lotion over my feet. 'Try to clear your mind.'

I stare dutifully up at the ceiling. Clear my mind.

What am I going to do about Elldridge? He'll be waiting for a response. What if he tells the other partners I was lax? What if it affects my chances of partnership? I feel a clench of alarm. Now is not the time to be leaving anything to chance.

'Try to let go of all your thoughts . . .' Maya is chanting.

Maybe I could send him a very quick email. Surreptitiously I reach down and feel the hard corner of my BlackBerry. Gradually I inch it out of my paper knickers. Maya is still massaging my feet, totally oblivious.

'Your body is growing heavy . . . your mind should be emptying . . .'

I edge the BlackBerry up onto my chest until I can just see the screen underneath the towel. Trying to keep my movements to a minimum, I furtively start typing an email with one hand.

'Imagine you're walking along a beach . . .' Maya is saying soothingly.

'Uh huh . . .' I murmur.

David, I'm typing. *Re ZFN Oil contract. I read through amendments. Feel our response should be*

'What are you doing?' says Maya, suddenly alert.

'Nothing!' I say, hastily shoving the BlackBerry back under the towel. 'Just . . . er . . . relaxing.'

Maya comes round the couch and looks at the bump in the towel where I'm clutching the BlackBerry.

'Are you hiding something?' she says in disbelief.

'No!'

From under the towel the BlackBerry emits a little bleep. Damn.

Maya's eyes narrow. 'Samantha,' she says in slow, ominous tones. 'Do you have a piece of electronic equipment under there?'

I have the feeling that if I don't confess she'll rip my towel off anyway.

'I was just sending an email,' I say at last and sheepishly produce the BlackBerry.

'You workaholics!' She grabs it out of my hand in exasperation. 'Emails can *wait*. It can all *wait*. You just don't know how to relax!'

'I'm not a workaholic!' I retort indignantly. 'I'm a lawyer! I can't just switch off! Especially not right now. I'm . . . well, I'm up for partnership at the moment. They make the decision tomorrow. If it happens, I'll be the youngest partner in the whole history of the firm. Do you know how big a deal that is? Do you have any idea—'

I stop with a squeak of surprise, as from inside my paper knickers there comes a judder. My mobile phone. I shoved it in there along with the BlackBerry and turned it on to 'vibrate' so it wouldn't make a noise.

Suspicion snaps through Maya's eyes. 'You smuggled in a *mobile phone as well*?'

'Look,' I say, trying to sound apologetic, 'I know you've got your rules and everything, which I do respect, but the thing is, I *need* my mobile.' I reach under the towel for the phone.

'*Leave it!*' Maya's cry takes me by surprise. 'Samantha, if you've listened to a single word I've said, you'll switch the phone off right now.'

The phone vibrates again in my hand. I look at the caller ID and feel a twist in my stomach. 'It's the office.'

'They can leave a message. They can wait. This is your own time.'

God, she really doesn't get it, does she? I almost want to laugh.

'I'm an associate at Carter Spink,' I explain. 'I don't *have* my own time.' I flip the phone open and an angry male voice bites down the line.

'Samantha, where the hell are you?'

It's Ketterman. The head of our corporate department. He must have a Christian name, but no one ever calls him anything except Ketterman.

'The Fallons deal is back on. Get back here now. Meeting at ten thirty.'

'I'll be there as soon as I can.' I snap the phone shut and give Maya a rueful glance. 'Sorry.'

I'M NOT *ADDICTED* to my watch.

But obviously I rely on it. You would too, if your time was measured in six-minute segments. For every six minutes of my working life, I'm supposed to bill a client. It all goes on a computerised time sheet, in itemised chunks.

> 11.00–11.06 Drafted contract for Project A
> 11.06–11.12 Amended documentation for Client B
> 11.12–11.18 Consulted on point for Agreement C

When I first started at Carter Spink it freaked me out slightly, the idea that I had to write down what I was working on, every minute of the day. I used to think, What if I do nothing for six minutes? What am I supposed to write down then?

> 11.00–11.06 Stared aimlessly out of window
> 11.06–11.10 Daydreamed about bumping into
> George Clooney in street
> 11.12–11.18 Attempted to touch nose with tongue

But the truth is, you get used to it. You get used to measuring your life in little chunks. And you get used to working. All the time.

If you're a lawyer at Carter Spink, you don't sit around. You don't stare out of the window or daydream. Not when every six minutes of your time is worth such a lot. Put it this way: if I let six minutes tick away without achieving anything, I've wasted the firm £50. Twelve minutes: £100. Eighteen minutes: £150.

Like I say, lawyers at Carter Spink don't sit around.

As I arrive at the office, Ketterman is standing by my desk, looking at the mess of papers and files strewn everywhere with distaste.

'Meeting in ten minutes,' he says, looking at his watch. 'I want the draft financing documentation ready.'

'Absolutely,' I reply, trying to stay calm. But just his presence is giving me the jitters.

Ketterman is unnerving at the best of times. He emanates scary, brainy power like other men emanate aftershave. But today is a million times worse, because Ketterman is on the decision panel. Tomorrow he and thirteen other partners decide on who will become a new partner.

Tomorrow I discover whether I've made it or whether my life has been one big useless failure. No pressure, or anything.

'The draft documentation is right here . . .' I reach into a pile of folders and pull out what feels like a box file with an efficient flourish.

It's an old box of Krispy Kreme doughnuts.

Hastily I shove it in the bin. 'It's definitely here somewhere . . .' I scrabble frantically and locate the correct file. Thank God. 'Here!'

'I don't know how you can work in this shambles.' Ketterman's voice is sarcastic. 'You know, the old rule was that desks were completely cleared every night by six. Perhaps we should reintroduce it.'

'Maybe!' I try to smile.

'Samantha!' A genial voice interrupts us and I look round in relief to see Arnold Saville approaching along the corridor.

Arnold is my favourite of the senior partners. He's got woolly grey hair which always seems a bit wild for a lawyer, and a flamboyant taste in ties. Today he's wearing a bright-red paisley affair, with a matching handkerchief in his top pocket. He greets me with a broad smile.

I'm sure Arnold's the one who's rooting for me to be made partner. Just as I'm equally sure Ketterman will be opposing it.

'Letter of appreciation about you, Samantha.' Arnold holds out a sheet of paper. 'From the chairman of Gleiman Brothers, no less.'

I take the headed sheet in surprise and glance down the handwritten note. '. . . *great esteem . . . her services always professional . . .*'

'I gather you saved him a few million pounds he wasn't expecting,' Arnold twinkles. 'He's delighted.'

'Oh, yes.' I colour slightly. 'Well, it was nothing. I just noticed an anomaly in the way they were structuring their finances.'

I glance at Ketterman, just to see if by any remote chance he might look impressed. But he's still wearing his impatient frown.

'I also want you to deal with this.' Ketterman plonks a file on my desk. 'I need a due diligence review in forty-eight hours.'

My heart sinks as I look at the folder. It'll take me hours to do this.

Ketterman's always giving me extra bits of mundane work he can't be bothered to do himself. In fact, all the partners do it. Even Arnold. Half the time they don't even tell me, just dump the file on my desk with some illegible memo and expect me to get on with it.

'Any problems?' His eyes are narrowing.

'Of course not,' I say in a brisk, can-do, potential-partner voice. 'See you at the meeting.'

As he stalks off I glance at my watch. Ten twenty-two. I have precisely eight minutes to make sure the draft documentation for the Fallons deal is all in order. I open the file and scan the pages swiftly, checking for errors. I've learned to read a lot faster since I've been at Carter Spink.

In fact, I do everything faster. I walk faster, talk faster, eat faster . . . have sex faster . . . Not that I've had much of that lately. But a couple of years ago I dated a senior partner from Berry Forbes. He was called Jacob and worked on huge international deals, and he had even less time than me. By the end, we'd honed our routine to about six minutes.

Anyway, then Jacob was made a huge offer and moved to Boston, so that was the end of it. I didn't mind very much. I didn't really fancy him.

'Samantha?' A voice interrupts my thoughts. It's my secretary, Maggie. She only started a few weeks ago and I don't know her very well yet. 'You had a message while you were out. From Joanne?'

'Joanne from Clifford Chance?' I look up, my attention grabbed.

'Not that Joanne,' says Maggie. 'Joanne your new cleaner. She wants to know where you keep your vacuum cleaner bags.'

'Why does the vacuum cleaner need to go in a bag?' I say, puzzled. 'Is she taking it somewhere?'

Maggie peers at me as though she's not sure if I'm joking.

'The bags that go *inside* your vacuum cleaner,' she says carefully. 'To collect the dust? Do you have any of those?'

'Oh!' I say, quickly. 'Oh, *those* bags. Er . . .'

'Maybe it's a Dyson,' suggests Maggie. 'They don't take bags. Is it a cylinder or an upright?' She looks at me expectantly.

I have no idea what she's talking about.

'I'll sort it,' I say in a businesslike manner, and start gathering my papers together. 'Thanks, Maggie.'

'She had another question.' Maggie consults her paper. 'How do you switch on your oven?'

For a moment I continue gathering my papers, as though I haven't quite heard. Obviously I know how to switch on my own oven.

'Well. You turn the er . . . knob,' I say at last, trying to sound nonchalant. 'It's pretty clear, really . . .'

'She said it has some weird timer lock.' Maggie frowns thoughtfully. 'Is it gas or electric?'

OK, I think I might terminate this conversation right now.

'Maggie, I really need to make a call,' I say regretfully.

'So what shall I tell your cleaner?' Maggie persists. 'She's waiting for me to call back.'

'Tell her to . . . leave it for today. I'll sort it out.'

As Maggie leaves my office I reach for a pen and memo pad.

1. How switch on oven?
2. Vacuum cleaner bags—buy

I put the pen down and massage my forehead. I really don't have time for this. I mean, vacuum bags. I don't even know what they look like, for God's sake, let alone where to buy them—

A sudden brainwave hits me. I'll order a new vacuum cleaner. That'll come with a bag already installed, surely.

'Samantha.'

'What? What is it?' I give a startled jump and open my eyes. Guy Ashby is standing at my door.

Guy is my best friend in the firm. He's six foot three with olive skin and dark eyes, and normally he looks every inch the smooth, polished lawyer. But this morning his dark hair is rumpled and there are shadows under his eyes.

'Relax.' Guy smiles. 'Only me. Coming to the meeting?'

'Oh. Er . . . yes I am.' I pick up my papers, then add carelessly, 'Are you OK, Guy? You look a bit rough.'

He broke up with his girlfriend. They had bitter rows all night and she's walked off for good . . . No, she's emigrated to New Zealand . . .

'All-nighter,' he says, wincing. 'Ketterman's inhuman.'

'Bummer.' I grin in sympathy, then push back my chair. 'Let's go.'

I've known Guy for a year, ever since he joined the corporate department as a partner. He's intelligent, and funny, and works the same way I do, and we just somehow . . . click.

And yes. It's possible that some kind of romance would have happened between us if things had been different. But there was a stupid misunderstanding, and. . . anyway. It didn't. The details aren't important. It's not something I dwell on. We're friends—and that's fine by me.

OK, this is exactly what happened.

Apparently Guy noticed me pretty much the first day at the firm, just like I noticed him. And he was interested. He asked if I was single. Which I was. This is the crucial part: I was single. I'd just split up with Jacob. It would have been perfect. But Nigel MacDermot, who is a stupid, stupid, *thoughtless* behind-the-times moron, told Guy I was attached to a senior partner at Berry Forbes. *Even though I was single.*

There was a slightly embarrassing few weeks where I smiled a lot at

Guy—and he looked awkward and started avoiding me.

I didn't understand what was going on, so I backed off. Then I heard on the grapevine he'd started going out with a girl called Charlotte who he'd met at some weekend party.

I mean, it's fine. Really. That's the way it goes. Some things happen— and some things don't. This one obviously just wasn't meant to be.

'So,' says Guy as we walk along the corridor to the meeting room. 'Partner.' He cocks an eyebrow.

'Don't say that!' I hiss in horror. 'He'll totally jinx it.'

'Come on. You know you've made it.'

'I don't know anything.'

'Samantha, you're the brightest lawyer in your year. And you work the hardest. Haven't you practised in the mirror for the firm's website?' Guy adopts a pose with his finger poised thoughtfully at his chin. 'Ms Samantha Sweeting, Partner.'

'I haven't even thought about it,' I say, rolling my eyes with disdain.

This is a slight lie. I've already planned how to do my hair for the photo. And which black suit to wear. And this time I'm going to smile. In the photo on my Carter Spink web page, I look way too serious.

'I heard your presentation blew their socks off,' says Guy seriously.

My disdain vanishes in a second. 'Really?' I say, trying not to sound too eager. 'You heard that?'

'And you put William Griffiths right on a point of law in front of everybody?' Guy folds his arms and regards me humorously. 'Do you ever make a mistake, Samantha Sweeting?'

'Oh, I make plenty of mistakes,' I say lightly. 'Believe me.'

Like not grabbing you and telling you I was single, the first day we met.

'A mistake isn't a mistake,' Guy pauses, 'unless it can't be put right.'

'Ready?' Ketterman's whiplash voice behind us makes us both jump and I turn to see a whole phalanx of soberly suited men, together with a pair of even more soberly suited women.

'Absolutely.' Guy nods at Ketterman, then turns back and winks at me.

Nine hours later we're all still in the meeting.

The huge mahogany table is strewn with photocopied draft con- tracts, financial reports, notepads covered in scribbles, polystyrene coffee cups and Post-its. Two of the lawyers from the opposition have got up from the table and are murmuring intently in the break-out room. Every meeting room has one of these: a little side area where you go for private conversations, or when you feel like breaking something.

The intensity of the afternoon has passed. It's like an ebb in the tide. Faces are flushed around the table, tempers are still high, but no one's shouting any more. The clients have gone. They reached agreement at about four o'clock, shook hands and sailed off in their shiny limos.

Now it's up to us, the lawyers, to work out what they said and what they actually meant (and if you think these are the same thing, you might as well give up law now), and put it all into a draft contract in time for the meeting tomorrow.

When they'll probably begin shouting some more.

The fluorescent lights are flickering in my eyes and I feel drained. It's seven nineteen, and in eleven minutes I'm supposed to be halfway across town, sitting down to dinner with my mother and brother Daniel.

I'll have to cancel. My own birthday dinner.

Even as I think the thought, I can hear the outraged voice of my oldest school friend Freya ringing in my mind.

They can't make you stay at work on your birthday!

What she doesn't understand is, the deadline comes first, end of story. Prior engagements don't count, birthdays don't count. Holidays are cancelled every week. Across the table from me is Clive Sutherland from the corporate department. His wife had twins this morning and he was back at the table by lunchtime.

'All right, people,' Ketterman's voice commands immediate attention. 'We have to adjourn.'

What? My head pops up.

Other heads have popped up too; I can detect the hope around the table. We're like school kids sensing a disturbance during the maths test, not daring to move in case we land a double detention.

'Until we have the documentation from Fallons, we can't proceed. I'll see you all tomorrow, here at nine a.m.' He sweeps out, and as the door closes, I exhale. I was holding my breath, I realise.

Clive Sutherland has already bolted for the door. People are already on their mobile phones all over the room, discussing dinner, films, uncancelling arrangements. There's a joyful lift to the proceedings. I have a sudden urge to yell 'Yippee!'

But that wouldn't be partner-like.

As my taxi edges through the traffic on Cheapside, I quickly rifle in my bag for my new make-up bag. I nipped into Selfridges in my lunch-hour the other day, when I realised I was still using the eyeliner and mascara I bought for my graduation six years ago. I didn't have time for a demonstration, but I asked the girl at the counter if she could just quickly sell me everything she thought I should have.

I didn't really listen as she explained each item, because I was on the phone to Elldridge about the Ukrainian contract. But the one thing I do remember is her insistence I should use something called bronzer powder. She said it might stop me looking so dreadfully—

Then she stopped herself. 'Pale,' she said at last.

I take out the compact and huge blusher brush, and start sweeping the powder onto my cheeks and forehead. Then, as I peer at my reflection in the mirror, I stifle a laugh. My face stares back at me, freakishly golden and shiny. I look ridiculous.

I mean, who am I kidding? A City lawyer who hasn't been on holiday for two years doesn't have a tan. Or even a glow.

I look at myself for a few more seconds, then take out a cleansing wipe and scrub the bronzer off until my face is white again, with shades of grey. Back to normal. The make-up girl kept mentioning the dark shadows under my eyes, too.

Thing is, if I *didn't* have shadows under my eyes, I'd probably get fired.

I'm wearing a black suit, as I always do. My mother gave me five black suits for my twenty-first birthday, and I've never broken the habit.

I free my hair from its elastic band, quickly comb it out, then twist it back into place. My hair has never exactly been my pride and joy. It's mouse colour, medium length, with a medium wave. At least, it was last time I looked. Most of the time it lives screwed up into a knot.

'Nice evening planned?' says the taxi driver.

'It's my birthday, actually.'

'Happy birthday!' He twinkles at me. 'You'll be partying, then.'

'Er . . . kind of.'

My family and wild parties don't exactly go together. But even so, it'll be really great for us to see each other. It doesn't happen very often.

It's not that we don't want to see each other. It's just we all have very busy careers. There's my mother, who's a barrister. She's quite well known, in fact. And then there's my brother Daniel, who is thirty-six and head of investment at Whittons. He was named last year as one of the top deal-makers in the City.

There's also my dad who lives in South Africa with his third wife. I haven't seen much of him since I was three. But that's OK. My mother's got enough energy for two parents.

We come to a halt outside the restaurant and I pay the taxi driver.

'Have a great evening, love!' he says. 'And happy birthday!'

'Thanks!'

As I hurry into Maxim's, I'm looking all around for Mum or Daniel, but I can't spot either of them.

'Hi!' I say to the maître d'. 'I'm meeting Ms Tennyson.'

That's Mum. She disapproves of a woman taking the name of her husband. She also disapproves of women staying at home, cooking, cleaning, or learning to type, and thinks all women should earn more than their husbands because they're naturally brighter.

The maître d' leads me to an empty table in the corner and I slide onto the suede banquette.

As I scan the menu I feel suddenly ravenous. I haven't had a proper meal for a week, and it all looks so yummy. Glazed *foie gras*. Lamb with spiced hummous. And on the specials board is chocolate-mint soufflé with two homemade sorbets.

'Miss Sweeting?' I look up to see the maître d' approaching, holding a mobile phone. 'I have a message. Your mother has been held up at her chambers.'

'Oh.' I try to hide my disappointment. But I can hardly complain. I've done the same thing to her enough times.

'I have her here on the telephone. Her secretary will put her through . . . Hello?' he says into the phone. 'I have Ms Tennyson's daughter.'

'Samantha?' comes a crisp, precise voice in my ear. 'Darling, I can't come tonight, I'm afraid.'

'You can't come at *all*?' My smile falters.

'Far too much to do. I'm in court tomorrow . . . No, get me the other file,' she adds to someone in her office. 'These things happen,' she resumes. 'But have a nice evening with Daniel. Oh, and happy birthday. I've wired three hundred pounds to your bank account.'

'Oh, right,' I say after a pause. 'Thanks.'

'Have you heard about the partnership yet?'

'Not yet.' I can hear her tapping her pen on the phone.

'How many hours have you put in this month?'

'Um . . . probably about two hundred . . .'

'Is that enough? Samantha, you don't want to be passed over.'

'Two hundred is quite a lot,' I explain. 'Compared to the others—'

'You have to be *better* than the others!' Her voice cuts across mine as though she's in a court room. 'You can't afford for your performance to slip below excellent. This is a *crucial time*—Not *that* file!' she adds impatiently to whoever it is. 'Hold the line, Samantha—'

'Samantha?'

I look up in confusion from the phone to see a girl in a powder-blue suit approaching the table. She's holding a gift basket adorned with a bow, and has a wide smile.

'I'm Lorraine, Daniel's PA,' she says. 'He couldn't make it tonight, I'm afraid. But I've got a little something for you—plus he's here on the phone to say hello.'

She holds out a lit-up mobile phone. In total confusion, I take it and press it to my other ear.

'Hi, Samantha,' comes Daniel's businesslike drawl. 'Look, sweets, we're on a mega deal. I can't be there.'

I feel a plunge of total dismay. *Neither* of them is coming?

'I'm really sorry, babe,' Daniel's saying. 'One of those things. But have a great time with Mum, won't you?'

I swallow several times. I can't admit she blew me out too. I can't admit that I'm sitting here all on my own.

'OK!' Somehow I muster a breezy tone. 'We will!'

'I've transferred some money to your account. Buy something nice. And I've sent some chocolates along with Lorraine,' he adds proudly. 'Picked them out myself.'

I look at the gift basket Lorraine is proffering. It isn't chocolates, it's soap.

'That's really lovely, Daniel,' I manage. 'Thanks very much.'

'*Happy Birthday to You . . .*'

There's sudden chorusing behind me. I swivel round to see a waiter carrying over a cocktail glass. A sparkler is fizzing out of it and 'Happy Birthday Samantha' is written in caramel on the steel tray, next to a miniature souvenir menu signed by the chef. Three waiters are following behind, all singing in harmony.

After a moment, Lorraine awkwardly joins in. '*Happy Birthday to You . . .*'

The waiter puts the tray down in front of me, but my hands are full of phones.

'I'll take that for you,' says Lorraine, relieving me of Daniel's phone.

'Samantha?' Mum is saying in my ear. 'Are you still there?'

'I'm just . . . they're singing Happy Birthday . . .'

I put the phone on the table. After a moment's thought, Lorraine puts the other phone carefully down on the other side of me.

This is my family birthday party. Two mobile phones.

I can see people looking over at the singing, their smiles falling a little as they see I'm sitting on my own. I can see the pity in the faces of the waiters. My cheeks are burning with embarrassment.

'So anyway . . .' Lorraine retrieves Daniel's mobile phone and pops it into her bag. 'Happy birthday—and have a lovely evening!'

As she tip-taps her way out of the restaurant, I pick up the other phone to say goodbye—but Mum's already rung off. The singing waiters have melted away. It's just me and a basket of soap.

It doesn't matter. The truth is, we were never all going to make a dinner. It was a fantasy idea. We shouldn't even have tried. We're all busy, we all have careers, that's just the way my family is.

As I stand outside the restaurant, a taxi pulls up right in front of me and I quickly stick my hand out. The rear door opens and a tatty beaded flip-flop emerges, followed by a pair of cut-off jeans, an embroidered kaftan, familiar tousled blonde hair . . .

'Stay here,' she's instructing the taxi driver. 'I'll be five minutes.'

'*Freya?*' I say in disbelief. She wheels round and her eyes widen.

'Samantha! What are you doing on the pavement?'

'What are *you* doing here? I thought you were going to India.'

'I'm on my way! I'm meeting Lord at the airport in about . . .' She looks at her watch. 'Ten minutes.'

She pulls a guilty face, and I can't help laughing. I've known Freya since we were both seven years old and starting boarding school together. On the first night she told me her family were circus performers and she knew how to ride an elephant and walk the tightrope. For a whole term I believed her and heard stories about her exotic circus life, until her parents arrived to pick her up and turned out to be a pair of accountants from Staines.

She has bright blue eyes and freckled skin, permanently tanned from her travels. Right now her nose is peeling slightly, and she has a new earring, right at the top of he ear. She has the whitest, most crooked teeth I've ever seen, and when she laughs one corner of her top lip rises.

'I'm here to gatecrash your birthday dinner.' Freya's eyes swivel to the restaurant in suspicion. 'But I thought I was late. What happened?'

'Well . . .' I hesitate. 'The thing was . . . Mum and Daniel . . .'

'Left early?' As she peers at me Freya's expression changes to one of horror. 'Didn't turn *up*? The bastards. Couldn't they just for once put you first instead of . . .' She breaks off, breathing hard. 'Sorry. I know. They're your family. Whatever.'

Freya and my mum don't exactly get on.

'It doesn't matter,' I say, with a rueful shrug. 'Really. I've got a pile of work to get through anyway.'

'*Work?*' She stares at me. 'Now? Are you serious? Doesn't it ever *stop*?'

'We're busy at the moment,' I say defensively. 'It's just a blip.'

'There's always a blip! There's always a crisis! Every year you tell me it'll get better soon. But it never does!' Her eyes are burning with concern. 'Samantha, what happened to your life?'

I stare back at her for a few moments, not sure how to reply. To be honest, I can't remember what my life used to be like.

'I want to be a partner of Carter Spink,' I say at last. 'That's what I want. You have to make sacrifices.'

'And what happens when you make partner?' she persists.

I shrug evasively. The truth is I haven't thought beyond making partner. It's like a dream. Like a shiny ball in the sky.

'You're twenty-nine years old!' Freya gestures with a bony, silver-ringed hand. 'You should be seeing the world!' She grabs my arm. 'Samantha, come to India. Now!'

'Do what?' I give a startled laugh. 'I can't come to *India*!'

'Take a month off. Why not? They're not going to fire you. Come to the airport, we'll get you a ticket . . .'

'Freya, you're crazy, but I love you.'

Slowly, Freya's grip on my arm loosens. 'Same,' she says. 'You're crazy, but I love you.'

Her mobile starts ringing, but she ignores it. Instead, she's rummaging in her bag. At last she produces a tiny, intricately worked silver perfume bottle, haphazardly wrapped in a piece of purple shot silk.

'Here.' She thrusts it at me.

'Freya,' I turn it over in my fingers, 'it's amazing.'

'I thought you'd like it.' She pulls her mobile out of her pocket. 'Hi!' she says impatiently into it. 'Look, Lord, I'll be there, OK?'

Freya's husband's full name is Lord Andrew Edgerly. Freya's nickname for him started as a joke and just kind of stuck. They met five years ago on a kibbutz and got married in Las Vegas. Technically, this makes her Lady Edgerly—but nobody can quite get their heads round this idea.

'Thanks for coming. Thanks for this.' I hug her. 'Have a fabulous time in India.'

'We will.' Freya is climbing back into her taxi. 'And if you want to come out, just let me know. Invent a family emergency . . . anything. Give them my number. I'll cover for you. Whatever your story is.'

'Go,' I say, laughing, and give her a little push. 'Go to India.'

The door slams, and she sticks her head out of the window.

'Sam . . . good luck for tomorrow.' She seizes my hand, suddenly serious. 'If it's really what you want, then I hope you get it.'

'It's what I want more than anything else.'

'You'll get it. I know it.' She waves goodbye. 'And don't go back to the office! Promise!' she shouts as her taxi roars off into the traffic.

'OK! I promise!' I yell back. I wait until she's disappeared, then stick my hand out for a taxi. 'Carter Spink, please,' I say as it pulls up.

I was crossing my fingers. Of course I'm going back to the office.

I arrive home at eleven o'clock, exhausted and brain dead, having got through only about half of Ketterman's file. Bloody Ketterman, I'm thinking, as I push open the main front door of the 1930s mansion block where I live. Bloody Ketterman. Bloody . . . bloody . . .

'Good evening, Samantha.'

I nearly jump a mile. It's Ketterman. Right there, standing in front of the lifts, holding a bulging briefcase. For an instant I'm transfixed in horror. What's he doing here?

'Someone told me you lived here.' His eyes glint through his spectacles. 'I've bought number 32 as a pied-à-terre. We'll be neighbours during the week.'

No. Please tell me this is not happening. He *lives* here?

'Er . . . welcome to the building!' I say, trying as hard as I can to sound like I mean it. The lift doors open and we both get in.

Number 32. That means he's only two floors above me.

As we rise up in silence I feel more and more uncomfortable. Should I make small talk? Some light, neighbourly chitchat?

'I made some headway on that file you gave me,' I say at last.

'Good,' he says shortly, and nods.

So much for the small talk. I should just cut to the big stuff.

Am I going to become a partner tomorrow?

'Well . . . good night,' I say awkwardly as I leave the lift.

'Good night, Samantha.'

The lift doors close and I emit a silent scream. I cannot live in the same building as Ketterman. I'm going to have to move.

I'm about to put my key in the lock when the door to the opposite flat opens a crack. 'Samantha?'

My heart sinks. As if I haven't had enough this evening. It's Mrs Farley, my neighbour. She has silver hair and an insatiable interest in my life. But she is very kind and takes in parcels for me, so I basically let her poke and pry at will.

'Another delivery arrived for you, dear,' she says. 'Dry-cleaning this time. I'll just fetch it for you.'

'Thanks,' I say gratefully, swinging my door open. A small pile of junk leaflets is sitting on the doormat and I sweep them aside, onto the bigger pile building up at the side of my hallway. I'm planning to recycle them when I get a moment. It's on my list.

'You're late home again.' Mrs Farley is at my side, holding a pile of polythene-covered shirts. 'You girls are so busy!' She clicks her tongue. 'You haven't been home before eleven this week!'

'Thanks very much.' I make to take my dry-cleaning, but Mrs Farley pushes past me into the flat, exclaiming, 'I'll carry it in for you!'

'Er . . . excuse the . . . er . . . mess,' I say as she squeezes past a pile of pictures propped against the wall. 'I keep meaning to put those up . . . and get rid of the boxes . . .'

I steer her hastily into the kitchen, away from the pile of takeaway menus on the hall table. Then I wish I hadn't. On the kitchen counter is a stack of old tins and packets, together with a note from my new cleaner, all in capitals:

DEAR SAMANTHA

1. ALL YOUR FOOD IS PAST ITS SELL-BY-DATES, SHOULD I THROW AWAY?
2. DO YOU HAVE ANY CLEANING MATERIALS?
3. ARE YOU COLLECTING CHINESE FOOD CARTONS FOR ANY REASON? DID NOT THROW THEM AWAY, JUST IN CASE.
YOUR CLEANER JOANNE

I can see Mrs Farley reading the note. I can practically *hear* the clucking going on in her head.

'So . . . thanks.' I hastily take the dry-cleaning from her and dump it on the hob, then usher her out to the front door, aware of her swivelling, inquisitive eyes. 'It's really kind of you.'

'It's no trouble.' She gives me a beady look. 'Not wishing to interfere, dear, but you know, you could wash your cotton blouses very well at home, and save on all that money.'

I look at her blankly. If I did that I'd have to iron them.

'And I *did* just happen to notice that one of them came back missing a button,' she adds. 'The pink and white stripe.'

'Oh, right,' I say. 'Well . . . I'll send it back. They won't charge.'

'You can pop a button on yourself, dear!' says Mrs Farley, sounding shocked. 'It won't take you two minutes. You must have a spare button in your work box?'

My what?

'I don't have a work box,' I explain as politely as I can. 'I don't really *do* sewing.'

'You can sew a simple button on, surely!' she exclaims.

'No,' I say, a bit rankled at her expression. 'But it's no problem. I'll send it back to the dry-cleaners.'

'In my day,' says Mrs Farley, shaking her head, 'all well-educated girls were taught how to sew on a button, darn a sock and turn a collar.'

None of this means anything to me. *Turn a collar*? It's gibberish.

'Well, in my day we weren't,' I reply politely. 'We were taught to study for our exams and get a career worth having.'

Mrs Farley looks me up and down for a few moments.

'It's a shame,' she says at last, gives me a sympathetic pat on the arm, and heads across the hallway to her flat.

I'm trying to keep calm, but the tensions of the day are rising inside me. I've had a non-existent birthday, I feel bone-tired and hungry . . . and now this old woman's telling me to sew on a *button*?

'How is it a shame?' I demand, stepping out of my doorway. 'How? OK, maybe I can't sew on a button. But I can restructure a finance agreement and save my client thirty million pounds. That's what I can do.'

Mrs Farley regards me from her doorway. If anything she looks more pitying than before. 'It's a shame,' she repeats, as though she didn't hear me. 'Good night.' She closes the door and I emit a squeal of exasperation.

Two

THIS IS IT. All the work, all the late nights . . . it's all been for this day.

Partner. Or not partner.

As I arrive at the office, I'm determined I'm not going to acknowledge this is any kind of special day. I'll just keep my head down and get on with my work.

But as I travel up in the lift, three people murmur 'Good luck'.

I head hurriedly into my office and close the door, trying to ignore the fact that through the glass partition I can see people talking in the corridor and glancing at me.

It's fine. I'll just start on some work, like any other day. I open Ketterman's file, find my place and start reading through a document on a five-year-old share transfer.

Somehow I get through the morning. I finish up on Ketterman's file and make a start on my report. I'm halfway through the third paragraph when Guy appears at my office door.

'You did it, Samantha,' he murmurs. 'You're a partner. You'll hear officially in an hour.'

A white dazzling heat shoots across my chest. I made it. *I made it.*

'You didn't hear it from me, OK?' Guy's face creases briefly in a smile. 'Well done.'

'Thanks . . .' I manage.

'I'll see you later. Congratulate you properly.' He turns and strides away, and I'm left staring unseeingly at my computer.

I made partner. Oh my God. *Oh my God.* Oh my GOD!

I take out a hand mirror and glance at my own exhilarated reflection. My cheeks are bright pink. I'm feeling a terrible urge to leap to my feet and cry out 'YES!' How do I survive an hour? How can I just sit here calmly? I can't possibly concentrate on Ketterman's report.

I stand up and walk over to my filing cabinet, purely for something to do. I open a couple of drawers at random, and close them again. Then, as I swivel round, I notice my desk, crammed with papers and files.

Ketterman's right. It is a disgrace. It doesn't look like a partner's desk.

I'll tidy it up. This is the perfect way to spend an hour.

I had forgotten how much I loathe and detest tidying.

All sorts of things are turning up as I sift through the mess on my desk. Company letters . . . contracts that need to be filed . . . memos . . . a Pilates pamphlet . . . last year's Christmas card from Arnold, which depicts him in a woolly reindeer costume . . . And . . . oh God, half a Snickers bar I obviously didn't finish eating at one time or another. I dump it in the bin and turn with a sigh to another pile of papers.

Partner! shoots through my mind. *PARTNER!*

Stop it, I instruct myself sternly. Concentrate on the task in hand. As I pull out an old copy of *The Lawyer* and wonder why on earth I was keeping it, some paper-clipped documents fall to the floor. I reach for them, and run my gaze down the front page, already reaching for the next thing. It's a memo, from Arnold.

Re: Third Union Bank.
    Please find attached debenture for Glazerbrooks Ltd. Please attend to registration at Companies House.

I peer at it without great interest. Third Union Bank are Arnold's client, and I've only dealt with them once. The deal is a loan for £50 million to Glazerbrooks, and all I have to do is register it within twenty-one days at Companies House. It's just another of the mundane jobs that partners are always dumping on my desk. Well, not any more, I think with a surge of determination. In fact, I think I'll delegate this to someone else, right now. I glance automatically at the date.

Then I look again. It's dated May 26.

Five weeks ago? That can't be right.

Puzzled, I flip quickly through the papers, looking to see if there's been a typo. There *must* be a typo—but the date is consistent. May 26.

I sit, frozen, staring at the document. Has this thing been on my desk for *five weeks*?

But . . . it can't. I mean . . . that would mean I'd missed the deadline.

I swallow hard. I have to be reading this wrong. I can't have made such a basic mistake. I cannot possibly have failed to register a charge before the deadline. I *always* register charges before the deadline.

My happy glow has gone. There's a kind of iciness about my spine. I'm trying desperately to remember if Arnold said anything about the deal to me. I can't even remember him mentioning it. But, then, why would he? It's one simple loan agreement. The kind of thing we do in our sleep. He would have assumed I'd carried out his instructions.

What am I going to do? A wall of panic hits me as I take in the consequences. Third Union Bank has lent Glazerbrooks £50 million. Without the charge being registered, this loan—this multi-million-pound loan—is unsecured. If Glazerbrooks went bust tomorrow, Third Union Bank would go to the back of the queue of creditors. And probably end up with nothing.

I bury my head in my hands. I'm trying to keep calm, but inside is a great well of terror. I have to face it. *I have made a mistake.*

What am I going to do?

Then suddenly Guy's words from yesterday ring in my ears, and I feel a flood of relief. *A mistake isn't a mistake unless it can't be put right.*

Yes. The point is, I can put this right. I can still register a charge.

It will be excruciating. I'll have to tell the bank what I've done—and Glazerbrooks—and Arnold—and Ketterman. I'll have to have new documentation drawn up. And, worst of all, live with everyone knowing I've made the kind of stupid, thoughtless error a trainee would make.

It might mean an end to my partnership, runs through my mind, but there's no other option. I have to put the situation right.

Quickly I log onto the Companies House website and enter a search for Glazerbrooks. As long as no other charge has been registered in the meantime, it will all come to the same thing . . .

I stare at the page in disbelief. No. It can't be.

A charge of £50 million was entered last week by BLLC Holdings. Our client has been bumped down the creditors' queue.

My mind is helter-skeltering. This isn't good. I have to do something before any more charges are made. I have to . . . call the bank.

I search through the attached contact sheet and find the name and number of the guy at Third Union. Charles Conway.

With trembling hands I dial the number. I feel as though I'm psyching myself up to dive into a noxious swamp full of leeches.

'Charles Conway.'

'Hi!' I say, trying to keep my voice steady. 'It's Samantha Sweeting from Carter Spink. I don't think we've met.'

'Hi, Samantha.' He sounds friendly enough. 'How can I help?'

'I was phoning on a . . . a technical matter. It's about . . .' I can hardly bear to say it. 'Glazerbrooks.'

'Oh, you've heard about that,' says Charles Conway.

The room seems to shrink. I grip the receiver more tightly. 'Heard . . . what?' My voice is higher than I'd like. 'I haven't heard anything.'

'Oh! I assumed that's why you were calling. They called in the receivers today. That last-ditch attempt to save themselves didn't work . . .'

He's still talking but I can't hear him. I feel light-headed. Black spots are dancing in front of my eyes.

Glazerbrooks is going bust.

I won't be able to register the charge.

I've lost Third Union Bank £50 million.

Charles Conway's voice suddenly hits my consciousness. 'It's a good thing you phoned.' I can hear him tapping at a keyboard, totally unconcerned. 'You might want to double-check that loan security.'

For a few moments I can't speak.

'Yes,' I say at last, my voice hoarse. I put down the receiver, shaking all over. I think I might throw up.

Barely knowing what I'm doing, I push back my chair. I have to get out. Away.

I walk through reception on autopilot. Out onto the sunny crowded lunchtime street, one foot in front of the other, just another office worker walking along.

Except I'm different. I've just lost my client £50 million.

I don't understand how it happened. My mind keeps turning it over. I never even saw the document. It must have been put on my desk, then covered up with something. A pile of contracts, a cup of coffee.

One error. One mistake. The only mistake I've ever made. I want to wake up and find this is all a bad dream, it happened in a movie, it happened to someone else.

But it was me. It is me. My career is over.

The last person at Carter Spink who made a mistake like this was Ted Stephens in 1983, who lost a client £10 million. He was fired on the spot.

My breaths are getting shorter; my head is dizzy; I feel like I'm being smothered. Suddenly I jump in terror as my mobile phone vibrates in my pocket. I pull it out and look at the caller ID. It's Guy.

I can't talk to him. I can't talk to anybody. Not right now.

A moment later, the phone tells me a message has been left. I lift the phone to my ear and press '1' to listen.

'Samantha!' Guy sounds jovial. 'Where are you? We're all waiting with the champagne to make the big partnership announcement!'

Partnership. I almost want to burst into tears. But . . . I can't. It's too big for that. I thrust my phone in my pocket. I begin to walk faster and faster, weaving through the pedestrians. I have no idea where I'm going. But I just can't stop.

At last, when my legs are starting to ache, I slow down and come to a halt. My mouth is dry; I need water. I look up, trying to get my bearings. Somehow I seem to have reached Paddington Station, of all places.

Numbly, I turn my steps towards the entrance and walk inside. The place is noisy and crowded with travellers. The fluorescent lights and air conditioning and the blaring announcements make me flinch. As I'm making my way to a kiosk selling bottled water, my mobile vibrates. I pull it out and look at the display. I have fifteen missed calls and another message from Guy. He left it about twenty minutes ago.

I hesitate, my heart beating with nerves, then press '1' to listen to it.

'Samantha, what *happened*?' He doesn't sound jovial any more, he sounds totally stressed. I feel prickles of dread all over my body.

'We know,' he's saying. 'OK? We know about Third Union Bank. Charles Conway called up. Then Ketterman found the paperwork on your desk. You have to come back to the office. Now. Call me back.'

They know. They all know.

As I'm standing there, something catches the corner of my eye. A familiar face is just visible through the crowd. I turn my head and squint at the man, trying to place him—then feel a fresh jolt of horror.

It's Greg Parker, one of the senior partners. He's striding along, holding his mobile phone. His brows are knitted together and he looks concerned. 'So where *is* she?' His voice travels across the concourse.

Panic hits me like a lightning bolt. I have to get out of his line of vision. I have to hide. I edge behind a vast woman in a beige mac and try to cower down so I'm hidden. But she keeps wandering about, and I keep having to shuffle along with her.

'Did you want something? Are you a beggar?' She suddenly turns and gives me a suspicious look.

'No!' I say in shock. 'I'm . . . er . . .' I can't say 'I'm hiding behind you.'

'Well, leave me alone!' She scowls and stalks off towards Costa Coffee. My heart is hammering in my chest. I'm totally exposed in the middle of the concourse. Greg Parker has stopped striding now. He's standing about fifty yards away, still talking on his mobile phone.

If I move, he'll see me. If I stay still . . . he'll see me.

Suddenly the electronic Departures display board renews itself with fresh information. A group of people who have been gazing up at it all pick up their bags and newspapers and head towards Platform Nine.

Without thinking twice I join the throng. I'm hidden in their midst as we sweep through the open barriers. I get on the train along with everyone else, walking swiftly down the carriage as far as I can.

The train pulls out of the station and I sink into a seat, opposite a family all wearing London Zoo T-shirts. They smile at me—and somehow I manage to smile back. I feel totally, utterly unreal.

'Refreshments?' A wizened man pushing a trolley appears in the carriage and beams at me. 'Hot and cold sandwiches, teas and coffees, soft drinks, alcoholic beverages?'

'The last, please.' I try not to sound desperate. 'A double. Of anything.'

No one comes to check my ticket. No one bothers me. The train seems to be some sort of express. Suburbs turn into fields, and the train is still rattling along. I've drunk three small bottles of gin, mixed with orange juice. My heart rate has subsided, but I have a throbbing headache. I feel weirdly distanced from everything.

I have made the biggest mistake of my career. I have quite possibly lost my job. I will never be a partner.

'Ladies and gentlemen . . .' The conductor is crackling over the loudspeaker. 'Unfortunately . . . rail works . . . alternative transport . . .'

I can't follow what he's saying. I don't even know where I'm headed. The train is pulling into a station. Lower Ebury. Everybody is gathering up their stuff and getting off.

Like an automaton I get up too. I follow the London Zoo family off the train and out of the station, and look around. I'm standing outside a tiny, twee country station, with a pub called The Bell over the road. The road bends round in both directions and I can glimpse fields in the distance. There's a coach standing on the side of the road, and all of the passengers from the train are piling onto it.

London Zoo mother is gesturing at me. 'You need to come this way,' she says helpfully. 'If you want the bus to Gloucester?'

The thought of getting on a coach makes me want to heave. I don't want the bus to anywhere. I just want a painkiller. My head feels like my skull is about to split open.

'Er . . . no, thanks. I'm fine here.' I smile as convincingly as I can and start walking down the road, away from the coach.

Inside my pocket, my phone suddenly vibrates. I pull it out. It's Guy. Again. This must be the thirtieth time he's rung. And every time he's left a message telling me to call him back; asking if I've got his emails.

I haven't got any of his emails. I was so freaked out, I left my BlackBerry on my desk. My phone is all I have. It vibrates again and I stare at it for a few moments. Then, my stomach clenched with nerves, I lift it to my ear and press Talk.

'Hi.' My voice is scratchy.

'Samantha?' His voice blasts down the line. 'Where *are* you?'

'I don't know. I had to get away. I . . . I went into shock . . .'

'Samantha, I don't know if you got my messages. But . . .' He hesitates. 'Everyone knows.'

'I know.' I lean against an old crumbling wall and squeeze my eyes shut, trying to block out the pain. 'I know.'

'How the hell did you make a simple error like that?'

'I don't know,' I say numbly. 'I just didn't see it. It was a mistake—'

'You never make mistakes!'

'Well, I do now!' I feel tears rising and fiercely blink them down. 'What's . . . what's happened?'

'It's not good.' He exhales. 'Ketterman's been having some damage-limitation talks with Glazerbrooks' lawyers and talking to the bank . . . and the insurers, of course.'

The insurers. The firm's professional indemnity insurance. I'm suddenly gripped by an almost exhilarating hope. If the insurers pay up without making a fuss, maybe things won't be as bad as I thought.

But even as I feel my spirits lift I know I'm like some desperate traveller seeing the mirage through the haze. Insurers never cough up the whole amount. Sometimes they don't cough up anything.

'What did the insurers say?' I gulp. 'Will they . . .'

'They haven't said anything yet.'

'Right.' I wipe my sweaty face, screwing myself up to ask the next question. 'And what about . . . me?'

Guy is silent.

As his meaning hits me I feel myself swaying as though I'm going to faint. There's my answer.

'It's over, isn't it?' I'm trying to sound calm but my voice is wobbling out of control. 'My career's over.'

'I . . . I don't know that. Listen, Samantha, you're freaked out. It's natural. But you can't hide. You have to come back.'

'I can't.' My voice rises in distress. 'I can't face everyone. I need some time . . .'

'Saman—' I flip my phone shut.

I feel faint. My head is bursting. I have to get some water. But the pub doesn't look open and I can't see any shops.

I totter along the road until I reach a pair of tall, carved pillars decorated with lions. Here's a house. I'll ring the bell and ask for a painkiller and a glass of water. And ask if there's a hotel near by.

I push open the wrought-iron gates and crunch over the gravel towards the heavy, oak front door. It's a rather grand house, made out of honey-coloured stone, with steep gables and tall chimneys and two Porsches on the drive. I raise a hand and tug the bell pull.

There's silence. I stand there for a while, but the whole house seems dead. I'm about to give up and trudge back down the drive, when all of a sudden the door swings open.

There before me is a woman with blonde, lacquered hair to her shoulders and long, dangly earrings. She has a cigarette in one hand and a cocktail in the other.

'Hello.' She drags on her cigarette and looks at me a bit suspiciously. 'Are you from the agency?'

I have no idea what this woman's talking about. My head's hurting so much, I can barely look at her, let alone take in what she's saying.

'Are you all right?' She peers at me. 'You look terrible!'

'I've got a rather bad headache,' I manage. 'Could I possibly have a glass of water?'

'Of course! Come in!' She waves her cigarette in my face and beckons me into a huge, impressive hall with a vaulted ceiling. 'You'll want to see the house, anyway. *Eddie?*' Her voice rises to a shriek. 'Eddie, another one's here! I'm Trish Geiger,' she adds to me. 'You may call me Mrs Geiger. This way . . .'

She leads me into a luxurious maple kitchen and tries a few drawers, apparently at random, before crying 'Aha!' and pulling out a plastic box. She opens it to reveal about fifty assorted bottles and packets of tablets.

'I've got aspirin . . . paracetamol . . . ibuprofen . . . *very* mild valium . . .' She hands me three green tablets and, after a few attempts, locates a cupboard full of glasses. 'Here we are. They'll zap any headache.' She runs me some iced water from the fridge. 'Drink that up.'

'Thanks,' I say, swallowing the tablets down with a wince. 'I'm so grateful. My head's just so painful. I can barely think straight.'

'Your English is very good.' She gives me a close, appraising look.

'Oh,' I say, thrown. 'Right. Well, I'm English. That's . . . you know, probably why.'

'You're *English?*' Trish Geiger seems galvanised by this news. 'Well! Come with me. Those'll kick in, in a minute.' She sweeps me out of the kitchen and back through the hall. 'This is the drawing room,' she says, gesturing around the large, grand room, dropping ash on the carpet. 'As you'll see, there's quite a lot of hoovering . . . dusting . . . silver to be kept clean . . .' She looks at me expectantly.

'Right.' I nod. I have no idea why this woman is telling me about her housework.

'We'll go in here.' She's leading me through another huge, grand room into an airy glassed conservatory furnished with opulent teak sunloungers, frondy plants and a well-stocked drinks tray.

'Eddie! Come in here!' She bangs on the glass and I look up to see a man in golfing slacks walking over the well-manicured lawn. He's tanned and affluent-looking, probably in his late forties.

Trish is probably in her late forties, too, I think, glimpsing her crow's-feet as she turns away from the window. Although something tells me she's going for thirty-nine and not a day older.

'Lovely garden,' I say.

'Oh.' Her eyes sweep over it without much interest. 'Yes, our gardener is very good. Now, sit down!' She makes a flapping motion with her hands and, feeling a little awkward, I sit down on a lounger. Trish sinks into a basket chair opposite and drains her cocktail.

'How's your head?' she demands and carries on before I'm able to reply. 'Better? Ah, here's Eddie!'

The door opens and Mr Geiger comes into the conservatory. He doesn't look quite as impressive close up as he did striding over the lawn. His eyes are a little bloodshot and he has the beginnings of a beer belly.

'Eddie Geiger,' he says, holding out his hand. 'Master of the house.'

'Eddie, this is . . .' Trish looks at me in surprise. 'What's your name?'

'Samantha,' I explain. 'I'm so sorry to bother you, but I had the most terrible headache . . .'

'I gave Samantha some of those prescription painkillers,' puts in Trish.

'Good choice.' Eddie unscrews a Scotch bottle and pours himself a drink.

I manage a half-smile. 'You've been very kind, letting me trespass on your evening.'

'Her English is good, isn't it?' Eddie raises his eyebrows at Trish.

'She's English!' says Trish triumphantly, as though she's pulled a rabbit out of a hat. 'Understands everything I say!'

I am really not getting something here. Do I *look* foreign?

'Shall we do the tour of the house?' Eddie turns to Trish.

My heart plummets. People who give tours of their houses should be abolished. The thought of trailing round, trying to find different things to say about each room, is unbearable. I just want to sit here and wait for the pills to kick in.

'Really, it's not necessary,' I begin. 'I'm sure it's beautiful—'

'Of course it's necessary!' Trish stubs out her cigarette. 'Come on.'

As I get up my head swims and I have to clutch onto a yucca plant to steady myself. This all feels like a bit of a dream.

OK, this woman cannot have a life. All she seems interested in is housework. As we trail round one splendid room after another she keeps pointing out things that need special dusting and showing me where the Hoover is kept. Now she's telling me about the washing machine.

'It seems . . . very . . . efficient,' I say, as she seems to be waiting for a compliment.

'We do like fresh linen *every* week. Well ironed, of course.' She gives me a sharp look.

'Of course.' I nod, trying to hide my bewilderment.

'Now upstairs!' She sweeps out of the kitchen.

Oh God. There's more?

'You come from London, Samantha?' says Eddie Geiger as we head up the stairs.

'That's right.'

'And you have a full-time job there?'

He's only asking to be polite—but for a few moments I can't bring myself to answer. Do I have a job?

'I did,' I say at last. 'To be honest . . . I don't know what my situation is at the moment.'

'What sort of hours did you work?' Trish wheels round.

'All hours.' I shrug. 'I'm used to working all day and into the night. Through the night, sometimes.'

The Geigers look absolutely stunned at this revelation. People just have no idea what the life of a lawyer is like.

'You used to work *through the night*?' Trish seems stupefied. 'On your own?'

'Me and the other staff. Whoever was needed.'

'So you come from . . . a big set-up?'

'One of the biggest in London.' I nod.

Trish and Eddie are darting glances at each other. They really are the weirdest people.

'Well, we're *far* more relaxed, you'll be glad to hear!' Trish gives a little laugh. 'This is the master bedroom . . . the second bedroom . . .'

As we walk down the corridor she opens and closes doors and shows me four-poster beds and handmade drapes, until my head swims even more. I don't know what was in those pills, but I'm feeling weirder by the minute. We descend a flight of stairs and I grab the wall to keep myself steady, but it seems to run away in a tangle of wallpaper flowers.

'Are you all right?' Eddie catches me as I'm about to topple to the floor.

'I think those painkillers were a bit strong,' I mumble.

'They *are* a bit vicious.' Trish gives me a considering look. 'You haven't drunk any *alcohol* today, have you?'

'Er . . . well, yes . . .'

She pulls a face. 'Well, it's all right as long as you don't start *hallucinating*. Then we'd have to call a doctor. And . . . here we are!' she continues, and opens the last door with a flourish. 'The staff accommodation.'

All the rooms in this house are huge. This one is about the size of my flat, with pale walls and stone mullioned windows overlooking the garden. It has the plainest bed I've seen yet in this house, vast and square and made up with crisp white bed linen.

'Lovely,' I say politely. 'It's a gorgeous room.'

'Good!' Eddie smacks his hands together. 'Well, Samantha, I'd say you've got the job!'

I look back at him through my daze. Job? What job?

'Eddie!' snaps Trish. 'You can't just offer her the job! We haven't finished the interview!'

Interview? Did I miss something?

'We haven't even given her a full job description!' Trish is still laying into Eddie. 'We haven't been through any of the details!'

'Well, go through the details, then!' retorts Eddie. Trish shoots him a look of fury and clears her throat.

'So, Samantha,' she says in formal tones, 'your role as full-time housekeeper will comprise all cleaning, laundry and cooking. You will wear a uniform and maintain a respectful . . .'

My role as—these people think I'm applying to be their *housekeeper*?

For a moment, I'm too dumbfounded to speak.

'. . . full board and lodging and four weeks holiday a year. Do you have any questions about the post?'

This is the moment where I have to explain there's been a big mistake. That I'm not a housekeeper, I'm a lawyer.

But nothing comes out of my mouth.

I could stay here one night, flashes through my brain. *Just one night. I could sort out the misunderstanding tomorrow.*

'Um . . . would it be possible to start tonight?' I hear myself saying.

'I don't see why not—' begins Eddie.

'Let's not jump ahead of ourselves,' Trish interrupts. 'We have had *quite* a few promising applicants for this post, Samantha. Several quite dazzling. One girl even had a diploma in French cordon bleu cookery!'

She drags on her cigarette, giving me a pointed look. And something inside me stiffens, like an automatic reflex. I can't help it. Is she implying that I might not *get* this job?

I regard Trish silently for a few moments. Somewhere, down inside my befuddled state of shock, I can feel a tiny flicker of the old Samantha returning. I can feel my ingrained ambition lifting its head and sniffing the air, rolling back its sleeves and spitting on its hands. I can beat some French-cordon-bleu-cookery girl.

I have never failed an interview in my life. I'm not about to start now.

'So.' Trish looks at her list. 'You're cordon bleu trained?'

'I trained under Michel de la Roux de la Blanc.' I pause gravely. 'His name obviously speaks for itself.'

'Absolutely!' says Trish, glancing uncertainly at Eddie.

We're sitting in the conservatory again. Trish is firing questions at me that sound like they come from a 'How To Hire Your Housekeeper' pamphlet. And I'm answering every single one with total confidence.

Deep down in my brain I can hear a little voice calling out, 'What are you doing? Samantha, what the hell are you *doing*?'

But I'm not listening. Somehow I've managed to block out real life, the mistake, my ruined career, the whole nightmare of a day . . . everything else in the world except this interview.

'Could you give us a sample menu?' Trish lights another cigarette. 'For a dinner party, say?'

Food . . . Impressive food . . . Suddenly I remember Maxim's, the night before. The souvenir birthday menu.

'I'll just consult my notes.' I unzip my bag and surreptitiously scan the Maxim's menu. 'For a formal dinner, I would serve . . . er . . . seared foie gras with an apricot glaze . . . lamb with spiced hummous . . . followed by chocolate-mint soufflé with two homemade sorbets.'

Take *that*, cordon bleu girl.

'Well!' Trish looks astounded. 'I must say, that's very impressive.'

'Marvellous!' Eddie looks like he's salivating.

Trish shoots him an annoyed look. 'I'm assuming you have a reference, Samantha?'

A reference?

'My referee is Lady Freya Edgerly,' I say, in sudden inspiration.

'*Lady* Edgerly?' Trish's eyebrows rise.

'I have been associated with Lord and Lady Edgerly for many years.' I nod. 'I know Lady Edgerly will vouch for me.'

Trish and Eddie are both staring at me, agog. Maybe I should add some housekeeperly detail.

'A lovely family,' I embellish. 'Quite a job it was, keeping the manor house clean. And . . . polishing Lady Edgerly's tiaras.'

Shit. I've gone a step too far with the tiaras.

But to my amazement, not a note of suspicion crosses either face.

'You cooked for them?' enquires Eddie. 'Breakfasts and so forth?'

'Naturally. Lord Edgerly was very fond of my Eggs Benedict.'

I can see Trish pulling what she clearly imagines are cryptic faces at Eddie, who is surreptitiously nodding back. They might as well have 'Let's Have Her!' tattooed on their foreheads. They look like all their Christmases have come at once.

Three

I WAKE THE NEXT MORNING to an unfamiliar, smooth white ceiling above me. I stare at it for a few moments in bewilderment, then lift my head a little. The sheets make a strange rumpling sound as I move. What's going on? My sheets don't sound anything like that.

But of course. They're the Geigers' sheets.

I sink comfortably back into my pillows—until another thought strikes me. Who are the Geigers?

I screw up my face, trying to remember. Snatches of yesterday are vivid in my mind, amidst a dense fog. I'm not sure what's real and what's a dream. I came on the train . . . yes . . . I had a headache . . . Paddington Station . . . walking out of the office . . .

Oh God. Oh please, no.

With a sickening whoosh the whole nightmare is back in my brain. The memo. Third Union Bank. Fifty million pounds. Asking Guy if I had a job left . . . His silence.

I lie very still for a while, letting it all sink in again. My career is wrecked. I have no chance of partnership. I probably have no job. Everything is over as I knew it. I squeeze my eyes tight shut, trying to escape the thoughts starting to float into my mind. Sickening, if-only thoughts. If I'd seen the memo earlier . . . If I had a tidier desk . . . If Arnold hadn't given that piece of work to me . . .

But there's no point. Ignoring my throbbing head, I walk to the window. What happened, happened. And now I find myself in a strange room in the middle of the countryside. With my career in ruins. Plus there's something nagging at me. A final piece of the jigsaw still missing in my dazed brain. It'll come to me in a minute.

I turn round and focus on a blue dress hanging on the wardrobe door. Some kind of uniform, with piping. Why would there be a—

It's coming back to me like some kind of terrible, drunken dream.

Did I take a job as a housekeeper?

For an instant I cannot move. What have I *done?*

My heart starts to thump as I take in my situation properly for the first time. I am staying in a strange couple's house under completely false pretences. I've slept in their bed. I'm wearing one of Trish's old T-shirts. They even gave me a toothbrush, after I invented a 'suitcase stolen on the train' story. The last thing I remember before crashing out is hearing Trish gloating on the phone. 'She's English!' she was saying. 'Yes, speaks English perfectly! *Super* girl. Cordon bleu trained!'

I'll have to tell them it was all lies.

There's a rapping at my bedroom door and I jump in fright.

'Samantha? May I come in?'

'Oh! Um . . . yes!'

The door opens and Trish appears, wearing pale pink exercise clothes with a diamanté logo.

'I've made you a cup of tea,' she says, handing me the mug. 'Mr Geiger and I would like you to feel very welcome in our house.'

'Oh!' I swallow nervously. 'Thanks.'

Mrs Geiger, there's something I need to tell you. I'm not a housekeeper.

Somehow the words don't make it out of my mouth.

Trish's eyes have narrowed as though she's already regretting her kind gesture. 'Don't think you'll be getting this every day, of course! But since you weren't feeling well last night . . .' She taps her watch. 'Now you'd better get dressed. We'll expect you down in ten minutes. We only have a light breakfast as a rule. Toast, coffee and whatnot. Then we can discuss the other meals of the day.'

'Er . . . OK,' I say feebly.

She closes the door and I put the tea down. What am I going to do?

OK. Calm down. Prioritise. I need to call the office. Find out exactly how bad the situation is. With a spasm of apprehension I reach inside my bag for my mobile phone.

The display is blank. The battery must have run out.

I stare at it in frustration. I must have been so spaced out yesterday I forgot to charge it. I pull out my charger, plug it into the wall and attach the phone. At once it starts charging up.

I wait for the signal to appear . . . but it doesn't. There's no signal.

I feel a thrust of panic. How am I going to call the office? How am I going to do *anything?* I cannot exist without my mobile phone.

Suddenly I remember passing a telephone on the landing. It was on a table in a little window bay. Maybe I could use that. I open my bedroom door and look up and down the corridor. No one's about. Cautiously I creep into the bay and lift the receiver. The dial tone rings calmly in my ear. I take a deep breath—then dial the direct line for Arnold.

'Arnold Saville's office,' announces the cheerful voice of his Lara, his secretary.

'Lara,' I say nervously, 'it's Samantha. Samantha Sweeting.'

'*Samantha?*' Lara sounds so gobsmacked, I wince. 'Oh my God! Where *are* you? Everyone's been—' She draws herself up.

'I . . . I'm out of London right now. May I talk to Arnold?'

'Of course. He's right here.' She disappears briefly into chirpy Vivaldi, before the line clears again.

'Samantha.' Arnold's friendly, assured voice booms down the line. 'My dear girl. You've got yourself in a pickle, haven't you?'

Only Arnold could describe the loss of a client's £50 million as a 'pickle'. In spite of everything, a tiny half-smile comes to my lips. I can just picture him, in his waistcoat, his woolly eyebrows knitted together.

'I know,' I say, trying to match his understated tones. 'It's not great.'

'I'm obliged to point out that your hasty departure yesterday did not help matters.'

'I'm so sorry. I just panicked.'

'Understandable. However, you left a bit of a mess behind.'

Underneath Arnold's jolly veneer I can detect unfamiliar levels of stress. Arnold never gets stressed. Things must be really bad.

'So—what's the latest situation?' I'm trying to sound composed. 'Is there anything the receivers can do?'

'I think it unlikely. They say their hands are tied.'

'Right.' It's like a hammer blow to the stomach. So that's it. The £50 million is gone for good. 'And the insurers?'

'That is the next step, of course. The money will be recovered eventually, I'm sure. But not without complications. As you will appreciate.'

For a few moments neither of us speaks. There's no good news, I realise with a dull ache of comprehension. There's no silver lining.

'Arnold,' I say, my voice quivering, 'I have no idea how I could have made such a . . . a *stupid* mistake. I don't understand how it happened. I don't even remember seeing the memo on my desk—'

'Where are you now?' Arnold breaks in.

'I'm . . .' I look helplessly out of the window. 'To be honest, I don't even know exactly where I am. But I can come in. I'll come back now.' My words come tumbling out. 'I'll get on the first train.'

'I don't think that's a good idea.' There's a new edge to Arnold's voice.

'Have I . . . have I been fired?'

'It hasn't been addressed yet.' He sounds testy. 'There have been slightly more pressing matters to consider, Samantha.'

'Of course. I'm sorry.' My throat is thickening. 'I've been with Carter Spink all my working life. All I ever wanted was . . .'

I can't even say it.

'Samantha, I know you're a very talented lawyer.' Arnold sighs. 'I'll do everything I can. I might as well tell you now, there's to be a meeting this morning to discuss your fate.'

'But you don't think I should come in?' I bite my lip.

'It might do more harm than good at the moment. Stay where you are. Leave the rest to me.' Arnold hesitates, his voice a little gruff. 'I'll do my best, Samantha. I promise.'

'I'll be waiting,' I say quickly. 'Thank you so much.' But he's gone. Slowly I put down the phone. I have never felt so powerless in my life. I have a sudden vision of them all sitting round a table: Arnold, Ketterman, maybe even Guy, deciding whether to give me a break.

'*Super* girl.'

I jump at the sound of Trish's approaching voice.

'Well, of course I'll check her references, but, Gillian, I am a *very* good judge of character. I'm not easily fooled—'

Trish rounds the corner, holding a mobile to her ear, and I quickly move away from the telephone.

'Samantha!' she says in surprise. 'What are you doing? Still not dressed? Buck up!' She heads off again and I scuttle back to my room. I close the door and stare at myself in the mirror.

I suddenly feel a bit bad.

In fact, I feel really bad. How are the Geigers going to react when I tell them I'm a total fraud? That I'm not a trained cordon bleu house-keeper at all, I just wanted a place to stay for the night?

I have a sudden image of them bundling me furiously out of the house. Feeling totally used. Maybe they'll even call the police. Have me arrested. Oh God. This could get really nasty.

But, I mean, it's not like I have any other option. It's not like I could actually . . . Could I?

I pick up the blue uniform and finger it, my mind whirling round and round. They've been pretty kind, putting me up. It's not like I'm doing anything else right now. It's not like I have anywhere else to go. Maybe it'll even take my mind off things, doing a little light housework.

Abruptly I come to a decision.

I'll busk it for a morning. It can't be that hard. I'll make their toast and dust the ornaments. I'll think of it as my little thank-you to them. Then as soon as I hear from Arnold I'll find a convincing excuse to leave. And the Geigers will never know I wasn't a proper housekeeper.

It'll be fine.

As I walk down the stairs, the Geigers are both standing at the bottom, looking up at me. I have never felt more self-conscious in my life.

I'm a housekeeper. I have to behave like a housekeeper.

'Welcome, Samantha!' says Eddie as I arrive down in the hall. 'Sleep all right?'

'Very well, thank you, Mr Geiger,' I reply demurely.

'That's good!' Eddie rocks back and forth on the soles of his feet. He seems just a little awkward. In fact, they both seem awkward.

'You'll be wanting to get to know your new kitchen!' says Trish brightly.

'Of course!' I say with a confident smile. 'I'm looking forward to it!'

It's only a kitchen. It's only one morning. I can do this.

Trish leads the way into the vast, maple kitchen, and this time I look around more carefully, trying to take in the details. There's a huge, hob-type thing set into the granite counter to my left. A bank of ovens built into the wall. Everywhere I look I can see shiny chrome gadgets plugged into sockets. Racks of saucepans and implements of all descriptions are hanging overhead in a jumble of stainless steel.

I have not one single clue what anything is.

'You'll want to get it the way you like it, of course,' says Trish.

'Absolutely,' I say in a businesslike way. 'Obviously I have my own . . . um . . . systems. That shouldn't be there, for example.' I point randomly at some gadget. 'I'll have to move it.'

'Really?' Trish looks fascinated. 'Why's that?'

There's a momentary beat of silence. Even Eddie looks interested.

'Kitchen . . . ergonomic . . . theory,' I improvise. 'So, you'd like toast for breakfast?' I add quickly.

'Toast for both of us,' says Trish. 'And coffee with skimmed milk.'

'Coming up.' I smile, feeling slight relief. I can make toast. Once I've worked out which of these things is the toaster.

'So, I'll just bring that through in a moment,' I add, trying to chivvy them out. 'Would you like to eat in the dining room?'

There's a small crash from the hall.

'That'll be the newspaper,' says Trish. 'Yes, you may serve breakfast in the dining room.' She hurries out, but Eddie loiters in the kitchen.

'You know, I've changed my mind.' He gives me a jovial smile. 'Forget the toast, Samantha. I'll have your famous Eggs Benedict. You whetted my appetite last night!'

Last night? What did I say last—

Oh no. Eggs Benedict. My famous signature dish as beloved by Lord Edgerly. What was I *thinking*?

I don't even know what Eggs Benedict *are*.

'Are you sure that's what you want?' I manage in a constricted voice.

'I wouldn't miss your speciality!' Eddie rubs his stomach appreciatively. 'It's my favourite breakfast.'

OK. Keep calm. It must be simple enough. Eggs and . . . something.

Eddie leans against the granite counter with an expectant look. I have a nasty suspicion he's waiting for me to start cooking. Hesitantly I get down a gleaming pan from the rack, just as Trish bustles in with the newspaper. She eyes me with bright curiosity.

'How will you be using the asparagus steamer, Samantha?'

Shit.

'I just wanted to . . . examine it. Yes.' I nod briskly, as though the pan has confirmed my suspicions, then hang it back on the rack again.

I'm feeling hotter and hotter. I have no idea even how to begin. Do I crack the eggs? Boil them? Throw them against the wall?

'Here are the eggs.' Eddie plonks a huge box on the counter and lifts the lid. 'Should be enough there, I'd imagine!'

I stare at the rows of brown eggs, feeling a little light-headed. What do I think I'm doing? I can't make Eggs Benedict. I can't make these people breakfast. I'm going to have to come clean.

I turn round and take a deep breath. 'Mr Geiger . . . Mrs Geiger . . .'

'Eggs?' Trish's voice cuts across mine. 'Eddie, you can't have eggs! Remember what the doctor said!' She looks at me, eyes narrowed. 'What did he ask you for, Samantha? Boiled eggs?'

'Er . . . Mr Geiger ordered Eggs Benedict. But the thing is—'

'You're not eating Eggs Benedict!' Trish practically shrieks at Eddie. 'It's full of cholesterol!'

'I'll eat what I like!' Eddie protests.

'The doctor gave him an eating plan.' Trish is dragging furiously on her cigarette. 'He's already had a bowl of cornflakes this morning!'

'I was hungry!' says Eddie, defensive. 'You had a chocolate muffin!'

Trish gasps as though he's hit her. Small red dots appear on her cheeks. For a few moments she seems unable to speak.

'We will have a cup of coffee each, Samantha,' she announces at last in dignified tones. 'You may serve it in the lounge. Use the pink china. Come along, Eddie.' And she sweeps out before I can say anything else.

Ten minutes later I've arranged a tray with a pink coffeepot, pink cups, creamer, sugar, and a sprig of pink flowers I snipped from a hanging basket outside the kitchen. I'm rather proud of it, if I say so myself.

I approach the sitting-room door, put the tray down on the table in the hall and knock cautiously.

'Come in!' Trish calls.

As I enter, she's sitting in a chair by the window, holding a magazine at a rather artificial angle. Eddie is on the other side of the room, examining a wooden carving.

'Thank you, Samantha.' Trish inclines her head graciously as I pour out the coffee. 'That will be all for the moment.'

I feel as though I've stumbled into a Merchant Ivory costume drama, except the costumes are pink yoga wear and golfing sweaters.

'Er . . . very good, madam,' I say, playing my part. Then, without meaning to, I bob a curtsy.

Both Geigers just gape at me in astonishment.

'Samantha, did you just . . . *curtsy*?' says Trish at last.

I stare back, frozen. What was I thinking? Housekeepers don't bloody curtsy. This isn't Gosford Park. They're still goggling at me. I have to say something. 'The Edgerlys liked me to curtsy. It's a habit I got into. I'm sorry, madam, I won't do it again.'

Trish's head is leaning further and further over, her eyes all screwed up. She's squinting at me as though she's trying to make me out.

She must realise I'm a fake, she *must*.

'I like it,' she pronounces at last, and nods her head in satisfaction. 'Yes, I like it. You can curtsy here, too.'

What? I can do *what*? This is the twenty-first century. And I am being asked to curtsy to a woman called Trish? I take a breath to protest—then close it again. It doesn't matter. It's not real. I can curtsy for a morning.

I can see *The Times* lying on the table. It's open at the business pages and a headline reads GLAZERBROOKS CALLS IN RECEIVERS.

My eyes run down the text but I can't see any mention of Carter Spink. The PR department must have managed to keep a lid on the story.

'Mr Geiger and I will be going out in a minute,' Trish says. 'Kindly prepare a light sandwich lunch for one o'clock, and get on with the downstairs cleaning. We'll talk about dinner later. I might tell you, we were both very impressed by your seared *foie gras* menu.'

'Oh . . . um . . . good!'

It's fine. I'll be gone by dinner time.

By 11.30 I'm a nervous wreck. My mobile's charged up and I've finally found a signal in the kitchen, but it hasn't rung. And there are no messages. I've checked it every minute.

I gave up on the 'light sandwich lunch' almost straight away. I sawed away at two loaves of bread—and ended up with ten huge, wonky slices, each one more misshapen than the last.

All I can say is, thank God for *Yellow Pages* and caterers. And

American Express. It's only going to cost me £45.50 to provide Trish and Eddie with a 'gourmet sandwich lunch' from Cotswold Caterers. To be honest, I would have paid twice that.

Now I'm just sitting on a chair, my hand clasped tightly over my mobile in my pocket, desperately willing it to ring. At the same time I'm utterly terrified that it will.

All of a sudden I can't bear the tension any more. I need something to relieve it. *Anything*. I wrench open the door of the Geigers' enormous fridge and pull out a bottle of white wine. I pour myself a glass and take an enormous, desperate gulp. I'm about to take another when I feel a tingling on the nape of my neck. As if . . . I'm being watched.

I swivel round. There's a man at the kitchen door. He's tall and broad, and deeply tanned, with intense blue eyes. His wavy hair is golden brown with bleached-blond tips. He's wearing old jeans and a torn T-shirt and the muddiest boots I've ever seen.

His eyes run doubtfully over the ten wonky, crumbly bread slices on the side, then onto my glass of wine.

'Hi,' he says at last. 'Are you the new cordon bleu cook?'

'Er . . . yes! Absolutely.' I smooth my uniform down. 'I'm the new housekeeper, Samantha. Hello.'

'I'm Nathaniel.' He holds out his hand and after a momentary pause I take it. His skin is so hard and rough, it's like shaking a piece of tree bark. 'I do the garden for the Geigers. You'll be wanting to talk to me about vegetables.'

I look at him uncertainly. Why would I want to talk to him about vegetables?

'I can supply pretty much anything,' he continues. 'Seasonal, of course. Just tell me what you want.'

'Oh, *vegetables*,' I say, suddenly realising what he means. 'For cooking. Er . . . yes. I'll be wanting some of those. Definitely.'

'They told me you trained with some Michelin-starred chef?' He gives a small frown. 'I don't know what kind of fancy stuff you use, but I'll do my best.' He produces a small, mud-stained notebook and a pencil. 'Which brassicas do you like to use?'

Brassicas? What are brassicas? They must be some kind of vegetable. I search my mind frantically but all I can see is an image of brassieres, waving on a washing line.

'I'd have to consult my menus,' I say at last with a businesslike nod.

'But just generally.' He looks up. 'Which do you use most? So I know what to plant.'

'I use . . . all sorts, really.' I give him an airy smile. 'You know how it is with brassicas. Sometimes you're in the mood for one . . . sometimes another!' I'm really not sure how convincing that sounded. Nathaniel looks baffled.

He puts down his notebook and surveys me for a moment. His attention shifts to my wineglass again. I'm not sure I like his expression.

'I was just about to put this wine in a sauce,' I say hastily. With a nonchalant air, I take a saucepan down from the rack, put it on the hob and pour the wine in. I shake in some salt, then pick up a wooden spoon and stir it.

'Where did you say you trained?' he says.

'At . . . cordon bleu school.' My cheeks are growing rather hot. I shake more salt into the wine and stir it briskly.

'You haven't turned the hob on,' Nathaniel observes.

'It's a cold sauce,' I reply, without lifting my head. I keep stirring for a minute, then put down my wooden spoon. 'So. I'll just leave that to . . . marinate now.'

At last I look up. Nathaniel is leaning against the doorframe, calmly watching me. There's an expression in his blue eyes that makes my throat tighten.

He knows. He knows I'm a fake. *Please don't tell the Geigers*, I silently transmit to him. *Please. I'll be gone soon.*

'Samantha?' Trish's head pops round the door and I start nervously. 'Oh, you've met Nathaniel! Did he tell you about his vegetable garden?'

'Er . . . yes.' I can't look at him. 'He did.'

'*Marvellous!*' She drags on a cigarette. 'Well, Mr Geiger and I are back now, and we'd like our sandwiches in twenty minutes.'

I feel a jolt of shock. Twenty minutes? But it's only ten past twelve. The caterers aren't coming till one o'clock.

'Would you like a drink first?' I suggest desperately.

'No, thanks!' she says. 'Just the sandwiches. We're both rather famished, actually, so if you could hurry up with them . . .'

'Right.' I swallow. 'No problem!'

I automatically bob a curtsy as Trish disappears and hear a kind of snorting sound from Nathaniel.

'You curtsy,' he says.

'Yes, I curtsy,' I say defiantly. 'Anything wrong with that?'

Nathaniel's eyes rest again on the misshapen bread slices lying on the breadboard. 'Is that lunch?' he says.

'No, that's not lunch!' I snap, flustered. 'And please could you get out of my kitchen? I need a clear space to work in.'

'See you around then. Good luck with the sauce.' He nods his head towards the pan of wine.

As he closes the kitchen door behind him I whip out my phone and speed-dial the caterers. But they've left their machine on.

'Hi,' I say breathlessly after the bleep. 'I ordered some sandwiches earlier? Well, I need them *now*. As soon as you can. Thanks.'

Even as I put the phone down I realise it's pointless. The caterers are never going to turn up in time. The Geigers are waiting.

Determination rises in me. OK. I can make a few sandwiches.

Quickly I pick up the two least wonky of my bread slices. I pick up the bread knife and start cutting off the crusts until they're about an inch square but presentable. There's a butter dish on the side and I gouge some out with a knife. As I spread it on the first slice the bread tears into two pieces.

I'll patch them together. No one'll notice.

I fling open a cupboard door and frantically root through pots of mustard . . . mint sauce . . . strawberry jam. Jam sandwiches it is. An English classic. I hastily smother one piece of bread with jam, spread some more butter on the other, and sandwich the two together. Then I stand back and look at it.

It's a total disaster. Jam is oozing out of the cracks. I've never seen a more revolting sandwich in my life.

Slowly I put the knife down in defeat. So this is it. Time for my resignation. As I stare at the jammy mess I feel strangely disappointed in myself. I would have thought I could last a morning.

A knocking sound breaks me out of my reverie. I whip round to see a girl in a blue velvet hairband peering through the kitchen window.

'Hi!' she calls. 'Did you order sandwiches for twenty?'

It all happens so fast. One minute I'm standing there looking at my botch of jam and crumbs. The next, two girls in green aprons are trooping into the kitchen with plates of professionally made sandwiches.

Clean-cut, white and brown sandwiches, stacked in neat pyramids, garnished with sprigs of herbs and slices of lemon. They even have little handwritten paper flags describing the fillings. *Tuna, mint and cucumber. Smoked salmon, cream cheese and caviar. Thai chicken with wild rocket.*

'I'm *so* sorry about the numbers mix-up,' the girl in the hairband says as I sign for them. 'It honestly looked like a twenty. And we don't often get an order for sandwiches for just two people . . .'

'It's fine!' I say, edging her towards the door. 'Really. Whatever. Just put it on my card.'

The door finally closes and I look around the kitchen, totally dazed. I've never *seen* so many sandwiches.

'Samantha?' I can hear Trish approaching. 'It's five past one, and I did ask *most* clearly for . . .'

Her voice trails off into silence as she reaches the kitchen door, and her whole face sags in astonishment. I turn and follow her gaze as she surveys the endless plates of sandwiches.

'My goodness!' At last Trish finds her voice. 'This is . . . impressive!'

'I wasn't sure what fillings you'd prefer,' I say. 'Obviously next time I won't make quite so many . . .'

'Well!' Trish appears totally at a loss.

'I'll put a selection on a plate for you,' I suggest. 'And bring it out to the conservatory.'

'*Marvellous*. Nathaniel!' Trish raps on the kitchen window. 'Come in and have a sandwich!'

I stop dead. No. Not him again.

'We don't want to waste them, after all.' She arches her eyebrows. 'If I did have a criticism, Samantha, it would be that you were a *little* profligate. Not that we're *poor*,' she adds suddenly. 'It isn't *that*.'

'Er . . . no, madam.'

'Mrs Geiger?' Nathaniel has appeared in the kitchen doorway again.

'Have one of Samantha's delicious sandwiches!' exclaims Trish, gesturing around the kitchen. 'Just look! Isn't she clever?'

There's total silence as Nathaniel surveys the endless mounds of sandwiches. I can't bring myself to meet his eye.

'That didn't take you long,' he says, a slight question in his voice.

'I'm pretty quick when I want to be.' I give him a bland smile.

'Samantha's wonderful!' says Trish, biting greedily into a sandwich and practically swooning. 'This Thai chicken is divine!'

Surreptitiously I pick up one from the pile and bite into it.

Bloody hell, that's good. Though I say it myself.

By half past two the kitchen is empty. Trish and Eddie devoured over half the sandwiches, and have now gone out. Nathaniel is back in the garden. I'm pacing up and down, looking at the clock every thirty seconds. Arnold will call soon. It's been hours.

Suddenly I feel my mobile vibrate and my whole chest seems to explode in painful fright. I grab the phone out of my uniform pocket with a suddenly trembling hand.

The caller ID tells me it's Ketterman.

As I stare at his name I feel real fear in a way I never have before.

'Hello.'

'Samantha. John Ketterman here.'

'Right.' My voice is scratchy with nerves. 'Hello.'

'Samantha, I'm ringing to tell you that your contract with Carter Spink has been terminated.'

I feel all the blood drain from my face.

'A letter is on its way to you giving the reasons.' His tone is distant and formal. 'Gross negligence compounded by your subsequent unprofessional behaviour. Your P45 will be sent to you. Your pass has been disabled. I don't expect to see you at the Carter Spink offices again.'

'Please don't . . .' My voice comes blurting out in desperation. 'Please give me another chance. I made one mistake. One.'

'Lawyers at Carter Spink don't make mistakes, Samantha. You have disgraced the reputation of the firm and yourself.' Ketterman's voice sharpens as though he, too, might be finding this difficult. 'You have lost fifty million pounds of a client's money through your own negligence. And subsequently absconded with no explanation. Samantha, you cannot have expected any other outcome, surely?'

There's a long silence. My forehead is pressed hard against the heel of my hand. I try to focus on breathing. 'No,' I whisper at last.

It's over. My entire career. Everything I've worked for since I was twelve years old. All gone. Everything ruined. In twenty-four hours.

At last I realise Ketterman has disappeared from the line. I get to my feet and stagger over to the shiny fridge. I look greenish-grey in its reflection. My eyes are huge, burning holes.

I've been fired. The phrase echoes round my mind. *I've been fired.*

Suddenly I hear the sound of a key in the front door. My eyes snap into focus and I move away from the fridge.

I can't be found like this. I can't face any probing; any sympathy. Otherwise I'm afraid I might just collapse into sobs and never stop. Distractedly I reach for a cloth and start sweeping it over the table.

'There you are!' Trish comes tripping into the kitchen on her high-heeled clogs, holding three bursting shopping bags. 'Samantha!' She stops at the sight of me. 'Are you all right? Is your headache back?'

'I'm . . . fine.' My voice shakes a little. 'Thanks.'

'You look *dreadful*! Goodness me! Have some more pills!'

'Really . . .'

'Go on! I'll have some too, why not?' she adds gaily. 'Now, sit down, and I'll make *you* a cup of tea!'

She plonks the bags down and switches on the kettle, then rootles around for the green painkillers.

'These are the ones you like, aren't they?'

'Um, I'd rather just have an aspirin,' I say quickly. 'If that's OK.'

'Are you quite sure?' She runs me a glass of water and gives me a couple of aspirin. 'Now, you just sit there. Relax. Don't even *think* of doing anything else! Until it's time to make the supper,' she adds.

'You're very kind,' I manage.

As I say the words I have the dim realisation that I mean them. Trish's kindness may be a bit warped, but it's real.

My mind is beating like a butterfly's wings. What am I going to do? *Go home.*

But the thought of returning to that flat, with Ketterman living two floors above, makes me sick. I can't face him. I can't do it.

Phone Guy. He'll have me to stay. They have that huge house in Islington with all those spare rooms. Then I'll sell my flat. Find a job.

What job?

'Here we are.' Trish puts a cup of tea down and scrutinises me for a few moments. 'This will cheer you up,' she says, patting the shopping bags with suppressed glee. 'After your *stunning* performance at lunch . . . I've been shopping. And I've got a surprise for you!'

'A surprise?' I look up, bewildered, as Trish starts producing packets from the bag.

'Foie gras . . . chick peas . . . shoulder of lamb . . .' She hefts a joint of meat onto the table and looks at me expectantly. Then she clicks her tongue at my bewildered expression. 'It's *ingredients*! Your dinner-party menu! We'll eat at eight, if that's OK?'

It'll be all right.

If I say it often enough to myself, it must be true.

I need to call Guy. I flip open my phone and dial Guy's number.

'Samantha.' He sounds guarded. 'Hi. Have you—'

'It's OK,' I squeeze my eyes shut. 'I've spoken to Ketterman. I know.'

'Oh, Samantha.' He exhales hard. 'I'm so sorry . . . All sorts of stories are going round.'

'Stories?' My heart is thudding. 'What . . . what stories?'

'There's a rumour you've skipped the country.' He sounds reluctant. 'Apparently people are saying you're . . . unreliable. That you've made errors before.'

I can't take all this in. I cannot stand his pity. If he says anything else I might burst into tears. 'It's fine,' I say, cutting him off. 'Really. Let's not talk about it. Let's just . . . look forward. I have to get my life on track.'

'Jesus, you're focused!' There's a note of admiration in his voice. 'You don't let anything faze you, do you?'

'I just have to . . . get on with things.' Somehow I keep my voice even and steady. 'I need to get back to London. But I can't go home. Ketterman bought a flat in my building. He *lives* there.'

'Yes, I heard about that.' I can hear the wince in Guy's voice.

'I just can't face him, Guy. So . . . I was wondering. Could I come and stay with you for a few days?'

There's silence. I wasn't expecting silence.

'Samantha, I'd love to help,' says Guy at last. 'But I'm not sure. We're having some work done to the bedrooms . . . it's not a good time . . .'

He sounds halting, as if he wants to get off the line. And suddenly it hits me. He doesn't want to be near me. It's as though my disgrace is contagious; as though his career might get blighted, too.

I know I should stay quiet, keep my dignity, but I just can't contain myself. 'You don't want to be associated with me, do you?' I burst out.

'Samantha!' His voice is defensive. 'Don't be ridiculous.'

'I'm still the same *person*. I thought you were my friend, Guy.'

'I am your friend! But you can't expect me to . . . Look, call me in a couple of days, maybe we can meet up for a drink . . .'

I try to control my voice. 'I'm sorry to have bothered you.'

I switch off my phone, light-headed with disbelief, wondering what to do next. When it suddenly vibrates in my hand, I nearly jump out of my skin. *Tennyson*, my display reads.

Mum. I feel a clutch of apprehension inside. I guess she's heard. I guess I could go and stay with her, it occurs to me. How weird. I didn't even think of that before. I open up the phone and take a deep breath.

'Hi, Mum.'

'Samantha.' Her voice pierces my ear with no preamble. 'How long were you going to leave it exactly before you told me about your debacle? I have to find out about my own daughter's disgrace from an *Internet joke*.' She utters the words with revulsion.

'An Internet joke?' I echo faintly. 'What do you mean?'

'You didn't know? Apparently in certain legal circles the new term for fifty million pounds is "a Samantha". I was not amused.'

'Mum, I'm so sorry—'

'Where are you?' She cuts across my faltering words.

'I'm . . . at someone's house. Out of London.'

'And what are your plans?'

'I don't know.' I rub my face. 'I need to . . . find a job.'

'Yes, and be thankful that I have acted for you. I've called in all my favours. It wasn't easy. But the senior partner at Fortescues will see you tomorrow at ten.'

'You've organised me a job interview?'

'Assuming all goes well, you will enter at senior associate level.' Her voice is crisp. 'You're being given this chance as a personal favour to me. As you can imagine, there are . . . reservations. So, if you want to progress, Samantha, you are going to have to perform. You're going to have to give more than you did at Carter Spink. No slacking. No complacency. You will have to prove yourself *doubly*. Do you understand?'

'Yes,' I say automatically. I shut my eyes, my thoughts whirling. I have a job interview. A fresh start. It's the solution to my nightmare. Why don't I feel more relieved? More happy?

More hours. More work. More late nights. It's almost as if I can feel the concrete blocks being loaded onto me again. Heavier and heavier.

'I mean, no,' I hear myself saying. 'No. I don't want it. It's too much . . .'

The words come out of my mouth all by themselves. I wasn't planning them; I've never even thought them before. But now they're out in the air they somehow feel . . . true.

'I'm *sorry*?' Mum's voice is sharp.

'I was thinking . . . I could take a break, maybe.'

'A break would finish your legal career.' Her voice snaps dismissively.

'I could do something else.'

'You wouldn't last more than two minutes in anything else!' She sounds affronted. 'Samantha, you're a *lawyer*.'

'There are other things than being a lawyer!' I cry, rattled.

'Samantha, if you're having some kind of breakdown—'

'I'm not!' My voice rises in distress. 'Just because I question my life, it doesn't mean I'm having a breakdown! I never *asked* you to find me another job. I need a bit of time to . . . to think.'

'You will be at that job interview, Samantha.' Mum's voice is like a whip. 'You will be there tomorrow at ten o'clock.'

'I won't!'

I switch off my phone, and almost savagely throw it down onto the table. My face is burning. Tears are pressing hotly at the back of my eyes. The phone starts vibrating angrily on the table but I ignore it. I'm not going to answer it. I'm not going to talk to anyone. I'm going to have a drink. And then I'm going to cook this bloody dinner.

I slosh some white wine into a glass and take several gulps. Then I address myself to the pile of raw ingredients waiting on the table.

I can cook. I can cook this stuff. Even if everything else in my life is in ruins, I can do this. I have a brain, I can work it out.

Without delay I rip the plastic covering off the lamb. This can go in the oven. In some kind of dish. Simple. And the chick peas can go in there too. Then I'll mash them and that will make the hummous.

I open a cupboard, select a baking tray and scatter the chick peas onto it. I grab a bottle of oil from the counter and drizzle it over the top. Already I'm feeling like a cook.

I shove the tray into the oven and turn it on full blast. Then I plonk the lamb in an oval dish and shove that in too.

So far so good. Now all I need to do is leaf through all Trish's recipe books and find instructions for seared *foie gras* with an apricot glaze.

By seven o'clock I'm still cooking.

At least I think that's what I'm doing. Both ovens are roaring with heat. Pots are bubbling on the hob. The electric whisk is whirring busily. I've burnt my right hand twice, taking things out of the oven.

I've been going for three hours. And I haven't yet made anything that could actually be eaten. So far I've discarded a collapsed chocolate soufflé, two pans of burnt onions, and a saucepan of congealed apricots that made me feel sick just to look at them.

The Geigers, meanwhile, have no idea. They're drinking sherry in the drawing room. They think everything is going splendidly.

A kind of frenzied hysteria has come over me. I know I cannot do this. But somehow I can't give up either. I keep thinking a miracle will happen. I'll pull it all together. I'll manage it somehow—

Oh God, the gravy's bubbling over.

I grab a spoon and start stirring it. It looks like revolting lumpy brown water. Frantically I start searching in the cupboards for something to chuck in. Flour. Cornflour. Something like that. This'll do. I grab a small pot and shake in vigorous amounts of the white powder, then wipe the sweat off my brow. OK. What now?

Suddenly I remember the egg whites, still whisking up in the food mixer. I grab the recipe book, running my finger down the page. I changed the dessert course to pavlova after I chanced upon the line in a recipe book: 'Meringues are so easy to make.'

So far so good. What next? 'Form the stiff meringue mixture into a large circle on your baking parchment.'

I peer at my bowl. *Stiff* meringue mixture? Mine's liquid.

It has to be right, I tell myself feverishly. It has to be. I followed the instructions. Maybe it's thicker than it looks. Maybe once I start pouring it out, it'll stiffen up by some weird culinary law of physics.

Slowly I start to pour it onto the tray. It doesn't stiffen up. It spreads in a white oozing lake and starts dripping off the tray onto the floor.

A big splodge lands on my foot and I give a frustrated cry. I feel near tears. Why didn't it work? A pent-up rage is rising up inside me: rage at myself, at my crappy egg whites, at cookery books, at cooks, at food . . . And most of all at whoever wrote that meringues were 'so easy to make'.

'They're not!' I hear myself yelling. 'They're bloody not!' I hurl the book across the kitchen, where it smashes against the kitchen door.

'What the hell—' a male voice exclaims in surprise.

The next minute the door flies open and Nathaniel is standing there, his hair glinting in the evening sun. A rucksack is hefted over his shoulder; he looks like he's on his way home. 'Is everything OK?'

'It's fine,' I say, rattled. 'Everything's fine. Thank you. Thank you so much.' I make a dismissive motion with my hand, but he doesn't move.

'I heard you were cooking a gourmet dinner tonight,' he says slowly, looking around at the mess.

'Yes. That's right. I'm just in the . . . most complex stage of the . . .' I glance down at the hob, and give an involuntary scream. 'The gravy!'

Brown bubbles are expanding out of my gravy saucepan, all over the cooker and down the sides onto the floor.

'Get it off the heat, for God's sake!' exclaims Nathaniel. He snatches up the pan and moves it. 'What on earth is in that?'

'Nothing!' I say. 'Just the usual ingredients . . .'

Nathaniel has noticed the little pot on the counter. He grabs it and stares at it incredulously. '*Baking soda?* You put baking soda in gravy? Is that what they taught you at—' He breaks off and sniffs the air. 'Hang on. Is something burning?'

I watch helplessly as he opens the bottom oven, grabs an oven glove with a practised air and hauls out a baking tray covered in what look like tiny black bullets. My chick peas. I forgot all about them.

'What are *these*?' he says incredulously. 'Rabbit droppings?'

'They're chick peas,' I retort. 'I drizzled them in olive oil and put them in the oven so they could . . . melt.'

Nathaniel stares at me. '*Melt?*'

'Soften,' I amend hurriedly.

Nathaniel puts down the tray and turns round, his face working with disbelief. 'You know bugger all about cooking! This is all a bluff! You're not a housekeeper. I don't know what the hell you're up to—'

'I'm not up to anything!' I reply, in shock.

'The Geigers are good people.' He faces me square on. 'I won't have them exploited.'

Suddenly, he looks really aggressive. Oh God. What does he think? That I'm some kind of confidence trickster?

I rub my sweaty face. 'I'm not trying to rip anyone off. OK, I can't cook. But I ended up here because of . . . a misunderstanding.'

'A misunderstanding?' He gives a suspicious frown.

'Yes,' I say, a little more sharply than I meant to. I sink down onto a chair. 'I was running away from . . . something. I needed a place to stay for the night. The Geigers assumed I was a housekeeper. And then in the morning I felt bad. I thought I'd do the job for a morning. But I'm not planning to stay. And I won't take any money from them, if that's what you're thinking.'

There's silence. At last I look up. Nathaniel is leaning against the counter, his huge arms folded. His wary frown has eased a little.

'What were you running from?' he says. 'A bad relationship?'

I think back over all my years at Carter Spink. All the hours I gave them; everything I sacrificed. Finished in a three-minute phone call.

'Yes,' I say slowly. 'A bad relationship.'

'How long were you in it?'

'Seven years.' To my horror I can feel tears seeping out of the corners of my eyes. 'I'm sorry,' I gulp. 'It's been quite a stressful day.'

Nathaniel tears off a square of kitchen towel from the wall-mounted roll behind him and hands it to me. 'If it was a bad relationship, you're well out of it,' he says calmly. 'No point staying. No point looking back.'

'You're right.' I wipe my eyes. 'Yes. I just have to decide what to do with my life. I can't stay here.'

'The Geigers are good employers,' says Nathaniel with a tiny shrug. 'You could do worse.'

'Yeah.' I raise a half-smile. 'Unfortunately I can't cook.'

'I could speak to my mum. She can cook. She could teach you.'

I look at him in astonishment, almost laughing. 'You think I should *stay*? I thought I was supposed to be a confidence trickster.' I shake my head. 'I have to go.'

'Shame. It would have been nice to have someone around who speaks English. And makes such great sandwiches,' he adds, totally deadpan.

I can't help smiling back. 'Caterers.'

'Ah. I wondered.'

A faint rapping at the door makes us both look up.

'Samantha?' Trish's voice outside is hushed and urgent. 'Don't worry, I won't come in. I don't want to disturb anything! You're probably at a very *crucial* stage.'

'Kind of . . .' I catch Nathaniel's eye and a sudden wave of hysteria rises through me.

'I just wanted to ask,' Trish continues, 'if you will be serving any kind of *sorbet* between the courses?'

I look at Nathaniel. His shoulders are shaking with silent laughter. I can't stop a tiny snort escaping. I clamp my hand desperately over my mouth, trying to get control of myself.

'Samantha?'

'Er . . . no,' I manage at last. 'There won't be any sorbet.'

Nathaniel has picked up one of my pans of burnt onions. He mimes taking a spoonful and eating it. *Yummy*, he mouths. Tears are streaming from my eyes. I'm almost asphyxiating, trying to keep quiet.

'Well! See you later!'

Trish tip-taps away and I collapse into helpless laughter. I've never laughed so hard in my life. My ribs hurt; I almost feel like I'll be sick.

At last I somehow calm down, wipe my eyes and blow my runny

nose. Nathaniel's stopped laughing too, and is looking around the bombshelled kitchen.

'Seriously,' he says, 'what are you going to do about this? They're expecting a fancy dinner.'

'I know.' I feel a fresh wave of hysteria and fight it down. 'OK.' I exhale with a little shudder and push back my damp hair. 'I'm going to rescue the situation.'

'You're going to rescue the situation.' He looks disbelieving.

'In fact I think this might solve everyone's problems.' I get to my feet and start busily sweeping packets into the bin. 'First I need to clear up the kitchen a bit . . .'

'I'll help.' Nathaniel stands up. 'This I have to see.'

Companionably, we empty pans and pots and packets into the bin. I open the oven and pull out the lamb in a cloud of smoke, then scrub all the smeared surfaces while Nathaniel mops up the meringue.

'How long have you worked here?' I ask him.

'Three years. Before that, I was working at Marchant House. It's a stately home, near Oxford. Before that, university.'

'University?' I say, my ears pricking up. 'I didn't know—'

I halt. I was about to say 'I didn't know gardeners went to university.'

'I did natural sciences.' Nathaniel gives me a look that makes me think he knew exactly what I was thinking.

I open my mouth to ask him where and when he was at university—then on second thoughts, close it and switch on the waste-disposal unit. I don't want to start getting into details, going down the 'Do we know anyone in common?' road. Right now, I could do without remembering the particulars of my life.

At last the kitchen looks a bit more normal. I take a deep breath.

'OK. Show time.'

'Good luck.' Nathaniel raises his eyebrows.

I open the kitchen door to see Trish and Eddie loitering in the hall.

'Ah, Samantha! Everything ready?' Trish's face is all lit up with anticipation, and I feel a huge twinge of guilt for what I'm about to do.

'Mr and Mrs Geiger.' I take a deep breath and put on my best breaking-bad-news-to-a-client face. 'I am devastated.' I look from one face to the other, then close my eyes and shake my head.

'Devastated?' echoes Trish nervously.

'I have done my best.' I open my eyes. 'But the dinner I created was not up to my own professional standards. I could not allow it out of the kitchen. I will of course reimburse all your costs—and offer my resignation. I will leave in the morning.'

There. Done. And no casualties.

'*Leave?*' Trish stares at me in consternation, her blue eyes practically bulging out of their sockets. 'You can't leave! You're the best housekeeper we've ever had! We'll give you a pay rise! Name your price!'

This conversation is really not going the way I planned.

'Well . . . we never actually discussed pay . . .'

'*Eddie!*' Trish rounds on him savagely. 'This is *your* fault! Samantha's leaving because you're not paying her enough!'

'I didn't say that—' I begin helplessly.

She digs Eddie in the ribs with her elbow. 'Say something!'

'Ah . . . Samantha.' Eddie clears his throat awkwardly. 'We'd be very happy if you would consider staying with us. We've been delighted with your performance and whatever your salary expectations are . . . we'll match them.' Trish digs him in the ribs again. 'Exceed them.'

They're both gazing at me with a kind of eager hope.

I glance at Nathaniel, who cocks his head as though to say 'Why not?'

The strangest feeling is coming over me. Three people. All telling me they want me within the space of ten minutes. I could stay. It's as simple as that. *I can't cook,* a little voice reminds me. *I can't clean. I'm not a housekeeper.* But I could learn. I could learn it all.

The silence is growing in tension. Even Nathaniel is watching me closely from the door.

'Well . . . OK.' I feel a smile coming to my lips. 'OK. If you want me to . . . I'll stay.'

Four

THE ONLY THING IS, now I actually have to be a housekeeper.

Having set my alarm early, the next morning I arrive downstairs in the kitchen before seven, in my uniform. The garden is misty and there are no sounds, except a couple of magpies chacking at each other on the lawn. I feel as though I'm the only person awake in the world.

Breakfast is a bit of a nightmare. It takes me three failed attempts before I realise how you're supposed to cut a grapefruit in half. You'd think they'd draw guidelines round them, or have perforations, or something. Meanwhile the milk for the coffee boils over—and when I plunge down the cafetière, the coffee explodes everywhere. Luckily Trish and Eddie are so busy arguing about where to go on their next holiday, they don't seem to notice what's going on in the kitchen.

On the plus side, I really think I'm getting the hang of the toaster.

When they've finished, I stack the dirty dishes in the dishwasher and am desperately trying to remember how I made it work yesterday, when Trish comes into the kitchen.

'Is everything all right?' she asks. 'Have you got your routine sorted, Samantha?'

'Absolutely.' I grope for a competent-sounding phrase. 'I'm pretty much . . . on top of everything.'

'Good!' she exclaims. 'I knew it! You don't need mollycoddling! You know your way around a house.'

'I should say so.'

Trish beams back. 'I expect you'll be tackling the laundry today.'

The laundry. I hadn't even thought about the laundry.

'Only I'd like you to change the sheets when you make the beds,' she adds.

Make the beds? That hadn't occurred to me either.

I feel a twinge of slight panic. Not only am I not remotely 'on top of everything', I don't have a clue what 'everything' is.

'Obviously I have my own . . . er . . . established routine,' I say, trying to sound casual. 'But it might be an idea if you give me a list of duties.'

'Oh.' Trish looks a little irritated. 'Well, if you think you need it. Now, Samantha, Mr Geiger would like to see you in his study. To discuss your pay and conditions. Don't keep him waiting!'

'Er . . . very good, madam.' I curtsy, then head out into the hall. I approach the door of Eddie's study and knock twice.

'Come in,' comes a jovial voice. As I walk into the room, Eddie is sitting behind his desk: a huge affair of mahogany and tooled leather with an expensive-looking laptop.

'Ah, Samantha.' Eddie gestures to an upright wooden chair and I sit down. 'Here we are. The document you've been waiting for.'

With a self-important air he hands me a folder marked HOUSEKEEPER'S CONTRACT. I open it up to find a title sheet on cream vellum paper produced to look like an old scroll. Printed in an ornate, medieval-style font are the words

CONTRACT OF AGREEMENT
Between Samantha Sweeting and Mr and Mrs Edward Geiger, this 2nd day of July in the year of our Lord two thousand and four.

'Wow,' I say in surprise. 'Did a . . . lawyer draw this up?'

I cannot imagine any lawyer I know drawing up a contract in Disney-medieval lettering. Let alone putting it all in a fake scroll.

'I didn't need a lawyer.' Eddie chuckles knowingly. 'I'm not playing at that game. Charge you an arm and a leg, those guys will, just for a bit of fancy Latin. Take it from me, Samantha, these things are simple enough to draw up if you've half a brain.' He gives me a wink.

'I'm sure you're right,' I say at last. I turn over the title sheet and run my eyes down the printed clauses.

Oh my God. What *is* this gibberish? I have to bite my lip as I take in phrases here and there.

. . . Insofar, notwithstanding the provision of culinary services, in a manner which shall be deemed, prima facie, to include yet not exclude light snacks and beverages . . .

My lips are clamped together. I must not laugh.

Pursuant to the aforetaining, ipso facto, all parties will retain the aforementioned rights beyond reasonable doubt.

The whole thing is a total nonsensical mishmash. Bits of legal jargon soldered together in meaningless, would-be-impressive phrases. I scan the rest of the page, desperately keeping a straight face, trying to think of a suitable response.

'Now, I know it looks frightening,' says Eddie, misinterpreting my silence. 'But don't be intimidated by all these long words. It's quite simple, really. Did you have a chance to look at the pay?'

My eye flicks to the figure quoted in bold under 'Weekly Salary'. It's slightly less than I charged per hour as a lawyer.

'It seems extremely generous,' I say after a pause.

'Is there anything you don't understand?' He beams jovially. 'Just say!'

Where do I start?

'Um . . . this bit.' I point to *Clause 7: Hours.* 'Does this mean I have the whole weekend off? Every weekend?'

'Of course.' Eddie seems surprised. 'We wouldn't expect you to give up your weekends! Unless it's a special occasion, in which case we'll pay you extra . . . you'll see in Clause 9 . . .'

I'm not listening. Every weekend free. I can't get my head round this. I don't think I've had a totally free weekend since I was twelve.

'That's great.' I look up, unable to stop myself smiling.

'I'll leave you alone to study the agreement before you sign.'

As Eddie disappears from the room, I look down at the contract again, rolling my eyes. I pick up a pencil and automatically start correcting the text, rephrasing, scoring out and adding queries in the margin.

Then, abruptly I stop myself. *What the hell am I doing?*

I grab a rubber and hastily erase all my amendments. I reach for a Biro and turn to the bottom of the page, where a cartoon owl in lawyer's garb is pointing to a dotted line.

Name: Samantha Sweeting.
Occupation:

I hesitate for a moment, then put *Domestic Help*.

As I write the words I have a fleeting blink of incredulity. I'm really doing this. I'm really taking this job, miles away from my former life in every sense. And no one knows what I'm doing. I have a sudden flash of the expression on my mother's face, if she knew where I was right now . . . if she could see me in my uniform . . . I'm almost tempted to call her up and tell her.

But I'm not going to. I have laundry to do.

It takes me two trips to bring down all the washing to the laundry room. I dump the overflowing baskets on the tiled floor and look at the high-tech washing machine. This should be simple enough.

I'm not exactly experienced in this area. At home I send everything except underwear to the dry-cleaners. But that doesn't mean I *can't* do it. Experimentally I open the door of the machine and at once an electronic display starts flashing at me. WASH? WASH?

Immediately I feel flustered. *Obviously* I want you to wash, I feel like snapping back. Just give me a chance to get the bloody clothes in.

I take a deep breath. Stay calm. One thing at a time. First step: fill the machine. I pick up a bundle of clothes—then stop myself.

No. First step: sort the clothes. Feeling pleased with myself for having thought of this, I start sorting out the dirty clothes into piles on the floor, consulting the labels as I go.

Whites 40.

Whites 90.

Wash inside out.

Wash colours separately.

Wash with care.

By the end of the first basket I'm totally bewildered. I've made about twenty different piles on the floor, most consisting of only one item. This is ridiculous. I can't put on twenty washes. It'll take all week.

OK . . . let's just be rational. People do washing every day, all over the world. It cannot be that hard. I'll just have to mix and match a bit.

I pick up a bundle of clothes from the floor and shove it into the drum. Then I open a nearby cupboard and grab a packet covered in pictures of white T-shirts, shake some powder into the little tray at the top. I close the door firmly. Now what?

WASH? the machine is still flashing at me. WASH?

'Er . . . yes!' I say. 'Wash them.' I jab randomly at a button.

ENTER PROGRAM? it flashes back.

Program? My eyes dart about for clues and I spot a manual tucked behind a spray bottle. I grab it and start leafing through.

The half-load option for small washes is only available for pre-wash programs A3–E2 and super rinse programs G2–L7 not including H4.

What? Come on. I have a degree from Cambridge. I know Latin, for God's sake. I can work this out. I flip to another page.

Programs E5 and F1 exclude spin cycle UNLESS button 'S' is depressed for five seconds before commencing.

I can't cope. My exam on international corporate litigation was a million times easier than this. OK, let's forget the manual. Let's just use common sense. I briskly press at the key pad in my best competent-housekeeper manner.

PROGRAM K3? the machine flashes at me. PROGRAM K3?

'No,' I say aloud, jabbing at the machine. 'I want something else.'

YOU HAVE CHOSEN PROGRAM K3 it flashes back.

'But I don't want program K3!' I say, flustered.

K3 COMMENCING, flashes the display. HEAVY DUTY UPHOLSTERY PROGRAM.

Heavy duty? *Upholstery?*

'Stop it,' I say under my breath, and start banging all the buttons. 'Stop!' I kick the machine in desperation. '*Stop!*'

'Everything all right?' comes Trish's voice from the kitchen and I leap away from the machine, smoothing my hair down.

'Er . . . fine! Fine!' I plaster on a professional smile as she appears at the door. 'Just . . . getting some washing on.'

'Well done.' She holds out a stripy shirt to me. 'Now, Mr Geiger needs a button sewn on this shirt, if you would be so kind . . .'

'Absolutely!' I take it from her with an inward gulp.

'And here's your list of duties!' She hands me a sheet of paper. 'It's by no means complete, but it should get you *started . . .*'

As I run my eyes down the endless list, I feel a bit faint.

Make beds . . . sweep and clean front steps . . . arrange flowers . . . polish all mirrors . . . store cupboards tidy . . . laundry . . . clean bathrooms daily . . .

'Now there's nothing here that should present you with a problem, is there?' adds Trish.

'Er . . . no!' My voice is a little strangled. 'No, it should all be fine!'

'But make a stab at the ironing *first*,' she continues firmly. 'There is quite a lot, I'm afraid.' For some reason, Trish is looking upwards. With foreboding, I follow her gaze. There, above us, is a mountain of crumpled shirts hanging on a wooden drying rack. At least thirty.

As I stare up at them, I feel wobbly. I can't iron a shirt. I've never used an iron in my life. What am I going to do?

'I expect you'll whip through these in no time!' she adds gaily. 'The ironing board's just there,' she adds with a nod.

'Um, thanks!' I manage.

The important thing is to look convincing. I'll get the ironing board out, wait till she leaves . . . then come up with a new plan.

I reach for the ironing board, trying to look matter-of-fact, as if I do this all the time. I tug briskly at one of the metal legs, but it won't move.

Trish takes the board from me, and in two movements has put it up. 'I expect you're used to a different model,' she adds as she clicks it shut. 'They all have their own little tricks.'

'Absolutely!' I say, seizing on this excuse in relief. 'Of course! I'm far more used to working with a . . . a . . . a Nimbus 2000.'

Trish peers at me in surprise. 'Isn't that the broomstick out of Harry Potter?'

Fuck. I knew I'd heard it somewhere.

'Yes . . . it is,' I say, my face flaming. 'And also a well-known ironing board. In fact, I think the broomstick was named *after* the ironing board.'

'Really?' Trish looks fascinated. 'I never knew that!' To my horror she leans expectantly against the door and lights a cigarette. 'Don't mind me!' she adds, her voice muffled. 'Just carry on!'

Carry on?

'There's the iron,' she adds with a gesture. 'Behind you.'

'Er . . . great! Thanks!' I take the iron and plug it in, as slowly as possible, my heart banging in fright.

'I expect the iron is hot enough by now,' said Trish helpfully.

'Right.' I give her a sick smile.

I have no choice. I'm going to have to start ironing. I reach for one of the shirts overhead, and spread it out awkwardly on the ironing board. Unable to believe what I'm doing, I pick up the iron. It's far heavier than I imagined and emits a terrifying cloud of steam. Very gingerly, I start lowering it towards the cotton fabric. I have no idea which bit of the shirt I'm aiming for. I think my eyes might be shut.

Suddenly there's a trilling from the kitchen. The phone. Thank God.

'Sorry, Samantha,' says Trish, frowning. 'I should get this . . .'

'That's fine!' My voice is shrill. 'No worries! I'll just get on . . .'

As soon as Trish is out of the room I put the iron down with a crash and bury my head in my hands. I must have been mad. This isn't going to work. I'm not made to be a housekeeper. The iron puffs steam in my face and I give a little scream of fright. I switch it off and collapse against the wall. It's only nine twenty and I'm already a total wreck.

And I thought being a lawyer was stressful.

Later, when time Trish comes into the kitchen I'm a little more composed. I can do this. It's not quantum physics. It's *housework*.

'Samantha, I'm afraid we're going to *desert* you for the day,' says Trish, looking concerned. 'Mr Geiger is off to golf and I'm going to see a *very* dear friend's new Mercedes. Will you be all right on your own?'

'I'll be fine!' I say, trying not to sound too joyful. 'Don't worry about me. Really. I'll just get on with things . . .'

'Is the ironing done?' She glances at the laundry room, impressed.

Done? What does she think I am, Wonder Woman?

'Actually, I thought I'd leave the ironing for now and tackle the rest of the house,' I say. 'That's my normal routine.'

'Absolutely.' She nods vigorously. 'Whatever suits you. Now, I won't be here to answer any questions, I'm afraid, but Nathaniel will!' She beckons out of the door.

'Oh,' I say as he walks in, wearing ripped jeans, his hair dishevelled. 'Er . . . hi, again.'

This is a bit weird. Seeing him this morning, after the drama of last night. As he meets my eye there's the twitch of a smile at his mouth.

'Hi,' he says. 'How's it going?'

'Great!' I say lightly. 'Really well.'

'Nathaniel knows *all* there is to know about this house.' Trish picks up her handbag. 'So if you can't find anything he's your man.'

'I'll bear that in mind,' I say. 'Thanks.'

'Toodle-oo!' calls Trish from the hall, and the front door bangs shut.

'Right!' I say. 'Well . . . I'll get on.'

I wait for Nathaniel to leave, but he leans against the table and looks at me quizzically. 'Do you have any idea how to clean a house?'

I'm starting to feel quite insulted here. Do I *look* like someone who can't clean a house?

'Of course I know how to clean a house.' I roll my eyes.

'Only I told my mum about you last night.' He gives a sudden smile, as though remembering the conversation, and I gaze at him suspiciously. What did he say? 'Anyway, she's willing to teach you cooking. And I said you'd probably need cleaning advice too—'

'I do not need cleaning advice!' I retort. 'I've cleaned houses loads of times. In fact, I need to get started.'

'Don't mind me.' Nathaniel shrugs.

I'll show him. In a businesslike manner I pick a can out of the cleaning cupboard and spray it onto the counter. There. Who says I don't know what I'm doing?

The spray has solidified into crystalline little grey droplets. I briskly rub them with a cloth—but they won't come off. Shit.

I look more closely at the can. 'DO NOT USE ON GRANITE'. *Shit.*

I hastily put the cloth down to hide the droplets. 'You're in my way.' I grab a feather duster from the blue tub and start brushing crumbs off the kitchen table. 'Excuse me . . .'

'I'll leave you then,' says Nathaniel, his mouth twitching again. He looks at the feather duster. 'Don't you want to be using a dustpan and brush for that?'

'I have my methods,' I say, lifting my chin. 'Thank you.'

'OK.' He grins. 'See you.'

I'm not going to let him faze me. I'm perfectly capable of cleaning this house. I just need . . . a plan. Yes. A time sheet, like at work.

As soon as Nathaniel's gone I grab a pen and piece of paper and start scribbling a list for the day.

9.30–9.36   Make beds
9.36–9.42   Take laundry out of machine and put in dryer
9.42–10.00 Clean bathrooms

I get to the end and read it over with a fresh surge of optimism. This is more like it. At this rate I should be done easily by lunchtime.

9.36 Fuck. I cannot make this bed. Why won't this sheet lie flat?

9.54 This is sheer torture. My arms have never ached so much in my entire life. The blankets weigh a ton, and the sheets won't go straight and I have no idea how to do the wretched corners. How do chambermaids do it? How?

10.30 At last. A whole hour of hard work and I have made precisely one bed. But never mind. Laundry next.

10.36 No. Please, no. I can hardly bear to look. It's a total disaster. Everything in the washing machine has gone pink. Every single thing. With trembling fingers I pick out a damp cashmere cardigan. It was cream when I put it in. It's now a sickly shade of candy floss. I knew K3 was bad news. I knew it—

Keep calm. There must be a solution. My eye starts flicking frantically over cans of products stacked on the shelves. Stain Away . . . Vanish. There has to be a remedy . . . I just need to think . . .

10.42 OK, I have the answer.

11.00 I've just spent £852 replacing all the clothes in the machine. Harrods personal-shopping department was very helpful, and will send them Express Delivery tomorrow.

11.06 The ironing. What am I going to do about that?

11.12 Right. I've looked in the local paper and I have a solution to that, too. A girl from the village will collect it, iron it all overnight at three pounds a shirt, and sew on Eddie's button.

So far this job has cost me nearly £1,000 pounds.

11.42 I've got the Hoover on, I'm cruising along nicely—

Shit. What was that? What just went up the Hoover? Why is it making that grinding noise? Have I broken it?

11.48 How much does a Hoover cost?

12.24 My legs are in total agony. I've been kneeling on hard tiles, cleaning the bath, for what seems like hours. All I want is a rest. But I have to keep moving. I can't stop for a moment. I am *so* behind . . .

12.30 What is wrong with this bleach bottle? Which way is the nozzle pointing, anyway? Why won't anything come out? OK, I'm going to squeeze it really, really hard—

12.32 Fuck. What has it done to my HAIR?

By three o'clock I am utterly knackered. I'm only halfway down my list and I can't see myself ever making it to the end. I don't know how people clean houses. It's the hardest job I've ever done, ever.

Right now I'm standing on a chair, cleaning the mirror in the drawing room. But the more I rub, the more smeary it gets.

I keep catching glances of myself in the glass. My hair is sticking out wildly, with a huge grotesque streak of greeny-blonde where I splashed the bleach. My face is bright red and sheeny, my hands are pink and sore from scrubbing and my eyes are bloodshot.

Why won't it get clean? Why? 'Get clean!' I cry, practically sobbing in frustration.

'Samantha.'

Abruptly I stop rubbing, to see Nathaniel standing in the doorway, looking at the smeary glass. 'Have you tried vinegar?'

'*Vinegar?*' I stare at him in suspicion.

'It cuts through the grease,' he adds. 'It's good on glass.'

'Oh. Right. Yes, I knew that.'

Nathaniel shakes his head. 'No, you didn't.'

I look at his adamant face. There's no point pretending any more. He knows I've never cleaned a house in my life.

'You're right,' I admit at last. 'I didn't.'

As I get down off the chair I feel wobbly with fatigue.

'You should have a break,' says Nathaniel firmly. 'You've been at it all day, I've seen you. Did you have any lunch?'

'No time.'

I sink down onto a chair, feeling suddenly too drained to move.

'It's . . . harder than I thought,' I say at last. 'A lot harder.'

'Uh huh.' He nods. 'What happened to your hair?'

'Bleach,' I say shortly. 'Cleaning the loo.'

He gives a muffled snort of laughter but I don't look up. To be honest, I'm beyond caring.

'I can't do it.' The words come out before I can stop them. 'I can't do this job. I'm . . . hopeless.'

'Sure you can.' He rifles in his rucksack and produces a can of Coke. 'Have this. You can't work on no fuel.'

'Thanks,' I say, taking it gratefully.

'The offer still stands,' he adds after a pause. 'My mother will give you lessons if you like.'

'Really?' I wipe my mouth, push back my sweaty hair and look up at him. 'She'd . . . do that?'

'She likes a challenge, my mum.' Nathaniel gives a little smile. 'She'll teach you your way around a kitchen. And anything else you need to know.' He glances quizzically towards the smeary mirror.

'That would be great,' I say humbly. 'I really appreciate it. Thanks.'

Five

I WAKE UP ON SATURDAY, heart pounding, and leap to my feet, my mind racing with everything I have to do . . .

And then it stops, like a car screeching to a halt. For a moment I can't move. Then, hesitantly, I sink back into bed, overcome by the weirdest, most extraordinary feeling I've ever experienced.

I have nothing to do. It's my day off. No one has any hold over me. This is my own time. *My own time.*

I check the time—and it's only 7.15 a.m. The whole day stretches before me like a clean sheet of paper. What shall I do?

I'm already sketching out a timetable for the day in my head. An hour wallowing in the bath and getting dressed. An hour lingering over breakfast. An hour reading the paper. I'm going to have the laziest, most indolent, most enjoyable morning I've ever had in my adult life.

As I head into the bathroom, I can feel muscles twinging with pain all over my body. They really should market house-cleaning as a work-out. I run a deep warm bath and slosh in some of Trish's bath oil, then step into the scented water and lie back happily.

I close my eyes, letting the water lap my shoulders, and let time waft past in great swathes. I think I even fall asleep for a while. I have never spent so long in a bath in my entire life.

At last I open my eyes, reach for a towel and get out again. As I'm starting to dry myself off I reach for my watch, just out of curiosity.

It's 7.30 a.m. *What?* I was only fifteen minutes?

I feel a flash of astonishment. How on earth can I have only taken fifteen minutes? I stand, dripping, in indecision for a moment, wondering if I should get back in again and do it all again, more slowly.

But no. That would be too weird. It doesn't matter. I'll just make sure I take my time properly over breakfast. Really *enjoy* it.

At least I have some clothes to put on. Trish took me out last night to a shopping centre a few miles away, so I could stock up on underwear and shorts and summer dresses. She told me she'd leave me to it—then ended up bossing me about and picking everything out for me . . . and somehow I finished up with not a single item in black.

I cautiously put on a pink slip dress and pair of sandals, and look at myself. I've never worn pink before in my life. But to my amazement I don't look too bad! Apart from the huge streak of bleach in my hair. I'm going to have to do something about that.

As I make my way along the corridor, there's no sound from the Geigers' bedroom. I move silently past the door, feeling suddenly awkward. It'll be a bit strange, being in their house all weekend, with nothing to do. I'd better go out later. Get out of their way.

The kitchen is as silent and gleamy as ever, but it's starting to feel slightly less intimidating. I know my way around the kettle and the toaster, if nothing else. I'll have toast for breakfast, with orange and ginger marmalade, and a nice cup of coffee. And I'll read the paper from cover to cover. That'll take me to about eleven o'clock and then I can think about what else to do.

I find a copy of *The Times* on the doormat, and bring it back to the kitchen just as my toast is popping up.

This is the life.

I sit by the window, crunching toast, sipping coffee and leafing through the paper in a leisurely way. At last, after devouring three slices, two cups of coffee and all the Saturday sections, I stretch my arms in a big yawn and glance at the clock.

I don't believe it. It's only 7.56.

What is wrong with me? I was supposed to take *hours* over breakfast. I was supposed to be sitting there all morning. Not get everything finished in twenty minutes flat.

OK . . . never mind. Let's not stress about it. What do people do on days off? My mind scrolls through a series of images from TV. I could make another cup of coffee? But I've already had two. I could read the paper again? But I have an almost photographic memory. So re-reading things is a bit pointless.

My gaze drifts outside to the garden, where a squirrel is perched on a stone pillar. Maybe I'll go outside. Enjoy the garden and the wildlife and the early-morning dew. Good idea.

Except the trouble with early-morning dew is it gets all over your feet. As I pick my way over the damp grass, I'm already wishing I hadn't put on open-toed sandals. Or that I'd waited till later for my little stroll.

The garden is a lot bigger than I'd appreciated. I walk down the lawn towards an ornamental hedge where everything seems to finish, only to realise there's a whole further section beyond it, with an orchard at the end and some sort of walled garden to my left.

It's a stunning garden. Even I can see that. The flowers are vivid without being garish, every wall is covered with some beautiful creeper or vine, and as I walk towards the orchard I can see little golden pears hanging from the branches of trees.

I stroll through the fruit trees towards a huge, square, brown patch of earth with plants growing in serried rows. These must be the vegetables. I prod one of them cautiously with my foot. It could be a cabbage or a lettuce. To be honest, it could be an alien. I have no idea.

I wander round a bit longer, then sit down on a wooden bench.

Now what? I look at my watch. Still only 8.16. I can't do this. I can't do nothing all day. I'll have to go and buy another paper from the village shop. If they've got *War and Peace*, I'll buy that too. I get up and am starting to head briskly back across the lawn when a bleep from my pocket makes me stop still.

It's my mobile. It's received a text. I pull it out and look at it, feeling edgy. I haven't had any contact with the outside world for over a day.

I know there are other texts in my phone—but I haven't read any of them. I know there are messages in my voicemail—but I haven't listened to a single one. I don't want to know. I'm blocking it all out.

I finger my mobile, telling myself to put it away. But now my curiosity has been sparked. As I stand there on the early-morning lawn, I can feel my mental self being dragged back to London, back to the office. A lot can happen in twenty-four hours. Things can change. Everything could have turned out positive in some way. Or . . . become even worse.

The tension is rising inside me. I'm gripping my phone more and more tightly. I have to know. Good or bad. I flip open the phone and find the text. It's from a number I don't even recognise.

Feeling a little sick, I press OK to read.

hi samantha, nathaniel here.

Nathaniel? *Nathaniel?* My relief is so huge, I laugh out loud. Of course! I gave him my mobile number yesterday for his mother. I scroll down to read the rest of the message.

if you're interested, mum could start cooking lessons today. nat

Cooking lessons. I feel a spark of delight. That's it. The perfect way to fill the day. I press Reply and quickly text:

would love to. thanks. sam

I send it with a little smile. This is fun. A minute or two later, the phone bleeps again.

what time? is 11 too early? nat

I look at my watch. Eleven o'clock is still two and a half hours away.

shall we make it 10? sam

At five to ten I'm ready in the hall. Nathaniel's mother's house is apparently tricky to find, so the plan is to meet here and he'll walk me over. As I check my reflection in the hall mirror, I wince. The streak of bleach is as obvious as ever. Maybe I could walk along with my hand carelessly positioned at my head, as if I'm thinking hard. I attempt a few casual, pensive poses in the mirror.

'Is your head all right?'

I swivel round in shock to see Nathaniel at the open door, wearing a plaid shirt and jeans.

'Er . . . fine,' I say, my hand still glued to my head. 'I was just . . .'

Oh, there's no point. I bring my hand down from my hair and Nathaniel regards the streak for a moment.

'It looks nice,' he says. 'Like a badger.'

'A badger?' I say, affronted. 'I don't look like a badger.'

'Badgers are beautiful creatures,' says Nathaniel with a shrug. 'I'd rather look like a badger than a stoat.'

Hang on. Since when was my choice between badger or stoat?

'Perhaps we should go,' I say with dignity. I pick up my bag and give one last glance in the mirror as I reach for the door.

OK. Maybe I look a little bit like a badger.

The summer air is already warming up outside, and as we turn out of the drive I realise this is the first time I've been out of the Geigers' grounds since I arrived here—apart from the shopping trip with Trish, when I was too busy scrabbling for her Celine Dion CD to notice my surroundings. Nathaniel has turned left and is striding easily along the road—but I can't move. I'm gazing at the sight in front of me, my jaw wide open. This village is absolutely *stunning*.

I look around, taking in the old, honey-coloured stone walls. The rows of ancient cottages have steeply pitched roofs. The river is lined with willow trees. Up ahead is the pub I noticed on the first day, decorated with hanging baskets. Everything is soft and mellow and feels like it's been here for hundreds of years.

'Samantha?'

Nathaniel has finally noticed I'm pinned to the spot.

'I'm sorry.' I hurry to join him. 'It's just such a beautiful place.'

'Didn't you see any of this as you arrived?' Nathaniel regards me with amusement. 'Did you just appear in a bubble?'

I think back to that panicked, dazed, desperate journey. Getting off the train, my head throbbing, my vision a blur.

'Kind of.' I try to match his relaxed pace. 'So, did you grow up here?'

'Yup. I came back when my dad got ill. Then he died, and I had to sort things out. Take care of Mum. Everything was in a mess.'

'I'm sorry,' I say awkwardly. 'Do you have any other family?'

'My brother Jake. He came back for a week.' Nathaniel hesitates. 'He runs his own business. Very successful.'

His voice is as easy as ever, but I can detect a thread of . . . something. Maybe I won't ask any more about his family.

'Well, *I'd* live here,' I say with enthusiasm.

Nathaniel gives me an odd look. 'You do live here,' he reminds me.

I feel a tweak of surprise. I suppose he's right. Technically, I do.

I walk on a few paces, trying to process this new thought. I've never lived anywhere except London before, apart from my three years at Cambridge. I've always had an NW postcode. An 0207 number. That's who I am. That's who I . . . was.

But already the old me is feeling more distant. I'm still feeling sore and bruised. But at the same time . . . I feel more alive with possibility than I have ever done. My ribcage expands widely as I breathe in the country air and I suddenly feel a wave of optimism.

'Here we are.' Nathaniel pushes open an old iron gate and gestures me to go up a stone path towards a little cottage with blue flowered curtains at the windows. 'Come and meet your cooking teacher.'

Nathaniel's mother is nothing like I expected. I was picturing some cosy Mrs Tiggywinkle character with grey hair in a bun and half-moon spectacles. Instead, I'm looking at a wiry woman with a vivid, pretty face. Her greying hair is in plaits either side of her face, she's wearing an apron over jeans, T-shirt and espadrilles.

'Mum.' Nathaniel grins and pushes me forward into the kitchen. 'Here she is. This is Samantha. Samantha . . . my mum. Iris.'

'Samantha. Welcome.' I can see her taking me in, head to foot. 'So, you want to learn how to cook.' Her tone is friendly but businesslike.

'Yes.' I smile. 'Please.'

'And how much cooking have you done before?' Iris smiles at me. 'What can you make? What are your basics?'

'Well . . . I can . . . I can make . . . um . . . toast,' I say.

'Toast?' She looks taken aback. 'Just toast?'

'And crumpets,' I add quickly. 'Tea cakes . . . anything that goes in a toaster, really . . .'

'But what about *cooking*?' She looks at me more carefully. 'What about, say . . . an omelette? Surely you can cook an omelette?'

I swallow. 'Not really.'

Iris's expression is so incredulous I feel my cheeks flame. 'I never did home economics at school,' I explain.

'But your mother, surely . . . or your grandmother . . .' She breaks off as I shake my head. '*Anyone?*'

I bite my lip. Iris exhales sharply as though taking in the situation for the first time. 'So you can't cook anything at all. And what have you promised to make for the Geigers?'

Oh God.

'Trish wanted a week's worth of menus. So I . . . um . . . gave her one based on this.' Sheepishly I get the crumpled Maxim's menu out of my bag and hand it to her.

'Braised lamb and baby onion assemblé with a fondant potato and goat's cheese crust, accompanied by cardamom spinach purée,' she reads out, in tones of disbelief.

I hear a snort and look up to see Nathaniel in fits of laughter.

'It was all I had!' I exclaim defensively. 'What was I going to say, fish fingers and chips?'

'"Assemblé" is just flannel.' Iris is still perusing the sheet. 'That's souped-up shepherd's pie. We can teach you that. And the braised trout with almonds is straightforward enough . . .' She runs her finger further down the page then at last looks up, a frown creasing her brow. 'I can teach you these dishes, Samantha. But it isn't going to be easy.'

'I'm a quick learner.' I lean forward. 'And I'll work hard.'

'All right,' says Iris at last. 'Let's get you cooking.'

She reaches into a cupboard for a set of weighing scales and I take the opportunity to delve into my bag for a pad of file paper and a pen. As Iris turns round and sees me, she looks bemused.

'What's that for?' She jerks her head at the file paper.

'So I can take notes,' I explain.

'Samantha, you're not going to be taking notes,' she says. 'Cooking isn't about writing down. It's about tasting. Feeling. Touching. Smelling.'

'Right.' I nod intelligently.

I must remember that. I quickly uncap my pen and scribble down *Cooking = all about tasting, smelling, feeling etc.* I cap my pen again and look up. Iris is regarding me with incredulity.

'Tasting,' she says, removing my pen and paper from my hands. 'Not writing. You need to use your senses. Your instincts.'

She lifts the lid off a pot gently steaming on the cooker and dips a spoon into it. 'Taste this.'

Gingerly I take the spoon in my mouth. 'Gravy,' I say at once.

Iris shakes her head. 'Don't tell me what you think it is. Tell me what you can taste.'

I stare at her, puzzled. 'I can taste . . . gravy.'

Her expression doesn't change. She's waiting for something else.

'Er . . . meat?' I hazard.

'Samantha, don't think about identifying the taste. Just tell me what the sensation is.' Iris holds the spoon out a second time. 'Taste it again—and this time close your eyes.'

'OK.' I take a mouthful and close my eyes obediently.

'Concentrate on the flavours. Nothing else.' Iris's voice is in my ear.

Eyes tight shut, I focus all my attention on my mouth.

'It's salty and meaty . . .' I say slowly, without opening my eyes. 'And sweet . . . and . . . and almost fruity? Like cherries?'

I open my eyes. Iris is scrutinising me intently. Behind her I suddenly notice Nathaniel, also watching. At the sight of him, I feel a tad flustered. Tasting gravy with your eyes closed is a fairly intimate thing to do, it turns out. I'm not sure I want anyone watching me.

Iris seems to understand. 'Nathaniel,' she says briskly, 'we're going to need ingredients for all these dishes.' She scribbles a long list and hands it to him. 'Run down and get these for us, love.'

As he leaves the room, she looks at me, a faint smile on her lips. 'That was much better. Here, get a pinny on.' She hands me a red-and-white striped apron and I tie it around myself.

'It's so kind of you to help me,' I say hesitantly as she gets out onions and some orange vegetable I don't recognise. 'I'm really grateful.'

'I like a challenge.' Her eyes sparkle at me. 'And I liked the sound of you.' Iris draws down a heavy wooden chopping board. 'Nathaniel told me how you got yourself out of your mess the other night. That took some spirit.'

'I had to do something.' I give her a rueful smile.

'And they offered you a pay rise as a result. Wonderful.' As she smiles, fine lines appear round her eyes. 'Trish Geiger is a very foolish woman.'

'I like Trish,' I say, feeling a stab of loyalty.

'So do I.' Iris nods. 'She's been very supportive to Nathaniel. But you must have noticed she has little or no brain.' She sounds so matter-of-fact I want to giggle. I watch as she puts a huge, gleaming pot on the stove, then turns and looks at me. 'So you've taken them in completely.'

'Yes.' I smile. 'They have no idea who I am.'

'And who are you?'

Her question takes me completely by surprise. I open my mouth but no words come out.

'Is your name really Samantha?'

'Yes!' I say in shock.

'That was a little blunt.' Iris lifts a hand in acknowledgment. 'But a girl arrives in the middle of the countryside out of nowhere and takes a job she can't do . . .' She pauses as though choosing her words. 'Nathaniel tells me you've got out of a bad relationship?'

'Yes,' I mumble. I can feel Iris's shrewd gaze, appraising me.

'You don't want to talk about it, do you?'

'Not really. No. I don't.'

As I look up there's a thread of understanding in her eyes.

'That's fine by me.' She picks up a knife. 'Now, let's start. Roll up your sleeves, tie back your hair and wash your hands. I'm going to teach you to chop an onion.'

We spend all weekend cooking.

I learn to slice an onion finely, turn it the other way and produce tiny dice. I learn to chop herbs with a rounded blade. I learn how to rub flour and ground ginger into chunks of meat, then drop the pieces into a spitting-hot, cast-iron pan. I learn the trick of blanching French beans in boiling water before sautéing them in butter.

A week ago I didn't know what 'sauté' even meant.

On Sunday afternoon, under Iris's calm guidance, I make roast chicken with sage and onion stuffing, steamed broccoli, cumin-scented carrots and roast potatoes. As I watch Nathaniel carrying the serving dish bearing the roast chicken, all crispy golden, to the table, I feel a glow of pride. My first roast chicken.

'Wine for the cooks,' says Iris, producing a bottle from the fridge and uncorking it. She pours me a glass, then gestures to the table. 'Sit down, Samantha. You've done enough for one weekend.'

As I sink down into the nearest chair, I realise for the first time how exhausted I am.

Nathaniel carves the chicken with expert ease, and Iris dishes out the vegetables. When we're all served she sits down and raises her glass.

'To you, Samantha. You've done splendidly.'

'Thanks.' I smile and am about to sip my wine when I realise the other two aren't moving.

'And to Ben,' Iris adds softly.

'On Sundays we always remember Dad,' Nathaniel explains.

'Oh.' I hesitate, then raise my glass.

'Now.' Iris's eyes glint and she puts her glass down. 'The moment of truth.' She takes a bite of chicken and I try to hide my nerves.

'Very good.' She nods at last. 'Very good indeed.'

I can't help a beam spreading across my face.

I sit in the glow of the evening light, not talking much but eating and listening to the other two chat. The atmosphere is so relaxed and easy, so different from any meal I've ever had at home. No one's on the phone. No one's rushing to get anywhere else. I could sit here all night.

As the meal is finally drawing to a close, I clear my throat.

'Iris, I just want to say thank you again.'

'I enjoyed it. Next weekend, we'll make lasagne. And gnocchi!' Iris takes a sip of wine. 'We'll have an Italian weekend.'

'*Next* weekend?' I stare at her. 'But—'

'You don't think you've finished, do you?' She hoots with laughter. 'I've only just started on you! Now, what else do you need help with? Cleaning? Washing?'

I feel a twinge of embarrassment. Iris clearly knows exactly how much of a mess I got myself into yesterday.

'I'm not really sure how to use the washing machine,' I admit at last.

'We'll cover that.' She nods. 'I'll pop up to the house when they're out and have a look at it.'

'And I can't sew on buttons . . .'

'Buttons.' She reaches for a piece of paper and a pencil, and writes it down, still munching. 'What about ironing?' She looks up, suddenly alert. 'You must have had to iron. How did you wriggle out of that one?'

'I'm sending it out to Stacey Nicholson,' I confess. 'In the village. She charges three pounds a shirt.'

'Stacey Nicholson?' Iris puts her pencil down. 'Samantha, you are *not* paying Stacey Nicholson to do your ironing. She's fifteen years old!' She pushes back her chair, looking galvanised. 'You're going to learn how to do it yourself. I'll teach you. Anyone can iron.' She reaches into a little side room, pulls out an old ironing board covered in flowery material and sets it up, then beckons me over. 'What do you have to iron?'

'Mr Geiger's shirts, mainly,' I say, nervously.

She plugs in an iron and turns the dial. 'Hot, for cotton. Wait for the iron to heat up. Now, I'll show you the right way to tackle a shirt . . .'

She rootles, frowning, in a pile of clean laundry in the little room. 'Shirts . . . shirts . . . Nathaniel, take off your shirt a moment.'

I stiffen. As I glance at Nathaniel I see he has stiffened too.

'Mum!' He gives an awkward laugh.

'Oh, don't be ridiculous, love,' says Iris impatiently. 'You can take off your shirt for a moment. No one's embarrassed. You're not embarrassed, are you, Samantha?'

'Um . . .' My voice is a little grainy. 'Um . . . no, of course not . . .'

'Now, this is your steam.' She presses a button on the iron and a jet of steam shoots into the air. 'Always check your steam compartment has water . . . Nathaniel! I'm waiting!'

Through the steam I can see Nathaniel slowly unbuttoning his shirt. I catch a flash of smooth tanned skin and hastily lower my gaze.

Let's not be adolescent about this. So he's taking off his shirt. It's no big deal.

He tosses the shirt to his mother, who catches it deftly. My eyes are studiously fixed downwards. I'm not going to look at him.

'Start with the collar . . .' Iris is smoothing the shirt out on the ironing board. 'Now, you don't have to press hard.' She guides my hand as the iron glides over the fabric. 'Keep a smooth touch . . .'

This is ridiculous. I'm an adult, mature woman. I can look at a man with no shirt on without falling to bits. What I'll do is . . . just take a casual peek. Yes. And get this out of my mind.

'Now the yoke.' Iris turns the shirt round on the board and I start pressing again. 'Very good . . . on to the cuffs now . . .'

I lift the shirt-tail to flip it over—and as I do so, accidentally-on-purpose raise my eyes. Sweet Jesus. I'm not sure the whole getting-it-out-of-my-mind plan is going to work after all.

'Samantha?' Iris grabs the iron from me. 'You're scorching the shirt!'

'Oh!' I come to. 'Sorry. I . . . I lost concentration.'

'Your cheeks seem very flushed.' Iris puts a curious hand to my cheek. 'Are you all right, sweetie?'

'Must be the . . . steam.' I start ironing again, my face like a furnace.

Iris continues to instruct me, but I don't hear a word. As I move the iron blindly back and forth, I'm pondering obsessively on a) Nathaniel, b) Nathaniel without his shirt on, c) whether Nathaniel has a girlfriend.

At last I shake out his ironed shirt, perfectly done with all the creases in the right places.

'Very good!' says Iris, applauding. 'After some practice you'll be able to do that in four minutes flat.'

'Looks great,' Nathaniel smiles, holding out a hand. 'Thanks.'

'That's OK!' I manage in a strangled squawk, and hastily look away again, my heart thumping.

Great. One glimpse of his body and I have a full-blown crush.

Six

HE DOESN'T HAVE a girlfriend. I managed to get that information out of Trish last night, under the guise of asking about all the neighbours. There was some girl in Gloucester, apparently—but that was all over months ago. The way is clear. I just need a strategy.

As I shower and get dressed the next morning, I'm totally fixated by thoughts of Nathaniel. I'm aware I've reverted to the behaviour of a fourteen-year-old adolescent; that next I'll be doodling *Samantha loves Nathaniel* with a love heart dotting the 'i'. But I don't care. It's not as though being a mature professional was working out so great for me.

I brush my hair, looking out at the misty green fields, and feel an inexplicable light-heartedness. I have no reason to feel so happy. On paper, everything is still catastrophic. My high-flying career is over. I'm earning a fraction of what I used to, for a job which involves picking other people's dirty underwear off the floor. And yet I can't help humming as I straighten my bed.

My life has changed and I'm changing with it. I've never gone after a man before. But then, until yesterday I'd never basted a chicken before.

If I can do that, I can ask a man out, surely? The old Samantha would have sat back and waited to be approached. Well, not the new Samantha. I've seen the dating shows on TV, it's all about looks and body language and flirty conversation.

I reach for my make-up bag, and spend about ten minutes alternately applying and removing make-up, until I've got something which looks natural and subtle, yet defined.

Now to the body language. I wrinkle up my forehead, trying to remember the rules from TV. If a woman is attracted to a man, her pupils will dilate. Also, she will unconsciously lean forward, laugh at his jokes and expose her wrists and palms. Experimentally I lean towards my reflection, holding out my hands as I do so. I try adding a flirty laugh. 'Ha ha ha!' I'm really not sure this is adding to my chances.

I head downstairs, draw back the curtains. Nathaniel is striding across the lawn. Oh no. Full, one hundred per cent crush alert.

I cannot take my eyes off him. The sunlight is catching the ends of his tawny hair and he's wearing ancient, faded jeans. As I watch, he picks up some huge sack of something, swings it round easily and throws it onto something that might be a compost heap.

My mind is suddenly filled with a fantasy of him picking me up in exactly the same way. Swinging me round easily in his big strong arms. I mean, I can't be *that* much heavier than a sack of potatoes—

'So, how was your weekend off, Samantha?' Trish breaks my thoughts. 'We barely saw you! Did you go into town?'

'I went to Nathaniel's house,' I reply without thinking.

'Nathaniel?' Trish sounds astonished. 'The *gardener*? Why?'

Immediately I realise my huge mistake. I can't exactly say 'To have cooking lessons'. I stare back at her foolishly for a few moments, trying to fabricate an instant, convincing reason.

'Just . . . to say hello, really . . .' I say at last, aware that I sound tongue-tied. And also that my cheeks are turning pink.

Trish's face suddenly snaps in comprehension and her eyes open very wide, like dinner plates. 'Oh, I *see*,' she says. 'How *adorable*!'

'No!' I say quickly. 'It's not . . . Honestly . . .'

'Don't worry!' Trish cuts me off emphatically. 'I won't say a *word*. I am discretion itself.' She puts a finger to her lips. 'You can rely on me.'

Before I can say anything else she picks up her coffee and heads out of the kitchen. That was awkward. But I suppose it doesn't really matter. As long as she doesn't say anything inappropriate to Nathaniel.

Then I realise I'm being stupid. Of *course* she'll say something inappropriate to Nathaniel. And then who knows what he'll think.

I must go and make the situation quite clear to him. That Trish misunderstood me, and I don't have a crush on him or anything like that.

Whilst, obviously, making it clear that I do.

I force myself to wait until I've done breakfast for Trish and Eddie, mixed up some olive oil and lemon zest, and put tonight's sea bream fillets into it, just as Iris taught me.

Then I hitch up my uniform a bit more, add some more eyeliner for luck, and head out into the garden, holding a basket I found in the larder. If Trish wants to know what I'm doing, I'm gathering herbs for cooking.

I find Nathaniel in the orchard, standing on a ladder, tying some rope round a tree. As I make my way towards him I suddenly start feeling ridiculously nervous. My mouth feels dry—and did I just feel my legs *wobble*?

Ignoring my jitters as best I can, I walk up to the ladder, toss back my hair and smile up at him, trying not to squint in the sun. 'Hi!'

'Hi.' Nathaniel smiles down. 'How's it going?'

'Fine, thanks! Much better. No disasters yet . . . I was after some . . . rosemary.' I gesture to my basket. 'If you have any?'

'Sure. I'll cut you some.' He jumps down off the ladder and we start walking along the path towards the herb garden.

It's totally silent, down here away from the house, apart from the odd buzzing insect and the crunch of gravel on the path. I try to think of something light and easy to say, but my brain is blank.

'Um . . . lovely herbs!' I manage at last, gesturing around the garden in genuine admiration. It's laid out in a hexagonal shape, with little paths between the sections. 'Did you do all this? It's amazing.'

'Thanks. I'm pleased with it.' Nathaniel smiles.

He pulls out a pair of secateurs from an old leather holster-type thing and starts clipping at a dark green, spiky bush.

My heart starts to thump. I have to say what I've come to say.

'So . . . um . . . it's really weird,' I begin as lightly as I can, fingering the scented leaves of some bushy plant. 'But Trish seems to have got the wrong idea about us! She seems to think we're . . . You know.'

'Ah.' He nods, his face averted.

'Which is obviously . . . ridiculous!' I add with another laugh.

'Mm-hmm.' He clips some more rosemary sprigs and holds them up. 'This enough for you?'

Mm-hmm? That's it? That's all he has to say on the subject?

'Actually, I'd like some more,' I say, and he turns back to the bush. 'So . . . isn't it ridiculous?' I add desperately, trying to prod him into a proper answer.

'Well, of course.' At last Nathaniel looks at me properly, his tanned forehead creased in a frown. 'You won't be wanting to get into anything for a while. Not so soon after a bad relationship.'

I look at him blankly. What on earth—oh yes. My bad relationship.

'Right,' I say after a pause. 'Yes, that.'

Dammit. Why did I invent a bad relationship? What was I *thinking*?

'Actually'—I force myself to sound careless—'the relationship wasn't *that* bad. In fact, I think I've pretty much got over it.'

'You've got over a seven-year relationship in a week?' Nathaniel puts a fragrant bundle of rosemary into my arms. He looks as though he's trying to fathom me out.

'Mum said . . .' He stops, looking awkward.

'What?' I say, a little breathless.

'Mum wondered if you'd been . . . badly treated.' He shifts his gaze away. 'You're so tense and twitchy.'

'I'm not tense and twitchy!' I retort at once.

Maybe that was a little tense and twitchy.

'I'm naturally twitchy,' I explain. 'But I wasn't badly treated or anything like that. I was just . . . I always felt . . . trapped.'

The word comes out to my own surprise.

I have a flash of my life at Carter Spink. Practically living at the office. Taking work home with me. Answering emails at every hour. Maybe I did feel a little bit trapped.

'But I'm fine now.' I shake back my hair. 'Ready to move on . . . and start a new relationship . . . or something more casual . . . whatever . . .'

A one-night stand would do . . .

I gaze up at him, trying to dilate my pupils.

'You probably shouldn't rush into anything new,' Nathaniel says. He moves away without meeting my eye and starts examining a shrub.

There's an awkwardness in his back. I feel a rush of blood to my face as it hits me. He doesn't want to go out with me.

Aargh. This is hideous. Here I am, with my hitched-up skirt and eyeliner, doing all the body language I know, just basically *offering* myself to him . . . And he's trying to let me know he's not interested.

I'm mortified. I have to get away from here. From him.

'You're right,' I say, flustered. 'It's . . . far too soon to think about anything like that. I'm just going to focus on my new job. Cooking and . . . and . . . so forth. I must get on. Thanks for the rosemary.'

'Any time,' says Nathaniel.

Clasping the bundle more tightly, I turn on my heel, and stride back along the gravel path up to the house.

I am *beyond* embarrassed. So much for a whole new Samantha.

Anyway, I don't care. It's for the best, really. Because I *do* have to concentrate on my work. As soon as I get back to the house I set up the ironing board, plug in the iron, turn on the radio and make a nice strong cup of coffee. This is going to be my focus from now on. Getting my tasks for the day done. Not some stupid ridiculous crush on the gardener. I'm being paid to do a job here and I'm going to do it.

By midmorning I've ironed ten shirts, put a load of laundry on and hoovered the conservatory. By lunchtime, I've dusted and hoovered all the downstairs rooms and polished all the mirrors with vinegar. By tea time, I've put on another load of laundry, shredded my vegetables in the food processor, measured out the wild rice to be steamed, and carefully prepared four filo pastry cases for my tartes de fruits, as Iris taught me.

By seven o'clock I've thrown away one lot of burnt filo cases, baked another four, topped them with strawberries and finished them with heated-up apricot jam. I've pan-fried the vegetable shreds in olive oil and garlic till they're soft. I've blanched my French beans. I've put the sea bream in the oven.

My face is bright red and my heart is beating fast and I'm moving round the kitchen in a kind of speeded-up reality . . . but I kind of feel OK. In fact, I feel almost exhilarated. Here I am, actually cooking a meal all on my own . . . and I'm just about on top of it!

I've laid the dining table with the best china I could find and put candles in the silver candlesticks. I've got a bottle of Prosecco waiting in the fridge and heated plates waiting in the oven, and I've even put Trish's CD of Enrique Iglesias love songs in the player. I feel like I'm throwing my first-ever dinner party.

With a pleasant flutter in my stomach, I smooth down my apron, push open the kitchen door and call 'Mrs Geiger? Mr Geiger?'

There's absolutely no reply. I would have thought they'd be hovering around the kitchen by now. Where *are* they?

I investigate the rooms on the ground floor, but they're all empty. Cautiously, I start to advance up the stairs.

'Er . . . Mrs Geiger?' I call hesitantly. 'Dinner's served.'

Suddenly a door is flung open violently. 'What about *Portugal*?' Trish shrieks. 'Do you remember *that*?' She strides out of the room in a whirlwind of pink and stops as she sees me.

'Um, dinner's ready,' I mumble, my eyes fixed on the carpet. 'Madam.'

'If you mention *bloody* Portugal one more *bloody* time—' Eddie comes marching out of the room.

'Eddie!' Trish cuts him off savagely, then gives a tiny nod towards me. '*Pas devant.*'

'What?' says Eddie, scowling.

'*Pas devant les . . . les . . .*' She wheels her hands, as though trying to conjure the missing word.

'*Domestiques?*' I offer awkwardly.

Trish shoots me a flinty look, then draws herself up with dignity. 'I shall be in my room.'

'It's my bloody room too!' says Eddie furiously, but the door has already banged shut.

'Um . . . I've made dinner . . .' I venture, but Eddie stalks to the stairs, ignoring me.

I feel a swell of dismay. If the sea bream isn't eaten soon it'll get all shrivelled.

'Mrs Geiger?' I knock on her door. 'I'm just worried the dinner will spoil—'

'So what?' comes back her muffled voice. 'I'm not in the mood for eating.'

I stare at the door in disbelief. I've spent all bloody day cooking dinner for them. The candles are lit, the plates are in the oven.

'You *have* to eat!' I cry out, and Eddie stops, halfway down the stairs. The bedroom door opens and Trish looks out in astonishment.

'What?' she says.

OK. Play this one carefully.

'Everyone has to eat,' I improvise. 'It's a human need. So why not discuss your differences over a meal? Or put them on hold! Have a glass of wine and relax and agree not to mention . . . er . . . Portugal.'

As I say the word, I can feel hackles rising.

'I'm not the one who mentioned it,' growls Eddie.

'I only mentioned it because you were so *insensitive* . . .' Trish's voice is rising and she brushes a sudden tear from her eye. 'How do you think *I* feel, being your . . . trophy wife?'

Trophy? I must not laugh.

'Trish.' To my astonishment, Eddie is hurrying up the stairs as fast as his paunch will allow. 'Don't you *ever* say that.' He grips her shoulders and looks her fiercely in the eye. 'We've always been a partnership. You know that.'

'I know,' whispers Trish.

She's gazing up at Eddie as though no one else exists, and I suddenly feel a little pang. They really are in love.

'Let's go and eat,' says Eddie finally. 'Samantha was right. We should have a nice meal together. Sit down and talk it over.'

Thank God for that. The sea bream will still be just about OK . . . I just need to put the sauce in a jug . . .

'All right, let's,' Trish sniffs. 'Samantha, we'll be out to dinner tonight.'

My smile freezes. 'But . . . I've cooked!' I say quickly. 'It's done.'

'Oh well, never mind.' Trish makes a flapping gesture. 'Eat it yourself.'

'But it's all ready for you! Roasted fish, julienned vegetables . . . '

'Where shall we go?' says Trish to Eddie, not listening to a word. 'Shall we try to get in at the Mill House?'

As I stand there in stupefaction, she disappears into the bedroom, followed by Eddie. The door closes and I'm left on the landing.

My dinner party's ruined.

When they've roared out of the drive in Eddie's Porsche, I go into the dining room and slowly clear everything up. I put away the crystal glasses and fold up the napkins and blow out the candles. Then I head back into the kitchen and look for a moment at all my dishes, set out ready for action. My sauce, still bubbling away on the hob. My carved-lemon-slice garnishes. I was so proud of everything.

Anyway, there's nothing I can do about it.

My sea bream are looking pretty sorry for themselves, but I put one onto a plate and pour myself a glass of wine. I sit at the table, cut myself a piece of bream and raise it to my mouth. Then I put my knife and fork down without even tasting it. I'm not hungry.

A whole wasted day. And tomorrow I've got to do it all over again.

What am I doing here?

I mean, really. What am I doing? Why am I not walking out right now and getting on a train back to London?

As I'm slumped there I become aware of a faint tapping at the open door. I look up to see Nathaniel leaning on the door frame, holding his rucksack. I feel a flash of embarrassment as I remember this morning's encounter.

'I thought I'd come and see if you needed any help.' His eyes travel around the kitchen, at the dishes of untouched food. 'What happened?'

'They didn't eat it. They went out to dinner.'

Nathaniel stares at me for a moment, then closes his eyes briefly and shakes his head. 'After you spent all day cooking for them?'

'It's their food. Their house. They can do what they like.'

I'm trying to sound careless and matter-of-fact. But I can still feel the disappointment, heavy inside me. Nathaniel puts down his rucksack, strides over to the cooker and inspects the sea bream. 'Looks good.'

'It looks like congealed, overcooked fish,' I correct him.

'My favourite.' He grins, but I'm not in the mood to smile back.

'Have some, then.' I gesture at the dish. 'No one else is going to eat it.'

'Well, then, shame to waste it.' He helps himself to everything, piling his plate ludicrously high, then pours himself a glass of wine and sits down opposite me at the table.

For a moment neither of us speaks. I'm not even looking at him.

'To you.' Nathaniel raises his wineglass. 'Congratulations.'

'Yeah, right.'

'Seriously, Samantha.' He waits patiently until I drag my eyes up from the floor. 'Whether they ate it or not, this is a real achievement. I mean, bloody hell.' His mouth twists humorously. 'Remember the last dinner you cooked in this kitchen?'

I give a reluctant smile. 'The lamb of doom, you mean.'

'The *chick peas*. I'll never forget those.' He takes a bite of fish, shaking his head incredulously. 'This is good, by the way.'

An image comes to me of those tiny blackened bullets; myself running around in frenzied chaos . . . and in spite of everything I want to giggle. I've already learned so much since then.

'Well, of course, I'd have been OK that night,' I say nonchalantly, 'if you hadn't insisted on *helping* me. I had it all under control till you got in my way.'

Nathaniel puts his fork down, still munching. For a few moments he looks at me, his blue eyes crinkled up with something—amusement, maybe. I can feel the heat rising in my cheeks, and as I glance downwards I notice that my hands are resting on the table, palms up.

And I'm leaning forward, I realise in sudden horror. My pupils are probably half a mile wide, too. I could not be any clearer if I wrote 'I fancy you' in felt-tip on my forehead.

I hastily move my hands to my lap, sit up straight and adopt a stony expression. I haven't got over this morning's mortification. In fact, I might take the opportunity to say something.

'So—' I begin, just as Nathaniel starts speaking too.

'Go on.' He gestures towards me and takes another bite of fish.

'Well.' I clear my throat. 'After our . . . conversation this morning, I was just going to say that you're right about relationships. Obviously I'm not ready for anything new yet. Or even interested. At all.'

There. That told him.

'What were you going to say?' I ask, pouring more wine into his glass.

'I was going to ask you out,' says Nathaniel, and I nearly flood the table with wine.

He what? The hands thing *worked*?

'But not to worry.' He takes a gulp of wine. 'I understand.'

Backtrack. I need to backtrack, very, very quickly. Yet subtly, so he doesn't actually *notice* I'm backtracking.

Oh, bugger it, I'll just be inconsistent. I'm a woman, I'm allowed to be.

'Nathaniel,' I force myself to say calmly, 'I'd love to go out with you.'

'Good.' He looks unperturbed. 'How's Friday night?'

'Perfect. I'll ask Trish and Eddie for the evening off.'

As I grin back I suddenly realise I feel hungry. I pull my plate of sea bream towards me, pick up my knife and fork and begin to eat.

Seven

I GET TO FRIDAY morning without any major calamities. At least, none that the Geigers know about.

There was the vegetable risotto disaster on Tuesday—but thank God I managed to get a last-minute substitute from the caterers. There was a peach camisole that, in hindsight, should have been ironed on a lower setting. There was the Dartington glass vase that I broke while trying to dust with the vacuum-cleaner attachment. But no one seems to have noticed it's gone yet. And the new one should arrive tomorrow.

So far, this week has only cost me £200, which is a vast improvement on last week.

I'm hanging out Eddie's damp underwear in the utility room, averting my eyes as best I can, when I hear Trish calling me.

'Samantha! Where *are* you?' She doesn't sound pleased, and I feel a quailing inside. What's she discovered? 'I *can't* have you walking around like that any more.' Trish arrives at the door of the utility room, shaking her head vigorously.

'I'm sorry?' I peer at her.

'Your *hair*.' She makes a face.

'Oh, right.' I touch the bleached patch with a grimace. 'I meant to get it done at the weekend—'

'You're having it done now,' she cuts across me. 'My *super* hairdresser's here.'

'Now?' I stare at her. 'But . . . I've got hoovering to do.'

'You can make up the hours later. And I'll take the money out of your wages. Come on. Annabel's waiting!'

I guess I have no choice. I dump the rest of Eddie's underpants on the rack and follow her up the stairs.

'Now, I've been meaning to mention my cashmere cardigan,' Trish adds sternly as we reach the top. 'The cream one?'

Shit. Shit. She's found out I replaced it.

'I don't know what you've done to it.' Trish pushes open her bedroom door. 'But it looks *marvellous*. That little ink stain on the hem has completely disappeared! It's like new!'

'Right.' I give a smile of relief. 'Well . . . all part of the service!'

I follow Trish into the bedroom, where a thin woman with big blonde hair, white jeans and a gold chain belt is setting up a chair in the middle of the floor.

'Hello!' She looks up, cigarette in hand, and I realise that she's about sixty years old. She comes forward, surveys my hair and winces.

'What's all this? Thought you'd try the streaky look?' She gives a raucous laugh at her own joke.

'It was a . . . bleach accident.'

'Accident!' She runs her fingers through my hair, clicking. 'Well, it can't stay this colour. We'd better go a nice blonde.'

'I've never been blonde,' I say in alarm. 'I'm not really sure—'

'You've got the colouring for it.' She's brushing my hair out.

'Well, as long as it's not *too* blonde,' I say hurriedly. 'Not . . . you know, that fake, tarty, platinum blonde . . .'

I trail off as I realise both the other women in the room have fake, tarty, platinum-blonde hair.

I sit down on the chair, wrap a towel round my shoulders and try not to flinch as Annabel briskly pastes some chemical-smelling mixture on my head and layers in what feels like a thousand bits of silver foil.

Blonde. Oh God. What am I *doing*?

Annabel puts a magazine in my hand. Behind, Trish is opening a bottle of champagne. 'You'll look lovely. Pretty girl like you should *do* something with her hair. Now, read us our signs.'

'Signs?' I say in bewilderment.

'Horoscopes!' Annabel clicks her tongue. 'Not the brightest penny, is she?' she adds in an undertone to Trish.

'She is a little dim,' Trish murmurs back. 'But *marvellous* at laundry.'

So this is what being a lady of leisure is like. Sitting with foil in your hair, drinking Buck's Fizz and reading glossy magazines. I haven't read any magazines except *The Lawyer* since I was about thirteen. Normally I spend hairdressers' appointments typing emails or reading contracts.

But I can't relax and enjoy myself. I'm feeling more and more apprehensive as I read 'Ten Ways To Know Your Bikini Is Too Small'. By the time I've got to 'Real-Life Holiday Romances' and Annabel is blow-drying my hair, my entire body is seized up in fear.

'There we are!' Annabel gives a final blast and switches the hair dryer off. There's silence. I can't open my eyes.

'*Much* better!' Trish says approvingly.

I slowly open one eye. Then the other.

My hair isn't blonde. It's caramel. It's warm caramel with streaks of honey and the tiniest threads of gold. As I move my head it shimmers.

I swallow a few times, trying to keep control of myself. I think I might cry. 'It's wonderful,' I say, finding my voice. 'Thank you so much.'

I'm entranced by my reflection. I can't take my eyes off my new, glowing, caramel, honey self. I look alive. I look *colourful*.

I'm never going back to the way I looked before. Never.

At seven o'clock that evening, I arrive downstairs to see Trish wandering out of the living room with a cocktail glass, bloodshot eyes and a high colour.

'So!' she says benevolently. 'You're going out with Nathaniel tonight.'

'That's right.' I glance at myself in the mirror. I've gone for a fairly informal outfit. Jeans, nice simple top, sandals. New shiny hair. *Flick*.

She eyes me inquisitively over the top of her glass. 'Is that what you're wearing?' She runs her eyes over my outfit. 'It's not very *jazzy*, is it? Let me lend you a little something.'

'I don't mind not being jazzy,' I begin, feeling a few qualms, but Trish has already disappeared up the stairs. A few moments later she appears, holding a jewel box.

'Here we are. You need a bit of *glitz*.' She produces a diamanté clip in the shape of a large jewelled beetle and clips it to my hair. '*Now*. You see how the emerald brings out your eyes?'

I gaze at myself. I cannot go out with a sparkly beetle on my head.

'And this is very glam!' Now she's garlanding a gilt chain round my waist. 'Let me just hang the charms on . . .'

Charms?

'Mrs Geiger . . .' I begin, flustered, as Eddie appears out of the study.

'Just got the quote in for the bathroom,' he says to Trish. 'Seven thousand, plus VAT.'

'Well, how much is it with VAT?' says Trish, rifling in her box.

I feel like a Christmas tree. She's hanging more and more glittery baubles off the belt, not to mention the beetle.

'I don't know!' retorts Eddie impatiently. 'What's seventeen and a half per cent of seven thousand?'

'One thousand, two hundred and twenty-five,' I respond absently.

There's a stunned silence.

Shit. That was a mistake. Trish and Eddie are goggling at me.

'Or . . . something.' I give a distracting laugh. 'Just a guess. So . . . have you got any more charms?'

Neither of them takes the slightest notice of me. Eddie's eyes are fixed on the paper he's holding. Very slowly he looks up.

'She's right,' he says in a strangled voice. 'She's bloody right. That's the correct answer.' He jabs the paper. 'It's here!'

'She's *right*?' Trish breathes in sharply. 'But how . . .'

'You saw her.' Eddie's voice rises to an incredulous squeak. 'She did it in her head!'

They both swivel round to gaze at me again.

'Is she *autistic*?' Trish seems beside herself.

Oh, for God's sake. *Rain Man* has a lot to answer for, if you ask me.

'I'm not autistic,' I say. 'I'm just . . . quite good with numbers.'

To my huge relief the doorbell rings, and I go to answer it. Nathaniel is standing on the doorstep, looking a little smarter than usual, in tan jeans and a green shirt.

'Hi,' I say hurriedly. 'Let's go.'

'Wait!' Eddie blocks my way. 'Young lady, you may be a lot brighter than you realise.'

Oh, no.

'What's going on?' asks Nathaniel.

'She's a mathematical genius!' says Trish. 'And we discovered it!'

I shoot Nathaniel an agonised 'she's talking nonsense' look.

'What formal education have you had, Samantha?' Eddie demands. 'Other than cooking.'

'I . . . um . . . here and there.' I spread my hands vaguely.

'It's the schools today.' Trish inhales sharply on her cigarette. 'Tony Blair should be *shot*.'

'Samantha,' Eddie says, looking self-righteous, 'I will take on your education. And if you're prepared to work hard—hard, mind—I'm sure we can get you some qualifications.'

'I don't really want any qualifications, sir,' I mumble, surreptitiously divesting myself of all the jewelled creatures and slipping them back into the jewellery box. Then I look at Nathaniel, who has been waiting on the doorstep. 'Shall we go?'

'So, what was all that about?' asks Nathaniel as we start walking along the village road. The air is soft and warm and my new hair is bouncing lightly. 'You're a mathematical genius?'

'No.' I can't help laughing. 'Of course not!'

'What *is* your background then?'

'Oh, you don't want to know.' I give him a brush-off smile. 'Very boring.'

'I don't believe that for a minute.' His tone is light but persistent. 'Did you have a career? Before you came here?'

I walk for a few paces without saying anything, my eyes on the ground, trying to think what to say. I can feel Nathaniel's eyes on me, but I twist my head away from his scrutiny.

'You don't want to talk about it,' he says at last.

'No! It's not that.' I push my hands through my hair. 'It's just . . . a long story.'

Nathaniel shrugs. 'We've got all evening.'

As I meet his steady gaze I feel a sudden pull, like a fishhook inside my chest. I want to unburden everything. Who I am, what happened, how hard it's been. He'd understand. He'd keep it secret.

'So.' He stops still in the street, his thumbs in his pockets. 'Are you going to tell me who you are?'

'Maybe,' I say at last, and find myself smiling. Nathaniel smiles back, his eyes crinkling with a slow, delicious ease.

'But not right now.' I look around the golden village street. 'It's too nice an evening to spoil. I'll tell you later.'

We walk on, passing an old stone wall covered with a profusion of climbing roses. And as I breathe in the delicious scent, I feel a sudden lightness; almost euphoria. The street is dappled with soft evening light and the last rays of sun are warm on my shoulders.

'Nice hair, by the way,' he says.

'Oh, thanks.' I give a nonchalant smile. 'It's nothing really.' *Flick.* 'So where are we going?'

'The pub,' he says. 'If that's OK?'

'Perfect!'

As we approach The Bell I see a small crowd of people outside: some standing by the door; others sitting at the wooden tables.

'What are they doing?' I say, puzzled.

'Waiting,' he says. 'Landlord's late.'

'Oh,' I say. I look around but all the tables are already taken. 'Well, never mind. We can sit here.'

I perch on an old barrel—but Nathaniel has already headed for the door of the pub.

And . . . that's weird. Everyone is standing back to let him through. I watch in astonishment as he reaches in his pocket and produces a big bunch of keys, then looks round to find me.

'Come on,' he beckons with a grin. 'Opening time.'

'You own a *pub?*' I say, as the initial melee of the evening dies down.

I've watched in wonderment for fifteen minutes as Nathaniel has pulled pints, bantered with customers, given instructions to the bar staff and made sure everyone is happy. Now the initial rush is over, he's come round to where I'm perched on a bar stool with a glass of wine.

'Three pubs,' he corrects me. 'It's our family business. The Bell, The Swan over in Bingley and The Two Foxes.'

'So you're not really a gardener!'

'I am really a gardener.' He looks down briefly. 'This is . . . business.'

There's a tone in his voice as though I've trodden on something sensitive. I look away—and my attention is caught by a picture on the wall of a middle-aged man. He has Nathaniel's strong jaw and blue eyes, and the same crinkles round his eyes as he smiles.

'That's your dad?' I say cautiously. 'He looks wonderful.'

'He was the life and soul.' Nathaniel's eyes soften. 'Everyone here, they all loved him.' He takes a deep slug of beer, then puts his glass down. 'But listen. We don't have to stay here. If you'd rather go somewhere else, somewhere smarter . . .'

I look around the bustling pub. Music is playing above the noise of talk and laughter. A group of regulars are greeting each other by the bar with cheerful insults. A pair of elderly American tourists in Stratford T-shirts are being advised on local beers by a barman with red hair and twinkling eyes. I can't remember the last time I was somewhere with such an easy, friendly atmosphere.

'Let's stay. And I'll help!' I slip off my stool and head behind the bar.

'Have you ever pulled a pint before?'

'No,' I say, picking up a glass and putting it under one of the beer taps. 'But I can learn.'

'OK.' Nathaniel comes round the bar. 'You tilt the glass like this . . . now pull.'

I pull the tap, and a burst of foam splutters out. 'Damn!'

'Slowly . . .' He puts his arms round me, guiding my hands.

Mmm, this is nice. He's saying something to me, but I'm not listening to a word. I'm in a blissful happy haze, enveloped in his strong arms.

'You know,' I begin, turning my head towards him. And then I stop as my eyes focus on something. There's an old wooden notice on the wall, stating *No Muddy Boots Please* and *No Working Clothes.* Underneath, another notice has been pinned. It's printed on yellowing paper in faded marker pen—and it reads: NO LAWYERS.

I stare at it, dumbfounded. No lawyers? Am I reading that correctly?

'There we are.' Nathaniel holds up the glass, full of a gleaming amber liquid. 'Your first-ever pint.'

'Er . . . great!' I say, then gesture casually at the sign. 'What's this?'

'I don't serve lawyers,' he says without a flicker.

'Nathaniel! Get over here!' someone calls from the other end of the bar and he clicks in annoyance.

'I'll only be a moment.' He touches my hand, then moves away.

OK . . . just calm down, obviously it's a joke. Everyone hates lawyers, just like everyone hates estate agents and tax collectors. It's an accepted fact of life. But they don't all put signs up in their pubs, do they?

As I'm standing there, the barman with red hair comes up to scoop some ice out of the tank.

'Hi,' he says, holding out his hand. 'I'm Eamonn.'

'Samantha.' I shake it with a smile. 'I'm here with Nathaniel.'

'He said.' His eyes twinkle. 'Welcome to Lower Ebury.'

As I watch him serving, it suddenly strikes me that this guy might know something about the sign.

'So,' I say carelessly when he comes back over, 'that sign about lawyers. It's a joke, right?'

'Not really,' Eamonn replies cheerfully. 'Nathaniel can't stand lawyers.'

'Right!' Somehow I manage to keep on smiling. 'Um . . . why's that?'

'There was some law suit between his dad and the council. Nathaniel says Ben got talked into doing it by the lawyers. He wasn't well anyway, and he got more and more stressed by it. Then he had a heart attack.'

'God, how awful,' I say in horror. 'And Nathaniel blamed the lawyers?'

'He reckons the case should never have been brought.' Eamonn hefts a crate of orange mixers onto the bar. 'The last lawyer came in this pub . . .' He leans conspiratorially across the bar, 'Nathaniel punched him.'

'He *punched* him?' My voice comes out a petrified squeak.

'It was on the day of his dad's funeral.' Eamonn lowers his voice. 'One of his dad's lawyers came in here and Nathaniel socked him one. We tease him about it now.'

He turns away to serve someone and I take a gulp of wine. Let's not freak out here. So he doesn't like lawyers. That doesn't mean *me*. Of course it doesn't. I can still be honest with him. I can still tell him about my past. He won't take it against me. Surely.

But what if he does?

'Sorry about that.' All of a sudden Nathaniel is in front of me, his face warm and friendly. 'Are you OK?'

'I'm fine!' I say over-brightly. 'Having a lovely time!'

By the end of the evening I've pulled about forty pints. I've had a plate of cod and chips and half a dish of sticky toffee pudding—and beaten Nathaniel at darts, to loud cheers from everyone watching.

At last Nathaniel rings last orders with a resounding clang of the bell, and a good hour later the final stragglers make it to the door, each pausing to say goodbye to Nathaniel as they leave.

'We'll clear up,' says Eamonn firmly. 'You'll want to be enjoying the rest of the evening.'

'Well . . . OK.' Nathaniel claps him on the back. 'Thanks, Eamonn.' He looks at me. 'Ready to go?'

Almost reluctantly I slide down off my bar stool. 'It's been an amazing evening,' I say to Eamonn. 'Brilliant to meet you.'

'Likewise.' He grins. 'Send us your invoice.'

I beam back. I've never had an evening out like this in my life.

No one in London ever took me to a pub for a date—let alone to the other side of the bar. On my first evening out with Jacob he took me to *Les Sylphides* at Covent Garden, then left after twenty minutes to take a call from the States and never returned. He said the next day he was so bound up in a point of commercial contract law, he forgot I was there.

And the worst thing is, instead of saying 'You bastard!' and punching him, I asked what point of commercial contract law.

After the beery warmth of the pub, the summer night is fresh and cool. There are no streetlamps; the only light comes from a big full moon and curtained cottage windows.

'Did you enjoy yourself?' Nathaniel sounds a bit anxious.

'I really, really loved it,' I say with enthusiasm. 'It's a great pub. And I can't get over how friendly it is. The way everyone knows you! And the village spirit. Everyone cares about each other. You can tell.'

'How can you tell that?' Nathaniel sounds amused.

'From the way everyone claps each other on the back,' I explain. 'Like, if someone were in trouble, everyone would rally round in a heart-warming way. You can just see it.'

I hear Nathaniel stifle a laugh. 'We did get the Most Heart-warming Village award last year,' he says.

'You can laugh,' I retort. 'But in London, no one's heart-warming. If you fell over dead in the street they'd just push you into the gutter. After emptying your wallet and stealing your identity.'

'I know about Londoners.' Nathaniel looks wry. 'I lived in London for a time.'

I gape at him in the moonlight. Nathaniel lived in London? I try, and fail, to picture him strap-hanging on the tube, reading *Metro*.

'Seriously?' I say at last, and he nods.

'And I hated it. Seriously.'

'But what—why . . .'

'I was a waiter on my year off before uni. My flat was opposite a twenty-four-hour supermarket. It was lit up all night with these bright fluorescent strips. And the noise . . .' He winces. 'In ten months of living there, I never had a single moment of total darkness or total quiet. I never heard a bird. I never saw the stars.'

Instinctively, I tilt my head back to look up at the clear night sky.

'How about you?' His voice brings me back to earth.

'What do you mean?'

'You were going to tell me your story,' he says.

'Oh.' I feel a spasm of nerves. 'Yes, right. So I was.'

I have to say something. Maybe I can keep it to a minimum. Tell the truth without mentioning the lawyer bit.

'Well,' I say at last. 'I was in London. In this . . . this . . .'

'Relationship,' he prompts.

'Er . . . yes.' I swallow. 'Well. Things went wrong. I got on a train . . . and I ended up here. That's it.'

'That's *it*?' Nathaniel sounds incredulous. 'That's the long story?'

'Look.' I turn to face him in the moonlight, my heart pumping. 'I know I was going to tell you more. But are the details really important? Does it matter, what I used to do . . . or be? The point is, I'm here. And I've just had the best evening of my life. Ever.'

I can see he wants to challenge me; he even opens his mouth to speak. Then he turns away without saying whatever it was.

I feel a plunge of despair. Maybe I've ruined everything.

We walk on again into the night without speaking. Nathaniel's shoulder brushes against mine. Then I feel his hand. His fingers graze against my own casually at first, as though by accident—then, slowly, entwine themselves round mine.

I feel an arching inside as my entire body responds, but somehow force myself not to catch my breath. Neither of us says a word. There's no sound except our footsteps on the road and a distant owl hooting. Nathaniel's hand is sure and firm round my own. I can feel the roughened callouses on his skin; his thumb rubbing over mine.

We come to a stop at the entrance to the Geigers' drive. He looks down at me silently, his expression almost grave. I can feel my breath thickening. I don't care if it's obvious I want him.

He releases my hand and puts both hands round my waist. Now he's slowly pulling me towards him. I close my eyes, prepared to lose myself.

'For goodness' sake!' comes an unmistakable voice. 'Aren't you going to *kiss* her?'

I jump and open my eyes. Nathaniel looks equally shocked, and takes an automatic step away. I swivel round—and to my utter horror,

Trish is leaning out of an upstairs window, looking straight down on us.

'I'm not a *prude*, you know,' she says. 'You are allowed to kiss!'

I shoot daggers at her. Has she never heard the word 'privacy'?

'Carry on!' Her cigarette end glows as she waves it. 'Don't mind me!'

Don't mind her? I'm sorry, but I am not doing this with Trish as a spectator. I glance at Nathaniel, who looks as nonplussed as I feel.

I meet his eye and suddenly feel uncontrollable laughter rising. This is disastrous. The mood is totally broken.

'Um . . . thanks for a great evening,' I say, trying to keep a straight face. 'I had a lovely time.'

'Me too.' His eyes are almost indigo in the shadows; his mouth twisted in amusement. 'So. Are we going to give Mrs Geiger her kicks? Or leave her in an unbearable frenzy of frustration?'

We both glance up at Trish, still leaning avidly out of her window.

'Oh . . . I think she probably deserves the unbearable frenzy of frustration,' I say with a tiny smile.

'So I'll see you tomorrow?'

'I'll be at your mum's at ten o'clock.'

'See you then.'

He holds out his hand and we barely brush fingertips before he turns and walks away. I watch him disappear into the darkness, then head down the drive to the house, my whole body still pulsating.

It's all very well, getting one over on Trish. But what about *my* unbearable frenzy of frustration?

Eight

I'M WOKEN THE NEXT DAY by Trish banging sharply on my door. 'Samantha! I need to speak to you! Now!'

It's not even eight o'clock on a Saturday morning. Where's the fire?

'OK!' I call blearily. 'Hang on a sec!'

I stumble out of bed, my head filled with delicious memories of last night. Nathaniel's hand in mine . . . Nathaniel's arms round me . . .

'Yes, Mrs Geiger?' I open my door to see Trish standing there in a silk dressing gown, her face flushed and her eyes bloodshot. She puts her hand over the cordless phone she's holding.

'Samantha.' There's a strange note of triumph in her voice. 'You've fibbed to me, haven't you?'

My mind frantically runs over all the fibs I've ever told Trish, up to and including 'I'm a housekeeper'. It could be something small and insignificant. Or she could have found out the whole lot.

'I don't know what you're referring to,' I say in a throaty voice. 'Madam.'

'Well.' Trish walks towards me, swishing her dressing gown crossly. 'As you can imagine, I'm *rather* upset that you never told me you'd cooked paella for the Spanish ambassador.'

My mouth hangs open. The Spanish what? Has she lost it?

'Mrs Geiger,' I say, a little nervously, 'would you like to sit down?'

'No, thank you,' she says crisply. 'I'm still on the phone with Lady Edgerly.'

The floor seems to wobble beneath me. *Freya's on the phone?*

'Lady Edgerly . . .' Trish lifts the phone to her ear. 'You're quite right, *far* too unassuming . . .' She looks up. 'Lady Edgerly would like to have a word with you.'

She hands me the phone and in a blur I lift it to my ear. 'Hello?'

'Samantha?' Freya's familiar, raspy voice erupts into my ear through a sea of crackle. 'Are you OK? What the *fuck* is going on?'

'I'm . . . fine!' I glance at Trish, who is standing approximately two metres away. 'I'll just . . . go somewhere a bit more . . .'

Ignoring Trish's laser-like eyes, I retreat into my bedroom and close the door tight. Then I lift the phone to my ear again.

'I'm fine!' I feel a rush of joy to be talking to Freya again.

'What on earth's going on?' she demands again. 'I got this message but it made no sense! You're a *housekeeper*? Is this some huge wind-up?'

'No.' I glance at the door, then move into the bathroom and switch on the fan. 'I'm a full-time housekeeper,' I say in a lower voice. 'I've left my job at Carter Spink.'

'You've *quit*?' says Freya incredulously. 'Just like that?'

'I didn't quit. I was . . . thrown out. I made a mistake and they fired me.' It's still hard to say it. Or even to think about it.

'You were thrown out for a simple *mistake*?' Freya sounds outraged.

'It wasn't a simple mistake. It was a really big, important mistake. Anyway, that's what happened. And I decided to do something different. Become a housekeeper for a bit.'

'You decided to become a housekeeper,' echoes Freya slowly. 'Samantha, did you totally lose your mind?'

'Why not?' I say defensively. 'You were the one who said I should have a break.'

'But a *housekeeper*? You can't cook!' She's giggling now. 'I've seen your cooking. And your non-existent cleaning.'

'I know!' A wave of hysteria is coming over me. 'It was a bit of a nightmare to begin with. But I'm learning. You'd be surprised.'

'Do you have to wear an apron?'

'I've got this hideous nylon uniform . . .' I'm snuffling with laughter now. 'And I call them madam . . . and sir . . . and I curtsy . . .'

'Samantha, this is insane,' says Freya between gurgles. 'You cannot stay there. I'm going to rescue you. I'll fly back tomorrow . . .'

'No!' I say with more vehemence than I intended. 'No! I'm . . . having a good time. It's fine.'

There's a suspicious silence down the phone. Dammit. Freya knows me far too well.

'With a man?' her teasing voice comes at last.

'Maybe.' I feel an unwilling grin come to my face. 'Yes.'

'Details?'

'It's early days. But he's . . . you know. Nice.' I beam foolishly at my own reflection in the bathroom mirror.

'Well, even so. You know I'm only a phone call away. You can stay at our place . . .'

'Thanks, Freya.' I feel a tug of affection for her.

'No problem. Samantha?'

'Yes?' There's a long silence, until I think the line must have cut out.

'What about the partnership?' says Freya at last. 'It was your dream. Are you just going to abandon it?'

I feel a twinge of deep, buried grief. 'That dream's over,' I say shortly. 'Partners don't make fifty-million-quid mistakes.'

'*Fifty million quid*? Jesus,' she breathes, sounding shocked. 'I can't imagine how you've coped with all this—'

'It's fine,' I cut her off. 'I've got over it. Really.'

'You know, I had a feeling something was up. I tried to send you an email via the Carter Spink website. But your page was gone.'

'Really?' I feel an odd little tweak inside.

'And then I thought—' She breaks off, and I can hear mayhem in the background. 'Our transport's here. Listen, I'll call you soon—'

'Wait!' I say urgently. 'Before you go, Freya, what on *earth* did you say to Trish about the Spanish ambassador?'

'Oh, that.' She giggles. 'Well, she kept asking questions, so I thought I'd better make some stuff up. I said you could fold napkins into a scene from *Swan Lake* . . . and make ice sculptures . . .'

'Freya . . .' I close my eyes.

'She lapped it up! I have to go, babe. Love you.'

'Love you too.'

The phone goes dead and I stand motionless, the bathroom suddenly very silent without Freya's husky voice amid the background clamour of India.

I look at my watch. Nine forty-five. I just have time to have a look.

Three minutes later I'm sitting at Eddie's desk, tapping my fingers as I wait for the Internet connection to work. I asked Trish if I could possibly send an email to Lady Edgerly, and she was only too eager to open up the study for me and loiter behind the chair, until I politely asked her to go away.

Eddie's home page opens and I type in www.carterspink.com.

As the familiar purple logo appears, I can feel all the old tensions rising. Taking a deep breath, I click swiftly past the Introduction, straight to Associates. The list comes up—and Freya's right. The names segue straight from Snell to Taylor. No Sweeting.

I exhale, telling myself to be rational. Of course they've taken me off. I've been fired, what else did I expect? I should just close down, go to Iris's house and forget about it. That's what I should do.

Instead, I find myself reaching for the mouse and tapping 'Samantha Sweeting' into the search box. 'No result' pings up a few moments later and I stare at it, taken aback.

No result? Nowhere on the whole *website*? But . . . what about in the Media section? Or News Archives?

I quickly click onto the Done Deals box, and search for 'Euro-Sal, merger, DanCo'. That was a big European deal last year and I handled the financing. The report appears on the screen, with the headline 'Carter Spink advises on £20bn merger'. My eyes run down the familiar text. 'The Carter Spink team was led from London by Arnold Saville, with associates Guy Ashby and Jane Smilington.'

I stop in disbelief, then go back and read the text more carefully, searching for the missing words—'and Samantha Sweeting', it should read. But the words aren't there. I'm not there.

My heart is thudding as I click from deal to deal, tracking back a year. Two years. Five years. They've wiped me out. Someone has gone painstakingly through the entire website and removed my name.

I take a breath, trying to stay calm. But anger is bubbling up, hot and strong. How dare they change history? I gave them seven years of my *life*. They can't just pretend I was never even on the payroll . . .

Then a new thought hits me. Why am I such an embarrassment? I slowly type in www.google.com and enter 'Samantha Sweeting' in the box, then press the return key.

A moment later the screen fills with text. As I scan the entries I feel as though I've been hit over the head.

. . . the **Samantha Sweeting** debacle . . .

. . . **Samantha Sweeting** went AWOL, leaving colleagues to . . .

. . . **Samantha Sweeting** jokes. What do you call a lawyer who . . .

. . . **Samantha Sweeting** fired from Carter Spink . . .

I can never go back. I knew that. But I don't think I really *knew* it. Not deep down in the pit of my stomach. Not where it counts.

I feel a wetness on my cheek and jump to my feet, shutting all the web pages down; I clear History in case Eddie gets curious. I shut down the computer and look round the silent room. This is where I am. Not there. That part of my life is over.

Iris's cottage is looking as idyllic as ever as I dash up to the front door, out of breath.

'Hello.' She looks up with a smile from where she's sitting with a mug of tea. 'You seem in a hurry.'

'I just wanted to get here on time.' I look round the garden, but I can't see any sign of Nathaniel.

'Nathaniel had to go and sort out a leaking pipe at one of the pubs,' says Iris, as though reading my mind. 'But he'll be back later. Meanwhile, we're going to make bread.'

'Great!' I say. I follow her into the kitchen and put on the same stripy apron as last time.

'I've started us off already,' says Iris, going to a large, old-fashioned mixing bowl on the table. 'Yeast, warm water, melted butter and flour. Mix together and you have your dough. Now, you're going to knead it.'

'Right,' I say again, looking blankly at the dough.

She shoots me a curious look. 'Are you all right, Samantha?'

'I'm fine.' I try to smile. 'Sorry.'

She hefts the dough onto the table and kneads it briskly. 'You see? Fold it over, make a quarter turn. You need to use a bit of energy.'

Cautiously I plunge my hands into the soft dough and try to imitate what she was doing.

'That's it,' says Iris, watching carefully. 'Get into a rhythm and really *work* it. Kneading's very good for releasing stress,' she adds wryly. 'Pretend you're bashing all your worst enemies.'

'I'll do that!' I manage a cheerful tone.

But there's a knot of tension in my chest, which doesn't dwindle away as I knead. I can't stop my mind flicking back to that website.

'The more you work the dough, the better the bread will be,' says Iris, with a smile. 'Can you feel it becoming warm and elastic in your hands?'

I look at the dough in my fingers, but I can't connect with it. My mind is skittering about like a bird on ice. My upper arms are aching; my face is sweating. How dare they wipe me out? I did things for that firm. I was a *good lawyer.*

'Would you like a rest?' Iris comes over and touches my shoulder. 'It's hard work when you're not used to it.'

'What's the point of all this?' My words shoot out before I can stop them. 'I mean, making bread. You make it and you eat it. Then it's gone.'

'You could say the same of all food,' Iris points out. 'Or of life itself.'

'Exactly.' I rub my forehead with my apron. 'Exactly.'

'I think that's enough kneading,' she says, taking the dough from me and patting it into a round shape.

'Shall I put it in the oven?' I say, trying to speak more normally.

'Not yet.' Iris places the dough back in the bowl and puts it on top of the stove. 'Now we wait.' She pops a tea towel over the bowl. 'Half an hour should do it. I'll make a cup of tea.'

'But . . . what are we waiting *for*?'

'For the yeast to rise and work its magic on the dough.' She smiles. 'Underneath that towel, a small miracle is happening.'

I look at the bowl, trying to think miracles. But it isn't working. I can't feel calm or serene. My body is wound up too far.

'I'm sorry,' I hear myself say. 'I can't do it.' I head for the kitchen door and out into the garden.

'Sweetie, what's wrong?' Iris comes after me.

'I can't do this!' I wheel round. 'I can't just . . . just sit around patiently, waiting for *yeast* to get its act together.'

'Why not?'

'Because it's such a waste of time!' I clutch my head in frustration.

'What do you think we should be doing instead?' she asks.

'Something . . . *important*. OK? Something constructive.'

Iris appears amused. 'What's more constructive than making bread?'

Oh *God*. I feel an urge to scream. It's OK for her, with her apron and no wrecked career on the Internet.

'You don't understand anything,' I say, close to tears.

'Samantha, you've had a trauma,' she says in kind, even tones. 'And it's affected you very deeply—'

'I *haven't* had a trauma! I just . . . I can't do this, Iris. I can't pretend to be this. I'm not a bread-maker, OK? I'm *not* a domestic goddess.' I look around the garden desperately, as though searching for clues. 'I don't know who I am any more. Or where I'm headed in life. Or anything.'

My energy's gone and I sink down on the dry grass. A few moments later Iris comes and squats down beside me.

'Don't beat yourself up for not knowing all the answers,' she says softly. 'Sometimes it's enough just to know what you're going to do next.'

'And what *am* I going to do next?' I say, with a hopeless shrug.

'You're going to help me shell the beans for lunch.' She sounds so matter-of-fact that I can't help half smiling.

When I've finished the beans we knead the dough again. We shape it into loaves, put them into loaf tins and then have to wait another half-hour for them to rise again. But somehow this time I don't mind. I sit at the table with Iris, hulling strawberries and listening to the radio until it's time to put the tins into the oven. Then Iris loads a tray with cheese, bean salad, biscuits and strawberries, and we take it outside to a table set under the shade of a tree.

'There,' she says, pouring some iced tea into a tumbler. 'Better?'

'Yes. Thanks,' I say awkwardly. 'I'm sorry about earlier. I just . . .'

'Samantha, it's all right.' She gives me a brief look, between slicing the cheese. 'You don't have to apologise.'

'But I do.' I take a deep breath. 'I'm really grateful, Iris. You've been so kind . . . and Nathaniel . . .'

'He took you to the pub, I heard.'

'It was amazing!' I say with enthusiasm. 'You must be so proud, to have that in your family.'

Iris nods. 'Those pubs have been run by Blewetts for generations.' She sits down and helps us both to bean salad, dressed with oil and speckled with herbs. I take a mouthful, and it's absolutely delicious.

'It must have been hard when your husband died,' I venture.

'Everything was in a mess.' Iris pauses. 'There were financial difficulties. I wasn't well. If it hadn't been for Nathaniel we might have lost the pubs. He made sure they got back on track. For his father's memory.' Her eyes cloud a little and she hesitates. 'You never know how things are going to turn out, however much you plan. But then you already know that.'

'I always thought my life would be a certain way,' I say, gazing down at my plate. 'I had it all mapped out.'

'But it didn't happen like that?'

For a few seconds I can't answer. I'm remembering the moment I heard I was going to be partner. That instant of undiluted, dazzling joy, when I thought my life had finally fallen into place.

'No,' I say, trying to keep my voice level. 'It didn't happen like that.'

'Don't be too hard on yourself, chicken,' she says. 'We all flounder.'

I can't imagine Iris ever floundering. She seems so calm.

'Oh, I floundered,' she says, reading my expression. 'After Ben went.

It was so sudden. Everything I thought I had, gone overnight.'

'So . . . what did you . . .' I spread my hands helplessly.

'I found another way,' she says. 'But it took time.' For a moment she holds my gaze, then looks at her watch. 'Speaking of which, I'll make some coffee. And see how that bread's getting on.'

I get up to follow her, but she bats me down again. 'Sit. Stay. Relax.'

I sit there in the dappled sunlight, sipping my iced tea, trying to relax. But emotions are still darting around me like unsettled fish. I clench my eyes shut, trying to clear my mind. I should never have looked at that website. I should never have read those comments.

'Hold out your arms, Samantha.' Iris's voice is suddenly behind me. 'Don't open your eyes. Go on.'

I have no idea what she's up to, but I hold out my arms. The next moment I feel something warm being put into them. A yeasty smell is rising up. I open my eyes to see a loaf of bread.

I stare at it in utter disbelief. It looks like the kind of bread you'd see in a baker's window. Fat and plump and golden brown, with a crusty, almost flaky top. It smells so delicious I can feel my mouth watering.

'Tell me that's nothing,' says Iris, squeezing my arm. 'You made that, sweetie. And you should be proud of yourself.'

I can't reply. Something hot is wadding my throat as I clutch the warm loaf. I made this bread. I made it. I, Samantha Sweeting, who gave up seven years of her life to be wiped out of existence. Who has no idea who she even is any more. I made a loaf of bread. Right now I feel like this is the only thing I have to hold on to.

To my horror a tear suddenly rolls down my cheek, followed by another. This is ridiculous. I have to get a grip on myself.

'Looks good,' comes Nathaniel's easy voice behind me, and I wheel round in shock. He's standing next to Iris, his hair glowing in the sun.

'Hi,' I say, flustered. 'I thought you were . . . fixing a pipe.'

'Still am.' He nods. 'I just popped home.'

'I'll go and get the other loaves out,' says Iris, patting me on the shoulder, and disappears over the grass towards the house.

I stand up and look at Nathaniel over the bread. Just the sight of him is adding all sorts of emotions into the mix.

'Are you all right?' he says, glancing at my tears.

'I'm fine. It's just been a weird day,' I say, brushing the tears away in embarrassment. 'I don't usually get so emotional about . . . bread.'

'Mum said you got a bit frustrated.' He raises his eyebrows. 'All that kneading?'

'It was the rising.' I raise a rueful smile. 'I've never been good at waiting.'

'Uh-huh.' Nathaniel's steady blue eyes meet mine.

'For anything.' Somehow I seem to be edging closer and closer to him, I'm not entirely sure how. 'I have to have things *now*.'

'Uh-huh.'

We're inches apart now. And as I gaze up at him, breathing hard, all the frustrations and shocks of the last couple of weeks seem to be distilling inside me. A huge block of pressure is growing, until I can't bear it. I need release. Unable to stop myself, I reach up and pull his face down towards mine.

I haven't kissed like this since I was a teenager. Arms wrapped round one another; oblivious of anything else in the world. Completely lost. Trish could be standing there with a video camera, issuing directions, and I wouldn't notice.

It seems hours later that I open my eyes and we draw apart. My lips feel swollen; my legs are staggery. Nathaniel looks equally shell-shocked. His eyes are opaque and he's breathing more swiftly.

The bread is totally squashed, I suddenly notice. I try to reshape it as best I can, putting it on the table like a deformed pottery exhibit while I gather my breath.

'I don't have long,' Nathaniel says. 'I have to get back to the pub.' His hand runs lightly down my back and I feel my body curving towards his.

'I don't take long,' I say, my voice husky with desire.

When did I become so brazen, exactly?

'I *really* don't have long.' He glances at his watch. 'About six minutes.'

'I only take six minutes,' I murmur with an enticing glance.

There's silence for a few moments. An incredulous expression is coming over Nathaniel's face. 'Well . . . round here we take things a bit slower,' he says at last.

'Right,' I say, trying not to look all disappointed. 'So . . . I'll see you,' I say, trying to sound casual. 'What are you doing tomorrow?'

'I'm not sure yet.' He gives a noncommittal shrug. 'Are you around?'

'I guess so. Maybe.'

'Well . . . I may see you.'

And with that he's striding away again over the grass, and I'm left with nothing but a misshapen loaf of bread and total confusion.

By the next morning I've thought long and hard and have got nowhere. Either a) Nathaniel was offended by my references to sex, and isn't interested any more, or b) he's fine, it's all still on, he was just being a man and not saying much, and I should stop obsessing.

Or somewhere in between.

Or some other option I haven't even considered. Or . . .

Actually, I think that might cover it. But still. I'm totally confused just thinking about it.

I stumble downstairs in my dressing gown at around nine, to find Trish in the hall, dressed in a white silk suit, with the biggest corsage of fake red roses I've ever seen.

'Morning, Samantha,' she says. 'We'll be out all day at my sister's party. Nathaniel will be coming over to work in the garden, but I expect you know that—'

'Nathaniel?' I feel an electric jolt. 'He's coming here?'

'He called this morning. The sweet peas need . . . stringing or looping or something?' She gets out a lip pencil and begins outlining her already lined lips. 'I heard he took you to his little pub?'

'Er . . . yes. He did.'

'I was *so* glad about that, really.' She takes out a mascara wand and starts adding more layers to her already spiky lashes. 'We nearly had to look for another gardener, can you *imagine*. Although of course it was a great shame for him. After all his plans.'

I look at her, nonplussed. What's she talking about?

'What was a shame?' I say.

'Nathaniel. His nursery. Plant thing.' She frowns at her reflection and flicks at a speck of mascara beneath her eye. 'Organic something or other. He showed us the business proposition. In fact, we were even considering backing him. We are very *supportive* employers, Samantha.' She fixes me with a blue gaze as though daring me to disagree.

'Of course!'

'Ready?' Eddie comes out of the study dressed very smartly in a blazer with shiny gold buttons and wearing a Panama hat. 'It's going to be bloody sweltering, you know.'

'Eddie, don't start,' snaps Trish, shoving her mascara wand back in the tube. 'We are going to this party and that's final.'

'And what happened?' I ask, trying to haul the conversation back on track. 'With Nathaniel's plans?'

Trish makes a small, regretful moue at herself in the mirror.

'Well, his father passed away very suddenly, and there was all that dreadful business with the pubs. And he changed his mind. Never bought the land.' She gives herself another, dissatisfied look. 'Should I wear my *pink* suit?'

'*No*,' Eddie and I say in unison. I glance at Eddie's exasperated face and stifle a giggle.

'You look lovely, Mrs Geiger,' I say. 'Really.'

Somehow, between us, Eddie and I manage to chivvy her away from the mirror, out of the front door and into Eddie's Porsche.

'What time will you be back?' I ask.

'Not until late this evening,' says Trish. 'Ah, Nathaniel, here you are.'

I look over the top of the car in slight apprehension. There he is, coming down the drive, in jeans and espadrilles and an old grey T-shirt, his rucksack over his shoulder. And here I am, in my dressing gown with my hair all over the place.

And still not sure how things have been left between us.

'Hi,' I say as he gets near.

'Hi.' Nathaniel's eyes crinkle in a friendly way, but he doesn't make any attempt to kiss me or even smile.

'So.' I wrench my eyes away and look at the gravel for a few moments. 'You're . . . working today.'

'I could do with some help,' he says casually. 'If you're at a loose end.'

I feel a dazzling leap of delight, which I attempt to hide with a cough.

'Right.' I shrug slightly, almost frowning. 'Well . . . maybe.'

'Great.' He nods to the Geigers and saunters off towards the garden.

Trish has been watching this exchange in increasing dissatisfaction.

'You're not very *affectionate* with each other, are you?' she says. 'You know, in *my* experience—'

'Leave them alone, for God's sake!' retorts Eddie, starting the engine. 'Let's get this bloody thing over with.'

'Eddie Geiger!' Trish shrills, swivelling round in her seat. 'This is my sister's party you're talking about! Do you realise—'

Eddie revs the engine, drowning out her voice, and with a spattering of gravel the Porsche disappears out of the drive.

Right. So . . . it's just Nathaniel and me. Alone together. Until eight o'clock this evening. That's the basic scenario.

Deliberately nonchalant, I turn on the gravel and make my way back towards the house. I force myself not to rush. I take a shower and get dressed and have breakfast, consisting of a cup of tea and an apple.

I've dressed low key. A T-shirt, a cotton skirt and flip flops. As I look in the mirror, I feel almost shivery with anticipation.

After the cool house, the garden feels scorching; the air still and almost shimmery. I stay in the shade, heading down the side path, not knowing where he's working; where I'm heading. And then I see him, in the midst of a row of lavender and lilac-coloured flowers, his brow furrowed against the sun as he knots a length of twine.

'Hi,' I say.

'Hi.' He looks up and wipes his brow. I'm half expecting him to drop what he's doing, come forward and kiss me. But he doesn't. He just carries on knotting, then cuts the twine off with a knife.

'I came to help,' I say after a pause. 'What are we doing?'

'Tying up the sweet peas.' He gestures at the plants, which are growing up what look like cane wigwams. 'They need support otherwise they just flop.' He throws a ball of twine over to me. 'Just tie them gently.'

He's not joking. I really *am* helping with the gardening. Cautiously I unwind a length of twine and follow what he's doing. The soft petals tickle me as I work and fill the air with an amazing sweet scent.

'How's that?'

'Let's see.' Nathaniel comes over to take a look. 'Yup. You could tie a little tighter.' His hand brushes briefly against mine as he turns away. 'Let's see you do the next one.'

My hand tingles at his touch. Did he mean to do that? Uncertain, I tie up the next plant, knotting harder than before.

'Yeah, that's good.' Suddenly Nathaniel's voice is behind me and I feel his fingers on the back of my neck, tracing around my earlobe. 'You need to do the whole row.'

He definitely meant to do that. No question. He has a game plan, I suddenly realise. OK, now I really am turned on.

The pulsating is growing stronger inside me as I move from plant to plant. There's silence except the rustling of leaves as I tie up three more plants and get to the end of the row.

'Done,' I say without turning round.

'Great, let's see.' He comes over to inspect my knotted twine. I can feel his other hand edging up my thigh, pushing up my skirt, his fingers feeling for my flesh. I can't move. I'm transfixed. Then suddenly he moves away, businesslike again, picking up a pair of trugs.

'What . . .' I can't even frame a sentence properly.

He kisses me briefly, hard on the mouth. 'Let's move on. Raspberries need picking.'

The raspberry cages are further down the garden, like rooms of green netting, with dry, earthy floors and rows of raspberry plants. As we enter there's no sound except that of buzzing insects. We work the first row wordlessly, intently, picking the fruit off the plants. By the end of the row my mouth is tangy with the taste of them; my hands are scratched and aching from the constant plucking and I'm sweating all over. The heat seems more intense in this raspberry cage than anywhere else in the garden.

We meet at the end of the row and Nathaniel looks at me a still second, sweat running down the side of his face.

'Hot work,' he says. He puts his trug down and strips off his T-shirt.

'Yes.' There's a still beat between us. Then, defiantly, I do the same.

I'm standing there in my bra, inches from him, my skin pale and milky compared to his. I meet his eyes and it's like we're playing truth or dare.

'I couldn't reach those.' I point at a cluster of fruit just out of reach.

'I'll help.' He leans over me, skin against skin, and I feel his mouth on my earlobe as he picks the fruit. My entire body responds. I can't bear this; I need it to stop. And I need it not to stop.

But it goes on. We move up and down the rows like two performers in a courtly dance. Outwardly concentrating on our moves yet aware only of each other. At the end of every row, he brushes some part of me with his mouth or fingers. I want to get at him, I want my hands all over him, but every time he turns away before anything can progress.

I'm starting to shiver all over with desire. He unhooked my bra two rows ago. I've discarded my knickers. He's unbuckled his belt. And still, *still* we're picking raspberries.

As I reach the end of the last row I put the heavy trug down and face him, unable to hide how desperate I am.

'Are we done?' My breath is coming in short, hot bursts.

'We've done pretty well.' His gaze drifts towards the other fruit cages. 'There's still more to do . . .'

'No,' I hear myself saying. 'No more.'

I stand there in the heat and the dusty earth, panting and aching. And just as I think I might explode, he comes forward and bends his mouth down to my nipple, and I nearly swoon. And this time he doesn't move away. This time is for real. His hands are moving over my body, my skirt is falling to the ground, his jeans are sliding off. Then I'm shuddering, and clutching him, and crying out. And the raspberries are forgotten, scattered on the ground, squashed, crushed beneath us.

We seem to lie still for hours afterwards. I feel numb with euphoria. There's dust and stones embedded in my back and knees and hands and raspberry stains all over my skin.

My head is on Nathaniel's chest, his heartbeat like a deep, comforting clock tick. The sun is hot on my skin. I have no idea what time it is. I don't care what time it is. I've lost all sense of minutes and hours.

At last Nathaniel shifts his head slightly. He kisses my shoulder, then smiles. 'You taste of raspberry.'

'That was . . .' I break off, almost too stupefied to frame any sensible words. 'You know . . . normally I . . .' A huge yawn suddenly overcomes me and I clap my hand over my mouth.

Nathaniel lifts a hand and traces lazy circles round my back.

'Six minutes isn't sex,' I hear him saying as my eyes crash shut. 'Six minutes is a boiled egg.'

By the time I wake up, the raspberry cages are in partial shade. Nathaniel has removed himself from underneath me, given me a pillow constructed from my crumpled, raspberry-stained skirt, put on his jeans and brought down some beer from the Geigers' fridge. I sit up, my head groggy, to see him leaning against a tree on the grass, swigging from the bottle.

'How long was I asleep?' I put my hand to my face and remove a small stone. I feel totally disorientated.

'Couple of hours. You want some of this?' He gestures to the bottle.

I get to my feet, brush myself down, put on my skirt and bra as a good compromise outfit and join him on the grass. He gives me the bottle and I take a swig. I sink back against the tree trunk, my bare feet in the cool grass.

'You're not as twitchy as you were,' says Nathaniel. 'You used to jump a mile whenever I spoke to you.'

'No, I didn't!'

'Uh huh, you did.' He nods. 'Like a rabbit.'

'I thought I was a badger.'

'You're a rabbit-badger cross. Very rare breed.' He grins at me and takes a swig of beer. For a while neither of us speaks.

'Mum says you've changed, too,' Nathaniel says at last, shooting me a swift, querying look. 'She says she reckons whoever you've run away from . . . whatever happened . . . they're losing their grip on you.'

The question is there in his voice, but I don't respond. I'm thinking of Iris, yesterday. Letting me take all my frustrations out on her. It's not like she's had it easy herself.

'Your mum's amazing,' I say at last.

'Yup.'

I put the bottle down and roll onto the grass, staring up at the blue sky. I have changed. I can feel it in myself. I feel . . . stiller.

'Who would you be?' I say, twisting a grass stem round my finger. 'If you could just run away. Become a different person.'

Nathaniel's silent for a moment, looking over his bottle at the garden.

'I'd be me,' he says at last with a shrug. 'I'm happy as I am. I like living where I live. I like doing what I do.'

I roll over onto my front and look up at him. 'There must be something else you'd like to do. Some dream you've got.'

He shakes his head, smiling. 'I'm doing what I want to do.'

'But what about the nursery you were going to set up?'

Nathaniel's face jolts in surprise. 'How did you—'

'Trish told me about it this morning. She said you had business plans and everything. What happened?'

For a moment he's silent, his eyes averted from mine. 'It was just an idea,' he says at last.

'You gave it up for your mum. To run the pubs.'

'Maybe.' He reaches for a low-growing branch and starts stripping it of leaves. 'Everything changed.'

'But do you really want to run the pubs?' I edge forward on the grass, trying to intercept his gaze. 'You said it yourself, you're not a landlord. You're a gardener.'

'It's not a question of *want*.' Nathaniel's voice has a sudden edge of frustration. 'It's a family business. Someone has to run it.'

'Why you?' I persist. 'Why not your brother?'

'He's . . . different. He does his own thing.'

'*You* could do your own thing!'

'I have responsibilities.' His frown grows heavier. 'My mum—'

'She'd want you to be happy in your life, not give it up for her.'

'I am happy. It's ridiculous to say—'

'But couldn't you be *happier*?'

There's silence in the garden. Nathaniel is looking away, his shoulders bent round as if he wants to shut out what I'm saying.

'Don't you ever want to ditch your responsibilities?' I throw my arms out wide. 'Just . . . walk out into the world and see what happens?'

'Is that what you did?' he demands, wheeling round, a sudden aggression in his voice.

I stare at him uncertainly. 'I . . . we're not talking about me,' I say at last. 'We're talking about you.'

'Samantha.' He exhales and rubs his brow. 'I know you don't want to talk about the past. But I want you to tell me one thing. And be truthful. Do you have kids?'

I'm so dumbfounded, I can't speak for a moment. He thinks I have *kids*? A gurgle of relieved laughter rises through me before I can stop it.

'No, I don't have kids! I mean . . . do I *look* like I've had five kids?' I can't help a note of indignation, and he starts to laugh too.

'Maybe not *five* . . .'

'What's that supposed to mean?'

I'm about to hit him with his shirt when a voice pierces the air. 'Saman*tha*?' It's Trish. Coming from the house. They're *home*?

My eyes swivel madly over the two of us. I'm naked except for a skirt and a bra, and covered in raspberry stains. Nathaniel is much the same, except in jeans.

'Quick! My clothes!' I hiss, scrabbling to my feet.

'Where are they?' says Nathaniel, looking around.

'I don't *know*!' I look at him helplessly.

'Samantha?' I can hear the conservatory doors being opened.

'Shit!' I squeak. 'She's coming!'

'It's fine,' says Nathaniel, retrieving his T-shirt from the raspberry cage. He pops it over his head and at once looks pretty normal. 'I'll create a diversion. You sneak up the side, behind the shrubs, go in the kitchen door, run upstairs and get changed. OK?'

'OK,' I say breathlessly. 'And what's our story?'

'Our story is . . .' He pauses as though thinking. 'We didn't shag in the garden or help ourselves to beer from the fridge.'

'Right.' I can't help giggling. 'Good plan.'

He kisses me, and I dart across the lawn and sneak up the side of the garden, keeping behind the shrubs. I feel about ten years old, playing hide-and-seek, the same mixture of terror and delight pounding in my heart. When I'm only ten yards or so from the house I crouch behind a shrub and wait. After a minute or two I see Nathaniel firmly leading the Geigers down the lawn towards the lily pond.

'I think we could have a case of powdery mildew,' he's saying.

I wait until they're well past, then sprint on light feet to the conservatory, in through the house and up the stairs. I hurry into the bathroom, turn on the shower full blast and stand under it for thirty seconds. Afterwards, I pull on clean underwear, a pair of fresh jeans and a demure long-sleeved top. I even add fresh lipstick. Then, slipping on a pair of espadrilles, I head downstairs and out into the garden.

Nathaniel and the Geigers are by now making their way back up to the house. Trish's heels are sinking into the lawn and both she and Eddie look hot and bothered.

'Hi,' I say casually as they approach. 'Did you enjoy the party?'

Too late I see Nathaniel making deathlike, finger-across-the-throat gestures behind their backs.

'Thank you for asking, Samantha.' Trish inhales sharply. 'But I'd rather not talk about the party, thank you.'

Eddie makes an incensed spluttering sound. 'You won't bloody give up, will you? All I said was—'

'It was the *way* you said it!' shrieks Trish. 'Sometimes I think your *sole* purpose in life is to embarrass me!'

Eddie huffs furiously and stalks off towards the house.

Uh-oh. I raise my eyebrows at Nathaniel, who grins back over Trish's quivering hairdo.

'Would you like a nice cup of tea, Mrs Geiger?' I say soothingly. 'Or . . . a Bloody Mary?'

'Thank you, Samantha,' she replies, lifting her chin in a dignified manner. 'A Bloody Mary would be very nice.'

As we walk up to the conservatory, Trish seems to calm down a little. Once inside, she even mixes her own Bloody Mary instead of bossing me around as I do it, and makes one each for me and Nathaniel, too.

'Now,' she says, after we've each taken a gulp and sat down among the frondy plants, 'there was something I needed to tell you, Samantha. My husband's niece is coming to stay tomorrow for a few weeks. She has some work to do, and it's *very* important she isn't disturbed. I'd like you to get the spare room ready for her.'

'Very good.' I nod dutifully.

'She's a very bright girl, Melissa.' Trish lights a cigarette with her Tiffany lighter. 'She's a lawyer.

A lawyer? This could be bad. In fact, this could be a disaster.

What if I *know* this lawyer?

'So . . . is she called Geiger too?' I ask casually.

'No, she's called Hurst.'

Melissa Hurst. It doesn't ring any bells.

'And where does she work?' *Please let it be abroad* . . .

'Oh, she's at some high-powered place in London.' Trish gestures vaguely with her glass.

OK, so I don't know her. But this is not looking good. If she's at any of the big London law firms she's bound to have heard about me. She's bound to know about the Carter Spink lawyer who lost £50 million and ran away. All it takes is for her to recognise my name, to put two and two together . . . and the whole story will come out. Everyone will know my lies. I glance at Nathaniel. I *can't* let things be spoilt. Not now.

He winks at me and I take a deep gulp of Bloody Mary. The answer is simple. I'll just have to do whatever it takes to keep my secret hidden.

Nine

THERE'S NO REASON why this lawyer should recognise my face. But just to be on the safe side, I opt for a simple disguise. After I've prepared the spare room the following afternoon, I hurry to my own room and pin my hair up on top of my head with artistic strands falling down and concealing my face. Then I add a pair of old sunglasses I found in the dressing-table drawer. They date from the 1980s and have big green frames that make me look like Elton John, but I'll live with that. The point is, I look nothing like my old self.

As I come downstairs, Nathaniel is heading out of the kitchen, looking pissed off. He looks up at me and stops dead in surprise.

'Are those *your* sunglasses?' He peers at me incredulously.

'I've got a headache. So . . . what's up?' I hastily change the subject.

'Trish.' He scowls. 'She's been lecturing me on noise. I can't mow the lawn between ten and two. Could I tiptoe on the gravel. *Tiptoe.*'

'Why?'

'Because of this blasted visitor. A bloody *lawyer.*' He shakes his head in disbelief. '*Her* work's important. *My* work's important!'

'She's coming!' Trish's voice suddenly shrills from the kitchen and she comes hurrying out. 'Are we all ready?' She flings open the front door and I hear the sound of a car door opening in the drive.

My heart starts to bang in my chest. This is it. If I recognise this woman I'll just keep my eyes down, mumble my words and play my part. I'm a housekeeper. I have never been anything but a housekeeper.

'You should get *lots* of peace here, Melissa,' I can hear Trish saying. 'I've instructed the staff to look after you with *extra* special care . . .'

I exchange looks with Nathaniel, who rolls his eyes.

I hold my breath. A moment later Trish enters the house, followed by a girl in jeans and a tight white top, dragging a suitcase.

This is the top, high-powered lawyer?

I stare at her in bewilderment. She has long dark hair and a pert, pretty face, and can't be much out of her teens.

'Melissa, this is our *wonderful* housekeeper—' Trish breaks off in surprise. 'Samantha, what are you wearing? You look like Elton John!'

'Hello,' I say awkwardly, taking the sunglasses off, but keeping my head down. 'It's very nice to meet you.'

'It's *fab* to be here.' Melissa has a boarding-school drawl and matching toss of the hair. 'London was, like *sooo* getting me down.'

'Mrs Geiger said you're a lawyer at some . . . big place in London?'

'Yah.' She gives me a smug smile. 'I'm at Chelsea Law School.'

What? She's not even a qualified lawyer. She's a law student. She's a *baby.* I cautiously raise my head and meet her eyes—but there's not a blink of recognition. Oh, for God's sake. I have nothing to worry about from this girl. I almost want to laugh.

'And who's this?' Melissa bats her mascaraed eyelashes alluringly at Nathaniel, whose scowl deepens.

'This is Nathaniel, our gardener,' says Trish. 'And he's under *strict* instructions not to disturb you.'

'Well, I've got *loads* of revision to do.' Melissa gives a world-weary sigh and pushes a hand through her hair. 'I've been *soooo* stressed.'

'I don't know how you do it!' Trish puts an arm around her shoulders. 'Now, what would you like to do first? We're *all* at your disposal.'

'Could you unpack my things?' Melissa turns to me. 'They'll be creased, so they'll all need ironing.'

I feel a slight jolt. I've turned into this girl's personal *maid*?

'Why don't you make us all some coffee first?' Trish says. 'We'll take it on the terrace. Bring some biscuits out, too.'

'Of course, Mrs Geiger,' I say, bobbing an automatic curtsy.

'Could you make mine half caffeinated, half decaf?' Melissa adds over her shoulder. 'I, like, don't want to get too wired.'

No, I bloody couldn't, you pretentious little cow.

'Of course.' I smile through gritted teeth. 'My pleasure.'

Something tells me this girl and I are not going to get along.

I dump the coffeepot on the counter with a bang.

'Don't let her wind you up.' Nathaniel comes over, puts his arms round me and kisses me. 'She's not worth it.'

'I know.' I nestle into his hold with a little smile, feeling myself relax. 'Mmm. I've missed you.'

He runs his hands down my back and I feel a tingle of delight. Last night I stayed over with Nathaniel at the pub and crept back to the Geigers at six o'clock in the morning. I have a feeling that this could become a regular pattern.

I take the coffee out to Trish, Melissa and Eddie on the terrace. They are sitting at the garden table, which is covered in papers and brochures.

'It's just *sooo* difficult,' Melissa is saying, as I pour. 'I mean, this is a decision that will affect my whole life. And you wouldn't believe my workload, Uncle Eddie.'

'It'll be worth it, love.' Eddie pats her hand reassuringly. 'When you're at . . .' He picks up a brochure from the table and peers at it through his reading glasses. 'Carter Spink.'

For a few moments I can't move. Melissa is going for a job at Carter Spink?

'Looks very swanky,' says Eddie, flipping over the glossy pages, each illustrated with a photograph. 'Look at these offices.'

As he flips through, I'm transfixed. There's a picture of the foyer. There's one of the floor I used to work on. I can't tear my eyes away— but at the same time I don't want to look. That's my old life. It doesn't belong here. And then suddenly, as Eddie flips another page over, I feel a jolt of disbelief. It's a picture of me. Me.

I'm in my black suit, my hair pinned up, sitting at a meeting-room table along with Ketterman, David Elldridge and a guy who was over from the States. I look so *pale*. I look so *serious*.

'And it's like . . . do I *want* to give up all my time?' Melissa is jabbing the page. 'These people work every night! What about a social life?'

My face is right there in full view. I'm just waiting for someone to frown in recognition. But no one does. Melissa is still rabbiting on: 'Although, you know, the money *is* really good . . .' She sighs, and flips the page. The picture's gone. I'm gone. I head back to the kitchen.

I don't see the Carter Spink brochure again for two weeks, when I'm drifting into the kitchen to make lunch.

I don't know what happened to time. I don't even wear a watch any more. The minutes and hours just ebb and flow and swirl around. Yesterday I lay in a field all afternoon with Nathaniel, watching dandelion seeds floating by, and the only ticking sound came from the crickets.

I barely recognise myself any more, either. I'm tanned from lying in the sun at lunchtimes. My arms are gaining muscles from all the polishing and kneading and carting heavy saucepans around.

Every morning, before breakfast, Nathaniel walks me back through the village to the Geigers' house—and even at that hour the air is already warming up. Everything seems slow and lazy, these days. Everyone's in holiday mood—except Trish, who is in full frenzy mood. She is holding a big charity lunch next week. From the fuss she's making you'd think it was a Royal wedding.

I'm tidying up the papers that Melissa has left on the table when I spot the Carter Spink brochure. I can't resist picking it up and leafing through the familiar pictures. There are the steps I went up every day for seven years. There's Guy, looking as dazzlingly handsome as ever.

'What are you doing?' Melissa has come into the kitchen without me hearing. She eyes me suspiciously. 'That's mine.'

'Just tidying your things,' I say pointedly, putting the brochure down. 'I've got to use this table.'

'Oh. Thanks.' Melissa rubs her face. She looks haggard, these days. There are shadows under her eyes and the sheen to her hair has gone.

'So are you applying to this law firm?' I ask casually. I look down at the Carter Spink brochure again. It's open at a picture of Arnold Saville. He's wearing a bright blue spotted tie and matching handkerchief and is beaming out at the world.

'Yup. They're the best.' Melissa is getting a Diet Coke from the fridge. 'That's the guy who was supposed to be interviewing me.' She jerks her head at the picture of Arnold. 'But he's leaving.'

I feel a jerk of astonishment. Arnold's leaving Carter Spink?

'Are you sure?' I say before I can stop myself.

'Yes.' Melissa gives me an odd look. 'What's it to you?'

'Oh, nothing,' I say hastily. 'I just meant . . . he doesn't look old enough to retire.'

'Well, he's going.' She shrugs and wanders out of the kitchen, leaving me staring down in puzzlement.

Arnold is leaving Carter Spink? But he's always boasted about lasting another twenty years. Why would he be leaving now? And what else has happened that I don't know about?

So that afternoon, when I've cleared up lunch, I slip into Eddie's study, switch on the computer and click on Google. I search for 'Arnold Saville'—and sure enough on the second page I come across a little diary item about his early retirement. I read the fifty-word piece, trying to glean clues. Why would Arnold retire early? Is he ill?

I search for further items, but that's the only one I can find. After a moment's hesitation, I go to the search box and, telling myself that I shouldn't, type in 'Samantha Sweeting'. Immediately a zillion stories about me pop up again on the screen. I don't feel so freaked out this time, though. It almost doesn't feel like me any more.

I scan entry after entry, seeing the same details replayed. After clicking through about five pages I add 'Third Union Bank' to my search, and scan the resulting entries. Then I type in 'Third Union Bank, BLLC Holdings', then 'Third Union Bank, Glazerbrooks'.

God, Google is addictive. I sit there, totally absorbed, clicking and typing and reading, gorging on endless web pages. After an hour I'm slumped in Eddie's chair like a zombie. My back is aching and my neck is stiff, and the words are all running into each other.

I rub my tired eyes and glance at the web page open in front of me, wondering what I'm even doing on it. It's some obscure list of guests at a lunch held earlier this year at the Painters Hall. About halfway down is the name BLLC Holdings, which must have been the link. On autopilot I move the cursor along the page—and into view comes the name *Nicholas Hanford Jones, director.*

Something chimes inside my addled brain. *Nicholas Hanford Jones.* Why do I know that name?

I screw my eyes up tight and concentrate as hard as I can. *Nicholas Hanford Jones.* I can almost see it in my mind's eye; I'm grasping at an association . . . an image . . . Come on, think . . . This is the trouble with having a nearly photographic memory. People think it must be useful, when in fact all it does is drive you insane.

And then suddenly it comes to me. The swirly writing of a wedding invitation. It was stuck up on the pinboard in Ketterman's office, about three years ago. I used to see it every time I went in.

> *Mr and Mrs Arnold Saville*
> *request the pleasure of your company*
> *at the wedding of their daughter Fiona*
> *to Mr Nicholas Hanford Jones.*

Nicholas Hanford Jones is Arnold Saville's son-in-law? Arnold has a family connection with BLLC Holdings?

I sink back in my chair, totally disconcerted. How come he never mentioned that?

And then another thought strikes me. I was on the BLLC Holdings Companies House page a minute ago. Why wasn't Nicholas Hanford Jones listed as a director? That's illegal, for a start.

I rub my brow, then out of curiosity type in 'Nicholas Hanford Jones'. A moment later the screen is full of entries, and I lean forward expectantly then start picking my way down, skimming each chunk of text, clicking onto the next page and the next. Just as I'm about to give up, my eye falls on an entry tucked away at the bottom of the page. *William **Hanford Jones**, Finance Director of Glazerbrooks, thanked **Nicholas** Jenkins for his speech . . .*

I stare at it for a few seconds in total disbelief. The finance director at Glazerbrooks is called Hanford Jones too? Are they from the same *family*? Feeling like some kind of private detective, I log onto Friends Reunited, and two minutes later I have my answer. They're brothers.

I feel a bit dazed. This is a pretty huge connection. The finance director of Glazerbrooks, which went bust owing Third Union Bank £50 million. A director of BLLC Holdings, which lent it £50 million three days before. And Arnold, representing Third Union Bank. All related; all in the same extended family.

Isn't it a potential conflict of interest? Shouldn't Arnold have disclosed the information straight away? Why on earth would he keep such an important thing secret? Unless—

No. It couldn't—he couldn't possibly . . .

I get up and thrust my hands through my hair. OK, let's just . . . stop all this, right now. This is Arnold I'm talking about. *Arnold.* I'm turning into some nutty conspiracy theorist.

With sudden resolution I get out my phone. I'll call Arnold. I'll wish him well in his retirement. Then maybe I can get rid of all these ridiculous ideas floating round my head.

After three rings the phone is picked up by Lara. 'Arnold Saville's office.'

'Hi, Lara,' I say. 'It's . . . Samantha. Samantha Sweeting.'

'*Samantha?*' Lara sounds poleaxed. 'Bloody hell! How are you?'

'I'm fine, thanks. Really good.' I quell a spasm of nerves. 'I just rang because I've heard that Arnold's leaving. Is it true?'

'It's true!' says Lara with relish. 'He's moving to the Bahamas.'

'The *Bahamas?*' I say in astonishment.

'He's bought a house there! Looks lovely. He leaves on Friday,' Lara continues. 'I'll be transferring to Derek Green's office, you remember him? Taxation partner? Very nice guy, though apparently he can have a bit of a temper—'

'Er . . . great!' I cut her off, suddenly remembering her ability to gossip for hours without taking a breath. 'Lara, I just wanted to give Arnold my best wishes. If you could possibly put me through?'

'Really?' Lara sounds surprised. 'That's incredibly generous of you, Samantha. After what happened.'

'Well, you know,' I say awkwardly, 'it wasn't Arnold's fault. He did what he could.'

There's a strange silence.

'Yes,' says Lara after a pause. 'Well. I'll put you through.'

After a few moments Arnold's familiar voice is booming down the line. 'Samantha, dear girl! Is it really you?'

'It's really me.' I manage a smile. 'I haven't *quite* disappeared off the face of the earth.'

'I should hope not! Now, you're all right, are you?'

'I'm . . . fine,' I say awkwardly. 'Thanks. I was just surprised to hear you're retiring.'

'I was never a glutton for punishment!' He gives an easy laugh. 'Thirty-three years at the coalface of law. That's enough for any human. Let alone any lawyer!'

Just his jovial voice is reassuring me. I must be crazy. Arnold couldn't be involved in anything untoward. He couldn't be hiding anything. He's *Arnold*. I'll mention it to him, I decide. Just to prove it to myself.

'Well . . . I hope it all goes well,' I say. 'And I . . . I guess you'll be seeing more of your family?'

'I'll be lumbered with the blighters, yes!' He laughs again.

'I never knew your son-in-law was a director of BLLC Holdings!' I attempt a casual tone. 'Quite a coincidence!'

There's a moment of silence.

'I'm sorry?' says Arnold. His voice is still as charming as ever, but the warmth has disappeared.

'BLLC Holdings.' I swallow. 'You know, the other company involved with the Third Union Bank loan? The one that registered a charge? I just happened to notice . . .'

'I have to go now, Samantha!' Arnold cuts me off smoothly. 'Delightful to chat, but I'm leaving the country on Friday and there's a lot to do. It's exceedingly busy here, so I wouldn't telephone again if I were you.'

The line goes dead before I can say any more. I slowly put down the receiver and stare at a butterfly fluttering outside the window.

That wasn't right. That wasn't a natural reaction. He got rid of me as soon as I mentioned his son-in-law.

Something is going on. Something is definitely going on.

What could it be? I have totally abandoned the housework for the afternoon and am sitting on my bed with a pad of paper and pencil, trying to work out the possibilities.

Who stands to gain? I stare at my scribbled facts and arrows yet again. Two brothers. Millions of pounds being transferred between banks and companies. Think. *Think* . . .

Let's get everything in logical order. Glazerbrooks went into receivership. Third Union Bank lost their money. BLLC Holdings jumped ahead in the queue . . .

I tap my pencil impatiently on the paper. But so what? They only get back the money they loaned. They don't get any advantage. Unless— what if they never paid over anything in the first place?

The thought hits my brain out of nowhere. I sit bolt upright, unable to breathe. What if that's it? *What if that's the scam?*

My mind starts to race. Suppose there are two brothers. They know that Glazerbrooks is in serious financial trouble. They know that the bank has just paid in £50 million but the bank's charge wasn't registered. That means there's a £50-million unsecured loan swilling around in the company, up for grabs by anyone else who registers a charge . . .

I can't sit down any more. I'm pacing back and forth, my brain sparking like an electrical circuit. It works. It works. They fiddle the figures. BLLC Holdings get the money that Third Union Bank paid over, Carter Spink's insurers foot the bill—

I pause in my striding. No. It doesn't work. I'm being stupid. The insurers are only covering the £50 million because I was negligent. That's the crucial element. The whole plan would have depended on me, Samantha Sweeting, making that particular mistake.

I mean . . . you can't plan a mistake in advance. You can't *make* someone forget to do something—

And then I stop dead. My skin suddenly feels clammy. The memo. I never saw that memo on my desk until it was too late.

What if—Oh my God. What if someone planted that memo on my desk? Slipped it into a pile of papers after the deadline had passed? *What if I didn't make a mistake?*

I assumed the memo was there all the time. I assumed it was my error. But what if it wasn't? Everyone at Carter Spink knew I had the messiest desk in the firm. It would be easy to slip the memo into a pile of papers. Make it look as if it had been there for weeks.

I'm breathing harder and harder, till I'm almost hyperventilating. I have lived with that mistake for two months. It's there every morning when I wake up and every day when I go to bed. Like a constant chorus in my head: Samantha Sweeting ruined her life.

But . . . what if I was used? *What if I didn't make a mistake after all?*

I have to know. I have to know the truth. Right now. With a shaking hand I reach for my mobile phone and punch in the number again.

'Lara, I need to speak to Arnold again,' I say, as soon as I'm connected.

'Samantha . . .' Lara sounds awkward. 'I'm afraid Arnold won't take any more calls from you. And he asked me to tell you that you're not to pester him about your job any more.'

I feel a flash of shock. 'Lara, I'm not pestering him about my job.' I try to keep my voice steady. 'I just need to talk to him about a . . . matter. If he won't talk to me, I'll come to the office. Can you make me an appointment, please?'

'Samantha . . .' She sounds even more embarrassed than before. 'Arnold told me to inform you . . . if you try to come here to the offices, Security will eject you.'

'*Eject* me?' I stare at the phone in disbelief.

'I'm sorry. I really am. And I don't blame you!' she adds fervently. 'I thought what Arnold did to you was really shocking! A lot of us do.'

I feel a fresh confusion. What he *did* to me? Does Lara know about the memo?

'What—what do you mean?' I stammer.

'The way he got you fired!' says Lara.

'What?' I feel like all the breath has been squeezed from my chest.

'I *did* wonder if you knew.' She lowers her voice. 'He's leaving now, so I can say it. I took the minutes at that meeting, after you ran off. And Arnold talked round all the other partners. He said you were a liability and they couldn't risk taking you back and all sorts. A lot of them wanted to give you another chance, you know.'

'Thanks for telling me, Lara. I . . . had no idea.'

I feel dizzy. Everything is turning out distorted. Arnold didn't fight my corner at all. He got me fired. With a sickening thud I suddenly recall him the day after it happened, insisting I should stay where I was, not come back. That's why. He wanted me out of the way so I couldn't fight for myself. So he could stitch me up.

And I trusted him. Totally and utterly. Like a stupid, gullible fool.

My chest is heaving painfully. All my doubts have disappeared. Arnold is in on something crooked. I know it. He set me up. He planted that memo, knowing it would destroy my career.

A bleeping from my mobile phone makes me jump, and I look up blearily. I'd almost forgotten where I was. I pick it up and see that I've got a text.

I'm downstairs. have a surprise to show you. nat

As I head downstairs, I'm really not with it. Flashes of anger keep overwhelming me as I think of Arnold's jocular smile, the way he told me he'd do his best for me, the way he listened as I blamed myself, as I apologised and grovelled . . .

'Hi.' Nathaniel waves a hand in front of my face. 'Earth to Samantha.'

'Oh . . . Sorry. Hi!' Somehow I muster a smile. 'What's the surprise?'

'Come this way.' He grins and ushers me out to his car, which is an ancient Beetle convertible. As usual, rows of seed pots are crowding the back seat and an old wooden spade is sticking out of the back.

'Madam.' He opens the door gallantly.

'So what are you showing me?' I ask as I get in.

'Magical mystery tour.' He gives an enigmatic smile, and starts up the engine.

We drive out of Lower Ebury and take a route through a tiny neighbouring village and up into the hills. Nathaniel seems in a cheerful mood and tells me stories about each farm and pub that we pass. But I barely hear a word. My mind is still churning.

I don't know what I can do. I can't even get into the building. I have no credibility. I'm powerless. And I only have three days. Once Arnold disappears off to the Bahamas that'll be it.

'Here we are!' Nathaniel turns off the road onto a gravel drive. He stops the engine. 'What do you think?'

With an effort I wrench my mind back to the present. 'Um . . .' I peer around blankly. 'Yes. Lovely.'

'Samantha, are you OK?' Nathaniel shoots me a curious glance.

'I'm fine.' I try to smile. 'Just a bit tired.'

I open the car door to get out, away from his gaze. I shut the door behind me, take a few steps forward and look around.

We're in some kind of courtyard, baking in the evening sun. There's a ramshackle house to the right, with a 'For Sale' post. Ahead are banks of greenhouses, glinting in the low sunlight. There are plots, filled with rows of vegetables, there's a Portacabin marked GARDEN CENTRE . . .

Hang on.

I swivel round in bewilderment to see that Nathaniel has got out of the car too. He's grinning at me and holding a sheaf of papers.

'A horticultural business opportunity,' he reads aloud. 'Four acres of land, with ten more available, subject to negotiation. Ten thousand square feet of glasshouses. Four-bedroom farmhouse, needs work . . .'

'You're *buying* this?' I say, my attention fully grabbed.

'I'm thinking about it. I wanted to show you first.' He spreads an arm out. 'It's a pretty good concern. Needs building up, but the land's there. We can get some polytunnels going, extend the offices . . .'

'But what about the pubs? How come you're suddenly—'

'It was you. What you said in the garden that day.' He pauses, the breeze ruffling his hair. 'I'm not a landlord, I'm a gardener. I'd be happier doing what I really want to do. So . . . I had a long talk with Mum and she understood. We both reckon Eamonn can take over. Not that he knows yet.'

'Wow.' I look around again, taking in a pile of wooden crates; stacks of seed trays; a tattered poster advertising Christmas trees. 'So you're really going to do it?'

Nathaniel shrugs, but I can see the excitement in his face. 'You only get one chance at life.'

'Well, I think it's fantastic.' I beam with genuine enthusiasm.

'And there's a house.' He nods towards it. 'Or at least, there will be a house. It's a bit run down.'

'Right.' I regard the ramshackle building with a grin. 'It does look a bit of a mess.'

'I wanted you to see it first,' says Nathaniel. 'Get your approval. I mean, one day you might . . .' He stops.

There's silence in the courtyard. All of a sudden my relationship sensors are swivelling round madly. What was he going to say?

'I might . . . stay over?' I supply at last, a little awkward.

'Exactly.' Nathaniel rubs his nose. 'Shall we have a look?'

The house is bigger than it looks from the outside, with bare boards and old fireplaces. One room has practically no plaster, and the kitchen is totally old-fashioned, with 1930s cupboards.

'Great kitchen.' I shoot him a teasing look.

'I'm sure I could refit it to your cordon bleu standards,' he returns.

We make our way upstairs and into a huge bedroom overlooking the rear of the house. From above, the vegetable plots look like an orderly patchwork quilt, stretching away into the green meadow beyond.

'It's a beautiful place,' I say, leaning on the window sill. 'I love it.'

Standing here, looking out at the view, Carter Spink and Arnold suddenly seem part of another life. I'm not just out of the loop, I'm off the string altogether. But even as I'm gazing out at the restful country scene, I can feel myself grasping for the end of it. I can't let it go. All it would take is one phone call to the right person . . . If I had some proof . . .

'What I was wondering is . . .'

Suddenly I become aware that Nathaniel is speaking. In fact I think he could have been speaking for a while—and I haven't heard a word. I hastily turn round, to see him facing me. His cheeks are flushed and he has an unfamiliar awkwardness about him. It looks like whatever he's been saying has required some effort.

'. . . do you feel the same way, Samantha?'

I stare back at him dumbly. Do I feel the same way about what?

Oh shit. Was he saying something really heartfelt and meaningful? Was he making some sort of speech of love? And I *missed* it?

This just teaches me to obsess. The man I'm secretly falling in love with just made a romantic speech to me—probably the only one I'll get in my whole life—and *I wasn't listening*?

And now he's waiting for me to reply. What am I going to do? He's just spilled his heart to me. I can't say, 'Sorry, I didn't quite catch that.'

'Um . . .' I push my hair back, playing for time. 'Well . . . you've given me quite a lot to think about.'

'But do you agree?'

Do I agree with what? Capital punishment for burglars? Threesomes?

OK, this is Nathaniel. I'm sure I agree with it, whatever it is.

'Yes.' I give him the most sincere look I can muster. 'Yes, I agree. Wholeheartedly. In fact . . . I've often thought so myself.'

A strange flicker passes over Nathaniel's face as he surveys me. 'You agree,' he says, as though to make sure. 'With everything?'

'Er . . . yes!'

'Even about the chimpanzees?'

'The *chimpanzees*?' I see Nathaniel's mouth twitching. He's twigged.

'You didn't listen to a word I was saying, did you?' he says.

'I didn't realise you were saying something important!' I wail, hanging my head. 'You should have warned me!'

Nathaniel looks at me incredulously. 'That took some nerve, you know, saying all that.'

'Say it again,' I beg. 'Say it all again! I'll listen!'

'Uh-huh.' He laughs, shaking his head. 'Maybe one day.'

'I'm sorry, Nathaniel. Really.' I turn away to stare out of the window again, pressing my head against the glass. 'I was just . . . distracted.'

'I know.' He comes over and puts his arms round me, over my own. I can feel his steady heartbeat against me, calming me down. 'Samantha, what's up? It's your old relationship, isn't it?'

'Yup,' I mutter after a pause.

'Why won't you tell me about it? I could help.'

I swivel round to face him. The sun is glowing in his eyes and on his burnished face. He's never looked more handsome. I have a sudden vision of him punching Arnold right in the face.

But I can't dump all this on him. It's too big. It's too . . . sordid.

'I don't want to bring that world into this one,' I say at last.

Nathaniel opens his mouth again but I turn away before he can speak. I stare out at the idyllic view again, blinking against the rays of the sun, my mind in turmoil.

Maybe I should just give up on the whole nightmare. Forget about it. Let it go. Close the door on my old life and leave it behind for ever. I have a job. I have Nathaniel. I have a possible future here.

But even as I'm thinking it—I know that's not what I'm going to do. I can't forget about it. I can't let go. There's one more chance and I have nothing left to lose.

Ten

OK. BEING BACK IN LONDON has thrown me a little bit. The city isn't the way I remember it. I can't believe how dirty it is. How *rushed* it is. Things I never noticed before. On automatic pilot I head down to the underground and onto a train. I can see my face in the window opposite, pale and expressionless.

As I walk back to my apartment building, my mind is buzzing. *Will he listen to me?*

I come out of the lift, two floors higher than usual. It's almost identical to my floor—same carpet, same wallpaper, same lamps. Just different numbers on the apartment doors: 31 and 32. I can't remember which one I want so in the end I plump for 31. It has a softer doormat. I sink down on the floor, put my bag down, lean against the door and wait.

My phone bleeps, but I ignore it. It'll be yet another message from

Trish. She was livid when I told her I had to go away for a couple of days; in fact she tried to stop me. So I told her I had a foot complaint which needed urgent attention from my specialist in London.

In hindsight this was a huge mistake, as she wanted to know every single gory detail. She even demanded I take off my shoe and show her. I had to spend ten minutes improvising about 'bone misalignment' while she peered at my foot and said 'it looks perfectly normal to me' in tones of great suspicion.

She looked at me mistrustfully for the rest of the day. Then she left a copy of *Marie Claire* casually open at the 'Pregnant? Need Confidential Advice?' advertisement. Honestly. I have to knock that one on the head or it'll be all over the village and Iris will be knitting bootees.

I look at my watch and feel a swoop of nerves. But all I can do is wait.

By the time Ketterman emerges from the lift I've been sitting here for three hours, without anything to eat or drink. But at the sight of him I scramble to my feet.

For a moment Ketterman looks shocked. Then he resumes his usual stony expression. 'Samantha. What are you doing here?'

I take a step forward. 'I know I'm the last person you want to see.' I rub my aching brow. 'Believe me, I don't want to be here either. Out of all the people in the world I could turn to for help . . . you would be the last. So the fact that I'm here, coming to you . . . should prove it to you.' I look at him desperately. 'I'm serious. I have something to tell you, and you have to listen. You have to.'

There's a long silence between us. Ketterman's face is rigid. I can't tell what he's thinking. Then, at last, he reaches into his pocket for a key. He walks past me, unlocks the door to flat 32—and turns.

'Come in.'

I wake up to the view of a cracked, grubby ceiling. My eyes run along to a huge cobweb in the corner of the room, then down the wall to a rickety bookshelf stuffed with books, tapes, letters, old Christmas decorations and the odd bit of discarded underwear.

How did I live in this mess for seven years? How did I not *notice* it?

I push back the cover, get out of bed and look around blearily. The carpet feels gritty under my feet and I wince. It needs a good hoover. I guess the cleaner stopped coming after the money stopped appearing.

I find a dressing gown, pull it on and head out to the kitchen. I'd forgotten how bare and cold and spartan it was in here. There's nothing in the fridge, of course. But I find a camomile teabag and fill the kettle, and perch on a bar stool, looking out at the brick wall opposite.

It's already nine fifteen. Ketterman will be at the office. He'll be taking whatever action he's going to take. I wait to feel the nerves rise . . . but they don't. I feel weirdly calm. Everything's out of my hands now; there's nothing I can do.

He listened to me. He actually listened, and asked questions, and even made me a cup of tea. I was there for over an hour. He didn't tell me what he thought or what he was going to do. He didn't even say whether he believed me or not. But something tells me he did.

The kettle's coming to the boil when the phone rings. I pick up the receiver, suddenly wondering how many people must have rung this number over the last few weeks. The machine is crammed with messages, but after listening to the first three, all from Mum and each more furious than the last, I gave up.

'Hello?'

'Samantha,' comes a businesslike voice. 'John Ketterman here.'

'Oh.' In spite of myself I feel a nervous swoop. 'Hi.'

'I'd like you to come to the Carter Spink offices,' he says. 'It may be necessary for you to speak to some people.'

'People?'

There's a slight pause, then Ketterman says, 'Investigators.'

Oh my God. Oh my *God*. I feel like punching the air or bursting into tears or something. But somehow I keep my composure.

'So have you found something out? Was my theory right?'

There's a crackling silence down the phone. I can't breathe.

'Not in every detail,' says Ketterman at last, and I feel a painful thrill of triumph. That means I was right in some details.

The phone goes dead. I put the receiver down and look at my reflection in the hall mirror. My cheeks are flushed and my eyes are bright.

I was right. And they know it.

They'll offer me my job back, it suddenly hits me. They'll offer me partnership. At the thought I'm seized with excitement—and at the same time, a kind of weird fear.

I'll cross that bridge when I come to it.

I spend three hours at the Carter Spink offices, talking in turn to a man from the Law Society, two of the senior partners and some guy from Third Union Bank.

I still haven't worked out exactly what's going on. Lawyers are so bloody discreet. I know someone's been to see Arnold at his home and that's about it. But even if no one's going to admit it, I know I was right. I've been vindicated.

After the last interview, a plate of sandwiches is brought to the room

I'm in, together with a bottle of mineral water and a muffin. I get to my feet, stretch, and wander over to the window. I feel like a prisoner in here. There's a tapping at the door and Ketterman comes into the room.

'Haven't I finished yet?' I say. 'I've been here hours.'

'We may need to speak to you again.' He gestures to the sandwiches. 'Have some lunch.'

I cannot stay in this room a moment longer. I have to stretch my legs, at least. 'I'll just go and freshen up first,' I say, and hurry out of the room before he can object.

As I enter the Ladies, all the women in there stop talking. I disappear into a cubicle and hear the sound of excited whisperings and murmurings outside. As I come out again, not one person has left the room. I can feel all the eyes on me, like sun lamps.

'So are you back now, Samantha?' says an associate called Lucy.

'Not exactly.' I turn away to the sink, feeling self-conscious.

'You look so *different*,' says another girl.

'Your arms!' says Lucy as I wash my hands. 'They're so brown. And *toned*. Have you been to a spa?'

'Er . . . no.' I give a mysterious smile. 'How's life been here?'

'Good.' Lucy nods a few times. 'Extremely busy. Clocked up sixty-six billable hours last week. Two all-nighters.'

'I had three,' puts in another girl. She speaks casually, but I can see the pride in her face. And the dark grey shadows under her eyes. Is that what I used to look like? All pale and strained and tense?

'Great!' I say politely, drying my hands. 'Well, I'd better get back now. See you.'

I exit the Ladies and am walking back to the interview room, lost in my own thoughts, when I hear a voice.

'Oh my God, *Samantha*?'

'*Guy*?' I look up in shock to see him hurrying down the corridor towards me, his smile even more dazzling than ever.

'Look at you!' He grips my shoulders tightly and scans my face. 'You look fantastic.' He lowers his voice. 'I've just been briefed on the situation. Bloody hell, Samantha, it's incredible. Only you could work all that out. *Arnold*, of all people. I was *shell-shocked*. Everyone is. Those who know,' he adds, lowering his voice still further. 'Obviously it's not out yet.'

'I don't even know what the "situation" is,' I reply, with a touch of resentment. 'No one's telling me anything.'

'Well, they will.' Guy reaches into his pocket, gets out his BlackBerry and squints at it. 'You are flavour of the month right now. I knew it all along.' He looks up. 'I knew you never made a mistake.'

I gape at him. How can he say that?

'No, you didn't,' I reply at last, finding my words. 'You said I was "unreliable".'

'I said *other* people had said you made errors.' Guy pauses in tapping at his BlackBerry and looks up, frowning. 'Shit, Samantha. I did stand up for you. I was on your side. Ask anyone!'

Yup. Sure. That's why you wouldn't have me to stay.

But I don't say anything out loud. I really don't want to get into it. It's history. 'Fine,' I say at last. 'Whatever.'

We start walking along the corridor together, Guy still engrossed in the BlackBerry. God, he's addicted to that thing, I think, with irritation.

'So where the hell did you disappear to?' At last he stops tapping. 'What have you been doing all this time?'

'I've got a job.'

'I knew you'd get snapped up.' He nods with satisfaction. 'Who's employed you?'

'Oh . . . no one you'd know,' I say after a pause.

'You're in the same area, though?' He puts his BlackBerry away. 'Doing the same kind of work?'

I have a sudden vision of me mopping Trish's bathroom floor.

'Er . . . as it happens, not really.' Somehow I keep a straight face.

Guy seems surprised. 'But you're still in banking law, right? Don't tell me you've made a complete change?' He suddenly looks galvanised. 'You haven't gone into commercial law, have you?'

'Um, no . . . not commercial law. I'd better go.' I cut him off and open the door to the interview room. 'See you later.'

I eat my sandwiches, I drink my mineral water. For half an hour no one disturbs me. I feel a bit like I'm in quarantine for some deadly illness. They could have given me some magazines, at least. I've developed quite a habit for gossip, after being surrounded by Trish's endless supply of *Heat* and *Hello!*.

At last I hear a knock at the door and Ketterman comes in.

'Samantha, we would like to see you in the boardroom.'

The *boardroom*? Blimey.

I follow Ketterman down the corridors, aware of the nudges and whisperings from everyone we pass. He opens the huge double doors to the boardroom and I walk in, to see about half the partners standing there, waiting for me. There's silence as Ketterman closes the doors.

Am I supposed to speak? Did I miss the instructions? Ketterman has joined the group of partners. Now he turns to face me.

'Samantha, as you know, an investigation of . . . recent events is under way. The results have not yet been fully determined.' He breaks off, looking tense, and I can see some of the others exchanging sober looks. 'However, we have come to one conclusion. You were wronged.'

I gape at him in stupefaction. He's *admitting* it? Getting a lawyer to admit they've made a mistake is like getting a movie star to admit they've had liposuction.

'Thank you.' I smile politely. 'I appreciate that.'

'And therefore.' Ketterman pauses. 'We would like to offer you full equity partnership in the firm. Effective immediately.'

I'm so shocked I nearly sit down on the floor. *Full equity partnership?*

I open my mouth—but I can't speak. I feel winded. Full equity partnership is the highest pinnacle. It's the most prestigious job in law. I never, ever, *ever* expected that.

'Welcome back, Samantha,' says one of the senior partners, Greg Parker.

'Welcome back,' chime in a few others. David Elldridge gives me a warm smile. Guy gives me the thumbs up.

'We have some champagne.' Ketterman nods to Guy, who opens the double doors. The next moment two waitresses from the partners' dining room are coming in with trays of champagne glasses. Someone puts one in my hand.

This is all going too fast. I have to say something.

'Er . . . excuse me?' I call out. 'I haven't said if I'll accept it yet.'

The whole room seems to freeze, like a videotape on pause.

'I'm sorry?' Ketterman's face contorts with incredulity.

Oh God. I'm not sure they're going to take this very well.

'The thing is . . .' I break off and take a sip of champagne for Dutch courage, trying to work out how to put this tactfully. I've been thinking about it all day. Being a partner at Carter Spink is the dream I've had all my adult life. The glittering prize. It's everything I ever wanted.

Except . . . all the things I never knew I wanted. Like fresh air. Like evenings off. Unburdened weekends. Making plans with friends.

I clear my throat and look round the room.

'It's a tremendous honour to be offered such an amazing opportunity,' I say earnestly. 'And I'm very grateful. Truly. However . . . the reason I came back wasn't to get my job back. It was to clear my name. To prove that I didn't make a mistake.' I can't help shooting a look at Guy. 'The truth is, since leaving Carter Spink I've . . . well . . . moved on. I have a job. Which I very much enjoy. So I won't be taking up your offer.'

There's a stunned silence.

'Is she *serious*?' says someone at the back.

'Samantha,' says Ketterman, coming forward, 'you may have found opportunities elsewhere. But you are a Carter Spink lawyer. This is where you trained, this is where you belong.'

'If it's a question of salary,' adds Elldridge, 'I'm sure we can match whatever you're currently . . .' he glances at Guy. 'Which law firm has she gone to?'

'Wherever you are, I'll speak to the senior partner,' says Ketterman in a businesslike way. 'The personnel director . . . whoever would be appropriate. If you give me a number.' He's taking out his BlackBerry.

My mouth twists. I desperately want to giggle.

'I never said I was working as a lawyer.'

It's as if I've said I think the world is flat. I have never seen so many flummoxed faces in my life.

'You're . . . not working as a lawyer?' says Elldridge at last. 'What are you working as, then?'

I was hoping it wouldn't come to this. But on the other hand, why shouldn't they know?

'I'm working as a housekeeper.' I smile.

'"Housekeeper"?' Elldridge peers at me. 'Is that the new jargon for troubleshooter? Is that what you mean?'

'No, it's not what I mean,' I say patiently. 'I'm a housekeeper. I make beds. I cook meals. I'm a domestic.'

For about sixty seconds nobody moves. God, I wish I had a camera. Their *faces*.

'You're literally . . . a *housekeeper*?' stutters Elldridge at last.

'Uh-huh.' I look at my watch. 'And I'm fulfilled and I'm relaxed and I'm happy. In fact, I should be getting back. Thank you,' I add to Ketterman, 'for listening to me.'

'You're turning down our offer?' says Greg Parker incredulously.

'I'm turning down your offer.' I give an apologetic shrug. 'Sorry.'

As I head out of the room I feel slightly wobbly about the legs. And slightly manic inside. *I turned it down.* I turned down senior partnership of Carter Spink.

What the hell is my mother going to say?

The thought makes me want to burst into hysterical laughter.

I feel too keyed up to wait for the lift so I head down the stairwell, clattering on the cold stone steps.

'Samantha!' Guy's voice suddenly echoes above me.

Oh, honestly. What does he want?

'I'm going!' I yell back. 'Leave me alone!' I can hear him accelerating down the steps, so I pick up speed myself.

'Samantha, this is crazy! I can't let you ruin your career out of . . . out of pique!' he calls.

I wheel round indignantly. 'I'm not doing this out of pique!'

'I know you're angry with us all!' Guy joins me on the staircase, breathing hard. 'I'm sure it makes you feel really good to turn us down, to say you're working as a housekeeper . . .'

'I *am* working as a housekeeper!' I retort. 'And I'm not turning you down because I'm angry, but because I don't want the job.'

'Samantha, you wanted partnership more than anything else in the world!' Guy grabs my arm. 'You can't throw it away! It's too valuable.'

'What if I don't value it any more?'

'It's only been a few weeks! Everything can't have changed!'

'It has. *I* have.' I swivel on my heel and start down the stairs again. I reach the bottom of the stairwell and burst into the foyer with Guy in hot pursuit. Hilary Grant, head of PR, is sitting on a leather sofa with some red-suited woman, and they both look up in surprise.

'Samantha, you cannot do this!' Guy is shouting after me as he emerges into the foyer. 'I cannot let you turn down senior partnership to be a . . . *housekeeper.*'

'Why not, if it's what I want to do?' I come to a halt on the marble and turn to face him. 'Guy, I've found out what it's like to have a life! I've found out what it's like, *not* working every weekend. Not feeling pressure all the time. And I like it!'

'You're going to stand there and tell me you prefer cleaning loos to being a partner of Carter Spink?' His face is flushed with outrage.

'Yes!' I say defiantly. 'Yes, I do!'

'Who's that?' says the woman in the red suit with interest.

'Samantha, you're making the biggest mistake of your entire existence!' Guy's voice follows me as I reach the doors. 'If you walk out now—'

I don't hear any more. I'm out of the door. Down the steps. Gone.

I might have just made the biggest mistake of my entire existence. As I sit on the train back to Gloucestershire, Guy's words keep ringing in my ears.

Once upon a time, just that thought would have sent me into a tailspin. But not any more. I almost want to laugh. He has no idea.

If I've learned one thing from everything that's happened to me, it's that there *is* no such thing as the biggest mistake of your existence. There's no such thing as ruining your life. Life's a pretty resilient thing, it turns out.

When I arrive at Lower Ebury I head straight to the pub. Nathaniel is behind the bar, talking to Eamonn. For a few moments I just watch him: his strong hands; the slant of his neck; the way his brow furrows as he nods. I can tell at once he disagrees with whatever Eamonn is saying. But he's waiting, wanting to be tactful about making his point.

Maybe I'm better at telepathy than I thought.

As if he's telepathic too, he looks up and smiles a welcome—but I can see the tension underneath. These last couple of days can't have been easy for him. Maybe he thought I wasn't coming back.

A roar goes up from the dartboard, and one of the guys turns and spots me walking towards the bar.

'Samantha!' he shouts. 'At last! We need you on our team!'

'In a sec!' I call over my shoulder. 'Hi,' I say as I reach Nathaniel.

'Hi,' he says casually. 'Good trip?'

'Not bad.' I nod. Nathaniel lifts up the bar for me to come through, his eyes searching my face as though for clues.

'So . . . is it over?'

'Yup.' I put my arms around him and hug him tight. 'It's over.'

And at that moment, I truly believe it is.

Eleven

NOTHING HAPPENS until lunchtime.

I make the breakfast for Trish and Eddie as usual. I hoover and dust as usual. Then I get out the chopping board and start squeezing oranges. I'm going to make bitter chocolate and orange mousse for the charity lunch tomorrow. We're going to serve it on a bed of crystallised orange slices, and each plate is going to be garnished with a real silver-leaf angel from a Christmas decoration catalogue.

This was Trish's idea. As are the angels hanging from the ceiling.

'How are we doing?' Trish comes tapping into the kitchen, looking flustered. 'Have you made the mousses yet?'

'Not yet,' I say, briskly squeezing an orange. 'Mrs Geiger, don't worry. It's all under control.'

'Do you know what I've *been* through, the last few days?' She clutches her head. 'More and more people keep accepting . . . I've had to change the seating plan . . .'

'It'll be fine,' I say soothingly. 'Try to relax.'

'Yes.' She breathes out slowly, holding her head between two lacquered fingernails. 'You're right. I'll just go and check the goody bags . . .'

I cannot believe how much Trish is spending on this lunch. Every time I question whether we really need to canopy the dining room in white silk, or give every guest an orchid buttonhole, she shrills 'It's all in a good cause!'

Which reminds me of something I've been meaning to ask her for quite a while now.

'Er . . . Mrs Geiger,' I say casually, 'are you charging your guests for entrance to the lunch?'

'Oh, no!' she says. 'I think that's rather *tacky*, don't you?'

'Are you holding a raffle?'

'I don't think so.' She wrinkles her nose. 'People *loathe* raffles.'

I hardly dare ask this next question. 'So . . . um . . . how exactly are you planning on making money for the charity?'

There's silence in the kitchen. Trish has frozen, her eyes wide.

'*Bugger*,' she says at last.

I knew it. She hadn't given it a thought. 'Perhaps we could ask for voluntary donations?' I suggest. 'We could hand round a little bag with the coffee and the mints?'

'Yes. Yes.' Trish peers at me as though I'm a genius. '*That's* the answer.' She exhales sharply. 'This is really very stressful, Samantha. I don't know how you stay so calm.'

I smile, feeling a sudden wave of fondness for her. When I arrived back at the house last night it was like coming home. Even though Trish had left a mountain of crockery on the counter for my return, and a note saying *Samantha, please polish all silver tomorrow.*

Trish heads out of the kitchen and I start whisking up egg whites for the mousse. Then I notice a man sidling down the drive. He's wearing jeans and an old polo shirt and has a camera slung round his neck. He disappears from view and I frown in puzzlement. Maybe he's a delivery man. I measure out the caster sugar, with half an ear out for the door-bell, and start folding it into the egg whites, just the way Iris taught me. Then, suddenly, the man is standing at the kitchen door, peering in through the window.

I'm not ruining my mixture for some door-to-door salesman. He can wait a few moments. I finish folding in the sugar—then head to the door and open it. 'Can I help?' I say politely.

The man gazes silently at me for a few seconds, glancing down every so often at a folded-up tabloid newspaper in his hand. 'Are you Samantha Sweeting?' he says at last.

I look back at him warily. 'Why?'

'I'm from the *Cheltenham Gazette*.' He flashes an ID card at me. 'I'm after an exclusive interview with you. "Why I chose the Cotswolds as my secret hideaway"—that kind of thing.'

I look at him blankly. 'Er . . . what are you talking about?'

'You haven't seen it?' He looks surprised. 'I take it this is you?'

He turns the newspaper round and as I see it, my stomach seizes up in shock.

It's a picture of me. In the newspaper. Me.

It's my official Carter Spink portrait. Above the picture, in bold black letters, is the headline: I'D RATHER CLEAN LOOS THAN BE A PARTNER AT CARTER SPINK.

With trembling hands I grab the paper and scan the text.

Top law firm Carter Spink is the most prestigious in the country. But yesterday one young woman turned down a high-ranking post as partner in order to work as a humble housekeeper.

GET A LIFE

Partners were left with egg on their faces as star £500-an-hour lawyer Samantha Sweeting rejected their offer, which carried a substantial six-figure salary. Having previously been fired, the high-flier apparently uncovered a financial scandal at the firm. However, when offered full equity partnership, Sweeting cited the pressure and lack of free time as reason for her decision.

'I've got used to having a life,' she said, as partners begged her to stay.

A former Carter Spink employee who declined to be named confirmed the brutal working conditions of the legal firm. 'They expect you to sell your soul,' he said.

A spokeswoman for Carter Spink defended the firm's practices. 'We are a flexible, modern firm with a sympathetic working ethos. We would like to talk to Samantha about her views and would certainly not expect employees to "sell their soul".'

VANISHED

She confirmed that Ms Sweeting's job offer is still open and Carter Spink partners are anxious to talk to her. However, in a further extraordinary twist, this modern-day Cinderella has not been seen since running away from the offices.

I stare at the page, numb with disbelief. How did— What did—?

A flash interrupts me and I look up in shock to see the guy pointing his camera at me.

'Stop!' I say in horror, putting my hands up in front of my face.

'Can I have a picture of you holding a toilet brush, love?' he says, zooming his lens in. 'They tipped me off at the pub it was you. Quite a scoop.' The camera flashes again and I flinch.

'No! You . . . you have made mistake.' I shove the paper back at him. 'This . . . Zees ees not me. My name is Martine. I no lawyer.'

The journalist looks at me suspiciously, and down at the photo again. I can see a flicker of doubt cross his face. I do look fairly different now from the way I did then, with my blonde hair and everything.

'That's not a French accent,' he says.

He has a point. Accents aren't exactly my strong point.

'Am . . . half Belgian.' I keep my eyes fixed on the floor. 'Please leave 'ouse now. Or I call police.'

I shove him off the doorstep, slam the door shut and turn the key. Then I pull the curtain across the window and lean back against the door, my heart thudding. What am I going to do?

OK. The important thing is not to panic. The important thing is to stay rational and take a balanced view of the situation.

On the one hand, my entire past has been exposed in a national tabloid. On the other hand, Trish and Eddie don't read that particular tabloid. Or the *Cheltenham Gazette*. It's one silly story in one silly paper and it will die away by tomorrow. There's no reason to tell them anything. I'll just carry on making my chocolate orange mousses as though nothing has happened. Yes. Total denial is the way forward.

Feeling slightly better I reach for the chocolate and start breaking chunks into a glass bowl.

OK. Denial's not going to work, because twenty minutes later there are three more journalists in the drive.

'Do you know what's going on, Samantha?' says Trish, coming into the kitchen carrying a book called *Your Elegant Luncheon Party*. 'There seems to be a bit of a *commotion* outside in the road.'

'Is there?' I say. 'I . . . I hadn't noticed.'

'It looks like a protest.' She wrinkles her brow. 'I do hope they're not still there tomorrow. Protesters are so *selfish* . . .'

I feel like I'm in some kind of parallel reality. Everything's going to come out. It's just a matter of time. What do I do?

'Have *you* seen this protest?' Trish demands as Eddie saunters into the kitchen. 'Outside our gates! I think we should tell these people to move on.'

'It's not a protest,' he says, opening the fridge. 'It's journalists.'

'*Journalists?*' Trish peers at him. 'What on earth would journalists be doing here?'

'Maybe we have a new celebrity neighbour?' suggests Eddie, pouring a beer into a glass.

At once Trish claps her hand over her mouth. 'Joanna Lumley! I *heard* a rumour she was buying in the village! Samantha, have you heard anything about this?'

'I . . . er . . . no,' I mumble, my face burning.

I have to say something. Come on. Say something. But what? Where do I start?

'Samantha, I need this shirt ironed by tonight.' Melissa comes wandering into the kitchen, holding out a sleeveless print shirt. 'And be really careful with the collar, OK?' she adds with a bad-tempered frown. 'The last one you did the creases weren't straight.'

'I'm not sure I'll have time—' I begin.

'*Make* time,' she snaps. 'What's going on outside?'

'We think it's Joanna Lumley!' says Trish excitedly.

Suddenly the doorbell rings.

My stomach seems to double over. For a moment I consider bolting out of the back door.

'I wonder if that's them!' exclaims Trish. 'Eddie, go and answer it. Samantha, put on some coffee.'

I'm totally paralysed. I need to speak. I need to explain. But my mouth won't move. Nothing will move.

'Samantha?' She peers at me. 'Are you all right?'

With an almighty effort I look up. 'Um . . . Mrs Geiger . . .' My voice comes out a nervous husk. 'There's something . . . I ought to . . .'

'Melissa!' Eddie's voice interrupts me. He's hurrying into the kitchen, a huge beam spread across his face. 'Melissa, love! They want you!'

'*Me?*' Melissa looks up in surprise. 'What do you mean, Uncle Eddie?'

'It's the *Daily Mail*. They want to interview you!' Eddie turns to Trish, glowing with pride. 'Did you know that our Melissa has one of the finest legal brains in the country?'

Oh no. Oh no.

'What?' Trish nearly drops her copy of *Your Elegant Luncheon Party*.

'That's what they said!' Eddie nods. 'They said it might come as quite a surprise to me to learn we had such a high-flying lawyer in the house. I said Nonsense!' He puts an arm round Melissa. 'We've always known you were a star!'

'Mrs Geiger,' I say urgently. No one takes any notice of me.

'It must be that prize I won at law school! They must have heard about it somehow!' Melissa is gasping. 'Oh my God! The *Daily Mail*!'

'They want to take photos!' puts in Eddie. 'They want an exclusive!'

'I need to put on some make-up!' Melissa looks totally flustered.

'Here!' Trish wrenches open her handbag. 'Here's some mascara . . . and lipstick . . .'

I have to stop this. I have to break it to them.

'Mr Geiger . . .' I clear my throat. 'Are you sure . . . I mean, did they ask for Melissa by . . . by name?'

'They didn't need to!' He twinkles at me. 'Only one lawyer in this house!'

'Make some coffee, Samantha,' instructs Trish sharply. 'And use the pink cups. Quickly! Wash them up.'

'The thing is . . . I have . . . I have something to tell you.'

'Not now, Samantha! Wash up those cups!' Trish thrusts the rubber gloves at me. 'I don't know *what's* wrong with you today.'

'But I don't think they've come to see Melissa,' I say desperately. 'There's something I . . . I should have told you . . .'

No one pays any attention. They're all focused on Melissa.

'How do I look?' Melissa smooths her hair back self-consciously.

'Lovely, darling!' Trish leans forward.

'Is she ready for the interview?' An unfamiliar woman's voice comes from the kitchen door and everyone freezes in excitement.

'In here!' Eddie pulls open the door to reveal a dark-haired woman in a trouser suit, whose eyes run appraisingly over the kitchen.

'Here's our legal star!' Eddie gestures to Melissa with a beam of pride.

'Hello.' Melissa tosses back her hair, then steps forward with an outstretched hand. 'I'm Melissa Hurst.'

The woman looks at Melissa blankly for a few moments. 'Not her,' she says. '*Her.*' And she points at me.

In puzzled silence, everyone swivels to stare at me.

'That's Samantha,' says Trish, looking perplexed. 'The housekeeper.'

'You're Samantha Sweeting, I take it?' The woman brings out her reporter's pad. 'Can I ask you a few questions?'

'You want to interview the *housekeeper*?' says Melissa, sarcastically.

The journalist ignores her. 'You *are* Samantha Sweeting, aren't you?' she persists.

'I . . . yes,' I admit at last, my face burning. 'But I don't want to do an interview. I don't have any comment.'

'*Comment?*' Trish's eyes dart around uncertainly. 'Comment on what?'

'What's going on, Samantha, love?' Eddie looks anxious. 'Are you in some kind of trouble?'

'You haven't *told* them?' The *Daily Mail* journalist looks up from her notepad. 'They have no idea?'

'Told us what?' says Trish, agitated. 'What?'

'Your "housekeeper" is a top City lawyer.' The woman throws down a copy of the tabloid onto the kitchen table. 'And she's just turned down a six-figure partnership to work for you.'

It's as though someone's thrown a grenade into the kitchen. Eddie visibly reels. Trish totters on her high-heeled clogs and grabs a chair for balance. Melissa's face looks like a popped balloon.

'I meant to tell you . . .' I bite my lip awkwardly as I look at their faces. 'I was . . . getting round to it . . .'

Trish's eyes are bulging as she reads the headline. Her mouth is opening and closing, but no sound is coming out.

'You're a . . . a *lawyer*?' she stutters at last.

'There's been a mistake!' Melissa's cheeks are bright pink. '*I'm* the lawyer. *I'm* the one who got a prize at law school! She's the *cleaner*.'

'She's the one who got three prizes at law school.' The journalist jerks her head towards me. 'And the highest law degree of her year.'

'But'—Melissa's face is darkening to an ugly purple—'It's impossible.'

'Youngest ever partner of Carter Spink . . .' The journalist consults her notes. 'Is that right, Ms Sweeting?'

'No!' I say. 'I mean . . . well . . . kind of. Can I make anyone a cup of tea?' I add desperately.

No one seems interested in tea.

'I don't understand.' Eddie turns to me. 'How did you combine being a lawyer with the housekeeping?'

'Yes!' exclaims Trish, coming to life. 'How on earth could you be a City lawyer and have time to train with Michel de la Roux de la Blanc?'

Oh God. They *still* don't get it?

'I'm not really a housekeeper,' I say desperately. 'I'm not really a cordon bleu cook. Michel de la Roux de la Blanc doesn't exist. I'm a . . . a fake.'

I can't look at either of them. Suddenly I feel terrible. 'I'll understand if you want me to leave,' I mumble.

'Leave?' Trish looks horrified. 'We don't want you to leave, do we, Eddie?'

'Absolutely not.' His face becomes even more ruddy. 'You've done a fine job, Samantha. You can't help it if you're a lawyer.'

'"I'm a fake",' says the journalist, writing it carefully down on her notepad. 'Do you feel guilty about that, Ms Sweeting?'

'Stop it!' I say. 'I'm not doing an interview.'

'Ms Sweeting says she'd rather clean loos than be a partner of Carter Spink,' says the journalist, turning to Trish. 'Could I see the loos in question?'

'*Our* loos?' Spots of pink appear on Trish's cheeks. 'Well, we did have the bathrooms refitted recently, they're all Royal Doulton . . .'

'Stop this!' I clutch my hair. 'Look, I'll . . . I'll make a statement to the press. And then I want you all to leave me and my employers alone.'

I hurry out of the kitchen, the *Daily Mail* woman following behind, and fling open the front door. The crowd of journalists is still there, behind the gate. Is it my imagination or are there more than before?

'It's Martine,' says the *Cheltenham Gazette* guy sardonically.

I ignore him. 'Ladies and gentlemen of the press,' I begin. 'I would be grateful if you would leave me alone. There isn't any story here.'

'Are you going to stay a housekeeper?' calls a fat guy in jeans.

'Yes, I am.' I lift my chin. 'I've made a personal choice, for personal reasons, and I'm very happy here.'

'What about feminism?' demands a young girl, as cameras flash. 'Women have fought for years to gain an equal foothold. Now you're telling them they should go back to the kitchen?'

'I'm not telling women anything!' I say, taken aback.

'Was Carter Spink a sexist hellhole?'

'Is this a bargaining ploy?'

'Could you pose for us in your pinny?' calls out the fat guy with a lascivious wink.

'No!' I say in horror. 'I have nothing else to say! Go away!'

Ignoring the cries and shouts of 'Samantha!' I turn and run with trembling legs back up the drive to the house.

I burst into the kitchen, to find Trish, Eddie and Melissa transfixed in front of the newspaper. All three of them raise their heads and regard me as though I'm some kind of alien.

'You charge five hundred pounds an hour?' Trish doesn't seem in control of her voice.

'They offered you full equity partnership?' Melissa looks green. 'And you said *no*? Are you *crazy*?'

'Don't read this stuff!' I try to grab the paper. 'Mrs Geiger, I just want to carry on as usual. I'm still your housekeeper—'

'You're one of the country's top legal talents!' Trish jabs the paper hysterically. 'It says so here!'

'Samantha?' There's a rapping at the door and Nathaniel comes into the kitchen, holding an armful of newly picked potatoes. 'Will this be enough for the lunch?'

I stare at him, feeling a clutch at my heart. He has no idea. Oh God. I should have told him. Why didn't I tell him? *Why didn't I tell him?*

'What are *you*?' says Trish, turning to him wildly. 'A top rocket scientist? A secret government agent?'

'I'm sorry?' Nathaniel shoots me a quizzical look but I can't raise a smile.

'Nathaniel . . .' I trail off, unable to continue.

Nathaniel looks from face to face, a crease of uncertainty deepening in his brow. 'What's going on?' he says at last.

I have never made such a hash of anything as I make of telling Nathaniel. I stammer, I stutter, I repeat myself and go round in circles.

Nathaniel listens in silence. He's leaning against an old stone pillar in front of the secluded bench where I'm sitting. His face is in profile, shadowed in the afternoon sun, and I can't tell what he's thinking.

At last I come to a finish and he slowly lifts his head. If I was hoping for a smile, I don't get it. 'You're a lawyer,' he says at last.

'Yes.' I nod shamefacedly.

'I thought you were in an abusive relationship.' He thrusts his hands through his hair. 'I thought that's why you didn't want to talk about your past. And you let me believe it.'

'I'm sorry.' I wince with guilt. 'I just didn't want you to know the truth.'

'Why not?' he retorts, and I can hear the hurt in his voice. 'What, you didn't trust me?'

'No!' I say in dismay. 'Of course I trust you! If it had been anything else . . .' I break off. 'Nathaniel, you have to understand. When we first met, how could I tell you? Everyone knows you hate lawyers. You even have a sign in your pub—No Lawyers!'

'That sign's a *joke*.' He makes an impatient gesture.

'It's not. Not completely.' I meet his gaze. 'Come on, Nathaniel. If I'd told you I was a City lawyer when we first met, would you have treated me in the same way?'

Nathaniel doesn't reply. I know he's too honest to give me the easy response. He knows as well as I do, the true answer is no.

'I'm the same person.' I lean forward and take his hand. 'Even if I used to be a lawyer . . . I'm still me.'

For a while Nathaniel says nothing, just stares down at the dirt. I'm holding my breath, desperate with hope. Then he looks up with a reluctant half-smile.

'So, how much are you charging me for this conversation, then?'

I exhale in a gust of relief. He's OK. He's OK about it.

'Oh, about a thousand pounds,' I say carelessly. 'I'll send you a bill.'

'Samantha Sweeting, corporate lawyer.' He surveys me for a few moments. 'Nope. I can't see it.'

'Me neither. That part of my life is over.' I squeeze his hand tightly. 'Nathaniel, I'm really sorry. I never meant any of this to happen.'

'I know.' He squeezes my hand back and I feel myself relax.

'So what happens now?' says Nathaniel.

'Nothing. The media interest will die down. They'll get bored.' I lean forward and rest my head on his shoulder, and feel his arms close round me. 'I'm happy in my job. I'm happy in this village. I'm happy with you. I just want everything to stay the same.'

I'm wrong. The media interest doesn't die down. I wake up the next morning to find twice as many journalists as yesterday camped outside, plus two TV vans. As I come into the kitchen, Eddie is sitting at the table, which is covered in newspapers.

'You're in every single paper,' he informs me. 'Look.' He shows me a double-page spread in the *Sun*. There's a picture of me superimposed on the background of a loo, and someone's drawn a toilet brush in one of my hands. 'I'd rather clean loos!' is in huge letters next to my face.

'Oh my God.' I sink into a chair and stare at the picture. '*Why?*'

'It's August,' says Eddie, flicking through the *Telegraph*. 'Nothing else in the news. Is it true you single-handedly uncovered Mafia connections at your law firm?'

'No!' I look up in horror. 'Who said that?'

'Can't remember where I saw it now,' he says, riffling through the pages. 'This one has a poll, look.' Eddie has opened another paper. '"Samantha Sweeting: Heroine or Fool? Phone or text your vote." Then they give a number to call.'

'Samantha! You're up!'

I raise my head to see Trish coming into the kitchen, holding a bundle of newspapers under her arm. As she looks at me she has the same shell-shocked expression of awe that she had yesterday, as though I'm a priceless work of art that has suddenly pitched up in her kitchen. 'I've just been reading about you.'

'Good morning, Mrs Geiger.' I hastily get to my feet. 'What can I get you for breakfast? Some coffee to begin with?'

'Don't *you* make the coffee, Samantha!' she replies, looking flustered. 'You're our guest. Eddie, *you* can make the coffee!'

'I'm not making the coffee!' objects Eddie.

'I'm not your guest!' I protest. 'I'm your housekeeper!'

I can see Eddie and Trish exchanging doubtful looks. What do they think? That I'm going to leave?

'Nothing's different!' I insist. 'I'm still your housekeeper! I've learned a lot, living here. I've changed as a person. And I've found a fulfilling way of life. Yes, I could make a lot more money being a lawyer in London. But it's not what I want.' I spread my arms around the kitchen. 'This is what I want to do. This is where I want to be.'

I'm half expecting Trish and Eddie to look moved by my little speech. Instead, they both peer at me in total incomprehension.

'I think you should consider the offer,' says Eddie. 'It says in the paper they're desperate to woo you back.'

'We won't be at *all* offended if you leave,' adds Trish, nodding emphatically. 'We'll *completely* understand.'

'I don't want to leave!' I say crossly. 'I want to stay here and enjoy a fulfilling life at a different pace.'

The telephone rings and Trish picks it up. 'Hello?' She listens for a moment. 'Yes, of *course*, Mavis. *And* Trudy. See you later.' She puts the receiver down. 'Two more guests for the charity lunch.'

'Right.' I glance at my watch. 'I'd better get going on the starters.'

As I'm getting out my pastry the phone rings again and Trish sighs. 'If this is more late guests . . . Hello?' As she listens, her expression changes and she puts her hand over the receiver.

'Samantha,' she hisses. 'It's an ad company. Are you willing to appear in a TV commercial for Toilet Duck? You'd wear a barrister's wig and gown, and you'd have to say—'

'No!' I say, recoiling. 'Of course not!'

'You should never turn down television,' says Eddie reprovingly. 'Could be a big opportunity.'

'No, it couldn't! I don't want to be in any commercials!' I can see Eddie opening his mouth to argue. 'I don't want to do any interviews,' I add quickly. 'I just want everything to go back to normal.'

By lunchtime everything is not back to normal. In fact everything is even more surreal than before.

I've had three more requests to appear on TV and Trish has given an exclusive interview to the *Mail*. Callers to a radio phone-in which Melissa insisted on listening to have described me as an 'antifeminist moron' and a 'parasite on the taxpayers who paid for my education'. I was so furious I almost phoned up myself.

But instead I switched the radio off and took three deep breaths. I'm not going to let myself get hassled. I have other things to think about. Fourteen guests have arrived for the charity lunch and are milling around on the lawn. I have wild-mushroom tartlets to bake, asparagus sauce to finish, and salmon fillets to roast.

I desperately wish Nathaniel was here to keep me calm. But he's gone off to Buckingham to pick up some koi carp for the pond, which Trish has suddenly decided she must have. Apparently they cost hundreds of pounds and all the celebrities have them. It's ridiculous. No one ever even *looks* in the pond.

The doorbell rings just as I'm opening the oven, and I sigh. Not another guest. We've had four late acceptances this morning, which has totally thrown my schedule.

I put the tray of tarts in the oven, gather up the remaining scraps of pastry, and start to wipe down my rolling pin.

'Samantha?' Trish taps at the door. 'We have another guest!'

'*Another* one?' I turn round, wiping flour off my cheek. 'But I've just put the starters in the oven . . .'

'It's a friend of yours. He says he needs to speak to you urgently. About business?' Trish raises her eyebrow at me significantly—then steps aside. And I freeze in astonishment.

It's Guy. Standing in Trish's kitchen. In his immaculate Jermyn Street suit. I stare at him, unable to speak, utterly flabbergasted.

Judging by his expression, he's pretty gobsmacked, too.

'Oh my God,' he says slowly, his eyes running over my uniform, my rolling pin, my floury hands. 'You really are a housekeeper.'

'Yes.' I lift my chin. 'I really am.'

'Samantha . . .' says Trish from the door. '*Not* that I want to interrupt, but . . . Starters in ten minutes?'

'Of course, Mrs Geiger.' I automatically bob a curtsy as Trish leaves and Guy's eyes nearly fall out of his head.

'You *curtsy*?'

'The curtsying was a bit of a mistake,' I admit. I catch his appalled eye and feel a giggle rising. 'Guy, what are you *doing* here?'

'I'm here to persuade you to come back.'

'I'm not coming back. Excuse me.' I get my asparagus sauce out of the fridge, pour it into a pan and and set it on a gentle heat.

Guy is watching in bemusement. 'Samantha,' he says. 'We need to talk.'

'I'm busy.' The kitchen timer goes off and I open the bottom oven to take out my rosemary garlic rolls. I feel a surge of pride as I see them, all golden brown and wafting a delicious, herby scent. I can't resist taking a nibble out of one, then offering it to Guy.

'You *made* these?' He looks astounded. 'I didn't know you could cook.'

'I couldn't. I learned.' I reach into the fridge again for some unsalted butter and break a knob into the foaming asparagus sauce.

'I have a job offer for you,' says Guy. He reaches into his inside pocket and produces a white letter. 'Here. Take a look.'

'I'm not interested!' I reply. 'Don't you understand?' I turn the hob down to a simmer and lean against the counter. 'I've learned a different way to live. I do my day's work, and I finish . . . and that's it. I'm *free*. I don't need to take paperwork home. I don't need to have my BlackBerry switched on twenty-four hours a day, seven days a week. I don't have that constant pressure any more. I'm not stressed out. And it suits me.'

I open the bottom oven, take out my trays of tartlets and start decanting them onto small warmed plates.

'I'll help,' says Guy, coming over.

'You can't *help*.' I roll my eyes.

'Of course I can.' To my astonishment he takes off his jacket, rolls up his sleeves and puts on a cherry-sprigged apron. 'What do I do?'

I can't help a tiny giggle. He looks so incongruous.

'Fine.' I hand him a tray. 'You can take in the starters with me.'

We head to the dining room, carrying the mushroom tartlets and the bread rolls. As we enter the white-canopied room, the chatter breaks off and fourteen dyed, lacquered heads turn. Trish's guests are seated round the table, sipping champagne, each wearing a suit of a different pastel colour. It's like walking into a Dulux paint chart.

'And this is Samantha!' says Trish, whose cheeks are a bright shade of pink. 'Our housekeeper . . . and also top lawyer!'

To my embarrassment a spattering of applause breaks out.

'We saw you in the papers!' says a woman in cream.

'This is Guy, who's helping me out today,' I say, beginning to serve the mushroom tarts.

'He's *also* a partner at Carter Spink,' adds Trish proudly.

I can see impressed glances being exchanged across the table. An elderly woman at the end turns to Trish, looking bewildered.

'Is *all* your help lawyers?'

'Not all,' says Trish airily. 'But having had a Cambridge-educated housekeeper, I could never go back.'

'Where do you get them from?' a red-haired woman asks avidly. 'Is there a special agency?'

'It's called Oxbridge Housekeepers,' says Guy, placing a mushroom tart in front of her. 'Only those with first-class honours can apply.'

'Shut *up*,' I mutter. 'Just serve the food.'

At last all the ladies are served and we retreat to the empty kitchen.

'Very funny,' I say, plonking the tray down with a crash.

'Well, for God's sake, Samantha. Do you expect me to take all this *seriously*?' He takes off the apron and throws it down on the table. 'Serving food to a bunch of airheads. You have more brains than anyone in that room, and you're serving them? You're *curtsying* to them? You're cleaning their *bathrooms*?'

He sounds so passionate, I turn round, shocked. His face is flushed and all traces of teasing have gone.

'Samantha, you're living in fantasyland!' he shouts. 'This is all fun because you've never done it before! But it'll wear off! Can't you *see*?'

I feel a pricking of uncertainty inside, which I ignore. 'No, it won't.' I give my asparagus sauce a determined stir. 'I love this life.'

'Will you still love it when you've been cleaning bathrooms for ten years? Get real.' He comes over to the cooker and I turn away. 'So you needed a break. Fine. But now you need to come back to real life.'

'This *is* real life for me,' I shoot back. 'It's more real than my life used to be. I'm not going back to that pressure. I worked seven days a week, for seven bloody years—'

'Exactly. Exactly! And just as you get the reward, you *bail out*?' He clutches his head. 'Samantha, do you realise how bad this all looks for Carter Spink? You have them over a barrel! They want the world to see you walking back into that office. They'll pay you whatever you want. You can earn enough to retire after ten years. You'll be set up for life! *Then* you can go and pick strawberries or sweep floors or whatever it is you want to do.'

I open my mouth automatically to respond . . . but all of a sudden my words have dried up. I can't quite track my thoughts. They're jumping about all over the place in confusion.

'You earned your partnership,' says Guy, his tone quieter. 'You earned it, Samantha. Use it.'

Guy doesn't say any more on the subject. He's always known exactly when to close an argument. He helps me serve the salmon, then gives me a hug and tells me to call him as soon as I've had time to think. And then he's gone, and I'm left alone in the kitchen, my thoughts churning.

I was so certain. I was so sure of myself. But now . . .

His arguments keep playing out in my mind. Maybe this is all a novelty. Maybe after a few years of a simpler life I won't be content.

I have a brain. I worked for my partnership. I earned it.

I bury my head in my hands, resting my elbows on the table, listening to my own heartbeat in my chest, thumping away like a question. *What am I going to do? What am I going to do?*

And yet all the time I'm being pushed towards one answer. The rational answer. The answer which makes most sense.

I know what it is. I'm just not sure I'm ready to face up to it yet.

It takes me until six o'clock. The lunch is over and I've cleared it away. Trish's guests have wandered round the garden and had cups of tea and melted away. As I walk out into the soft, balmy evening, Nathaniel and Trish are standing by the pond, with a plastic tank by Nathaniel's feet.

'This is a kumonryu,' Nathaniel is saying as he scoops something out of the tank with a big green net. 'Want to have a look?' As I get nearer I see an enormous patterned fish flapping noisily in the net. He offers it to Trish and she reels back with a little shriek.

'Get it away! Put it in the pond!'

'It cost you two hundred quid,' says Nathaniel with a shrug. 'I thought you might want to say hello.'

'Put them all in.' Trish shudders. 'I'll come and see them when they're swimming about.' She turns and heads back towards the house.

'All right?' Nathaniel looks up at me. 'How was the charity lunch?'

'It was fine.'

'Did you hear the news?' He scoops another fish into the pond. 'Eamonn's got engaged! He's having a party next weekend at the pub.'

'That's . . . that's great.' My mouth is dry. Come on. Just tell him.

'Nathaniel, I'm going back.' I close my eyes, trying to ignore the stab of pain inside. 'I'm going back to London.'

For a moment he doesn't move. Then very slowly he turns round, the net still in his hand, his face expressionless. 'Right,' he says.

'I'm going back to my old job as a lawyer.' My voice shakes a little. 'Guy from my old firm came down today, and he made me realise . . .' I break off and gesture helplessly.

'Realise what?' Nathaniel says, his brow furrowing a little.

'I can't be a housekeeper all my life.' I sound more defensive than I'd like. 'I'm a trained lawyer. I have a brain.'

'I know you have a brain.' Now *he* sounds defensive. Oh God. I'm not managing this well.

'I've earned partnership. Full equity partnership at Carter Spink.' I gaze up at him, trying to convey the significance of this. 'It's the most prestigious . . . lucrative . . . amazing . . . I can make enough money in a few years to retire.'

Nathaniel doesn't seem too impressed. 'At what cost?'

'What do you mean?'

'I mean that when you turned up here, you were a nervous wreck. You were like some freaked-out rabbit. White as a sheet. Stiff as a board. You looked like you hadn't ever seen the sun, you looked like you hadn't ever *enjoyed* yourself—'

'You're exaggerating.'

'I'm not. Can't you *see* how much you've changed? You're not edgy any more. You're not a bundle of nerves.'

'OK, so I've relaxed a bit!' I throw up my hands. 'I know I've calmed down and I've learned to cook and iron and pull pints . . . and I've had a wonderful time. But it's like a holiday. It can't last for ever.'

Nathaniel shakes his head in despair. 'So after all this you're just going to go back and carry on as though nothing happened?'

'It'll be different this time! I'll make it different. I'll keep a balance.'

'Who are you kidding?' Nathaniel grips my shoulders. 'Samantha, it'll be the same stress, the same lifestyle—'

I feel a sudden surge of anger towards him for not understanding.

'Well, at least I *tried* something new!' My words pour out in a torrent.

'At least I went out and tried the challenge of a different life for a bit.'

'What's that supposed to mean?' His grasp loosens in shock.

'It means, what have *you* ever tried, Nathaniel?' I know I sound shrill and aggressive but I can't help myself. 'You live in the same village you grew up in, you run the family business, you're buying a nursery down the road . . . you're practically still in the *womb*. So before you lecture me on the way to live my life, try living one of your own, OK?'

I break off, panting, to see Nathaniel looking as though I've slapped him. 'I . . . didn't mean it,' I mumble.

I take a few steps away, feeling near to tears. This isn't the way things were supposed to go. Nathaniel was supposed to support me and give me a hug and tell me I was making the right decision. Instead, here we are, standing yards apart, not even looking at each other.

'I thought about spreading my wings.' Nathaniel's voice sounds stiff. 'There's a nursery in Cornwall I'd die to own. Fantastic piece of land, fantastic business . . . but I didn't look at it. I preferred not to be six hours' drive away from you.' He shrugs.

I don't know how to reply. For a while there's silence, except for the cooing of pigeons down at the end of the garden.

'Nathaniel . . . I have to go back.' My voice isn't quite steady. 'I don't have any choice. But we can still be together. The two of us. We can still make it work. We'll have holidays . . . weekends . . . I'll come back for Eamonn's party . . . You won't know I've gone!'

He's silent for a moment, fiddling with the handle of the bucket. When at last he looks up, his expression makes my heart constrict.

'Yeah,' he says in a quiet voice. 'I will.'

Twelve

THE NEWS MAKES the front page of the *Daily Mail*. I am a genuine celebrity: SAMANTHA CHOOSES LAW OVER LOOS. As I come downstairs and enter the kitchen the next morning, Trish is poring over it, with Eddie reading another copy.

'Trish's interview has been printed!' he announces. 'Look!'

'"I always knew Samantha was a cut above the average house-keeper," says Trish Geiger, thirty-seven,' reads out Trish proudly. '"We often discussed philosophy and ethics together over the Hoover.'''

She looks up and her face changes. 'Samantha, are you all right? You look absolutely washed out.'

'I didn't sleep that well,' I admit, and flick on the kettle.

I spent the night at Nathaniel's. We didn't talk any more about my going. But at three o'clock, when I looked over at him, he was awake too, staring up at the ceiling.

'You need energy!' says Trish, perturbed. 'It's your big day! You need to look your best!'

'I will.' I try to smile. 'I just need a cup of coffee.'

It's going to be a huge day. The Carter Spink PR department swung into action as soon as I made my decision, and have turned my return into a full media event. There's going to be a big press conference at lunchtime in front of the Geigers' house, where I'll say how delighted I am to be going back to Carter Spink. Several of the partners are going to shake my hand for the photographers and I'll give a few short interviews. And then we're all going back to London on the train.

'So,' says Eddie as I spoon coffee into the pot. 'All packed up?'

'Pretty much. And, Mrs Geiger . . . here.' I hand Trish the folded blue uniform which I've been carrying under my arm. 'It's clean and pressed. Ready for your next housekeeper.'

As Trish takes the uniform she looks suddenly stricken. 'Of course,' she says, her voice jumpy. 'Thank you, Samantha.' She clasps a napkin to her eyes.

'There, there,' says Eddie, patting her on the back. He looks rather moist around the eyes himself. Oh God, now I feel like crying myself.

'I'm really grateful for everything,' I gulp. 'And I'm sorry for leaving you in the lurch.'

'We know you've made the right decision.' Trish dabs her eyes.

'We're very proud of you,' chips in Eddie gruffly.

'Anyway!' Trish pulls herself together and takes a sip of coffee. 'I've decided to make a *speech* at the press conference. I'm sure the press will be expecting me to speak.'

'Absolutely,' I say, a little nonplussed. 'Good idea.'

'After all, now we're becoming media personalities—'

'Media personalities?' interrupts Eddie incredulously. 'We're not media personalities.'

'Of course we are! I'm in the *Daily Mail*!' A faint flush comes to Trish's face. 'This could be just the beginning for us, Eddie. If we hired the right publicist we could be on reality TV. Or . . . advertise Campari.'

'Campari?' expostulates Eddie. 'Trish, you don't *drink* Campari.'

'I could!' Trish is saying defensively as the doorbell rings. 'Or they could use coloured water . . .'

Smiling, I head into the hall, pulling my dressing gown around myself. Maybe it's Nathaniel, come to wish me luck.

But as I open the door, I see the entire PR team from Carter Spink standing on the doorstep, all in identical trouser suits.

'Samantha.' Hilary Grant, head of PR, runs her eyes over me. 'Ready?'

By twelve o'clock I'm wearing a black suit, black tights, black high heels, and the crispest white shirt I've ever seen. I've been professionally made up and my hair has been scraped back into a bun.

Hilary brought the clothes and the hairdresser and make-up artist. Now we're in the drawing room while she preps me on what to say to the press. For the thousand millionth time.

'What's the most important thing to remember?' she's demanding.

'Not to mention loos,' I say wearily.

'And if they ask about recipes?'

'I answer, "I'm a lawyer. My only recipe is the recipe for success."' Somehow I manage to utter the words straight-faced.

'The *News Today* team will follow you back to London.' Hilary consults her BlackBerry. 'We've given them access for the rest of the day.'

I cannot believe how big this has become. A news programme actually wants to do a fly-on-the-wall TV documentary section about my return to Carter Spink. Is there nothing else happening in the world?

The door opens and I hear Melissa's voice coming from the hall.

'So I can call you at the office to talk about my career plan?'

'Absolutely. Er . . . good idea.' Guy appears in the room and quickly shuts the door before Melissa can follow him in. 'Who the hell's *that*?'

'Melissa.' I roll my eyes heavenwards. 'Don't ask.'

'She says you taught her everything she knows.' Guy gives an amused grin. 'Would that be in corporate law—or scone-baking?'

'Ha ha,' I say politely.

'So,' Guy raises his eyebrows. 'How are you? Excited?'

'Yes.' I smile.

'You made the right decision, you know,' says Guy.

'I know.' I brush a fleck of cotton off my skirt.

Hilary taps her watch. 'It's nearly time.'

The entire world seems to have descended on the Geigers' house. As I venture out of the front door with Hilary and two PR managers, there are what looks like hundreds of people in the drive. A row of TV cameras is trained on me, photographers and journalists are in a crowd behind, and Carter Spink PR assistants are milling around and handing out coffee from a refreshments stand that has sprung up from nowhere.

I can see David Elldridge and Greg Parker standing by the cappuccino machine, both typing on their BlackBerries. The PR department wanted as many partners as possible for the photocall, but none of the others could make it.

'Samantha.' I look up to see Nathaniel coming across the gravel. His face is shadowed and his blue eyes are tense. 'How are you doing?'

'I'm . . . fine.' I look at him for a couple of seconds. 'It's all a bit crazy.'

I feel his hand clasping mine and intertwine my fingers between his as tightly as I can. I can feel his thumb rubbing mine, just like he did that first evening we had together. Like some private language.

'Are you going to introduce me, Samantha?' Guy saunters over.

'This is Guy,' I say reluctantly. 'I work with him at Carter Spink. Guy . . . Nathaniel.'

'Delighted to meet you!' Guy holds out his hand and Nathaniel is forced to let go of mine to shake it.

'So you look after the garden.' Guy looks around the drive. 'Very nice.'

I can see Nathaniel's fist forming at his side.

Please don't punch him, I pray urgently. *Don't* punch him—

To my relief I notice Iris coming through the gate, peering at all the journalists with interest.

'Look!' I say quickly to Nathaniel. 'Your mum.'

I greet Iris with a wave. As she reaches me she just looks at me for a few moments: at my bun, my black suit, my high-heeled shoes. 'Goodness,' she says at last.

'I know.' I give an awkward laugh. 'A bit different.'

'So, Samantha.' Her eyes rest softly on mine. 'You found your way.'

'Yes.' I swallow. 'Yes, I did. This is the right way for me, Iris. I'm a lawyer. I always was. It's a great opportunity.'

Iris nods, her expression guarded. 'Nathaniel told me all about it. I'm sure you've made the right decision.' She pauses. 'Well . . . goodbye, chicken. And good luck. We'll miss you.'

As I lean forward to hug her, I feel tears pricking my eyes. 'Iris . . . I don't know how to thank you,' I whisper. 'For everything you did.'

'You did it all yourself.' She squeezes me tight. 'I'm proud of you.'

'And it's not really goodbye.' I wipe my eyes with a tissue, praying my make-up hasn't run. 'I'll be back before you know it. I'm going to visit as many weekends as I can . . .'

'Samantha?' Hilary calls me from the refreshments stand, where she's talking to David Elldridge and Greg Parker. 'Can you come over here?'

'I'll be right there!' I call back.

'Samantha, before you go . . .' Iris takes hold of both my hands, her face twisted a little in anxiety. 'Sweetie, I'm sure you're doing what's best for you. But just remember, you only get your youth once.' She looks at my hand, smooth against hers. 'You only get these precious years once.'

'I'll remember.' I bite my lip. 'I promise.'

'Good.' She pats my hand. 'Off you go.'

As I walk over to the refreshments stand, Nathaniel's hand is tightly in mine. We're going to have to say goodbye in a couple of hours.

No. I can't think about that.

Hilary is looking a little stressed as I approach. 'Got your statement?'

'All set.' I take out the folded sheet of paper. 'Hilary, this is Nathaniel.'

Hilary's eyes run over him without interest. 'Hello,' she says. 'Now, Samantha, we'll start in about three minutes. The team are just distributing press packs . . .'

Three more minutes. Three minutes before my old life begins again.

'So . . . I'll be back for Eamonn's party,' I say, still clutching Nathaniel's hand. 'It's only a few days away. I'll catch the train down on Friday night, spend the weekend . . .'

'Not next weekend,' chips in Guy, shaking chocolate onto a cappuccino. He looks up. 'You'll be in Hong Kong.'

'What?' I say stupidly.

'Samatron are delighted you're back and they've asked for you on this merger. We're flying to Hong Kong tomorrow. Has no one told you?'

'No,' I say, staring at him in shock. 'No one's even mentioned it. So when will we be back?'

Guy shrugs. 'Couple of weeks?'

'Samantha!' says Elldridge, coming up. 'Has Guy mentioned, we want you on a corporate shooting weekend at the end of September? Up in Scotland, should be fun.'

'Right. Um, yes, that sounds great. The only thing is, I'm trying to keep some weekends free . . . keep a bit of balance in my life . . .'

Elldridge looks puzzled. 'You've *had* your break, Samantha,' he says jovially. 'Now it's back to work.'

'Realistically, I'd say you're not going to have a free weekend till Christmas,' puts in Guy.

Everything's moving too fast. I thought it would be different this time. I thought I'd have more control.

'Christmas,' echoes Nathaniel at last, looking thunderstruck.

'No,' I say at once. 'He's exaggerating. It won't be that bad.' I rub my brow. 'I'll be back before Christmas. I promise. Whatever it takes.'

A strange flicker passes over his face. 'Don't turn it into a duty.'

'*Duty?*' I stare at him. 'That's not what I meant.'

'Samantha!' snaps Hilary. 'You *really* don't have time for this.'

'You should go.' Nathaniel gestures with his head. 'You're busy.'

This is awful. It feels like everything is disintegrating between us. I have to do something. Reach out to him.

'Nathaniel, just tell me.' My voice trembles. 'Tell me before I go. That day in the farmhouse . . . what did you say to me?'

Nathaniel looks at me for a long moment, then something in his eyes seems to close up. 'It was long and boring and badly put.' He shrugs.

'Right! I'm going to announce you,' says Hilary.

She marches onto the lawn. 'Ladies and gentlemen of the press!' Hilary's voice is blaring through the microphone. 'I'm delighted to welcome you all here this morning. And to introduce our newest partner at Carter Spink, Samantha Sweeting!'

Applause breaks out as I cross the lawn but it barely touches my consciousness. All of a sudden I'm stranded in front of the nation's press and I don't know what I want. I don't know what I should do.

Slowly I unfold my statement and smooth it down.

'Good morning,' I say into the microphone, my voice stilted. 'I am delighted to be able to share my exciting news with you. After being made a wonderful offer by Carter Spink, I will be returning to the firm today as a partner. Needless to say . . . I'm thrilled.'

Somehow I can't make my voice sound thrilled. I glance across to where Nathaniel and Guy are standing together. Guy's talking and Nathaniel is listening, his face taut. What's Guy saying?

'I have been overwhelmed by the warmth and generosity of the Carter Spink welcome,' I continue hesitantly, 'and am honoured to be joining such a prestigious partnership of . . .'

My eyes return to Guy and Nathaniel but Nathaniel's vanished. Where's he gone? I can't concentrate on what I'm saying.

'Talent and excellence!' snaps Hilary from the sidelines.

'Um . . . yes.' I find my place on the sheet. 'Talent. And excellence.'

A titter goes through the journalists. I'm not doing a good job here.

'Carter Spink's quality of service is . . . um . . . second to none,' I continue, trying to sound convincing.

'Better quality than the toilets you used to clean?' calls out a journalist with ruddy cheeks.

'We are not taking questions at this stage!' says Hilary crossly. 'And we are taking no questions on the subject of toilets, bathrooms, or any other form of sanitary ware. Samantha, carry on.'

'Unspeakable, were they?' laughs the ruddy-cheeked guy.

'Samantha, carry *on*,' spits Hilary, looking livid.

'They certainly were not unspeakable!' Trish comes striding onto the lawn, her fuchsia heels sinking into the grass. 'I will not have my toilets maligned! They're all Royal Doulton. They're Royal Doulton,' she repeats into the microphone. 'Highest quality. You're doing very well, Samantha.' She pats me on the shoulder.

All the journalists are laughing by now. Hilary's face is puce.

'Excuse me,' she says to Trish with suppressed fury. 'We are in the middle of a press conference here. Could you please leave?'

'This is my lawn,' says Trish, lifting her chin. 'The press want to hear from me, too. Eddie, where's my speech?'

'You're not making a *speech*,' says Hilary in horror, as Eddie darts onto the lawn with a printed scroll sheet.

'I would like to thank my husband Eddie for all his support,' begins Trish, ignoring Hilary. 'I would like to thank the *Daily Mail* . . .'

'This isn't the bloody Oscars.' Hilary looks apoplectic.

'Don't swear at me,' retorts Trish sharply. 'I am the owner of this residence, I'd like to remind you.'

'Mrs Geiger, have you seen Nathaniel?' I look desperately around the crowd for the millionth time. 'He's disappeared.'

'Who's Nathaniel?' asks one of the journalists.

'He's the gardener,' puts in the ruddy-faced guy. 'Lover boy.'

'Samantha,' says Hilary furiously. 'Please get back to the official statement.' She pushes Trish away from the microphone.

'Don't you touch me!' shrills Trish. 'I'll sue. Samantha Sweeting is my lawyer, you know.'

'Oy, Samantha! What does Nathaniel think about you going back to London?' shouts someone.

'Have you put your career over love?' chimes in a bright-faced girl.

'No,' I say desperately. 'I just . . . I need to talk to him. Where *is* he? Guy?' I hurry towards him over the grass. 'What did you say to Nathaniel? You have to tell me.'

'I advised him to keep his dignity.' Guy gives an arrogant shrug. 'To be honest, I told the him the truth. You won't be back.'

'How *dare* you?' I gasp in fury. 'How *dare* you say that? I will be back! And he can come to London—'

'Oh, please.' Guy raises his eyes. 'He doesn't want to hang around like some sad bastard, getting in your way, embarrassing you . . .'

'Embarrassing me?' I stare at Guy, aghast. 'Is that what you *said* to him? Is that why he left?'

'For God's sake, Samantha,' snaps Guy impatiently. 'He's a *gardener*.'

My fist acts before I can think. It hits Guy right on the jaw.

I can hear gasps and shouts and cameras snapping all around, but I don't care. That is the best thing I have ever done.

'Ow! Fuck!' He clasps his face. 'What the fuck was that for?'

The journalists are all crowding round now, hurling questions at us, but I ignore them.

'It's you who embarrass me,' I spit at Guy. 'You're worth nothing compared to him. *Nothing*.' To my horror I can feel tears coming to my eyes. I have to find Nathaniel. Right now.

'Everything's fine! Everything's fine!' Hilary comes thundering across the grass, a blur of pinstripe trouser suit. 'Samantha's a little over-wrought today.' She grabs my arm in a vice-like grip, her teeth bared in a rictus smile. 'Just a friendly disagreement between partners. Samantha is looking forward to the challenges of leading a world-renowned legal team. Aren't you, Samantha?' Her grip tightens. '*Aren't you, Samantha?*'

'I . . . don't know,' I say in despair. 'I just don't know. I'm sorry, Hilary.' I wrench my arm out of hers and start running over the grass, towards the gates.

'Stop her!' Hilary is yelling to all the PR staff. 'Block her way!'

Girls in trouser suits start coming at me from all directions like some kind of SWAT team. Somehow I dodge them. One makes a grab for my jacket and I wriggle out of it. I throw off my high heels too, and pick up my pace, barely wincing at the gravel under my soles as I push open the gate and run down the street, not looking back.

By the time I arrive at the pub my tights have been torn to shreds on the road, my hair has come out of its bun and half fallen down my back, my make-up is swimming in sweat, and my chest is burning with pain. But I don't care. I have to find Nathaniel. I have to tell him he's the most important thing in my life, more important than any job.

I have to tell him I love him.

I don't know why I didn't realise it before, why I never said it before. It's so obvious. It's so blinding.

'Eamonn!' I call urgently as I approach, and he looks up in surprise from where he's collecting up glasses. 'I have to talk to Nathaniel. Is he here?'

'Here?' Eamonn appears lost for words. 'Samantha, you've missed him. He's already gone.'

'Gone?' I come to a halt, panting. 'Gone where?'

'To look at this business he wants to buy.'

'The one in Bingley?' I gulp in relief, still out of breath.

'That's not where . . .' Eamonn looks awkward. I stare at him, feeling a sudden foreboding. 'Samantha . . . he's gone to Cornwall. He said he might be down there a couple of weeks. I thought he'd have told you.'

'Um, no,' I say, my voice barely working. 'He didn't.'

Suddenly my legs feel like jelly. I sink down onto one of the barrels, my head pounding. He's gone to Cornwall, just like that. Without even saying goodbye. Without even talking about it.

'He left a note in case you dropped by.' Eamonn feels in his pocket and produces an envelope.

'Thanks, Eamonn.' I take the envelope and pull out the paper.

S, I think we both know this is the end of the line. Let's quit while we're ahead. Just know that this summer was perfect. N

Tears are flooding down my cheeks as I read it, over and over. I can't believe he's gone. How can he have given up on us? Whatever Guy said to him, whatever he thought. How can he have just *left*?

I hear a sound and look up to see Guy and a crowd of journalists gathered around me. I hadn't even noticed.

'Samantha,' says Guy, his voice low and conciliatory. 'Things may seem bad at the moment.' He glances at the note. 'But you have a fantastic career to get on with.'

I don't answer. My shoulders are hunched over, my nose is running and my hair is falling around my face in lacquered strands.

'There's nothing to keep you here now.' Guy takes a step forward and puts my glossy high-heeled shoes on the table beside me. 'Come on, partner. Everyone's waiting.'

Thirteen

I FEEL NUMB. It really is all over. I'm sitting in a first-class compartment on the train to London, with the other partners. It's an express train. In a couple of hours we'll be back. I have a new pair of tights on. My make-up has been repaired. I've even given a fresh statement to the press, hastily constructed by Hilary: 'Although I will always feel affection for my friends in Lower Ebury, nothing is more exciting and important in my life right now than my career with Carter Spink.'

I said it pretty convincingly. I even found a smile from somewhere as

I shook David Elldridge's hand. It's just possible they might print a picture of that, rather than the one of me punching Guy. You never know.

Wedged in the corner opposite me is the TV cameraman for the news documentary, together with the producer, Dominic, a guy with trendy glasses and a denim jacket. I can feel the camera lens on me, following every move, zooming in and out, catching every expression.

'And so lawyer Samantha Sweeting leaves the village where she was known only as a domestic help,' Dominic is saying into his microphone in a low, TV-commentary voice. 'The question is . . . does she have any regrets?' He gives me a questioning glance.

'I thought you were supposed to be fly-on-the-wall,' I snap with a baleful look.

'Here you go!' Guy dumps a heavy set of contracts on my lap. 'Here's the Samatron deal. Get your teeth into that.'

I look at the pile of paper, inches thick. Once upon a time, seeing a brand-new, fresh contract gave me a rush of adrenaline. Now I feel blank.

I leaf through the contract, trying to summon up some enthusiasm.

'From cookery books to contracts,' murmurs Dominic into his microphone. 'From wooden spoons to writs.'

This guy is really starting to piss me off.

I turn back to my contract, but the words are jumbling in front of my eyes. All I can think about is Nathaniel. I've tried calling him but he isn't answering. Or replying to texts. It's like he doesn't want to know any more. My eyes are starting to blur with tears again and I blink them away furiously. I can't cry. I'm a partner. Partners do not cry. Trying to get a grip on myself, I look out of the window instead. We seem to be slowing down, which is a bit weird.

'An announcement for all passengers . . .' A voice comes crackling out of the loudspeakers. 'This train has been rescheduled as a slow train. It will be stopping at Hitherton, Marston Bridge, Bridbury . . .'

'What?' Guy looks up. 'A *slow* train?'

'. . . and will arrive at Paddington half an hour after the scheduled time,' the voice is saying. 'Apologies for any . . .'

'*Half an hour?*' David Elldridge whips out his mobile phone, looking livid. 'I'm going to have to reschedule my meeting.'

'I'll have to put off the Pattinson Lobb people.' Guy looks equally pissed off, and is already jabbing at the speed-dial on his phone.

'Davina,' Greg Parker is saying into his phone. 'Tell the team I'll be half an hour late, I'm sending an email—' He puts down his phone and immediately starts typing into his BlackBerry.

I'm watching all this frenzied action incredulously. They all look so stressed. So the train's going to be late. It's *half an hour*. That's thirty minutes. How can anyone get so het up over just thirty minutes?

The train pulls into Hitherton station and comes slowly to a halt. I glance out of the window—then gasp aloud. A huge hot-air balloon is hovering in the air, just a few feet above the station building. It's bright red and yellow, with people waving from a basket.

'Hey, look!' I exclaim. 'Look at that! It's amazing!'

No one lifts their head. They're all frantically tapping their keyboards. No one is interested in anything except the contents of their BlackBerry. Is this what I'm supposed to be like? Because I've forgotten how. I look at them all, the cream of the legal world, dressed in their handmade suits, holding state-of-the-art computers. Missing out. Not even *caring* that they're missing out. Living in their own world.

I don't belong here. That's not my world any more. *I'm not one of them*.

I suddenly know it, with the deepest certainty I've ever felt. I don't fit. Maybe I did once, but not any more. I shouldn't be here. This isn't what I want from my life. This isn't who I want to be.

I have to get out. Now.

Up and down the train people are stepping in and out, banging doors, hefting bags. As calmly as I can I reach for my suitcase, pick up my bag and stand up.

'I'm sorry,' I say. 'I made a mistake. I've only just realised.'

'*What?*' Guy looks up.

'I'm sorry I've wasted your time.' My voice wavers slightly. 'But . . . I can't stay. I can't do this.'

'Is this to do with the gardener?' Guy sounds exasperated. 'Because quite frankly—'

'No! It's to do with *me*! I just . . .' I hesitate, searching for the words. 'I don't want to be someone who doesn't look out of the window.'

Guy's face doesn't register an iota of understanding.

'Goodbye.' I open the train door and step out, but Guy grabs me roughly.

'Samantha, stop this crap. I *know* you. And you're a *lawyer*.'

'You *don't* know me, Guy.' My words burst out in a surge of sudden anger. 'Don't define me. I'm not a lawyer. I'm a *person*.'

I pull my arm out of his and slam the door shut, shaking all over. The next moment it opens again and Dominic and the cameraman pile out after me.

'And so!' Dominic is murmuring excitedly into his microphone. 'In a shock turn of events, Samantha Sweeting has rejected her glittering legal career!'

I am really going to thump him in a minute.

'This morning she was devastated to lose the man she loved. Now she has no career either.' He pauses, then adds in sepulchral tones, 'Who knows what dark thoughts are going through her mind?'

What's he trying to imply? That I'm going to throw myself under the next train? He'd love that, wouldn't he? He'd probably win an Emmy.

'Do you have a plan, Samantha?' asks Dominic, thrusting his microphone at me. 'A goal?'

'Sometimes you don't need a goal in life,' I say defensively. 'You don't need to know the big picture. You just need to know what you're going to do next.'

'And what are you going to do next?'

'I'm . . . working on it.' I turn and march away from the camera, towards the waiting room. As I near it, I see a guard coming out.

'Um, hello,' I say. 'I'd like to know how to get to . . .' I trail off, uncertainly. Where am I going? 'To . . . um . . . Cornwall,' I hear myself saying.

'*Cornwall?*' He looks taken aback. 'Whereabouts in Cornwall?'

'I don't know.' I swallow. 'Not exactly. But I need to get there, as quickly as possible.'

There can't be that many nurseries for sale in Cornwall. I'll track down the right one. I'll find him. Somehow.

'Well.' The guard's brow creases. 'I'll have to consult the book.' He disappears into his room. I can hear Dominic whispering feverishly into his microphone, but I don't care.

'Here we are.' The guard emerges, holding a piece of paper covered in pencil. 'Six changes, I'm afraid, to Penzance. And it'll be one hundred and twenty pounds. Train'll be a while,' he adds. 'Platform Two.'

'Thanks.' I pick up my suitcase and head over the footbridge. I can hear Dominic hurrying after me with the cameraman.

'Samantha appears to have taken leave of her senses,' he's panting into his microphone. 'Who knows what rash move she will make next?'

He *so* wants me to jump, doesn't he? I'm just going to ignore him.

'With no address,' I hear him continuing, 'Samantha is setting off on a long and uncertain journey to find the man who rejected her this morning. Is this a wise plan?'

OK, I've had enough.

'Maybe it isn't a wise plan!' I turn to face him. 'Maybe I won't find him. Maybe he won't even want to know. But I have to try.'

Dominic opens his mouth again to speak.

'Shut up,' I say. 'Just shut up.'

It seems like hours before I hear the sound of the train in the distance. But it's the wrong side. It's another train for London. As it pulls in

I can hear the doors opening and people piling on and off.

'London train!' the guard is shouting. 'Platform One.'

My eyes move idly over the windows, at people in their seats, talking, sleeping, reading, listening to iPods—

And then everything seems to freeze. Am I *dreaming*?

It's Nathaniel. On the London train. He's three yards away, sitting in a window seat, staring ahead rigidly.

What—Why is he—

'Nathaniel!' I try to shout, but my voice has turned into a husk. 'Nathaniel!' I wave my arms frantically, trying to get his attention.

'It's him!' exclaims Dominic. 'Nathaniel!' he yells, his voice like a foghorn. 'Over here, mate!'

'Nathaniel!' At last my voice is working. 'Na-than-iel!'

At my desperate scream he finally looks up and jolts with shock as he sees me. For a moment his expression is sheer disbelief. Then his whole face seems to expand in a slow explosion of delight.

I can hear the train doors slamming. It's about to leave.

I can see him getting up inside the train, grabbing his rucksack, squeezing past the woman in the next seat. Then he disappears from view, just as the train starts pulling out of the station.

'Too late,' says the cameraman lugubriously. 'He'll never make it.'

My chest is too tight for me to answer. All I can do is stare at the departing train, moving past carriage by carriage, speeding up, faster and faster . . . until finally it's gone.

And Nathaniel is standing on the platform. He's there.

Without moving my eyes from his I begin to walk along the platform, speeding up as I reach the footbridge. On the opposite side he does the same. We reach the top of the steps, walk forward a way and both come to a halt, a few feet apart.

'I thought you were going down to Cornwall,' I say at last. 'To buy your nursery.'

'I changed my mind. Thought I might . . . visit a friend in London instead.' He glances at my suitcase. 'Where were you going?'

I clear my throat. 'I was thinking . . . Cornwall.'

'Cornwall?' He stares at me.

'Uh huh.'

Nathaniel leans against the barricade, his thumbs in his pockets, and surveys the wooden slats of the bridge. 'So . . . where are your friends?'

'Gone. And they're not my friends. I punched Guy,' I add proudly.

Nathaniel throws back his head and laughs. 'So they fired you.'

'I fired them,' I correct him.

'You did?' says Nathaniel in amazement. He reaches out for my hand but I don't take it. Underneath my joy I'm still feeling unsettled. The hurt of this morning hasn't gone. I can't pretend everything's OK.

'I got your note.' I lift my eyes to his and Nathaniel flinches.

'Samantha . . . I wrote you a different one on the train. In case you wouldn't see me in London.'

He fishes awkwardly in his pocket and pulls out a letter, several sheets long; both sides of the paper covered in writing. I hold it for a few moments without reading it.

'What does it say?' I raise my eyes.

'It's long and boring.' His gaze burns into mine. 'And badly put.'

I turn the pages slowly over in my fingers. Here and there I glimpse words that make my eyes fill instantly.

'So,' I manage.

'So.' Nathaniel's arms come round my waist; his warm mouth lands on mine. As he holds me tight I can feel the tears spilling onto my cheeks. This is where I belong. This is where I fit. I finally draw away and look up at him, wiping my eyes.

'Where now?' He looks down over the bridge and I follow his gaze. The railway track extends in both directions, way into the distance. 'Which way?'

I look along the endless line, squinting in the sunshine. I'm twenty-nine years old. I can go anywhere. Do anything. Be anyone I like.

'There's no rush,' I say at last and reach up to kiss him again.

Sophie Kinsella

Sophie Kinsella wrote her first novel under her real name, Madeleine Wickham, at the age of twenty-four, whilst she was working as a financial journalist and *The Tennis Party* was an immediate success. She wrote five further novels under this name but then decided that she wanted to write in a totally different style. She submitted her first 'Sophie Kinsella' novel anonymously to her existing publishers and it was snapped up without her editors knowing that she was already one of their authors. It wasn't until the appropriately titled *Can You Keep a Secret?* was published that Madeleine/Sophie revealed her true identity for the first time.

In September 2000, Sophie published her first novel in the *Shopaholic* series—*The Secret Dreamworld of a Shopaholic*. The book's heroine, Becky Bloomwood—a fun and feisty financial journalist who loves shopping but is hopeless with money—captured the hearts of readers worldwide and she has since featured in five further adventures and was brought to the big screen in 2009 with the hit Disney movie, *Confessions of a Shopaholic*.

The Undomestic Goddess is one of Sophie's stand alone novels and the author explains how it came about. 'The novel came from two ideas that were in my head. I am completely useless domestically and I've always thought it would be a good source of comedy. I can't iron, find tidying up soul-destroying and I have to psyche myself up to cook. I can make easy family meals but I'm not brave enough to host a proper grown-up dinner party!' So would she get caterers in, as Samantha does in the novel, and try to pass the food off as her own? 'I'd love to try but I know I couldn't carry it off—my friends know me too well, sadly. No, I'm not a good cook—although I did learn to bake bread for this novel. I have a good friend who is a domestic goddess and we spent the day baking bread and it was fantastic fun and very therapeutic. We made four gorgeous loaves, ate one for tea—hoovering it all up in minutes with her homemade jam—and I could see that the other three would be gone equally quickly and I kept thinking, God, now we need to do it all over again! For that day it was lovely, but never again.

'And then I've always loved the concept of making a horrendous mistake and running away. I thought that was really interesting because you hear about someone being dishonest, embezzling and trying to cover it up, but you don't hear about someone basically making an honest mistake.'

Sophie Kinsella is married with four sons but even with a demanding family she has never taken time away from her writing. 'I am not someone who can just switch off and not think about books for six months. When I'm not writing, I'm thinking—and shopping, of course, lots and lots of shopping! Well, a girl has to do her research, doesn't she?'

Also from Sophie Kinsella:

Fiction:
Writing as Madeleine Wickham:
The Tennis Party, A Desirable Residence, Swimming Pool Sunday, The Gatecrasher, The Wedding Girl, Cocktails for Three, Sleeping Arrangements.

Writing as Sophie Kinsella:
Shopaholic Series: *The Secret Dreamworld of a Shopaholic, Shopaholic Abroad, Shopaholic Ties the Knot, Shopaholic and Sister, Shopaholic and Baby, Mini Shopaholic.*

Stand Alone Sophie Kinsella novels:
Can You Keep A Secret?, The Undomestic Goddess, Remember Me?, Twenties Girl.

Movies:
Confessions of a Shopaholic.

PHILIPPA GREGORY

the Queen's Fool

In Tudor England it is a crime to follow the Jewish religion, and from an early age Hannah Green has learned to hide her faith. She also has the troubled gift of second sight. Both things make her vulnerable to accusations of heresy and witchcraft.

In the treacherous world of the Tudor court, Hannah desperately needs to find a protector.

SUMMER 1548

THE GIRL, GIGGLING and overexcited, was running in the sunlit garden, running away from her stepfather, but not so fast that he could not catch her. Her stepmother, seated in an arbour with Rosamund roses in bud all around her, caught sight of the fourteen-year-old girl and the handsome man chasing round the broad tree trunks on the smooth turf and smiled, determined to see only the best in both of them: the girl she was bringing up and the man she had adored for years.

He snatched at the hem of the girl's swinging gown and caught her up to him for a moment. 'A forfeit!' he said, his dark face close to her flushed cheeks.

They both knew what the forfeit would be. Like quicksilver she slid from his grasp and dodged to the far side of an ornamental fountain with a broad circular bowl. Elizabeth's excited face was reflected in the surface of the water as she leaned forward to taunt him.

'Can't catch me!'

''Course I can.'

She leaned low so that he could see her small breasts at the top of the square-cut green gown. She felt his eyes on her and the colour in her cheeks deepened. He watched, amused and aroused, as her neck flushed rosy pink.

'I can catch you any time I want to,' he said.

'Come on then!' she said, not knowing exactly what she was inviting, but knowing that she wanted to hear his feet pounding the grass behind her, and, more than anything else, to feel his arms round her, pulling her against the fascinating contours of his body, the scratchy embroidery of his doublet against her cheek. She gave a little scream and dashed away again down an *allée* of yew trees, where the Chelsea garden ran down to the river.

The queen, smiling, looked up from her sewing and saw her beloved stepdaughter racing between the trees, her handsome husband a few easy strides behind. She looked down again at her sewing and did not see him catch Elizabeth, whirl her round, and put her back to the red papery bark of the yew tree.

Elizabeth felt the smooth sweep of his moustache against her lips. She closed her eyes and tipped back her head to offer her lips, her neck to his mouth. When she felt his sharp teeth graze her skin, she was no longer a giggling child, she was a young woman in the heat of first desire.

Gently he loosened his grip on her waist, and his hand stole up the firmly boned stomacher to the neck of her gown, where he could slide a finger down inside her linen to touch her breasts. Her nipple was hard and aroused; when he rubbed it she gave a little mew of pleasure that made him chuckle at the predictability of female desire.

Elizabeth pressed herself against the length of his body, feeling his thigh push between her legs in reply. She had a sensation like an overwhelming curiosity. She longed to know what might happen next.

All at once he caught at the hem of her brocade skirt and pulled it up and up until he could get at her, sliding his practised hand up her thighs, underneath her linen shift. At his teasing touch, she melted and he could feel her almost dissolve beneath him. She would have fallen if he had not had a firm arm round her waist, and he knew at that moment that he could have the king's own daughter, Princess Elizabeth, against a tree in the queen's garden. The girl was a virgin in name alone. In reality, she was little more than a whore.

A light step on the path made him quickly turn, dropping Elizabeth's gown and putting her behind him, out of sight. He was afraid it was the queen, his wife, whose love for him was insulted every day that he seduced her ward under her very nose: Queen Catherine, who had been entrusted with the care of her stepdaughter the princess, who had sat at Henry VIII's deathbed but dreamed of this man.

But it was not the queen who stood before him on the path. It was only a girl, a little girl of about nine years old, with big, solemn dark eyes and a white Spanish cap tied under her chin. She carried two books strapped with bookseller's tape in her hand.

'How now, sweetheart!' he exclaimed, falsely cheerful. 'You gave me a start. I might have thought you a fairy, appearing so suddenly.'

She frowned at his rapid, over-loud speech, and then she replied, very slowly with a strong Spanish accent. 'Forgive me, sir. My father told me to bring these books to Sir Thomas Seymour.'

She proffered the package of books, and Tom Seymour was forced to step forward and take them from her hands. 'You're the bookseller's daughter,' he said cheerfully. 'The bookseller from Spain.'

She bowed her head in assent, not taking her scrutiny from his face.

'What are you staring at, child?' he asked, conscious of Elizabeth hastily rearranging her gown behind him.

'I was looking at you, sir, but I saw something most dreadful.'

'What?' he demanded, afraid she would say that she had seen him with a princess of England backed up against a tree like a common doxy.

'I saw a scaffold behind you,' said the surprising child, and then she turned and walked away.

Tom Seymour whirled back to Elizabeth. 'Did you hear that?'

The princess was trying to comb her disordered hair with fingers still shaking with desire. 'No,' she said silkily. 'Did she say something?'

'She only said that she saw the scaffold behind me!' He was more shaken than he wanted to reveal.

At the mention of the scaffold Elizabeth was suddenly alert. 'Why?' she snapped. 'Why should she say such a thing?'

'God knows,' he said. 'Probably mistook the word—she's foreign. Probably meant throne. Probably saw the throne behind me.'

But in Elizabeth's imagination the throne and the scaffold were always close neighbours. The colour drained from her face. 'Who is she?' Her voice was sharp with nervousness.

He turned to look for the child but the *allée* was empty. At the distant end of it he could see his wife, Catherine, walking slowly towards them, her back arched to carry the pregnant curve of her belly.

'Not a word,' he said quickly to the girl at his side. 'Not a word of this, sweetheart. You don't want to upset your stepmother.'

He hardly needed to warn her. The girl was always conscious that she must play a part. She might be only fourteen, but she had been trained in deceit for twelve long years since the death of her mother. She might feel desire, but she was always more alert to danger or ambition than to lust.

He took her cold hand and led her up the *allée* towards his wife. He tried for a merry smile. 'I caught her at last!' he called out. He glanced around. He could not see the child. 'We had such a race!' he cried.

I was that child, and that was the first sight I ever had of the Princess Elizabeth: panting with lust, damp with desire, rubbing herself like a cat against another woman's husband. But it was the first and last time I saw Tom Seymour. Within a year, he was dead on the scaffold, charged with treason, and Elizabeth had denied three times having anything more than the most common acquaintance with him.

WINTER 1552–3

'I REMEMBER THIS!' I said excitedly to my father, turning from the rail of the Thames barge as we tacked our way upstream. 'Father! I remember these gardens running down to the water, and the great houses, and the day you sent me to deliver some books to the English lord, and I came upon him in the garden with the princess.'

He found a smile for me, though his face was weary from our long journey. 'Do you, child?' he asked quietly. 'That was a happy summer for us. She said . . .' He broke off. We never mentioned my mother's name, even when we were alone. At first it had been a precaution to keep us safe from those who had killed her and would come after us, but now we were hiding from grief as well as from the Inquisition.

'Will we live here?' I asked hopefully.

'Nowhere as grand as this,' he said gently. 'We will have to start small, Hannah, in just a little shop. We have to make our lives again. And when we are settled then you will come out of boy's clothes, and dress as a girl again, and marry young Daniel Carpenter.'

'And can we stop running?' I asked, very low.

My father hesitated. We had been running from the Inquisition for so long that it was almost impossible to hope that we had reached a safe haven. We ran away the very night that my mother was found guilty of being a Jew—a false Christian, a 'Marrano'—by the Church court, and we were long gone when they released her to the civil court to be burned alive at the stake. First over the border to Portugal, then overland to Paris, all the way pretending to be something that we were not: a merchant and his young apprentice lad, pilgrims on the way to Chartres, a scholar and his tutor going to the great university of Paris.

We met my mother's cousins in Paris, and they sent us on to their kin in Amsterdam, where they directed us to London. We were to hide our race under English skies; we were to become Protestant Christians. We would learn to like it. I must learn to like it.

The kin—the People whose name cannot be spoken, whose faith is hidden, the People who are condemned to wander, banned from every country in Christendom—were thriving in secret in London as in Paris, as in Amsterdam. We all lived as Christians and kept the Sabbath in secret, and then, the very next day, went to Mass with a clean conscience. Our family helped us to London with letters of introduction to the d'Israeli family, who went here by the name of Carpenter, organised my betrothal to the Carpenter boy, financed my father's purchase of a printing press and found us rooms over a shop off Fleet Street.

In the months after our arrival my father set up his print shop with a determination to survive and to provide for me. At once, his stock of texts was much in demand, especially his copies of the gospels that he had brought inside the waistband of his breeches and now translated into English. He bought the books and manuscripts which had once belonged to the libraries of religious houses—destroyed by Henry, the king before the young king, Edward. My father went out daily and came back with something rare and precious, and when he had tidied it, and indexed it, everyone wanted to buy. At night, even when he was weary, he set print and ran off short copies of the gospels and simple texts for the faithful to study, all in English, all clear and simple. We sold them cheaply, at little more than cost price, to spread the word of God. We let it be known that we believed in giving the Word to the people. We could not have been better Protestants if our lives had depended on it.

Of course, our lives did depend on it.

I ran errands, read proofs, helped with translations, set print. On days when I was not busy in the print shop I stood outside to summon passers-by, still dressed in the boy's clothes I had used for our escape.

As I lounged against the wall of our shop, drinking in the weak English sunshine, I heard the ring of a spur against a cobblestone and I snapped my eyes open and leapt to attention. Before me, casting a long shadow, was a richly dressed young man, a tall hat on his head, a cape swinging from his shoulders, a thin silver sword at his side. He was the most breathtakingly handsome man I had ever seen.

Behind him was an older man, near thirty years of age, with the pale skin of a scholar, and dark, deep-set eyes. He was a writer—I saw the ink stain on the third finger of his right hand—and he was something greater even than this: a thinker, a man prepared to seek out what was hidden. He was a dangerous man, a man not afraid of heresies, not afraid of questions, a man who would seek the truth behind the truth.

I had been so interested in these two, the young man like a god, the older man like a priest, that I had not looked at the third. This third man was all dressed in white, gleaming like enamelled silver. I could hardly see him for the brightness of the sun on his sparkling cloak. I blinked, but still I could not see his face. Then I realised that the men were looking in the doorway of the bookshop next door.

Cursing myself for an idle fool, I jumped into their path and said clearly, in my newly acquired English accent, 'Good day to you, sirs. Can we help you? We have the finest collection of pleasing and moral books you will find in London, at the fairest of prices and—'

'I am looking for the shop of Oliver Green,' the young man said.

At the moment his dark eyes flicked to mine, I felt myself freeze, as if all the clocks in London had suddenly stopped still. I wanted to hold him: there, in his red slashed doublet in the winter sunshine, for ever. I wanted him to look at me and see me, me, as I truly was: not an urchin lad with a dirty face, but a girl, almost a young woman. But his glance flicked indifferently past me to our shop, and I came to my senses and held open the door for the three of them.

'This is the shop of the scholar and bookmaker Oliver Green. Step inside, my lords,' I invited them, and I shouted into the inner dark room: 'Father! Here are three great lords to see you.'

I heard the clatter as he pushed back his high printer's stool and came out, wiping his hands on his apron. 'Welcome,' he said. 'I am Oliver Green. And I will serve you in any way that I can do. Any way that is pleasing to the laws of the land, and the customs—'

'Yes, yes,' the young man said sharply. 'We hear that you are just come from Spain, Oliver Green.'

My father nodded. 'I am just come to England indeed, but we left Spain three years ago, sir.'

'Your name? It is a very English name?'

'It was Verde,' he said with a wry smile. 'It is easier for Englishmen if we call ourselves Green.'

'And you are a Christian? And a publisher of Christian theology and philosophy?' the young man asked.

I could see the small gulp in my father's throat at the dangerous question, but his voice was steady when he answered. 'Most certainly, sir.'

'And are you of the reformed or the old tradition?'

My father did not know what answer they wanted to this, nor could he know what might hang on it. Actually *we* might hang on it, or burn for it, or go to the block for it, however it was that they chose this day to deal with heretics in this country under the young King Edward.

'The reformed,' he said tentatively. 'Though christened into the old faith in Spain, I follow the English church now.'

I could smell the sweat of his terror, acrid as smoke. 'It's all right,' I said in a quick undertone in Spanish. 'I'm sure they want our books, not us.'

My father nodded to show he had heard me. But the young lord was onto my whisper at once. 'What did the lad say?'

'I said that you are scholars,' I lied in English.

'Go inside, *querida*,' my father said quickly to me. 'You must forgive the child, my lords. My wife died just three years ago and the child is a fool, only kept to mind the door.'

'The child speaks only the truth,' the older man remarked pleasantly as I hovered in the doorway. 'For we have not come to disturb you; there is no need to be afraid. I am a scholar, not an inquisitor. I only wanted to see your library.' He turned to me. 'But why did you say three lords?' he asked. 'There are only two of us, lad. How many can you see?'

I looked from the older man to the handsome young man and saw that there were, indeed, only two of them. The man in white had gone.

'I saw a third man behind you, sir,' I said to the older one. 'Out in the street. I am sorry. He is not there now.'

'She is a fool but a good girl,' my father said, waving me away.

'No, wait,' the young man said. 'Wait a minute. I thought this was a lad. A girl? Why d'you have her dressed as a boy?'

'And the third man?' his companion asked me. 'What was he like?'

'All in white,' I said through half-closed lips. 'And shining.'

'What did he wear?'

'I could only see a white cape.'

'And on his head?'

'I could only see the whiteness.'

'And his face?'

'I couldn't see his face for the brightness of the light.'

'D'you think he had a name, child?'

I could feel the word coming into my mouth though I did not understand it. 'Uriel.'

The man looked into my face as if he would read me like one of my father's books. 'Uriel?'

'Yes, sir.'

The younger man turned to my father. 'When you say she is a fool, d'you mean that she has the Sight?'

'She talks out of turn,' my father said stubbornly. 'Nothing more.'

'She has the Sight,' the older man breathed. 'Praise God, I come looking for manuscripts and I find a girl who sees Uriel and knows his holy name.' He turned to my father. 'Does she have any knowledge of sacred things? Has she read your books?'

'Before God, no,' my father said earnestly, lying with every sign of conviction. 'I swear to you, my lord, I have brought her up to be a good ignorant girl. She knows nothing, I promise you. Nothing.'

The older man shook his head. 'Please,' he said gently to my father, 'do not fear me. You can trust me. This girl has the Sight, hasn't she?'

'No,' my father said baldly, denying me for my own safety. 'She's nothing more than a fool. She's not worth your attention . . .'

'Peace,' the young man said. 'We did not come to distress you. This gentleman is John Dee, my tutor. I am Robert Dudley.'

At their names my father grew even more anxious, as well he might. The handsome young man was the son of the greatest man in the land: Lord John Dudley, protector of the King of England himself. If they took a liking to my father's library then we could find ourselves supplying books to the king, a scholarly king, and our fortune would be made. But if they found our books seditious or blasphemous or heretical, then we could be thrown into prison or into exile again or to our deaths.

'May I see your library?' John Dee asked.

I saw my father's reluctance to let the man browse the shelves and drawers of his collection. I knew that the books of secret wisdom in Greek and Hebrew were always hidden, behind the sliding back of the bookshelf. But even the ones on show might lead us into trouble.

'Of course, my lord,' he surrendered. 'It will be an honour to me.' He led the way into the inner room and John Dee followed him.

The young lord, Robert Dudley, took a seat on one of the stools and looked at me with interest. 'Twelve years old?'

'Yes, sir,' I lied promptly, although in truth I was nearly fourteen.

'And a maid, though dressed as a lad.'

'Yes, sir.'

'No marriage arranged for you?'

'Not straight away, sir.'

'But a betrothal in sight?'

'Yes, sir.'

'And who has your father picked out for you?'

'I am to marry a cousin from my mother's family when I am sixteen,' I replied. 'I don't particularly wish it.'

'You're a maid,' he scoffed. 'All young maids say they don't wish it.'

I shot a look at him which showed my resentment too clearly.

'Oho! Have I offended you, Mistress Boy?'

'I know my own mind, sir,' I said quietly. 'And I am not a maid like any other.'

'Clearly. So what is your mind, Mistress Boy?'

'I don't wish to marry.'

'And how shall you eat?'

'I should like to have my own shop, and print my own books.'

'And do you think a girl, even a pretty one in breeches, could manage without a husband?'

'I am sure I could,' I said. 'Widow Worthing has a shop.'

'A widow has had a husband to give her a fortune; she didn't have to make her own.'

'A girl can make her own fortune,' I said stoutly. 'I should think a girl could command a shop.'

'And what else can a girl command?' he teased me. 'A ship? An army? A kingdom?'

'You will see a woman run a kingdom better than any in the world before,' I fired back, and then checked at the look on his face. I put my hand over my mouth. 'I didn't mean to say that,' I whispered.

He looked at me as if he would hear more. 'Do you think, Mistress Boy, that I will live to see a woman rule a kingdom?'

'In Spain it was done,' I said weakly. 'Once. Queen Isabella.'

He nodded and let it go, as if drawing us both back from the brink of something dangerous. 'So. D'you know your way to Whitehall Palace, Mistress Boy?'

'Yes, sir.'

'Then when Mr Dee has chosen the books he wants to see, you can bring them there, to my rooms. All right?'

I nodded.

'How is your father's shop prospering?' he asked. 'Selling many books? Many customers coming?'

'Some,' I said cautiously. 'But it is early days for us yet.'

'Your gift does not guide him in his business, then?'

I shook my head. 'It is not a gift. It is more like folly, as he says.'

'You speak out? And you can see what others cannot?'

'Sometimes.'

'And what did you see when you looked at me?'

His voice was pitched very low, as if he would lead me to whisper a reply. I took a quiet breath. 'I think that you would trouble a young woman who was not in breeches.'

He laughed out loud at that. 'Please God that is a true seeing. But I never fear trouble with girls; it is their fathers who strike me with terror.'

I smiled back, I could not help myself. There was something about the way his eyes danced when he laughed that made me want to laugh too.

'And have you ever foretold the future and it came true?' he asked, suddenly serious.

The question itself was dangerous in a country that was always alert for witchcraft. 'I have no powers,' I said quickly.

'But without exerting powers, can you see the future? It is given to some of us, as a holy gift, to know what might be. My friend here, Mr Dee, believes that angels guide the course of mankind and may sometimes warn us against sin, just as the course of the stars can tell a man what his destiny might be.'

I shook my head at this dangerous talk, determined not to respond.

He looked thoughtful. 'Can you dance or play an instrument? Learn a part in a masque and say your lines?'

'Not very well,' I said unhelpfully.

He laughed at my reluctance. 'Well, we shall see, Mistress Boy. We shall see what you can do.'

Next day, carrying a parcel of books and a carefully rolled scroll of manuscript, I walked to Whitehall Palace, my cap pulled over my ears against the icy wind. I had never been inside a royal palace before, and I had thought I would just give the books to the guards on the gate, but when I showed them the note that Lord Robert had scrawled, with the Dudley seal of the bear and staff at the bottom, they bowed me through as though I were a visiting prince, and ordered a man to guide me.

Inside the gates, the palace was like a series of courtyards, each beautifully built, with a great garden in the middle set with apple trees and arbours and seats. The soldier led me across the first garden and gave me no time to stop and stare at the finely dressed lords and ladies who, wrapped in furs and velvets against the cold, were playing at bowls on the green. Inside the door, swung open by another pair of soldiers, there were more fine people in a great chamber, and behind that great room another, and then another. My guide led me through door after door until we came to a long gallery, and Robert Dudley was at the far end of it.

I was so relieved to find him that I ran a few steps towards him and called out: 'My lord!'

The guard hesitated, as if he would block me from getting any closer, but Robert Dudley waved him aside. 'Mistress Boy!' he exclaimed. He got to his feet and then I saw his companion. It was the young king, King Edward, fifteen years of age and beautifully dressed in plush blue velvet but with a face the colour of skimmed milk.

I dropped to my knee, holding tight to my father's books and trying to doff my cap at the same time, as Lord Robert remarked: 'This is the girl-boy. Don't you think she would be a wonderful player?'

I did not look up but I heard the king's voice, thinned with pain. 'You take such fancies, Dudley. Why should she be a player?'

'Her voice,' Dudley said. 'Such a voice, very sweet, and that accent, part Spanish and part London, I could listen to her for ever. And she holds herself like a princess in beggar's clothes.'

I kept my head down so that he should not see my delighted beam.

The young king returned me to the real world. 'It's against Holy Writ for a girl to dress as a boy.' His voice tailed away into a cough which shook him like a bear might shake a dog.

I looked up as the king took his handkerchief from his mouth and I saw a glimpse of a dark stain. Quickly, he tucked it out of sight.

'It's no sin,' Dudley said soothingly. 'She's no sinner. The girl is a holy fool. She saw an angel walking in Fleet Street. Can you imagine it?'

The younger man turned to me at once, his face brightened with interest. 'Did you see an angel?'

I nodded, my eyes downcast. I could not deny my gift. 'Yes, sire. I—'

'What can you see for me?' he interrupted.

I looked up. Anyone could have seen the shadow of death on his face, in his waxy skin, in his swollen eyes, in his bony thinness, even without the evidence of the stain on his handkerchief and the tremor of his lips. I tried to tell a lie but I could feel the words coming despite myself. 'I see the gates of heaven opening.'

The young king was not angry. He smiled. 'This child tells the truth when everyone else lies to me,' he said. 'All the rest of you run around finding new ways to lie. But this little one . . .' He lost his breath and gestured to me. 'Stay at court. You shall be my fool.'

'I have to go home to my father, Your Grace,' I said as quietly and as humbly as I could, ignoring Lord Robert's glare. 'I only came today to bring Lord Robert his books.'

'You shall be my fool and wear my livery,' the young man ruled. 'Robert, I am grateful to you for finding her for me. I shan't forget it.'

It was a dismissal. Robert Dudley bowed and snapped his fingers for me, turned and went from the room. I hesitated, wanting to refuse the king, but there was nothing to do but bow to him and run after Dudley like some pet greyhound scampering at his master's heels. He went down a long gallery, towards double doors guarded by soldiers with pikes, who flung them open as we approached. Finally we came to a great pair of doors where the soldiers wore the Dudley livery, and we went in.

'Father,' Dudley said, and dropped to one knee.

There was a man at the fireplace of the great inner hall, looking down into the flames. He turned and made an unemotional blessing over his son's head with two fingers. I dropped to my knee too, and stayed down even when I felt Robert Dudley rise up beside me.

'How's the king this morning?'

'Worse,' Robert said flatly. 'Cough bad, he brought up some black bile, breathless. Can't last, Father.'

'And this is the girl?'

'This is the bookseller's daughter, dresses like a lad but certainly a girl. Has the Sight, according to John Dee. I took her into the king as you ordered, begged her for a fool. She told him that she saw the gates of heaven opened for him. He liked it. She is to be his fool.'

'Good,' the duke said. 'And have you told her of her duties?'

'I brought her straight here.'

'Stand, fool.'

I rose to my feet and took my first look at Robert Dudley's father, the Duke of Northumberland, the greatest man in the kingdom. I took him in: a long bony face like a horse, dark eyes, balding head half hidden by a rich velvet cap with a big silver brooch of his coat of arms: the bear and staff. I looked into his eyes and saw—nothing. This was a man whose face could hide his thoughts.

'What's your name?' he asked of me.

'Hannah Green, my lord.'

'Listen, Hannah the Fool, you have been begged for a fool and the king has accepted you. D'you know what that means?'

I shook my head.

'You become his, like one of his puppies. Your job is to be yourself. Speak as your gift commands you. Say the first thing that comes into your head. It will amuse him. You will be paid to be his fool.'

I waited.

'Do you understand, fool?'

'Yes. But I don't accept.'

'You can't accept or not accept. You were your father's property, now you are ours. And we have begged you for a fool to the king. He owns you. D'you understand?'

'My father would not sell me,' I said stubbornly.

'He cannot stand against us,' Robert said quietly behind me. 'And I promised him that you would be safer here than out on the street. I gave him my word and he accepted. The business was done while we ordered the books, Hannah. It is finished.'

'Now,' continued the duke. 'Not like a puppy, and not like a fool, you have another task. You are to be our vassal.'

At the strange English word I glanced at Robert Dudley.

'Servant to command, servant for life,' he explained.

'Everything you hear, everything you see, you tell me, or Robert here. You are our eyes and our ears at his side. Understand?'

'My lord, I have to go home to my father,' I said desperately. 'I cannot be the king's fool. I have work to do at the bookshop.'

The duke raised one eyebrow at his son. Robert leaned towards me and spoke very quietly.

'Mistress Boy, I think your father is not a good Christian from a good Christian family at all, but a Jew.'

I opened my mouth to deny it, but I could not speak for fear.

'Now, luckily for you, your Sight has won you the safest and highest place that you might dream of. Serve the king well, serve our family well and your father is safe. Fail us in any one thing and he is tossed in a blanket till his eyes fall backwards in his head, and you are married to a red-faced chapel-going Luther-reading pig herder. You can choose.'

There was the briefest of moments. Then the Duke of Northumberland waved me away. He did not even wait for me to make my choice. He did not need the Sight to know what my choice would have to be.

'**A**nd you are to live at court?' my father confirmed.

We were eating our dinner, a small pie brought in from the bake-house at the end of the street.

'I am to sleep with the maidservants,' I said glumly. 'And wear the livery of the king's pages. I am to be his companion.'

'It's better than I could have provided for you,' my father said, trying to be cheerful. 'We won't make enough money to pay the rent on this house next quarter, unless Lord Robert orders some more books.'

'I can send you my wages,' I offered. 'I am to be paid.'

He patted my hand. 'You're a good girl. Never forget that. Never forget your mother, never forget that you are one of the children of Israel.'

I nodded. 'I am to go the palace tomorrow. I am to start at once. Father . . .'

'I will come to the gate and see you every evening,' he promised. 'Have courage, daughter. You are one of the Chosen.'

'How will I keep the fast days?' I demanded in sudden grief. 'They will make me work on the Sabbath. They will make me eat pork!'

He met my gaze and then he bowed his head. 'I shall keep the law for you here,' he said. 'God is good. He understands. I will pray for you, Hannah. And even if you are praying on your knees in the Christian chapel God still sees you and hears your prayer.'

'Father, Lord Robert threatened me. He knows we are Jews and he said that he would keep our secret as long as I obey him.'

'Daughter, we are safe nowhere. And you at least are under his patronage. He swore to me that you would be safe in his household.'

'Father, how could you let me go? Why did you agree that they could take me away from you?'

'Hannah, how could I stop them?'

In the lime-washed room under the eaves of the palace roof I turned over the pile of my new clothes and read the inventory from the office of the Master of the Household: *One pageboy livery in yellow. One pair of hose, dark red. One pair of hose, dark green. One surcoat, long. Two linen shirts. Two pairs of sleeves, one pair red, one pair green. One black hat. One black cloak for riding. One pair of slippers for dancing. Two pairs of boots, one pair for riding, one pair for walking. Everything used but clean and darned and delivered to the king's fool, Hannah Green.*

'I shall look a fool indeed,' I said to myself.

That night I whispered an account of my day to my father as he stood at the postern gate and I leaned against the doorway. 'There is a fool at court already, a man called Will Somers. He was kind to me, and showed me where I should sit. He is a witty man; he made everyone laugh.'

'And what do you do?'

'Nothing as yet. I have thought of nothing to say.'

My father glanced around. 'Can you think of something? Won't they want you to think of something?'

'Father, I cannot command the Sight.'

'Did you see Lord Robert?'

'He winked at me.' I leaned back against the cold stone and drew my warm new cloak round my shoulders.

'The king?'

'He was not even at dinner. He was sick, they sent his food to his rooms. The duke took his place at the head of the table.'

'And does the duke have his eye on you?'

'He did not seem to see me at all.'

'Has he forgotten you?'

'He doesn't have to look to know who is where, and what they are doing. He will not have forgotten me. He is not a man who forgets.'

The duke had decided that there was to be a masque at Candlemas and gave it out as the king's command, so we all had to wear special costumes and learn our lines. Will Somers, the king's fool who had come to court twenty years ago when he was a boy, was to introduce the piece and recite a rhyme, the king's choristers were to sing, and I was to recite a poem, specially composed for the occasion. My costume was to be a new livery, specially made for me in the fool's colour of yellow.

The Master of the Revels gave me a little sword and ordered that Will and I should prepare for a fight, which would fit somewhere into the story of the masque.

We met for our first practice in one of the antechambers off the great hall. I was awkward and unwilling; I did not want to learn to fight with swords like a boy. No man at court but Will Somers could have persuaded me to it, but he treated our lesson as if he had been hired to improve my understanding of Greek. He behaved as if it was a skill I needed to learn, and he wanted me to learn well.

He started with my stance. Resting his hands on my shoulders, he gently smoothed them down, took my chin and raised it up. 'Hold your head high, like a princess,' he said. Then he showed me the swordsman's stance, hand on my hip for balance, how to slide forward with my leading foot always on the floor so that I should not trip or fall, how to move behind the sword and to let it retreat to me. Then we started on the feints and passes. Will commanded me to stab at him.

I hesitated. 'What if I hit you?'

'Then I shall take a splinter, not a deadly cut,' he pointed out. 'It's only wood, Hannah.'

'Get ready then,' I said nervously, and lunged forward.

To my amazement Will sidestepped me and was at my side, his wooden sword to my throat. 'You're dead,' he said. 'Not so good at foresight after all. Try again.'

The next time I lunged with a good deal more energy and caught the hem of his coat as he flicked to one side.

'Excellent,' he said breathlessly. 'And again. We have to plan how you are going to murder me amusingly by Candlemas.'

We had our sword dance planned in good time and it did seem very funny. At least two practices ended in us both having fits of giggles as we mistimed a lunge and cracked heads together. But one day the Master of the Revels put his head into the room and said: 'You won't be needed. The king is not having a masque.'

I turned with the play-sword still in my hand. 'But we're all ready!'

'He's sick,' the Master said dourly.

'And is the Lady Mary still coming to court?' Will asked.

'Said to be,' the Master said. 'She'll get better rooms and a better cut of the meat this time, don't you think, Will?'

He shut the door before Will could reply, and so I turned and asked, 'What does he mean?'

'He means that those of the court who move towards the heir and away from the king will be making their move now.'

'Because?'

'Ah, child. Lady Mary is the heir. She will be queen if we lose the king, God bless him, poor lad.'

'But she's a heret—'

'Of the Catholic faith,' he corrected me smoothly.

'And King Edward . . .'

'His heart will break to leave the kingdom to a Catholic heir but he can do nothing about it. It's how King Henry left it. God bless him, he must be rolling in his shroud to see it come to this. It makes you think, doesn't it? Is England ever to get any peace? Two young lusty kings: Henry's father, Henry himself, handsome as the sun, each of them, lecherous as sparrows, and they leave us with nothing but a lad as weak as a girl, and an old maid to come after him?'

'And what will happen to us?' I demanded. 'If the young king dies and his sister takes the throne?'

Will grinned. 'Then we shall be Queen Mary's fools,' he said simply. 'And if I can make her laugh it will be a novelty indeed.'

My father came to the side gate that night and he brought someone with him, a young man dressed in a worsted cape, dark ringlets of hair falling to his collar, dark eyes and a shy, boyish smile. It took me a moment to recognise him; he was Daniel Carpenter, my betrothed.

He was twenty years old, training to be a physician like his father, who had died only last year. I had seen Daniel only once before, when he and his mother welcomed us to England with a gift of bread and some wine, and I knew next to nothing about him.

'Daniel asked to see you alone,' my father said awkwardly, and he stepped back a little, out of earshot.

'I heard that you had been begged for a fool,' Daniel said. At first glance he looked more Portuguese than Jewish, but the heavy-lidded eyes would have betrayed him to one who was looking.

I slid my gaze from his face and took in a slight frame with broad shoulders, narrow waist, long legs: a handsome young man.

'Yes,' I said shortly. 'I have a place at court.'

'When you are sixteen you will have to leave court and come home again,' he said.

I raised my eyebrows at this young stranger. 'Who gives this order?'

'I do.'

'I don't believe you have any command over me.'

'When I am your husband . . .'

'Then, yes.'

'I am your betrothed. You are promised to me. I have some rights.'

I showed him a sulky face. 'I am commanded by the king, I am commanded by the Duke of Northumberland, I am commanded by his son Lord Robert Dudley, I am commanded by my father; you might as well join in. Every other man in London seems to think he can order me.'

He gave a little gulp of involuntary laughter and clipped me gently on my shoulder as if I were his comrade. I found I was smiling back at him. 'Oh, poor maid,' he said. 'Poor set-upon maid.'

I shook my head. 'Fool indeed.'

'When I have served my apprenticeship and I am a physician I will make a home for us.'

'And when will that be?' I asked him.

'Within two years,' he said stiffly. 'I shall be able to keep a wife by the time you are ready for marriage.'

'Come for me then,' I said unhelpfully. 'Come with your orders then, if I am still here.'

'In the meantime, we are still betrothed,' he insisted. 'I have waited for you and your father to come from Amsterdam. When you finally came to England I thought you would be glad of . . . be glad of . . . a home. And then I hear you and your father are to set up house together, you are not coming to live with Mother and me, and you have not put aside your boy's costume. Then I hear you are working for him like a son. And then I hear you have left the protection of your father's house. And now I find you at court.'

It was not the Sight that helped me through all of this, but the sharp intuition of a girl on the edge of womanhood. 'You thought you would rescue me, that I would be a fearful girl longing to cling to a man!'

The sudden darkening of his flush and the jerk of his head told me that I had hit the mark.

'Well, learn this, young apprentice physician, I have seen sights and travelled in countries that you cannot imagine. I have been afraid and I have been in danger, and I have never for one moment thought that I would throw myself at a man for his help.'

'You are not . . .' He was lost for words, choking on a young man's indignation. 'You are not . . . maidenly.'

'I thank God for it.'

'You are not . . .' His temper was getting the better of him. 'You would not be my first choice!'

That silenced me, and we looked at each other in some sort of shock.

'Do you want another girl?' I asked, a little shaken.

'I don't know another girl,' he said sulkily. 'But I don't want a girl who doesn't want me.'

'It's not you I dislike,' I volunteered. 'It's marriage itself.'

My father glanced over curiously and saw the two of us, face to face, aghast in silence. Daniel turned away from me and took two paces to one side, I leaned against the cold stone of the doorpost and wondered if this would be the last I would see of him.

Daniel mastered himself, and came back to me. 'You do wrong to taunt me, Hannah Green,' he said, his voice trembling with his intensity. 'Whatever else, we are promised to one another. We can make a home here. You and I can be married and have children who will be English children. They will know nothing but this life. We need not even tell them of your mother, of her faith. Nor of our own.'

'Oh, you'll tell them,' I predicted. 'You say you won't now, but once we have a child you won't be able to resist it. And you'll find ways to light the candle on Friday night and not to work on the Sabbath. You'll be a doctor then, you will circumcise the boys in secret and teach them the prayers. You'll have me teach the girls to make unleavened bread and to keep the milk from the meat and to drain the blood from the beef. And so it goes on, like some sickness that we pass on, one to another.'

'It's no sickness,' he whispered passionately. 'It is our gift, we are chosen to keep faith.'

I would have argued for the sake of contradicting him, but it went against the deeper grain of my love for my mother and her faith. 'Yes,' I admitted. 'It is not a sickness, but it kills us just as if it were. My grandmother and my aunt died of it, my mother too. And this is what you propose to me. A lifetime of fear, not Chosen so much as cursed.'

'If you don't want to marry me, then you can marry a Christian and pretend that you know nothing more,' he pointed out. 'You can deny the faith that your mother and your grandmother died for. Just say the word and I shall tell your father that I wish to be released.'

I hesitated. I wanted to be free. I did not want to be cast out. 'I don't know,' I said, a girl's plea. 'I'm not ready to say . . .'

'Then be guided by those who do,' he said flatly. He saw me bridle at that. 'Look, you can't fight everyone,' he advised me. 'You have to choose where you belong and rest there.'

'It's too great a cost for me,' I whispered. 'For you it is a good life. For me it is to lose everything I might be and everything I might do, and become nothing but your servant.'

'This is not being a Jew; this is being a girl,' he said. 'Would you deny your sex as well as your religion?'

I said nothing.

'You are not a faithful woman,' he said. 'You would betray yourself.'

'That's a dreadful thing to say,' I whispered.

'But it is true,' he maintained. 'You are a Jew and you are a woman and you are my betrothed, and all these things you would deny. Who do you work for in the court? The king? The Dudleys? Are you faithful to them?'

I thought of how I had been begged as a fool and appointed as a spy.

'I just want to be free,' I said. 'I don't want to be anybody's anything.'

I saw my father looking towards us. I saw him make a little tentative move as if to interrupt us, but then he waited.

'Shall I tell them that we cannot agree and ask you to release me from our betrothal?' Daniel asked tightly.

Wilfully, I was about to agree, but his silence, his patient waiting for my reply made me look at Daniel Carpenter more closely. The light was going from the sky and in the half-darkness I could see the man he would become. He would be handsome, he would have a dark mobile face, a quick observing eye, a sensitive mouth, thick black hair like mine. And he would be a wise man; he was a wise youth, he had seen me and understood me and contradicted my very core, and yet still he stood waiting. He would be a generous husband.

'Leave me now,' I said feebly. 'I can't say now. I have said too much already. I am sorry for speaking out. I am sorry if I angered you.'

But his anger had left him as quickly as it had come, and that was another thing that I liked in him.

'Shall I come again?'

'All right.'

'Are we still betrothed?'

I shrugged. 'I haven't broken it,' I said.

He nodded. 'I shall need to know,' he warned me. 'I shall want to marry within two years—you, or another girl.'

My father came up beside Daniel before I could reply, and put a hand on his shoulder. 'And so you two are getting acquainted,' he said hopefully. 'What d'you make of your wife-to-be, Daniel?'

I expected Daniel to complain of me to my father, but he gave me a small rueful smile. 'I think we are coming to know each other,' he said gently. 'We have overleapt being polite strangers and reached disagreement very quickly, don't you think, Hannah?'

'Commendably quick,' I said, and was rewarded by his smile.

Lady Mary came to London for the Candlemas feast, as had been planned; it seemed that no one had told her that her brother was too sick to rise from his bed. She rode in through the palace gate of Whitehall with a great train behind her, and was greeted at the very threshold of the palace by the duke, with his sons, including Lord Robert, at his side, and the council of England bowing low before her. As I watched her seated high on her horse, looking down at the sea of humbly bowing heads, I thought I saw a smile of pure amusement cross her lips before she put down her hand to be kissed.

I had heard so much about her, the beloved daughter of the king who had been put aside on the word of Anne Boleyn, the whore. The princess who had been humbled to dust, the mourning girl who had been forbidden to see her dying mother. I had expected a figure of tragedy, but what I saw was a stocky little fighter with enough wit about her to smile at the court, knocking their noses on their knees because, suddenly, she was the heir with formidable prospects.

The duke treated her as if she were queen already. She was helped from her horse and led in to the banquet. The king was in his chamber, coughing and retching in his little bed, but they had the banquet anyway, and I saw the Lady Mary look round at the beaming faces as if to note that, when the heir was in the ascendant, a king could lie sick and alone, and no one mind at all.

There was dancing after dinner but she did not rise from her seat, though she tapped her foot and seemed to enjoy the music. Will made her laugh a couple of times, and she smiled on him as if he were a familiar face in a dangerous world.

I looked her over, as did the court: this woman who might be my next mistress. She was a woman in her thirty-seventh year, but she still had the pretty colouring of a girl. She wore her hood set back off her square, honest face and showed her hair, dark brown with a tinge of Tudor red. Her smile was her great charm; it came slowly, and her dark eyes were warm. But what struck me most about her was her air of honesty. She looked as if she said nothing that she did not mean.

She had a great jewelled cross at her throat as if to flaunt her religion in this most Protestant court, and I thought that she must be either very brave or very reckless to insist on her faith when her brother's men were burning heretics for less. But then I saw the tremor in her hand when she reached for her golden goblet, and I imagined that like many women she had learned to put on a braver face than she might feel.

When there was a break in the dancing, Robert Dudley was at her side, whispering to her, and he beckoned me forward.

'I hear you are from Spain, and my brother's new fool,' she said in English.

I bowed low. 'Yes, Your Grace.'

'Speak Spanish,' Lord Robert commanded me, and I bowed again and told her in Spanish that I was glad to be at court.

When I looked up I saw the delight in her face at hearing her mother's language. 'What part of Spain?' she asked eagerly in English.

'Castile, Your Grace,' I lied at once. I did not want any enquiries made of us and of my family's destruction in our home of Aragon.

'And why did you come to England?'

I was prepared for the question. My father and I had discussed the dangers of every answer and settled on the safest. 'My father is a scholar,' I said. 'He wanted to print books from his library of manuscripts, and he wanted to work in London, which is such a centre of learning.'

'And you are my brother's holy fool,' she said. 'D'you have any words of wisdom for me?'

I shook my head helplessly. 'I wish I could see at will, Your Grace. I am much less wise than you, I should think.'

'She told my tutor, John Dee, that she could see an angel walking with us,' Robert put in.

The Lady Mary looked at me with more respect.

'This is a good little maid,' he continued, 'and I think she does have a true gift. She has been a great comfort to your brother in his illness. She has a gift of seeing the truth and speaking true, and he likes that.'

'That alone is a rare gift to find at court,' the Lady Mary said. She nodded kindly to me and I stepped back and the music started up again. I kept my eye on Robert Dudley as he led out one young lady and then another to dance before the Lady Mary, and I was rewarded when he glanced over to me and gave me a hidden approving smile.

The Lady Mary did not see the king that night but the chambermaids' gossip was that when she went into his room the next day she came out again, white as a winding sheet. She had not known till then that her little brother was so near to his death.

After that, there was no reason for her to stay. She rode out as she had come, with a great retinue following behind, and all the court bowing low, praying silently that, when she came to the throne, she would be blessed with forgetfulness and overlook the priests they had burned at the stake, and the churches they had despoiled.

I was watching this charade of humility from one of the palace windows when I felt a gentle touch on my sleeve. I turned, and there was Lord Robert, smiling down at me.

'My lord, I thought you would be with your father, saying goodbye to the Lady Mary.'

'No, I came to find you to ask if you would do me a service?'

I felt my colour rise to my cheeks. 'Anything . . .' I stammered.

He smiled. 'Just one small thing. Would you come with me to my tutor's rooms, and see if you can assist him in one of his experiments?'

I nodded and Lord Robert took my hand and, drawing it into the crook of his arm, led me to the Northumberland private quarters.

John Dee was seated in the library overlooking an inner garden. He raised his head as we came into the room. 'Ah, Hannah Verde.'

It was so odd for me to hear my real name, given in full, that for a moment I did not respond, and then I dipped a little bow. 'Yes, sir.'

'She says she will help. But I have not told her what you want,' Lord Robert said.

Mr Dee rose from the table. 'I have a special mirror,' he said. 'I think it possible that one with special sight might see rays of light that are not visible to the ordinary eye, d'you understand?'

I did not.

'Just as we cannot see a sound or a scent, but we know that something is there, I think that the planets and the angels send out rays of light, which we might see if we had the right glass to see them in.'

'Oh,' I said blankly.

The tutor broke off with a smile. 'No matter. You need not understand me. I was only thinking that since you saw the angel Uriel that day, you might see such rays in this mirror.'

'I don't mind looking, if Lord Robert wishes it,' I volunteered.

He nodded. 'I have it ready. Come in.' He led the way to an inner chamber. The window was shielded by a thick curtain, all the cold winter light blocked out. A square table was placed before it, the four legs standing on four wax seals. On top of the table was an extraordinary mirror of great beauty. I stepped up to it and saw myself, reflected in gold, looking not like the boy-girl I was, but like a young woman.

'I want you to close your eyes,' Dee said, 'and listen carefully to the prayer that I am going to read. When you say "amen" you can open your eyes again and tell me what you see. Are you ready?'

I closed my eyes and I could hear him softly blowing out the few candles illuminating the shadowy room. 'I am ready,' I whispered.

It was a long prayer in Latin; I understood it despite Mr Dee's English pronunciation of the words. It was a prayer for guidance and for the angels to come and protect the work we would do. I whispered 'amen' and then I opened my eyes.

The candles were all out. The mirror was a pool of darkness, black reflected in black, I could see nothing.

'Show us when the king will die,' Mr Dee whispered from behind me.

I watched, waiting for something to happen, my eyes staring into the blackness. I could see nothing. I waited. Nothing came to me. I stared into the darkness until I knew that far from being a holy fool I was a fool pure and simple, looking at a reflection of nothing.

I had to say something. They knew who I was. They had bought me and now they expected some benefit for their bargain.

'July,' I said quietly, as good a reply as any.

'Which year?' Mr Dee prompted me, his voice silky and quiet.

Common sense alone suggested that the young king could not live much longer. 'This year,' I said unwillingly.

'The day?'

'The sixth,' I whispered in reply.

'Tell the name of the next ruler of England,' Mr Dee whispered.

I was about to reply 'Queen Mary', echoing his own tranced tone. 'Jane,' I said simply, surprising myself.

I turned to Lord Robert. 'I don't know why I said that. I am most sorry, my lord. I don't know—'

John Dee quickly grasped my jaw, and turned my head back to the mirror. 'Don't talk!' he ordered. 'Just tell us the king who comes after Jane. Look, Hannah. Tell me what you see. Does Jane have a son?'

I would have said 'yes' but my tongue would not move in my dry mouth. 'I cannot see,' I said humbly. 'Truly, I cannot see.'

'A closing prayer,' Mr Dee said, gripping my shoulders. He prayed again in Latin that the visions should be true, and that no one in this world nor in any other should be harmed by our scrying.

'Amen,' I said, more fervently now that I knew this was dangerous work, perhaps even treasonous work.

'She has the Sight,' Mr Dee said. 'She has it indeed.'

Lord Robert looked at his tutor. 'Will this make a great difference to your work?'

The older man shrugged. 'Who knows? We are all children in darkness. But she has the Sight.' He paused, and then turned to me. 'Hannah Verde, I must tell you one thing.'

'Yes, sir?'

'You have the Sight because you are pure in heart. Please, for yourself and for the gift you bear, refuse any offers of marriage, resist any seduction, keep yourself pure.'

Behind me, Lord Robert gave a snort of amusement.

I felt my colour rise from my neck to my ear lobes. 'I have no carnal desires,' I said in a low whisper. I did not dare to look at Lord Robert.

'Then you will see true,' John Dee said.

'But I don't understand,' I protested. 'Who is Jane? It is Lady Mary who will be queen if His Grace dies.'

Lord Robert put his finger on my lips and at once I was silent. 'Mistress Boy, you must say not a word of this. It is treason to cast the horoscope of a king, and the punishment for treason is death. D'you want to see me on the scaffold?'

'No! I—'

'Do you want to die yourself?'

'No!' I could hear a quaver in my voice. 'My lord, I am afraid.'

'Then never say one word of this to anyone. Not even to your father. Just forget all you saw, forget the mirror, forget the room.' He gave me his sweet seductive smile. 'I ask it of you as your friend. I have put my life in your hands.'

I was lost. 'All right,' I said.

The court moved to Greenwich Palace later that February and it was given out that the king was better. But he never asked for me, nor for Will Somers. He did not ask for music nor for company, nor did he ever come to the great hall for dinner. The physicians, who had been waiting in every corner of the court, talking among themselves and giving guarded replies to all enquiries, seemed to slip away as the days wore on and there was no news of his recovery, and not even their cheerful predictions about leeches cleansing the king's blood and carefully administered poison killing his disease seemed to ring true. Lord Robert's father, the Duke of Northumberland, was all but king in Edward's place, seated at the right hand of an empty throne at dinner, taking the chair at the head of the council table every week.

I said nothing. I was being paid as a fool to say surprising and impertinent things but I could think of nothing more impertinent and surprising than the truth—that the young king was half-prisoner to his protector, that he was dying without companions or nursing, and that this whole court was thinking of the crown and not of the boy, left to die alone. I would be a fool indeed to tell the truth in this court of liars.

I had new work to do. Lord Robert's tutor, Mr Dee, sought me out and asked if I would read with him. His eyes were tired, he said, and my father had sent him some manuscripts that could be more easily deciphered by young sight.

'I don't read very well,' I said cautiously.

He smiled. 'You are a very careful young woman,' he said. 'And that is wise in these changing times. But you are safe with me and with Lord Robert. I imagine you can read English and Latin fluently, am I right?'

I nodded.

'And Spanish, of course, and perhaps French?'

I kept my silence.

Mr Dee came a little closer and bent his head to whisper in my ear. 'Can you read Greek? I need someone who can read Greek for me.'

If I had been older and wiser I would have denied my knowledge. But I was only fourteen and proud of my abilities.

'Yes,' I said. 'I can read Greek and Hebrew.'

'Hebrew?' he exclaimed, his interest sharpened. 'I guessed you had fled Spain as soon as I saw you,' he continued gently. 'I guessed you were Conversos. But it was not for me to say. You go to church, don't you? You believe in Jesus Christ and his mercy?'

'Oh yes, my lord. Without fail.' There was no point in telling him that there was no more devout Christian than a Jew trying to be invisible.

Mr Dee paused. 'As for me, I believe there is a creator, a great creator who has given us a world full of mysteries. I believe that God made this world as a great and glorious mechanical garden, one that works to its own laws and that we will one day come to understand it. Alchemy— the art of change—is how we shall come to understand it, and when we know how things are made, we can make them ourselves, we will have the knowledge of God . . .' He broke off. 'You shall come every morning and read with me for an hour and we shall make great progress.'

'If Lord Robert says I may,' I said.

Mr Dee smiled at me again. 'Young lady, you are going to help me to understand the meaning of all things. There is a key to the universe and we are just beginning to grasp at it. There are rules, unchangeable rules, which command the courses of the planets, the tides of the sea, and the affairs of men, and I know, I absolutely know, that all these things are linked: the sea, the planets and the history of man. With God's grace and with the skill we can muster we will discover these laws and when we know them . . .' He paused. 'We will know everything.'

SPRING 1553

I WAS ALLOWED to go home to my father in April and I took him my wages for the quarter.

'What news of the court?' my father asked.

'Everyone says that the king is growing stronger with the warmer weather.' I did not add that everyone was speaking a lie.

'God bless him and keep him,' my father said piously. He looked at me as if he would know more. 'And Lord Robert. Do you see him?'

I felt myself colour. 'Now and then.' I could have told him to the very hour and the minute when I had last seen Lord Robert. He had been mounted on his horse, about to go hawking for herons along the mud flats of the river shore. He was wearing a black cape and a black hat with a dark feather pinned to the ribbon with a jet brooch. He had a beautiful hooded falcon on his wrist and he rode with one hand out-stretched to keep the bird steady and his other hand holding the curvetting horse. He looked like a prince in a storybook.

'There is to be a great wedding,' I said to fill the pause. 'Lord Robert's father has arranged it.'

'Who is to marry?' my father asked with a gossip's curiosity.

I ticked off the three couples on my fingers. 'Lady Catherine Dudley is to marry Lord Henry Hastings, and the two Grey sisters are to marry Lord Guilford Dudley and Lord Henry Herbert. They say that Lady Jane does not want to marry; she lives only to study her books. But her mother and her father have beaten her till she agreed.'

My father nodded, the forcible ordering of a daughter was no surprise. 'And what else?' he asked. 'What of Lord Robert's father, the Duke of Northumberland?'

'He's very much disliked,' I whispered. 'But he is like a king himself. He goes in and out of the king's bedroom and says that this or that is the king's own wish. What can anyone do against him?'

'They took up our neighbour the portrait painter only last week,' my father remarked. 'Mr Tuller. They said he was a Catholic and a heretic. Took him off for questioning, and he has not come back.'

We both glanced towards the door.

'D'you think we should leave?' I asked, very low.

'Not yet,' he said cautiously. 'Besides, where could we go that was safe? I'd rather be in Protestant England than Catholic France. We are good reformed Christians now. You go to church, don't you?'

'Twice, sometimes three times a day,' I assured him.

'I make sure I am seen to go. And I give to charity, and I pay my parish dues. We can do nothing more. We've both been baptised. What can any man say against us?'

I said nothing. We both knew that anyone could say anything against anyone. In the countries that had turned the ritual of the church into a burning matter, no one could be sure that they would not offend.

'If the king falls ill and dies,' my father whispered, 'then Lady Mary takes the throne, and she is a Roman Catholic. Will she make the whole country become Roman Catholic again?'

'Who knows what will happen?' I asked, thinking of my naming the next heir as 'Jane' and Robert Dudley's lack of surprise.

'Don't worry, *querida*. Everyone in the country will have to change, not just us. Everyone will be the same.'

I glanced over to where the Sabbath candle burned under the upended pitcher, its light hidden but its flame burning for our God. 'But we're not the same,' I said simply.

John Dee and I read together every morning like devoted scholars. Mostly he commanded me to read the Bible in Greek and then the same passage in Latin so that he might compare the translations.

In the afternoons Will Somers and I practised our sword fighting, leaving aside the comical tricks and concentrating on proper fighting, until he told me that I was a commendable swordsman for a fool. Although I was glad to learn a useful skill, we thought that the lessons would have been for nothing since the king continued to be so sick. In May, however, we were commanded to entertain at the great wedding feasts at Durham House in the Strand.

'You would think it a royal wedding,' Will said slyly to me.

'How, royal?' I asked.

He put his finger to his lips. 'Jane's mother, Frances Brandon, is King Henry's niece. Jane and Catherine are royal cousins.'

'Yes,' I said. 'And so?'

'And Jane is to marry a Dudley.'

'Yes,' I said, following this not at all.

'Who more royal than the Dudleys?' he demanded.

'The king's sisters,' I pointed out. 'Jane's own mother. And others too.'

'Not if you measure in terms of desire,' Will explained sweetly. 'In terms of desire there is no one more royal than the duke.'

Our sword fight was preceded by dancers and a masque and followed by jugglers, and we acquitted ourselves well. The guests roared with laughter at Will's tumbles and my triumphant skill, and the contrast between our looks: Will so tall and gangling, thrusting his sword wildly this way and that, and me, neat and determined, dancing round him and stabbing with my little sword, and parrying his blows.

The chief bride was as white as the pearls embroidered on her gold gown. Her bridegroom sat closer to his mother than to his new bride and neither bride nor groom spoke so much as one word to each other. Jane's sister had been married to her betrothed in the same ceremony, and she and he toasted each other and drank amorously from the same loving cup. But when the shout went up for a toast for Jane and Guilford, I could see that it cost Lady Jane an effort to raise her golden goblet to her new husband. Her eyes were red and raw, the shadows under them were dark with fatigue, and there were marks on either side of her neck that looked like thumbprints.

'What d'you think, Hannah the Fool?' the Duke of Northumberland shouted down the hall to me. 'Shall she be a lucky bride?'

My neighbours turned to me, and I felt the old swimming sensation that was a sign of the Sight coming. I tried to fight it off; this court would be the worst place in the world to tell the truth. I could not stop the words coming. 'Never more lucky than today,' I said.

Lord Robert flashed a cautionary look at me but I could not take back the words. I had spoken as I felt, not with the skill of a courtier. My sense was that Jane's luck, at a low ebb when she married with a bruise on her throat, would now run ever more swiftly downhill. But the duke took it as a compliment to his son and raised his goblet.

The court danced until late, as if there were great joy from such weddings, and then the three couples were taken to their bedrooms and put to bed with much throwing of rose petals and sprinkling of rosewater. But it was all show, no more real than Will and I fighting with wooden swords. None of the marriages was to be consummated yet, and the next day Lady Jane went home with her parents to Suffolk Place, Guilford Dudley went home with his mother, and Lord Robert and the duke were up early to return to the king at Greenwich.

'Why does your brother not make a house with his wife?' I asked Lord Robert. I met him at the gateway of the stable yard, and he waited beside me while they brought out his great horse.

'Well, it is not unusual. I do not live with mine,' he remarked.

I saw the roofs of Durham House tilt against the sky, as I staggered and held on to the wall till the world steadied again. 'You have a wife?'

'Oho, did you not know that, my little seer? Oh yes, I have been married since I was a lad. And I thank God for it because if I had not been married already, it would have been me married to Jane Grey and dancing to my father's bidding.'

'Does your wife never come to court?'

'Almost never. She lives in the country; she has no liking for London.'

'What's her name?'

'Amy,' he said casually. 'Why?'

I had no answer. Numbly, I shook my head.

'You don't like the thought of me married, Mistress Boy?'

'I was surprised, only.'

Lord Robert put his gloved hand under my chin and turned my face up to him so that I was forced to meet his dark eyes. 'Tell me the truth. Are you troubled with the desires of a maid, my little Mistress Boy?'

I was too young to hide it. I felt the tears come into my eyes and I stayed still, letting him hold me.

He saw the tears and knew what they meant. 'Desire? And for me?'

Still I said nothing, looking at him through my blurred vision.

'I promised your father that I would not let any harm come to you,' he said gently.

'It has come already,' I said, speaking the inescapable truth.

He shook his head, his dark eyes warm. 'Oh, this is nothing. This is young love, greensickness. The mistake I made in my youth was to marry for such a slim cause. It is not love that matters, Mistress Boy; it is what you choose to do with it. What d'you choose to do with yours?'

'I could serve you.'

He took one of my cold hands and took it up to his lips, a touch as intimate as any kiss on the lips. 'Yes,' he said gently, not raising his head, 'you could serve me. A loving servant is a great gift for any man. Will you be mine, Mistress Boy? Heart and soul? And do whatever I ask of you?'

'Yes,' I said, hardly grasping the enormity of my promise.

'Whatever I ask of you?'

'Yes.'

At once he straightened up, suddenly decisive. 'Good. Then I have a new post for you, new work.'

'You begged me to the king,' I reminded him. 'I am his fool.'

His mouth twisted in a moment's pity. 'The poor lad won't miss you,' he said. 'I shall tell you all of it. Come to Greenwich tomorrow, with the rest of them, and I'll tell you then.'

I clattered into the courtyard of the palace at Greenwich riding astride one of the cart-horses pulling the wagon with supplies. It was a beautiful spring day, the fields running down to the river were a sea of gold and silver daffodils. As I paused, feeling the breeze against my face, one of the Dudley servants shouted towards me: 'Hannah the Fool?'

'Yes?'

'Go to Lord Robert and his father in their privy rooms at once. At once, lad!'

I nodded and went into the palace at a run, past the royal chambers to the ones that were no less grand, guarded by soldiers in the Dudley livery. They swung open the double doors for me and I was in the presence room where the duke would hear the petitions of common people. I went through another set of doors, and another, the rooms getting smaller and more intimate, until the last double doors opened, and there was Lord Robert leaning over a desk with a manuscript scroll spread out before him, his father looking over his shoulder. I recognised at once that it was Mr Dee's writing, and that it was a map that he had made partly from ancient maps of Britain borrowed from my father, and partly from calculations of his own based on the sailors' charts of the coastline. Mr Dee had prepared the map because he believed that England's greatest fortune were the seas around the coast, but the duke was using it for a different purpose.

He had placed little counters in a crowd at London, and more in the painted blue sea. A set of counters of a different colour was in the north of the country—Scots, I thought—and another little group in the east of the country. I made a deep bow to Lord Robert and to his father.

'It has to be done at speed,' the duke remarked, 'before anyone has a chance to protest, then we can deal with the north, with the Spanish, and with those of her tenants who stay loyal, in our own time.'

'And she?' Lord Robert asked quietly.

'She can do nothing,' the duke said. 'And if she tries to run, your little spy will warn us.' He looked up at me on those words. 'Hannah Green, I am sending you to wait upon the Lady Mary. You are to be her fool until I summon you back to court. My son assures me that you can keep your counsel. Is he right?'

The skin on the back of my neck went cold. 'I can keep a secret,' I said unhelpfully. 'But I don't like to.'

Robert smiled. 'Hannah will keep our secrets,' he said gently. 'She is mine, heart and soul.'

The duke nodded. 'Well, then. Tell her the rest.'

Lord Robert came round the table and took my hand. He stood close to me and when I looked up from my study of the floor I met his dark gaze. 'Mistress Boy, I need you to go to the Lady Mary and write to me and tell me what she thinks, and where she goes, and whom she meets.'

I blinked. 'Spy on her?'

He hesitated. 'Befriend her.'

'Spy on her. Exactly,' his father said brusquely.

'Will you do this for me?' Lord Robert asked. 'It would be a very great service to me. It is the service I ask of your love.'

'Will I be in danger?' I asked. In my head I could hear the knock of the Inquisition and the trample of their feet over our threshold.

'No,' he promised me. 'I have guaranteed your safety while you are under my protection. No one can hurt you if you are a Dudley.'

'What must I do?'

'Watch the Lady Mary and report to me.'

'You want me to write to you? Will I never see you?'

He smiled. 'You shall come to me when I send for you,' he said. He put his hand into his jacket and brought out a letter. It was from my father to the duke, promising him the delivery of some manuscripts. 'Here is a mystery for you,' Lord Robert said gently. 'See the first twenty-six letters of the first sentence?'

I scanned them. 'Yes.'

'They are to be your alphabet. When you write to me I want you to use these. Where it says "My Lord", that is your ABC. The M for "my" is your A, the Y is your B, and so on. Do you understand? When a letter occurs twice you use it only once. Use the first set for your first letter to me and your second set for your second letter, and so on. I have a copy of the letter and when your message comes to me I can translate it.'

'Will you reply to me?'

'Only if I need to ask you something, and if I do, I will use this almanac also. Burn my letters as soon as you have read them.'

I nodded.

'Do you promise to do this exactly as I ask?'

'Yes,' I said miserably. 'When do I have to go?'

'Within three days,' the duke said from his place behind the table. 'There's a cart going to the Lady Mary with some goods for her. You can ride alongside that. You shall have one of my ponies, girl, and you can keep her at Lady Mary's house for your return. And if something should happen that you think threatens me or Lord Robert, something very grave indeed, you can ride to warn us at once. Will you do that?'

'Yes, sir,' I said obediently.

Lord Robert said that I might send for my father to say goodbye to him and he came downriver to Greenwich Palace in a fishing smack on the ebbing tide, with Daniel seated beside him.

'You!' I said without any enthusiasm, when I saw him help my father from the bobbing boat.

'Me,' he replied with the glimmer of a smile. 'Constant, aren't I?'

I went to my father and felt his arms come round me. 'Oh, Papa,' I whispered in Spanish. 'I have to go to the Lady Mary and I am afraid of the journey, and afraid of living at her house, I am afraid of . . .' I broke off, tasting the many lies on my tongue and realising that I would never be able to tell anyone the truth about myself ever again.

'Daughter, come home to me. I will ask Lord Robert to release you, we can leave England. You are not trapped here . . .'

'Lord Robert himself asked me to go,' I said simply. 'And I already said I would.'

His hand caressed my cropped hair. '*Querida*, I shall be here, and if you send for me I shall come to you. Or Daniel will come and fetch you away. Won't you, Daniel?'

I turned in my father's arms to look at my betrothed. He was leaning against the wooden railing that ran round the jetty.

'I would rather fetch you away now.'

My father released me and I took a step towards Daniel.

'I have agreed to go to serve Lady Mary,' I said quietly to him.

'She is a Papist in a Protestant country,' he said. 'You could not have chosen a place where your faith and practices will be more scrutinised. What are you to do for Lady Mary?'

He stepped closer to me so we could whisper.

'I am to be her companion, be her fool.' I paused and decided to tell him the truth. 'I am to spy for Lord Robert and his father.'

His head was so close to mine that I could feel the warmth of his cheek against my forehead as he leaned closer to speak into my ear.

'And you have agreed?'

I hesitated. 'They know that Father and I are Jews,' I said.

He was silent for a moment. I felt the solidity of his chest against my shoulder. His arm came around my waist to hold me closer to him and I felt the warmth of his grip. A rare sense of safety came over me as he held me, and for a moment I stood still.

'You are a hostage.'

'In a way. It feels more as if Lord Robert knows my secret and trusts me with his. I feel bound to him.'

He nodded. I craned my neck to look up into his scowling face. At first I thought he was angry, then I realised that he was thinking hard.

'Does he know my name?' he demanded.

'He knows I am betrothed, but not your name, and nothing of your family,' I said. 'I have not brought danger to your door.'

'No, you keep it all to yourself,' he said with a brief unhappy smile. 'Hannah, I beg you not to go. This road leads straight into danger.'

'I am in danger whatever I do. This way, Lord Robert will protect me.'

'But only while you do his bidding.'

I nodded. I could not tell him that I had volunteered to walk into this danger, and I would have risked worse for love of Lord Robert.

'This is a burden that you shouldn't have to bear alone,' he said. 'If you are in danger, send for me and I will help you escape.'

'I promise that I will.'

Gently he kissed me, full on the lips, and I felt the warmth of his mouth on mine. He released me and stepped back to the boat.

I found I was slightly dizzy, as if I had gulped down strong wine. 'Oh, Daniel!' I breathed, but he was climbing into the boat and did not hear me. I turned to my father and caught him hiding his smile.

'God bless you, daughter, and bring you home safe to us,' he said quietly. I knelt on the wooden pier for my father's blessing and felt his hand come down on my head in the familiar, beloved caress. He took my hands and raised me up. 'He is an attractive young man, isn't he?' he demanded, a chuckle behind his voice. Then he wrapped his cape around himself and went down the steps to the fishing smack.

SUMMER 1553

LADY MARY WAS at her house at Hunsdon, in the county of Hertfordshire. It took us three days to get to her, riding northwards out of London, on a winding road through muddy valleys and then climbing arduously through hills called the North Weald. We stayed overnight on the road, once at an inn, once at a grand house that had been a monastery and was now in the hands of the man who had cleansed it of heresy at some profit to himself. These days they could offer us no rooms better than a hayloft over the stable, and the carter complained that in the old days this had been a generous house of good monks where any traveller might be sure of a good dinner and a comfortable bed. It was the same story all round the country. All the monasteries and abbeys were now in the possession of the great lords, the men of court who had made their fortunes by advising that the world would be a better place if wealth was stripped from the English church and poured into their own pockets.

'If the poor king dies then Lady Mary will come to the throne and turn it all back,' the carter said. 'She will be a queen for the people. A queen who returns us to the old ways.'

Since I had not known the England that he said was lost, I could not feel as he did. I rode ahead of the cart, and it was such an adventure to travel so freely in a strange country that I was sorry when the carter whistled to me and called out, 'Here's Hunsdon now.' I realised that these carefree days were over, that I had to return to work, and that now I had two tasks: one as a holy fool, and the other as a spy.

Lady Mary was in her chamber sewing blackwork, the famous Spanish embroidery of black thread on white linen, while one of her ladies read aloud to her. The first thing I heard, on reaching her presence, was a Spanish word, mispronounced, and she gave a merry laugh when she saw me wince.

'Ah, at last! A girl who can speak Spanish!' she exclaimed and gave me her hand to kiss. 'If you could only read it!'

'I can read it,' I said, considering it reasonable that the daughter of a bookseller should be able to read her native tongue.

'Oh, can you?' She turned to her maid in waiting. 'You will be pleased to hear that, Susan! Now you will not need to read to me in the afternoons.'

Susan did not look at all pleased, but she took herself off to the bay window with the other ladies and took up some sewing.

Lady Mary gestured that I should sit on a cushion close by her feet. 'Tell me all the news of the court. Do you have a message from my brother the king?'

'No, Lady Mary,' I said, and saw her disappointment.

'I was hoping he would have thought of me more kindly, now he is so ill,' she said. 'When he was a little boy I nursed him through half a dozen illnesses. I hoped he would remember that and think that we . . .' She tapped her fingertips together as if to draw herself back from memories. 'No matter,' she said. 'Any other messages?'

'The duke asked me to give you this letter.'

She took it and broke the seal and smoothed it out. I saw her smile and then I heard her warm chuckle. 'You bring me very good news, Hannah the Fool,' she said. 'This is a payment under the will of my late father which has been owed to me since his death. I thought I would never see it, but here it is, a draft on a London goldsmith. I can pay my bills and face the shopkeepers of Ware again.'

'I am glad of it,' I said awkwardly, not knowing what else to say.

'Yes,' she said, then paused, thoughtful. 'The question which remains is why I am suddenly to be so well treated.' She looked speculatively at me. 'Tell me, child, tell me the truth. Is my little brother dying?'

I hesitated, unsure if it was treason to tell of the death of the king.

She took my hand and I looked into her square, determined face. Her eyes, dark and honest, met mine. She looked like a woman you could trust, a mistress you could love. 'You can tell me. I can keep a secret,' she said. 'I have kept many many secrets.'

'Since you ask it, I will tell you: I am certain that he is dying,' I admitted quietly. 'But the duke denies it.'

She nodded. 'And this wedding of Lady Jane Grey to the duke's son. What do they say about it at court?'

'That she was unwilling, and he not much better.'

'And why did the duke insist?' she asked.

'It was time that Guilford was married?' I hazarded.

She looked at me, bright as a knife blade. 'They say no more than that?'

I shrugged. 'Not in my hearing, my lady.'

'And what of you? Did you ask to come to this exile?' Her wry smile indicated to me that she did not think it likely.

'Lord Robert told me to come,' I confessed. 'And his father, the duke.'

'Did they tell you why?'

I wanted to bite my lips to hold in the secret. 'No, my lady. Just to keep you company.'

'What are you afraid of?' she asked bluntly.

For a moment I was so taken aback I could have told her. I was afraid of arrest, of the Inquisition, of the torture chamber and the heretic's death. I was afraid of betraying others to their deaths, afraid of the very air of conspiracy itself. 'I am just a little nervous,' I said quietly. 'I am new to this country, and to court life.'

She let the silence run and then she looked at me more kindly. 'Poor child, you are very young to be adrift, all alone in these deep waters.'

'I am Lord Robert's vassal,' I said. 'I am not alone.'

She smiled. 'Perhaps you will be very good company,' she said finally. 'There have been days and months and even years when I would have been very glad of a merry face and an uplifted voice.'

'I am not a witty fool,' I said cautiously. 'I am not supposed to be especially merry.'

Lady Mary laughed aloud at that. 'And I am not supposed to be given especially to laughter,' she said. 'Perhaps you will suit me very well.'

The household at Hunsdon turned out to be a melancholy place. Lady Mary was plagued with headaches, which often came in the evening, darkening her face as the light drained from the sky. Her ladies would notice her frown, but she never mentioned the pain and never drooped in her wooden chair. She sat as her mother had taught her, upright like a queen, and she kept her head up, even when her eyes were squinting against dim candles.

The mornings were the best times for her. After she had been to Mass and broken her fast she liked to walk, and often she chose me to walk with her. One warm day in late June she commanded me to walk at her side and to name the flowers in Spanish. I had to keep my steps short so that I did not stride ahead of her, and she often stopped with her hand to her side, the colour draining from her face.

'Are you not well this morning, my lady?' I asked.

'Just tired,' she said. 'I did not sleep last night.' She smiled at the concern on my face. 'Oh, it is no worse than it has always been. I should learn to have more serenity. But not to know . . . and to have to wait . . . and to know that he is in the hands of advisers who have set their hearts . . .'

'Your brother?' I asked when she fell silent.

'I have thought of him every day from the day he was born!' she burst out passionately. 'Such a tiny boy and so much expected of him.

So quick to learn and so—I don't know—so cold in his heart where he should have been warm. Poor boy, poor motherless boy! All three of us, thrown together, and none of us with a mother living, and none of us knowing what would happen next.

'I had more care of Elizabeth than I did of him, of course. And now she is far from me, and I cannot even see him. Of course I worry about him: about what they are doing to his body and his soul . . . and about what they are doing to his will,' she added very quietly.

'His will?'

'It is my inheritance,' she said fiercely. 'If you report, as I imagine you do, tell them I never forget that.'

'I don't report!' I exclaimed, shocked. It was true, I had sent no report, there was nothing in our dull lives to report.

'Whether or no,' she dismissed my defence, 'nothing and no one can deny me my place. My father himself left it to me. It is me and then it is Elizabeth. We are three heirs, taking precedence one after another to honour our father. Elizabeth knows that I am the next heir after Edward: he came first as the boy; I come second as the first legitimate princess. And since you promise that you don't report, you can make this reply if anyone asks you: tell them that I will keep my inheritance. I am an English queen-to-be. No one can put me aside.'

Her face was illuminated with her sense of destiny. 'It is the purpose of my life,' she said. 'Nobody will pity me ever again. They will see that I have dedicated my life to being the bride of this country. I will be a virgin queen. I shall have no children but the people of this country. I shall be their mother. I shall live for them. It is my holy calling. I shall give myself up for them.'

She turned from me and strode back to the house, and I followed her at a distance. The morning sun burning off the mist made a lightness in the air all around her, and I had a moment's dizziness as I realised that this woman would be a great queen for England, a queen who would bring back the richness and beauty and charity that her father had stripped out from the churches and from the daily life. The sun was so bright around her yellow silk hood that it was like a crown, and I stumbled on a tussock of grass and fell.

She turned and saw me on my knees. 'Hannah?'

'You will be queen,' I said simply, the Sight speaking in my voice. 'The king will die within a month. Long live the queen.'

In a second she was by my side, holding me up. 'What did you say?'

'You will be queen,' I said. 'He is sinking fast now.'

I lost my senses for a moment and then I opened my eyes again and she was looking down at me, still holding me closely.

'Can you tell me any more?' she asked me gently.

I shook my head. 'I am sorry, Lady Mary, I barely know what I said. It was not said knowingly.'

She nodded. 'It is the Holy Spirit which moves you to speak such news to me. Will you swear to keep it secret between us?'

For a moment I hesitated, thinking of the complicated webs of loyalties that were interwoven around me. I nodded. It was no disloyalty not to tell Lord Robert something he must already know. 'Yes, Lady Mary.'

I tried to rise but I dropped back to my knees with dizziness.

'Wait,' she said. 'Don't get up till your head is clear.' She sat beside me on the grass and gently put my head in her lap. 'Close your eyes.'

I wanted to sleep as she held me. 'I am not a spy,' I said.

Her finger touched my lips. 'Hush,' she said. 'I know that you work for the Dudleys. And I know you are a good girl. Who better than I to understand a life of complicated loyalties? After my father sent my mother away from me there was no one near me who did not try to persuade me that Anne Boleyn was the true queen and her bastard child the true heir. They made me deny my mother, they made me deny my faith, they threatened me with death on the scaffold. I was a girl of twenty and they made me proclaim myself a bastard and my faith a heresy. You need not fear, little Hannah. I understand.'

I felt her soft touch on my hair. I felt my eyes close and the sinews of my back and neck unknot as I realised I was safe with her.

We sat in silence, and then I heard the door of the house bang open. I sat up and saw one of Lady Mary's ladies burst out of the shadowy interior and look wildly around for her. Lady Mary waved and the girl ran over. It was Lady Margaret. As she came close I felt Lady Mary's back straighten, as she steadied herself for the news I had foretold.

'Lady Mary! Oh!'

The girl was almost speechless with her desire to tell, and breathless from her run. 'At church just now . . .'

'What?'

'They didn't pray for you.'

'Pray for me?'

'No. They prayed for the king and his advisers, same as always, but where the prayer says "and for the king's sisters", they missed you out.'

Lady Mary's gaze swept the girl's face. 'Both of us? Elizabeth too?'

'Yes!'

Lady Mary rose to her feet, her eyes narrowed with anxiety. 'Send out Mr Tomlinson into Ware. Tell him to get reports from other churches. See if this is happening everywhere.'

The girl bobbed a curtsy and ran back into the house.

'What does it mean?' I asked, scrambling to my feet.

She looked at me without seeing me. 'It means that Northumberland has started to move against me. First he does not warn me how ill my brother is. Then he commands the priests to leave Elizabeth and me from the prayers. Next he will command them to mention another, the king's new heir. Then, when my poor brother is dead, they will arrest me, arrest Elizabeth, and put their false prince on the throne.'

'Who?' I asked.

'Edward Courtenay,' she said decisively. 'My cousin. He is the only one Northumberland would choose, since he cannot put himself or his sons on the throne.'

I suddenly saw it. The wedding feast, the white face of Lady Jane Grey, the bruises at her throat as if someone had taken her by the neck to shake their ambition into her. 'Oh, but he can: Lady Jane Grey,' I said.

'Newly wed to Northumberland's son Guilford,' Lady Mary agreed. She paused for a moment. 'I would not have thought they would have dared. Her mother, my cousin, would have to resign her claim for her daughter. But Jane is a Protestant, and Dudley's father commands the keys to the kingdom.'

Her pale face suddenly drained even paler and I saw her stagger. 'My God, what of Elizabeth? He will kill us both,' she whispered. 'He will have to. Otherwise there will be rebellions against him from both Protestant and Catholic.' She turned towards the house. 'Come, Hannah!' she threw over her shoulder. 'Come quickly!'

She wrote to warn Elizabeth; she wrote for advice. I did not see either letter, but that night I took the manuscript Lord Robert had given to me and wrote a message, using my father's letter as the base of the code: 'M is alarmed that she is left out of the prayers. She believes Lady J will be named heir. She has written to Eliz to warn her. And to the Sp ambassador for advice.'

I paused then. It was arduous work, translating every letter into another, but I wanted to write something, a line, a word, to remind him of me, not as his spy, not as a fool, but as me, myself, a girl who had promised to serve him heart and soul, for love.

'I miss you,' I wrote, and then I scratched it out, not even troubling to translate it into code.

'When can I come home?' went the same way.

'I am frightened,' was the most honest of all the confessions.

In the end I wrote nothing, there was nothing I could think of that would turn Lord Robert's attention to me, while the boy king was dying and his own young, white-faced sister-in-law was stepping up to the throne of England and bringing the Dudley family to absolute greatness.

There was nothing to do but to wait for news of the death of the king to come from London. Lady Mary had her own private messages coming and going, and optimistic letters from the duke. Then, in the first days of July, one letter made her snatch her breath and put a hand to her heart.

'How is the king, my lady?' I asked her. 'Not worse?'

Her colour burned in her cheeks. 'The duke says that he is better, and that he wants to see me.' She rose to her feet and paced across to the window.

'Shall we go?' I asked. I was on my feet already at the thought of returning to London, to court, to see Lord Robert again, to see my father, and Daniel.

I saw her shoulders straighten as she took the decision. 'If he asks for me, of course I have to go. We'll leave tomorrow.'

Next day we were on the road, Lady Mary's pennant before us, her soldiers around us, and the country people tumbling out of their houses to call out blessings on her name.

Riding towards London with the people of England cheering her on, Lady Mary looked like a true princess. She wore a deep red gown and jacket, which made her dark eyes shine. She rode well, one hand in a worn red glove on the bridle, the other waving to everyone who called out to her, her head up, her courage high, her weariness all gone.

We rode hard along the London road, splashing through the fords at their summertime low, cantering where the tracks were soft enough. Just after midday we came into the town of Hoddesdon, weary of the saddle and hoping for a good dinner and a rest before we continued the journey. Without warning, a man stepped out from a doorway and put his hand up to signal to her. Clearly she recognised him: she waved him forward so he could speak to her privately. He was brief, and kept his voice low. Then he stepped back and Lady Mary snapped an order to halt, and tumbled down from her saddle so fast that her Master of Horse could scarcely catch her. She ran into the nearest inn, shouting for paper and pen, and ordering everyone to drink, eat, see to their horses and be ready to leave again within the hour.

'Mother of God, I can't,' Lady Margaret said pitifully as her royal mistress strode past. 'I'm too tired to go another step.'

'Then stay behind,' snapped Lady Mary, who never snapped. That sharpness of tone warned us that the hopeful ride to London, to visit the young, recovering king, had suddenly gone terribly wrong.

When she came out of the parlour she was pale and her eyes were red, but she was not softened by grief. She was sharp with decision, and she was angry.

She sent one messenger flying south down the road to London to find the Spanish ambassador, to beg for his advice and to alert the Spanish emperor that she would need his help to claim her throne. She took another messenger aside for a verbal message for Lady Elizabeth. 'Speak only to her when you are alone,' she emphasised. 'Tell her not to go to London; it is a trap. Tell her to come at once to me for her own safety.'

She sent a further message to the duke himself, swearing that she was too ill to ride to London but would rest quietly at Hunsdon. Then she ordered the main group to stay behind. 'I'll take you, Lady Margaret, and you, Hannah,' she said. She smiled at her lady in waiting and closest friend, Jane Dormer. 'Follow us,' she said, and she leaned forward to whisper our destination in her ear. 'You must bring this company on behind us. We are going to travel too fast for everyone to keep pace.'

She picked six men to escort us, gave her followers a brief leave-taking and snapped her fingers for her Master of Horse to help her into the saddle. She wheeled her horse round and led us out of Hoddesdon, back the way we had come. But this time we took the great road north.

'Where are we going, Lady Mary? It's getting dark,' Lady Margaret asked plaintively. 'We can't ride in the dark.'

'Kenninghall,' Lady Mary crisply replied.

'Where's Kenninghall?' I asked, seeing Lady Margaret's aghast face.

'Norfolk,' she said as if it were the end of the world. 'God help us, she's running away.'

'Running away?' I felt my throat tense.

'It's towards the sea. She'll get a ship out of Lowestoft and run to Spain. Whatever that man told her must mean that she's in such danger that she has to get out of the country altogether.'

It was a punishing ride. We did not check until it was fully night, when we paused at the home of a gentleman, John Huddlestone, at Sawston Hall. I begged a piece of paper and a pen from the house-keeper and wrote a letter, not to Lord Robert, whose address I did not dare to give, but to John Dee.

'My dear tutor,' I wrote, hoping this would mislead anyone who opened my letter, 'this little riddle may amuse you.' Then underneath I wrote the coded letters in the form of a serpentine circle, hoping to make it look like a game that a girl of my age might send to a kind scholar. It simply read: 'She is going to Kenninghall.'

The housekeeper promised to send it to Greenwich by the carter who would pass by tomorrow, and I had to hope that it would find its destination and be read by the right man. Then I lay down to sleep on a little truckle bed that they had pulled out beside the kitchen fire.

I woke painfully early, at five in the morning, to find the kitchen lad clattering pails of water and sacks of logs past my head. Lady Mary heard Mass in John Huddlestone's chapel, as if it were not a forbidden ceremony, broke her fast, and was back in the saddle by seven in the morning, riding in the highest of spirits away from Sawston Hall with John Huddlestone at her side to show her the way.

I was riding at the back, the dozen or so horses clattering ahead of me, my little pony too tired to keep pace, when I smelt an old terrible scent on the air. I could smell smoke, the scent of heresy, a fire burning up someone's faith, burning up someone's house . . . I turned in the saddle and saw the glow on the horizon where the house we had just left, Sawston Hall, was being torched.

'My lady!' I called out. She heard me, and turned her head and then reined in her horse, John Huddlestone beside her.

'Your house!' I said simply to him.

He looked beyond me, squinting his eyes to see. He couldn't tell for sure; he could not smell the smoke as I had done.

Lady Mary looked at me. 'Are you sure, Hannah?'

I nodded. 'I can smell it. I can smell smoke.' I heard the quaver of fear in my voice. 'Your house is being burnt out, sir.'

He turned his horse as if he would ride straight home, then he remembered the woman whose visit had cost him his home. 'Forgive me, Lady Mary. I must go home . . . My wife . . .'

'Go,' she said gently. 'And be very well assured that when I come into my own, I will give you another house, a bigger and richer house than this one you have lost for your loyalty to me. I shall not forget.'

He nodded, half deaf with worry, and then set his horse at a gallop to where the blaze of his house glowed on the horizon.

His groom rode up beside Lady Mary. 'D'you want me to guide you, my lady?' he asked.

'Yes,' she answered. 'Can you take me to Bury St Edmunds?'

'Through Mildenhall and Thetford forest? Yes, m'lady.'

She gave the signal to move on and she rode without once looking back. I thought that she was a princess indeed, if she could see last night's refuge burnt to the ground and think only of the struggle ahead of her and not of the ruins left behind.

That night we stayed at Euston Hall near Thetford, and I lay on the floor of Lady Mary's bedroom, wrapped in my cape, still fully dressed, waiting for the alarm that I was sure must come. All night I did little more than doze, waiting for a Protestant mob. I could not close my eyes for fear that I would be wakened by the smell of smoke, so that it was almost a relief near dawn when I heard the sound of a horse's hoofs on cobbles. I was up at the window in a second, my hand outstretched to Lady Mary as she woke, cautioning her to be quiet.

'What can you see?' she demanded from the bed, as she pulled back the covers. 'How many men?'

'Only one horse. He looks weary.'

'Go and see who it is.'

I hurried down the wooden stairs to the hall. The porter had the spy-hole opened and was arguing with the traveller, who seemed to be demanding admission to stay the night. I touched the porter on the shoulder and he stood aside.

'And who are you?' I demanded, my voice as gruff as I could make it.

'Who are you?' he asked back.

'You'd better tell me what you want,' I insisted.

He came closer to the spyhole and lowered his voice to a whisper. 'I have important news for a great lady. It is about her brother. D'you understand me?'

There was no way of knowing whether or not he was sent to entrap us. I took the risk, stepped back and nodded to the porter. 'Let him in, and then bar the door behind him again.'

He came in.

'What's the message?' I asked.

'I shall tell it to no one but herself.'

There was a rustle of silken skirts and Lady Mary came down the stairs. 'And you are?' she asked.

It was his response to the sight of her that convinced me that he was on our side, and that the world had changed for us, overnight. Fast as a stooping falcon, he dropped down to one knee, pulled his hat from his head, and bowed to her, as to a queen.

God save her, she did not turn a hair. She extended her hand as if she had been Queen of England for all her life. He kissed it reverently, and then looked up into her face.

'I am Robert Raynes, a goldsmith of London, sent by Sir Nicholas Throckmorton to bring you the news that your brother Edward is dead, Your Grace. You are Queen of England.'

'God bless him,' she said softly. 'God save Edward's precious soul.'

There was a short silence.

'Did he die in faith?' she asked.

He shook his head. 'He died as a Protestant.'

She nodded. 'And I am proclaimed queen?' she demanded.

He shook his head. 'The king died in much pain on the night of the sixth,' he said quietly.

'The *sixth*?' she interrupted.

'Yes. Before his death he changed his father's will. You are denied the succession, the Lady Elizabeth also. Lady Jane Grey is named heir.'

'And what about me?'

'You are named as a traitor to the throne. Lord Robert Dudley is on his way now to arrest you and take you to the Tower.'

'Lord Robert is coming?' I asked.

'He will go to Hunsdon first,' Lady Mary reassured me. 'I wrote to his father that I was staying there. He won't know where we are.'

I did not contradict her, but I knew that John Dee would send my note on to him this very day and that, thanks to me, he would know exactly where to look for us.

Her concern was all for her sister. 'And Lady Elizabeth?'

He shrugged. 'I don't know. She may be arrested already.'

'And when was the king's death announced? And Lady Jane falsely proclaimed?'

'Not when I left.'

She took a moment to understand, and then she was angry. 'He has died, and it has not been announced? My brother is lying dead, unwatched? Without the rites of the church? Without any honours done to him at all?'

'His death was still a secret when I left.'

She nodded, her eyes suddenly veiled and cautious. 'I thank you for coming to me,' she said. 'You can sleep here tonight. Go back to London in the morning and convey my thanks to Sir Nicholas. He has done the right thing to inform me. I am queen, and I will have my throne.'

She turned on her heel and swept up the stairs, and I followed. As soon as we got into her room she closed the door behind us, and threw aside her regal dignity.

'Get me the clothes of a serving girl, and wake John Huddlestone's groom,' she said urgently. 'Then go to the stables and get two horses ready, one with a pillion saddle for me and the groom, one for you.'

'My lady?'

'You call me Your Grace now,' she said grimly. 'I am Queen of England. Now hurry.'

'What am I to tell the groom?'

'Tell him that we have to get to Kenninghall today. That I will ride behind him; we will leave the rest of them here. You come with me.'

I nodded and hurried from the room. The serving maid who had waited on us last night was sleeping with half a dozen others in the attic bedrooms. I shook her awake, put my hand over her mouth and hissed in her ear: 'I've had enough of this; I'm running away. I'll give you a silver shilling for your gown and cape. You can say I stole them.'

'Two shillings,' she said instantly.

'Agreed,' I said. 'Give them me, and I'll bring you the money.'

She bundled them up for me with her cap and I went light-footed downstairs to Lady Mary's room.

'Here,' I said. 'They cost me two shillings.'

She found the coins in her purse. 'No boots.'

'Please wear your own boots,' I said fervently. 'I've run away before, I know what it's like. You'll never get anywhere in borrowed boots.'

She smiled at that. 'Hurry,' was all she said.

I ran back upstairs with the two shillings and then I found Tom, John Huddlestone's groom, and sent him down to the stables to get the horses ready. I crept down to the bakery just outside the kitchen door, and found, as I had hoped, a batch of bread rolls baked in the warmth of the oven last night. I stuffed my breeches pockets and my jacket pockets with half a dozen of them so that I looked like a donkey with panniers, and then I went back to the hall.

Lady Mary was there, dressed as a serving maid, her hood pulled over her face. The porter was arguing, reluctant to open the door to the stable yard for a maidservant. She turned with relief as she heard me approach.

'Come on,' I said reasonably to the man. 'She is a servant of John Huddlestone. His groom is waiting. He told us to leave at first light.'

He complained, but he opened the door and Lady Mary and I slipped through. Tom was in the yard, holding one big hunter with a pillion saddle on its back and a smaller horse for me.

He got into the saddle and took the hunter to the mounting block. I helped the Lady Mary scramble up behind him. She took a tight grip round his waist and kept her hood pulled forward to hide her face. I had to take my horse to the mounting block too. I had never ridden such a big horse before, and I was frightened of him, but no smaller animal could manage the hard ride we must make today.

Tom led the way out of the yard. I turned after him and heard my heart pounding and knew that I was on the run, once again, and afraid, once again, and that this time I was perhaps in a worse case because this time I was running with the pretender to the throne of England, with Lord Robert Dudley and his army in pursuit, and I was his vassal sworn; her trusted servant, and a Jew; but a practising Christian, serving a Papist princess in a country sworn to be Protestant. Little wonder that my heart was in my mouth and beating louder than the clopping of the hoofs of the horses as we went down the road to the east.

When we reached Kenninghall at midday, I saw why we had ridden till the horses foundered to get here. It was a solid moated house, with a drawbridge that could be raised and a portcullis above it that could be dropped down to seal the only entrance. It was built in warm red brick, a deceptively beautiful house that could be held in a siege.

Lady Mary was not expected, and the few servants who lived at the house to keep it in order came tumbling out of the doors in a flurry of surprise. After a nod from Lady Mary I quickly told them of the astounding news from London as they took our horses into the stable yard and a cheer went up as they heard of her accession to the throne.

As they pulled me down, I let out a yelp of pain. The inner part of my legs had been skinned raw from three days in the saddle, and my back and shoulders were locked tight from the jolting ride.

Lady Mary must have been near-dead with exhaustion, after sitting pillion for all that long time, but only I saw the grimace of pain as they lifted her down to the ground. Everyone else saw the tilt of her chin as she heard them shout for her, and the charm of the Tudor smile as she welcomed them all into the great hall and bade them good cheer. She took a moment to pray for the soul of her dead brother, and then she raised her head and promised them that, just as she had been a fair landlord and mistress to them, she would be a good queen.

That earned her another cheer and the hall started to fill with people, workers from the fields and woods and villagers from their homes, and the servants ran about with flagons of ale and cups of wine and loaves of bread and meat. The Lady Mary took her seat at the head of the hall and smiled on everyone as if she had never been ill in her life, then after an hour of good company, she laughed out loud and said she must get out of this cloak and this poor gown, and went to her rooms.

The few house servants had flung themselves into getting her rooms ready and her bed was made with linen. They brought in a bathtub, lined it with sheets to protect her from splinters, and filled it with hot water. And they found some old gowns, which she had left behind when she was last at this house, and laid them out on the bed for her.

'You can go,' she said to me, as she threw the servant girl's cloak from her shoulders, and turned her back to the maid to be unlaced. 'Find something to eat and go straight to bed. You must be tired out.'

'Thank you,' I said, hobbling for the door.

'And, Hannah?'

'Yes, my lady . . . Yes, Your Grace?'

'You have been a good friend to me this day. I will not forget it.'

I paused, thinking of the two letters I had written to Lord Robert that would bring him hard on our heels, thinking what would happen to this determined, ambitious woman when he caught us. It would be the Tower for her, and probably her death for treason. I had been a spy in her household and the falsest of friends.

If I could have confessed to her then, I would have done. I wanted to tell her that I had been put into her household to work against her, but that now that I knew her, and loved her, I would do anything to serve her. I wanted to tell her that Robert Dudley was my lord and I would always be bound to do anything he asked me. I wanted to tell her that everything I did seemed to be always full of contradictions: black and white, love and fear, all at once.

But I could say nothing, and so I just dropped to one knee before her and bowed my head.

She did not give me her hand to kiss, like a queen would have done. She put her hand on my head like my own mother used to do and she said, 'God bless you, Hannah, and keep you safe from sin.'

At that moment, at that particular tenderness, I felt the tears well up in my eyes. I got myself out of the room and into my own small attic bedchamber and into my bed without bath or dinner, before anybody should see me cry like the little girl I still was.

We were at Kenninghall for three days on siege alert, but still Lord Robert and his company of cavalry did not come. The gentlemen from the country all around the manor came pouring in with their servants and their kinsmen, some of them armed, some of them bringing black-smiths to hammer out spears and lances from the pruning hooks, spades and scythes they brought with them. Lady Mary proclaimed herself as queen in the great hall, despite the advice of the Spanish ambassador. He had written to tell her that Northumberland had sent warships into the French seas off Norfolk, to prevent the Spanish ships from rescuing her. She must surrender to the duke and give up her claim to the crown, and throw herself on his mercy.

'What can you see, Hannah?' she asked me. It was early morning, and she had just come from Mass, her rosary beads still in her fingers, her forehead still damp with holy water. It was a bad morning for her, her face, sometimes so illuminated and merry with hope, was grey and tired. She looked sick of fear itself.

I shook my head. 'I have only seen for you once, Your Grace, and I was certain then that you would be queen. And now you are. I have seen nothing since.'

'I am queen indeed now,' she said wryly. 'I am proclaimed queen by myself at least. I wish you had told me how long it would last, and if anyone else would agree with me.'

'I wish I could,' I said sincerely. 'What are we going to do?'

'My Spanish kinsmen tell me to surrender,' she said simply. 'They tell me that I will be executed if I continue with this course, that it's a battle I can't win. The duke has the Tower, he has London, he has the country, he has the warships at sea and an army of followers and the royal guard. He has all the coin of the realm at the Mint, he has all the weapons of the nation at the Tower. I have this one castle, these few loyal men and their pitchforks. And somewhere out there is Lord Robert and his troop coming towards us.'

'Can't we get away?' I asked.

She shook her head. 'Not fast enough, not far enough. If I could have got on a Spanish warship then, perhaps . . . but the duke has the sea between here and France held down by English warships, he was ready for this, and I was unprepared. I am trapped.'

I remembered John Dee's map spread out in the duke's study and the little counters that signified soldiers and sailors on ships all around Norfolk, and Lady Mary trapped in the middle of them.

'Will you have to surrender?' I whispered.

I had thought she was frightened; but at my question the colour rushed into her cheeks and she smiled as if I had suggested a challenge, a great gamble. 'You know, I'm damned if I will!' she swore. She laughed aloud as if it was a bet for a joust rather than her life on the table. 'I have spent my life running and lying and hiding. Just once, *just once* I should be glad to ride out under my own standard and defy the men who have denied my right and denied the authority of the church and God Himself.'

I felt my own spirits leap up at her enthusiasm. 'My la . . . Your Grace,' I stumbled.

Lady Mary gathered her rosary beads, tucked them into the pocket of her gown and strode towards the door of the great hall, where her armies of gentlemen and soldiers were breaking their fast. She entered the head of the hall and mounted the dais. 'Today we move out,' she announced, loud and clear for the least man at the back of the hall to hear. 'We go to Framlingham, a day's ride, no more than that. I shall raise my standard there. If we get there before Lord Robert we can hold him off in a siege. We can hold him off for months. I can fight a battle from there. I can collect troops.'

There was a murmur of surprise and then approbation.

'Trust me!' she commanded them. 'I will not fail you. I am your proclaimed queen and you will see me on the throne, and then I will remember who was here today. I will remember and you will be repaid many times over for doing your duty to the true Queen of England.'

Mary raised her standard at Framlingham Castle, a fortress to match any in England, and unbelievably half the world turned up on horseback and on foot to swear allegiance to her. I walked beside her as she went down the massed ranks of the men and thanked them for coming to her and swore to be a true and honest queen to them.

We had news from London at last. The announcement of King Edward's death had been made shamefully late. After the poor boy had died, the duke had kept the corpse hidden in his room while the ink dried on his will, and the powerful men of the country considered where their best interests lay. Lady Jane Grey had to be dragged onto the throne by her father-in-law. They said she had cried and said that she could not be queen, and that the Lady Mary was the rightful heir. It did not save her from her fate. They unfurled the canopy of state over her bowed head, they served her on bended knee despite her tearful protests, and the Duke of Northumberland proclaimed her as queen.

The country was launched into civil war, against us, the traitors. Lady Elizabeth had not replied to Lady Mary's warnings. She had taken to her bed when she heard of her brother's death and was too sick even to read her letters. When Lady Mary learned of that, she turned away to hide the hurt in her face. She had counted on Elizabeth's support, the two princesses together defending their father's will. To find that Elizabeth was hiding under the bed covers rather than racing to be with her sister, was a blow to Mary's heart as well as to her cause.

We learned that Windsor Castle had been fortified and provisioned for a siege, the guns of the Tower of London were battle-ready and turned to face inland, and Northumberland himself had raised an army and was coming to root out our Lady Mary, who was now officially named as a traitor to Queen Jane.

But then, in the middle of July, it all fell apart for the duke. His alliances, his treaties, could not hold against the sense that every Englishman had that Mary, Henry's daughter, was the rightful queen. Northumberland was hated by many and it was clear that he would rule through Jane as he had ruled through Edward. The people of England, from lords to commoners, muttered and then declared against him.

The accord he had stitched together to darn Queen Jane into the fabric of England all unravelled. More and more men declared in public for Lady Mary, and Lord Robert himself was defeated by an army of outraged citizens, who just sprang up from the ploughed furrows, swearing that they would protect the rightful queen. Lord Robert declared for the Lady Mary and deserted his father but, despite turning his coat, was captured at Bury by citizens who declared him a traitor. The duke himself, trapped at Cambridge, his army disappearing like the morning mist, announced suddenly that he too was for Lady Mary and sent her a message explaining that he had only ever tried to do his best for the realm.

'What does this mean?' I asked her, seeing the letter shaking so violently in her hand that she could hardly read it.

'It means I have won,' she said simply. 'Won by right, accepted right and not by battle. I am queen and the people's choice.'

'And what will happen to the duke?' I asked, thinking of his son, Lord Robert, somewhere a prisoner.

'He's a traitor,' she said, her eyes cold.

I said nothing. I waited for a moment, a heartbeat, a girl's heartbeat. 'And what will happen to Lord Robert?' I asked, my voice very small.

Lady Mary turned. 'He is a traitor and a traitor's son. What do you think will happen to him?'

Lady Mary took her big horse and, riding sidesaddle, set off on the road to London, a thousand, two thousand men riding behind her, and their men, their tenants and retainers and followers coming on foot behind them. The Lady Mary, in her old red riding habit, with her head held high, rode her big horse like a knight going into battle, a queen going to claim her throne. She had won the greatest victory of her life by sheer determination and courage.

Everyone thought that her coming to the throne would be the return of the good years, rich harvests, warm weather, and an end to the constant epidemics of plague. Everyone thought that she would restore the wealth of the church, the beauty of the shrines and the certainty of faith. Everyone was glad to see her, with her army of men behind her, their bright faces showing the world that they were proud to serve such a princess and to bring her to her capital city, which was ringing the bells in every church tower to make her welcome.

Lady Elizabeth, too sick to rise from her bed during the days of danger, managed to get to London before us. She came riding out from the city to greet us, at the head of a thousand men, all in the Tudor colours of green and white, riding in her pride as if she had never been sick with terror and hiding in her bed. She came out as if she were Lord Mayor of London, coming to give us the keys to the city, with the cheers of the Londoners all around her.

I reined in my horse and fell back a little so that I could see her. I remembered the girl in the garden that I had seen running from her stepfather and making sure that he caught her. I was desperately curious to see how that girl had changed.

She was young, only nineteen years old, yet she was imposing. I saw at once that she had arranged this cavalcade—she knew the power of appearances and she had the skill to design them. The green of her livery had been chosen to suit the flaming brazen red of her hair, which she wore loose beneath her green hood as if to flaunt her youth and maidenhood beside her older spinster sister. Against her radiance, the Lady Mary, drained by the strain of the last two months, faded into second place.

Lady Elizabeth's entourage halted before us and Lady Mary started to dismount as Lady Elizabeth flung herself down from her big white gelding, almost as grand as a man's warhorse, as if she had been waiting all her life for this moment. At the sight of her, the Lady Mary's face lit up, as a mother will smile on seeing her child. Lady Mary held out her arms, Elizabeth plunged into her embrace and Lady Mary kissed her warmly.

Elizabeth welcomed her sister to the city and congratulated her on her great victory. 'A victory of hearts,' she said. 'You are queen of the hearts of your people, the only way to rule this country.'

'Our victory,' Mary said generously at once. 'Northumberland would have put us both to death. I have won the right for us both to take our inheritance. You will be an acknowledged princess again, my sister and my heir, and you will ride beside me when I enter London.'

'Your Grace honours me too much,' Elizabeth said sweetly.

The Lady Mary gave the signal to mount and Elizabeth turned to her horse as her groom helped her into her saddle. She smiled around at us and saw me, riding astride in my pageboy livery. Her gaze went past me, utterly uninterested. She did not recognise me as the child who had seen her with Tom Seymour in the garden, so long ago.

But I was interested in her. From the first glimpse I had of her, up against a tree like a common whore, she had haunted my memory. There was something about her that fascinated me. When I saw her, in her green gown on that huge white horse, I saw a woman who was proud of her beauty and beautiful in her pride, and I longed to grow into a woman like that. I had been an unhappy girl for so long, and then a boy for so long, and a fool for so long that I had no idea how to be a woman—the very idea baffled me. But when I saw Lady Elizabeth, high on her horse, blazing with beauty and confidence, I thought that this was the sort of woman that I might one day become.

I looked from her to Lady Mary, the mistress I had come to love, and I thought that it would be better for her if she made plans to marry off Lady Elizabeth at once, and send her far away. No household could be at peace with this firebrand in its midst, and no kingdom could settle with such an heir burning so brightly beside an ageing queen.

AUTUMN 1553

As Lady Mary became established in her new life as the next Queen of England, I realised that I must speak to her about my own future. I chose my time carefully, just after Mass when the Lady Mary walked back from her chapel at Richmond in a mood of quiet exaltation. It was then that I fell into step beside her.

'Your Grace?'

'Yes, Hannah?' she smiled at me. 'Do you have any words of wisdom for me?'

'I am a most irregular fool,' I said. 'I see that I pronounce very rarely.'

'You told me I would be queen, and I held that to my heart in the days when I was afraid,' she said. 'I can wait for the gift of the Holy Spirit to move you.'

'It was that I wanted to speak to you about,' I said awkwardly. 'I came into the king's service when I was begged as a fool to him by the Duke of Northumberland, who then sent me as a companion to you. You, er . . . you don't have to have me.'

As I spoke, we turned into her private apartments and it was as well, for she gave a most unqueenly gurgle of laughter. 'You are not, as it were, compulsory?'

I found I was smiling too. 'Please, Your Grace. I have been in your household without you ever asking for my company. I just wanted to say that you can release me.'

She sobered at once. 'Do you want to go home, Hannah?'

'Not especially, Your Grace,' I said tentatively. 'I love my father very well but at home I am his clerk and printer. It is more enjoyable at court.'

'Hannah, would you like to stay with me?' she asked sweetly.

I knelt at her feet. 'I would,' I said, speaking from my heart. I thought I might be safe with her. 'But I cannot promise to have the Sight.'

'I know that,' she said gently. 'It is the gift of the Holy Spirit, which blows where it lists, I don't expect you to be my astrologer. I want you to be my little maid, my little friend. Will you be that?'

'Yes, Your Grace, I should like that,' I said, and felt the touch of her hand on my head.

She was silent for a moment, her hand resting gently as I knelt before her. 'It is very rare to find one that I can trust,' she said quietly. 'I know that you came into my household paid by my enemies, but I think your gift comes from God, and I believe that you came to me from God. And you love me now, don't you, Hannah?'

'Yes, Your Grace,' I said simply. 'I don't think anyone could serve you and not come to love you.'

These were not easy days for the Lady Mary. She was preparing for her coronation but the Tower, where the kings of England usually spent their coronation night, was filled with traitors who had armed against her only a few months before. Her advisers told her that she should execute at once everyone who had been involved in the rebellion.

'I will not have the blood of that foolish girl on my hands,' the Lady Mary said.

Lady Jane had written to her cousin and confessed that she had been wrong to take the throne but that she had acted under duress.

'I know Cousin Jane,' the Lady Mary said quietly to Jane Dormer one evening. 'I have known her since she was a girl. She would never have put herself before one of my father's named heirs. The sin was done by the Duke of Northumberland and by Jane's father between them.'

'You can't pardon everyone,' Jane Dormer said bluntly. 'And she was proclaimed queen and sat beneath the canopy of state. You can't pretend it did not happen.'

Lady Mary nodded. 'The duke had to die,' she agreed. 'But there it can end. I shall release Jane's father, the Duke of Suffolk, and Jane and her husband Guilford can stay in the Tower until after my coronation.'

'And Robert Dudley?' I asked in as small a voice as I could make.

She looked around and saw me, seated on the steps before her throne, her greyhound beside me. 'Oh, are you there, little fool?' she said gently. 'Yes, your old master shall be tried for treason but held, not executed, until it is safe to release him. Does that content you?'

'Whatever Your Grace wishes,' I said obediently, but my heart leapt at the thought of his survival.

'It won't content those who want your safety,' Jane Dormer pointed out bluntly. 'How can you live in peace when those who would have destroyed you are still walking on this earth? How will you make them stop their plotting? D'you think they would have pardoned and released *you* if they had won?'

The Lady Mary smiled and put her hand over the hand of her best friend. 'Jane, this throne was given to me by God. I shall show His mercy whenever I can. Even to those who know it not.'

I sent a note to my father that I would come on Michaelmas Day, and I collected my wages and strode out through the darkening streets in my good-fitting boots and with a little sword at my side.

The door of the bookshop was closed, candlelight showing through the shutters. I tapped on the door and he opened it cautiously. It was Friday night and the Sabbath candle was hidden under a pitcher beneath the counter, burning its holy light into the darkness.

He was pale as I came into the room and I knew, with the understanding of a fellow refugee, that the knock on the door had startled him.

'Father, it is only me,' I said gently and I knelt before him, and he blessed me and raised me up.

'So, you are in service to the royal court again,' he said, smiling. 'How your fortunes do rise, my daughter.'

'She is a wonderful woman,' I said. 'I would rather serve her than anyone else in the land.'

'Rather than Lord Robert?'

I glanced towards the closed door. 'Only the Tower guards can serve him and I pray that they do it well.'

My father shook his head. 'I remember him coming here that day, a man you would think could command half the world, and now . . .'

'She won't execute him,' I said. 'She will be merciful to all now that the duke himself is dead.'

My father nodded. 'Dangerous times,' he said. 'Mr Dee remarked the other day that dangerous times are a crucible for change.'

'You have seen him?'

He nodded again. 'He is a most profound student and thinker. A great man. Oh! And I nearly forgot. He has ordered some books to be delivered to Lord Robert in the Tower.'

'Has he?' I said. 'Shall I take them for him?'

'As soon as they arrive,' my father said gently. 'And, Hannah, if you see Lord Robert . . .'

'Yes?'

'*Querida*, you must ask him to release you from your service to him and bid him farewell. He is a traitor sentenced to death. We cannot be associated with him.'

I bowed my head.

'Daniel wishes it too.'

My head came up at that. 'Why, whatever would he know about it?'

My father smiled. 'He is not an ignorant boy, Hannah.'

'He is not at court. He does not know the way of that world.'

'He is going to be a very great physician,' my father said gently. 'He is a thoughtful young man, and a hard worker, and he has a gift for study.

He comes here twice a week to read. And he always asks for you.'

'Does he?'

My father nodded. 'He calls you his princess,' he said.

I was so surprised for a moment that I could not speak. 'His princess?'

'Yes,' my father said, smiling at my incomprehension. 'He speaks like a young man in love. He comes to see me and he asks me, "How is my princess?"—and he means you, Hannah.'

The coronation of my mistress, Lady Mary, was set for the first day of October and the whole court, the whole city of London and the whole country had spent much of the summer preparing for the celebration that would bring Henry's daughter to his throne at last. There were faces missing from the crowds that lined the London streets. Devoted Protestants, mistrusting the queen's sincere promise of tolerance, had already fled into exile. But the rest of the court, city and country turned out in their thousands to greet the new queen.

It was a fairy-tale coronation, a spectacle like something out of one of my father's storybooks. A princess in a golden chariot, wearing blue velvet trimmed with white ermine, riding through the streets of her city, which were hung with tapestries, past fountains running with wine so that the very air was heady with the warm scent of it, past crowds who screamed with delight at the sight of their princess, their virgin queen.

In the second carriage was Princess Elizabeth and Henry's neglected queen, Anne of Cleves, fatter than ever, with a ready smile for the crowd. And behind that chariot came forty-six ladies of the court and country, on foot and dressed in their best, and flagging a little by the time we had processed from Whitehall to the Tower.

Behind them, in the procession of officers of the court, came all the minor gentry and officials. I walked among them with Will Somers, the witty fool, beside me, and my yellow cap on my head and my fool's bell on a stick in my hand. I marched with my head up and thought myself an Englishwoman that day, and a loyal Englishwoman at that, with a proven love for my queen and for my adopted country.

We slept that night in the Tower, and the next day Lady Mary was crowned Queen of England, with her sister Elizabeth carrying her train, and the first to kneel to her and swear allegiance. I could hardly see them; I was crammed at the back of the Abbey, peering round a gentleman of the court. In any case, my sight was blinded with tears at the knowledge that my Lady Mary had come to her throne, and her lifelong battle for recognition and justice was over at last. God (whatever His name might be) had finally blessed her; she had won.

WINTER 1553

IT WAS AS DARK as midnight, though it was still only six in the evening, the mist peeling like a black shroud off the corpse of the cold river. The smell in my nostrils was the scent of despair from the massive, wet, weeping walls of the Tower of London, surely the gloomiest palace that any monarch ever built. I presented myself to the postern gate and the guard held up a flaming torch to see my white face.

'A young lad,' he concluded.

'I've got books to deliver to Lord Robert,' I said.

He withdrew the torch and the darkness flooded over me, then the creak of the hinges warned me that he was opening the gate.

'Let me see them,' he said.

I proffered the books readily enough. They were works of theology defending the Papist point of view, licensed by the Vatican and authorised by the queen's own council.

'Go through,' the guard said.

I walked on the slippery cobblestones to the guardhouse, and from there along a causeway, and then up a flight of wooden steps to the high doorway in the fortress wall of the white tower.

Another soldier was waiting in the doorway. He led me inside and then rapped at an inner door and swung it open to admit me.

At last I saw him, my Lord Robert, leaning over his papers, a candle at his elbow, the golden light shining on his dark head, on his pale skin, and then the slow-dawning radiance of his smile.

'Mistress Boy! Oh! My Mistress Boy!'

I dropped to one knee. 'My lord!' was all I could say before I burst into tears.

He laughed, pulled me to my feet, put his arm around my shoulders, wiped my face, all in one dizzying caress. 'Come now, child, come now. What's wrong?'

'It's you!' I gulped. 'You being here. And you look so . . .' I could not bear to say 'pale', 'ill', 'tired', 'defeated', but all those words were true. 'Imprisoned,' I found at last.

He laughed and led me over to the fire, seated himself on a chair and pulled up a stool so that I was facing him, like a favourite nephew.

'It was a great gamble,' he said softly. 'And we lost, and the price we will pay is a heavy one.'

'Will they . . .?' I could not bear to ask him if it was his own death that he was facing with this indomitable smile.

'Oh, I should think so,' he said cheerfully. 'Very soon. I would, if I were the queen. Now tell me the news. Tell me everything.'

'The queen is considering if she should marry; you'll know that, I suppose,' I said, low-voiced. 'And she has been ill. They have proposed one man after another. The best choice is Philip of Spain. The Spanish ambassador tells her that it will be a good marriage, but she is afraid. She knows she cannot rule alone but she is afraid of a man ruling over her.'

'And Lady Elizabeth?'

I glanced at the thick wooden door and dropped my low voice to an even quieter murmur. 'She and the queen cannot agree these days,' I said. 'Lady Elizabeth is no longer the little girl of the queen's teaching, and she goes to Mass only when she has to. And everyone says . . .'

'What do they say, my little spy?'

'That she is sending out letters to true Protestants, that she has a network of supporters. That the French will pay for an uprising against the queen. And that, at the very least, she only has to wait until the queen dies and then the throne is all hers anyway, and she can throw off all disguise and be a Protestant queen as she is now a Protestant princess.'

'And the queen believes all this slander?'

I looked up at him, hoping that he would understand. 'She thought that Elizabeth would be a sister to her,' I said. 'Elizabeth went with her into London at the very moment of her greatest triumph. She was at her side then, and again at the day of her coronation. She was first to kneel before the new queen and put her hands in hers and swear to be a true and faithful subject. She swore fidelity before God. How can she now plot against her?'

He sat back in his chair and observed my heat with interest. 'Is the queen angry with Elizabeth?'

I shook my head. 'No. It's worse than anger. She is disappointed in her. She is lonely, Lord Robert. She wanted her little sister at her side. She singled her out for love and respect. She can hardly believe now that Elizabeth would plot against her.'

'And yet the queen does nothing against her?'

'She wants to bring peace,' I said. 'She won't act against Elizabeth unless she has to. She says that she won't execute Lady Jane, or your brother . . .' I did not say 'or you' but we were both thinking it. 'She wants to bring peace to this country.'

'Well, amen to that,' Lord Robert said. He rose to his feet and looked out of the window at the dark courtyard below, where his own father had been executed. 'And shall I stay here till I rot?' he asked quietly.

'I once asked her directly. She said that she wanted no blood spilt that could be spared. She won't execute you and she must let you go free when Lady Jane goes free.'

'I wouldn't if I were her,' he said quietly. 'If I were her, I would rid myself of Elizabeth, of Jane, of my brother and of me, and name Mary Stuart as the next heir, French or not. One clean cut. That's the only way to get this country back into the Papist church and keep it there, and soon she will realise it.'

I crossed the room and stood behind him. Timidly I put my hand on his shoulder.

'And you?' he asked gently. 'Safe in royal service now?'

'I am never safe,' I said in a low voice. 'I love the queen and no one questions who I am or where I have come from. I should feel safe, but I always feel as if I am creeping across thin ice.'

He nodded. 'I'll take your secret with me to the scaffold if I go that way,' he promised. 'You have nothing to fear from me, child.'

I nodded. When I looked up he was watching me, his dark eyes warm. 'You've grown, Mistress Boy,' he remarked. 'Soon be a woman. I shall be sorry not to see it.'

I had nothing to say. He smiled as if he knew only too well the churn of my emotions. 'Ah, little fool. I should have left you in your father's shop that day, and not drawn you into this.'

'My father told me to bid you farewell.'

'Aye, he is right. You can leave me now. I release you from your promise to love me. You are no longer my vassal. I let you go.'

It was little more than a joke to him. He knew as well as I did that you cannot release a girl from her promise to love a man. She either gets herself free or she is bound for life.

'I'm not free,' I whispered. 'My father told me to come to see you and to say goodbye. But I am not free. I never will be.'

'Would you serve me still?'

I nodded.

Lord Robert smiled and leaned forward, his mouth so close to my ear that I could feel the warmth of his breath. 'Then do this one last thing for me. Go to Lady Elizabeth. Tell her to study with my old tutor, John Dee. Then find John Dee and tell him to make contact with his old master, Sir William Pickering. Tell him to meet also with James Crofts and Tom Wyatt. I think they are engaged in an alchemical experiment that is near to John Dee's heart. Edward Courtenay can make a chemical wedding. Can you remember all of that?'

'Yes,' I said. 'But I don't know what it means.'

'All the better. They are to make gold from the basest of metal, and cast down silver to ash. Tell him that. He'll know what I mean. And tell him that I will play my part in the alchemy, if he will get me there.'

'Where?' I asked.

'Just remember the message,' he said. 'Tell it back to me.'

I repeated it, word for word, and he nodded. He then put his lips to my neck, just below my ear, a little brush of a kiss, a little breath of a kiss. 'You're a good girl,' he said. 'And I thank you.'

He let me go then, and I stepped backwards from him as if I could not bear to turn away. I tapped on the door behind me, and the guard swung it open. 'God bless you and keep you safe, my lord,' I said.

'God speed, lad,' he replied evenly, to the closing door, and then it was shut and I was in the darkness and without him once more.

As fool to the queen I was expected to be in her chambers every day, at her side. But as soon as I could be absent for an hour without attracting notice, I took a chance, and went to the old Dudley rooms to look for John Dee. I tapped on the door and a man in strange livery opened it and looked suspiciously at me.

'I thought the Dudley household lived here,' I said timidly.

'Not any more,' he said smartly.

'Where will I find them?'

He shrugged. 'The duchess has rooms near the queen. Her sons are in the Tower. Her husband is in hell.'

'The tutor?'

He shrugged. 'Gone away. Back to his father's house, I should think.'

I nodded and took myself back to the queen's rooms, and sat by her feet on a small cushion. Her little dog, a greyhound, had a cushion that matched mine, and dog and I sat, watching with the same brown-eyed incomprehension, while the courtiers came and made their bows and applied for land and places and favours of grants of money, and sometimes the queen patted the dog and sometimes she patted me.

When they were all gone, she walked over to the window and rested her head against the thick pane of glass. The door opened and Jane Dormer beckoned two porters into the room, carrying a frame between them, swathed in linen cloth.

'Something for you, Your Grace!' she said with a roguish smile.

'What is it, Jane? I am weary now.'

In answer, Mistress Dormer waited till the men had leaned their burden against the wall, and then took the hem of the cloth and turned to her royal mistress. 'Are you ready?'

The queen was persuaded into smiling. 'Is this the portrait of Philip?' she asked. 'I won't be taken in by it. You forget, I am old enough to remember when my father married a portrait but divorced the sitter.'

In answer, Jane Dormer swept the cloth aside. I heard the queen's indrawn breath, and then heard her little girlish giggle. 'My God, Jane, this is a man!' she whispered.

Jane Dormer collapsed with laughter, dropped the cloth and dashed across the room to stand back to admire the portrait.

He was indeed a handsome man. He was young, in his mid-twenties, brown-bearded with dark smiling eyes, a full sensual mouth, broad shoulders and slim strong legs. He was wearing dark red with a dark red cap at a rakish angle on his curly brown hair.

'What d'you think, Your Grace?' Jane demanded.

The queen said nothing. I looked from the portrait back to her face again. She was gazing at him. For a moment I could not think what she reminded me of. Then I knew it. It was my own face in the looking glass when I thought of Robert Dudley.

'He's very . . . pleasing,' she said.

Jane Dormer met my eyes and smiled at me.

I wanted to smile back but my head was ringing with a strange noise, a tingling noise like little bells. I put my hands over my ears but the sound echoed louder inside my head.

'And see? A gold cross on a chain,' Jane cooed. 'Thank God, there will be a Catholic Christian prince for England once more.'

It was too much to bear now. I twisted round, trying to shake the terrible ringing out of my ears. Then I burst out, 'Your Grace! Your heart will break!' and at once the noise was cut off short and there was silence, and the queen was looking at me, and Jane Dormer was looking at me, and I realised I had spoken out of turn, shouted out as a fool.

'What did you say?' Jane Dormer challenged me to repeat my words, defying me to spoil the happy mood of the afternoon.

'I said, "Your Grace, your heart will break",' I repeated. 'But I cannot say why.'

Jane turned to the queen. 'Your Grace, pay no heed to the fool.'

The queen's face, which had been so bright and so animated, suddenly turned sulky. 'You can both leave,' she said flatly. She hunched her shoulders and turned away. I knew that she had made her choice and that no fool's words would change her mind.

While the long negotiations about the marriage went on between the queen's council, sick with apprehension at the thought of a Spaniard on the throne of England, and the Spanish representatives, eager to add another kingdom to their sprawling empire, I found my way to the home of John Dee's father, a small house in the city close by the river. I tapped on the door and at first no one answered. Then a window above the front door opened and someone shouted down: 'Who is it?'

'Mr Dee, it is me. Hannah the Fool,' I called up. 'I was looking for you.'

'Hush,' he said quickly and slammed the casement window shut. I heard his feet echoing on the wooden stairs inside the house and the noise of the bolts being drawn, and then the door opened inwards to a dark hall. 'Come in quickly,' he said.

He slammed the door shut after me and bolted it.

'Did anyone follow you?'

My heart thudded at the question. 'No, sir. I don't think so.'

John Dee nodded, and then he turned and went upstairs without a word to me. I hesitated, then followed him.

At the top of the stairs the door was open and he beckoned me into his room. At the window was his desk with a beautiful strange brass instrument in pride of place.

'Are you a wanted man, Mr Dee? Should I go?'

He smiled and shook his head. 'I'm overcautious,' he said frankly.

'You are sure?' I pressed him.

He gave a little laugh. 'Hannah, you are like a young doe on the edge of flight. Be calm. You are safe here.'

I steadied myself and started to look around. He saw my gaze go back to the instrument at the window.

'What d'you think that is?' he asked.

I shook my head. It was a beautiful thing, made in brass, a ball as big as a pigeon's egg in the centre on a stalk, and around it a brass ring cunningly supported by two other stalks, which meant it could swing and move, a ball sliding around on it. Outside there was another ring and another ball, outside that, another. They were a series of rings and balls and the farthest from the centre was the smallest.

'This,' he said softly, 'is a model of the world. This is how the creator made the world and then set it in motion. This holds the secret of how God's mind works.' He leaned forward and gently touched the first ring. As if by magic they all started to move slowly, each going at its own pace, each following its own orbit, sometimes passing, sometimes overtaking each other. Only the little gold egg in the centre did not move; everything else swung round it.

'Where is our world?' I asked.

He smiled at me. 'Here,' he said, pointing to the golden egg at the centre of all the others. He pointed to the next ring with the slowly circling ball. 'This the moon.' He pointed to the next. 'This the sun.' He pointed to the next few. 'These are the planets, and beyond them these are the stars.' He put a hand on one ring to steady it and I watched the instrument slow and stop. Then, as if he suddenly remembered me, 'And you? What did you come here for?' he asked in quite a different tone of voice.

'I have a message. From Lord Robert.'

'What does Lord Robert want?'

'He gave me two tasks. One, to tell Lady Elizabeth to seek you out and ask you to be her tutor, and the other to tell you to meet with some men.'

'What men?'

'Sir William Pickering, Tom Wyatt and James Crofts,' I recited. 'And he said to tell you this: that they are engaged in an alchemical experiment to make gold from base metal and to refine silver back to ash and you should help them with this. Edward Courtenay can make a chemical wedding. And I am to go back and tell him what will come to pass.'

Mr Dee glanced at the window as if he feared eavesdroppers on the very sill outside. 'These are not good times for me to serve a suspect princess and a man in the Tower for treason, and three others whose names I may already know, whose plans I may already doubt. What is he thinking of, exposing you to such danger?'

'I am his to command,' I said firmly. 'I have given my word.'

'He should release you,' he said gently. 'He cannot command anything from the Tower.'

'He has released me.'

'Hannah, will you look in the mirror again and see for me?' he asked.

I hesitated. I was afraid of the dark mirror, afraid of the things that might come through to haunt us. 'Mr Dee, last time I did not have a true seeing,' I confessed awkwardly.

'You said the date of the king's death. You predicted the next queen would be Jane. Your answers were true,' he observed.

'They were nothing more than guesses,' I said.

He smiled. 'Then just do that again,' he said. 'Just guess for me.'

'Very well.'

'We'll do it now,' he said. He took my hand and led me into a small box-room. The same mirror we had used before was leaning against a wall. He lit two candles and put them before the mirror, so that they seemed like innumerable candles disappearing into infinite distance.

I drew a long breath to ward off my fear and seated myself before the mirror. I heard his muttered prayer and I repeated: 'Amen'. Then I gazed into the darkness of the mirror.

I could hear myself speaking but I could hardly make out the words.

I could hear the scratching of his pen as he wrote down what I was saying. I could hear myself reciting a string of numbers, and then strange words, like a wild poetry that had a rhythm and a beauty of its own, but no meaning that I could tell. Then I heard my voice say very clearly in English: 'There will be a child, but no child. There will be a king but no king. There will be a virgin queen all-forgotten. There will be a queen but no virgin.'

'And Lord Robert Dudley?' he whispered.

'He will have the making of a prince who will change the history of the world,' I whispered in reply. 'And he will die, beloved by a queen, safe in his bed.'

When I recovered my senses, John Dee was standing by me with a drink that tasted of fruit with a tang behind it of metal.

'Are you all right?' he asked me.

I nodded. 'Yes. A little sleepy.'

'You had better go back to court,' he said. 'You will be missed.'

It was hard to find a way to speak with the Lady Elizabeth without half the court remarking on it. I could not simply go to her rooms and ask to see her. I would be reported to the queen. But one day, as I was walking behind her in the gallery, she stumbled for a moment. I went to help her, and she took my arm.

'I have broken the heel on my shoe,' she said.

'Let me help you to your rooms,' I offered, and added in a whisper, 'I have a message for you, from Lord Robert Dudley.'

She did not even flicker a sideways glance at me, and in that absolute control I saw at once that she was a consummate plotter.

'I can receive no messages without my sister's blessing,' Elizabeth said sweetly. 'But I would be very glad if you would help me to my chamber; I wrenched my foot when the heel broke.'

She bent down and took off her shoe. I gave her my arm. A courtier passing looked at us both. 'The princess has broken the heel of her shoe,' I explained. He nodded, and went on. He, for one, was not going to trouble himself to help her.

Elizabeth limped slightly on her stockinged foot and it made her walk slowly. She gave me plenty of time to deliver the message that she had said she could not hear without permission.

'Lord Robert asks you to summon John Dee as your tutor,' I said.

'You can tell him that I will not do anything that would displease my sister the queen,' she said easily. 'But I have long wanted to study with Mr Dee and I was going to ask him to read with me.'

We were at the door of her rooms. A guard stood to attention as we approached and swung the door open. Elizabeth released me. 'Thank you for your help,' she said coolly, and went inside. As the door shut behind her I saw her bend down and put her shoe back on. The heel was perfectly sound.

I went home to my father leaving a court humming with gossip, walking through a city seething with rebellion. Rumours of a secret army mustering to wage war against the queen were everywhere. Ballads were sung against the marriage; the braver preachers thundered against the match; chapbooks abused the queen for even considering the Spanish prince. England was not some dowry to be handed over to Spain. The very notion was treason.

My father had company in the bookshop. Daniel Carpenter's mother was perched on one of the stools at the counter, her son beside her. I knelt for my father's blessing, and then made a little bow to Mrs Carpenter and to my husband-to-be.

'I waited to see you and hear the news from court,' Mrs Carpenter said. 'And Daniel wanted to see you, of course.'

The glance that Daniel shot at her made it clear that he did not wish her to explain his doings to me.

'Is the queen's marriage to go ahead?' my father asked.

'Without doubt,' I said. 'The queen is desperate for a helper and a companion, and it is natural she should want a Spanish prince.'

My father glanced at Mrs Carpenter. 'Please God it makes no difference to us,' he said. 'Please God she does not bring in Spanish ways.'

She leaned forward and patted my father's hand. 'We have lived in England for three generations,' she said reassuringly. 'Nobody can think that we are anything but good Christians and good Englishmen.'

'I cannot stay if it is to become another Spain,' my father said in a low voice. 'You know, every Sunday, every saint's day, they burned heretics, sometimes hundreds at a time. And those of us who had practised Christianity for years were put on trial alongside those who had hardly pretended to it. And no one could prove their innocence! I knew one day they would come for me, and I started to prepare. But I did not think they would take my parents, my wife's sister, my wife before me . . .' He broke off. 'I should have thought of it. We should have gone earlier.'

'Papa, we couldn't save her,' I said, comforting him with the same words that he had used to me when I had cried that we should have stayed and died beside her.

'Old times,' Mrs Carpenter said briskly. 'And they won't come here. Not the Holy Inquisition, not in England.'

'Oh yes, they will,' Daniel asserted.

It was as if he had said a foul word. A silence fell at once. His mother and my father both turned to look at him.

'A Spanish prince, a half-Spanish queen—she must be determined to restore the church. How better to do it than to bring in the Inquisition to root out heresy?'

'She's too merciful to do it,' I said. 'She has not even executed Lady Jane, though all her advisers say that she should. I think she will restore this country to the true faith by gentle means. Already, half the country is glad to return to the Mass; the others will follow later.'

'I hope so,' Daniel said. 'But we should be prepared. I don't want to hear a knock on the door one night and know that we are too late to save ourselves.'

'Where would we go?' I asked. I could feel that old feeling of terror in the pit of my belly, the feeling that nowhere would ever be safe for me.

'First Amsterdam, and then Italy,' he said firmly. 'You and I will marry as soon as we get to Amsterdam and then continue overland. We will travel all together. Your father and my mother and my sisters with us. I can complete my training as a physician in Italy, and there are Italian cities that are tolerant of Jews, where we could live openly in our faith. Your father can sell his books, and my sisters could find work. We will live as a family.'

'See how he plans ahead,' Mrs Carpenter said in an approving whisper to my father.

'We are not promised to marry till next year,' I said. 'I'm not ready to marry yet.'

'Oh, not again,' said my father.

'All girls think that,' said Mrs Carpenter.

Daniel said nothing.

I slid down from my stool. 'May we talk privately?' I asked.

'Go into the printing room,' my father told Daniel. 'Your mother and I will take a glass of wine out here.'

He poured wine for her and I caught her amused smile as Daniel and I went into the inside room where the big press stood.

'Mr Dee tells me that I will lose the Sight if I marry,' I said earnestly. 'He believes it is a gift from God, I cannot throw it away.'

'It is guesswork and waking dreams,' Daniel said roundly.

It was so close to my own opinion that I could hardly argue. 'It is beyond our understanding,' I said stoutly. 'There are secrets I cannot tell you,' I said, and then I added: 'And that is another reason that I cannot be your wife. There should not be secrets between man and wife.'

He turned away with an exclamation of irritation. 'Don't be clever with me,' he said. 'You are so full of trickery that you will talk yourself out of happiness and into heartbreak.'

'How should I be happy if I have to be a nothing?' I asked. 'I am the favourite of Queen Mary. I am highly paid. The greatest philosopher in the land thinks I have a gift from God to foretell the future. And you think my happiness lies in walking away from all this to marry an apprentice physician!'

He caught my hands, which were twisting together, and pulled me towards him. His breath was coming as quickly as my own. 'Enough,' he said angrily. 'You have insulted me enough, I think. You need not marry an apprentice physician. You can be Robert Dudley's whore or his tutor's adept. You can think yourself the queen's companion but everyone knows you as the fool. You make yourself less than what I would offer you. You could be the wife of an honourable man who would love you and instead you throw yourself into the gutter for any passer-by to pick up.'

'I do not!' I gasped, trying to pull my hands away.

Suddenly he pulled me towards him and wrapped his arms around my waist. His dark head came down, his mouth close to mine. I could smell the pomade in his hair and the heat of the skin of his cheek. I shrank back even as I felt the desire to go forward.

'Do you love another man?' he demanded urgently.

'No,' I lied.

'Do you swear, on all you believe, whatever that is, that you are free to marry me?'

'I am free to marry you,' I said, honestly enough, for God knew as well as I did that no one else wanted me.

'With honour,' he specified.

I could have spat at him in my temper. 'Of course, with honour,' I said. 'Have I not told you that my gift is dependent on my virginity? Have I not said that I will not risk that?' I pulled away from him but his grip on me tightened. Despite myself, my body took in the sense of him: the strength of his arms, his thighs pressing against me, the scent of him and, for some odd reason, the feeling of absolute safety that he gave me. I realised that I wanted to mould myself around him, put my head on his shoulder, let him hold me against him and know that I was safe—if only I would let him love me, if only I would let myself love him.

'If they bring in the Inquisition, we will have to leave, you know that.'

'Yes, I know that,' I said, only half hearing him, feeling him with every inch of my body.

'If we leave, you will have to come with me as my wife, I will take you and your father to safety under no other condition.'

'Yes.'

'Then we are agreed?'

'If we have to leave England then I will marry you,' I said.

'And in any case we will marry when you are sixteen.'

I nodded, my eyes closed. Then I felt his mouth come down onto mine and I felt his kiss melt every argument away.

He released me, and smiled as if he knew that I was dizzy with desire. 'As to Lord Robert, it is my request that you serve him no longer,' he said. 'He is a convicted traitor, and you endanger yourself and us all by seeking his company.' His look darkened. 'And he is not a man I would trust with my betrothed.'

'He thinks of me as a child and a fool,' I corrected him.

'You are neither,' he said gently. 'And neither am I. You are half in love with him, Hannah, and I won't tolerate it.'

I hesitated, ready to argue, and then I felt the most curious sensation of my life: the desire to tell the truth to someone.

'If I tell you the truth about something, will you help me?' I asked.

'I will give you the best help I can,' he said, drawing me back to him.

'Daniel, this is the truth. I saw that the king would die, I named the day. I saw that Jane would be crowned queen. I saw that Queen Mary would be queen, and I have seen a glimpse of her future, which is heartbreak. John Dee says I have a gift of Sight. He tells me it comes in part from me being a virgin and I want to honour the gift. And I want to marry you. And I desire you. And I cannot help but love Lord Robert. All those things. All at once.' I held him close, while he considered the rush of truths I had told him. Moments later he eased me back from him and looked into my eyes.

'Is it an honourable love, as a servant to a master?' he asked.

I felt my lip quiver and the tears come to my eyes. 'It's all muddled up,' I said weakly. 'I love him for what he is . . .' I was silenced by the impossibility of conveying to Daniel the desirability of Robert Dudley; his looks, his clothes, his wealth, his boots, his horses were all beyond my vocabulary. 'I love him for what he might become—he will be freed, he will be a great man, a great man, Daniel. He will be the maker of a Prince of England. And tonight he is in the Tower, waiting for the sentence of death, and I think of him, and I think of my mother waiting, like he is waiting, for the morning when they took her out . . .' I lost my voice, I shook my head.

He held me for a few more seconds and then he coldly put me from him. 'This is not your mother. There is no reason to love a man who has plotted and intrigued his way to treason. He would have put Lady Jane on the throne and beheaded the mistress that you say you love: Queen Mary. He is not an honourable man.'

I opened my mouth to argue but there was nothing I could say.

'And you are all mixed up with him, with his treasonous plans, and with your feeling for him. I won't call it love because if I thought for one moment it was anything more than a girl's fancy I would go out now to your father and break our betrothal. But I tell you this. You have to leave the service of Robert Dudley, whatever future you have seen for him. You have to avoid John Dee and you have to surrender your gift. You can serve the queen until you are sixteen but you have to be my betrothed in word and in every act you take. And in eighteen months' time, when you are sixteen, we will marry and you will leave court.'

'Eighteen months?' I said, very low.

'Eighteen months,' he said flatly. 'Or I swear I will take another girl to be my wife and throw you away to whatever future the soothsayer, the traitor and the queen make up for you.'

It was a cold winter, and not even Christmas brought any joy to the people. The queen held Christmas at Whitehall and appointed a Lord of Misrule and demanded a merry court in the old ways, but it was no good. The missing places at the Christmas feast told their own story: Lady Elizabeth stayed at Ashridge, her house on the Great North Road, ideally placed to advance on London as soon as someone gave the word. Half a dozen of the queen's council were unaccountably missing; the French ambassador was busier than any good Christian should be at Christmastide. It was clear that there was trouble brewing right up to the very throne, and the queen knew it; we all of us knew it.

'It's not very merry, is it, Hannah?' she asked me sadly. 'I have waited for this Christmas all my life, and now it seems that people have forgotten how to be happy.'

'Next year it will be better,' I said. 'When you are married and Prince Philip is here.'

At the very mention of his name the colour rose up in her pale cheeks. 'Hush,' she said, gleaming. 'I would be wrong to expect it of him. He will have to be often in his other kingdoms. There is no greater empire in the world than the one he will inherit, you know.'

Suddenly, there was a knock from the guards outside and the double doors were thrown open. The noise startled me and I was on my feet in an instant, my heart pounding. A messenger stood in the doorway, the Lord Chancellor, Bishop Gardiner, with him, and the veteran soldier Thomas Howard, Duke of Norfolk, beside him, their faces grim.

I fell back, certain that they had somehow discovered who I was, and had a warrant for my arrest as a heretic Jew. Then I saw they were not looking at me. They were looking at the queen and their jaws were set and their eyes cold.

'Oh, no,' I whispered.

She must have thought it was the end for her, as she rose slowly to her feet and looked from one stern face to another. She knew that the duke could turn his coat in a moment; the council could have mustered a swift plot. But the face she turned to them was as serene as if they had come to invite her to dine. In that moment I loved her for her courage, for her determination never to show fear. 'How now, my lords?' she said pleasantly. 'I hope you bring me good news for all you seem so severe.'

'Your Grace, it is not good news,' Bishop Gardiner said flatly. 'The rebels are marching against you. My young friend Edward Courtenay has seen the wisdom to confess to me and throw himself on your mercy.'

'And Edward tells you?'

'That a plot is in train to march on London, to put you in the Tower and to set the Lady Elizabeth on the throne in your place. We have the names of some of them: Sir William Pickering, Sir Thomas Wyatt in Kent and Sir James Crofts.'

I kept back behind her. These were the very men that my lord had named to me, that he had asked me to name to John Dee. These were the men who were to make a chemical wedding and to pull down silver and replace it with gold. Now I thought I knew what he meant. I thought I knew which queen was silver and which was gold in his metaphor. And I thought that I had again betrayed the queen while taking her wage, and that it would not be long before someone discovered who had been the catalyst in this plot.

She took a breath to steady herself. 'Any others?'

'The Duke of Suffolk is not at his house in Sheen, and no one knows where he has gone.'

If the Duke of Suffolk had disappeared then it could mean only one thing: he was raising his hundreds of tenants and retainers to restore the throne to his daughter Jane. We were faced with an uprising for Elizabeth and a rebellion for Queen Jane. Those two names could turn out more than half of the country, and all the courage and determination that Queen Mary had shown before could come to nothing now.

'And Lady Elizabeth? Does she know of this? Is she at Ashridge still?'

'Courtenay says that she was on the brink of marriage with him, and the two of them were to take your throne and rule together. Thank God the lad has seen sense and come over to us in time. She knows of everything; she is waiting in readiness. The King of France will support her claim and send a French army to put her on the throne. She may even now be riding to head the rebel army.'

I saw the queen's colour drain from her face.

The duke stepped forward. 'You must go to Framlingham at once, Your Grace. And we will have a warship standing by to take you out of the country to Spain. This is a battle you cannot win. Once you're safe in Spain perhaps you can regroup, perhaps Prince Philip . . .'

I saw her grip on the back of her chair tighten. 'It is a mere six months since I rode into London *from* Framlingham,' she said. 'The people wanted me as queen then.'

'You were their choice in preference to the Duke of Northumberland with Queen Jane as his puppet,' he brutally reminded her. 'Not instead of Elizabeth. The people want the Protestant religion and the Protestant princess. They won't have you with Prince Philip of Spain as king.'

'I won't leave London,' she said. 'I have waited all my life for my mother's throne; I shan't abandon it now.'

'You have no choice,' he warned her. 'They will be at the gates of the city within days.'

'I will wait till that moment.'

'You are gambling with your life as well as your throne,' the duke almost shouted at her.

'I know that!' she exclaimed.

He took a breath. 'Do I have your command to muster the royal guard and the city's trained bands and lead them out against Wyatt in Kent?'

'Yes. But there must be no sieges of towns and no sacking of villages.'

'It cannot be done!' he protested. 'In battle, one cannot protect the battleground.'

'These are your orders,' she insisted icily. 'I will not have a civil war fought over my wheat fields, especially in these starving times.'

For a moment he looked as if he would argue. Then she leaned towards him. 'Trust me in this,' she said persuasively. 'I know. I am a virgin queen; my only children are my people. They have to see that I love them and care for them. I cannot get married on a tide of their innocent blood. This has to be gently done, and firmly done. Can you do it for me?'

He shook his head. 'No,' he said. He was too afraid to waste time in flattery. 'Nobody can do it. They are gathering in their hundreds, in their thousands. These people understand only one thing and that is force. They understand gibbets at the crossroads and heads on pikes. You cannot rule Englishmen and be merciful, Your Grace.'

'You are mistaken,' she said, as determined as he was. 'I came to this throne by a miracle and God does not change his mind. We will win these men back by the love of God. It has to be done as God would have it, or His miracle cannot take place.'

The duke looked as if he would have argued.

'It is my command,' she said flatly.

He shrugged and bowed. 'As you command then,' he said. 'Whatever the consequences.'

The Duke of Norfolk took the apprentice boys from London and the queen's own guard, and marched them down to Kent to meet Wyatt's force in a set-piece battle, which should have routed the men from Kent in a day. But when our forces, who had sworn to protect the queen, faced Wyatt's men and saw their honest faces and their determination, they threw their caps in the air and shouted 'We are all Englishmen!'

Not a shot was fired. They embraced each other as brothers and turned against their commander, united against the queen. The duke hared back to London, having done nothing but add a trained force to Thomas Wyatt's raggle-taggle army, which came onwards, even more determined than before. Swelled by recruits from every village on the London road, they reached the south bank of the Thames on a wave of enthusiasm, and found London Bridge raised against them, and the guns of the Tower trained on the southern bank ready for them.

'They are not to open fire,' the queen ruled.

'Your Grace, for the love of God. The rebels are encamped within range now. We could destroy them in one cannonade.'

'They shall stay there until we can raise an army to drive them away.'

'Your Grace, you have no army.'

She was pale but she did not waver. 'I have no army *yet*,' she emphasised. 'But I will raise one from the good men of London.'

Against her council's advice, the queen put on her great gown of state and went to the Guildhall to meet the Mayor and the people. Jane Dormer, her other ladies and I went in her train.

Of all of the queen's council and certainly of all of her ladies in waiting, only Jane and I had any hopes of getting out of London alive, but Jane and I had seen her at Framlingham, and we knew that this was a queen to back against all odds. She was at her very best when she and her God stood against disaster. With an enemy at the gates of London, you would want no other queen.

They had set up a throne for her in the Guildhall and half of London came from sheer curiosity, crowding to hear the queen argue for her life. When she stood, a small figure under the weighty golden crown, draped in the heavy robes of state, I thought for a moment that she would not be able to convince them to keep their faith with her.

She opened her mouth to speak and there was no sound. I thought she had lost her voice from fear itself, and Wyatt might as well march into the hall now and claim the throne for the Lady Elizabeth. But then her voice rang out, clear and sweet as if she were a chorister singing in the chapel on Christmas Day.

She told them everything. She told them that she was a king's daughter and she claimed her father's power, and their fealty. She reminded them that she was a virgin without a child of her own and that she loved the people of the country as only a mother can love her child, and that she could not doubt but that they loved her in return.

She was seductive. Our Mary blazed with passion until they caught her fire and were part of it. She swore to them that she was marrying solely to give them an heir, and if they did not think it was the best choice then she would die a virgin for them; that she was their queen— it meant nothing to her whether she had a man or not. What was important was the throne. Nothing else mattered. She would be guided by them in her marriage, as in everything else. She was theirs, they were hers, and there was nothing that could change it.

'And now, good subjects, pluck up your hearts and like true men face up against these rebels and fear them not, for I assure you I fear them nothing at all!'

She was tremendous. They threw their caps in the air, and cheered her as if she were the Virgin Mary herself. And they raced outside and took the news to all those who had not been able to get into the Guildhall. London went mad for Mary. The men volunteered to march against the rebels; the women tore up their best linen into bandages and baked bread for the volunteer soldiers to take in their knapsacks. The battle was won, not when Wyatt's army was defeated just a few days later, but in that single afternoon, by Mary, standing on her own two feet, head held high, blazing with courage.

Once again the queen learned that holding the throne was harder than winning it. She spent the days after the uprising struggling with her conscience, faced with the agonising question of what should be done with the rebels who had been so dramatically defeated. Clearly, God would protect this Mary on her throne, but God was not to be mocked. Mary must also protect herself. There could be no more mercy from a tenderhearted queen. It did not matter that Jane had not led this rebellion; hers was the head that they would crown, and so hers was the head that must be struck off the body.

'She would do the same to you, Your Grace,' they murmured to her.

'She is a girl of sixteen,' the queen replied.

'Her father joined the rebels for her cause. The others joined for the Princess Elizabeth. Both young women were born to be your enemies. Their existence means that your life is in perpetual danger. Both of them must be destroyed.'

The queen took their hardhearted advice to her prie-dieu. 'Jane is guilty of nothing but her lineage,' she whispered, looking up at the statue of the crucified Christ.

She waited, as if hoping for the miracle of a reply.

'And You know, as I do,' she said, very low, 'that Elizabeth is guilty indeed. But how can I send my cousin and my sister to the scaffold?'

Jane Dormer shot me a look and the two of us moved so as to block the view and the hearing of the other ladies in waiting. The queen should not be overheard consulting the only adviser she truly trusted.

We did not live like a victorious court in a victorious city. It was a court hanging on a thread of its own indecision, sick with worry. Every day, after Mass and breakfast, Queen Mary walked by the side of the river, her hands dug deep in her muff, her steps hastened by the cold wind blowing her skirts forward.

I knew she was troubled and so I dogged her footsteps two steps behind her because I knew she had taken so many lonely walks that now she liked the comfort of knowing that someone was keeping vigil with her.

The wind coming off the river was too cold for her to walk for long, even with a thick cape and a fur collar at her neck. She turned on her heel and I nearly bumped into her.

'I beg pardon, Your Grace,' I said, stepping out of her way.

'You can walk beside me,' she said.

I fell into step, saying nothing, but waiting for her to speak. She was silent till we came to the small garden door where the guard swung it open before her. Inside, a maid was waiting to take her cloak and to offer her a pair of dry shoes. I swung my cloak over my arm and stamped my feet on the rushes to warm them.

'Come with me,' the queen said over her shoulder, and led the way up the winding stone stairs to her apartments. The stairs emerged into a little lobby room, which led to the queen's private chamber. Jane Dormer was sewing in the window seat, half a dozen women working alongside her; one of the queen's ladies was reading from the Book of Psalms. The queen gave a little nod of pleasure. Philip of Spain, when he finally came, would find a sober and devout court.

'Come, Hannah,' she said, taking a seat at the fireside and gesturing to me to sit on a stool nearby.

I sat down, folded my knees under my chin and looked up at her.

'I want you to look at something for me.'

'Look at something?'

'Look with your gift, with your inner eye.'

I hesitated. 'Your Grace, you know it is not at my command.'

'No, but you have seen the future twice with me; once you spoke of my becoming queen and once you spoke to warn me of heartbreak. Now I want you to warn me again.'

'Warn you against what?' My voice was as low as hers. No one in the room could have heard us over the crackle of the logs in the fireplace.

'Against Elizabeth,' she breathed.

'Your Grace, there are wiser heads than mine to advise you,' I said.

'None I trust more. None who comes with your gift.'

I hesitated. 'Is she coming to court?'

Mary shook her head. 'She won't come. She says she is near death with sickness, a swelling of the belly and of her limbs. She is too ill to be moved. It is an old illness of hers, a real one, I believe. But it always comes on at certain times.'

'Certain times?'

'When she is very afraid,' Mary said quietly, 'and when she has been caught out. The first time she was sick like this was when they executed Thomas Seymour. Now I think she fears being accused of another plot. I am sending my doctors to see her, and I want you to go too.'

'Of course.' I did not know what else I could say.

'Sit with her, read to her, be her companion as you have been mine. If she is well enough to come to court, you can travel with her. If she is dying you can comfort her, send for a priest and try to turn her thoughts to her salvation. It is not too late, even now, for her to be forgiven by God.'

'Anything else?' My voice was a thread of sound.

'Spy on her,' she said flatly. 'Everything she does, everyone she sees, every name you hear mentioned. Write to me every day and tell me what you have learned. I have to know if she is plotting against me. I have to know if she is my enemy and will stop at nothing till my death. You shall be my eyes and ears at her bedside and God will guide you.'

I surrendered to her conviction. 'When do I leave?'

'Tomorrow at dawn,' the queen said.

I rose to my feet and gave her a little bow. She put out her hand to me. 'Hannah,' she said quietly.

'Yes, Your Grace?'

'I wish you could see into her heart and see that she is able to love me, and able to turn to the true faith.'

'I hope I see that too,' I said fervently.

Her mouth was working, holding back tears. 'But if she is faithless, you must tell me, even though it will break my heart.'

'I will.'

It took us three days to travel the thirty miles to Ashridge, struggling, heads bowed through a storm of freezing cold sleet. We reached the house by noon and we were glad to see the curl of smoke from the tall chimneys. We clattered round to the stable yard and found no grooms to take the horses. Lady Elizabeth kept only a small staff, and none of them was ready to greet a train such as ours. We trooped round to the front door of the house.

The princess's own cousin, Lord William Howard, hammered on the door and tried the handle. It was bolted and barred from the inside. He stepped back and looked around for the captain of the guard. At that moment I realised that his orders were very different from mine. I was here to look into Elizabeth's heart, to restore her to the affection of her sister. He was here to bring her to London, alive or dead.

'Knock again,' he said grimly. 'And then break it down.'

At once the door yielded, swung open by an unenthusiastic pair of menservants, and we marched into the great hall without invitation.

The place was in silence, extra rushes on the floor to muffle the sound of the servants' feet, a strong smell of mint purifying the air.

A redoubtable woman, Mrs Kat Ashley, Elizabeth's best servant and protector, was at the head of the hall, her hands clasped together under a solid bosom. She looked the royal train up and down as if we were a pack of pirates. 'I shall tell my lady that you are here but she is too sick to see anyone,' she said flatly. 'I will see that you are served such dinner as we can lay before you, but we have not the rooms to accommodate such a great company as yourselves.'

'We will stay at Hillham Hall,' Sir Thomas Cornwallis said helpfully.

Mrs Ashley raised her eyebrow as if she did not think much of his choice, and turned to the door at the head of the hall. I fell into step behind her. She rounded on me. 'And where d'you think you're going?'

I looked up at her, my face innocent. 'To the Lady Elizabeth.'

'She'll see no one,' the woman ruled. 'She is too ill.'

'Then let me pray at the foot of her bed,' I said quietly.

'If she is so very ill she will want the fool's prayers,' someone said from the hall. 'That child can see angels.'

Kat Ashley, caught out by her own story, nodded briefly and let me follow her out of the door, through the presence chamber and into Elizabeth's private rooms.

There was a heavy curtain over the door to shut out the noise from the presence chamber. Candles illuminated the room and showed the princess, red hair spread like a haemorrhage on the pillow, her face white.

At once I could see she was ill indeed. Her belly was as swollen as if she were pregnant but her hands as they lay on the embroidered coverlet were swollen too, as if she were an old lady. Her lovely face was puffy. Even her neck was thick.

'What is the matter with her?' I demanded.

'Dropsy,' Mrs Ashley replied. 'Worse than she has ever had it before. She needs rest and peace.'

'My lady,' I breathed.

The princess peered at me from under swollen eyelids. 'Who?'

'The queen's fool,' I said. 'Hannah.'

She veiled her eyes. 'A message?' she asked, her voice a thread.

'No,' I said quickly. 'I am come to you from Queen Mary. She has sent me to be your companion.'

'I thank her,' Elizabeth said, her voice a whisper. 'You can tell her that I am sick indeed and need to be alone.'

'She has sent doctors to make you better,' I said.

'I am too sick to travel,' she said, speaking strongly for the first time.

I bit my lip to hide my smile. She was ill; no one could manifest a swelling to escape a charge of treason. But she would play her illness as the trump card it was.

'She has sent her councillors to accompany you,' I warned her.

'Who?'

'Your cousin, Lord William Howard, among others.'

I saw her swollen lips twist in a bitter smile. 'She must be very determined against me if she sends my own kin to arrest me,' she remarked.

'May I be your companion during your illness?' I suggested.

She turned her head away. 'I am too tired,' she said. 'You can come back when I am better.'

I rose from my kneeling position by the bed and stepped backwards. Kat Ashley jerked her head towards the door to send me from the room.

Then we waited. Good God, how we waited. She was the absolute mistress of delay. When the physicians said she was well enough to leave, she could not choose the gowns she would bring, then her ladies could not pack them in time for us to set off before dusk. Then everything had to be unpacked again since we were staying another day, and then Elizabeth was so exhausted she could see no one at all the next day, and the merry dance of Elizabeth's waiting began again.

During one of these mornings, when the big trunks were being laboriously loaded into the wagons, I went to Lady Elizabeth to see if I could assist her. She was lying on a day bed, in an attitude of exhaustion.

'It is all packed,' she said. 'And I am so tired I do not know if I can begin the journey.'

The swelling of her body had reduced but she was clearly still unwell. She would have looked better if she had not powdered her cheeks with rice powder and, I swear, darkened the shadows under her eyes.

'The queen is determined that you shall go to London,' I warned her.

She bit her lip. 'Do you know if she will accuse me when we get there?' she asked, her voice very low.

'She loves you,' I reassured her. 'I think she would take you back into her favour even now, if you would just accept her faith.'

Elizabeth looked into my eyes, that straight honest Tudor look, like her father, like her sister. 'Are you telling me the truth?' she asked. 'Are you a holy fool or a trickster, Hannah Green?'

'I am neither,' I said, meeting her gaze. 'I was begged for a fool by Robert Dudley, against my wishes. I have a gift of Sight which comes to me unbidden.'

'You saw an angel behind Robert Dudley,' she reminded me.

I smiled. 'I did.'

'What was it like?'

I giggled, I couldn't help it. 'Lady Elizabeth, I was so taken with Lord Robert that I hardly noticed the angel.'

She sat up, quite forgetting her pose of illness, and laughed with me. 'He is very . . . he is so . . . he is indeed a man you look at.'

'And I only realised it was an angel afterwards,' I said.

'And do your visions come to pass?' she asked keenly.

'Some things that I see have come to pass,' I said, honestly enough. 'But sometimes the very things I need to know, I cannot tell. Then it is a useless gift. If it had warned me—just once—'

'What warning?' she asked.

'The death of my mother,' I said. I would have bitten back the words as soon as they were spoken.

'I did not know,' she said gently. 'Did she die in Spain? You came from Spain, did you not?'

'In Spain,' I said. 'Of the plague.' I felt a sharp twist of pain in my belly at lying about my mother.

'I am sorry,' she said, very low. 'It is hard for a young woman to grow up without a mother.'

I knew she was thinking of herself, and of the mother who had died on the scaffold with the names of witch, adulteress and whore. She put away the thought. 'But what made you come to England?'

'We have kin here. And my father had arranged a marriage for me.'

'And your betrothed? Do you like him?'

'Well enough as a cousin. Not enough for a husband.'

'And do you have any choice in the matter?'

'Not much,' I said shortly.

She nodded. 'It's always the same for all women,' she said, a hint of resentment in her voice. 'The only people who can choose their lives are those in breeches. You do right to wear them.'

'I'll have to put them aside soon,' I said. 'I was allowed to wear them when I was little more than a child but I . . .' I checked myself. I did not want to confide in her.

'When I was your age, I thought I would never know how to be a young woman,' she said. 'All I wanted to do was to be a scholar. I hoped that I might become a great and learned lady and be allowed to stay at court. When my father died I thought I would be always at court: my brother's favourite sister, and aunt to his many children, and together we would see my father's work complete.' She shook her head. 'Indeed, I should not want your gift of Sight,' she said. 'If I had known that I would come to this, under the shadow of my sister's displeasure, and my beloved brother dead, and my father's legacy thrown away . . .'

Elizabeth broke off and then turned to me, her dark eyes filled with tears. 'Even if the Vatican named me a saint, Mary would not be happy,' she said. 'And I will tell you why. She will never forgive me for what they did to her mother, and for what they did to her. She will never forgive me for being my father's best beloved daughter. And the last thing she wants at court is a younger sister to show her up.'

I said nothing. It was too shrewd an assessment.

'A younger sister who is prettier than she. A younger sister who looks like a pure Tudor and not like a half-caste Spaniard.'

I turned my head. 'Have a care, Princess.'

Elizabeth laughed, a wild little laugh. 'She sent you here to see into my heart. Didn't she? She has great faith in God working his purpose in her life, telling her what is to be. But her God is very slow in bringing her joy, I think. That long wait for the throne and then a rebellious kingdom at the end of it. And now a wedding, but a bridegroom who is in no hurry to come but instead stays at home with his mistress. What do you see for her, fool?'

I turned my head, afraid that my face might show the sudden vivid image I had in my mind's eye, the dark mirror, and the words spilling out of my mouth, telling of the two queens who would rule England. A child, but no child, a king but no king, a virgin queen all-forgotten, a queen but no virgin. 'Nothing, Your Grace. I cannot see to command.'

She half closed her eyes and smiled. 'Not a fool at all then, Hannah.'

The next day she could resist no longer. The wagons with her trunks, furniture and linens had already gone. The queen's own litter with cushions and rugs of the warmest wool was standing at the door, four white mules harnessed to it. As the doctors bundled Elizabeth into the litter, she cried out as if in pain, but I thought it was fear that was choking her.

We travelled slowly. At every halt the princess delayed, complaining of the jolting pace. She rose later every morning, too pained with her aching joints to face the litter until midday. Whenever we stopped to dine she sat late at the table and was reluctant to get back into the litter.

'What do you think to gain from this delay, Princess?' I asked her on the third morning, when Lord Howard had sent me into her bedchamber for the tenth time to ask when she would be ready to come.

She was standing stock-still, while one of her ladies slowly wound a scarf round her throat. 'I gain another day,' she said.

'But to do what?'

She smiled at me, though her eyes were dark with fear. 'Ah, Hannah, you have never longed to live as I long to live if you do not know that another day is the most precious thing. Every day we do not reach London is another day that I am alive. Every morning that I wake, every night that I sleep is a victory for me.'

On the fourth day into the journey a messenger met us, carrying a letter for Lord William Howard. His lordship read it and tucked it into the front of his doublet, his face grim. Elizabeth waited till he was looking away and then beckoned to me. I drew up my horse beside her.

'I would give a good deal to know what was in that letter,' she said. 'Go and listen for me. They won't notice you.'

My opportunity came when we stopped to dine. Lord Howard and the other councillors were watching their horses being taken into the stalls. I saw him pull the letter from inside his doublet and I paused beside him to straighten my riding boot.

'Lady Jane is dead,' he announced baldly. 'Executed two days ago. Guilford Dudley before her.'

'And Robert Dudley?' I demanded urgently.

Much was always forgiven a fool. 'I have no news of him,' he said. 'I should think he was executed alongside his brother.'

I felt the world become blurred around me and I realised I was about to faint. I plumped down onto the cold step and put my head in my hands. 'Lord Robert,' I whispered into my knees. 'My lord.'

It was impossible that he was dead, that bright, dark-eyed vitality gone for ever. Who could bring themselves to kill bonny Robin? Who could sign such a warrant, what headsman could bear to do it? And it was all the more impossible since I had seen the prophecy in his favour.

I had been shown that he would be beloved by a queen, that he would die in his bed. If my Lord Robert was dead then not only was the great love of my life dead, but also I had been taught, in the hardest way, that my gift was a delusion. Everything was over in one sweep of the axe.

I got to my feet and staggered back against the stone wall.

'Are you sick, fool?' came the cool voice of one of Lord Howard's men. His Lordship glanced over indifferently.

I gulped down the lump that was in my throat. 'May I tell Lady Elizabeth about Lady Jane?' I asked him. 'She will want to know.'

'You can tell her,' he said.

'The charge?' I asked, although I knew the answer.

'Treason,' he said flatly. 'Tell her that. And pretending to the throne.'

Without another word being said, everyone turned to the litter where Lady Elizabeth was laboriously descending.

'So die all traitors,' said her cousin, looking at the white-faced girl who had been a friend to every man who now swung on the gibbet.

I waited till she had dined before I found my way to her side.

'The letter?' she asked me.

'I am sorry to tell you, Lady Elizabeth,' I said, 'that your cousin Lady Jane Grey has been executed and her husband . . . and Lord Robert Dudley too.'

'She has done it then,' she observed quietly. 'The queen. She has found the power of the axe. Thank God I am innocent of any wrongdoing.'

Ten days after we had first set off we arrived at the house of a private gentleman in Highgate, late in the evening.

I was housed with Lady Elizabeth's ladies, and they were up at dawn preparing for her entry into London. As I saw the virginal white gown being brushed and pressed and carried into her chamber I remembered the day that she greeted her sister into the city of London, wearing the Tudor colours of white and green. Now she was driven snow, all in white, a martyr-bride. When the litter came to the door she was ready; there was no delaying when there was a crowd collecting to see her.

'You'll want the curtains closed,' Lord Howard said gruffly to her.

'Keep them back,' she said. 'The people can see what condition I am in when forced out of my house for a fortnight's journey in all weathers.'

'Ten days,' he said gruffly. 'And could have been done in five.'

She did not deign to answer him, but lay back on her pillows and lifted her hand to indicate that he could go. I heard him swear briefly under his breath and then swing into the saddle of his horse. I pulled my horse up behind the litter and the little cavalcade turned out of the courtyard to the London road and into the city.

Elizabeth kept her eyes straight to the front and did not look left or right, but she sensed the dangling bodies on the gallows at every corner; half of them were known to her, and all of them had died in a rebellion that they believed she had summoned.

A few people called out 'God save Your Grace!' to her, and she raised a weak hand to them. She looked like a martyr being dragged to her death and, under this avenue of gallows, no one could doubt her fear.

At Whitehall, Elizabeth straightened up in the litter and looked towards the great steps of the palace. Queen Mary was not there to greet her sister, and neither was anyone of the court. She arrived to silent disgrace. A single gentleman-server was on the steps and he spoke to Lord Howard, not to the princess, as if they were her gaolers.

Lord Howard came to the litter and put out his hand for her. 'An apartment has been prepared for you,' he said shortly. 'You may choose two attendants to take with you.'

'My ladies must come with me,' she argued instantly. 'I am not well.'

'The orders are two attendants and no more,' he said coldly. 'Choose.'

'Mrs Ashley and . . .' Elizabeth looked around and her eye fell on me. I stepped back, as anxious as any other turncoat not to be linked with this doomed princess. But she knew through me she had a chance to reach the queen. 'Mrs Ashley and Hannah the Fool,' she said.

Lord Howard laughed. 'Three fools together then,' he muttered.

I did not wait to see Elizabeth settled in her rooms before I sought out my fellow fool Will Somers. He was dozing in the great hall on one of the benches. I sat beside him, wondering if I might wake him.

Without opening his eyes he remarked: 'A pair of fools we must be: parted for weeks and we don't even speak,' and he sat bolt upright and hugged me round the shoulders.

'I thought you were asleep,' I said.

'I was fooling,' he said with dignity. 'I have decided that a sleeping fool is funnier than one who is awake. The princess has come, has she?'

I nodded.

'Ill?'

'Very. Truly ill, I think.'

'The queen could offer her an instant cure for all pain. She has become a surgeon. She specialises in amputations.'

'Please God it does not come to that,' I said quickly. 'But, Will, tell me—did Robert Dudley make a good death? Was it quick?'

'Still alive,' he said. 'Against all the odds.'

I felt my heart turn over. 'Dear God, I thought he was dead.'

'He should be dead, God knows. He's seen his father and his brother and his poor sister-in-law all taken out and executed underneath his window, and yet he's still there.'

'Could I visit him without trouble?'

Will laughed. 'The Dudleys always bring trouble.'

'I mean without being suspected.'

He shook his head. 'This is a court gone dark,' he said sadly. 'Nobody can do anything without being suspected. That is why I sleep. I cannot be accused of plotting in my sleep.'

SPRING 1554

IN THE DAYS that followed I went between the queen's apartments and Lady Elizabeth's, but in neither place could I be comfortable.

The cold days turned warmer in March and the skies grew pale earlier in the mornings and later at night. The court stayed on tiptoe, watching to see what would happen to the princess. She was examined almost daily by the councillors but the queen would not see her face to face. 'I cannot,' she said shortly, and I knew that she was nerving herself to send Elizabeth to trial, and from there it would be a short walk to the scaffold.

They had enough evidence to hang her three times over but still the queen waited. Just before Easter I was glad to get a letter from my father asking me if I could absent myself from court for a week and come to the shop. He said he was unwell, but I was not to worry, it was just a passing fever and Daniel came every day.

I took the letter to the queen and when she gave me leave, made my way to the princess's apartment.

'I have been given leave to go to my home, to my father,' I said as I knelt before her.

'Going? When will you return?' Elizabeth asked.

'Within the week, your ladyship.'

She nodded, turned away and brushed her eyes with the back of her hand. 'Good God, I am weak as a child losing a nursemaid!'

'What's the matter?' I asked. I had never seen her so low.

'I am frozen to my very bones with fear,' Elizabeth said. 'I tell you, Hannah, if fear is cold and darkness I am living in the wastes of the

Russias. My only friends have been exiled, imprisoned or beheaded. I am twenty years old and I am utterly alone. I have no one's love and care. No one comes near me but Kat and you, and now you are leaving.'

'I have to see my father,' I said. 'But I'll come back as soon as he is well.'

The face she turned to me was not that of the defiant princess, the hated Protestant enemy, but that of a young woman trying to find the courage to face a death that must come soon. 'You will come back to me, Hannah? I have become accustomed to you. I ask it of you as a friend, not a princess. You will come back?'

'Yes,' I promised. I took her cold hand. 'I swear I will come back.'

My father's shop had the shutters up though it was only early in the afternoon. Daniel was putting the bolt on the last shutter and he turned round at the sound of my footsteps.

'Good,' he said shortly. 'Come inside.'

I put my hand on his arm. 'Daniel, is he very ill?'

He covered my hand briefly with his own. 'Come inside.'

I went into the shop. The counter was bare of books, the printing room quiet. I went up the rickety stairs at the rear of the shop and looked towards the little truckle bed in the corner of the room, fearing that I would see him there, too ill to stand.

The bed was heaped with papers and a small pile of clothes. My father was standing before it. I recognised at once the signs of packing for a long journey.

'Oh, no,' I said.

My father turned to me. 'It's time for us to go,' he said. 'Did they give you permission to come away for a week?'

'Yes,' I said. 'But they expect me back. I came running down here in terror that you were ill.'

'That gives us a week,' he said, disregarding my complaint. 'More than enough time to get to France.'

'Not again,' I said flatly. 'You said we were to stay in England.'

'It's not safe,' Daniel insisted, coming into the room behind me. 'The queen's marriage is to go ahead, and Prince Philip of Spain will bring in the Inquisition. Already the gallows are up on the street corners, and there is an informer in every village. We cannot stay here.'

'You said we would be English.' I appealed past him to my father. 'And the gallows are for traitors, not for heretics.'

'She will hang traitors today and heretics tomorrow,' Daniel said firmly. He took my hand and led me to the bed, which was covered with rolls of manuscript. 'See these? Every one is now a forbidden book. When your father came to England these were his library, his great collection, now they would serve only as evidence against him. What are we to do with them? Burn them before they burn us?'

'Keep them safe for better times,' I said, incurably the daughter of a librarian.

He shook his head. 'There is nowhere safe for them, and there is nowhere safe for their owner in a country ruled by Spain. We have to go away and take them with us.'

'But where do we have to go now?' I cried. It was the wail of a child who has been too long travelling.

'Venice,' he said shortly. 'France, then Italy, and then Venice. I shall study at Padua, your father will be able to open a print shop in Venice, and we will be safe there.'

I waited. I knew what was coming next.

'And we will marry,' he said, 'as soon as we arrive in France.'

'And your mother and your sisters?' I asked. It was living with them that I dreaded as much as marriage.

'They are packing now,' he said.

'When do we leave?'

'In two days' time, at dawn. Palm Sunday.'

'Why so soon?' I gasped.

'Because they have come asking questions already.'

I stared at Daniel, filled with horror as my worst fears started to take shape. 'They came for my father?'

'They came to my shop looking for John Dee,' my father said quietly. 'They knew that he sent books to Lord Robert. They knew that he had seen the princess. They knew that he had foretold the young king's death, and that is treason. They wanted to see the books that he asked me to store here.'

I was twisting my hands together. 'Why are you storing forbidden books?' I cried out in frustrated anger.

His face was gentle. 'Because all books are forbidden when a country turns to terror. The scaffolds on the corners, the list of things you may not read. These things always go together. John Dee and Lord Robert and even Daniel here and I, even you, my child, are all scholars steeped in knowledge that has suddenly become against the law.'

'We are not guilty of treason,' I said stubbornly. 'Lord Robert is still alive, John Dee too. The queen is merciful . . .'

'And what happens when Elizabeth confesses?' Daniel snapped at me. 'When she names her fellow traitors, not just Thomas Wyatt but Robert Dudley, John Dee, perhaps even you. Have you never taken a message or run an errand for her? Could you swear to it?'

I hesitated. 'She would never confess.'

'She is a woman.' He dismissed her. 'They will frighten her and then promise her forgiveness, and she will confess to anything. And she is enmeshed with Dudley and Dee and Wyatt and the rest of them. I warned you of this. I told you that if you played a double game at court you would bring danger to our door.'

I was breathless with rage. 'What door?' I demanded. 'We have no door. We have the open road, because you, like a coward, are afraid of your own shadow.'

For a moment I thought Daniel would strike me. His hand flew up and then he froze. 'I am sorry you call me a coward before your father's face.' He spat out the words. 'I am sorry you think so lowly of me, your husband-to-be. But whatever you think of me, I am commanding you to help your father pack and be ready.'

I drew myself up and faced him. 'I will not come.'

'Then our betrothal will be ended.'

My father raised a hand in dissent, but he said nothing.

'So be it,' I said. I felt cold. 'I release you from your promise to me, and I ask you to release me.'

'That's easily done,' he flared. 'I release you, Hannah, and I hope that you never regret this decision.' He turned on his heel and clattered down the stairs. We heard the shop door bang, and he was gone.

Over the next two days we worked in an almost unbroken silence. I helped my father tie his books together, the manuscripts we rolled into scrolls and packed in barrels, and pushed them behind the press in the printing room. He could take only the core of his library; the rest of the books would have to follow later.

'I wish you would come too,' he said earnestly. 'You're too young to be left here on your own.'

'I'm under the protection of the queen,' I said.

We worked all through the last night, and when he would not stop to eat I knew that he was mourning for me as a daughter that he had lost. At dawn I heard the creaking of wheels in the street and I looked out of the downstairs window, and there was the dark shape of the wagon lumbering towards us with Daniel leading a stocky pair of horses.

'Here they are,' I said quietly to my father, and started to heave the boxes of books through the door.

The wagon halted beside me and Daniel gently put me aside. 'I'll do that,' he said. He lifted the boxes into the back of the cart, where I saw the glimpse of four pale faces: his mother and his three sisters.

'Hello,' I said awkwardly, and then went back to the shop. I felt so wretched I could hardly carry the boxes from the rear of the printing shop out to the cart and hand them over to Daniel.

My father did nothing. He stood with his forehead leaning against the wall of the house. 'The press,' he said quietly.

'I will see that it is taken down, sheeted and stored safely,' I promised. 'Along with everything else. And when you decide to come back, it will be here for you and we can start again.'

'We won't come back,' Daniel said. 'This country is going to be a Spanish dominion. How can we be safe here? How can you be safe here? Do you think your names are not on Inquisition records as heretics and runaways? Newly arrived from Spain? Named Verde? Do you really think you will pass as an English girl called Hannah Green? With your speech, and your looks?'

I put my hands to my face. It was unbearable.

'Daughter,' my father said.

'All right,' I said furiously, in anger and despair. 'Enough! I'll come.'

Daniel said nothing in his triumph; he did not even smile. My father muttered, 'Praise God,' and picked up a box as if he were a twenty-year-old porter and loaded it on the back of the wagon. Within minutes everything was done.

'We'll pay the rent for the next year,' Daniel decided. 'Then we can fetch the printing press and the rest of the manuscripts.'

My father climbed in the back of the wagon and held out his hand for me. I hesitated. The three white faces of Daniel's sisters turned to me, blank with hostility. 'Is she coming now?' one of them asked.

'You can help me with the horses,' Daniel said quickly and I left the tailgate of the wagon and went to the head of the nearest horse.

'Where are we going?' I asked.

'To the docks,' he said. 'A ship is waiting on the tide. I have booked our passage to France. I already paid for you. I knew you would come.'

I gritted my teeth at his arrogance and tugged on the reins of the big horse and said, 'Come on then!' as if the horse were to blame, and as it felt the even ground of the street under its hoofs it started a steady walk and I swung up onto the driving box of the wagon.

A few moments later, Daniel joined me. 'I did not mean to taunt you,' he said stiffly. 'I only meant that I knew you could not leave your father and your People, and choose to live among strangers for ever.'

I shook my head. In the cold morning light with the fog curling off the Thames I could see the great palaces that faced out over the river, their pleasure gardens running down to the water's edge. All of them were places I had enjoyed, a favoured guest in the queen's train. We entered the city, just stirring to start the day, and I saw the smoke from the ovens uncurling from the bakers' chimneys, past the church of St Paul's scented once more with incense, and then we headed along the familiar route towards the Tower.

Daniel knew I was thinking of Robert Dudley as I looked up, past the wall to where the great white tower pointed like a raised fist.

'Perhaps he'll slither free,' Daniel said.

I turned my head away. 'I'm leaving, aren't I?' I said inconsequentially. 'That should be enough for you.'

I looked at the thickness of the walls and the forbidding gated entrances as we skirted round the breadth of the Tower and came back to the riverside at last.

One of Daniel's sisters poked her head up from the back of the wagon. 'Are we nearly there?' she asked, her voice sharp with fear.

'Nearly,' Daniel said gently. 'Greet your new sister, Hannah. This is Mary.'

'Hello, Mary,' I said.

She nodded, and stared as if I were some freak show at Bartholomew's fair. She took in the richness of my cloak and the fine quality of my linen, then her eyes went down to my embroidered hose and breeches. Without another word she dropped down to the body of the wagon and whispered to her sisters, and I heard their muffled laughter.

'She's shy,' Daniel said. 'She doesn't mean to be rude.'

I was certain that she was determined to be rude but there was no point in telling him. Instead I watched the dark flow of the water as we plodded down the road to the dockside.

I glanced back upriver and then I saw a sight that made me put my hand out to Daniel. 'Stop!'

He did not tighten the rein. 'Why? What is it?'

'Stop, I say!' I said abruptly. 'I have seen something on the river.'

He paused then, and I could see the royal barge, but with no standard flying, the drumbeat keeping the rowers in time, a dark figure at the front of the boat, two hooded men, one at the rear, one at the prow, scanning the banks in case of trouble.

'They must have Elizabeth,' I guessed.

'You can't possibly tell,' Daniel said. 'And if they do have her? It's nothing to do with us. They'd be bound to arrest her now that Wyatt . . .'

'If they turn into the Tower then they have her on board and they are taking her to her death,' I said flatly. 'And Lord Robert will die too.'

He went to flick the reins to make the horse move on, but I clamped my hand on his wrist. 'Let me see, damn you,' I spat at him.

He waited for a moment. As we watched, the barge turned, struggled against the onrush of the tide and then headed towards the Tower. The dark water gate—a heavy portcullis that protected the Tower from the river—rolled up; this visit was prearranged to be secret and silent. The barge went in, the water gate came down, there was utter silence except for the plash of dark water running by us. It was as if the hushed barge and the two dark watching men at prow and stern had never been.

I slipped down from the wagon and I leaned back against the forewheel, closing my eyes. I could imagine the scene as brightly as if it were noon: Elizabeth arguing and delaying and struggling for every extra minute, all the way from the water gate to the room they would have prepared for her in the Tower. I could see her fighting for every grain of sand in the hour glass. And finally, I could see her in her room, looking down on the green where her mother had her head swept from her body with the sharpest French sword they could find, and I could see her watching them build the scaffold that would be her own death place.

Daniel was by my side. 'I have to go to her,' I said. I opened my eyes as if I had wakened from a dream. 'I have to go. I promised I would go back to her, and I cannot betray a promise to a dying woman.'

'You will be identified with her and with him,' he whispered passionately. 'When they come to hang the servants you will be among them.'

I did not even answer him, something nagged in my mind. 'What was that you said about Wyatt?'

He flushed. I had caught him out. 'He has been tried and found guilty and sentenced to death. They have his confession to convict Elizabeth.'

'You knew this? And kept it from me?'

'Yes.'

I drew my cloak round my dark breeches, and went round to the back of the wagon.

'Where are you going?' He grabbed me at the elbow.

'I am getting my bag, I am going to the Tower, I am going to Elizabeth,' I said simply. 'I will stay with her till her death and then I will come to find you.'

'You cannot defy me like this,' he said in sudden rage. 'You are my betrothed. I have told you what we are doing. See, my sisters, my mother, all obey me. You have to do the same.'

I gritted my teeth and squared up to him as if I were in truth a young man and not a girl in breeches. 'See, I do not obey you,' I said bluntly. 'See, I am not a girl like your sisters. See, even if I were your wife you would not find me biddable. Now take your hand off my arm!'

My father climbed out of the wagon and Daniel's sister Mary tumbled out after him, her face bright with excitement.

'What is happening?' my father asked.

'The Lady Elizabeth has just been taken to the Tower,' I explained.

'We saw the royal barge go in by the water gate. I am certain she was on board. I promised I would go back to her. I was going to break that promise to come with you. But now she is in the Tower and under sentence of death, I am honour bound to go to her.'

My father turned to Daniel, waiting for his decision.

'It is nothing to do with Daniel,' I went on, trying to keep the rage from my voice. 'There is no need to look to him. This is my decision.'

'We will go to France as we planned,' Daniel said steadily. 'But we will wait at Calais for you. We will wait for Elizabeth's execution, and then you will come to us.'

I hesitated. Calais was an English town, part of the remaining English settlement in France. 'Don't you fear the Inquisition in Calais?' I asked. 'If they come here, their writ will run there too.'

'If it comes, we can get away to France,' he said. 'And we should have warning. Do you promise you will join us?'

'Yes,' I said, feeling my rage and my fear roll away from me. 'Yes, I can promise I will come when it is over, when Elizabeth is safe or dead.'

'I shall come back for you when I hear that she is dead,' he said. 'We can collect the printing press and the other papers at the same time.'

My father took my hands in his. 'You will come, *querida*?' he asked. 'You won't fail?'

'I love you, Father,' I whispered. 'Of course I will come to you. But I love Lady Elizabeth too, and I promised to stay near her.'

'What is she doing now?' one of Daniel's sisters demanded in a delighted hiss from the rear of the wagon. Mary stepped up to the side, and I heard their scandalised whispers.

'Give me my bag and let me go,' I said shortly to Daniel. I stepped up to the rear of the wagon and said, 'Goodbye,' to the lot of them.

Daniel dropped my bag on the cobbles. 'I will come for you,' he reminded me.

'Yes, I know,' I said, with as little warmth in my voice as in his.

My father kissed my forehead, and put his hand on my head to bless me, then he turned without another word and got back into the wagon. Daniel waited till he was seated inside, and then he reached for me, pulled me close and kissed me fiercely on the mouth. It was a kiss so full of desire and anger that I flinched away from him and only when he abruptly let me go and swung onto the driver's box did I realise that I wanted that kiss from him, and that I wanted more. But it was too late to say anything, too late to do anything. Daniel flicked the reins and the wagon rolled past me, and I was left in the cold London morning with nothing but a small bag at my feet, a hot bruised mouth and a promised duty to a traitor.

SUMMER–AUTUMN 1554

THOSE DAYS and then weeks in the Tower with the princess were the worst ones of my life in England, the worst days for Elizabeth too. She went into a sort of trance of unhappiness and fear which nothing could lift. She knew that she was going to die. Philip of Spain had sworn that he would not come to England while the Protestant princess was alive.

In the middle of May, the proposed month of the queen's wedding, as the weather grew warmer, still the scaffold was not built for Elizabeth; still Philip of Spain did not come. Then, one day, there was a sudden change at the Tower. A Norfolk squire and his blue-liveried men marched into the Tower to make it their own. Elizabeth went from door to window in a frenzy of fear, craning her head at the arrow slit, peering through the keyhole of the door trying to see what was happening.

Finally, she sent me out to ask if he had come to oversee her execution. 'I have to prepare,' she said. 'I am not ready to die tomorrow.'

I nodded, and went out. The green was empty; there were no sawn planks awaiting a carpenter. She was safe for another day. I stopped at the water gate and fell into conversation with one of the blue-liveried men. The gossip he told me sent me flying back to the princess.

'You're saved,' I said briefly, coming in through the door of her cramped room. Kat Ashley looked up and made the sign of a cross, the old habit forced out of her by her fear.

Elizabeth, who had been kneeling up at the window, looking out at the circling gulls, turned round, her face pale, her eyelids red. 'What?'

'You're to be released to Sir Henry Bedingfield,' I said. 'And to go with him to Woodstock Palace.'

There was no leap of hope in her face. 'And what then?'

'House arrest,' I said.

'I am not declared innocent? I am not received at court?'

'You're not on trial and you're not executed,' I pointed out. 'And you're away from the Tower.'

'They will bury me at Woodstock,' she said. 'This is a trick to get me away from the city so I can be forgotten. They will poison me when I am out of sight and bury me far from court.'

'If the queen wanted you dead she could have sent for a swordsman,'

I said. 'This is your freedom, or at least a part-freedom. I should have thought you would be glad.'

Elizabeth's face was dull. 'D'you know what my mother did to Mary's mother?' she asked in a whisper. 'Queen Catherine died in poverty and hardship while her daughter was a servant in my nursery, waiting on me. Don't you think that daughter remembers that? Don't you see this is Mary's revenge?'

'But, Lady Elizabeth,' I pleaded with her. 'You said to me, every moment you have is a moment you have won. When you leave here, you have won yourself another moment.'

'When I leave here I go to a secret and shameful death,' she said flatly.

I knew I could not leave the Tower without trying to see Lord Robert. I was searched before I was allowed to his door, and I was not left alone with him. My service to Elizabeth had tainted my reputation of loyalty to the queen.

When they swung open the door he was at his desk at the window, reading. He turned in his seat as the door opened and looked to see who was coming in. When he saw me he smiled, a world-weary smile. I stepped into the room and took in the difference in him. He was heavier, his face puffed up with fatigue and boredom, his skin pale from his months of imprisonment, but his dark eyes were steady and his mouth twisted upwards in what had once been his merry smile.

'It is Mistress Boy,' he said.

'The queen commanded me to bear the Lady Elizabeth company,' I said, coming into the room, awkwardly conscious of the guard behind me. 'So I have been in the Tower with you all this time.'

His dark glance flared with interest. 'And is she well?' he asked.

'She has been ill and very anxious,' I said. 'I came to see you now because tomorrow we leave. She is to be released under house arrest to Sir Henry Bedingfield and we are to go to Woodstock Palace.'

'Released,' he said quietly. 'Why would Mary be merciful?'

I shrugged my shoulders. It was against the queen's interest, but it was typical of her nature. 'She has a tenderness for Elizabeth even now,' I volunteered. 'Not even to please her new husband can she send her sister to the scaffold.'

'Elizabeth was always lucky,' he said.

'And you, my lord?' I could not keep the love from my voice.

He smiled at me. 'I am more settled,' he said. 'Whether I live or die is beyond my command, and I understand that now.'

'My lord,' I whispered earnestly. 'You cannot die. Your tutor and I looked in the mirror and saw your fortune. He said that you are to die safe in your bed, and that you will be the beloved of a queen and the making of a prince who will change the history of the world.'

He frowned. 'Are you sure? What d'you mean?'

The guard cleared his throat. 'Nothing in code.'

Lord Robert shook his head at the idiocy of the man but curbed his impatience. 'Well,' he said. 'It's good to know that you think I will not follow my father out there.' He nodded at the green beyond the window.

There was a tap on the door behind us. 'I can't go yet!' I exclaimed, turning, but it was not another guard who stood there; it was a woman.

She was a pretty brown-haired woman with a creamy skin and soft brown eyes. She was dressed richly; I noticed the embroidery on her gown and the slashing of velvet and silk on her sleeves. She took in the scene, me with my cheeks flushed and my eyes filled with tears, my master Lord Robert smiling in his chair, and then she stepped across the room and he rose to greet her. She kissed him coolly on both cheeks.

'And who is this?' she asked. 'Ah! You must be the queen's fool.'

There was a moment before I replied. I had never before minded my title. But the way she said it gave me pause. 'And you must be Lady Dudley,' I said bluntly.

She nodded. 'You can go,' she said, and turned to her husband.

He stopped her. 'I have not yet finished my business with Hannah Green.' He seated her in his chair at his desk and drew me to the other window, out of earshot.

'Hannah, if anything changes between the princess and the queen, if you should chance to meet with our friend John Dee, I should be glad to know of everything.'

I smiled at his touch on my hand, at his words that told me that he was alive and yearning for life again.

'I shall write to you,' I promised him. 'I shall tell you everything that I can. I cannot be disloyal to the queen—'

'Nor now to Elizabeth either?' he suggested with a smile.

'She is a wonderful young woman,' I said. 'You could not be in her service and not admire her.'

He laughed. 'Child, you want to love and be loved so much that you are always on all sides at once. I've known Elizabeth all her life. I taught her to jump with her first pony. She was a most impressive child,' he said fondly. 'Give her my love and my loyalty. Tell her that if I could have dined with her I would have done.'

I nodded.

'You had better go,' he said quietly. 'Do not forget me, Hannah.'

I nodded again and went to the door. The guard swung it open for me. I bowed to Lady Dudley and she gave me a brief, dismissive nod.

Woodstock turned out to be a crumbling old palace that had been neglected for years. It was better than the Tower but Elizabeth was still undoubtedly a prisoner. At first she was allowed access to only the four rooms of the gatehouse, but she extended her parole until she could walk in the gardens, and then in the orchard.

She became increasingly confident that she would not be assassinated by Sir Henry, and instead of fearing him she became contemptuous of him. He, poor man, was worn thin by her peremptory demands.

Then, one day in early summer, a messenger came from London, with a bundle of business for Elizabeth and a letter for me, addressed to 'Hannah Green, with Lady Elizabeth at the Tower of London'.

Dear Hannah,

This is to inform you that your father is safely arrived in Calais. We have rented a house and a shop and he is buying and selling books and papers. My mother is keeping house for him and my sisters are working, one at a milliner's, one for a glover and one as a housekeeper. I am working for a surgeon, and I am learning much from him.

I am sorry that you did not come with us, and I am sorry that I spoke to you in such a way that did not convince you. I understand that you will not do as I command; I understand that you do not see why I should command. It is unmaidenly, but it is the truth of you.

Let me be clear with you. I cannot become a cat's-paw. I cannot do as you desire and hand over the mastery of our family. It is my responsibility and duty; it cannot be yours. But I will make a good husband to you. I regret that I released you from our betrothal and this letter is to ask you to promise yourself to me once more. I wish to marry you, Hannah.

I think about you all of the time. I want to see you, to touch you. When I kissed you goodbye I am afraid I was rough with you and you did not want my kiss. I felt anger and desire, all mixed up at that moment, and had no care what you might be feeling. I hope the kiss did not frighten you. You see, Hannah, I think I am in love with you.

I tell you this because I do not know what else to do with this hot stir of feelings in my heart and in my body. I cannot sleep and I cannot eat. Forgive me if this offends you, but what am I to do? Surely I should tell you? If we were married we would share this secret in the marriage bed—but I cannot even think about being wedded and bedded with you; it heats my blood to think of you as my wife.

Please write back to me as soon as you read this and tell me what you want. I wish to God you would write to me soon. I wish to God I could make you understand the fever that I am in.

Daniel

A woman ready for love would have replied at once. A girl ready for womanhood would have at least sent some sort of reply. I read it through very carefully, and then I put it at the back of a fire and burned it, as if I would burn my desire to ashes, along with his letter. At least I had the honesty to recognise my desire. I had felt it when he had held me in the shadowy press room; it had blazed up when he had crushed me to him when we parted at the wagon. But I knew that if I replied to him he would come to fetch me, and then I would be his wife, and I was not yet ready to be an obedient wife.

Besides, I had no time to think about Daniel, or about my future. The messenger from London had brought papers for Elizabeth as well as me. When I entered her rooms I found her wound up to breaking pitch at the prospect of her sister's marriage, and her own disinheritance. She was stalking the room like a furious cat. She had received a cold message from the queen's chamberlain that Philip of Spain had left his country and was sailing for England, that the court would meet him at Winchester—but Elizabeth herself was not invited. And to add insult to her hurt pride, she was to send me to join the queen and the court at once. The fool was valued more than the princess.

'This is to insult me,' she spat. 'She does not dare to meet Philip of Spain with me at her side! She knows he will look from the old queen to the young princess and prefer me!'

'He is betrothed to her,' I said quietly. 'It's not a matter of desire.'

'Then why am I not summoned to court? It's all right for you,' she said nastily. 'You're not a prisoner. You're not even my servant. You can come and go as you please. She wants you at her side. You will be able to see all your friends again when you meet them at Winchester for the wedding feast. No doubt you will be in the queen's train.'

'Perhaps.'

'Hannah, you can't leave me,' she said flatly.

'Lady Elizabeth, I have to go. The queen commands me.'

'She said you were to be my companion.'

'And now she says I am to leave.'

'Hannah!' She broke off, near to tears. 'I am ruined. If she bears a son to him, I am ruined. A son,' she muttered, cautious even in her chagrin to keep her voice low. 'A damned Spanish son. A damned Catholic Spanish son. And England an outpost of the Spanish empire, England, my England, a cat's-paw of Spanish policy. And the priests back, and the burnings beginning, and my father's faith and my father's legacy torn out of English earth before it has time to flower. Damn her. Damn her to hell and her misconceived child with her.'

'Lady Elizabeth!' I exclaimed. 'Don't say that!'

She rounded on me, her hands up, her fists clenched. 'Damn her, and damn you too for standing her friend.'

'You must have thought it might happen,' I started. 'The marriage was agreed; he would not delay for ever . . .'

She let out a wail at that and dropped to the floor.

I knelt beside her and took her hands. They were icy. 'Lady Elizabeth,' I said soothingly. 'Be calm. It is a marriage which is bound to take place and there is nothing you can do about it.'

'But not even invited . . .' She gave another little wail.

'It is hard. But she has been merciful to you.' I paused. 'Remember, he would have had you beheaded.'

'And I am to be grateful for that?'

'You could be calm. And wait.'

The face she turned up to me was suddenly glacial. 'If she bears him a son then I will have nothing to wait for but a forced marriage to some Papist prince, or death.'

'You said to me that any day you could stay alive was a victory,' I reminded her.

She shook her head. 'Staying alive is not important,' she said quietly. 'It never was. I was staying alive for England. Staying alive to be England's princess. Staying alive to inherit.'

'You must do that,' I said soothingly. 'Stay alive for England. Wait.'

I could not see much of the actual wedding service. I had a glimpse of Prince Philip as he stepped towards the blaze of gold of the altar of Winchester Cathedral, heard the soaring voices of the queen's choristers singing the wedding mass, and then the soft gasp as Bishop Gardiner raised the couple's clasped hands to show that the wedding was completed and England's virgin queen was now a married woman.

I thought I would see the prince clearly at the wedding feast, but as I was hurrying on my way to the hall I heard the rattle of the weapons of the Spanish guard and I stepped back into a window embrasure as the men at arms marched down, and after them the bustle of his court with the prince himself at the centre. And then, amid all this hustle of excitement, something happened to me. I could see the flurry of silks and velvets, hear the tap of swords against the stone walls, smell the pomade they wore in their hair and beards, and I stumbled back, feeling for the cold wall behind me to steady me, almost fainting, overwhelmed with a homesickness and a longing for Spain. I think I even cried out, and one man turned dark familiar eyes and looked towards me.

'What is it, lad?' he asked, seeing my golden pageboy suit.

'It's the queen's holy fool,' one of his men remarked in Spanish. 'Some toy that she affects. A boy-girl, a hermaphrodite.'

'Good God, a wizened old maid served by no maid at all,' someone quipped. The prince said 'Hush,' but absent-mindedly, as if he was not defending a new wife but reprimanding a familiar offence.

'Are you sick, child?' he asked me in Spanish.

One of his companions stepped forward and took my hand. 'The prince asks are you sick?' he demanded in careful English.

'I am not sick,' I said in English, hoping that no one would hear the vestiges of my accent. 'I was startled by the prince.'

'You startled her only,' he laughed, turning to the prince and speaking in Spanish. 'God grant that you may startle her mistress.'

'She's more likely to startle him,' someone remarked. 'God save us, how are we to put our prince to bed with such an aged dame?'

'And a virgin,' someone else replied. 'Not even a willing widow.'

'And she's so dull,' the first one persisted.

'Enough,' the prince said clearly, speaking in Spanish, thinking that only they would understand. 'I have wedded her, and I shall bed her, and if you hear that I cannot do it you can speculate then as to the cause.'

I had not forgotten Daniel Carpenter and his letter to me for all that I had thrown it in the fire after one reading. I might as well have folded it and kept it, close to my heart, for I remembered every word that he had written, as if I reread it like a lovesick girl every night.

I found that I was thinking of him more often since the arrival of the Spanish court. No one could have thought badly of marriage who could see the queen; from the morning that she rose from her married bed, she glowed with a warmth that had not been seen in her before. She looked like a woman who has found a safe haven at last. She was a woman in love, a beloved wife; she had a councillor she could trust, a powerful man devoted to her well-being. I thought that if a woman as fiercely virginal and as intensely spiritual as the queen could find love, then so perhaps could I. A woman might blossom into being a wife, not be trimmed down to fit. And this made me think that Daniel might be the man I could turn to, could trust. Daniel, who loved me.

He also came to my mind for his fears and his cautions, even though I had scoffed at them at the time. Though the Spanish court drew me in, I knew that Daniel had been right to take his family and my father out of the country. These were early days, but there were signs that the queen's fabled mercy—so generous to those who challenged her throne—might not extend to those who insulted her faith.

I thought I should write to Daniel, and to my father, and send the letter by some of the many soldiers who were going to Calais to refortify the town against the French, now doubly our enemy since we had a Spanish king.

Dear Daniel,

I did not reply to you earlier because I did not know what to say. Besides, I have been with the princess at Woodstock and could not have got a letter to you. I am now with the queen at Winchester and we will soon go to London when I can send you this letter.

I am very glad that your business took you to Calais, and I propose to join you and my father when matters change here for me, just as we agreed. I think you judged rightly when you should leave and I am ready to join you in good time.

I read your letter very carefully, Daniel, and I think of you often. To answer you with honesty, I am not eager for marriage as yet, but when you speak to me as you did in your letter, and when you kissed me on parting, I felt a delight I cannot name. You did not frighten me, Daniel; I liked your kiss. I would have you as my husband, when I am released from court, when the time is right and we are both equally ready. I accept your proposal that we should be betrothed but I need to see my way clear to marriage.

I do not want to turn you into a cat's-paw in your own home; you are wrong to fear that and to reproach me with a desire I do not have. I do not want to rule over you, but I do not want you to rule over me. I need to be a woman in my own right, and not only a wife. I have travelled far and lived according to my own means, and I seem to have adopted a lad's pride along with breeches. I would not mislead you in this, Daniel. I cannot be a servant to a husband; I would have to be his friend and comrade. I write to ask you if you could have a wife like this.

I enclose a letter for my father. He will tell you the rest of my news. I do not forget that I went from you only to bear the princess company in the Tower. She is now released from the Tower but she is still a prisoner. I know if I were an ordinary betrothed girl I would have no obligations but to you— but, Daniel, I am not a girl like that. I want to complete my service to the princess and to the queen and then, and only then, come to you. I hope you can understand this.

But I should like to be betrothed to you, if we can agree . . .
Hannah

I folded the letter up and put it away, ready to send to Daniel when the court moved to London in August.

The queen and her new husband settled into the Palace of Whitehall and started to establish the routines of a joint court.

I was in her chamber early one morning, waiting for her to come to Mass, when she emerged in her nightgown and knelt in silence before the prie-dieu. Something in her silence told me that she was deeply moved, and I knelt behind her, bowed my head and waited. Jane Dormer came from the queen's bedroom where she slept when the king was not with his wife and knelt down too, her head bowed. After a good half-hour of silent prayer, the queen still rapt on her knees, I shuffled cautiously towards Jane and whispered in a voice so low that it could not disturb the queen. 'What's happening?'

'She's missed her course,' Jane said, her voice a tiny thread of sound.

'She is with child?' I could hardly believe it. And I did not feel the joy I would have expected at the prospect of Mary's dreams coming true. 'Really with child?'

She heard the doubt in my voice and turned a hard gaze on me. 'What is it you doubt, fool? My word? Hers?'

'I doubt no one,' I said quickly. 'Please God it is so. And no one could want it more than I.'

Jane shook her head. 'No one could want it more than she,' she said, nodding towards the kneeling queen, 'for she has prayed to carry a son for England since she was old enough to pray.'

The queen said nothing to the king nor to the court, but Jane watched her with the devotion of a mother and next month, in September, when the queen did not bleed, she gave me a small triumphant nod and I grinned back. The queen told the king in secret, but anyone seeing his redoubled tenderness towards her must have guessed that she was carrying his child, and that it was a great hidden joy to them both.

Their happiness illuminated the palace, and for the first time I lived at a royal court that was alive with flirtation and music and dancing and parties and in the heart of it all was the queen, serene and smiling, with her young husband always lovingly at her side. We were the richest, most elegant court in the whole of Christendom, and we knew it. With Queen Mary glowing at the head of this radiant court we danced at a very pinnacle of self-satisfied pleasure.

In October the queen was informed that Elizabeth was sick again. Woodstock, and Elizabeth, and Elizabeth's many ploys for attention seemed far away as the queen gazed dreamily out of the window at the garden where the trees were turning yellow and golden and bronze. 'She can see my doctors if she insists,' she said absently to me. 'Would you go with them, Hannah? And see if she is as bad as she claims? I don't want to be unkind to her. If she would just admit her part in the plot I would release her. I am carrying an heir to the throne, an heir for England and for the whole Spanish empire. This will be the greatest prince the world has ever known. Elizabeth can admit her fault and I will forgive her. And then she should be married; the king has suggested his cousin, the Duke of Savoy. Tell Elizabeth that this time of waiting and suspicion can be at an end; tell her I am with child. Tell her I shall have my baby in early May. Any hopes she had of the throne will be over by next summer. Make sure she understands, Hannah. There has been bad blood between us but it can be over as soon as she consents.'

I knelt to her and bowed my head. 'I shall miss being with you,' I said honestly. 'Especially now that you are so happy.'

She put her hand on my head. 'I shall miss you too, my little fool,' she said. 'But you shall come back in time for the Christmas feast, and after that you shall bear me company when I am confined.'

'Your Grace, I shall be so pleased to bear you company.'

'A spring baby,' she said dreamily. 'A little spring lamb of God. Won't that be wonderful, Hannah? An heir for England and for Spain.'

At Woodstock I found Elizabeth very ill. No one could have doubted her frailty. She was in bed, exhausted and fat, and looked years older than twenty-one. With her jowls bloated by illness Elizabeth bore a startling resemblance to the portraits of her father in his later years.

I waited till the physicians had seen her and bled her and she had rested before I went into her bedchamber.

'Lady Elizabeth,' I said and dropped to my knees by the bed.

'Faithless,' she said, hardly opening her eyes.

I had to choke back a giggle at her tendency to drama. 'Oh, my lady,' I said reproachfully. 'You know I have to go where I am bid.'

'I know you went dancing off to Winchester for the wedding and I have not seen you since.' Her voice rose to match her temper.

'The queen commanded me to go with her to London and now she has sent me to you. And I bring a message.'

She raised herself a little on her pillows. 'I am almost too sick to listen, so tell me briefly. Am I to be released?'

'If you will admit your fault.'

Her dark eyes flared under the puffy eyelids. 'Tell me what she said.'

I recited to her what the queen had offered. I spared her nothing, not the news of the pregnancy, her sister's willingness to be friends again.

I thought she would rage when she heard the queen was with child, but she did not even comment. 'I will think about what you have told me,' she said, following her usual instinct to buy time. 'Are you to stay with me? Or take an answer back to her?'

'I am not to go back to court until Christmas,' I said. Temptingly, I added: 'If you were to beg her forgiveness perhaps you could be at the court for Christmas. It's very gay now, Princess, the court is filled with handsome grandees and there is dancing every night.'

'I'm not a child to tempt with toys,' she said with quiet dignity. 'And I am not a fool. You can go now, Hannah, you have served her and done her bidding. But for the rest of your stay here you shall serve me.'

WINTER 1554–SPRING 1555

CHRISTMAS CAME AND WENT and Elizabeth would not confess. There was no joy for me either, as I was ordered to stay with her until she begged for forgiveness. Woodstock was a malevolent house in winter, freezing cold and damp. I had been in good health when I arrived, and yet even I could feel myself growing weak. For Elizabeth, it was a nightmare.

But to everyone's surprise, the queen weakened first. As the bitter winter melted into a wet spring, Elizabeth was bidden to court, without having to confess, and I was ordered to ride in her train. It was not the return she might have wanted; she was brought in almost as a prisoner. We skirted the city—the queen had ordered that Elizabeth should not ride down the great roads of London—but as we went through the little lanes I felt my heart skip a beat in terror, and I pulled up my horse in the middle of the lane and made the princess stop.

'Go on, fool,' she said ungraciously. 'Kick him on.'

'God help me, God help me,' I babbled.

'What is it?'

Seeing me stock-still, Sir Henry Bedingfield's man turned his horse and came back. 'Come on now,' he said roughly, taking the bridle and pulling my horse forward. 'Orders are to keep moving.'

'My God,' I said again. It was all I could say.

Elizabeth came up alongside. 'Look, she's white as a sheet and shaking. Hannah? What is it?'

'Smoke,' was all I could say. 'Fire.'

'Oh, it's the Smithfield fires,' the soldier said. 'That's upset the lass. It's that, isn't it, bairn?'

At Elizabeth's quick look of enquiry he explained. 'New laws. Heretics are put to death by burning. They're burning today in Smithfield. I can't smell it, but your lass here can. It's upset her.'

'Burning?' Elizabeth demanded. 'Burning heretics? You mean Protestants? In London? Today?' Her eyes were blazing black with anger, but she did not impress the soldier.

'Aye,' he said briefly. 'It's a new world. A new queen on the throne, a new king at her side, and a new law to match. We've had nothing but foul weather and bad luck since King Henry broke with the Pope. But now the Pope's rule is back and the Holy Father will bless England again and we can have a son and heir and decent weather.'

Elizabeth said not one word. She took her pomander from her belt, put it in my hand and held my hand up to my nose so I could smell the aromatic scent of dried orange and cloves.

We rode to Hampton Court in an icy silence and we were greeted as prisoners with a guard. They bundled us in the back door as if they were ashamed to greet us. But once the door of her private rooms was locked behind us, Elizabeth turned and took my cold hands in hers.

'I could not smell smoke,' she said. 'Nobody could. The soldier only knew that they were burning today; he could not smell it.'

Still I said nothing.

'It was your gift, wasn't it?' she asked curiously.

I cleared my throat. 'Yes,' I admitted.

'You were sent by God to warn me that this was happening,' she said.

I nodded, though I knew that it was my own terror she had seen, the horror I had felt as a child when they had dragged my own mother from our house to tie her to a stake and light the fire under her feet.

Princess Elizabeth went to the window, knelt and put her bright head in her hands. 'Dear God, thank you for sending me this messenger with this vision,' I heard her say softly. 'I understand it, I understand my destiny today as I have never done before. Bring me to my throne that I may do my duty for you and for my people. Amen.'

She rose to her feet. 'You have given me a vision today, Hannah. I knew it before, but now I have seen it in your eyes. I have to be queen of this country and put a stop to this horror.'

In the evening, before dinner, I was summoned to the queen's rooms and found her in conference with the king and with the new arrival and greatest favourite: the archbishop and papal legate, Cardinal Reginald Pole. I was in the presence chamber before I saw him, for if I had known he was there I would never have crossed the threshold. I was immediately, instinctively afraid of him.

He glanced up as I came into the room and his gaze flicked indifferently over me, but the queen held out her hands in greeting. I ran to her and dropped to my knee at her feet.

'Your Grace!'

'My little fool,' she said tenderly.

I looked up at her and saw at once the changes in her appearance made by her pregnancy. Her colour was good, she was rosy-cheeked, her face plumper and rounder, her eyes bright from good health. Her belly was a proud curve only partly concealed by the loosened panel of her stomacher and the wider cut of her gown, and I thought how proudly she must be letting out the lacing every day to accommodate the growing child.

With her hand resting on my head in blessing she turned to the two other men. 'This is my dear little fool Hannah, who has been with me since the death of my brother. She is a faithful, loving girl and I use her as my little emissary with Elizabeth, who trusts her too.' She turned to me. 'She is here?'

'Just arrived,' I said.

She tapped my shoulder to bid me rise and I warily got to my feet and looked at the two men.

'You see visions?' the cardinal asked. 'Hear voices?'

'Very rarely,' I said shortly, trying to keep my accent as English as possible. 'And unfortunately, never at times of my choosing.'

'She saw that I would be queen,' Mary said. 'And she foretold my brother's death. And she came to the attention of her first master because she saw an angel in Fleet Street.'

The cardinal smiled at the king. 'Can you advise us, holy fool? We are about God's business as it has not been done in England for generations. We are bringing the country back to the church. We are making good what has been bad for so long.'

I hesitated. It was clear to me that this was more rhetoric than a question demanding an answer. But the queen looked to me to speak.

'I would think it should be done gently,' I said. 'But that is my opinion, not the voice of my gift. I just wish that it could be done gently.'

'It should be done quickly and powerfully,' the queen said. 'The longer it takes the more doubts will emerge.'

'One should never offend more men than one can persuade,' her husband, ruler of half of Europe, told her.

I saw her melt at his voice, but she did not change her opinion. 'These are a stubborn people,' she said. 'Given a choice they are like children who will go from apple to plum and take a bite out of each, and spoil everything.'

The cardinal nodded at the king. 'Her Grace is right,' he said. 'Best that we should root out heresy, destroy it, and have the country at peace and in the old ways in one move.'

The king looked thoughtful. 'We must do it quickly and clearly, but with mercy,' he said. He turned to the queen. 'You have to be a gentle mother to your people. They have to be persuaded, not forced.'

Sweetly, she put her hand on her swelling belly. 'I want to be a gentle mother indeed,' she said.

He put his hand over her own. 'I know it,' he said. 'Who should know better than I? And together we will make a holy Catholic inheritance for this young man of ours so that when he comes to his throne, here, and in Spain, he will be doubly blessed with the greatest lands in Christendom and the greatest peace the world has ever known.'

SPRING–SUMMER 1555

AT HAMPTON COURT PALACE they made the room ready for the queen's confinement. The privy chamber behind her bedroom was hung with tapestries especially chosen for their holy and encouraging scenes. The windows were bolted shut so that not a breath of air should come into the room. They tied the posts of the bed with straps that she might cling to while her labour tore her thirty-nine-year-old body apart. The bed was dressed with a magnificent counterpane which the queen and her ladies had been embroidering since her wedding day. There were great log piles beside the fireplace so that the room could be heated to fever pitch. They shrouded the floors with carpets so that every sound should be muffled and they brought in the magnificent royal cradle with a 240-piece layette for the boy who would be born within the next six weeks.

In the first week of May, the queen said farewell to the court and went through the doors of her privy chamber to the darkened interior where she must stay until the birth of her boy, and for six weeks after that, before being churched. The only people to see her would be her ladies; the queen's council would have to take their orders from the king, acting in her stead.

The baby was a little late; the weeks came and went with no sign of him. The midwives predicted a stronger baby for taking his own time and an easier labour when it started. But as May went by they started to remark that it was an exceptionally late baby.

While the long hot dull weeks of waiting dragged on, I sat with Queen Mary in the shrouded room. Sometimes I read to her from the Bible in Spanish, sometimes I gave her little pieces of news about the court, or told her Will Somers's latest nonsense. I took flowers in for her, hedgerow flowers like daisies, and then the little roses in bud.

She took them with a smile of pleasure. 'Are the roses in bud already?'

'Yes, Your Grace.'

'I shall be sorry to miss the sight of them this year.'

As I had feared, the darkness and quietness of the room was preying on her spirits. I had seen her unhappy and fearful before and I recognised the gauntness of her face as the shine was rubbed off her.

Elizabeth, in contrast, was now free to go where she would, and grew more and more confident as the summer drew on. She had lost the fleshiness that had come with her illness; she was filled with energy and zest for life. The Spanish adored her—her colouring alone was fascinating to them. When she rode her great grey hunter in her green riding habit with her copper hair spread out on her shoulders, they called her Enchantress, and Beautiful Brass-head. Elizabeth would protest at the fuss they made, and so encourage them even more.

King Philip never checked them, though a more careful brother-in-law would have guarded against Elizabeth's head being turned by the flattery of his court. Nor did he speak now of her marrying and going away from England. Indeed, he made it clear that Elizabeth was an honoured member of the court and heir to the throne.

I thought this was mostly policy on his part, but then one day I was looking from the palace window to a sheltered lawn on the south side of the palace and I saw a couple walking, heads close together, half hidden and then half revealed by the dark strong yew trees. I smiled as I watched this clandestine courtship.

But then the girl turned her head and I saw a flash from under her dark hood, the unmistakable glint of copper hair. The girl was Elizabeth, and the man walking beside her, close enough to touch but not touching, was Mary's husband.

I put myself outside Elizabeth's door that night and waited for her and her ladies to go to dinner.

'Ah, fool,' she said pleasantly as she came out of her rooms. 'Are you dining with me?'

'If you wish, Princess,' I said politely, falling into her train. 'I saw a curious thing today in the garden.'

'In which garden?' she asked.

'The summer garden,' I said. 'I saw two lovers walking side by side.'

'Not lovers,' she said easily. 'You lack the Sight if you saw lovers, my fool. That was the king and I, walking together.'

'You looked like lovers,' I said flatly, 'from where I was standing. You looked like a courting couple. And if the queen had seen you and her husband today, she would banish you to Woodstock in a moment.'

Elizabeth gave a dizzy laugh. 'Oh no, for he would not let her.'

'He? He does not give the orders here.'

'He is king,' she pointed out. 'He told her I should be treated with respect, and I am. He told her that I should be free to come and go as I wish, and I am. He will tell her that I am to stay at court, and I will. And, he will tell her that I shall be free to meet whom I choose, and talk with whom I choose, and, in short, do anything at all that I choose.'

I gasped that she could leap so far in her confidence. 'You will always be under suspicion.'

'Not I,' she said. 'Not any more. I could be caught with a dozen pikes in my laundry basket tomorrow, and I would not be charged. He will protect me.'

'Princess, this is the most dangerous game you are playing,' I warned her. 'I have never heard you so reckless before.'

'If he loves me then nothing can touch me,' she said, her voice very low. 'And I can make him love me.'

'He cannot intend anything but your dishonour, and her heartbreak,' I said fiercely.

'Oh, he intends nothing at all.' She was gleaming with pleasure. 'He is beyond intentions. I have him on the run. D'you not know the pleasure of turning a man's head, Hannah? Let me tell you, it is better than anything. And when the man is the most powerful man in Christendom, the King of England and Prince of Spain, and the husband of your icy, arrogant, tyrannical ugly old sister, it is the greatest joy that can be had!'

In mid-June the queen, still pregnant, broke with convention to release herself from the confinement chamber. The physicians could not say that she would be any worse for being outside. In the cool of the morning or in the shadowy evening she would stroll slowly in her private garden, attended only by her ladies and the members of her household.

'Your Grace.' I dropped to one knee as I met her in the privy garden one day. She had been looking at the fast flow of the river past the boat pier, looking, and yet not seeing. A brood of ducklings was playing in the current, their mother watchful nearby, surveying the little bundles as they paddled and bobbed. Even the ducks on the Thames had young, but England's cradle was still empty.

She turned an unseeing dark gaze to me. 'Oh, Hannah.'

'Are you well, Your Grace?'

She tried to smile. 'No, my child. I am not very well.'

'Are you in pain?'

She shook her head. 'I should be glad of pain, of labour pains. No, Hannah. I feel nothing, not in my body, not in my heart.'

I drew a little closer. 'Perhaps these are the fancies that come before birth,' I said soothingly.

She shook her head. 'No, I don't think so.' She held out her hands to me, as patient as a sick child. 'Can't you see, Hannah? With your gift? Can you see, and tell me the truth?'

Almost unwillingly I took her hands, and at her touch I felt a rush of despair as cold as if I had fallen into the river that flowed beneath the pier. She saw the shock in my face, and read it rightly at once.

'He's gone, hasn't he?' she whispered. 'I have somehow lost him.'

'I wouldn't know, Your Grace,' I stumbled. 'I'm no physician. I do not have the skill to judge . . .'

She shook her head, the bright sunlight glinting on the rich embroidery of her hood, on the gold hoops in her ears, all this worldly wealth encasing heartbreak. 'I knew it,' she said. 'I had a son in my belly and now he is gone. I feel an emptiness where I used to feel a life.'

'Oh, Your Grace!' I cried out. 'There can be another child. Where one has been made you can make another.'

She did not even seem to hear me. She let her hands lie in mine and she looked towards the river as if she would want it to wash her away.

'Your Grace?' I whispered, very quietly. 'Queen Mary? Dearest Mary?'

When she turned her face to me her eyes were filled with tears. 'It's all wrong,' she said, and her voice was low and utterly desolate. 'It has been going wrong since Elizabeth's mother took my father from us and broke my mother's heart, and nothing can put it right again. It's been going wrong since Elizabeth's mother won my father to sin and led him from his faith so that he lived and died in torment. It's all wrong, Hannah, and I cannot put it right though I have tried and tried. It is too much for me. And now Elizabeth has taken my husband, the only joy of my life, the only person I have ever loved since I lost my mother. She has taken him from me. And now my son has gone from me too.'

I gripped her hands as if she were a drowning woman. 'Mary!'

Gently she pulled her hands from me, and walked away, alone again, as she always had been, as now she thought she always must be. I knew that she was walking with the tears streaming down her cheeks. She could not ask for help; she could not receive help. The pain in her heart was that of loss. She had lost the love of her father; she had lost her mother. Now she had lost her child, and every day, in full view of the court, she was losing her husband to her pretty younger sister.

In July the court should have been on progress, travelling round the great houses of England, enjoying the hunting and the parties and the pleasures of the English summer, but our setting out had been delayed, waiting for the birth of the prince, and now, twelve weeks late, nobody truly believed that the prince would come.

Nobody said anything to the queen—that was the worst of it. She had lost a child which meant more to her than the world itself, and nobody comforted her. She was surrounded by a wall of polite silence, but they smiled when she had gone by, and some of them laughed behind their hands and said that she was an old and foolish woman and that she had mistaken the drying up of her courses for a pregnancy! and what a fool she was! and what a fool she had made of the king!

She must have known how they spoke of her, and the bitter twist of her mouth showed her hurt, but she walked with her head high through a summertime court that was buzzing with malice and gossip, and she still said nothing. At the end of July, the midwives packed up their dozens of bandages, put away the embroidered white silk layette, packed away the bonnets, the little bootees, the petticoats and the swaddling bands and finally carried the magnificent wooden cradle from the birthing room. The servants took down the tapestries from the windows and the walls, the thick Turkish rugs from the floor, the straps and the rich bedding from the bed. Without any word of explanation the matter was closed. The court moved in an almost silent procession to Oatlands Palace and took up residence so quietly that you would have thought that someone had died in hiding, of shame.

I had a letter from my father in August, asking me when I would join them at Calais. Indeed, I was anxious to go. I wanted to be with my father. I wanted to be far from the smoke of Smithfield.

I went to Elizabeth first. 'Princess, my father asks me to join him in Calais. Do I have your permission to go?'

Her pretty face scowled at once. Elizabeth was a great collector of servants, she never liked anyone to leave. 'Hannah, I have need of you.'

'God bless you, Princess, but I think you are well served,' I said with a smile. 'And you did not give me a very warm welcome when I came to you at Woodstock.'

'I was ill then,' she said irritably. 'And you were Mary's spy.'

'I have never spied on anyone,' I said, conveniently forgetting my work for Lord Robert. 'The queen sent me to you, as I told you. Now I see that you are respected and well-treated at court, I can leave you, you don't need me.'

'I shall decide what service I need and what I can do without,' she said at once. 'Not you.'

I made my little pageboy bow. 'Please, Princess, let me go to my father and my betrothed.'

She was diverted by the thought of my marriage, as I knew she would be. She smiled at me, the true Tudor charm shining through her irritability. 'Is that what you are after? Ready to put off your motley and go to find your lover? Do you think you are ready to be a woman, little fool? Have you studied me enough?'

'You would not be my study if I wanted to be a good wife,' I said.

She gave a ripple of laughter. 'Thank God, no. But what have you learned from me?'

'How to torment a man to madness, how to make a man follow you without even turning your head, and how to get down from your horse so you press against every inch of him.'

She threw back her head and laughed, a loud genuine laugh. 'You've learned well,' she said. 'I only hope you get as much joy from these skills as I do.'

'But what profit?' I asked.

The glance Elizabeth shot me was one of acute calculation. 'Some amusement,' she conceded. 'And real profit. You and I have slept safer in our beds because the king is in love with me, Hannah. And my path to the throne has been a little clearer since the most powerful man in the world swore he would support me.'

'You have his promise?' I asked, amazed at her.

She nodded. 'Oh, yes. My sister is betrayed more deeply than she knows. Half her country is in love with me, and now her husband too. My advice to you, as you go to your husband, is never to trust him and never love him more than he loves you.'

I shook my head, smiling. 'I mean to be a good wife,' I said. 'He is a good man. I mean to leave this court and go to him and become a good and steady wife to him.'

'Ah, you can't be that,' she said bluntly. 'You're not a woman grown yet. You're afraid of your own power.. You're afraid of his desire. You're afraid of your own desire. You're afraid of being a woman.'

I said nothing, though it was the truth.

'Oh, go then, little fool. But when you are bored, and you will be bored, you can come back to me again. I like having you in my service.'

I bowed and took myself off to the queen's rooms.

The moment I opened the door I knew that there was something wrong. Queen Mary was crouched on the floor, doubled up, folded over her knees, her forehead pressed on the cold hearthstone at the empty fireside. Only Jane Dormer was with her, seated in the shadows behind her, in stubborn silence. When I went to the queen and knelt before her I saw her face was wet with tears.

'Your Grace!'

'Hannah, he is leaving me,' she said.

'Leaving you?'

Her eyes were sightless, filled with tears, fixed on the empty hearth. 'He is going to the Low Countries. Hannah, he is leaving me . . .'

I went over to Jane Dormer, who was stabbing her needle into a linen shirt in the window seat. 'How long has she been like this?'

'Since he told her his news, this morning. He has broken her heart, as you predicted,' she said flatly. 'Don't you remember it? I do. When I brought her the portrait and I was so hopeful and she was so taken with him. You said he would break her heart and he has done so. Him with his baby that was there and then gone. Now he has told her he is going to war against the French, and she can say nothing but that he is leaving her, leaving her. And she cries as if she would die of grief.'

I went to the queen and knelt down beside her where she keened, soundlessly, her forehead knocking against the hearthstone as she rocked forward and back. 'Your Grace, I'm going down to the kitchen. Can I bring you anything to eat or drink?'

She sat back on her heels but did not look at me. Her gaze remained fixed on the empty hearth, but she put out her cold little hand and took mine. 'Don't leave me,' she said. 'Not you as well. He's leaving me, Hannah. He's leaving me, and I don't know how I can bear to live.'

Dear Father,

Thank you for your blessing in your letter to me. I am glad that you are well and that the shop in Calais is doing so well. I should have been glad to obey your command and come to you at once but when I went to the queen for permission to leave her service I found her so ill that I cannot leave her, at least for this month. The king has set sail for the Lowlands and she is quite desolate without him. We have come to Greenwich and it is like a court in mourning. I will stay with her until he returns, which he has promised, on his word of honour, will be very soon. When he comes back I shall come to you without delay.

I send you my love and duty and hope to see you soon—

Your Hannah

Dear Daniel,

Forgive me, I cannot come yet. The queen is in a despair so great that I dare not leave her. The king has left and she is clinging to all her other friends. She is so bereft that I fear for her mind. Forgive me, love, I will come as soon as I can. He has sworn it is a brief absence, merely to protect his interests in the Low Countries, and so we expect him back within the month. September or October at the latest, I will be able to come to you. I want to be your wife, indeed I do.

Hannah

AUTUMN–WINTER 1555

THE QUEEN RETREATED into a private world of silent misery in the palace that had been the happiest of them all: Greenwich. The king had hidden from her despair in the elaborate formality of leave-taking. Once he was gone she kept to her darkened rooms and would be served only by Jane Dormer or me, and the court became haunted by her unhappiness. She hid her face from us, deep in despair and filled with shame at how low she had been brought by love.

When she emerged to sit on her throne in the empty room it was to find that the Spaniards were openly rebelling against being forced to stay, and all the English men and women of the court were angry too. Life in the queen's service was not what it had been when the king had arrived, not what a court should be. It was like a nunnery ruled by a mortally sick abbess. No one spoke above a whisper, no feasts ever took place, there were no entertainments or gaiety, and the queen sat on her throne with a face of blank misery and retired to her rooms to be on her own whenever she could. Life at court had become long days of hopeless waiting for the king to return. We all knew that he never would.

With no man to torment, and no chance of making the queen more miserable than she was already, Princess Elizabeth took the opportunity to go to her palace at Hatfield. The queen let her go without a word of affection. Any love she had felt for Elizabeth the child had been worn out by the disloyalty of Elizabeth the young woman.

I went down to the great gate to bid the princess farewell. She gave me a roguish wink as she put her boot in a stablelad's cupped hands and let him throw her up into the saddle.

'I wager you'd rather come with me,' she said wickedly. 'I don't see you having a very merry Christmas here, Hannah.'

'I will serve my mistress in good times and bad,' I said steadily.

'You're sure your young man will wait for you?' she teased me.

I shrugged my shoulders. 'He says he will.'

'Well, you can come to me, at any time, if you wish,' she said.

'Thank you, Princess,' I said and was surprised by my pleasure in her invitation, but nobody could resist Elizabeth's charm.

'Don't leave it too late,' she warned me with mock seriousness.

'Too late?'

'When I am queen they will all be rushing to serve me. You want to be at the head of that queue,' she said frankly.

'It could be years yet,' I rejoined.

She shook her head. She was supremely confident on this crisp autumn morning. 'Oh, I don't think so,' she said. 'The queen is not a strong or a happy woman. In King Philip's absence I think my poor sister will fade away with grief. And when that happens they will find me, studying my Bible, and I will say—' She broke off for a moment. 'What did my sister plan to say when they told her she was queen?'

I hesitated. I could remember vividly her words in those optimistic days when Mary had promised she would be the virgin queen and restore the England of her mother to its true faith and happiness. 'She was going to say: "This is the Lord's doing; it is marvellous in our eyes", but in the end they told her when we were on the run and she had to fight on her own for her throne, rather than be granted it.'

'I say, that's good,' Elizabeth said with appreciation. '"This is the Lord's doing; it is marvellous in our eyes." That's excellent. I'll say that. You'll want to be with me when that happens, won't you?'

I glanced around to make sure we were not overheard but Elizabeth knew there was no one in earshot. She never put herself at risk—it was always her friends who ended up in the Tower.

The small cavalcade was ready to go. Elizabeth looked down at me, her smiling face bright under her black velvet hat. 'So you'd better come to me soon,' she reminded me.

'If I can come, I will. God keep you, Princess.'

She leaned down and patted my hand as a gesture of farewell. 'I shall wait,' she said, her eyes dancing. 'I shall survive.'

King Philip wrote frequently, but his letters were no reply to Mary's tender promises of love and demands that he should come back to her. They were letters of business and instructions as to how the council should decide one matter or another, and the queen was forced to go to council meetings with his letter in her hands and lay before them the orders of a man who was king only in name, and force them through on her own authority. They did not welcome her as she came red-eyed into the chamber, and they were openly doubtful that a prince of Spain, fighting his own wars, had English interests at heart.

In October I was looking for Jane Dormer before dinner, and failing everywhere else I put my head round the door to the queen's chapel in case the lady in waiting had taken a few moments for prayer. To my surprise I saw Will Somers, kneeling before a statue of Our Lady, lighting a candle at her feet, his fool's peaked hat crumpled in his hand.

I had never thought of Will as a devout man. I stepped back and waited for him at the doorway. With a heavy sigh, he got to his feet and came down the aisle, looking older than his thirty-five years.

'Will?' I said, coming to meet him.

'Child.' His habitual sweet smile came readily to his lips but his eyes were still dark.

'Are you in trouble?'

'Ah, I wasn't praying for me,' he said shortly.

'Then who?'

He glanced around the empty chapel and then drew me into a pew. 'D'you have any influence with Her Grace, d'you think, Hannah?'

I thought for a moment, then honestly, regretfully, I shook my head. 'She listens only to the king,' I said. 'And to her own conscience.'

'If you spoke from your gift, would she listen to you?'

'She might,' I said cautiously. 'But I cannot command it to serve me, Will. You know that.'

'I thought you might pretend,' he said bluntly.

I recoiled. 'It's a holy gift! It would be blasphemy to pretend!'

'Child, this month there are three men of God in prison charged with heresy, and if I am not mistaken they will be taken out and burned to death: poor Archbishop Cranmer, Bishop Latimer and Bishop Ridley.'

I waited.

He looked at me and he put his arm around my shoulder and hugged me. 'Tell her that you have had a gift of Sight and that they must be sent into exile,' he urged me. 'Hannah, if these men die then the queen will make an enemy of every man of compassion. They must not die on the queen's order. She will be shamed for ever if she does this.'

I hesitated. 'I dare not, Will. You told me yourself never to meddle,' I whispered. 'Your master beheaded two wives, never mind bishops, and you didn't stop him.'

'And he'll be remembered as a wife-killer,' Will predicted. 'And they will forget that he brought peace and prosperity to the country, that he made an England that we could all love. All they will remember of him will be that he had six wives and beheaded two of them. And all they will remember of this queen is that she brought the country floods and famine and fire. She will be remembered as England's curse when she was to have been our virgin queen, England's saviour.'

I rose up from the pew and found my knees were shaking. 'I am afraid, Will,' I said in a small voice. 'I cannot have her accusing me. I cannot have anyone asking where I came from, who my family is . . .'

He fell silent. 'Jane Dormer will not speak with her,' he said. 'I already tried her. The queen has no other friend but you.'

I paused, I could feel his will and my conscience pressing against my head, forcing me to do the right thing despite my fears. 'All right. I'll speak with her,' I burst out. 'I'll do the best I can.'

I waited till the queen was going to bed that evening and was kneeling before her prie-dieu in the corner of her bedroom. I knelt beside her but I did not pray. I was going over in my mind what I could say to persuade her not to do this dreadful thing.

Finally she rose from her knees and went to her chair at the fireside. I drew the poker from the embers where it had been heating, and thrust it into the mug of ale to warm it for her. When I put it in her hands her fingers were icy-cold.

'Your Grace, I have something to ask you,' I said very quietly.

She looked at me as if she hardly saw me. 'What is it, Hannah?'

'I have heard that your prisons are holding three good men on charges of heresy: Bishop Latimer, Bishop Ridley and Archbishop Cranmer.'

'Yes. It is true that those men are charged.'

'I want to ask you to show mercy,' I said simply. 'It is an awful thing to put a good man to death. And everyone says that these are good men. Just mistaken men, just disagreeing with the church's teaching. But they were good bishops to your brother, Your Grace, and they are ordained bishops in the Church of England.'

She said nothing for a long time. I did not know whether to press the case or to leave it. The silence started to frighten me a little. I sat back on my heels and waited for her to speak and I could feel my own danger coming towards me.

When she turned to me, she was not like the Mary I loved at all. Her face was like a mask of snow. 'They are *not* good men, for they deny the word of God and the rule of God, and they win others to their sin,' she hissed at me. 'It is men like them that have brought down the wrath of God on England. God must be appeased. Only when this sin is rooted out of the country will I be able to conceive a child and be able to give birth. No holy prince could come to a country such as this. The wrong that my father started, which my brother continued, has to be reversed. It all has to be turned back.'

She broke off, panting. I said nothing; I was stunned by her passion.

'Sometimes I don't think I have the strength to do it,' she went on. 'But God gives me the strength. He gives me the resolution to order these dreadful judgments, to send sinners to the fires so that the land may be cleansed. And then you—who I have trusted!—you come here to me when I am praying, to tempt me into error, into weakness, asking me to deny God and my holy work for Him.'

'Your Grace . . .' My voice caught in my throat. She rose to her feet and I jumped up. I had cramp in my right leg from kneeling for so long and it gave way beneath me so I sprawled on the floor.

She looked at me as if God Himself had struck me down. 'Hannah, my child, you are halfway to mortal sin yourself to ask this of me. Don't take one step further, or I shall send for the priests to wrestle with your soul.'

I could smell the smoke. I tried to tell myself it was from the fire in the grate, but I knew it was the smoke of my mother burning, the smoke of the other English men and women burning in the market-places up and down the countryside.

I scrabbled at the queen's feet like a cripple and she pulled her skirts away from me as if she could not bear me to touch her, and she went from the room without another word, leaving me on the floor, smelling smoke and crying for sheer terror.

Christmas was celebrated at court with much weighty ceremony but no joy, just as Elizabeth had predicted. Everyone remembered that last year Queen Mary had swirled around the court with her stomacher unlaced and her big belly carried proudly before her. Last year we had been waiting for our prince. This year we knew that there could not be one, for the king had left the queen's bed and her red eyes and thin body attested to the fact that she was sterile and alone. All autumn there had been rumours of plots and counterplots. It was said that the English people could not tolerate to be ruled by a Spanish king. Philip's father was going to hand over the empire to his son and then most of Christendom would be under his command. People muttered that England was an outlying island to him, that he would rule it through the barren queen, who did not cease to adore him though everyone knew he had taken a mistress and would never come home to her again.

The queen must have heard at least half of this gossip; the council kept her informed of the threats that were made against her husband, against herself, against her throne. She grew very quiet and withdrawn and determined. She held to her vision of a peaceful religious country where men and women would be safe in the church of their fathers, and she tried to believe that she could bring this about if she did not waver from her duty, however much it might cost her. The queen's council passed a new law which said that a heretic who repented on the stake had changed his mind too late—he should still be burned to death. Also, anyone who sympathised with his fate would be burned too.

SPRING 1556

THE COLD WET WINTER turned to a wetter spring. The queen waited for letters which came infrequently and brought her little joy.

One evening in early May she announced her intention of spending the whole night in prayer and sent me and all her ladies away. I was glad to be excused from yet another long, silent evening when we sewed by the fireside and tried not to notice when the queen's tears drenched the linen shirt that she was stitching for the king.

I was walking briskly to the chamber that I shared with three of the other maids when I saw a shadow by a doorway in the gallery. I did not hesitate. I would never pause for someone waiting to speak to me, and he had to fall into step beside me and keep to my rapid pace.

'You must come with me, Hannah Verde,' he said.

Even at the sound of my full name I did not pause.

'I only obey the queen.'

He held before me a rolled scroll and dropped one end to let it fall open. Almost despite myself I felt my feet slow and stop. I saw the seals at the bottom and my name at the top: Hannah Verde, alias Hannah Green, alias Hannah the Fool.

'What is this?' I asked, though I knew.

'A warrant for your arrest, for heresy,' he said.

'Heresy?' I breathed, as if I had never heard the word before, as if I had not been waiting for this moment every day since they took my mother.

'Yes, maid, heresy,' he said, taking my arm in a grip that I could not have fought even if my strength had not been bleeding away in my terror.

'The queen will intercede for me!' I whimpered, hearing my voice as weak as a child's.

'This is a royal warrant,' he said simply. 'You are to be arrested for questioning and she has given her authority.'

They took me to St Paul's in the city and they kept me overnight in a prison room with a woman who had been racked so badly that she lay like a rag doll in the corner of the cell, her arm and leg bones broken. With us also was a woman whose nails had been pulled from her fingers. She nursed her broken hands in her lap and did not look up when they turned the key in the door and thrust me inside. Her mouth was pursed in a funny little grimace, and I realised they had also cut out her tongue.

I hunkered down like a beggar on the threshold, my back to the door. In my terror, I watched the moonlight stroll across the floor, illuminating first one woman then the other. The night passed in the end, though I thought that it would last for ever. In the morning the door swung open and neither woman raised her head.

'Hannah Verde,' the voice outside said.

I tried to rise to my feet in obedience but my legs buckled beneath me from sheer terror. I knew that I could not have my fingernails torn out without screaming for mercy, telling everything I knew. I could not be tied to the rack without betraying my lord, Elizabeth, John Dee, every name I had ever heard whispered.

The guard dragged me along, my feet scrabbling like a drunkard's on the stones behind us.

'Where?' I said faintly.

'Bishop Bonner,' he said. 'God help you.'

'Amen,' I said promptly, as if accurate observation now would save me. 'Dear God, amen.'

I knew I was lost. I could not speak, let alone defend myself. I thought what a fool of a girl I had been not to go with Daniel when he would have saved me. What an arrogant child I had been to think that I could weave my way through these plots and not attract notice. Me, with olive skin and dark eyes, and a name like Hannah?

We came to a panelled door, monstrous with hammered nails. He tapped on it, opened it at a call from within, and walked in, arms tight around me as if we were mismatched lovers.

The bishop was sitting at a table facing the door; his clerk had his back to the door. A chair was set at a distance facing both table and bishop. The gaoler dumped me roughly into it and stood back, closed the door and set himself before it.

'Name?' the bishop asked wearily.

'Hannah Verde,' the gaoler answered, while I searched for my voice and found it was lost in terror.

'Age?'

He reached forward and prodded my shoulder.

'Seventeen,' I whispered.

'What?'

'Seventeen,' I said, a little louder. I had forgotten the meticulous record-keeping of the Inquisition, the bureaucracy of terror. They would take my name, my age, my address, my occupation, the names of my father and mother, their address, their occupations, and only when they had everything named and labelled would they torture me until I spilled out everything I knew, everything I could imagine.

'Occupation?'

'Fool to the queen,' I said.

There was a splashing noise in the room, a childish damp warmth in my breeches and a shameful stable smell. I had pissed myself for fear. I bowed my head, mortification overlaying my terror.

The clerk raised his head as if alerted by the warm, sharp smell. He turned and observed me. 'Oh, I can vouch for this girl,' he said as if it were a matter of very little interest.

It was John Dee.

I was beyond wondering how he came to be the bishop's clerk. I just met his neutral look with the blank eyes of a girl too frightened to think for herself.

'Can you?' asked the bishop doubtfully.

John Dee nodded. 'She is a holy fool,' he said. 'She once saw an angel in Fleet Street.'

'That must be heretical,' the bishop maintained.

John Dee considered it for a moment, as if it were not a matter of life and death to me. 'No, a true vision I think, and Queen Mary thinks the same. She will not be best pleased when she discovers we have arrested her fool.'

That gave the bishop pause. I could see him hesitate. 'The queen's orders to me are to root out heresy wherever I find it, and to show no favour. The girl was arrested with a royal warrant.'

'Oh well, as you wish,' John Dee said negligently.

I opened my mouth to speak but no words came. I could not believe that he would defend me so half-heartedly. Yet here he was, turning his back to me once more and copying my name into the Inquisition's ledger.

'Details,' Bishop Bonner said.

'Subject was seen to look away at the elevation of the Host on the morning of 27 December,' John Dee read in a clerkly mutter. 'Subject asked the queen to show mercy to heretics. Subject is a familiar to Princess Elizabeth. Subject has a knowledge of learning and languages unbecoming in a woman.'

'How d'you plead?' Bishop Bonner asked me.

'I did not look from the elevation of the Host . . .' I started, my voice weary and hopeless.

'Oh! This is nothing but malice,' John Dee exclaimed impatiently.

'Eh?' the bishop said.

'Malicious complaint,' John Dee said briskly and pushed the ledger away. 'We are supposed to be rooting out heresy here, and they bring us the quarrels of waiting maids.'

The bishop glanced at the paper. 'Sympathy with heretics?' he queried. 'That's enough for burning.'

John Dee raised his head and smiled confidently at his master. 'She's a holy fool,' he said, laughter in his voice. 'It's her task in life to ask the questions that no sane man would ask.'

'Let her go?' the bishop asked, his eyebrows raised.

'Sign here,' John Dee said, sliding a paper across the desk. 'Let's get rid of her and get on with our work. The child is a fool; we would be fools to question her.'

I held my breath.

The bishop signed.

'Take her away,' John Dee said wearily. He swung round in his seat to face me. 'Hannah Verde, also known as Hannah the Fool, we are releasing you from an inquiry into heresy. No charge to answer. D'you have wit enough to understand that, child?'

'Yes, sir,' I said very quietly.

John Dee nodded to the gaoler. 'Release her.'

I pushed myself up from the chair. My legs were still too weak to hold me. The guard slid a hand round my waist and kept me on my feet.

I bowed my head to the bishop, and to the man I had once been honoured to know, and I left them with their bloodstained hands to interrogate innocent people and send them out to be burned.

When they turned me roughly out into the dirty street, I wandered around at the back of St Paul's and stumbled blindly until I felt I had put a safe distance between the tower's ominous reaching shadow and my frightened weaving steps.

The bright sunshine burned in my face and showed me that it was past midday. Step by step I went on, pausing when my legs buckled underneath me, until I found my way to our little shop off Fleet Street and hammered on our neighbour's door.

'Dear God, what has become of you?'

I managed a twisted smile. 'I have a fever,' I said. 'I forgot my key, and lost my way. Would you let me in?'

He stepped back from me. In these times of hardship everyone was afraid of infection. 'Do you need food?'

'Yes,' I said, too low for pride.

'I will leave you something on the doorstep,' he said. 'Here's the key.'

I took it wordlessly, and staggered to the shop. It turned in the lock and I stepped into the shuttered room. At once the precious scent of printers' ink and dry paper surrounded me. I stood, inhaling it, the very perfume of heresy, the familiar beloved odour of home.

I heard the scrape and clink of a dish on the doorstep and went to fetch a pie and a little mug of ale. I ate sitting on the floor behind the counter, hidden from the shuttered windows.

As soon as I had eaten, I put the bowl back on the doorstep and locked the door. Then I went into my father's print shop and store-room, cleared the volumes from the bottom shelf of his book collection and put myself to sleep on the shelf. I curled up in the shape of a G and closed my eyes and slept.

In the morning, when I woke, I was determined on my future. I found a piece of manuscript paper and wrote a letter to Daniel, a letter I thought I would never write.

> Dear Daniel,
>
> It is time for me to leave the court and England. Please come for me and the printing press at once. If this letter miscarries or I do not see you within a week, I shall come on my own.
>
> Hannah

When I sealed it up I was certain, as I had known in my heart for the last few months, that there was no safety for anyone in Queen Mary's England any more.

There was a tap at the door. My heart plunged with the familiar terror, but then I could see, through the shutters, the silhouette of our next-door neighbour.

I opened the door to him. 'Slept well?' he demanded.

'Yes,' I said. 'Thank you.'

'Ate well? They are a good baker's.'

'Yes. Thank you.'

'Are you going back to court today?'

For a moment I hesitated, then I realised that there was nowhere else for me to go. If I went missing from court it was tantamount to a confession of guilt. I had to go back and act the part of an innocent woman rightly freed, until Daniel came for me.

'Yes, today,' I said brightly.

'Would you see this gets to the queen?' he asked, abashed but determined. He handed me a trade card, an illustrated label which assured the reader that he could supply all the books that were moral and improving and approved by the church.

'I will put it in her hands,' I lied to him. 'You can depend upon it.'

I put Daniel's letter in the hands of a shipmaster who was sailing to Calais that morning, and came back to a subdued court. The maids in waiting had thought I had gone to my father's shop. The queen had not missed me. Only Will Somers cocked an enquiring eyebrow at me when I came in to dinner. He made his way to my bench and sat down beside me.

'Are you well, child? You're white as a sheet.'

'I've just got back,' I said shortly. 'I was arrested.'

Any other person in the court would have found an excuse to move elsewhere to take his dinner. Will planted both elbows on the table. 'Never!' he said. 'How come you got out again?'

A little unwilling giggle escaped me. 'They said I was a fool, and could not be held responsible.'

His crack of laughter made all the neighbouring tables turn their heads and smile. 'You! Well that's good news for me. I shall know what to plead. And that's what they truly said?'

'Yes. But, Will, it is no laughing matter. I was most afraid.'

His warm big hand took my cold fingers in a gentle grasp. 'Child, we are all of us afraid. Better times coming, eh?'

'When will they come?' I whispered.

He shook his head without saying anything, but I knew that he was thinking of Elizabeth and when her reign might begin. And if Will Somers was thinking of Elizabeth with hope, then the queen had lost the love of a man who had been a true friend indeed.

I decided that if I heard nothing from Daniel within seven days I would go to the shop, pack the most precious books and manuscripts in as large a box as I could manage, and take a passage to Calais on my own.

In the meantime I had to wait. I attended Mass in the queen's train; I read the Bible to her in Spanish in her room every day after dinner; I prayed with her at her bedtime. I watched her unhappiness turn to a solid-seated misery, a state that I thought she would live and die in.

One morning, as we were coming out of Mass, the queen leading the way and her ladies behind her, one of the queen's newest maids in waiting fell into step beside me.

'Have you heard? Have you heard?' the girl whispered to me as we turned into the queen's presence chamber. The gallery was crowded with people who had come to see the queen, most of them to ask for clemency for people on trial for heresy.

'Heard what?' I asked.

'The Princess Elizabeth is accused of treason!' the maid in waiting hissed at me. 'Her servants are all arrested. They're tearing her London house apart, searching it.'

Despite the heat of the crowd, I felt myself freeze, right down to my toes in my boots. 'Elizabeth? What treason?' I whispered.

'A plot to kill the queen,' the girl said in a breath of ice.

'Who else with her?'

'Nobody knows! Kat Ashley, for certain. Perhaps all of them.'

I nodded. I knew somebody who would know. I extricated myself from the train that was following the queen into her presence chamber. She would be in there for at least two hours. She would not miss me while I ran down the gallery to the great hall.

Will was not there. A soldier directed me to the stable yard and I found him in a loose box, playing with one of the deerhound puppies. The animal, all long legs and excitement, clambered all over him.

'Will, they're searching the Princess Elizabeth's London house.'

'Aye, I know,' he said, lifting his face away from the puppy, which was enthusiastically licking his neck.

'What are they looking for?'

'Doesn't matter. What matters is what they found.'

'What did they find?'

'Letters and pamphlets and all sorts of seditious nonsense in Kat Ashley's box. A May Day plot cooked up between her and the princess's new Italian lute player and Dudley—' He broke off as he saw my aghast face. 'Oh, not your lord. His cousin, Sir Henry.'

'Lord Robert is not under suspicion?' I demanded.

'Should he be?'

'No. How could he do anything? And anyway, he is loyal to the queen.'

'As are we all. Even Tobias the hound, here. Well, Tobias is more loyal because he can't say one thing and think another. He gives his love where he eats his dinner, which is more than others I could mention.'

I flushed. 'If you mean me, I love the queen and I always have done.'

His face softened. 'I know you do. I meant her pretty little sister who has not the patience to wait her turn, but has been plotting again.'

'She's guilty of nothing,' I said at once, my loyalty to Elizabeth as reliable as my love of the queen.

Will laughed. 'She's an heir in waiting. She'd attract trouble like a tall tree attracts lightning. So Kat Ashley and the lute player are for the Tower.'

I said nothing, my throat tightening with fear.

'What's the matter, child?' Will's tone was kindly. 'You're white as snow.'

'I have not been well this last week. A touch of fever.'

'Let's hope it doesn't spread,' Will said wryly.

I held to my lie of fever and took to my bed. I thought of Elizabeth, who seemed to be able to summon ill health as an alibi when she needed one, and I knew the pangs of a terror that made me sweat so much that I would have passed for a sick girl indeed.

I heard the news from the maids in waiting. Cardinal Pole headed the inquiry into the conspiracy and every day another man was arrested and taken for questioning. Kat Ashley's box in Elizabeth's London house held the first draft of a pamphlet urging Englishmen to rise up against the Catholic queen and put the Protestant princess on the throne.

Cardinal Pole started to look around Elizabeth's friends for who might have a press that would have printed such a pamphlet in secret. I thought of the sheeted press in the printer's shop off Fleet Street and wondered how soon it would be before they came for me.

I spent three days in bed, staring at the white ceiling, shivering with fear though the sunshine was bright on the lime-washed walls and bees bumbled against the glass of the window. Then in the evening of the third day, I got up from my bed. I knew the queen would be preparing to walk into the great hall and sit before a dinner that she could not bear to eat. I got myself to her rooms as she rose from her prie-dieu.

'Hannah, are you better now?' The words were kind but her eyes were dead. She was trapped in her own world of grief.

'I am better, but I have been much distressed by a letter which came to me this day,' I said. The strain on my white face supported my story. 'My father is ill, near to death, and I would like to go to him.'

'Is he in London?'

'In Calais, Your Grace. He has a shop in Calais, and lives with my betrothed and his family.'

She nodded. 'You can go to him, of course. And come back when he is well again, Hannah. You can go to the Household Exchequer and get your wages to date; you will need money.'

'Thank you, Your Grace.' I felt my throat tighten at the thought of her kindness to me when I was running from her.

She reached out to me and I knelt and kissed her fingers. For the last time, her gentle touch came on my head. 'God bless you, Hannah, and keep you safe,' she said with all her old sweetness. She gave me a weary little smile as she went to the double doors and they threw them open for her, and then she went out, her head high, her face drained, her eyes dark with sadness, to face the court that no longer respected her.

As soon as I heard the court settle to their dinner, I put on my dark green livery, my new riding boots, my cape and my cap. I took my little knapsack from my box and put in the wages I had from the Exchequer. I crept down the side stairs and hesitated at the entrance to the great hall. I could hear the familiar sound of the household at dinner. It was the sound of my life for the past three years. I could not believe that this was no longer my home, my haven. I could not believe that this was increasingly the most dangerous place for me to be.

I turned on my heel and dashed out of the door, careless of who saw me. I headed for the river, as my quickest and least noticeable route into the city, and made my way to our shop at a dawdle. I wanted to see that the place was untouched before I approached it. Suddenly, I came to an abrupt standstill. To my horror, as I turned the corner I could see that it had been broken and entered. The door was thrown wide open; the dark entrance was lit with a flickering light as two men, three men moved about inside. Outside waited a wagon with two horses. The men were taking away great barrels of goods. I recognised the packed manuscripts that we had stored away when my father left, and I knew they would be evidence enough to hang me twice over.

I was just about to slide backwards into the alley when one of the shadows inside the shop came out with a big box and loaded it into the wagon. Something about the profile was familiar: the scholar's bend of the shoulders, the thinness of his frame below his worn cape.

I felt my heart thud with hope and fear but I did not step out until I was sure. Then the two other men came out, carrying a well-wrapped piece of the printing press. The man in front was our next-door neighbour, and the man carrying the other end was my betrothed, Daniel.

'Father! My father!' I cried out softly, and sprang from the dark doorway into the shadowy street.

His head jerked up at the sound of my voice and his arms opened wide. I was in his embrace in a moment, feeling his warm, strong arms wrapped around me, hugging me as if he would never let me go again.

'Hannah, my daughter, my girl,' he said, kissing the top of my head.

I looked up into his face, worn and older than I remembered, and saw him too tracing my features. We both spoke at once:

'I got your letter. Are you in danger?'

'Father, are you well? I am so glad . . .'

We laughed. 'Tell me first,' he said. 'Are you in danger? We have come for you.'

I shook my head. 'Thank God,' I said. 'They arrested me for heresy, but I was released.'

At my words, he glanced quickly around. I thought anyone in England would have known him for a Jew now, that furtive ever-guilty glance of the People with no home and no welcome among strangers.

Daniel crossed the cobbled street, strode over the drain and came to an abrupt halt before us.

'Hannah,' he said awkwardly.

I had summoned him to save me. By rights he should have something more from me than a down-turned face and a mumbled: 'Hello, Daniel.'

'Hello,' he said, equally inadequate.

'Let's go into the shop,' my father said, casting another cautious glance up and down the street. He shut the door behind us. 'We were packing up first and then Daniel was going to fetch you. Why are you here?'

'I was running away from court,' I said. 'I didn't dare wait for you to come. I was coming to you.'

'Why?' Daniel asked. 'What has happened?'

'They are arresting men for plotting to overthrow the queen,' I said. Daniel's glance at me was acute. 'Were you involved in the plot?'

'No,' I said.

He gave me a hard, sceptical look, then asked, 'Have you dined?'

'I'm not hungry,' I said. 'I can help to pack.'

'Good, for we have a ship that leaves on the one o'clock tide.'

I set to work with Daniel, my father and our next-door neighbour, carrying the boxes and barrels and pieces of the press to the wagon.

It was near ten o'clock at night by the time we had finished, and a late spring moon was lighting the street. My father swung himself into the back of the wagon; Daniel and I rode on the box. Our neighbour shook hands all round and bade us farewell. At Daniel's signal, the horses leaned against the traces and the wagon eased forward.

'This is like last time,' he remarked. 'I hope you don't jump ship again.'

I shook my head. 'I won't.'

'No outstanding promises?' Daniel smiled.

'No,' I said sadly. 'The queen does not want anyone but the king, and I think he will never come home to her. And though the Princess Elizabeth's household is charged with treason, she has the favour of the king. She might be imprisoned but she won't be killed now.'

He took my hand and brought it to his lips. The touch of his mouth on my fingers was warm, I could feel his breath on my skin, and for a moment I could think of nothing but his touch.

'I cannot go on living without you,' he said softly.

Our road took us past the Tower. I felt, rather than saw, Daniel stiffen as the lowering shadow of Robert Dudley's prison fell on us.

'You know, I could not help loving him,' I said in a small voice. 'When I first saw him I was a child, and he was the most beautiful man I had ever seen in my life and the son of the greatest man in England.'

'Well, now you are a woman and he is a traitor,' Daniel said flatly. 'And you are mine.'

I shot a sideways smile at him. 'As you say, husband,' I said meekly.

The ship was waiting as Daniel had arranged and we had a few hours of hard work loading the pieces of the dismantled press and the barrels and boxes of books and papers before finally we were all aboard and the sailors cast off, the barges took us in tow, and the ship went slowly downriver, helped by the ebbing tide. My father had brought a hamper of food and we sat on the deck and ate cold chicken with a strange, strong-tasting cheese and a hard, crunchy bread.

'You'll have to get used to this fare,' Daniel laughed at me. 'This is Calais food.'

'Shall we stay in Calais?' I asked.

He shook his head. 'It's not safe for us for ever,' he said. 'Soon Queen Mary will turn her attention there too. The place is riddled with all sorts of heretics.' Daniel smiled at me and put his hand over my own. 'I have found a home for us. We are going to go to Genoa.'

'Genoa?'

'They are making a community of Jews there,' he said, his voice very low. 'They want the trade contacts and the gold and trustworthy credit that the People bring with them. We'll go there. A doctor can always find work, and a bookseller can always sell books to the Jews.'

'And shall we live as Jews or Gentiles?' I asked.

His smile at me was infinitely warm. 'We shall live as suits us,' he said. 'I won't have the Christian rules that forbid my learning; I won't have Jewish rules that forbid my life. I shall accept no prohibitions on my thoughts or my actions except those that make sense to me.'

'And shall I?' I asked.

'Yes,' he said simply. 'Everything you have ever said makes sense to me only if I see you as my partner in this venture. Yes. You shall find your own way and I hope we will agree.'

My father, seated a little away from us and carefully not listening to our conversation, enacted an unconvincing yawn. 'I'm for sleep,' he said. He put his hand on my head. 'Bless you, child. It is good to have you with me once more.' He wrapped his cape round himself and laid down on the cold deck.

Daniel stretched out his arm to me. 'Come here and I will keep you warm,' he said.

I was not in the least cold but I did not tell him that as I went into the circle of his arm and let myself stretch out against the mystery of his male body. I felt him gently kissing my cropped hair and then I felt and heard his breath against my ear.

'Oh, Hannah,' he whispered. 'I have dreamed of having you for so long I could cry like a girl for desire.'

I giggled. 'Daniel,' I said, trying the unfamiliar name on my lips. I turned my face up towards him and felt the warmth of his mouth on mine, a kiss that melted the very marrow of my bones. Under his cape his hands caressed my back and then fumbled under my jerkin and linen and stroked my breasts, my throat, my belly, and I stretched out like a petted cat and whispered 'Daniel' once more. This time it was an invitation. Gently, his hands explored the contours of my body. Shyly but with gathering curiosity I let my fingers explore the soft fine hair of his chest, the warmth of his skin beneath his breeches.

Under Daniel's cloak we slid our breeches down and coupled with an easy confident delight that started breathless and became ecstasy. I had not known that it could feel like that. Watching other women and men court, even trembling beneath Lord Robert's touch, I had not known that such pleasure was possible. We parted only to doze and within an hour we woke and moved together again. Only when we saw the sky lighten through the ropes to our left did I drift from arching desire and satisfaction into exhausted sleep.

I woke to a cold morning, and had to scramble into my clothes before the sailors could see what we had been about. At first I could see nothing but the dark outline of the land, and then slowly it became clearer to me. A solid fort guarded the entrance to the harbour.

'Fort Risban,' Daniel said, standing behind me. 'Do you see the port beyond? The canals flow from it all round the city, so it is a moated city as well as a walled one.'

As the ship came into port I stayed at the side, watching the features of this town where I would make my home. The cobbled streets between the high houses would be my routes to and from the baker, from the market, to my house. This strange smell of a working port: old fish, the tarry odour of drying nets, the clean tang of salt wind, all this would become the familiar taste on my lips and the perfume of my woollen cape. In a little while I would cease to wonder how the queen was this morning, how Elizabeth was faring, and how my lord was, watching the sun rise from the arrow-slit window of his prison. All of those thoughts and loves and loyalties I must put behind me. Now I would live for my husband and my father and I would learn to belong to this new family: a husband, three sisters and my mother-in-law.

'My mother is waiting for us.' Daniel's breath was warm against my hair as he leaned against me at the rail of the ship. I looked to where he was looking and saw her, formidable, arms folded across a broad chest, scrutinising the deck of the ship as if to see whether her reluctant daughter-in-law had done her duty and arrived this time.

When she saw Daniel she raised a hand in greeting, and I waved back. I was too far away to see her face, but I imagined her carefully schooling her expression.

'Welcome to Calais,' she said to me as we came down the gangplank. Daniel she wordlessly enfolded into an adoring embrace.

He struggled to be free. 'I have to see to them unloading the press,' he told her, and went back on board and swung down into the hold. Mrs Carpenter and I were left alone in awkward silence on the quayside.

'He found you then,' she said eventually, with no great pleasure.

'Yes,' I said.

'And are you ready to marry him now?'

'Yes.'

'You'll have to get out of those clothes,' she said. 'They're respectable people in Calais; they won't like the sight of you in breeches.'

'I know,' I said. 'I left in a hurry or I would have changed before I came.'

Daniel appeared and looked pleased that we were talking. 'I think I have everything unloaded,' he said. 'Your father is going to stay here with the things while I fetch a wagon.'

'I'll wait with him,' I said hastily.

'No,' he said. 'Go home with Mother. She can show you our house and you can get warm.'

He wanted to ensure that I was comfortable. He did not know that the last thing I wanted to do was to go home with his mother and sit with his sisters and wait for the men to finish their work and come home. 'I'll get the wagon with you then,' I said. 'I'm not cold.'

At a glance from his mother he hesitated. 'You can't go to the carter's yard dressed like that,' she said firmly. 'You will shame us all. Wrap your cloak around you and come home with me.'

Home was a pretty enough little house in London Street, squashed in beside others in a row near the south gate of the town. The top floor was divided into three bedrooms; Daniel's three sisters shared the big bed in the room that faced the back of the house, his mother had a tiny room all to herself, and my father had the third. Daniel mostly lived with his tutor, but would sleep on a truckle bed in my father's room when he stayed overnight. The next floor served as a dining room and sitting room for the family, and the ground floor was my father's shop facing the street, and at the back a little kitchen and scullery. In the yard behind, Daniel and my father had built and thatched a roof, and the printing press would be reassembled and set up in there.

All three of Daniel's sisters were waiting to greet us in the living room at the top of the stairs. I was acutely conscious of my travel-stained clothes and dirty face and hands, as I saw them look me up and down and then glance in silence at each other.

'Here are my girls,' their mother said. 'Mary, Sarah and Anne.'

The three of them rose and dipped a curtsy as one, and sat down again. In my pageboy livery I could not curtsy so I made a little bow.

'I'll put the kettle on,' Mrs Carpenter said.

'I'll help,' Anne said and dived out of the room. The other two and I regarded each other with silent dislike.

'Did you have a good crossing?' Mary asked.

'Yes, thank you.' The tranced night on the deck and Daniel's insistent touch seemed to be a long way away now.

'And are you going to marry Daniel now?'

'Mary! Really!' her sister protested.

'I don't see why I shouldn't ask. It's been a long enough betrothal.'

'Yes, I am,' I said.

They turned their bright inquisitive faces towards me. 'Indeed,' Mary said. 'You've left court then?'

'Yes.'

'And will you not go back?' the other one, Sarah, asked.

'No,' I said, keeping the regret from my voice.

'Won't you find it awfully dull here, after living at court?'

'I shall help my father in the shop, I expect,' I said.

'Where are you and Daniel going to sleep?' Mary asked.

'Mary! Really!'

'Well, they can hardly bed down on the truckle bed,' she pointed out reasonably. 'And Mother can't be asked to move. And we have always had the best back bedroom.'

'Daniel and I will decide,' I said with an edge to my voice. 'And if there is not enough room for us here we will set up our own house.'

Mary gave a little scream of shock as her mother came up the stairs.

'What is it, child?' she demanded.

'Hannah has not been in the house five minutes and already she says she and Daniel will live elsewhere!' Mary exclaimed, halfway to tears. 'Already she is taking Daniel away from us! Just as I knew she would! Just as I said—she will spoil everything!' She leapt to her feet, tore open the door and ran up the stairs leading to her room.

'Oh, really!' her mother exclaimed in indignation. 'How could you upset Mary on your very first day? You will have to learn to mind your tongue, Miss Hannah. You are living with a family now. You have not the right to speak out like a fool any more.'

For one stunned moment I said nothing to defend myself. Then: 'I am sorry,' I said through my teeth.

SUMMER 1556

IT WAS A LONG HOT SUMMER, that first summer in Calais. I loitered in the squares, and dawdled at the fish quay to see the dazzle of sunlight on the ripples of the harbour. They called it *le Bassin du Paradis*, and in the bright sunlight I thought it was paradise indeed. But for me it was a breathtakingly tedious season. Daniel and I were under the same roof, but we had to live as maid and suitor; we were hardly ever left alone together. I longed for his touch, for his kiss, and for the pleasure that he had given me on the night that we sailed to France. But he could hardly bear to come near me, knowing that he must always step back, knowing that he must never do more than kiss my lips or my hand.

I was out of my breeches and into a gown in the first week and soon experiencing a constant tuition in how a young lady should behave. Daniel's mother had awarded herself the task of 'taking me in hand'.

She found a sulky and unwilling pupil. I was not naturally gifted at housekeeping. I did not want to know how to scour a brass pan with sand so that it glittered. I did not want to take a scrubbing brush to the front step. I did not want to peel potatoes so that there was no waste at all. I wanted to know none of these things, and I did not see why I should learn them.

'As my wife you will need to know how to do such things,' Daniel said reasonably enough. I had slipped out to waylay him before he entered the house and we both fell under his mother's rule.

'Why should I know? You don't do them.'

'Because I will be out at work and you will be caring for our children and preparing their food,' he said.

'I thought I would keep a printing shop, like my father.'

'And who would cook and clean for us?'

'Couldn't we have a maid?'

He laughed. 'Perhaps, later on. But I couldn't afford to pay wages for a maid at first, you know, Hannah. I am not a wealthy man. When I set up in practice on my own we shall have only my fees to live on.'

'And will we have a house of our own then?'

He drew my hand through his elbow as if he were afraid that I might pull away at his answer. 'No,' he said simply. 'We will find a bigger house, perhaps in Genoa. But I will always offer a house to my sisters and to my mother, to your father too. Surely you would want nothing less?'

I hesitated. 'I don't get on very well with your sisters, and your mother does not approve of me,' I said quietly.

He nodded, I was telling him nothing he did not know. 'They'll come round,' he said warmly.

'I hope so,' I said and watched him smile.

We were married in late June, as soon as all my gowns were made and my hair long enough for me to be—as Daniel's mother said—passable, at l'Eglise de Notre Dame, the great church of Calais. It was a Christian wedding with a Mass afterwards and every one of us was meticulous in our observation of the rituals in church. Afterwards, in the privacy of the little house in London Street, Daniel's sisters held a shawl as a chuppah over our heads as my father repeated the seven blessings for a wedding, as far as he could remember them, and Daniel's mother put a wrapped glass at Daniel's feet for him to stamp on. Then we drew back the shutters, opened the doors and held a wedding feast for the neighbours with gifts and dancing.

The vexed question of where we would sleep as a married couple had been resolved by my father moving to a bunk alongside the printing press in the little room created by thatching the back yard. Daniel and I slept in Father's old room on the top floor, a thin plaster wall between us and his sleepless mother on one side, and his curious sisters, awake and listening, on the other side.

On our wedding night we fell upon each other as a pair of wanton lovers, longing for an experience too long denied. They put us to bed with much laughter and jokes and pretended embarrassment, and as soon as they were gone Daniel bolted the door, closed the shutters and drew me into the bed. Desperate for privacy we put the covers completely over our heads and kissed and caressed in the hot darkness, hoping that the blankets would muffle our whispers. But the pleasure of his touch overwhelmed me and I gave a breathy little cry. At once, I stopped short and clapped a hand over my mouth.

'It doesn't matter,' he said, prising my fingers from my lips to kiss them again.

'It does,' I said, speaking nothing but the truth.

'Kiss me,' he begged me.

'Well, very quietly . . .'

I kissed him and felt his mouth melt under mine. He rolled underneath me and guided me to mount him. At the first touch of his hardness between my legs I moaned with pleasure and bit the back of my hand, trying to stay silent. He turned me so that I was underneath him.

'Put your hand over my mouth,' I urged him.

He hesitated. 'It feels as if I am forcing you,' he said uncomfortably.

I gave a little breathy laugh. 'If you were forcing me I would be quieter,' I joked, but he could not laugh. He pulled away from me, dropped onto his back and pulled me to lie beside him, my head on his shoulder.

'We'll wait till they are all asleep,' he said.

We waited and waited but his mother's heavy tread did not come up the stairs until late, and then we heard, with embarrassing clarity, her sigh as she sat on the side of her bed, the 'clip, clop' as she dropped one wooden clog then another on the floor. Then we heard with a sharpness that showed us how thin the walls must be, the rustle of her undressing and then the creak of the bed as she got under the covers.

After that it was impossible. If I even turned the bed creaked so loud that I knew she would hear it. I pressed my mouth to his ear and breathed, 'Let us make love tomorrow when they are all out,' and I felt the nod of his silent assent. Then we lay, sleepless with lust, not touching, not even looking at each other, on our bridal night.

They came for the sheets in the morning, and would have flown them like a bloodstained flag from the window to prove the consummation of the marriage but Daniel stopped them. 'There's no need,' he said. 'And I don't like the old ways.'

The girls said nothing but they raised their eyebrows at me as if they well knew that we had not bedded together at all, and suspected that he could not feel desire for me. His mother, on the other hand, looked at me as if it proved to her that I was not a virgin and that her son had brought a whore into her home.

Within a few days I had learned to lie like a stone beneath my husband, and he had learned to take his pleasure as quickly as he could in silence. Within a few weeks we made love as seldom as possible. The early promise of our night of lovemaking on the boat that had left me dizzy with satisfied desire could not be explored or fulfilled in a bedroom with four nosy women listening.

As the summer wore on and Daniel's mother gave me the pick of the food, the breast of the scrawny French chickens, the fattest sweetest peaches, I realised that she was waiting for me to speak to her. In the last days of August she could not bear to wait any longer.

'Have you got something to tell me, daughter?' she asked. 'A little news that would make an old woman very, very happy?'

I realised what she was after. 'No,' I said shortly.

'Not yet sure?'

'Sure I am not with child, if that is what you mean,' I said flatly.

The Queen's Fool | 419

'Well, what is the matter with you?' she demanded. 'Daniel has had you at least twice a week ever since your wedding day. No one can doubt him. Are you ill?'

'No,' I said through cold lips. She would, of course, know exactly how often we made love.

'Then what is the matter?' she repeated. 'I have been waiting for you to tell me that you are with child any day these last two months.'

'Then sorry I am, to so disappoint you,' I said, as cold as Princess Elizabeth in one of her haughty moods.

'You're not taking something?' she hissed. 'You've not got some draught to take to stop a child coming? Some slut's trick?'

'Of course not!' I said, roused to anger. 'Why would I?'

'God knows what you would or would not do!' she exclaimed in genuine distress. 'Why would you go to court? Why would you not come with us to Calais? Why be so unnatural, so unwomanly, more like a boy than a girl? Why come now, too late, when Daniel could have had his pick of any girl in Calais? Pretty girls and fertile girls too. A girl who has a baby in the cradle this summer and knows her place, and would be glad enough to be in my house, and proud to call me mother.'

I felt very cold, like fear, like a dreadful uncertainty. 'I thought you were talking in general,' I said. 'D'you mean that Daniel has a woman he likes, here in Calais?' I asked.

'He never offered her marriage,' she said grudgingly. 'He always said that you and he were betrothed and that he was promised.'

'Is she Jew, or Gentile?' I whispered.

'Gentile. But she would take our religion if Daniel married her.'

'Married her?' I exclaimed. 'But you just said he always said he was betrothed to me!'

'It was nothing,' she said, trying to slide away from her own indiscretion. 'Only something she once said to me.'

'You spoke to her about Daniel marrying her?'

'I had to!' she flared up. 'She came to the house, her belly before her, wanting to know what would be done for her.'

'Her belly?' I repeated numbly. 'She is with child?'

'She has his son,' Daniel's mother said. 'And a fine healthy boy, the very picture of him as a baby.'

I sank to the stool at the table and looked up at her in bewilderment. 'Why did he not tell me?'

She shrugged. 'Why would he tell you? Did you tell him everything in all these long years when you made him wait for you?'

I thought of Lord Robert. 'I did not lie with another and conceive a child,' I said quietly.

'Daniel is a handsome young man,' she said. 'Did you think he would wait like a nun for you? Or did you not think of him at all, while you played the fool and dressed like a whore and ran after who knows who?'

I said nothing, listening to the resentment in her tone, observing the rage in her flushed cheeks.

'Does he see his child?'

'Every Sunday at church,' she said. I caught her quickly hidden smile of triumph. 'And twice a week, when he tells you he is working late, he goes to her house to dine with her and to see his child.'

I rose up from the table.

'Where are you going?' she asked, suddenly alarmed.

'I am going to meet him as he walks home,' I said.

'Don't upset him,' she said. 'Don't tell him that you know of this woman. Better women than you have turned away and seen nothing.'

I thought of the look of blank pain on Queen Mary's face when she heard Elizabeth's lilting laugh at the king's whisper in her ear.

I stormed from the house and across the marketplace, not seeing the stalls and the usual traders. I came to the door of the physician's house in a rush and then realised that I could not hammer on it and demand to see Daniel. I would have to wait. I hitched myself up onto a low stone wall of the opposite house and settled down to wait for him.

I did not plan what I might say or do. I just waited.

I heard the clock strike four and then half past before the side door opened and Daniel came out, calling a farewell and closing the door behind him. At once I crossed the road and ran up to him. 'Daniel!'

'Hannah!' His pleasure in seeing me was unfeigned. But after one glance at my white face he said: 'Is there something wrong? Are you ill?'

'No,' I said, my lip trembling. 'I just wanted to see you.'

'And now you do,' he said. He drew my hand through his arm. 'Shall I walk you home round the city walls, m'lady? Get a breath of sea air?'

I tried to smile at him but I was too heartsore. I let him lead me to the end of the street and then along a lane. At the very end of the lane was the towering wall of the town, shallow stone steps running up the inside. We climbed them, up and up, until we got to the ramparts and could look north towards the horizon where England lay—England, the queen, the princess, my lord: all such a long way away. It seemed to me in that moment that I had known a better life as a fool to a queen than I had being a fool to Daniel and to his stone-hearted mother and his poisonous sisters.

'Now,' he said, matching his steps to mine as we walked along the wall. 'What is the matter, Hannah?'

I did not turn the conversation round and round. I went straight to the heart of it, as if I were still a troubled pageboy and not a betrayed wife. 'Your mother tells me that you have got a Calais woman with child,' I said bluntly. 'And that you see her and her child three times a week.'

I could feel his stride falter, and when I looked up at him he had lost the colour from his cheeks. 'Yes,' he said. 'That's true.'

'You should have told me.'

He nodded, marshalling his thoughts. 'I suppose I should have done. But if I had told you, would you have married me?'

'I don't know. No, probably not.'

'Then you see why I did not tell you.'

'You cozened me and married me on a lie.'

'I told you that you were the one great love of my life, and you are. I told you that I thought we should marry to provide for my mother and for your father, and I still think that we did the right thing. I told you that we should marry so that we might live together, as the Children of Israel, and I could keep you safe.'

'You lied to me,' I said again.

'Yes,' he said simply. 'I had to.'

'Do you love her?' I asked. I could hear the pitiful note in my own voice and I pulled my hand from his arm, filled with resentment that love should have brought me so low that I was whimpering at betrayal.

'No,' he said bluntly. 'But when we first came to Calais, I was lonely and she was pretty and warm and good company. If I had any sense I would not have gone with her, but I did.'

'More than once?' I asked, wounding myself.

'More than once.'

'And I suppose you didn't make love to *her* with a hand over her mouth so your mother and sisters couldn't hear?'

'No,' he said shortly.

'And her son?'

His face warmed at once. 'He is five months old. Strong and lusty.'

'Does she take your name?'

'No. She keeps her own.'

'Does she live with her family?'

'She is in service.'

'They allow her to keep her child?'

'They have a kindness for her, and they are old. They like to have a child about the house.'

'They know that you are the father?'

He nodded his head.

I rocked with shock. 'Everyone knows? Your sisters, the priest? The people who came to our wedding feast and wished me well? Everyone?'

Daniel hesitated. 'It's a small town, Hannah. Yes, I should think everyone knows of it.'

'Does she know you are married?'

'Yes, she knew I was betrothed when we first met. I told her I was going to England to fetch you and we would marry when we returned.'

'Does she not mind?'

'Not now,' he said. 'She has become accustomed.'

I said nothing. I thought it most unlikely that a woman who had fallen in love with a man and borne his child would become accustomed within a year to him marrying someone else.

'Did you not want to marry her when you knew she was carrying your child?'

'She is not one of the People,' Daniel said simply. 'And, in any case, I wanted to marry you. When I knew she was with child I was ashamed of what I had done, but she knew I did not love her, and that I was promised to you. She did not expect me to marry her. So I gave her money for a dowry and I pay her every month for the boy's keep.'

'What's the child named?'

He took a breath. 'Daniel,' he said and saw me flinch.

'I am sorry,' he said again. 'But we can overcome this. She makes no claims against me. I will support the child but I need not go and see her. I shall miss the boy; I hoped to see him grow up, but I will understand if you cannot tolerate me seeing her. I will give him up. You and I are young. You will forgive me, we will have a child of our own, we will find a better house. We will be happy.'

'No,' I said shortly.

'What?'

'I said, "No". Tomorrow I shall buy a boy's suit and my father and I will find new premises for the bookshop. I shall work as his apprentice again. I shall never trust a man again, as long as I live. You have hurt me, Daniel, and betrayed me and I will never forgive you.'

He went very white. 'You cannot leave me,' he said. 'We are married in the sight of God, our God. You cannot break an oath to God. You cannot break your pledge to me.'

I rose to it as if it were a challenge. 'I care nothing for your God, nor for you. I shall leave you tomorrow.'

We spent a sleepless night. There was nowhere to go but home and we had to lie side by side, stiff as bodkins in the darkness with his mother alert behind one wall, and his sisters agog on the other side. In the morning I took my father out of the house and told him that my mind was made up and that I would not live with Daniel as his wife.

'Hannah, what will you do with your life?' he said anxiously. 'I cannot be always with you. Who will protect you when I am gone?'

'I shall go back to royal service. I shall go to the princess or to my lord,' I said.

'Your lord is a known traitor and the princess will be married to one of the Spanish princes within the month.'

'Not her! She's not a fool. She would not marry a man and trust him! She knows better than to put her heart into a man's keeping.'

'She cannot live alone any more than you can live alone.'

'Father, my husband has betrayed me and shamed me. I cannot take him back as if nothing had happened. I cannot live with his sisters and his mother all whispering behind their hands every time he comes home late. I cannot live as if I belonged here.'

'My child, where do you belong if not here? If not with me? If not with your husband?'

I had my answer: 'I belong nowhere.'

My father shook his head. A young woman always had to be placed somewhere. She could not live unless she was bolted down in one service or another.

'Father, please let us set up a little business on our own, as we did in London. Let me help you in the printing shop. Let me live with you and we can be at peace and make our living here.'

He hesitated for a long moment, and suddenly I saw him as a stranger might see him. He was an old man and I was taking him from a home where he had become comfortable.

'What will you wear?' he asked finally.

I could have laughed out loud, it mattered so little to me. But I realised that it signified to him whether he had a daughter who could appear to fit into this world or whether I would be eternally out of step with it.

'I will wear a gown if you wish,' I said to please him. 'But I will wear boots underneath it. I will wear a jerkin and a jacket on top.'

'And your wedding ring,' he stipulated. 'You will not deny your marriage.'

'Father, he has denied it every day.'

'Daughter, he is your husband.'

I sighed. 'Very well. But we can go, can we? And at once?'

He rested his hand on my face. 'Child, I thought that you had a good husband who loved you and you would be happy.'

I gritted my teeth so the tears did not come to my eyes and make him think that I might soften, that I might still be a young woman with a chance of love. 'No,' I said simply.

AUTUMN 1556

THE FIRST MONTH in our little shop at the south city gate, I rejoiced in my escape from the Carpenter household. Every morning I awoke with an utter exultation that I need not fit myself to someone else's pattern.

Most Sundays at church I would glimpse Daniel, meticulously observant to every movement of the Mass. In their pew his mother and his sisters stole little glances at me, and once I saw them with a pretty, vapid-looking, fair-haired young woman with a baby on her hip and I guessed that she was the mother of Daniel's child.

I turned my head away from their curious glances but I felt an odd swimmy feeling that I had not known for years. I leaned forward and gripped the smooth, time-worn wood of the pew and waited for the sensation to pass. But it grew stronger. The Sight was coming to me.

The last thing I wanted was to make a spectacle of myself in church, especially when the woman was there with her child, but the waves of darkness seemed to engulf me.

I could hear the sound of a battle and someone screaming: 'Not my baby! Take him! Take him!' and at that moment there was a dreadful crash like a forest falling, and a rush of horses and men and danger, and I wanted to run but there was nowhere to run, and I cried out with fear.

'You're all right now,' came a voice and it was Daniel's beloved voice and I was in his arms, and the sun was shining warmly on my face, and there was no darkness, nor terror, nor the clatter of hoofs on stones.

'I fainted,' I said. 'Did I say anything?'

'Only "I can't take him",' he said. 'Was it the Sight, Hannah?'

I nodded. I should have pulled away from him but I rested against his shoulder and felt the seductive sense of safety that he always gave me.

'A warning?' he asked.

'Something awful,' I said. 'But I don't know what. That's what it's like, I see enough to feel terror but not enough to know.'

'I had thought you would lose the Sight,' he said quietly.

'It seems not. It's not a vision I would want.'

'Hush then,' he soothed. He turned his face to one side and said, 'I will take her home. You can leave us. She needs nothing.'

At once I realised that a small circle of people had gathered behind him to see the woman who had cried out and fainted in church.

My father appeared beside Daniel. 'Could you walk if we both helped you?' he asked. 'Or shall I fetch a litter?'

'I can walk,' I said. 'I am not ill.'

The two of them helped me to my feet and we went down the narrow path to the lane that led to the city gate and our shop. At the corner I saw a knot of women waiting, Daniel's mother, his three sisters, and the woman with a baby on her hip. She was staring at me just as I stared at her, each of us measuring the other. She gave me a smile, a shy smile, half apologetic, half hopeful. The baby she held against her was a true Jewish boy, dark-haired, dark-eyed, solemn-faced, with sweet olive skin. I would have known him for Daniel's child the moment I had seen him, even if Mrs Carpenter had not betrayed the secret.

As I looked at her I saw a shadow behind her, a shadow that was gone as quickly as I turned my gaze to it. I had seen something like a horseman, riding behind her, bending low towards her. I blinked. There was nothing there but this young woman, her baby held close, and Daniel's womenfolk looking at me, looking at them.

'Come on, Father,' I said, very weary. 'Get me home.'

WINTER 1556–SPRING 1557

WITHIN DAYS THE WORD was out that I had fainted in church because I was pregnant, but by winter they had to acknowledge that they were wrong and that the bookseller's daughter had not yet received her comeuppance. By Christmas it was all but forgotten, and by the long, cold spring I was almost accepted as yet another eccentric in this town of runaways, vagabonds, ex-pirates and chancers.

The spring storms kept ships in port and made news from England late and unreliable. I was not the only person who waited every day on the quayside and called to incoming ships: 'What's the news? What's the news in England?' We had learned that King Philip's long desire to drag his wife's country into war against France had finally triumphed over her better sense, and England and France were declared enemies.

The spring gales threw rain and salt water against the tiles and windows of the house and chilled my father to his very bones. Some days he was too cold and weary to get out of bed at all and I would kindle a little fire in the grate in his bedroom and sit by his bed and read to him in Hebrew from the precious scraps of our Bible. He smiled to hear the old words that promised the land to the People, and safety at last.

In March, as the town went mad for King Philip, who travelled through the port on his way to Gravesend, I paid little attention to the rumours of his plans for war and his intentions towards the Princess Elizabeth. I was growing very anxious for my father, who did not seem to be getting any stronger. After two weeks of worry, I swallowed my pride and sent for the newly licensed Dr Daniel Carpenter, who had set up an independent practice at a little shop on the far side of the quay. He came the moment that the street urchin delivered my message.

'How long has he been ill?' he asked me.

'He is not really ill. He seems tired more than anything else,' I said, taking his wet cape from him and spreading it before the little fire to dry. 'He doesn't eat much, just soup and dried fruit. He sleeps day and night.'

'His urine?' Daniel asked.

I fetched the flask that I had kept for his diagnosis and he took it to the window and looked at the colour in the daylight.

'Is he upstairs?'

'In the back bedroom,' I said, and followed him up the stairs.

I waited outside while Daniel took my father's pulse and laid his cool hands on my father's forehead, and asked him gently how he did.

When Daniel came out, his face was grave and tender. He ushered me downstairs and did not speak until we were in the shop once more.

'Hannah, I could cup him, and physic him, and torment him a dozen different ways, but I don't think I or any other doctor could cure him.'

'Cure him?' I repeated stupidly. 'He's just tired.'

'He is dying,' my husband said gently.

For a moment I could not take it in. 'But, Daniel, that's not possible! There's nothing wrong with him!'

'He has a growth in his belly which is pressing against his lungs and his heart,' Daniel said quietly. 'He can feel it himself; he knows it.'

'He is just tired,' I protested.

'And if he feels any worse than tired, if he feels pain, then we will give him physic to take the pain away,' Daniel assured me.

'I thought he was just tired,' I said again, stupidly.

'I know,' Daniel said.

'How long d'you think?' I thought he would say months, a year.

'Days,' he said quietly. 'Perhaps weeks. But no more, I don't think.'

'Days?' I said uncomprehendingly. 'How can it be days?'

He shook his head, his eyes compassionate. 'I am sorry, Hannah. But he is in no pain. And he is not afraid. He is prepared for his death. He is only anxious about you.'

'Me!' I exclaimed.

'Yes,' he said steadily. 'You should assure him that you are provided for, that you are safe.'

I hesitated.

'I myself have sworn to him that if you are in any difficulty or in any danger that I will care for you before any other. I will protect you as my wife for as long as you live.'

I held on to the door handle so that I did not pitch myself into his arms and wail like a bereaved child. 'That was kind of you,' I managed to say. 'I don't need your protection, but you were kind to reassure him.'

'You have my protection whether you need it or not,' Daniel said. 'I am your husband, and I do not forget it.' He took up his cape from the stool before the fire and swung it round his shoulders. 'I shall come tomorrow, and every day at noon,' he said. 'And I shall find a woman to sit with him so that you can rest.'

I nodded; I could not trust myself to speak. Then he went out of the door into the rain and I went upstairs to my father.

As Daniel had predicted, my father slipped away very quickly. True to his word, Daniel brought a night nurse, Marie, so that my father was never alone. In the day I found a lad to mind the shop while I sat with my father and read to him in Hebrew. In April I found a new volume which had a small surviving snippet of the prayers for the dead. I saw his smile of acknowledgment. He raised his hand. I fell silent.

'Yes, it is time,' was all he said. His voice was a thread. 'You will be well, my child?'

I put the book on the seat of my chair and knelt at his bedside. Effortfully he put his hand on my head for a blessing. 'Don't worry about me,' I whispered. 'I will be all right. I have the shop and the press; I can earn a living, and Daniel will always look after me.'

He nodded. Already he was drifting away, too far to give advice, too far to remonstrate. 'I bless you, *querida*,' he said gently.

'Father!' My eyes were filled with tears. I dropped my head to his bed.

'Bless you,' he said again and lay quietly.

I levered myself back to my chair and blinked my eyes. Through the blur of tears I could hardly see the words. Then I started to read. '"Magnified and sanctified be the name of God throughout the world which He has created according to His will. May He establish His kingdom during the days of your life and during the life of all of the house of Israel, speedily, yea soon; and say ye, Amen."'

Daniel cared for me as he had promised he would. As son-in-law, all my father's goods became his by right, but he signed them over to me in the same day and he asked Marie to stay on for the next few months. She could sleep downstairs in the kitchen, and would keep me safe at nights. Mrs Carpenter frowned her disapproval but held her peace.

She made the preparations for the requiem mass and then the secret Jewish ceremony, done the same day, behind our closed door. When I thanked her she waved me away. 'These are the ways of our People,' she said. 'We have to remember them. If we forget them, we forget ourselves. And now you know how it is done, you can teach your children, and the way of our People can be handed down.'

Daniel did not ask me if I would forgive him and if we could start again as man and wife. He did not ask me if I was longing for a touch, for a kiss, longing to feel alive like a young woman in springtime and not always like a girl fighting against the world. He did not ask me if I felt, since my father was dead, that I was terribly alone in the world, and that I would always be Hannah alone, neither of the People, nor a wife, and now, not even a daughter. He did not ask me these things; I did not volunteer them. And so we parted kindly on my doorstep, with a sense of sadness and regret, and I imagine he went home and called on the way at the house of the plump fair-haired mother of his son, and I went into my house and closed my door and sat in darkness for a long time.

SUMMER 1557

By EARLY SUMMER the streets were filled with the sound of recruiting officers marching along, drumming and whistling for lads to volunteer for the English army to fight the French. The harbour was a continual bustle of ships coming and going, unloading weapons and gunpowder and horses. In the fields outside the city, a little camp had sprung up and soldiers were marched here and there, and bawled at, and marched back again. All I knew was that the extra traffic through the city gate did not bring much extra trade. The town became unruly with the hundreds of extra men coming through and I took to wearing a pair of dark breeches, tucked my hair up under my cap, and donned a thick jerkin, despite the summer heat. I carried a dagger in my boot and I would have used it if anyone had come against me or broken into the shop. I kept Marie, my father's nurse, as my lodger and she and I bolted the door at six o'clock every night and did not open it until the morning, blowing out our candles if we heard brawling in the street.

The harbour was almost blocked by incoming ships; as soon as the men marched from the fields outside the town towards the outlying forts, the camp immediately filled with more soldiers. The day the cavalry troops clattered through the town I thought that our chimney pot would be shaken from the roof by the noise. Other women of my age lined the streets, cheering and waving as the men went by, but I kept my head down. I had seen enough death; my heart did not leap to the whistle of the pipes and the urgent rattle of the drums.

By midsummer the English army, marshalled, half trained and wholly wild for a fight, moved out of Calais, led by King Philip himself. They launched an attack on St Quentin, and in August stormed the town and won it from the French. It was a resounding victory against a hated enemy. The citizens of Calais, ambitious to reclaim the whole of the lost English lands in France, went mad with joy at this first sign, and every returning soldier was laden with flowers and had a horn of wine pressed into his willing hand and was blessed as the saviour of his nation.

I saw Daniel at church on Sunday when the priest preached the victory of God's chosen people over the treacherous French, and then, to my amazement, he prayed for the safe delivery of the queen of a son and heir to the throne. For me, it was better news even than the taking of St Quentin, and for the first time in long months I felt my heart lift. When I thought of Mary carrying a child in her womb again I felt my down-turned face lift up and smile. I knew how glad she must be, how this must bring her back to the joy she had felt in early marriage, how she must think now that God had forgiven the English and she might become a gentle queen and a good mother.

When Daniel came up to me after church he saw the happiness on my face and smiled. 'You did not know of the queen's condition?'

'How could I know?' I said. 'I see nobody. I hear only the most general of gossip.'

'There is news of your old lord too,' he said levelly. 'Have you heard?'

'Robert Dudley?' I felt the shock of his name. 'What news?'

'Good news,' Daniel said quietly, though I could see it brought little joy for him. 'He and half a dozen other men accused of treason were released some time ago and fought with the king.'

'He came through the town? And I didn't know?'

'He fought at St Quentin and was mentioned in dispatches for his bravery,' Daniel said shortly.

I felt myself glow with pleasure. 'Oh! How wonderful!'

'Yes,' Daniel said without enthusiasm. 'You won't try to find him, Hannah? The countryside is unsafe.'

'Will he go home through Calais, when the French sue for peace?'

'I should think so.'

'I will try to see him then. Perhaps he'll help me return to England.'

Daniel went pale, his face even graver than before. 'You cannot risk going back while the rules against heresy are so strong,' he said quietly.

'If I were under my lord's protection I would be safe,' I said with simple confidence.

It cost him a good deal to acknowledge Lord Robert's power. 'I suppose so. But please, talk to me before you take a decision. His credit may not be so good. It is only one act of bravery in a long life of treason.'

I let the criticism go.

'Can I walk you to your door?'

He offered me his arm and I took it and fell into step beside him. For the first time in months I felt a little of my own darkness lift and dissolve. The queen was with child, Lord Robert was free and honoured for his bravery, England and Spain in alliance had defeated the French army. Surely things would start coming right for me too.

'Mother tells me that she saw you in the marketplace in breeches,' Daniel remarked.

'Yes,' I said carelessly. 'When there are so many soldiers and rough men and women on the streets I feel safer like that.'

'Would you come back to my house?' Daniel asked. 'I would like to keep you safe. You could keep the shop on.'

'It's making no money,' I conceded honestly. 'I don't stay away from you for the sake of the shop. I can't come back to you, Daniel. I have made up my mind and I will not change it.'

We had reached my door. 'But if you were in trouble or danger you would send for me,' he pressed me.

'Yes.'

'And you wouldn't leave for England, or meet with Lord Robert, without telling me?'

I shrugged. 'I have no plans, except I should like to see the queen again. She must be so happy now, expecting her child.'

'Perhaps when the peace treaty is signed,' he suggested, 'I could take you to London for a visit and bring you back, if you would like that.'

I looked at him attentively. 'Daniel, that would be kind indeed.'

'I would do anything to make you happy,' he said gently.

I opened my door. 'Thank you,' I said quietly and slipped away from him before I should make the mistake of stepping into his arms.

WINTER 1557–8

THERE WERE RUMOURS that the defeated French army was regrouping on the borders of the English Pale and every stranger who came into Calais for the Christmas market was regarded as a spy. The French must come against Calais in revenge for St Quentin, but the French must know, as we all knew, that the town could not be taken.

Then in the night, without warning, Fort Nieulay fell. It was one of the eight forts that guarded Calais, and as such was only a small loss. But Nieulay was the fort on the River Hames that controlled the sea gates, which were supposed to flood the canals round the town so that no army could cross. With Nieulay in French hands we had nothing to defend us but the other forts and the great walls. We had lost the first line of defence.

The very next day we heard the roar of cannon and then a rumour swept through the town. Fort Risban, the fort that guarded the inner harbour of Calais, had fallen too, even though it was newly built and newly fortified. Now the harbour itself lay open to French shipping.

'What shall we do?' Marie asked me.

'It's only two forts,' I said stoutly, trying to hide my fear. 'The English army will know we are under siege and come to rescue us.'

But it was the French army that drew up in lines before the walls of Calais, and it was the French harquebusiers who flung a storm of arrows that arched over the top of the walls and killed people at random as they ran through the streets, desperate to get back inside their houses.

'The English will come,' I said. 'Lord Robert will come and attack the French from the rear.'

We bolted the shutters on the shop and shrank inside to the back room, in a terror that the great south city gate, so close to our little shop, would be a focus for attack. The French brought up siege engines. Even hidden in the back room of the shop I could hear the pounding of the great ram against the barred gates.

Then the clatter of hundreds of horses' hoofs was in the street outside our door, and I realised that the English army, garrisoned inside the town, was gathering for a counterattack. They must think that if they could dislodge the French from the city gates, the surrounding countryside could be retaken and the pressure relieved from the town defences.

We could hear the horses go by and then the silence while they assembled at the gate. I realised that, for them to get out, the gate would have to be thrown open, and for that time my little shop would be right in the centre of the battle.

It was enough. I whispered to Marie in French, 'We have to get out of here. I am going to Daniel. D'you want to come with me?'

'I'll go to my cousins. They live near the harbour.'

I crept to the door and opened it a crack. The sight as I peered through was terrifying. The street outside was absolute chaos, with soldiers running up the stone steps to the ramparts laden with weapons, wounded men being helped down.

I threw open the door and almost at once heard a most dreadful cry from the walls immediately above the shop as a hail of arrows found an unprotected band of men. Marie and I fled into the street. Behind us, and then all around us, came a dreadful crash. The French siege engine had catapulted a great load of stone and rubble over the wall. It rained down on our street like a falling mountain.

'I'm off!' Marie shouted to me, plunging down a lane to the fish quay.

I could not even shout a blessing; the smell of the smoke—the very scent of my nightmares—filled the air, filled my nostrils, my lungs, even my eyes, so that I could not breathe and my eyes were filled with tears so that I could not see.

From the ramparts above me I heard a high shriek of terror and I looked up to see a man on fire, the burning arrow still caught in his clothing, as he dived to the floor and rolled, trying to extinguish the flames, screaming like a heretic as his body burned.

I ducked from the doorway and started to run, anywhere to get away from the smell of a man burning. I wanted to find Daniel. He seemed like the only safe haven in a world turned into a nightmare.

I pressed myself back against the walls of the houses as a company of horse mustered in the street. Then I found the courage to dart round the dangerous hoofs and duck into a refuge further down the street as a great charge of horsemen came thundering by. I looked up and saw the standard they were carrying before them—the bear and staff embroidered on the bright ground—and I called out: 'Robert Dudley!'

A man looked over at me. 'At the head, where he always is.'

I pushed my way back, afraid of nothing now, turning horses' heads to one side, sliding between their big flanks. 'Let me by, let me by, sir. I am going to Robert Dudley.'

It became like a dream. The great horses with the men mounted as high as centaurs above me. Their heavy armour shining in the sunshine, clashing when they brushed one against another, sounding like cymbals when they hammered their halberds on their shields.

I found myself at the head of the square and there was his standard-bearer, and beside him . . .

'My lord!' I yelled.

The helmeted head turned slowly towards me, the visor down so he could not see me. I pulled the cap from my head, my hair tumbled down and I lifted my face towards the dark knight, high on his horse.

'My lord! It's me! Hannah the Fool.'

His gauntleted hand lifted the false face of metal, but the shadow of the helmet left his face in darkness and still I could not see him. His head was turned towards me. I could feel his eyes on me, sharp under the sharp points of the helmet. 'Mistress Boy?'

It was his voice, coming from the mouth of this man-god, this great man of metal. But it was his voice, as intimate and warm and familiar as if he had come from dancing at King Edward's summer feast.

The horse sidled. I stepped back on a doorstep; it raised me up four inches, nothing more. 'My lord, it is me!'

'Mistress Boy, what the devil are you doing here?'

'I live here,' I said, half laughing and half crying at seeing him again. 'What of you?'

'Released, fighting, winning—perhaps losing at the moment. Are you safe here?'

'I don't think so,' I said honestly. 'Can we hold the town?'

He pulled the gauntlet from his right hand, twisted a ring from his finger, threw it towards me. 'Take this to the *Windflight*,' he said. 'My ship. Go now, get aboard. We are to make a charge.'

'My lord . . .'

'It's an order!' he shouted at me. 'Go!'

I gasped, pushing the ring on my finger. It had been on his little finger, it fitted my third, just above my wedding ring.

'My lord!' I cried out again. 'Come back safe.'

The bugle played so loud that no one could be heard. They were about to charge. He dropped his visor over his face, pulled his gauntlet back on his hand, lifted his lance from its place, tipped it to his helmet in a salute to me, and wheeled his horse round to face his company.

'A Dudley!' he shouted. 'For God and the queen!'

'For God and the queen!' they roared back at him. 'For God and the queen! Dudley! Dudley!'

They moved towards the city walls, out of the square, and like a camp follower, disobedient to his order, I moved after them. The roar of the siege grew louder as they got near to the gate, and at the sound of French rage I shrank back, looked behind for the way to the harbour.

Then I saw her. Daniel's woman, bedraggled with her pretty dress half dragged from her shoulder, exposing her breast. Her child was on her hip, clinging to her, his dark eyes wide. Her hair was tumbling down, her eye blacked, her face anguished, running like a hunted deer, skipping and stumbling on the cobbles of the street.

She recognised me at once. She had watched me, as I had watched her, every Sunday at Mass.

'Hannah,' she called out to me. 'Hannah!'

'What is it?' I shouted irritably. 'What d'you want with me?'

She showed me her child. 'Take him!'

At once I remembered the intensity of my vision in church, the first time I had seen her. Then as now there was a screaming and a thundering noise. Then, in my nightmare, she had called out 'Take him!' As she cried out the sky suddenly grew dark with a hail of missiles and I ducked into a doorway, but on the other side of the street she came on, dodging through the falling rocks. 'Hannah! Hannah! I need your help.'

'Go home,' I shouted unhelpfully. 'Go to a cellar or somewhere.'

The last of the horses was moving out of the square. We heard the groan of the counterweights as they pulled back the gate for Lord Robert and his cavalry to charge out, and the great roar of rage as they thundered out to meet the French army.

'They are leaving us?' she screamed in horror. 'Running away?'

'No, going out to fight. Find yourself a refuge . . .' I yelled impatiently.

'God save us. They need not go out to fight them; they are in the town already! We are lost!' Daniel's woman shouted. 'It was them . . .'

Her words suddenly penetrated my mind, and I whirled round to look at her again. At once I realised the significance of her black eye and her torn gown. The French were in the city, and they had raped her.

'They came in through the harbour! Ten minutes ago!' she screamed at me, and as she shouted the words I saw coming down the street behind her a tide of French cavalry, in the streets and behind my lord, cutting off him and his men from the harbour. The first rank was on us in a moment, a lance plunging down towards me, and without thinking I snatched the dagger from my boot and with the short blade I parried the thrust. The shock of the blow jarred my blade from my hand, but saved my life as it threw me back against the door of the house behind me. I felt it yield and I fell back into the darkness of an unknown house as I heard Daniel's woman scream: 'Save my baby! Take him! Take him!'

Even as she ran towards me with him held out before her, even as she thrust him into my hands, and he came all warm and soft and heavy, I heard myself say: 'I can't take him.'

I saw the lance run her through, spearing her spine, as she cried out again: 'Take him! Take him!' and at that moment there was a dreadful crash like a forest falling down all at once and a rush of horses and men and danger, and I stumbled back into the dark interior of the house with the boy held tight against me, and the door swung shut on the street with a bang like a thunderclap.

I turned to thank whoever had saved me, but before I could speak there was a roar of flames and a sudden blast of hot smoke, and someone pushed past me and threw open the door again.

The thatched roof of this temporary refuge was alight, blazing up like kindling in seconds. Everyone who had been hidden in the house was pushing past me to the street outside, and I, smelling smoke, dashed out after them, the child tight against my shoulder.

Mercifully, the streets were clear for the moment. The French horsemen had chased after Lord Robert's troop in one mad, dangerous dash. But Daniel's woman was where they had left her with two great lance thrusts through her body.

At the sight I snatched her child closer to me and started to run down the street, down the stone steps to the harbour. I could not wait to look for Daniel; I could not do anything but take the chance I had been given with Lord Robert's ring.

The boats were tied by just one rope, all sails furled ready to go at a moment's notice. I looked desperately around for Lord Robert's standard and saw it, at the prime position, at the very end of the pier where it would be easiest to slip away. I ran down the pier, my feet thudding on the wooden boards, and skidded to a halt when a sailor leapt from the ship and stood before the gangplank with a shining cutlass out of its scabbard, pointing at my throat. 'No further, lad,' he said.

'Lord Robert sent me,' I panted.

He shook his head. 'We could all say that. What's happening in town?'

'Lord Robert led his company out in a charge but the French are in the town already, at his back.'

'Can he turn?'

'I don't know. I didn't see it.'

He shouted an order over his shoulder. The men on deck stood by the ropes for the sails and two men vaulted ashore and held the rope ready to cast off.

I held out my hand to show Lord Robert's ring gripped tight on my finger, above my wedding ring.

The sailor looked at it carefully. 'His ring,' he said.

'His own. He gave it me himself. He saw me before he led them out. I am his vassal. I was Hannah the Fool before I came here.'

'I'd not have recognised you,' he said. 'And this? Your son?'

'Yes.' The lie was said before I had time to think, and then I would not have recalled it.

He stepped to one side and nodded me up the narrow gangplank, then positioned himself square at the foot again.

The winter afternoon grew dark and no one could tell us whether Lord Robert had broken the French ranks or whether they had entered the town behind his back and cut him down. Then we saw the town lit up from one point to another as the French besieging army broke through the walls and fired one thatched roof and then another.

Suddenly there was a rush of men and horses down to the quayside and a flurry as they flung themselves from the saddle, threw off their armour and hared up to the waiting ships.

Then I saw my lord. I would have recognised him in any crowd. He was walking, broadsword in one hand, helmet in the other, trailing his feet like a defeated man. Behind him came a train of men, limping, bleeding, heads bowed. He led them to the ship and stood aside as they went up the gangplank and threw themselves down on the deck.

'That's enough, sir,' the sailor said to him quietly when we were fully loaded. My lord looked up, like a man newly wakened from sleep, and said: 'But we have to take the rest. I promised they would serve me and I would take them to victory. I can't leave them here now.'

'We'll come back for them,' the sailor said gently. He put one strong arm round my lord's shoulders and drew him firmly up the gangplank. 'We'll come back for the rest of them and then we'll retake Calais. Never doubt it, sir. Never doubt it.'

Lord Robert went to the stern of the boat, scanning the harbour, seeing the disorderly retreat. We could smell the smoke drifting in a pall across the water from the burning buildings. We had lost. The English had lost. It was as simple and as brutal as that, and the path of a true man was to consider how to win the next battle.

He spent the whole voyage gazing over the stern towards the coast of France. I knew, because I was watching him, as I sat on a coil of rope at the mast, just behind him. We made an odd trio: a renegade Jew with a Gentile bastard on her hip, and a newly released traitor who had led his men to defeat.

I had not expected his wife Amy at the quayside, but she was there, hand over her eyes, scanning the deck for him. I saw her before she saw him and said, 'Your wife,' in his ear.

He went quickly down the gangplank to her. He did not take her in his arms nor greet her with any sign of affection, but he listened intently to her and then he turned to me.

'I have to go to court to explain to the queen what has happened at Calais,' he said briefly. 'Heads will have to roll for this, perhaps mine.'

'My lord,' I breathed.

'Yes,' he said savagely. 'I don't seem to have done much to advance my family. Hannah, you go with Amy. She is staying with friends in Sussex. I shall send for you there.'

'My lord.' I went a little closer. 'I don't want to live in the country,' was all I could say.

Robert Dudley grinned at me. 'I am sure, sweetheart. I cannot stand it myself. But you must endure it for a month or two. If the queen beheads me, then you can make your own way where you please. All right? But if I survive this, I will open my London house and you shall come back to my service. Whatever you wish. How old is the child?'

I hesitated. 'He's nearly two,' I said.

'You married his father?' he asked.

I looked him in the face. 'Yes.'

'And named him?'

'Daniel, for his father.'

He nodded. 'Amy will take care of you,' he said. 'She likes children.' A snap of his fingers summoned his wife to his side. I saw her shake her head in disagreement, and then lower her eyes when she was over-ruled. When she shot me a look of pure hatred, I guessed that he had ordered her to care for me and my son.

She had brought his horse. I watched him swing up into his saddle, his men mount up around him. 'London,' he said succinctly and rode his horse north towards whatever fate had for him.

I could not get the measure of Amy Dudley as we rode through the icy countryside of England in those cold days of January 1558. She was a good rider but she seemed to take little pleasure in it, even on the days when the sun rose like a red disc on the horizon and when a few robins hopped and hid in the leafless hedgerows. I thought it was the absence of her husband that made her so sulky, but her companion, Mrs Oddingsell, did not try to cheer her; they did not even speak of him. They rode in silence, as women accustomed to it.

I had to ride behind them, all the way from Gravesend to Chichester, with the baby strapped on my back, and every evening I was aching from my buttocks to my neck with the strain. The extraordinary child had barely made a noise from the moment that his mother had half flung him at me as the French cavalry rode her down. Sleeping, he had rested against me, nestled in as if he were my own; awake, he sat on my lap or on the floor at my feet, or stood, one hand holding firmly on to my breeches. He said not one word, not in French, nor in English. He regarded me with solemn dark eyes and said nothing.

I was not a naturally maternal woman, yet I could not help but admire this small person's tenacity. I started to like the feeling of his fat little hand stretching trustfully up for mine. I started to sleep well with him nestled against my side.

I went down the empty roads with my eyes on the country that was bleak and so cursed, but my mind was on my husband and the town I had left. Now that our flight was over and we had arrived in a comparative safe haven, I was sick with fear for Daniel. I did not even know if he was alive. I knew that worrying about him helped neither of us, but it was impossible to stop myself. I could not get a letter into Calais until some sort of peace was declared, and that would not be for months. Worse, I could not expect to hear from him; he would have no idea where I had gone or even if I were alive. When he went to my shop in the city wall to look for me, as he surely would do, he would find the place sacked or burnt out, and not even Marie, supposing she had survived, would be able to tell him where I was. And then he would find that little Daniel's mother was dead and that the boy was missing too. He would have no reason to guess that I and his son were together in safety in England. He would think that he had lost his wife and his child in one dreadful battle.

I could not enjoy my safety when I knew that he might still be in danger. There could be no happiness for me until I knew that he was alive. Somewhere on the road—in Kent, I think—it came to me with the simple brightness of the wintry sun lying on the horizon and shining blindingly into my eyes. I could not settle without Daniel, because I loved him. I had loved him perhaps from the moment I had seen him at the gates of Whitehall Palace where we had quarrelled at our meeting, and I had loved his steadiness and his fidelity and his patience with me ever since. I felt as if I had grown up with him. He had seen me begged as a fool to the king, devoted to the queen and entranced by the Princess Elizabeth. He had seen my schoolchild adoration of my master, and he had seen me struggle with myself to become the woman I now was. The only thing he had not seen was the resolution of this inner battle: the moment when I could say, 'Yes, I am a woman, and I love this man.'

Everything that had happened in Calais melted away before this one fact. The intrusion of his mother, the malice of his sisters and his own innocent stupidity. Nothing seemed to matter but that I knew now that I loved him, and that it might be too late for me ever to tell him.

If he were dead then it did not seem to matter very much that he had lain with another girl; the greater loss quite concealed the smaller betrayal. As I mounted my horse in the morning and dismounted wearily at night, I realised that I was indeed the widow I announced myself to be. I had lost Daniel, and only now did I have the sense to find that I had loved him all along.

We were to stay in a great house, north of Chichester, and I was glad to clatter into the stable yard at midday and hand over my tired horse to one of the grooms. I was weary as I followed Lady Dudley up the steps to the great hall, and apprehensive. I followed Mrs Oddingsell with Danny on my hip, and there was our hostess, Lady Philips, with a hand held out for Lady Dudley and a deep curtsy.

'You shall have your usual room overlooking the park,' she said, and then she turned to Mrs Oddingsell and me with a smile.

'This is Mrs Carpenter. She can share with your housekeeper,' Lady Dudley said abruptly. 'She is a woman known to my lord, that he rescued from Calais. I dare say he will let me know what she is to do, shortly.'

Lady Philips raised an eyebrow at Amy's abrupt tone, which all but named me as Robert Dudley's whore. Mrs Oddingsell curtsied and went to the stairs, but I did not immediately follow her.

'I need some things for the child,' I said uncomfortably.

'There are some clothes in the paupers' cupboard,' Lady Philips said.

I curtsied. 'It was very kind of his lordship to give me a place on his ship from Calais,' I said clearly. 'The more so since he had not seen me for so long, since I had been in royal service to the queen. But I am a married woman now, my husband a doctor in Calais, and this is my husband's son.' I saw that they both understood me and had heard the reference to royal service.

'My lord is always good to his servants, however lowly,' Amy Dudley said unpleasantly, and waved me away.

'And I need proper clothes for my son,' I said, standing my ground. 'Not from the paupers' cupboard.'

Both women looked at me with renewed attention.

'I need clothes for a gentleman's son,' I said simply.

Lady Philips, not at all sure now what cuckoo she had welcomed into her house, gave me a cautious smile. 'I have some things put by,' she said carefully. 'My sister's boy wore them.'

'I am sure they will suit the purpose excellently,' I said with a pleasant smile. 'And I thank you, your ladyship.'

Within a week I was desperate to leave. The bleak countryside of Sussex in winter seemed to press on my face like a pane of cold glass. The sky above the hills was iron grey, filled with snow.

Amy Dudley was a welcome and regular guest here. There was some debt between Sir John Philips and my lord that was repaid by his hospitality to Lady Dudley.

'Does she not have a house of her own?' I demanded of Mrs Oddingsell in frustration.

'Not one that she chooses to use,' she said shortly.

Without a house to command or lands to farm, Lady Dudley was a woman of complete idleness. There was nothing that brought her alive. She was in a state of obedient waiting. Then I realised what she was waiting for. She was waiting for a sign from Robert.

But there was no sign of him, though January went into February. No sign of Robert, though he clearly had not been arrested by the queen. Whatever the blame for the loss of Calais, it was not to be laid at his door.

In the absence of any work to do in the household, I found that I spent all my time with the child, Danny, and all my thoughts were with his father. I decided to write to Daniel and address the letter to my father's old shop in London. If Daniel came looking for me, or sent anyone to seek me, that would be one of the places he would visit first. I would send a copy of it to my lord and ask him to forward it to Calais. Surely there must be emissaries going to the city?

> *Dear husband,*
>
> *It is strange that after all we have been through we should once more be separated, and once again I am in England and you in Calais, but this time I think you are in greater danger than I. I pray every night that you are safe.*
>
> *I had the good fortune to be offered a place on the English ship belonging to Lord Robert and in the hurry of battle I thought it best to take it. I wish now I had found my way to you, but, Daniel, I did not know what to do. Also, I had another life to consider. The mother of your child was killed by a French horseman before me, and her last act was to put your son in my hands. I have him with me now and I am caring for him as my own. He is safe and well though he does not speak yet. He is eating well and growing well, and learning to walk more strongly.*
>
> *We are living at Chichester in Sussex with Lord Dudley's wife until I can find myself a place. I am thinking of going to court or to the Princess Elizabeth, if she will have me.*
>
> *I pray that you are safe and well, Daniel, and I tell you now, as I should have told you before, that I never stopped loving you, even when I left your home. I loved you then, I love you now. If God ever grants me another*

chance with you, Daniel, I would want to be your wife once more.
Your wife (if you will let me call myself that)
Hannah Carpenter

I sent the letter to my lord, with a covering note.

My lord,
Your wife has been very kind to me but I am trespassing on her hospitality
here. Please give me permission to come to court or to see if the Princess
Elizabeth will take me into her service.
Hannah Green

I heard nothing from Daniel, and I had hardly hoped for it, though I could not tell if it was the silence of distance or the silence of death.

But, at last, a note came from court.

I shall be with you next week. RD

Amy Dudley reacted coolly, with great dignity. She saw that the silver plate and the pewter trenchers were given an extra polish, and that the best linen was laid out for her bed, but other than that, she made no special provision for the return of the lord. Only I saw that she was waiting like a dog waits for his master's step on the threshold. No one else would have noticed the tension in her body every day, from daybreak, when he might come early, till dusk, when he might arrive late.

Finally, on Friday, when there was nothing to put before him but carp from the moat, we saw his train coming down the lane, his standard at the head of a trotting column of riders, smartly in step, two by two, all bright in his livery, and Robert before them all, like a young king. Riding behind him—I squinted my eyes against the low winter sun shining towards me—was John Dee, the reverend and respected Catholic chaplain to Bishop Bonner.

I stepped up to the window of the upper gallery where I had been playing with Danny, so that I could see Robert Dudley's welcome. The front door of the house was torn open and Amy Dudley was on the top step, her hands clasped before her, the picture of demure self-control, but I knew she was raging to be with him.

Lord Robert pulled up his horse, jumped from the saddle, threw the reins to a waiting groom, tossed some remark over his shoulder to John Dee and bowed and kissed his wife's hand as if he had been away for a couple of nights and not for most of their married life.

I picked up Danny, who came to me eagerly with his beaming smile but saying nothing, and made my way down the great stairs to the hall. The household was assembled, lined up as if they were an army for inspection, Sir John Philips and his lady at the head. My lord stood illuminated in the doorway, his broad shoulders brushing the door frame, his smile confident and challenging.

The years of imprisonment had scarred him with nothing worse than a deep groove on either side of his mouth and a hardness at the back of his eyes. Apart from that shadow, he was the same young man whom I had seen walking with an angel in Fleet Street five years ago.

'I'm very glad to be with you,' he said to them all. 'And I thank you all for the good service you have done to me and mine while I have been away.' He paused. 'You will be anxious for news of the queen.' He glanced up the stairs and saw me dressed as a woman, for the first time ever. His amazed stare took in the cut-down gown that I had sewn with the help of Mrs Oddingsell, my dark hair smoothed back under my hood, the dark-headed child on my hip. Comically, he looked and then looked again at the sight of me, recognised me despite the gown, and then shook a baffled head, but continued his speech.

'The queen is in her confinement chamber and expecting to give birth to a son. The king will return to England when the baby is born. In the meantime he is protecting the borders of his Spanish lands in the Low Countries, and has sworn to retake Calais for England. The Princess Elizabeth has visited her sister and wished her well. The princess is in good health, good spirits and great beauty, praise God. She has told the queen that she will not marry any Spanish prince, nor anyone of the king's choosing. She will remain a bride of England.'

There was a little murmur at the news and the servants began to disperse. Robert shook John Philips warmly by the hand, kissed Lady Philips on her cheek and then turned to me.

'Hannah? Is that really you?'

I came down the stairs slowly, conscious of his wife behind him, still standing in the doorway.

'My lord,' I said. I reached the bottom step and dropped him a curtsy.

'I would never have known you,' he said incredulously. 'You are more than a girl, Hannah. You are a woman grown, and out of your breeches at last! And a babe in your arms? This is a transformation!'

I smiled but I could feel Amy's eyes boring into me. 'This is my son,' I said. 'I thank you for saving us from Calais.'

His face clouded over. 'I wish I could have saved them all.'

'Have you any news from the town?' I asked him. 'My husband and his family may still be there. Did you send my letter onward?'

'I gave it to my pageboy and told him to give it to a fisherman who goes out deep into the French seas and ask him to pass it to a French ship if he met with one, but I could do no more for you. We have heard nothing of the men who were captured. King Philip will keep us at war with France for as long as he can, and the queen is in no position to argue. There will be some exchange of prisoners, and men sent home, but God knows when.' He shook his head as if to dislodge the memories of the fall of the infallible castle. 'I have never seen you in a gown before. You are transformed!'

I tried to laugh but I could see Amy coming to claim her husband.

'You will want to change out of your riding clothes and wash,' she said firmly. 'There is hot water in your bedchamber.'

'Then I'll go up.' He glanced over his shoulder. 'And someone must show Dee where he is to lodge.' I shrank back, but my lord did not notice. He called out: 'Here, John—look at who we have here!'

John Dee came forward and I saw that he was more changed than Robert. His hair was greying at the temples, his eyes were dark with fatigue. But his confidence and inner peace were as strong as ever.

'Who is this lady?' he asked.

'I am Hannah Carpenter, Mr Dee,' I said guardedly. I did not know whether he was going to acknowledge that we had last met in the most terrible place in England when I was on trial for my life and he was my judge. 'I was Hannah Green. The queen's fool.'

He looked quickly at me again and then a slow, sweet smile spread from his eyes to his lips and I knew he would never speak of it. 'Ah, Hannah, I would not have known you in your gown.'

'And he is Dr Dee now,' my lord said. 'Bishop Bonner's chaplain.'

'Oh,' I said guardedly.

'And is this your son?' John Dee asked.

'Yes. This is Daniel Carpenter,' I said proudly, and John Dee reached forward and touched my little boy's fingers with his own.

'How old is he?'

'Nearly two.'

'And his father?'

I frowned. 'I parted from my husband at Calais. I don't know if he is safe,' I said.

'You have no . . . sense of him?' John Dee asked me, his voice low.

I shook my head.

'Dr Dee, Hannah will show you to your chamber.' Amy's voice broke in abruptly, speaking of me as if I were her servant.

I led the way up the stairs to one of the small bedchambers on the first floor, John Dee following me. Lord Robert sprang up the stairs two at a time behind us. We heard the door bang as he went into his room.

I had barely showed John Dee where he was to sleep, the cupboard where he could put his clothes, and poured hot water for him to wash, when the chamber door opened and Lord Robert came in.

'Hannah, don't go,' he said. 'I want to hear your news.'

'I have none,' I said coolly. 'I have been here, as you know, all this long while, with your wife, doing nothing.'

He gave a short laugh. 'Have you been bored, Mistress Boy? It cannot be worse than married life, surely?'

I smiled. I was not going to tell Lord Robert that I had parted from my husband within a few months of our marriage.

'And have you kept your gift?' John Dee asked quietly. 'I always thought that the angels would only come to a virgin.'

'It comes so rarely that it is hard to tell,' I said, my voice very small. 'But I had a true seeing in Calais, after my wedding: I foresaw the horsemen riding through the streets.' I shut my eyes against the memory.

'You saw the French coming into Calais?' Lord Robert asked incredulously. 'Dear God, why didn't you warn me?'

'I would have done if I had known what it was,' I replied. 'Don't doubt me. I would have come at once if I had understood what I was seeing.'

Robert shook his head and turned to look out of the window. 'I wish to God I had been warned,' he said moodily.

'Will you scry for me again?' John Dee asked. 'So that we can see if your gift remains true?'

I looked at him in utter disbelief. 'Are you seeking the advice of angels?' I asked the Inquisitor's chaplain. 'You? Of all men?'

John Dee was not at all perturbed by the sharpness of my tone. 'I do not change my beliefs. And we need guidance all the more, in these troubled times. But we must ask discreetly. There is always danger for those who seek knowledge. But if we could know that the queen will give birth to a healthy child we would be better able to plan for the future. If she is to be blessed with a son, then Princess Elizabeth should change her plans.'

'And I should change mine,' Lord Robert remarked wryly.

'I don't know if I can do it,' I said. 'I have seen the future only once, in all the time I was in Calais.'

'Shall we try this evening?' Lord Robert asked. 'Will you try and see if it comes easily, Hannah? For old times' sake?'

'If you will ask a question for me,' I bargained.

'What is it?' John Dee asked.

'If my husband is alive or dead,' I said. 'It's all I want to know. I don't even ask the future, if I shall see him again. I would be happy just to know that he is alive.'

'You love him so much?' Lord Robert asked sceptically.

'I do,' I said simply. 'I cannot rest until I know that he is safe.'

'I shall ask the angels and you shall scry for me,' John Dee promised. 'Tonight?'

'When Danny is asleep,' I said.

'At eight o'clock?' Lord Robert asked. 'Here?'

John Dee glanced around. 'I will ask the men to bring up my table and my books.'

Amy had hoped to sit up late with her husband, or to go to bed early together, but at eight o'clock he made excuses and he and John Dee and I gathered in John Dee's room with the door closed, the shutters across the window and only one candle lit and glowing in the mirror.

'Are you happy to do this?' John Dee asked.

'What are you going to ask?'

'If the queen will have a boy child,' Robert said. 'There is nothing more important to know than this. And if we can win back Calais.'

I looked towards John Dee. 'And if my husband lives,' I reminded him.

'We will see what is given us,' he said gently. 'Watch the flame and tell us what you hear or what you see.'

The candle flame bobbed in a little draught; its brightness filled my mind. It was like the summer sunshine of Spain, and I thought I heard my mother calling me, her voice happy and filled with confidence that nothing would ever go wrong. Then abruptly I heard a tremendous banging that made me gasp and leap to my feet, jolted out of my dream with my heart thudding in fear of arrest.

John Dee was white-faced. We were discovered and ruined. Lord Robert had his sword from his belt and a knife from his boot.

'Open up!' came the shout from the barred door and there was a great blow against the wood which made it rock inwards. I was certain that it was the Inquisition. I crossed the room to Lord Robert. 'Please, my lord,' I said rapidly. 'Don't let them burn me. Run me through, before they take me, and save my son.'

In one fluid movement he was up on the window seat, pulled me up beside him and kicked out the windowpane. 'Jump out,' he advised me. 'And run if you can. I'll hold them for a moment.' There was another terrible blow on the door. He nodded at John Dee. 'Open up,' he said.

John Dee flung open the door and Lady Amy Dudley fell into the room. 'You!' she exclaimed as soon as she saw me, half out of the window. 'As I thought! Whore!'

A servant behind her raised a mace in a half-apologetic gesture. The Philipses' elegant linenfold door panels were splintered beyond repair. Robert slammed his sword back into the scabbard and gestured to

John Dee. 'Please, John, do shut what is left of the door,' he said wearily.

'What are you doing here?' Amy demanded, her eyes taking in the table, the candles, the holy symbols. 'What foul lechery?'

'Nothing,' Robert said wearily.

'What is she doing here with you? And him?'

He stepped forward and took her hands. 'My lady, this is my friend and this my loyal servant. We were praying together for my prosperity.'

She broke from his grasp and struck at him, her hands clenched into fists, pounding against his chest. 'She is a whore and he is a dealer in black arts!' she cried. 'And you are a false deceiver who has broken my heart too many times to count!'

Robert caught her hands. 'She is a good servant of mine and a respectable married woman,' he said quietly. 'And Dr Dee is chaplain to one of the most important churchmen in the land. Madam, I beg you to compose yourself.'

'I hate you!' she suddenly screamed. With a wail she tore herself from his grip and threw herself face down on the bed. She was screaming with grief, quite beside herself. John Dee and my lord exchanged an aghast look. There was a little tearing noise and I realised she had bitten the counterpane and was ripping it with her teeth.

'Oh, for the sake of God!' Robert took her shoulders and pulled her up from the bed. At once she went for his face with her nails. Robert grabbed her hands and bore her down till she fell on the floor, kneeling at his feet, her wrists in his grip.

'I know you!' she swore up at him. 'If it is not her, then it is another. There is nothing about you but pride and lust.'

His face, suffused with temper, slowly calmed, but he kept a tight hold of her hands. 'I am a sinner indeed,' he said. 'But thank God, I at least am not crazed.'

Her mouth trembled and then she let out a wail, looking up into his flinty face, the tears pouring from her eyes, her mouth drooling sobs. 'I am not crazed. I am ill, Robert,' she said despairingly. 'I am sick of grief.'

He met my eyes over her head. 'Fetch Mrs Oddingsell,' he said briefly. 'She knows what to do.'

I nodded and went from the room. Half the household was busy on the landing outside the chamber. 'Go to your work!' I said abruptly, and then I ran down the long gallery to find Mrs Oddingsell seated before a mean fire at the cold end of the chamber.

'Her ladyship is crying, and his lordship sent for you,' I said baldly.

She got to her feet at once, without surprise, and went quickly down the room. I half ran beside her. 'Has this happened before?' I asked.

She nodded.

'Is she ill?'

'Easily distressed by him.'

I took that in, made allowances for a servant's loyal lies. 'Was she always like this?'

'When they were young and in love it passed for passion. But she was only at peace when he was in the Tower—except for when the princess was imprisoned too.'

'What?'

'She was ill with jealousy, then.'

'They were prisoners!' I exclaimed.

Mrs Oddingsell nodded. 'In her mind they were lovers. And now, he is free to come and go. And she knows that he is seeing the princess. He will break her heart. It is no figure of speech. She will die of this.'

We were at Dr Dee's door. I put a hand on her arm. 'Are you her nurse?' I asked.

'More like her keeper,' she said and quietly went in.

Lady Amy Dudley kept to her room for the next three days while Robert and John Dee rode out hunting, read in the library, gambled small sums of money, and talked, at dinner and at play, of what the future of the country might be, what shape the nobility and the parliament should take, how far the borders might extend overseas.

On the evening of the third day of their visit, my lord had a message from Dover, and left me and John Dee alone in the library. John Dee had drawn a map of the world after the model of his friend Gerardus Mercator and tried to explain to me that I must think of the world as round, and think of this map as the skin of the world peeled off, like the skin peeled off an orange and laid flat.

He struggled to make me see it until he laughed and said that I must be content to see angels; I clearly could not see longitude. He took up his maps and went with them to his room as Lord Robert came into the library with a piece of paper in his hand.

'At last I have news of your husband. He is safe,' he said.

I jumped to my feet and found I was trembling. 'My lord?'

'He was taken by the French who suspected him as a spy, but they are holding him with other English soldiers,' he told me. 'I dare say I can arrange for him to be exchanged for other prisoners of war, or ransomed, or something.'

'He is safe?' I asked. 'Not sick, nor injured?'

'See for yourself,' he said, handing over the three scrawled lines on the sheet of paper.

'Thank you,' I said. I read and reread the letter. It said nothing more than he had already told me, but somehow in words of black ink on travel-stained paper it seemed more true. 'Thank God.'

'Thank God indeed,' said my lord with a smile.

Impulsively I took his hand. 'And thank you, my lord,' I said fervently. 'You are kind to take the trouble for me. I know it. I am grateful.'

Gently he drew me in, put a warm hand on my waist. 'Sweetheart, you know I would do anything in my power to make you happy.'

I hesitated. His hand was light, I could feel the heat of his palm through the fabric of my gown. I felt myself lean towards him. He stole a quick glance up and down the empty gallery and then his mouth came down towards mine. He hesitated, he was such a practised seducer that he knew the power of delay to increase desire. Then he bent a little lower and he kissed me, tenderly and then with increasing passion until my arms were round his neck and he had me pressed against a wall, my head tipped back, my eyes closed, quite given up to the delicious sensation of his touch.

'Lord Robert,' I whispered.

'I'm for bed. Come with me, sweetheart mine.'

I did not hesitate. 'I am sorry, my lord, no.'

'You are sorry, my lord, no?' he repeated comically. 'What d'you mean, Mistress Boy?'

'I shall not lie with you,' I said steadily.

'Why not? Don't tell me it is not your desire, for I shan't believe you. I can taste it on your lips. You want me as much as I want you. And that is a good deal, tonight.'

'It is my desire,' I admitted. 'And if I were not a married woman I would be glad to be your lover.'

'Oh, Hannah, a husband such a long way away and safely in prison need not concern you. A word from you to me, and he can stay there until there is a general amnesty. Come to bed with me, now.'

Steadfastly I shook my head. 'No, my lord. It is not that he might catch me,' I said. 'It is that I do not want to betray him.'

'You betray him in your heart,' Robert said cheerfully. 'You lean back against my arm, you tip your head, you open your mouth for my kisses. He is betrayed already, Mistress Boy. The rest is just enacting the desire.'

I smiled at his persuasive, self-serving logic. 'Perhaps, but it is wrong. My lord, I tell you true, I have adored you since the day I first saw you. But I love Daniel with a true and honourable love, and I want to be a good wife to him, and faithful to him.'

'But you would so enjoy a night with me, you know,' he said, partly from vanity, partly as a final attempt.

'I am very sure of it,' I said, as shameless as he. 'And if I cared for nothing but pleasure then I would be begging you for tonight and every night after. But I have fallen in love, my lord, and no one but my lover will do for me.'

He stepped back and swept me a beautiful courtly bow, as low as if for a queen. 'Mistress Boy, you always exceed my expectations. I knew you would make a wonderful woman but I never expected you would make a surprising and honourable woman. I hope your husband is worthy of you, I do indeed. And if he is not . . .'

I laughed. 'If he breaks my heart a second time then I will come back to you as heartless as you are yourself, my lord,' I said.

'Oh well, it is agreed,' he said with a laugh, and went to his bed alone.

SPRING 1558

WITHIN A FEW DAYS his lordship and John Dee returned to court. I waited for news, but heard nothing except common gossip. The baby, which was due in March, was late, and by April people were starting to say that the queen had made a mistake again, and there was no child. I could not imagine how she would be able to bear it if she were to be once more disappointed. I knew her for a courageous woman, but to come out of confinement for a second time and tell the world that there was no baby—I could not see how any woman could bear the humiliation of it, least of all the Queen of England. Then I received word from my lord.

Mistress Boy,
The queen is to come out of her confinement soon, and I need you here to advise me. You may bring me my blue velvet missal which I left in the chapel at my seat and come at once. Robt.

I went to the chapel, with Danny walking before me. I had to stoop low so that he could hold my fingers with both his hands, and walk with my support. My back ached by the time we got to the chapel and I sat in Robert's chair and let Danny make his way down one of the pews, steadying himself on the seat. I would never have believed that I would have stooped till my back ached for the amusement of a small boy, and yet when I had the missal and we walked back to our chamber I bent low again to let Danny hold on to my fingers. I prayed in silence that perhaps, even now, the queen might have a son and might know joy like this, such a strange, unexpected joy—the happiness of caring for a child whose whole life was in my hands.

He was not an ordinary child. Even I, who knew so little about children, could tell that. Like a house with shuttered windows the child had shielded himself, and had shut himself away from the life of the world outside. I felt that I was standing outside, calling for a response that might never come. But I was determined to go on calling to him.

The court was at Richmond, and the moment I arrived I knew that something had happened. There was an air of suppressed excitement in the stables. Everyone was gossiping in corners and there was no one to take our horses, not even the Dudley grooms.

I threw the reins to the nearest young man, and with Danny on my hip strode up the path to the garden entrance of the palace, to the inner hall, looking for someone I could trust. At the back of the hall, Will Somers was sitting all alone. I went up to him and touched him on the shoulder.

His dull gaze went first to Danny and then to me. He did not recognise me. 'Mistress, I can do nothing for you,' he said shortly, and turned his head away. 'I have no spirits for jests today.'

'Will, it's me.'

He looked at me more closely. 'Hannah? Hannah, the Invisible Fool?'

I nodded at the implied reproach. 'Will, what has happened?'

He did not remark on my clothes, on my child, on anything. 'It's the queen,' he said.

'Oh, Will, she's not dead?'

He shook his head. 'Not yet. But it can only be a matter of time.'

'The baby?' I asked with a swift sure painful knowledge.

'It's happened again,' he said. 'There was no baby. Again. And again she is the laughing stock of Europe.'

Without thinking I stretched out my hands to him for comfort and he gripped them tightly. 'Is she ill?' I whispered after a moment.

'Her women say that she will not rise up from the floor,' he said. 'She sits, hunched on the floorboards like a beggar woman. I don't know how it can have happened, Hannah . . . What will happen next?'

'Why? What will happen next?' I repeated, aghast.

He hunched a shoulder and gave me a crooked sad smile. 'Nothing much here,' he said dismissively. 'It's at Hatfield that it will all happen. There is the heir; clearly, we can't make one here. *She'll* have her speech ready, I don't doubt. She'll be all prepared for the day when they tell her that the queen is dead and she is the new queen.'

'You're right.' I shared his bitterness. 'And she has her speech ready. She's going to say: "This is the Lord's doing; it is marvellous in our eyes".'

Will gave a bitter crow of laughter. 'How d'you know that?'

'Oh, Will! She asked me what the queen was going to say at her accession, and when I told her she thought it so good she said she would use it herself.'

'Well, why not?' he asked, suddenly bitter again. 'She will have taken everything else. Queen Mary's own husband, the people's love, the throne, and now the very words out of her sister's mouth.'

I nodded. 'Do you think I can see the queen?'

He smiled. 'She won't recognise you. You've become a beautiful woman, Hannah. Is it just the gown? Was it your dressmaker who transformed you?'

I shook my head. 'Love, I think.'

'For your husband? You found him, did you?'

'I found him, and then I lost him almost at once, Will, because I was a fool, filled with pride and jealousy. But I have his son, and he has taught me to love without thinking of myself. I love him more than I thought possible. More than I knew I could love anyone. This is my son, Danny. And if we ever see his father again I will be able to tell him that I am a woman grown at last, and ready for love.'

Will smiled at Danny, who shyly dipped his head and then looked into Will's kindly creased face and smiled back.

'Can you hold him for me, while I ask if I may see the queen?'

Will held out his arms and Danny went to him with the easy trust that Will inspired in everyone. I went up the sweep of stairs to the queen's presence chamber and then to the closed door of her private rooms. My name got me as far as her privy chamber, and then I saw Jane Dormer standing at the closed door.

'Jane, it is me,' I said. 'Hannah.'

It was a sign of the depth of the queen's grief and Jane's despair that she did not remark on my unexpected return, nor on my new costume.

'Perhaps she'll speak to you,' she said quietly, alert for eavesdroppers. 'Be careful what you say. Don't mention the king, nor the baby.'

Jane opened the door for me with one hand and thrust me into the room with the other. I stumbled in and dropped to a curtsy and heard the door close softly behind me.

The room was in deep shade, still shuttered for confinement. I looked around. The queen was not seated on any of the looming chairs nor crumpled in the great bed. She was not on her knees before her prie-dieu. I could not see her anywhere.

Then I heard a little noise, a tiny sound, like a child catching her breath after a bout of sobbing.

'Mary,' I whispered. 'Where are you?'

As my eyes grew accustomed to the darkness I finally made her out. She was lying on the floor amid the rushes, face turned towards the skirting board, hunched like a starving woman will hunch over her empty belly. I crawled on my hands and knees across the floor towards her, and gently touched her shoulders.

She did not respond. I don't think she even knew I was there. She was locked in a grief so deep and so impenetrable that I thought she would be trapped in that inner darkness for the rest of her life.

I stroked her shoulder as one might stroke a dying animal. Since words could do nothing, I thought a gentle touch might help, but I did not know if she could even feel that. Then I lifted her shoulders gently from the floor, put her head in my lap and took her hood from her poor weary head and wiped the tears as they poured from her closed eyelids down her tired, lined face. I sat with her in silence until her deeper breathing told me that she had fallen asleep. Even in her sleep the tears still welled up from her closed eyelids and ran down her wet cheeks.

When I came out of the queen's rooms, Lord Robert was there.

'You,' I said, without much pleasure.

'Aye, me,' he said. 'And no need to look so sour. I am not to blame.'

'You're a man,' I observed. 'And men are mostly to blame for the sorrow that women suffer.'

He gave a short laugh. 'I am guilty of being a man, I admit it. You can come and dine in my rooms. Your boy is there too. Will has him.'

I went with him, his arm round my waist.

'Is she ill?' he asked, his mouth to my ear.

'Brokenhearted,' I said shortly.

He nodded at that and swept me into his rooms. As we went in Danny looked up from Will's lap and made a little crow, the greatest noise he ever made, and stretched up for me. I took him in my arms.

'Thank you,' I said to Will.

'He was a comfort to me,' he said frankly.

'You can stay, Will,' Robert said. 'Hannah is going to dine with me.'

'I have no appetite,' Will said. 'I have seen so much sorrow in this country that my belly is full of it. I am sick of sorrow. I wish I could have a little joy for seasoning.'

'Times will change,' Robert said encouragingly. 'Changing already.'

'You'd be ready for new times, for one,' Will said, his spirit rising up. 'Since in the last reign you were one of the greatest lords and in this one you were a traitor waiting for the axe. I imagine change would be very welcome to you. What d'you hope from the next, my lord? What has the next queen promised you?'

'Nothing but good for the country,' Robert said easily with a pleasant smile. 'Come and dine with us, Will. You're among friends.'

'All right,' he said, seating himself at the table. I hitched Danny onto the chair beside me so that he could eat from my bowl and I took a glass of wine that Lord Robert poured for me.

'Here's to us,' Robert said, raising his glass in an ironic toast. 'A heart-broken queen, an absent king, a lost baby, a queen in waiting and two fools and a reformed traitor. Here's health.'

'Three fools together,' Will said, raising his glass.

SUMMER 1558

ALMOST BY DEFAULT, I found myself back in the queen's service. She was so anxious and suspicious of everyone around her that she would be served only by people who had been with her from the earliest days. She hardly seemed to notice that I had been away from her for more than two years, and was now dressed like a woman. She liked to hear me read to her in Spanish, and she liked me to sit by her bed while she slept. The deep sadness that had invaded her with the failure of her second pregnancy meant that she had no curiosity about me. I told her that my father had died, that I had married my betrothed, and that we had a child. She was interested only that my husband and I were separated: he in France—safe, I hoped—while I was in England.

'How can you bear not to be with your husband?' she asked suddenly, after three long hours of silence one grey afternoon.

'I miss him,' I said, startled at her suddenly speaking to me. 'But I hope to find him again. I will go to France as soon as it is possible. I will go and look for him. Or I hope he will come to me.'

She turned towards the window and looked out at the river. 'I keep a fleet of ships ready for the king to come to me,' she said. 'And horses and lodgings all along the road from Dover to London. They are all waiting for him. A small army of men does nothing but wait for him. I, the Queen of England, his own wife, waits for him. Why does he not come?'

There was no answer that I could give her. There was no answer that anyone could give her. When she asked the Spanish ambassador, he bowed low and murmured that the king had to be with his army. She must understand the need of that—the French were still threatening his lands. It satisfied her for a day, but the next day, when she looked for him, the Spanish ambassador had gone.

'Where is he?' the queen asked. I was holding her hood, waiting for her maid to finish arranging her hair. Her beautiful chestnut hair had gone grey and thin now. When it was brushed out it looked sparse and dry. The lines on her face and the weariness in her eyes made her seem far older than her forty-two years.

'Where is who, Your Grace?' I asked.

'The Spanish ambassador, Count Feria?'

I handed her hood to her maid, then I gritted my teeth and told her the truth. 'I believe he has gone to see the princess.'

The queen turned round to look at me, her eyes shocked. 'Why? Hannah? Why would he do that?'

I shook my head. 'How would I know, Your Grace? Does he not go to present his compliments to the princess now and then?'

'No. He does not. For most of his time in England she has been under house arrest, a suspected traitor, and he himself urged me to execute her. Why would he go to pay his compliments now?'

None of us answered. She took the hood from the waiting woman's hands and put it on, meeting her own honest eyes in the mirror. 'The king will have ordered him to go.'

She was silent for a moment, thinking what she should do. I kept my gaze down. I could not bear to look up and see her, facing the knowledge that her own husband was sending messages to her heir, to her rival, to his mistress.

When she turned back to us her expression was calm. 'Hannah, a word with you, please,' she said, extending her hand.

I went to her side and she took my arm and leaned on me slightly as we walked from the room to her presence chamber. 'I want you to go to Elizabeth,' she said quietly, as they opened the doors. There was hardly anyone outside waiting to see her. They were all at Hatfield. 'Just go as if for a visit. Tell her you have recently come back from Calais and wanted to see how she did. Can you do that?'

'I would have to take my son,' I stipulated.

'Take him,' she nodded. 'And see if you can find out from Elizabeth herself, or from her ladies, what Count Feria wanted with her. It may be that the king is pressing her to marry the Prince of Savoy. She has sworn to me that she will not have him but Elizabeth has no principles, only appearances. If the king promised to support her claim to be my heir, she might think it worth her while to marry his cousin. I have to know.'

'When d'you want me to go?' I asked unwillingly.

'At first light tomorrow,' she said. 'And don't write to me; I am surrounded by spies. I will wait for you to tell me what she is planning when you come back to me.'

It was a merry ride to Hatfield for Danny and me. He rode the horse astride before me until he grew too tired, and then I strapped him to my back and he slept, rocked by the jolting.

The old palace at Hatfield had been the royal nursery for generations, chosen for its clean air and proximity to London. It was an old building, small-windowed and dark-beamed, and the escort of two men led the way to the front door so that Danny and I might dismount and go inside while they took the horses away.

There was no one in the hall to greet us but a boy bringing in logs for the fire, which was kept going, even in midsummer. 'They're all in the garden,' he said. 'Acting a play.'

His gesture directed me to a door at the rear of the hall, and with Danny in my arms I opened it, followed the stone corridor to another door and then stepped out into the sunshine.

What play-acting there had been was clearly over, and what was left was a romp. Veils of cloth of gold and silver and overturned chairs were scattered around the orchard, and Elizabeth's ladies were running in all directions from a man in the centre of the circle with a dark scarf over his face to blindfold him. As I watched he caught a flying skirt and drew a girl to him, but she wriggled free and ran away laughing. They gathered round him and with much giggling and cooing they turned him round and round until he was dizzy and then they retreated. Again he dashed and lunged, while they ran this way and that, giggling with that heady mixture of girlish playfulness and female arousal. Among them, her red hair flying loose, her face flushed and laughing, was the princess. She was not the Elizabeth I had seen white-faced with terror. She was not the princess I had seen bloated on her bed, sick to her very bones with fear. She was a princess coming into the midsummer of her life, coming into her womanhood, coming to the throne. She was a fairy-tale princess, beautiful, powerful, wilful, infallible.

As I watched she tapped the blindfolded man on the shoulder and made to run back again. This time he was too quick for her. As his hand flashed out, she sprang back just too slowly; he snatched her at the waist and though she struggled he held her close.

'I have caught you!' he called out. 'Who is it?'

'You have to guess! You have to guess!' the ladies cried.

He ran his hand over her forehead, her hair, her nose, her lips. 'A beauty,' he said certainly.

Impertinently, he let his hand stray down over her chin, down her neck, he took her throat in his hand. I saw the colour flame into Elizabeth's cheeks and I realised she was on fire with desire at his touch. She did not step back from him or move to check him. She was ready to let him finger her all over, watched by all her court.

He held her firmly, and there was a little whisper as he gripped her with one hand at the waist, and with the other traced the border of the neck of her gown, his fingertips brushing the tops of her breasts. Slowly, tantalisingly, he slid his hand down the front of her gown over the embroidered stomacher, past the girdle at her waist, over the thick skirt of her gown at the front, and then round the back to take hold of her buttocks, as if she were his own woman.

Elizabeth gave a little soft moan and twisted from his grip, almost falling back among her ladies. 'Who was it? Who was it?' they chanted, relieved that she had freed herself from his embrace.

'I give up,' he said. 'I cannot play some foolish game. I have touched the very curves of heaven.'

He pulled the blindfold from his eyes and I saw his face. His eyes met Elizabeth's. He knew exactly who it had been in his arms. He had known from the moment he had caught her, as he had intended to do, as she had intended him to do. He had caressed her in front of all the court, caressed her as an accepted lover, and she had let him stroke her as if she were a whore. She smiled at him, her knowing, desirous smile, and he smiled back.

Of course, the man was my lord Robert Dudley.

'**A**nd what are you doing here, child?' he asked me before dinner, walking on the terrace.

'Queen Mary sent me to pay her compliments to Elizabeth.'

'Oho, my little spy, are you at work again?'

'Yes, and most unwillingly.'

'And what does the queen want to know?'

'She wants to know what Count Feria was doing here,' I said simply. 'Is he here?'

'Left yesterday.'

'What did he want?'

'He brought a message from the king. Queen Mary's own beloved husband. A faithless dog, isn't he, the randy old Spaniard?'

'Why d'you say that?'

'Mistress Boy, I have a wife who does me no service, and shows me no kindness, but not even I would court her own sister under her nose and shame her while she was still living.'

'He is courting Elizabeth?'

'The Pope has been approached to give permission for their marriage,' he said flatly. 'If the queen lives then it's my guess that Philip will apply for an annulment of their marriage and marry Elizabeth. If the queen dies, then Elizabeth is heir to the throne and an even richer plum for the picking. He will snap her up within the year.'

I looked at him, my face quite blank with horror. 'This cannot be,' I said, appalled. 'It's a betrayal. It's the worst thing he could do to her.'

'It's an unexpected move,' he said. 'Disagreeable for a loving wife.'

'The queen would die of grief and shame. To be put aside, as her mother was put aside? And for Anne Boleyn's daughter?'

He nodded. 'As I said, a faithless Spanish dog.'

'And Elizabeth?'

He glanced over my shoulder. 'You can ask her yourself.'

I slid into a curtsy, and then came up. Elizabeth's black eyes snapped at me. She did not like to see me with Robert Dudley.

'Princess.'

'I heard you were back. My lord said that you had become a woman. I did not expect to see you quite so . . .'

I waited.

'Fat,' she said.

Instead of being insulted, as she intended, I giggled out loud at the childish jealous rudeness of her.

At once her eyes danced too. Elizabeth never sulked.

'Whereas you, Princess, are more beautiful than ever,' I said smoothly.

'I hope so. And what were you talking about with your heads so close together?'

'About you,' I said simply. 'The queen sent me to find out how you did. And I was glad to come and see you.'

'I warned you not to leave it too late,' she said, her gesture taking in the waiting women, the courtiers from London.

'I see your ladyship keeps a merry court,' I said evenly. 'As you should. And I cannot join you, even if you would condescend to have me. I have to serve your sister. She does not have a merry court; she has few friends. I would not leave her now.'

'Then you must be the only person in England who has not deserted her,' she said cheerfully. 'I took on her cook last week. Does she get anything to eat at all?'

'She manages,' I said drily. 'And even the Spanish ambassador, Count Feria, her trusted councillor, was missing from court when I left.'

She shot a quick look at Robert Dudley and I saw him nod permission for her to speak.

'I refused his request,' she said gently. 'I have no plans to marry anyone. You can assure the queen of that, for it is true.'

I gave her a little curtsy. 'I am glad not to have to take her any news that would make her yet more unhappy.'

The next day we rode back to the queen, and I found her walking by the river, no more than a handful of courtiers behind her, one being faithful Will Somers, who called himself a fool but had never, in my hearing, said a foolish word.

'Your Grace,' I said, and swept her my curtsy.

The queen took in my appearance, the mud on my cloak, the child at my side. 'You have come straight from Hatfield?'

'As you commanded.'

'Can someone take the child?'

Will stepped forward and Danny beamed. I set him down and he gave his quiet little gurgle of pleasure and toddled towards Will.

'I am sorry to bring him to Your Grace. I thought you might like to see him,' I said awkwardly.

She shook her head. 'No, Hannah, I do not ever want to see him.' She gestured for me to walk beside her. 'Did you see Elizabeth?'

'Yes.'

'And what did she say of the ambassador?'

'I spoke to one of her women.' I was anxious not to identify Lord Robert as the favourite at this treacherous alternative court. 'She said that the ambassador had visited to pay his compliments.'

'And what else?'

I hesitated. My duty to be honest to the queen and my desire not to hurt her seemed to be in utter conflict. I could not bring myself to tell her that her own husband was proposing marriage to her own sister.

'He was pressing the suit of the Duke of Savoy,' I said. 'Elizabeth herself assured me that she would not marry him.'

'The Duke of Savoy?' she asked.

I nodded.

The queen reached out her hand and I took it and waited, not knowing what she would say to me. 'Hannah, you have been my friend for many years, and a true friend, I think.'

'Yes, Your Grace.'

She lowered her voice to a whisper. 'Hannah, answer me a question and then I will never think of this again. But answer me truly.'

I gulped, wondering what terror was opening up beneath my feet. 'I will, Your Grace.' Inwardly I promised myself that if the question endangered me, or Danny, or my lord, I would allow myself to lie.

'Was there any suggestion that the king was pressing his own suit?' she whispered, so low that I could hardly hear her. 'Even though he is my husband, even though he is forsworn before God, the Pope, and our two kingdoms? Please tell me, Hannah. I know that it is the question of a madwoman. I know that I am his wife and he could not be doing this. But I have become filled with the thought that he is courting her, not as a flirtation, but for his wife. I have to know. I am tortured by this fear.'

I bit my lip, and she needed nothing more. With the quick apprehension of a woman seeing her worst fear, she knew it at once.

'Dear God, it *is* so,' she said slowly. 'I thought that my suspicion of him was part of my illness, but it is not. I can see it on your face. He is courting my sister for marriage. My own sister? And my own husband?'

I clasped her cold hand between my own. 'Your Grace—'

'Dearest God, this is the very worst thing that could ever have happened to me,' she said quietly. 'I saw my mother pushed from her throne and shamed by a younger woman who took the king from her and laughed as she did it. And now this woman's bastard daughter does just the same thing to me.' She broke off and looked at me. 'No wonder I couldn't believe it. It is the thing I have feared all my life. Ending up like my own mother, neglected, abandoned, with a Boleyn whore in triumph on the throne.'

I gave her hand a little tug. 'Your Grace, don't give way. Not here. Not here before all these people.'

I was thinking of her, and I was thinking of Elizabeth's court who would laugh till they cried if they heard that the queen had broken down because she had heard at last what all of Europe had known for months—that her husband had betrayed her.

She shook from head to toe with the effort, but she drew herself up, she blinked back the tears. 'You are right,' she said. 'I will not be shamed. I will say nothing more. I will think nothing more. Walk with me, Hannah.'

I glanced back at Danny. Will was seated on the ground with the boy astride his knees, showing him how he could wiggle his ears. Danny's chuckle was delighted. I took the queen's arm and matched my stride to her slow pace. The court fell in behind us, yawning.

'You know,' the queen whispered to me, 'you know, Hannah, I loved him from the moment I first saw his portrait. D'you remember?'

'Yes,' I said, remembering my warning that he would break her heart.

'I adored him when I met him. D'you remember our wedding day, when he looked so handsome and we were so happy?'

I nodded again.

'I worshipped him when he took me to bed. He gave me the only joy I had known in my life. Nobody will ever know how much I have loved him. And now he is planning to marry my worst enemy when I am dead. He is looking forward to my death and his life after it.'

She stood quietly for a few moments as her court halted aimlessly behind her, looking from her to me and wondering what fresh bad news I had brought. Then I saw her stiffen, and her hand went to her eyes, as if she had a sudden pain. 'Unless he does not wait for my death,' she said quietly.

A quick glance at my white face told her the rest of the story. She shook her head. 'No, never,' she whispered. 'Not this. He would never divorce me? Not as my father did to my mother? With no grounds except lust for another woman?'

I said nothing.

She did not cry. She was Queen Mary who had been Princess Mary, who had learned as a little girl to keep her head up and her tears back. She just nodded, as if she had taken a hard knock to the head.

AUTUMN 1558

IN SEPTEMBER WE MOVED to Hampton Court in the hopes that the fresh air would clear the queen's breathing, which was hoarse and sore. The doctors offered her a mixture of oils and drinks, but nothing seemed to do her any good. She was reluctant to see them, and often refused to take her medicine. I thought she was remembering how her little brother had been all but poisoned by the physicians who tried one thing and then another, but then I realised that she could not be troubled with physic; she no longer cared for anything, not even her health.

I rode to Hampton Court with Danny in a pillion saddle behind me for the first time. He was old enough and strong enough to ride astride and to hold on tightly to my waist for the short journey. He was still mute, but he was as peaceful and as smiling as he had always been. I could tell by the tight grip on my waist that he was excited at the journey and at riding properly for the first time. The horse was steady and we ambled along beside the queen's litter down the damp dirty lanes between the fields where they were trying to harvest the wet rye crop.

Danny looked around him, never missing a moment of this, his first proper ride. He waved at the people in the field; he waved at the villagers who stood at their doorways to watch as we went by. I thought it spoke volumes for the state of the country that a woman would not wave in reply to a little boy, since he was riding in the queen's train. The country had turned against Mary and would not forgive her.

The queen rode with the curtains of the litter drawn, in rocking darkness, and when we got to Hampton Court she went straight to her rooms and had the shutters closed so that she was plunged into dusk.

Danny and I rode into the stable yard, and a groom lifted me down from the saddle. I turned and reached up for Danny. For a moment I thought he would cling and insist on staying on horseback.

'Do you want to pat the horse?' I tempted him.

His face lit up at once and he reached out his little arms for me and came tumbling down. I held him to the horse's neck and let him pat the warm, sweet-smelling skin. The horse, a handsome big-boned bay, turned its head to look at him. Danny, very little, and horse, very big, stared quite transfixed by each other, and then Danny gave a deep sigh of pleasure and said: 'Good.'

It was so natural and easy that for a moment I did not realise he had spoken. When I did realise, I hardly dared to take a breath in case I prevented him speaking again.

'He *was* a good horse, wasn't he?' I said with affected nonchalance. 'Shall we ride him again tomorrow?'

Danny looked from the horse to me. 'Yes,' he said decidedly.

I held him close to me and kissed his silky head. 'We'll do that then,' I said gently. 'And we'll let him go to bed now.'

My legs felt weak as we walked from the stable yard, Danny at my side, his little hand reaching up to hold mine. I could feel myself smiling, though tears were running down my cheeks. Danny would speak, Danny would grow up as a normal child. I had saved him from death in Calais, and I had brought him to life in England. I had justified the trust of his mother, and perhaps one day I would be able to tell his father that I had kept his son safe for love of him, and for love of the child. It seemed wonderful to me that his first word should be: 'good'. Perhaps it was a foreseeing. Perhaps life would be good for my son Danny.

For a little while the queen seemed better, away from the city. She walked by the river with me in the mornings or in the evenings; she could not tolerate the brightness of midday. But Hampton Court was filled with ghosts. It was on these paths and in these gardens where she had walked with Philip when they were newly married. It was here that she had whispered to him that she was with child, and gone into her first confinement, certain of her happiness, confident of having a son. And it was here that she came out from her confinement, childless and ill, and saw Elizabeth growing in beauty and exulting in her triumph, another step closer to the throne.

'I feel no better here at all,' she said to me one day as Jane Dormer and I came in to say good night. She had gone to bed early again, almost doubled up with pain from the ache in her belly and feverishly hot. 'We will go to St James's Palace next week. We will spend Christmas there. The king likes St James's.'

Jane Dormer and I exchanged one silent glance. We did not think that King Philip would come home to his wife for Christmas when he had not come home when she had lost their child, when he had not come home after she wrote to him that she was so sick that she did not see how to bear to live.

As we had feared, it was a depleted court at St James's Palace. My Lord Robert had bigger and better rooms, not because his star was rising but simply because there were fewer men at court. I saw him at dinner on some days, but generally he was at Hatfield, where the princess kept her merry circle about her.

Lord Robert saw me only rarely, but he had not forgotten me. He came looking for me, one day in September. 'I have done you a great favour, I think,' he said with his charming smile. 'Are you still in love with your husband, Mrs Carpenter? Or shall we abandon him in Calais?'

'You have news of him?' I asked. I put my hand down and felt Danny's hand creep into my own.

'I might have,' he said provocatively. 'But you have not answered my question. Do you want him home, or shall we forget all about him?'

'I cannot jest about this, and especially not before his son,' I said. 'I want him home, my lord. Please tell me, do you have news of him?'

'His name is on this list.' He flicked the paper at me. 'Soldiers to be ransomed, townspeople who are to be returned to England. The whole of the English Pale outside Calais is to come home. If the queen can find some money in the treasury we can get them all back.'

I could feel my heart thudding. 'There is no money in the treasury,' I said. 'The country is all but ruined.'

He shrugged. 'There is money to keep the fleet waiting to escort the king home. There is money for his adventures abroad. Mention it to her as she dresses for dinner tonight, and I will speak with her after dinner.'

I waited until the queen had dragged herself up from her bed and was seated before her mirror, her maid behind her brushing her hair. Jane Dormer, who was usually such a fierce guardian of the queen's privacy, had taken the fever herself, and was lying down. It was just the queen and I and some unimportant girl from the Norfolk family.

'Your Grace,' I said simply. 'I have had news of my husband.'

She turned her dull gaze on me. 'I had forgotten you are married. Is he alive?'

'Yes,' I said. 'He is among the English men and women hoping to be ransomed out of Calais.'

She was only slightly more interested. 'Who is arranging this?'

'Lord Robert. His men have been held captive too.'

The queen sighed. 'Are they asking very much?'

'I don't know,' I said frankly.

'I will speak with Lord Robert,' she said, as if she were very weary. 'I will do what I can for you and your husband, Hannah.'

I knelt before her. 'Thank you, Your Grace.'

When I looked up I saw that she was exhausted. 'I wish I could bring my husband home so easily,' she said. 'But I don't believe he will ever come home to me again.'

The queen was too ill to transact the business herself—the fever was always worse after dinner and she could barely breathe for coughing— but she scrawled an assent on a bill on the treasury for money and Lord Robert assured me that the business would go through. We met in the stable yard. He was riding to Hatfield and in a hurry to be off.

'Will he come to you here at court?' he asked casually.

I hesitated. I had not thought of the details of our meeting. 'I suppose so,' I said. 'I should leave a message for him at my old shop in Fleet Street.'

I said nothing more, but a deeper worry was starting to dawn on me. What if Daniel's love for me had not grown, like mine, in absence? What if he had decided that I was dead and that he should make a new life elsewhere in Italy or France as he had so often said? Worse than that: what if he thought I had run away with Lord Robert and chosen a life of shame without him? What if he had cast me off?

'Can I get a message to him as he is released?' I asked.

Lord Robert shook his head. 'You will have to trust that he will come and find you,' he said cheerfully. 'Is he the faithful type of man?'

I thought of his years of steady waiting for me, and how he had watched me come to my love of him, and how he had let me go and return to him. 'Yes,' I said shortly.

Lord Robert sprang up into the saddle. 'If you see John Dee, would you tell him that Princess Elizabeth wants that map of his?' he said.

'Why would she want a map?' I asked, immediately suspicious.

Lord Robert winked at me. He leaned from his horse and spoke very low. 'If the queen dies without naming Elizabeth as her heir then we may have a battle on our hands.'

His horse shifted and I stepped back quickly. 'Oh, not again,' I said.

'No fight with the people of England,' he assured me. 'They want the Protestant princess. But with the Spanish king. D'you think he'd let such a prize slip away if he thought he could come claim it for himself?'

'You are arming and planning for war *again*?' I asked.

'Why else would I want my soldiers back?' he demanded. 'Thank you for your help with that, Hannah.'

I choked on my shock. 'My lord!'

He patted the horse's neck and tightened the rein. 'It's always a coil,' he said simply. 'And you are always in it, Hannah. You cannot live with a queen and not be enmeshed in a dozen plots. You live in a snake pit and I tell you frankly, you have not the aptitude for it. Now go to her. I hear she is worse.'

'Not at all,' I said stoutly. 'You can tell the princess that the queen has rallied and is better today.'

He nodded. He did not believe me at all. 'Well, God bless her anyway,' he said kindly. 'For whether she lives or dies she has lost Calais, she has lost her babies, lost her husband, lost the throne and lost everything.'

Lord Robert was gone for more than a week and so I could have no news of the release of the English captives. I went to our old print shop and pinned a note on the door. The times were so bad and rents so poor in London that still no one had taken the shop, and many of my father's books and papers would still be stacked, untouched, in the cellar. I thought that if Daniel did not come to me, and if the queen did not recover, then I might set up as a bookseller once again and hope for better times.

When I got back to court there was a scurry around the queen's apartments. She had collapsed while dressing for dinner and been put to bed. The doctors had been called and were bleeding her. Quietly, I handed Danny to Will Somers, who was in the privy chamber, and I went inside the guarded doors to the queen's bedchamber.

Jane Dormer, white as a sheet and visibly ill herself, was at the head of the bed, holding the queen's hand as the physicians were picking fat leeches off her legs and dropping them back into their glass jar. The queen's thin legs were bruised where their vile mouths had been fixed on her. The maid twitched down the sheet. The queen's eyes were closed in shame at being so exposed, her head turned away. The doctors bowed and got themselves out of the room.

'Go to bed, Jane,' the queen said weakly. 'You are as sick as I am.'

'Not until I have seen Your Grace take some soup.'

The queen shook her head and waved her hand to the door. Jane curtsied and went out, leaving the queen and me alone.

'Is that you, Hannah?' she asked without opening her eyes.

'Yes, Your Grace.'

'Will you write a letter for me, in Spanish? And send it to the king without showing it to anyone?'

'Yes, Your Grace.'

I took some paper and a pen from the table, drew up a little stool and sat beside her bed. She dictated to me in English and I translated it into Spanish as I wrote. The sentences were long and fluent. I knew that she had been waiting a long time to send him this letter. In all the nights when she had wept for him, she had composed this letter to be sent from her deathbed. She wrote him a letter like the one her mother wrote to her father from her deathbed: a letter of love and constancy to a man who had offered nothing but heartache.

Dearest Husband,

Since it has pleased you to stay far from me in my illness and my sorrow, I write to you these words which I wish I might have said to your beloved face.

You could not have had and never will have a more loving and faithful wife. The sight of you gladdened my heart every day that we were together. My only regret is that we spent so much time apart.

It seems very hard to me that I should face death as I have faced life: alone and without the one I love. I pray that you may never know the loneliness that has walked step by step with me every day of my life.

This may be my last chance to bid you farewell and to send you my love. May we meet in heaven, though we could not be together on earth, prays

Your wife

Mary R.

The tears were running down my cheeks by the time I had written this to her dictation, but she was calm.

'You will get better, Your Grace,' I assured her.

'No,' she said simply. There was not a trace of self-pity in her tone. It was as if she were weary of the world. 'No. I don't think so.'

WINTER 1558

LORD ROBERT CAME TO COURT with the queen's council to press her to sign her will and name her heir. Every man in the council had been at Hatfield the previous month. All their advice for Queen Mary had been dictated by the queen in waiting.

'She is too sick to see anyone,' Jane Dormer said truculently.

She and I stood shoulder to shoulder in the doorway to the queen's apartments. Lord Robert winked at me but I did not smile back.

'This is her duty,' said the Lord Chancellor. 'She has to make a will.'

'She made one,' Jane said abruptly. 'Before she went into confinement last time.'

He shook his head and looked embarrassed. 'She named her child as heir, and the king as regent,' he said. 'But there was no child. She has to name the Princess Elizabeth now, and no regent. She has a duty to her country and you should not stand in her way.'

We wavered, and they saw it. 'Stand aside,' said the duke, and Jane and I stood unwillingly back and let them walk in to the queen.

They did not take very long, and when they were gone I went in to see her. She was lying propped up on her pillows, a bowl at her side to catch the black bile that spewed from her mouth when she coughed, a jug of squeezed lemons and sugar to take the taste from her lips, a maid in attendance but no one else. She was as lonely as any beggar coughing out her life on a stranger's doorstep.

'Your Grace, I sent your letter to your husband,' I said quietly. 'Pray God he reads it and comes home to you and you have a merry Christmas with him after all.'

Queen Mary did not even smile at the picture I painted. 'He will not,' she said dully. 'And I would rather not see him ride past me to Hatfield.' She coughed and held a cloth to her mouth. The maid stepped forward and took it from her, offered her the bowl, and then took it away.

'I have another task for you,' she said when she could speak again. 'I want you to go with Jane Dormer to Hatfield.'

I waited.

'Ask Elizabeth to swear on her immortal soul that if she inherits the kingdom she will keep the true faith,' she said, her voice a tiny thread but the conviction behind the words as strong as ever.

I hesitated. 'She will not swear,' I said, knowing Elizabeth.

'Then I will not name her my heir,' she said flatly. 'Mary Stuart in France would claim the throne with French blessing. Elizabeth has the choice. She can fight her way to the throne if she can find enough fools to follow her, or she can come to it with my blessing. But she has to swear to uphold the faith. And she has to mean it.'

'How will I know if she means it?' I asked.

She was too weary to turn her head to me. 'Look at her with your gift, Hannah,' she said. 'This is the last time I will ask you to see for me. Look at her with your gift and tell me what is the best for my England.'

I would have argued, but simple pity for her made me hold my tongue. This was a woman clinging on to life by the thinnest thread.

I bowed and went from the room.

Jane Dormer, still recovering from her own fever and exhausted from nursing the queen, riding in a litter, and I, with Danny astride before me, made our way north to Hatfield and noted sourly the number of fine horses that were going in the same direction as us, from the ailing queen to the thriving heir.

The old palace was ablaze with lights. There was some sort of banquet in progress as we arrived. 'I cannot break bread with her,' Jane said shortly. 'Let us ask to see her, and leave.'

'Of course we can dine,' I said practically. 'You must be starving. I am, and Danny needs to eat. You go and eat in the kitchen if it pleases you. I am going in to dine.'

I could have laughed at her astounded face. I lifted Danny up onto my hip and, braced against his weight, I walked into the dining hall at Hatfield.

Elizabeth had the trappings of queenship already, as if she were an actor practising a part in full costume. She had a gold canopy over a wooden chair so thickly carved and heavy it might almost have been a throne. On her right hand she had the Spanish ambassador, as if to flaunt that connection; on her left hand was seated the most favoured lord at this court, my Lord Robert. Beside him was the right-hand man of the Grand Inquisitor of London, the scourge of Protestantism, Dr John Dee; on the other side of the Spanish ambassador was the princess's cousin, who had once arrested her, now dearly beloved to his kin. Beyond him was a quietly ambitious man, a staunch Protestant: William Cecil. I looked at Elizabeth's table and smiled. Nobody would be able to guess which way this cat might jump, judging by those honoured with seats beside her. She had put Spanish and English, Catholic and Protestant advisers side by side. Who could deduce what was in her mind?

John Dee, looking down the hall, caught my smile and raised his hand to me in greeting. Lord Robert followed the direction of his gaze, saw me, and beckoned me forward. I threaded my way through the court and dropped a curtsy to the princess, who shot me a gleaming smile from her eyes like a jet arrow.

'Ah, it is the girl who was so afraid of being a woman that she first became a fool, and then became a widow,' she said acidly.

'Princess Elizabeth,' I said, curtsying as the words hit home.

'Have you come to see me?'

'Yes, Princess.'

'Have you a message for me from the queen?'

'Yes, Princess.'

There was a little ripple of attention all along the table.

'Is Her Majesty in good health?' The Spanish ambassador, Count Feria, leaned forward, taking the heat from the exchange.

'You would surely know better than I,' I said with a sourness that came easily to me, seeing him at Elizabeth's table. 'Since she writes intimately to only one person, since she loves one man in all the world, and he is your master.'

Elizabeth and my lord exchanged a hidden smile at my rudeness. The count turned his head away.

'You may take a seat with my ladies and see me privately after dinner,' the princess ruled. 'Did you come alone with your son?'

I shook my head. 'Jane Dormer came with me. She is dining alone. She did not want to keep this company.'

'I see you are not so choosy,' Elizabeth taunted me.

I met her bright black gaze without shrinking. 'Dinner is dinner, Princess. And both of us have gone hungry in the past.'

She laughed at that and nodded at them to make a space for me. 'She has become a witty fool,' she said to Lord Robert. 'I am glad of it. I never had much faith in seeings and predictions.'

'Once she told me a pretty vision,' he said, his voice very low, his eyes on me but his smile for her.

'Oh?'

'She told me I would be adored by a queen.'

They both laughed, that low-voiced chuckle of conspiring lovers, and he smiled down the hall at me. I met his gaze with a face like flint.

What is the matter with you?' Elizabeth demanded of me after dinner. We were standing in an alcove in the gallery at Hatfield.

'I don't like Count Feria,' I said bluntly.

'You made that clear enough. Do you really think I will allow you to come into my dinner and insult my guests? You took off a fool's livery; you will have to behave like a lady.'

I smiled. 'Since I carry a message that you want to hear, I think you will listen to it before you have me thrown out of the gates, whether I am a fool or a lady.'

She laughed at my impertinence.

'And I doubt that you like him either,' I said boldly. 'First he was your enemy, now he is your friend. There are many such as him around you now, I should imagine.'

'Most of this court. And you among them.'

I shook my head. 'I have always admired you both.'

'You love her more than you love me,' she insisted jealously.

I laughed aloud at her childishness, and Lord Robert, standing near, turned to look at me with a smile.

'But, Princess, she loves me,' I said, 'and you have never done anything but abuse me and accuse me of being her spy.'

Elizabeth laughed too. 'Yes. But I don't forget that you came to serve me in the Tower. And I don't forget that you brought me a true vision. When you smelt the smoke from the burnings I knew then that I must become queen and bring peace to this country.'

'Well, amen to that,' I said.

'And what is your message?' she asked more soberly.

'Can we talk in your privy chamber? And can I bring Jane Dormer to you?'

'With Lord Robert,' she stipulated. 'And John Dee.'

I bowed my head and followed her as she walked down the gallery to her chamber. The court billowed into bows as she went past as if she were queen already. I smiled, remembering a day when she had limped with her shoe in her hand and no one had offered her an arm. Now they would lay down their cloaks in the mud to keep her feet dry.

We went into her chamber and Elizabeth took a small wooden chair by the fireside. She gestured that I could pull up a stool and I took it to the other side of the fire, put Danny on my knee and leaned back against the wooden panelling. The queen wanted me to advise her if Elizabeth would keep the true faith. I had to listen through the words to the meaning behind them. I had to look through the mask of her smiling face and into her heart.

The door opened and Jane came into the room. She swept Elizabeth a scant curtsy and stood before her. Elizabeth gestured her to sit.

'I will stand, if it please you,' Jane said stiffly.

'You have business with me.' Elizabeth invited her to begin.

'The queen has asked Hannah and me to come to you and put a question to you. The queen requires you to make your answer in very truth. She would want you to swear on your soul that the answer you give is the truth and the whole truth.'

'And what is this question?'

'The queen bid me tell you that she will name you as her heir, her one true heir, and you will be queen on the throne of England without a word of dissent if you will promise her that you will cleave to the true faith,' Jane said quietly.

John Dee drew in a sharp breath, but the princess was absolutely still.

'And if I do not?'

'Then she will name another heir.'

'Mary Stuart?'

'I do not know and I will not speculate,' Jane replied.

The princess nodded. 'Am I to swear on a Bible?' she asked.

'On your soul,' Jane said. 'On your immortal soul before God.'

It was a solemn moment. Elizabeth glanced towards Lord Robert and he took a little step towards her, as if he would protect her.

'And does she swear to name me as heir in return?'

Jane Dormer nodded. 'If you are of the true faith.'

Elizabeth took a deep breath. 'I will swear,' she said.

She rose to her feet. I did not rise as I should have done; I stayed completely still, my eyes fixed on her pale face as if I would read her like a clean page of text, fresh off the press, with the ink still drying.

Elizabeth raised her hand. 'I swear, on my immortal soul, that I shall keep this country in the true faith,' she said. Her hand trembled slightly. She brought it down and clasped her hands together before her, and turned to Jane Dormer.

'Did she ask for anything more?'

'No more,' Jane said, her voice very thin.

'So you can tell her I have done it?'

Jane's eyes slid towards me, and the princess was onto her at once.

'Ah, so that is what you are here for.' She rounded on me. 'My little seer-spy. You are to make a window into my soul and see into my heart and tell the queen what you imagine you saw.'

I said nothing.

'You will tell her that I swore her oath,' she commanded me.

I rose to my feet, Danny's little head lolling sleepily against my shoulder. 'If we may, we shall stay here tonight and return to the queen tomorrow,' I said, avoiding answering. 'We shall leave at dawn,' I said, thinking of the frailty of the queen's health. I knew that she would be hanging on to hear that England was safe within the true faith, that whatever else was lost, she had restored England into grace.

'Then I will bid you good night and God speed now,' Elizabeth said sweetly. She let us get to the door and saw Jane Dormer go through ahead of me, before she said, so quietly that only I, listening for her summons, could have heard it: 'Hannah.'

I turned.

'I know you are her loyal friend as well as mine,' she said gently. 'Do this last service for your mistress and take my word as true, and let her go to her God with some comfort. Give her peace, and give peace to our country.'

I bowed to her and went out.

I thought we would leave Hatfield without another farewell, but when I went for my horse on a frosty cold morning with the sun burning red like an ember on the white horizon, there was Lord Robert looking handsome and smiling, wrapped in a dark red velvet cloak with John Dee at his side.

'The men are to be released from Calais within a week,' Robert said. 'They will be collected by a ship that will bring them into Gravesend.'

I felt my heart beat faster.

'You are blushing like a girl,' Lord Robert said, gently mocking.

'Do you think he will have had my letter, which I sent when I first came home?' I asked.

Lord Robert shrugged. 'He may have done. But you can tell him yourself, soon enough.'

I drew a little closer to him. 'You see, if he did not receive it then he will not know that I escaped out of Calais. He might think I am dead. He might not come to England, he might go to Italy or somewhere.'

'Someone would have looked for you,' he said. 'If you had been killed they would have found your body.'

I shifted awkwardly. Daniel came to me and stretched out his arms. 'Dan'l up!' he commanded.

'Wait a moment,' I said absently. I turned back to Lord Robert. 'If someone told him that I left with you . . .'

'Then he would know that you are alive, and where to find you,' he said logically. Then he checked and slapped his forehead. 'Mistress Boy, you have played me for an idiot all along. You are estranged from him, aren't you? And you fear that he will think you ran away with me? And he won't come for you because he has cast you off? And now you don't want me, but you've lost him, and all you've got is his son . . .' He broke off, struck with sudden doubt. 'He *is* your husband's son, isn't he?'

'Yes,' I said staunchly.

'Is he yours?' he said, some sense warning him that there was a lie hidden away somewhere near.

'Yes,' I said without wavering.

Lord Robert laughed aloud. 'My God, girl, you are a fool indeed. You did not love him till you lost him.'

'Yes,' I admitted through gritted teeth.

'Well, more a woman than a fool,' he said fairly. 'I would say women love men most when they have lost them, or cannot get them. Well-a-day, my pretty fool. You had best get a ship and set sail for your Daniel as soon as you can. Otherwise he will be out of prison and free as a bird flying away, and you will never find him at all.'

'Can I get a ship to Calais?' I asked blankly.

He thought for a moment. 'Not very readily, but you could go over with the ship that is going to fetch my soldiers home. I'll write you a note.' He snapped his fingers to a stableboy and sent him running for a clerk with pen and paper. When the lad came he dictated three lines to give me a free pass on the boat for myself and my son.

I curtsied low to him in genuine gratitude. 'Thank you, my lord,' I said. 'I do thank you very deeply.'

He smiled his heart-turning smile. 'My pleasure, dearest little fool. But the ship sails within a week. Will you be able to leave the queen?'

'She's sinking fast,' I said slowly. 'That's why I was in such a hurry to leave at once. She was holding on for Elizabeth's answer.'

'Well, thank you for that information,' he said.

I bit my lip as I realised that to tell him was to tell Elizabeth, and those planning her campaign.

'No harm done,' he said. 'Half of her doctors are paid by us to let us know how she is.'

John Dee drew closer. 'And could you see into the princess's heart?' he asked gently. 'Could you tell if she was sincere in her oath for keeping the true faith? Do you believe she will be a Catholic queen?'

'I don't know,' I said simply. 'I shall pray for guidance on the way home.'

Robert would have said something, but John Dee put a hand on his arm. 'Hannah will say the right thing to the queen,' he said. 'She knows that it is not one queen or another that matters; it is not one name of God or another. What matters most is to bring peace to this country so that a man or woman in danger of cruelty or persecution can come here and be certain of a fair hearing.' He paused, and I thought of my father and me, coming to this England and hoping for a safe haven.

'What matters is that a man or woman can believe what they wish, and worship how they wish, to a God whom they name as they wish. What matters is that we make a strong country here that can be a force for good in the world, where men and women can question and learn freely. This country's destiny is to be a place where men and women can know that they are free.'

He stopped. Lord Robert was smiling down at me.

'I know what she will do,' Lord Robert said sweetly. 'Because she is my tenderhearted Mistress Boy still. She will say whatever she has to say to comfort the queen in her final hours. God bless her, the poor lady.'

I leaned down and scooped Daniel up into my arms. The grooms brought my horse from the stables and Jane Dormer came from the house and got into the litter without a word to either man.

'Good luck in Calais,' Robert Dudley said, smiling. 'Few women succeed in finding the love of their life. I hope you do, little Mistress Boy.'

It was a cold long ride back to St James's palace, but Danny's little body, wrapped in a thick jerkin of wool, was warm as he rode before me, and now and then I could hear a delighted little carol of song from him.

When we got to the palace the hall was subdued, the few guards playing cards, the firelight flickering, the torches burning low. Will Somers was in the queen's presence chamber, with half a dozen others, mostly paid court officials and physicians. There were no friends or beloved kin waiting to see the queen, praying for her in her illness. She was not England's darling any more, and the chamber rang with emptiness.

Danny spotted Will and sprang towards him.

'You go in,' Will said. 'She has been asking for you.'

'Is she any better?' I asked hopefully.

He shook his head. 'No.'

Cautiously I opened the door to her privy chamber and went in. Two of her women were seated at the fireside, enjoying a gossip when they should have been watching her. They jumped up guiltily as we went past them into the queen's bedchamber.

Mary was curled up in the bed like a little girl, her hair in a cloud around her face. She did not turn her head at the sound of the opening door, so deep was she in her grief.

'Your Grace?' Jane Dormer said, her voice cracking. 'It is I. And Hannah the Fool. We have come back from Princess Elizabeth.'

The queen sighed deeply and turned her head wearily towards us.

'She took the oath,' Jane said. 'She swore she would keep the country in the true faith.'

I stepped to the bedside and took Queen Mary's hand. It fluttered in mine like a dying bird.

'I saw Elizabeth take the oath,' I started. I was about to tell her the kindest lie that I could form. But gently, irresistibly, I told her the truth, as if the Sight was speaking the truth through me. 'Mary, she will not keep it. But she will do better than keep it, I hope you can understand that now. She will become a better queen than she is a woman. She will teach the people of this country that each man and woman must consider his or her own conscience, must find their own way to God. And she will bring this country to peace and prosperity. You did the very best that you could do for the people of this country, and you have a good successor. Elizabeth will never be the woman that you have been, but she will be a good queen to England, I know it.'

She raised her head a little and her eyelids fluttered open. She looked at me with her straight honest gaze once more, and then she closed her eyes and lay still.

I did not stay to watch the rush of servants to Hatfield. I packed my bag and took Danny by the hand and took a boat down the river to Gravesend. I had my lord's letter to show to the ship's captain, and he promised me a berth as soon as they sailed. We waited a day or two, and then Danny and I boarded the little ship and set sail for Calais.

Danny was delighted by the ship, the moving deck beneath his feet, the slap and rush of the waves, the creaking of the sails and the cry of the seagulls. 'Sea!' he exclaimed, over and over again. He took my face in both of his little hands and gazed at me with his enormous dark eyes, desperate to tell me the significance of his delight. 'Sea. Mamma! Sea!'

'What did you say?' I said, taken aback. He had never spoken my name before; I had expected him to call me Hannah. I had never thought he would call me mother.

'Sea,' he repeated obediently, and wriggled to be put down.

Calais was a different place with the walls breached and the sides of the castle smeared with black oil from the siege, the stones darkened with smoke from the fire. The captain's face was grim when we came into the harbour and saw the English ships, which had been fired where they were moored. He tied up with military smartness and slapped down the gangplank. I took Danny in my arms and went with the captain and the armed guard up to the castle under our white pennant of truce.

We were expected; the commander came out civilly enough and spoke to the captain in rapid French. The captain bridled, understanding perhaps one word in three, and then leaned forward and said very loudly and slowly: 'I have come for the English men, as has been agreed, and I expect them forthwith.'

When he had no response, he said it again, pitched a little higher.

'Captain, would you like me to speak for you? I can speak French,' I offered.

He turned to me with relief. 'Can you? That might help.'

I stepped forward a little and said to the commander in French: 'Captain Gatting offers his apologies but he cannot speak French. I can translate for you. I am Madame Carpenter. I have come for my husband, who has been ransomed, and the captain has come for the other men. We have a ship waiting in the harbour.'

He bowed slightly. 'Madame, I am obliged to you. The men are mustered and ready. The civilians are to be released first and then the soldiers will march down to the harbour. Their weapons will not be returned. It is agreed?'

I translated for the captain and he scowled at me. 'We ought to get the weapons back,' he said.

I shrugged. All I could think of was Daniel, waiting somewhere inside the castle for his release. 'We can't.'

'Tell him very well, but tell him that I'm not best pleased,' the captain said sourly.

'Captain Gatting agrees,' I said smoothly in French.

'Please come inside.' The commander led us over the drawbridge and into the inner courtyard. Another thick curtain wall with a portcullis doorway led to the central courtyard where about two hundred men were mustered, the soldiers in one block, the civilians in another. I raked the ranks for Daniel but I could not see him.

'Commandant, I am seeking my husband, Daniel Carpenter, a civilian,' I said. 'I cannot see him, and I am afraid of missing him in the crowd.'

'Daniel Carpenter?' he asked. He turned and snapped an order at the man guarding the civilians.

'Daniel Carpenter!' the man bawled out.

In the middle of one of the ranks a man came forward. 'Who asks for him?' said Daniel, my husband.

I closed my eyes for a moment as the world seemed to shift all around me.

'I am Daniel Carpenter,' Daniel said again, not a quaver in his voice, stepping forward on the very brink of freedom, greeting whatever new danger might threaten him without a moment's hesitation.

The commander beckoned him to come forward and moved to one side so that I could see him. Daniel saw me for the first time and I saw him go very pale. He was older-looking, a little weary, thinner, but nothing worse than winter-pale and winter-thin. He was the same. He was my beloved Daniel with his dark curling hair and his dark eyes and his kissable mouth and that particular smile which was my smile: it only ever shone on me; it was at once desiring, steadfast and amused.

'Daniel,' I whispered. 'My Daniel!'

'Ah, Hannah,' he said quietly. 'You.'

Behind us, the civilians were signing their names and marching out to freedom. I did not hear the shouted orders or the tramp of their feet. All I could see, all I could know, was Daniel.

'I ran away,' I said. 'I am sorry. I was afraid and I did not know what to do. Lord Robert gave me safe passage to England and I went back to Queen Mary. I wrote to you at once. I would not have gone without you if there had been any time to think.'

Gently, he stepped forward and took my hand. 'I have dreamed and dreamed of you,' he said quietly. 'I thought you had left me for Lord Robert when you had the chance.'

'No! Never. I knew at once that I wanted to be with you. I have been trying to get a letter to you. I have been trying to reach you. I swear it, Daniel. I have thought of nothing and no one but you, ever since I left.'

'Have you come back to be my wife?' he asked simply.

I nodded. At this most important moment I lost all my fluency. I could not speak. I could not argue my case, I could not persuade him in any one of my many languages. I could not even whisper. I just nodded emphatically, and Danny on my hip, his arms round my neck, gave a gurgle of laughter and nodded too, copying me.

I had hoped Daniel would be glad and snatch me up into his arms, but he was sombre. 'I will take you back,' he said solemnly. 'And I will not question you, and we will say no more about this time apart. You will never have a word of reproach from me, I swear it, and I will bring this boy up as my son.'

For a moment I did not understand what he meant, and then I gasped. 'Daniel, he is your son! This is your son by your woman. This is her son. We were running from the French horsemen and she fell, she gave him to me as she went down. I am sorry, Daniel. She died at once. And this is your boy; I passed him off as mine. He is my boy now. He is my boy too.'

'He is mine?' he asked wonderingly. He looked at the child for the first time and saw, as anyone would have to see, the dark eyes that were his own, and the brave little smile.

'He is mine too,' I said jealously. 'He knows that he is my boy.'

Daniel gave a little half-laugh, almost a sob, and put his arms out. Danny reached for his father and went confidently to him, put his plump little arms round his neck, looked him in the face and leaned back so he could scrutinise him. Then he thumped his little fist on his own chest and said, by way of introduction: 'Dan'l.'

Daniel nodded, and pointed to his own chest. 'Father,' he said.

Danny's little half-moon eyebrows raised in interest.

'*Your* father,' Daniel said.

He took my hand and tucked it firmly under his arm, as he held his son tightly with the other. He walked to the dispatching officer and gave his name and was ticked off their list. Then together we walked towards the open portcullis.

'Where are we going?' I asked, although I did not care. As long as I was with him and Danny, we could go anywhere in the world, be it flat or round, be it the centre of the heavens or wildly circling around the sun.

'We are going to make a home,' he said firmly. 'For you and me and Daniel. We are going to live as the People, you are going to be my wife, and his mother, and one of the Children of Israel.'

'I agree,' I said, surprising him again.

He stopped in his tracks. 'You agree?' he repeated comically.

I nodded.

'And Daniel is to be brought up as one of the People?' he confirmed.

I nodded again.

He drew a breath. 'Hannah, in all my dreams, I did not dream of this.'

I pressed against his side. 'Daniel, I did not know what I wanted when I was a girl. And then I was a fool in every sense of the word. And now that I am a woman grown, I know that I love you and I want this son of yours, and our other children who will come. I have seen a woman break her heart for love: my Queen Mary. I have seen another break her soul to avoid it: my Princess Elizabeth. I don't want to be Mary or Elizabeth; I want to be me: Hannah Carpenter.'

'And we shall live somewhere that we can follow our beliefs without danger,' he insisted.

'Yes,' I said, 'in the England that Elizabeth will make.'

Philippa Gregory

Philippa Gregory's love for history and commitment to factual accuracy are the hallmarks of her writing and over the years she has written about many periods of history. Her first novel about the reign of the Tudors, *The Other Boleyn Girl*, was made into a television drama and a major film. *The Queen's Fool* was set in the same period but how long does it take Philippa to research her novels? 'Usually about two and a half years but a little less time for *The Queen's Fool* because, obviously, I used a lot of the research from *The Other Boleyn Girl*. At that time I had come across accounts of a network of Jewish families living undercover in Europe and was interested in pursuing that—which gave me extra research to do! Amazingly, I came across a book written in 1932 called *A History of the Marranos* and in the foreword the Jewish researcher had written: "Well, at least now in 1932 we have a Europe that is safe for Jewish people and we can live at peace with our neighbours at last." It was so poignant to read that and I found it so very moving. Anti-Semitism is still a live issue and that, in a sense, is why I love history so much. The past gives you an added insight into the world today.'

Philippa Gregory had also chanced upon a reference in a historical document about a woman who had been fool to both Queen Mary and Queen Elizabeth. 'I read up about fools and discovered that there were two different sorts. One type was comical like Will Somers in the book, and the other type was what they called holy fools, or innocent fools—people who were perhaps even mentally ill—who either had "the sight", or visions. So I made Hannah both Jewish and a holy fool. When you are writing a historical novel you have to first ground yourself in the facts, then answer the question: "If I was her, at that time, how would I react to this situation? The historical records never tell you *why* people do things, only what they do. The novelist can go further than the historian by attempting to explain the human motives.'

To keep track of the wealth of research she gathers, Philippa Gregory keeps a large time-chart in her study, detailing the events of every week and every day during the period covered by the novel. The walls, too, are plastered with portraits of the characters she is writing about, the plans of their houses, and the details of their daily lives—even the weather. 'Readers want accurate historical fiction. This is a wonderful thing to write and should be equally wonderful to read. One of the nice things people say is that reading my books is a very intense, real experience. For me it's got to be like that too.'

Also from Philippa Gregory:

Fiction:
15th Century Plantagenet:
The Red Queen, The White Queen.

16th Century Tudor:
The Constant Princess, The Other Boleyn Girl, The Boleyn Inheritance, The Queen's Fool, The Virgin's Lover, The Other Queen, The Wise Woman.

17th Century:
Earthly Joys, Virgin Earth.

18th Century:
Wideacre, The Favoured Child, Meridon, A Respectable Trade.

20th Century:
Fallen Skies, Zelda's Cut, The Little House, Alice Hartley's Happiness, Perfectly Correct.

Short Stories:
Bread and Chocolate.

Movies:
The Other Boleyn Girl.

TV Adaptations:
The Other Boleyn Girl, A Respectable Trade, The Little House.

PS, I love you

Cecelia Ahern

Holly, Sharon and Denise have been friends since school. And of the three, Holly has always been the one to do things first: the first to fall in love, the first to get married.

But into every life a little rain must fall and Holly is discovering what it is like to be the first to learn life's hardest lesson.

One

HOLLY HELD the blue cotton sweater to her face and the familiar smell struck her immediately, an overwhelming grief knotting her stomach and pulling at her heart. Pins and needles ran up the back of her neck and a lump in her throat threatened to choke her. Panic took over. Apart from the low hum of the fridge and the occasional moaning of the pipes, the house was quiet. She was alone. Bile rose to her throat and she ran to the bathroom, where she collapsed to her knees before the toilet.

Gerry was gone and he would never be back. That was the reality. She would never again run her fingers through his soft hair, never share a secret joke across the table at a dinner party, never cry to him when she got home from a hard day at work and just needed a hug; she would never share a bed with him again, never be woken up by his fits of sneezes each morning, never laugh with him so much her stomach would ache, never fight with him about whose turn it was to get up and turn the bedroom light off. All that was left was a bundle of memories, and an image of his face that became more and more vague each day.

Their plan had been very simple. To stay together for the rest of their lives. A plan that anyone within their circle would agree was accomplishable. They were best friends, lovers and soul mates, destined to be together, everyone thought. But, as it happened, one day destiny changed its mind.

The end had come all too soon. After complaining of a migraine for a few days, Gerry had agreed to Holly's suggestion that he see his doctor.

This was done one Wednesday on a lunch break from work. The doctor thought it was caused by stress and agreed that at the very worst he might need glasses. Gerry had been upset about the idea he might need glasses. He needn't have worried, since as it turned out it wasn't his eyes that were the problem. It was the tumour growing inside his brain.

Holly flushed the toilet and shakily steadied herself to her feet. Gerry had been thirty years old. By no means had he been the healthiest man on the earth, but he'd been healthy enough. When he was very sick he would joke bravely about how he shouldn't have lived life so safely. Should have have drunk more, should have travelled more, should have jumped out of aeroplanes while waxing his legs . . . Even as he laughed about it, Holly could see the regret in his eyes. Regret for the things he'd never made time to do, the places he'd never seen. Did he regret the life he'd had with her? Holly never doubted that he loved her, but feared he felt he had wasted precious time.

Growing older became something he wanted desperately to accomplish, rather than merely a dreaded inevitability. How presumptuous they had been never to consider growing old as an achievement.

Holly drifted from room to room while she sobbed her fat, salty tears. Her eyes were red and sore. None of the rooms provided her with any solace. Gerry would not be happy with this, she thought. She dried her eyes and tried to shake some sense into herself.

Just as she had done every night for the past two months, Holly fell into a fitful sleep in the early hours of the morning. Each day she woke to find herself sprawled uncomfortably across some piece of furniture; today it was the couch. Once again it was the phone call from a concerned friend or family member that roused her. They probably thought that all she did was sleep.

'Hello,' she answered. Her voice was hoarse from all the tears, but she had long since stopped caring about maintaining a brave face.

'Oh, sorry, love, did I wake you?' Every morning Holly's mother called to see if she had survived the night alone.

'No, I was just dozing, it's OK.'

'Your dad and Declan have gone out and I was thinking of you, pet.'

Why did that sympathetic voice always send tears to Holly's eyes? Her mother shouldn't have to be worried. Everything should be normal. Gerry should be here, rolling his eyes up to heaven and trying to make Holly laugh while her mother yapped on. So many times she would have to hand the phone to Gerry as her fit of giggles took over. Then he would chat away, ignoring Holly as she jumped round the bed pulling her silliest faces just to get back at him. It seldom worked.

'It's a lovely day, Holly. It would do you the world of good to go out for a walk. Get some fresh air.'

'Um, I suppose.'

'Maybe I'll call round later and we can have a chat.'

'No, thanks, Mum. I'm OK.'

Silence. Then, 'Well, all right, then. Give me a ring if you change your mind. I'm free all day.'

'OK. Thanks, though.'

'Right then . . . take care, love. Oh, I almost forgot. That envelope is still here on the kitchen table. It's been here for weeks.'

'It's probably just another card.'

'No, I don't think it is, love. Above your name it says . . . oh, hold on while I get it . . .' The phone was put down, then picked up again. 'OK, it says at the top "The List". I'm not sure what that means, love. It's worth just taking a . . .'

Holly dropped the phone.

'**G**erry, turn off the light!' Holly giggled as she watched her husband undress before her. He danced round the room performing a striptease, slowly unbuttoning his white shirt with his long slender fingers. He raised his left eyebrow towards Holly and allowed the shirt to slide from his shoulders, caught it in his right hand and swung it over his head.

Holly giggled again.

'Turn off the light? What, and miss all this?' he grinned cheekily while flexing his muscles. He wasn't a vain man but had much to be vain about, thought Holly. His body was strong and perfectly toned. He wasn't a very tall man, but he was tall enough to make Holly feel safe when he stood protectively beside her five-foot-five body. When she hugged him her head would rest neatly just below his chin.

He lowered his boxers, caught them on the tips of his toes and flung them at Holly, where they landed on her head.

'Well, at least it's darker under here anyway,' she laughed.

Gerry dived into bed, snuggled up beside her and tucked his freezing-cold feet underneath her legs.

'Aaaagh! Gerry, your feet are like ice cubes.' Holly knew he had no intention of budging an inch. 'Gerry!'

'Holly!' he mimicked.

'Didn't you forget something?'

'No, not that I know of.'

'The light?'

'Ah yes, the light,' he said sleepily and pretended to snore loudly.

'Gerry!'

'I had to get out and do it last night, as I remember.'

'Yeah, but you were right beside the switch a second ago!'

'Yes . . . just a second ago,' he repeated sleepily.

Holly sighed. She hated having to get out of bed when she was nice and snug, step onto the cold wooden floor, then fumble around in the darkness on the way back. She tutted.

'I can't do it all the time you know, Hol. Someday I might not be here and then what will you do?'

'Get my new husband to do it,' Holly huffed, trying her best to kick his cold feet away from hers.

'Ha!'

'Or just remember to do it myself before I get into bed.'

'Fat chance, my dear. I'll have to leave a message on the light switch before I go just so you'll remember.'

'How thoughtful of you, but I would rather you just leave me your money.'

'And a note on the immersion. And on the milk carton.'

'Gerry. You're a very funny man. Hey, why don't you just leave me a list in your will of things to do if you think I'll be so incompetent?'

'Not a bad idea,' he laughed.

'Fine, then, I'll turn off the bloody light.' Holly grudgingly got out of bed, and switched the light off. She held out her arms in the darkness and slowly began to find her way back.

'Hello?!!! Holly, did you get lost? Is there anybody out there, there, there, there?' Gerry shouted out to the black room.

'Yes, I'm hhhhowwwwwwcch!' she yelped as she stubbed her toe against the bedpost.

Gerry snorted and sniggered underneath the duvet. 'Number two on my list: Watch out for bedpost—'

'Oh, shut up, Gerry, and stop being so morbid,' Holly snapped back, cradling her poor foot in her hand.

'Want me to kiss it better?' he asked.

'No, it's OK,' Holly replied sadly. 'If I could just put them here so I can warm . . .'

'Aaaaah! Bloody hell, they're freezing!!'

Which made her laugh again.

So that was how the joke about the list had come about. It was soon shared with their closest friends, Sharon and John McCarthy. It was John who had approached Holly in the school corridor when they were just fourteen and muttered the famous words, 'Me mate wants to know if you'll go out with him.' After days of emergency meetings with her friends, Holly eventually agreed.

'Aah, go on, Holly,' Sharon had urged, 'he's such a ride.'

How Holly envied Sharon right now. Sharon and John had married the same year as Holly and Gerry. Holly was the baby of the bunch at twenty-three, the others were twenty-four. Some said she was too young and she should be travelling the world and enjoying herself. Instead, Gerry and Holly travelled the world together. It made far more sense that way because when they weren't together . . . well, Holly just felt like she was missing a vital organ from her body.

Tears rolled down Holly's face and she realised she had been day-dreaming again. She sat frozen on the couch with the phone still off the hook beside her. The hours just seemed to pass her by these days without her knowing what time or even what day it was. She seemed to be numb to everything but the pain in her heart, in her bones, in her head. She was just so tired . . . Her stomach grumbled and she realised she couldn't remember the last time she had eaten.

She shuffled into the kitchen wearing Gerry's dressing gown and her favourite pink 'disco diva' slippers, which he had bought her. She was his disco diva, he used to say. Always the first on the dance floor, always the last out of the club. Huh, where was that girl now?

She opened the fridge and stared in at the empty shelves. Just vegetables and yoghurt long past its sell-by date. She smiled weakly as she shook the milk carton. Empty. Third on his list . . .

Christmas two years ago, Holly had gone shopping with Sharon for a dress for the annual ball they attended at the Burlington Hotel. Shopping with Sharon was always a dangerous outing, and Holly spent a disgraceful amount of money in Brown Thomas on the most beautiful white dress she had ever seen.

'Sharon, this will burn a huge hole in my pocket,' Holly said guiltily, running her fingers over the soft material.

'Aah, don't worry, Gerry can stitch it up for you,' Sharon replied, followed by her infamous cackle. 'Buy the damn thing, Holly. It's Christmas, after all, the season of giving and all that.'

'God, you are so evil, Sharon. I'm never shopping with you again. This is like, half my month's wages.'

'Would you rather eat, or look fab?' Was it even worth thinking about?

The dress was cut low, which showed off Holly's chest perfectly, and it was split to the thigh, displaying her slim legs. Gerry hadn't been able to take his eyes off her. It wasn't because she looked so beautiful, however. He just couldn't understand how on earth that little slip of material had cost so much. Once at the ball, Ms Disco Diva overindulged in alcoholic beverages and succeeded in destroying her dress by spilling red wine down her front. While the men at the table drunkenly informed their partners that number fifty-four on the list prevented you from drinking red wine while wearing an expensive white dress, Gerry knocked his pint over, causing it to dribble off the table onto Holly's lap, and she tearfully announced, 'Rule fitty-fife: *neffer, effer* buy a 'spensive white dress.'

Was it possible that Gerry had kept his word and written a list for her before he died? She had spent every minute of every day with him up until his death, and he had never mentioned it. No, Holly, pull yourself together. She so desperately wanted him back that she was imagining all kinds of crazy things. He wouldn't have. Would he?

Holly was walking through an entire field of pretty tiger lilies; the wind was blowing gently, causing the silky petals to tickle the tips of her fingers as she pushed through long strands of bright green grass. All around her, birds whistled as they went about their business. The sun was so bright she had to shield her eyes, and with each brush of wind that passed her face, the sweet scent of the lilies filled her nostrils. She felt so . . . happy, so free.

Suddenly the Caribbean sun disappeared behind a looming grey cloud. The wind picked up and the air chilled. The petals of her tiger lilies were racing through the air wildly, blurring her vision. With every step, sharp stones scraped her feet. Something was wrong, and she felt afraid. In the distance a grey stone was visible. She wanted to run back, but she needed to find out what was ahead.

Bang! Bang! Bang! She raced over the sharp stones, collapsed to her knees in front of the grey slab and let out a scream of pain as she realised it was Gerry's grave. *Bang! Bang! Bang!* He was trying to get out! She could hear him!

Holly jumped from her sleep to a loud banging on the front door. 'Holly! Please let me in!' *Bang! Bang! Bang!* Confused and half asleep, she made her way to the door to find a frantic-looking Sharon.

'Holly, I've been banging on the door for ages!'

Holly looked around outside, still not fully alert. It was bright and slightly chilly—must be morning.

'Well, aren't you going to let me in?'

'Yeah, Sharon, sorry. I was just dozing on the couch.'

'God, you look terrible, Hol.' Sharon studied her face before giving her a big hug.

'Wow, thanks.' Holly rolled her eyes and turned to shut the door. Sharon was never one to beat about the bush, but that was why she loved her so much, for her honesty. That was also why Holly hadn't been round to see Sharon for the past month.

'It's so stuffy in here, when's the last time you opened a window?' Sharon marched round the house opening windows and picking up empty cups and plates. She brought them into the kitchen, where she then proceeded to tidy up.

'Oh, you don't have to do it, Sharon,' Holly protested. 'I'll do it.'

'When? Next year? I don't want you slumming it while the rest of us pretend not to notice. Why don't you go upstairs and shower, and we'll have a cup of tea when you come down.'

A shower. When was the last time she had even washed? Sharon was right, she must look disgusting with her greasy hair and dirty dressing gown. Gerry's dressing gown. But that was something she never intended to wash. She wanted it exactly as Gerry had left it.

'OK, but there's no milk. I haven't got round to . . .' There was no way she was letting Sharon look inside that fridge.

'Ta-da!' Sharon sang, holding up a bag Holly hadn't noticed her carrying in. 'Don't worry, I took care of that.'

'Thanks, Sharon.' Tears welled in Holly's eyes.

'Hold it! There will be no tears today! Just fun and laughter and general happiness, my dear friend. Now shower, quick!'

Holly felt almost human when she came back downstairs. She was dressed in a blue track suit and had allowed her long blonde hair to fall down on her shoulders. She gasped as she looked round the house. She couldn't have been half an hour, but Sharon had tidied and polished, vacuumed and plumped. She followed the noise she could hear to the kitchen, where Sharon was scrubbing the hobs.

'Sharon, you absolute angel! I can't believe you did all this! And in such a short space of time!'

'Ha! I was beginning to think you'd fallen down the plughole. You would and all, the size of you.' She looked Holly up and down. 'OK, so there's cheese and yoghurts, pasta and tinned foods. And microwave dinners in the freezer. How much weight have you lost?' Holly looked down at her track suit, sagging at the hips. 'There's biscuits to go with your tea. Jammy Dodgers, your favourite.'

That did it. The Jammy Dodgers were the icing on the cake. Holly felt the tears start to run down her face. 'Oh, Sharon,' she wailed, 'thank you so much. You've been so good to me and I've been such a horrible bitch of a friend.' She sat at the table and grabbed Sharon's hand. 'I don't know what I'd do without you.' This is what Holly had been dreading, breaking down in front of people, but she didn't feel embarrassed. Sharon sat opposite her patiently holding her hand as if it were normal.

'I'm your best friend, Hol. If I don't help you, then who will?' Sharon gave her an encouraging smile.

'Suppose I should be helping myself.'

'Pah!' Sharon waved her hand dismissively. 'Whenever you're ready. Grieving is all part of helping yourself anyway.'

'Thanks for coming round, Sharon, I really enjoyed the chat.' Holly gratefully hugged her friend, who had taken the day off work to be with her. 'I feel better already.'

'It's good to be around people, Hol. Friends and family can help.'

'Oh, I realise that now. I just thought I could handle it on my own.'

'Promise me you'll call round. Or at least get out of the house once in a while?'

'Promise.' Holly sighed. 'You're beginning to sound like my mum.'

'We're all just looking out for you. OK, see you soon, and *eat!*' Sharon added, poking her in the ribs.

Holly waved as Sharon pulled away in her car. It was nearly dark. They had spent the day laughing and joking about old times, then crying, followed by some more laughing, then more crying again. It had been good being with the living again instead of moping around with the ghosts of her past. Tomorrow was a new day and she intended to begin it by collecting that envelope.

Two

HOLLY STARTED her Friday morning well by getting up early. However, although she had gone to bed full of optimism, she was struck afresh by the harsh reality of how difficult every moment would be. Once again she woke to a silent house, but there was one small breakthrough. For the first time, she had woken up without the aid of a telephone call. She adjusted her mind, as she did every morning, to the fact that the dreams of Gerry and her being together that had lived in her mind for the past ten hours were just that—dreams.

She showered and dressed comfortably in blue jeans, trainers and a

T-shirt. She made a face at her reflection in the mirror. She had black circles under her eyes, her lips were chapped and chewed on and her hair was a disaster. First thing to do was to go down to her local hair-dressers' and pray that Leo could fit her in.

Holly bounced out of the salon with delight. Without Gerry beside her, a few men looked her way, something that was alien to her and made her feel uncomfortable, so she ran to the safety of her car and pre-pared herself for her parents' house. So far, today was going well. It had been a good move to visit Leo.

She pulled up to the kerb outside her parents' house in Portmarnock and took a deep breath. To her mother's surprise Holly had called first thing to arrange a time to meet up. It was three thirty now, and Holly sat outside in the car with butterflies in her tummy. Apart from visits her parents had paid her over the past two months, Holly had barely spent any time with her family. She didn't want all the attention; she didn't want the intrusive questions about how she was feeling and what she was going to do next. However, it was time to put that fear aside.

Her parents' house was situated directly across the road from Portmarnock beach, the blue flag bearing testament to its cleanliness. She parked the car and stared across the road to the sea. She had lived here from the day she was born till the day she moved out to live with Gerry. She had loved waking up to the sound of the sea lapping against the rocks and the excited call of the seagulls. Sharon had lived round the corner, and on the hottest days of the year, the girls would venture across the road in their summer's best and keep an eye out for the good-looking boys. Sharon with her brown hair, fair skin and huge chest, Holly with her blonde hair, sallow skin and small chest. Sharon would shout to the boys and call them over. Holly would just fix her eyes on her favourite and not move them till he noticed.

Holly didn't intend to stay long, just long enough to have a little chat and collect the envelope. She rang the doorbell.

'Hi, love! Come in, come in!' said her mother with the welcoming, loving face that Holly just wanted to kiss every time she saw her.

'Hi, Mum.' Holly stepped into the house. 'You on your own?'

'Yes, your father's out with Declan, buying paint for his room.'

'Don't tell me you're still paying for everything for him?'

'Well, your father might be, but I'm not. He's working nights now so he has a bit of pocket money. Although we don't see a penny of it.' She chuckled and brought Holly to the kitchen, where she put the kettle on.

Declan was Holly's youngest brother and the baby of the family, a twenty-two-year-old studying film production at college. He constantly had a video camera in his hand.

'What job has he got now?'

Her mother rolled her eyes to heaven. 'He's joined some band. The Orgasmic Fish, I think they call themselves. Holly, if he goes on one more time about how famous they're going to be, I'll go mad.'

'Ah, poor Deco, don't worry, he'll find something eventually.'

'I know, and it's funny, because of all you darling children, he's the last one I worry about. He'll find his way.'

They brought their mugs into the living room and settled down in front of the television. 'You look good, love. Any luck with a job yet?'

'No, not yet, Mum. I haven't even started looking.'

Her mother nodded. 'Take your time and think about what you like, or else you'll end up rushing into a job you hate, like the last time.'

The last job Holly had had was working as a secretary for an unforgiving slimeball in a solicitor's office. She'd been forced to leave when the little creep failed to understand she needed time off to be with her dying husband. Now she had to look for a new job.

Holly and her mother relaxed, falling in and out of conversation until Holly finally built up the courage to ask for the envelope.

'Oh, of course, love. I hope it's nothing important, it's been there for a long time.'

'I'll find out soon enough.'

They said their goodbyes and Holly couldn't get out of the house quickly enough. Perching herself on the grass overlooking the sand and sea, Holly ran her hands over the thick brown envelope. Above the address label were two handwritten words, thick and bold:

THE LIST.

Her stomach did a little dance. Her trembling fingers gently tore at the package. She turned it upside-down and shook the contents out. Out fell ten tiny little envelopes, the kind you would expect to find on a bouquet of flowers, each with a different month written on it. Her heart missed a few beats as she saw a loose page underneath the pile.

With tears in her eyes, she read the familiar handwriting, knowing that the person who had sat down to write to her would never be able to do so again. She ran her fingers over his words, knowing that the last person to have touched the page was him.

My darling Holly,

I don't know where you are or when exactly you are reading this. I just hope it finds you safe and healthy. You whispered not long ago that you couldn't go on alone. You can, Holly.

You are strong and brave and you can get through this. We shared some beautiful times together and . . . you made my life. I have no regrets. But I am just a chapter in your life, there will be many more. Remember our wonderful memories, but please don't be afraid to make some more.

Thank you for doing me the honour of being my wife. For everything, I am eternally grateful..

Whenever you need me, know that I am with you.
Love for ever,
Your husband and best friend, Gerry

PS, I promised a list, so here it is. The envelopes must be opened when labelled and must be obeyed. I'm looking out for you, so I will know . . .

Holly broke down, sadness sweeping over her. Yet she felt relief that Gerry would somehow be with her for another little while. She leafed through the small white envelopes. It was April now. She had missed March, and so she delicately opened it. Inside was a small card with Gerry's handwriting on it:

Save yourself the bruises and buy yourself a bedside lamp!
PS, I love you . . .

Her tears turned to laughter. Gerry was back!

Holly read his letter over and over in an attempt to summon him to life again. Eventually, when she could no longer see the words through her tears, she closed her eyes and breathed in and out along with the gentle sighing of the waves. It was as though the sea were taking big deep breaths, pulling the water in while it inhaled and pushing it all back up onto the sand as it exhaled. She thought about how she used to lie by Gerry's side during his final days and listen to the sound of his breathing. She had been terrified to leave him just in case that was the time he chose to leave her. When she returned to his bedside she would sit frozen in a terrified silence and watch his chest for any movement.

But he always managed to hang on, baffling the doctors with his determination to live. Gerry kept his good humour right up until the end. He was so weak and his voice so quiet, but Holly had learned to understand his babbling new language. They would giggle together late into the night, and other nights they would hold each other and cry. Holly remained strong for him. Looking back on it, she knew that she needed him more than he needed her, needed to feel she wasn't just standing by helpless.

On February 2nd at four in the morning, Holly held Gerry's hand tightly as he took his last breath. She didn't want him to be afraid, and she didn't want him to feel that she was afraid, because at that moment she wasn't. She had felt relief that his pain was gone, and that she had been there with him. She felt relieved to have known him, to have loved him and to have been loved by him, and relief that the last thing he saw was her smiling face assuring him it was OK to let go.

The days after that were a blur. She occupied herself making funeral arrangements and greeting his relatives and old schoolfriends. She was thankful that after months his suffering was over. It didn't occur to her to feel the anger or bitterness she felt now. That feeling didn't arrive until she went to collect her husband's death certificate.

As she sat in the crowded health clinic waiting for her number to be called, she wondered why on earth Gerry's number had been called so early in his life. She sat sandwiched between a young couple and an elderly couple, and it all just seemed unfair. Squashed between the shoulders of her past and her lost future, she felt suffocated. She shouldn't have had to be there.

None of her friends had to be there.

None of her family had to be there.

It didn't seem fair. Because it just wasn't fair.

After presenting the official proof of death to bank managers and insurance companies, Holly returned home to her nest and locked herself away from the world. That was two months ago and she hadn't left the house until today. And what a welcome she had been given, she thought, smiling down at the envelopes. Gerry was back.

'Wow!' was all Sharon and John could say as the three of them sat round Holly's kitchen table in silence, staring at the contents of the package. Conversation between them had been minimal for the last few minutes as they all tried to decide how they felt. It had gone something like this:

'But how did he manage to . . .?'

'But why didn't we notice him . . . well . . .?'

'When do you think . . .? He was on his own sometimes . . .'

Holly and Sharon just sat looking at each other while John tried to figure out how his terminally ill friend had managed to carry out this idea all alone.

'Wow,' he eventually repeated after coming to the conclusion that Gerry had done just that.

'Are you OK, Holly?' Sharon asked. 'I mean, how do you feel about all this? It must be . . . weird.'

'I feel fine. Actually, I think it's the best thing that could have happened right now. It's funny, though, how amazed we are, considering how much we all went on about this list.'

'I think Gerry was the only person who took it really seriously,' Sharon said.

There was a silence. 'Well, let's study this more closely,' John said. 'There's how many envelopes?'

Holly sorted through the pile. 'There's March, which is the lamp one, April, May, June, July, August, September, October, November and December. A message for every month left in the year.'

'Hold on!' John's blue eyes twinkled. 'It's April now.'

'Oh, I forgot about that. Oh, no, should I open it now?'

'Go on,' encouraged Sharon.

Holly picked up the envelope and slowly began to open it. She wanted to treasure every second before it became another memory. She pulled out the little card.

A disco diva must always look her best. Go shopping for an outfit, as you'll need it for next month!
PS, I love you . . .

'Ooooh,' John sang with excitement. 'He's getting cryptic!'

Holly lay on her bed like a demented woman, switching the lamp on and off with a smile on her face. She and Sharon had gone shopping in Bed Knobs and Broomsticks in Malahide, and had eventually agreed on a beautifully carved wooden stand and cream shade, which matched the cream and wooden furnishings of the master bedroom. And although Gerry hadn't physically been there with her as she bought it, she felt as though they had made the purchase together.

She had drawn the curtains of her bedroom in order to test her new merchandise. How easily this could have ended their nightly arguments, but perhaps neither of them had wanted to end them. It had become a routine, something familiar that made them feel closer. How she would gladly get out of her cosy bed for him now, gladly walk on the cold floor, gladly bruise herself on the bedpost while fumbling in the dark. But that time was gone.

The sound of Gloria Gaynor's 'I Will Survive' snapped her back to the present. Her mobile phone was ringing.

'Hello?'

'G'day, mate, I'm hooooome!' shrieked a familiar voice.

'Oh my God, Ciara! I didn't know you were coming home!'

'Neither did I, actually,' said Holly's younger sister. 'But I ran out of money and decided to surprise you all!'

'Wow, I bet Mum and Dad were surprised all right.'

'Well, Mum's organising dinner tonight to celebrate. The whole family.'

'Did I mention that I'm going to the dentist to have all my teeth pulled out? Sorry, I can't make it.'

'I know, I know, I said the same thing to Mum, but we haven't all been together for ages. Sure, when's the last time you've even seen Richard and Meredith?'

'Oh, Richard was in flying form at the funeral. Had lots of comforting things to say like, "Did you not consider donating his brain to medical science?" Yes, he's a fantastic brother all right.'

'Oh, gosh, the funeral. I'm sorry I couldn't make it.'

'Ciara, don't be silly, it was far too expensive, flying from Australia. So when you say the whole family you mean . . .?'

'Yes, Richard and Meredith are bringing our little niece and nephew. And Jack and Abbey are coming. Declan will be there in body, and Mum, Dad and me, of course, and you *will* be there.'

Holly groaned. As much as she moaned about her family she had a great relationship with her brother Jack. He was only two years older than her so they had always been close growing up, always getting up to mischief (usually aimed at their eldest brother, Richard). Jack was similar to Holly in personality, and she considered him to be the most normal of her siblings. It also helped that she got along with Abbey, and when Gerry was alive the four of them often met up for dinner and drinks. When Gerry was alive . . . God, that didn't sound right.

Ciara was a whole different kettle of fish. Jack and Holly were convinced she was from the planet Ciara, population: one. Ciara had the look of her father: long legs and dark hair. She also had various tattoos and piercings as a result of her travels. A tattoo for every country, her dad joked. A tattoo for every man, Holly and Jack were convinced.

Of course this carry-on was all frowned upon by the eldest of the family, Richard, who had been born with the serious illness of being an eternal old man. His life revolved around regulations and obedience. When he was younger he had one friend and they had a fight when they were ten. After that Holly could never remember him bringing anyone home or going out to socialise. She and Jack thought it was a wonder he had even met his equally joyless wife, Meredith. Probably at an anti-happiness convention.

It wasn't as though Holly had the *worst* family in the world, it was just that they were such a strange mix. These huge clashes of personalities usually led to arguments at the most inappropriate times. They *could* get along, but that was with everyone really being on their best behaviour.

So was Holly looking forward to tonight? Absolutely not.

Holly reluctantly knocked on the door to her family home and immediately heard the pounding of tiny feet followed by a voice that should not belong to a child.

'Mummy! Daddy! It's Auntie Holly, it's Auntie Holly!'

It was nephew Timothy, nephew Timothy.

His happiness was suddenly crushed by a stern voice. 'Timothy! What did I tell you about running in the house! Go and stand in the corner and think about what I said. Do I make myself clear?'

'Yes, Mummy.'

'Ah, come on, Meredith, will he hurt himself on the carpet?'

Holly laughed to herself; Ciara was definitely home.

The door swung open and there stood Meredith, looking even more sour-faced than usual. 'Holly.' She nodded.

'Meredith,' Holly imitated.

Once in the living room, Holly looked round for Jack, but to her disappointment he was nowhere to be seen. Richard stood in front of the fireplace with his hands in his pockets, rocking back and forth from his heels to the balls of his feet like a man in mid-lecture. His lecture was aimed at their father, Frank, who sat in his favourite armchair, looking like a chastised schoolboy. Richard was so lost in his story he didn't see Holly enter the room. She blew her poor father a kiss, not wanting to be brought into their conversation. He smiled and pretended to catch it.

Declan was slumped on the couch wearing his ripped jeans and South Park T-shirt, puffing furiously on a cigarette, while Meredith invaded his space and warned him of the dangers of smoking. Ciara was hiding behind the couch throwing pieces of popcorn at Timothy who stood facing the wall in the corner, too afraid to turn round. Abbey was pinned to the floor by five-year-old Emily and an evil-looking doll.

'Hi, Ciara.' Holly approached her sister, who jumped up and gave her a big hug. 'Nice hair.'

'You like it?'

'Yeah, pink is really your colour.'

Ciara looked satisfied. 'That's what I tried to tell them,' she said, squinting her eyes at Richard and Meredith. 'So how's my big sis?'

'Oh, you know.' Holly smiled weakly. 'I'm hanging in there.'

'Jack's in the kitchen helping your mum if you're looking for him, Holly,' Abbey announced.

Holly raised her eyebrows. 'Really? Well, isn't he great?'

Holly's dad shifted in his seat. 'And all this happens in just one tiny test tube?'

Richard let out a disapproving sigh. 'Yes, but you have to understand these are so minuscule, Father, it's rather fascinating. The organisms combine with the . . .' And away he went.

Holly tiptoed into the kitchen, where she found her brother munching on some food. 'Ah, here he is, the Naked Chef himself.'

Jack smiled. 'There's my favourite sister.' He held out his arms to offer her one of his big bear hugs. 'How are you?' he said quietly into her ear.

'I'm OK, thanks.' Holly smiled sadly and kissed him on the cheek. 'Darling Mother, I am here to offer my services.' She planted a kiss on her mother's flushed cheek.

'Oh, aren't I just the luckiest woman in the world having such caring children,' Elizabeth said sarcastically. 'I hope you two won't be getting up to any mischief tonight. I would like this to be an argument-free zone for a change.'

'Mother, I am shocked the thought even crossed your mind.' Jack winked across to Holly.

'All right,' Elizabeth said, not believing a word of it. 'Well, sorry, there's nothing to be done here. Dinner will be ready in a few minutes.'

Elizabeth joined her children at the table and the three of them stared at the kitchen door, all thinking the same thing.

'No, Abbey,' squealed Emily, 'you're not doing what I tell you.' This was followed by a loud guffaw; Richard must have cracked a joke because he was the only one laughing.

'But I suppose it's important that we all stay here and keep an eye on the dinner,' Elizabeth added.

Everyone oohed and aahed as Elizabeth brought out the food and the aroma filled the room. Holly had always loved her mother's cooking; she was never afraid to experiment with new flavours and recipes.

'Hey, poor little Timmy must be starving out there,' Ciara exclaimed to Richard. 'He must have done his time by now.'

She knew she was skating on thin ice but she loved the danger of it, and more important, she loved to wind Richard up. After all, she had to make up for lost time, she had been away for a year.

'Ciara, it's important that Timothy should know when he has done something wrong,' explained Richard.

'Yeah, but couldn't you just tell him?'

The rest of the family tried hard not to laugh.

'He needs to know that his actions will lead to serious consequences.'

'Ah well.' Ciara raised her voice a few octaves. 'He's missing all this yummy food. Mmm-mmm-mmm.'

'Stop it, Ciara,' Elizabeth snapped.

'Or you'll have to stand in the corner,' Jack added sternly.

The table erupted with laughter, bar Meredith and Richard, of course.

'So, Ciara, tell us about your adventures.' Frank moved swiftly on.

Ciara's eyes lit up. 'Oh, I had the most amazing time, Dad. I'd definitely recommend Australia to anyone.'

'Awful long flight, though,' Richard said.

'Did you get any more tattoos?' Holly asked.

'Yeah, look.' With that, Ciara stood up and pulled down her trousers, revealing a butterfly on her behind.

Mum, Dad, Richard and Meredith protested in outrage, while the others sat in convulsions of laughter. This carried on for a long time. Finally, when Ciara had apologised and Meredith had removed her hands from Emily's eyes, the table settled down.

'They are revolting things,' Richard said in disgust.

'I think butterflies are pretty, Daddy,' said Emily.

'Emily, I'm talking about tattoos. They can give you all sorts of diseases.' Emily's smile faded.

'Hey, I didn't get this done in a dodgy place sharing needles with drug dealers. The place was perfectly clean.'

'Well, that's an oxymoron,' Meredith said with disgust.

'Been in one recently, Meredith?' Ciara asked forcefully.

'I have never been in one, thank you.' Then she turned to Emily. 'They are dirty, horrible places, Emily, where only dangerous people go.'

'Is Aunt Ciara dangerous, Mummy?'

'Only to five-year-old girls,' Ciara said, and Emily froze.

'Richard, dear, do you think that Timmy might want to come in now for some food?' Elizabeth asked politely.

'It's Timothy,' Meredith interrupted.

'Yes, Mother, I think that would be OK.'

A very sorry little Timothy walked into the room with his head down and took his place silently. Holly's heart leapt out to him. How cruel to treat a child like that . . . Her sympathetic thoughts diminished immediately as she felt his little foot kick her shin underneath the table.

'So, Ciara, come on, did you do anything wild and wonderful out there?' Holly pushed for more information.

'Oh, yeah, I did a bungee jump actually, well, I did a few. I have a photo here.' She took out her wallet and passed the photo round the table. 'The first one I did was off a bridge and my head hit the water . . .'

'Oh, Ciara, that sounds dangerous,' her mother said.

'Oh, no, it wasn't dangerous at all,' she reassured her.

'Holly, what are you doing for your birthday?' Abbey asked.

'Oh, that's right!' shouted Ciara. 'You're gonna be thirty!'

'I'm not doing anything big,' Holly warned everyone. 'I don't want any party or anything, *please.*'

'Oh, you have to—' said Ciara.

'She doesn't have to if she doesn't want to,' Frank said.

'Thank you, Dad. I'm just going to have a girlie night out clubbing or something. Nothing mad, nothing wild.'

'Yes, I agree with you, Holly,' said Richard. 'Those birthday celebrations are always a bit embarrassing. Grown adults acting like children, drinking too much. You're quite right.'

'Well, I actually quite enjoy those parties, Richard,' Holly shot back. 'I just don't feel in the mood, that's all.'

There was silence for a moment before Ciara piped up: 'A girlie night it is then.'

'Can I tag along with the camera?' asked Declan.

'For what?'

'Just for some footage of clubs and stuff for college.'

'As long as you know I won't be going to trendy places.'

'No, I don't mind where you g—OW!' he shouted and stared menacingly at Timothy.

Timmy stuck out his tongue and the conversation continued on.

Three

ON HER BIRTHDAY, Holly stood in front of the full-length mirror and inspected herself. She had carried out Gerry's orders and had purchased a new outfit. What for, she didn't know, but several times every day she had to drag herself away from opening the envelope for May. There were only two days left until she could, and the anticipation left her no room to think of anything else.

She had settled on wearing an all-black outfit to suit her current mood. Black fitted trousers slimmed her legs and were tailored perfectly to sit over her black boots. A black corset, which made her look like she had a bigger chest, finished the outfit off perfectly. Her hair was tied up, allowing strands to fall in loose waves around her shoulders.

She didn't feel thirty. But then again, what was being thirty supposed to feel like? When she was younger, she'd thought that a woman of that age would be wise and knowledgeable, settled in her life with a husband and children and a career. She had none of those things. There was nothing about being thirty worth celebrating.

The doorbell rang and Holly could hear excited chatter outside. She took a deep breath and plastered a smile on her face.

'Happy birthday!' Sharon, Abbey, Ciara and Denise—who she hadn't seen in ages—all yelled in unison.

She stared back at their happy faces and was immediately cheered up by their enthusiasm. She ushered them into the living room and waved hello to the camera being brandished by Declan.

'No, Holly, you're supposed to ignore him!' Denise dragged Holly by the arm onto the couch, where they all surrounded her and immediately started thrusting presents in her face.

'Open mine first!' squealed Ciara.

'I think we should pop open the bubbly first and *then* open the pressies,' said Abbey.

'Ciara, I promise to open yours first,' Holly said.

Abbey raced into the kitchen and returned with a tray full of champagne flutes. 'Anyone for champers, sweetie darlings?'

'Holly, you can do the honours.' Abbey handed her the bottle and everyone ran for cover.

'Hey, I'm not that bad!' Holly said, as she began to remove the cork.

The girls all cheered as they heard the pop, and crawled out of their hiding places.

'OK,' said Sharon. 'Here's to my bestest friend in the whole world who has had such a difficult year, but throughout everything has been the bravest and the strongest person I've ever met. She's an inspiration to us all. Here's to her finding happiness for the next thirty years! To Holly!'

'To Holly,' they all chorused, holding up their glasses. Everyone's eyes were sparkling with tears as they all took sips of their drinks, except for Ciara, who had knocked back her glass of champagne and was scrambling to give her present to Holly.

'OK, first you have to wear this tiara because you are our princess for the night, and second here's my present!'

The girls helped Holly put on the sparkling tiara that luckily went perfectly with her black, glittery corset. She carefully removed the tape from the parcel and looked inside the box. 'What is it?'

'Read it!' Ciara said excitedly.

Holly began to read aloud from the box, 'It's a battery-operated . . . Oh my God! Ciara! You naughty girl!' Holly and the girls laughed hysterically. 'Well, I'll definitely need this.'

Declan looked like he was about to throw up.

Holly gave her sister a hug.

'OK, me next,' Abbey said, putting her parcel on Holly's lap.

Holly opened Abbey's present. 'Oh, Abbey, it's beautiful!' She held up the sterling silver-covered photo album.

'For your new memories,' Abbey said softly.

'It's perfect,' Holly said, wrapping her arms around Abbey and squeezing her. 'Thank you.'

'Mine is less sentimental.' Denise handed her an envelope.

'Oh, brilliant!' Holly exclaimed as she opened it. 'A weekend of pampering in Haven's Health and Beauty Clinic! Oh, Denise, thank you!' Holly winked at Sharon. 'OK, last but not least . . .'

It was a large silver frame with a photograph of Sharon, Denise and Holly at the Christmas Ball two years ago.

'Oh, I'm wearing my 'spensive white dress!' Holly walked over to the fireplace. That had been the last ball that she and Gerry had been to. 'Well, this will take pride of place,' she announced, placing it beside her wedding photo on the mantelpiece.

'OK, girls,' screamed Ciara, 'let's get some serious drinking done!'

Two bottles of champagne and several bottles of wine later, the girls stumbled out of the house and piled into a taxi. Holly insisted on sitting in the passenger seat and having a heart-to-heart with Nick the driver.

'Bye, Nick!' they all shouted before falling out onto the kerb. They had decided to chance their luck at Dublin's most stylish club, Boudoir. It was reserved for the rich and famous only, and it was a well-known fact that if you weren't rich and famous, you had to have a member's card. Denise walked up to the door coolly waving her video store card in the bouncers' faces. Amazingly, they stopped her.

The only famous faces they saw as they fought to get in were a few newsreaders from the national TV station, to whom Denise kept repeating, 'Good evening,' very seriously. Unfortunately, after that Holly remembered no more.

Holly woke with her head pounding. Her mouth was dry. She leaned up on one elbow and tried to open her eyes, which were somehow glued together. She squinted round the room. It was bright, very bright, and it seemed to be spinning. Something very odd was going on. Holly caught sight of herself in the mirror and startled herself. Had she been in an accident last night? She collapsed flat on her back again. Suddenly the house alarm began wailing. Oh, take whatever you want, she thought, just bring me a glass of water before you go. After a while she realised it wasn't the alarm but the phone ringing beside her bed.

'Hello?' she croaked.

'Good, I'm not the only one,' said a desperately ill-sounding voice.

'Who are you?' croaked Holly again.

'Sharon, I think. The man beside me in bed seems to think I know him.' Holly heard John laughing loudly.

'Sharon, what happened last night? Please enlighten me.'

'Alcohol happened last night. Lots and lots of alcohol.'

'Any other information?'

'Nope,' Sharon said drowsily.

'Know what time is it?'

'Two o'clock. It's afternoon, Holly.'

'Oh. How did that happen?'

'Gravity or something. I was out that day from school.'

'Oh God, I think I'm dying. I think I'll go back to sleep. Maybe when I wake up, the ground will have stopped moving.'

'Good idea. Oh, and, Holly, welcome to the thirties club.'

Holly groaned. ''Night.' Seconds later she was asleep.

Eventually, at nine o'clock that night, she decided to treat herself to a Chinese takeaway. She sat snuggled up on the couch in her pyjamas watching Saturday night TV. Holly was surprised. It was the first time since Gerry had died that she was at ease with her own company.

Later that night Jack called. 'Hey, sis, what are you doing?'

'Watching TV, having a Chinese,' she said.

'Well, you sound in good form. Unlike my poor girlfriend.'

'I'm never going out with you again, Holly,' she heard Abbey scream weakly in the background.

'She says she can't remember anything.'

'Neither can I. Maybe it happens as soon as you hit thirty.'

'Or maybe it's just an evil plan you all hatched so you wouldn't have to tell us what you got up to.' He laughed. 'Anyway, I was ringing to ask if you're going to Declan's gig tomorrow night.'

'Where is it?'

'Hogan's pub.'

'No way. There is no way I'm ever setting foot in a pub again, especially to listen to some loud rock band.'

'Don't drink then. Please come, Holly, we hardly got a chance to talk at dinner.'

'Well, we're hardly going to have a heart-to-heart with The Orgasmic Fish banging out their tunes,' she said sarcastically.

'They're actually called Black Strawberries now, which has a nice sweet ring to it I think,' he laughed.

Holly groaned, 'Oh, please don't make me go, Jack.'

'You're going. Declan will be chuffed when I tell him, the family never usually goes to these things.'

504 | Cecelia Ahern

Holly arrived at Hogan's pub feeling a lot fresher than the day before. It was a popular three-storey club situated in the centre of town and even on a Sunday the place was packed.. The first floor was a trendy nightclub that played all the latest music from the charts, where the young, beautiful people went. The ground floor was a traditional Irish pub for the older crowd. The basement was dark and dingy and it was where bands usually played. The tiny bar in the corner was surrounded by a huge crowd of young students in scruffy jeans and ripped T-shirts, pushing to be served. The bar staff also looked like they should be at college, and were rushing around with sweat dripping from their faces.

The basement was stuffy and Holly was finding it difficult to breathe in the smoky air. She waved at Declan to let him know she was there, but decided not to make her way over as he was surrounded by a crowd of girls. She wouldn't want to cramp his style. Holly had missed out on the whole student scene, having decided not to go to college and instead working as a secretary. Gerry had studied marketing at Dublin City University but he never socialised much with his college friends.

Finally, Declan made his way over.

'Well, hello, Mr Popular, I feel privileged you chose to speak to me.'

Declan rubbed his hands together cheekily. 'I know! This band business is great.' He scoured the crowds. 'And we were told there might be a record company guy coming to see us tonight.'

'Oh, cool!' Holly's eyes widened with excitement for her brother. She glanced around and tried to spot someone who might be a record company person. What would they look like? Finally, her eyes fell upon a man who seemed older than the rest of the crowd, more her own age. He was dressed in a black leather jacket, black slacks and a black T-shirt and had stubble round his jaw. He stood staring at the stage.

'Over there, Deco!' Holly pointed at the man.

Declan looked excited and his eyes followed to where her finger pointed. Then his smile faded as he obviously recognised the man. 'No, that's just *Danny*!' he yelled, and he wolf-whistled to grab his attention.

Danny twirled round and nodded his head in recognition before making his way over. 'Hi, Declan, how are you set?'

'Yeah, OK.' Declan nodded unenthusiastically. Somebody must have told him acting like you didn't care was cool.

'Sound check go OK?'

'There were a few problems but we sorted them out.'

'Good.' He turned to Holly. 'Sorry for ignoring you. I'm Daniel.'

'Nice to meet you. I'm Holly.'

'Oh, sorry,' Declan interrupted. 'Holly, this is the owner; Daniel, this is my sister.'

'Hey, Deco, we're on!' yelled a blue-haired boy.

'See you two later,' and Declan ran off.

'Good luck!' yelled Holly. 'So you're a Hogan,' she said.

Daniel smiled. 'Well, no, actually, I'm a Connelly. I just took over the place a few weeks ago.'

'Oh.' Holly was surprised. 'So are you going to change it to Connelly's?'

'Can't afford all the lettering on the front, it's a bit long.'

Holly laughed. 'Well, everyone knows the name Hogan's; it would probably be stupid to change it.'

Daniel nodded. 'That was the main reason actually.'

Suddenly Jack appeared at the entrance and Holly waved him over. 'I'm so sorry I'm late,' he said, giving her a hug. 'Did I miss anything?'

'Nope. He's about to go on. Jack, this is Daniel, the new owner.'

'Nice to meet you,' Daniel said, shaking his hand.

'Are they any good?' Jack asked him, nodding at the stage.

'To tell you the truth, I've never heard them play.'

'That was brave of you!' laughed Jack.

'I hope not too brave,' Daniel said as the boys took to the stage.

The crowd cheered and Declan took on his moody persona as he lifted his guitar strap over his shoulder. The music started and after that there was no chance of conversation. The crowd began to jump up and down, and once too often Holly's foot was stomped on.

'*Can I get you two a drink?*' Daniel yelled.

Jack asked for a pint of Budweiser and Holly settled for a 7UP. They watched Daniel battle through the crowds and climb behind the bar to fix the drinks. He returned minutes later with their glasses and a stool for Holly. She and Jack turned their attention back to the stage and watched their brother perform.

After four songs Holly had had enough, and she gave Jack a kiss goodbye. '*Nice meeting you, Daniel! Thanks for the drink!*' she screamed and made her way back to civilisation and cool, fresh air.

Her ears continued to ring all the way home in the car. It was ten o'clock by the time she got there. Only two more hours till May. And that meant she could open another envelope.

Holly sat at her kitchen table nervously drumming her fingers. She gulped back her third cup of coffee and uncrossed her legs. It was 11.30 p.m. and she had the envelope on the table in front of her.

She picked it up and ran her hands over it. Who would know if she opened it early? No one would care.

But that wasn't true. Gerry would know. Each time Holly held the envelopes in her hand she felt a connection with him. She felt like they were playing a game together, even though they were in two different worlds. He'd know if she cheated.

The small hand of the clock eventually struck midnight. Once again she treasured every moment of the process. She carefully tore open the seal, slid the card out and opened it.

> Go on, Disco Diva! Face your fear of karaoke at Club Diva this month and, you never know, you might be rewarded . . .
> PS, I love you . . .

The corners of her lips lifted into a smile and she began to laugh. Holly kept repeating 'no way!' whenever she caught her breath. Finally she calmed down. 'Gerry! You bastard! There is absolutely no way I am going through with this!'

She felt Gerry watching her. He laughed.

'You know how I feel about this, and I refuse to do it.'

'You have to do it, you know,' laughed Gerry.

'I do not have to do this!'

'Do it for me.'

'I am not doing it for world peace. I hate karaoke!'

'Do it for me,' he repeated.

The sound of the phone caused Holly to jump in her seat. It was Sharon. 'OK, it's five past twelve, what did it say?'

'What makes you think I opened it?'

'Ha!' Sharon snorted. 'Twenty years of friendship qualifies me as being an expert on you; now come on, tell me.'

'I'm not doing what he wants me to do,' Holly stated bluntly.

'Why, what is it?'

'Oh, just Gerry's *pathetic* attempt at being *humorous*,' she snapped.

'Holly, spill the beans.' John was on the downstairs phone.

'OK . . . Gerry wants me to . . . sing at a karaoke.'

The others burst out laughing so loud, Holly had to remove the phone from her ear. 'Phone me back when the two of you shut up,' she said angrily, hanging up.

A few minutes later they called back.

'OK.' Sharon had an overly serious 'let's get down to business' tone in her voice. 'I'm fine now. Don't look at me, John,' she said away from the phone. 'Holly, I'm sorry, but I kept thinking about the last time you—'

'Yeah, yeah, yeah,' Holly interrupted. 'It was *the most embarrassing day of my life* so I just happen to remember it. That's why I'm not doing it.'

'Oh, Holly, you can't let a stupid thing like that put you off! It was only a little fall—'

'Yes, thank you! I remember it just fine. Anyway I can't even sing,

Sharon; I think I established that fact marvellously the last time!'

Sharon was very quiet.

'Sharon? Sharon, are you still there?'

There was no answer.

'Sharon, are you laughing?' Holly gave out.

Holly heard a little squeak and then the line went dead. 'What wonderfully supportive friends I have,' she muttered.

'Happy birthday, Holly! Or should I say happy belated birthday?' Richard laughed nervously. Holly's mouth dropped open in shock at the sight of her older brother standing on her doorstep. This was a rare occurrence; in fact, it may have been a first.

'I brought you a mini Phalaenopsis orchid,' he said, handing her a plant. 'Shipped fresh, budding and ready to bloom.'

Holly fingered the tiny pink buds. 'Gosh, Richard, orchids are my favourite!'

'Well, you have a nice big garden here anyway, nice and'—he cleared his throat—'green. Bit overgrown, though . . .' He began that annoying rocking thing he did with his feet.

'Would you like to come in or are you just passing through?' Please say no, please say no. Despite the thoughtful gift, Holly was in no mood for Richard's company.

'Well, yes, I'll come in for a little while so.' He wiped his feet for a good two minutes at the door. He reminded Holly of her old maths teacher at school, dressed in a brown cardigan with brown trousers that stopped just at the top of his neat brown shoes.

Richard never seemed comfortable in his own skin. He looked like he was being choked to death by his tie, and his smile never managed to reach his eyes. Holly led him into the living room and placed the ceramic pot on the television.

'No, no, Holly,' he said, wagging a finger. 'It needs a cool, draught-free location away from sunlight and heat vents.'

'Oh, of course.' Holly picked the pot back up and searched the room for a suitable place.

'That little table in the centre, it should be safe there.'

Holly placed the pot on the table. 'Can I get you a tea or coffee?'

'Yes, great,' he said, clapping his hands together, 'tea would be splendid. Just milk, no sugar.'

Holly returned with two mugs of tea and placed them down on the coffee table. She hoped the steam rising from the mugs wouldn't murder the poor plant.

'You just need to water it regularly and feed it during the months of spring.' He was still talking about the plant. Holly nodded, knowing full well she would not do either of those things.

'I didn't know you had green fingers, Richard.'

'Only when I'm painting with the children. At least that's what Meredith says,' he laughed, cracking a rare joke.

'Do you do much work in your garden?'

'Oh, yes, I love to work in the garden.' His eyes lit up. 'Saturdays are my garden days,' he said, smiling into his mug of tea.

Holly felt as if a complete stranger were sitting beside her. She realised she knew very little about Richard and that equally he knew very little about her. But that was the way Richard had always liked to keep things. He never shared news with the family. The first time the family had even heard of Meredith was the day they both came over for dinner to announce their engagement. Unfortunately, at that stage it was too late to convince him not to marry the flame-haired, green-eyed dragon. Not that he would have listened.

'So,' she announced, far too loudly, 'anything strange or startling?' Like why are you here?

'No, no, nothing strange.' He took a sip of tea. 'I just thought I would pop in and say hello while I was in the area.'

'Ah, right. What brings you to the dark and dangerous world of the north side?'

'Oh, you know, just a little business.'

'How are Emily and Timmy, sorry, I mean Timothy?'

His eyes lit up. 'Oh, they're good, Holly. Worrying, though.'

'What do you mean?' Holly asked.

'Oh, there isn't one thing in particular, Holly. Children are a worry in general.' He looked her in the eye. 'But I suppose you're glad you'll never have to worry about this children nonsense.'

Holly felt like she had been kicked in the stomach.

'So have you found a job yet?' he continued on.

Holly sat frozen with shock. She was insulted and hurt and she wanted him out of her house. 'No,' she spat out.

'So what are you doing for money? Have you signed on the dole?'

'No, Richard,' she said. 'I get widow's allowance.'

'Ah, that's a great, handy thing, isn't it?'

'Handy is not a word I'd use. Devastatingly depressing is more like it.'

The atmosphere was tense. Suddenly he slapped his leg. 'I better motor on so and get back to work,' he announced, standing up. 'Anyway, nice to see you and thank you for the tea.'

'You're welcome, and thank you for the orchid,' Holly said through gritted teeth. He marched down the path to his brown family car.

Holly fumed as she watched him drive away, and then banged the door shut. That man made her blood boil so much she felt like knocking him out. He just hadn't a clue . . . about anything.

'**O**h, Sharon, I just *hate* him,' Holly moaned to her friend on the phone later that night.

'Just ignore him, Holly, he's an idiot.'

'But that's what annoys me. He's thirty-six. He should bloody well know when to keep his mouth shut. He says things deliberately.'

'I don't think he does it deliberately, Holly. I genuinely think he called round to wish you a happy—'

'Yeah! And what's that about?' Holly ranted. 'Since *when* has he ever called round to give me a birthday present? *Never!*'

'Well, thirty is more of a big deal than any other . . ..'

'Not in his eyes it's not! He even said so at dinner the other day.' She mimicked his voice. '*I don't agree with silly celebrations blah-blah-blah, I'm a sap blah-blah-blah.*'

Sharon laughed. 'OK, so he's an evil monster!'

Holly paused. 'Well, I wouldn't go that far, Sharon.'

Sharon laughed. 'Oh, I just can't please you at all, can I?'

Holly smiled weakly. Gerry would know exactly how she was feeling, he would know exactly what to say and he would know exactly what to do. He would give her one of his hugs and all her problems would melt away. She grabbed a pillow from her bed and hugged it tight.

'Helloooo? Earth to Holly? Am I talking to myself again?'

'Oh, sorry, Sharon, what did you say?'

'Have you given any more thought to this karaoke business?'

'Sharon!' Holly yelped. 'No more thought is required!'

'OK, calm down, woman! I was just thinking that we could hire out a karaoke machine. What do you think?'

'No, Sharon, he wants me to do it in Club Diva.'

'Ah! So sweet! Because you're his disco diva?'

'I think that was the general idea,' Holly said miserably.

'Ah! That's lovely, although Club Diva? Never heard of it.'

'Well, if no one knows where it is, then I just can't do it, can I?' Holly said, satisfied she had found a way out.

They both said their goodbyes and Holly hung up. It was back to her empty, silent house.

Holly woke up the next morning still fully dressed and lying on her bed. She could feel herself slipping into her old habits again. All her positive thoughts were melting away. It was so bloody tiring trying to be happy all the time. Who cared if the house was a mess? Nobody but she was going to see it. Who cared if she didn't wear make-up or wash for a week? *Who bloody cared?* Her mobile phone vibrated, signalling a message. It was from Sharon:

> club diva no 36700700
> think bout it. wud b fun.
> do it 4 gerry?asg

Gerry's bloody dead, she felt like texting back. But ever since she had begun opening the envelopes he didn't feel dead to her. It was as if he were just away on holiday and writing her letters, so he wasn't *really* gone. Well, the least she could do was ring the club and suss out the situation. It didn't mean she had to go through with it.

She dialled the number and a man answered. She couldn't think of anything to say so she quickly hung up again. Oh, come on, Holly, she told herself, it's really not that difficult.

Holly pressed redial. The same voice answered, 'Club Diva.'

'Hi, I was wondering if you do karaoke nights there?'

'Yes, we do, they are on a . . .' she heard him leafing through some pages, 'yeah, sorry, they're on a Tuesday night.'

'OK, em, well, I was wondering if, em . . .' Holly took a deep breath. 'My friend might be interested in singing and she was wondering what she would have to do?'

There was a long pause on the other end.

'Hello?' Was this person stupid?

'Yeah, sorry, I don't organise the karaoke nights, so . . .'

'OK.' Holly was losing her temper. It had taken courage to make the call and some underqualified little twit wasn't going to ruin it. 'Is there anyone who might have a clue?'

'Eh, no, there isn't, the club isn't actually open yet, it's very early in the morning still,' came the sarcastic response.

'Well, thank you very much, you've been a terrific help,' she said, matching his sarcasm.

'Excuse me, if you can just bear with me for a moment, I'll try to find out for you.' Holly was put on hold and forced to listen to 'Greensleeves' for five minutes. 'Hello? Are you still there?'

'Barely,' she said angrily.

'OK, I just made a phone call. What's your friend's name?'

Holly froze. 'Em, her name is Holly Kennedy.'

'OK, well, it's actually a karaoke competition on Tuesday nights. It goes on for a month and every week two people out of ten are chosen till the last week of the month, when six people sing in the final.'

Holly gulped. She didn't want to do this.

'But unfortunately,' he continued, 'the names have all been entered in advance. Your friend could try again at Christmas. That's when the next competition is on.'

'Oh, OK.'

'By the way, the name Holly Kennedy rings a bell. Would that be Declan Kennedy's sister?'

'Eh, yeah. Why, do you know her?' asked a shocked Holly.

'I met her briefly here the other night with her brother.'

Was Declan going round introducing girls as his sister? The sick and twisted little . . . No, that couldn't be right.

'Declan played a gig in Club Diva?'

'No, no.' The man laughed. 'He played with his band downstairs in the basement.'

'Is Club Diva in Hogan's?'

He laughed again. 'Yeah, it's on the top floor. Maybe I should advertise a bit more!'

'Is that Daniel?' Holly blurted out, and then kicked herself.

'Eh, yeah, do I know you?'

'Em, no! Holly just mentioned you in conversation, that's all.' Then she realised how that sounded. 'Very briefly in conversation,' she added.' Holly began hitting her head softly on the wall.

Daniel chuckled. 'Oh, OK, well, tell her if she wants to sing at Christmas I can put her name down now for it. You wouldn't believe the amount of people that want to sign up.'

'Really,' Holly said weakly. She felt like a fool.

'Oh, by the way, who am I speaking to?'

Holly paced her bedroom floor. 'Em . . . you're speaking to Sharon.'

'OK, Sharon, well, I have your number on caller ID so I'll call you if anyone backs out.' He hung up.

Holly leapt into bed, throwing the duvet over her head as she felt her face burn with embarrassment. She hid under the covers, cursing herself for being such a bimbo. Ignoring the ringing phone, she tried to convince herself she hadn't been a complete idiot. Eventually, after she had persuaded herself she could show her face in public again (it took a long time), she crawled out of bed and hit the button on her answering machine. The electronic voice announced she had one message.

'Hi, Sharon, I must have just missed you. It's Daniel here from Club Diva.' He paused. 'Em, I was just looking through the list and it seems somebody entered Holly's name a few months back, unless it's another Holly Kennedy . . . Anyway, call me back so we can sort it out. Thanks.'

Holly sat shocked on the edge of her bed, unable to move.

Four

HOLLY AND SHARON went to Bewley's Café overlooking Grafton Street, where they met up with Denise on her lunch break. Sharon said it was the best window-shopping she could ever do, as she had a bird's-eye view of all her favourite shops.

After lunch, the three girls linked arms and walked down the street, headed towards the clothes shop where Denise was manager. 'Right, you ladies of leisure, I'd better get back to work,' Denise said, pushing the door to her shop open. As soon as her staff saw her they stopped gossiping and began to tidy the clothes rails. Holly and Sharon tried not to laugh. They said their goodbyes and both headed up to Stephen's Green to collect their cars.

It was four o'clock by the time Holly eventually got out of town and began to drive in the direction of Swords. Sharon had convinced her to go shopping, which had resulted in her splashing out on a ridiculous top she was far too old to wear. She really needed to watch her spending from now on; her funds were running low, and without regular income she could sense tense times ahead. She had to start thinking about getting a job, but she was finding it hard enough to get out of bed in the morning as it was. Another boring nine-to-five job wasn't going to help matters. But it would pay the bills. Holly sighed loudly. The thought of it was just depressing her. She phoned her mum and checked if it was all right for her to call round.

'Of course you can, love.' Then Elizabeth lowered her voice. 'Just as long as you know that Richard is here.' What was with all the little visits all of a sudden?

Holly contemplated going straight home, but he was her brother. As annoying as he was, she couldn't avoid him for ever.

She arrived to an extremely loud and crowded house, and it felt like old times again. Her mum was setting an extra place at the table just as she walked in. 'Oh, Mum, you should have told me you were having supper,' Holly said, giving her a hug and a kiss.

'Why, have you eaten already?'

'No, but I hope you didn't go to too much trouble.'

'No trouble at all, dear, it just means that poor Declan will have to go without food for the day, that's all,' she said, teasing her son who was taking his seat. He made a face at her.

'So, Mr Hard Worker, why aren't you in college?' Holly said.

'I've been in college all morning,' Declan replied. 'And I'm going back in at eight o'clock, actually.'

'That's very late,' said her father, pouring gravy all over his plate. Frank always ended up with more gravy than food on his plate.

'Yeah, but it was the only time I could get the editing suite.'

'Is there only one editing suite, Declan?' piped up Richard.

'Yeah.' Ever the conversationalist.

'And how many students are there?'

'It's only a small class, there are just twelve of us.'

'Don't they have the funds for any more?'

'For what, students?' Declan teased.

'No, for another editing suite.'

'No, it's only a small college, Richard.'

'I suppose the bigger universities would be better equipped.'

And there was the dig they were all waiting for.

'No, the facilities are top of the range. And the lecturers are a bonus because they work in the industry. It's not just textbook stuff.'

Good for you, Declan, Holly thought.

'I wouldn't imagine they get paid well doing that.'

'Richard, working in film is a very good job; people have spent years studying for master's—'

'Oh, you get a degree for that, do you?' Richard was amazed. 'I thought it was just a little course you were doing.'

Declan stopped eating and looked at Holly in shock. Funny how Richard's ignorance still amazed everyone.

'What's your project on, Declan?' Frank asked.

'Oh, basically it's on club life in Dublin.'

'Oooh, will we be in it?' Ciara asked excitedly.

'I might show the back of your head or something,' he joked.

'Well, I can't wait to see it,' Holly said encouragingly.

'Thanks.' Declan started laughing. 'Hey, what's this I hear about you singing in a karaoke competition next week?'

'What?' Ciara's eyes nearly popped out of her head.

Holly pretended not to know what he was talking about.

'Ah, come on, Danny told me.' Declan turned to the rest of the table and explained, 'Danny owns the place where I did the gig and he told me Holly entered a karaoke competition in the club upstairs.'

Everyone oohed and aahed about how great it was.

Holly refused to give in. 'Declan, Daniel's just playing games with you. Sure, if I was in a karaoke competition I *think* I would tell you all.'

Declan laughed. 'I saw your name on the list! Don't lie!'

'Holly, why didn't you tell us?' her mother asked.

Holly put her knife and fork down. 'Because I can't sing!'

'Then why are you doing it?' Ciara burst out laughing.

She might as well tell them, she figured; otherwise Declan would beat it out of her and she didn't like lying to her parents.

'OK, basically Gerry entered my name in the competition months ago because he really wanted me to do it, and as much as I *don't* want to do it, I feel I have to go through with it. It's stupid, I know.'

Her family stared at her.

'Well, I think that's a wonderful idea,' her dad announced.

'Yes,' added her mum, 'and we'll all be there to support you.'

'No, Mum, you really don't have to be. It's no big deal.'

'There's no way my sister is singing in a competition without me being there,' declared Ciara.

'Here, here,' said Richard. 'We'll all go so. I've never been to a karaoke before. When is it on?' He took out his diary.

'Eh . . . Saturday,' Holly lied, and Richard began writing it down.

'It is not!' Declan burst out. 'It's next Tuesday, you liar!'

Holly could not stop going to the toilet. She was nervous and had had ~~had~~ practically no sleep the night before. And she looked how she felt. There was no better laxative than fear.

The big day had arrived—her worst nightmare, singing in public.

Her friends and family had been as supportive as ever, sending her Good Luck cards. Sharon and John had even sent her a bouquet of flowers, which she placed on the draught-free, heat-vent-free coffee table beside her half-dead orchid.

Holly dressed in the outfit Gerry had told her to buy in April and cursed him throughout. She piled on waterproof mascara because she could foresee the night ending in tears.

John and Sharon collected her in a taxi and she refused to talk to them, cursing everyone for forcing her to do this.

'Relax, Holly,' Sharon said, 'everything will be fine.'

'Bug off,' she snapped.

They finally reached Hogan's and, much to her horror, the club was packed. Her family had saved a table beside the Ladies, as requested.

Richard was sitting awkwardly on a stool, looking out of place in a suit. 'Tell me about these rules, Father. What will Holly have to do?'

Frank explained the 'rules' to Richard and Holly's nerves began to build even more.

'Gosh, that's terrific,' Richard said, staring round the club in awe. Holly didn't think he'd ever been in a nightclub before.

Jack was sitting with his arm draped round Abbey's shoulders; they both gave her a supportive smile.

'Hi, Holly,' Daniel said, approaching with a clipboard. 'OK, the order of the night is: first up is Margaret, then Keith and then you. OK?'

'That's all I need,' Holly snapped rudely. She just wished that everyone would leave her alone to wish evil thoughts on them all, but Daniel was still talking.

'Look, Holly, I'm really sorry to disturb you again, but could you tell me which of your friends is Sharon?'

'Over there.' Holly pointed to Sharon. 'Hold on, why?'

'Oh, I just wanted to apologise for the last time we spoke.'

'Why?' Holly said with panic in her voice.

'Oh, we just had a minor disagreement on the phone.' He headed over to Sharon. Holly leapt from her stool.

'Sharon, hi, I'm Daniel. I just wanted to apologise about the confusion on the phone last week.'

Sharon looked at him as though he had ten heads. 'Confusion? On the phone? What's your name again?'

'Em, it's Daniel.'

'And we spoke on the phone?' Sharon said politely.

Holly gestured wildly to her behind Daniel's back. He cleared his throat nervously. 'Yes, you called the club?'

'No, sweetie, you've got the wrong girl,' Sharon said.

Daniel appeared confused. Holly nodded her head frantically.

'Oh . . .' Sharon said, looking like she finally remembered. 'Oh, Daniel! God, I am so sorry, my brain cells seem to be going a bit dead. Must be too much of this,' she laughed, picking up her drink.

Relief washed over Daniel's face. 'Good, so you remember us having that conversation?'

'Oh, *that* conversation. Listen, don't worry about it.' She waved her hand dismissively.

'It's just that I only took over the place recently and I wasn't too sure of the arrangements for tonight.'

'Oh, don't worry, we all need time to adjust . . . you know?' Sharon looked at Holly to see if she had said the right thing.

'OK, then, well, it's nice to finally meet you in person,' Daniel said.

John and Sharon stared at him as he walked away.

'What was that all about?' Sharon asked Holly.

'Oh, I'll explain it to you later,' said Holly as their karaoke host for the evening was just stepping up onstage.

'Good evening, ladies and gentlemen!' he announced.

'Good evening!' shouted Richard, looking excited.

'We have an exciting night ahead of us . . .' He went on and on in his DJ voice. 'First up we have Margaret from Tallaght, to sing the theme to *Titanic*, "My Heart Will Go On" by Celine Dion. Please put your hands together for Margaret!' The crowd went wild. Holly's heart raced.

When Margaret began to sing, the room became so quiet you could almost hear a pin drop. Her eyes were closed and she sang with such passion it seemed she had lived every line of the song.

'Wasn't that incredible?' the DJ announced as Margaret tripped back to her seat. The crowd cheered again. 'Next up we have Keith, you may remember him as last year's winner, and he's singing "America" by Neil Diamond. Give it up for Keith!'

Holly didn't need to hear any more and rushed into the toilet. She paced up and down trying to calm herself. Her knees were knocking, her stomach was twisted in knots. She looked at herself in the mirror and tried to take big deep breaths. The crowd applauded outside and Holly froze. She was next.

'Wasn't Keith terrific, ladies and gentlemen?' Lots of cheers again. 'Well, it doesn't get any better than that! Next we have a newcomer to the competition. Please put your hands together for Holly!'

Holly ran to the cubicle and locked herself in.

It was three years ago that Holly had taken to the stage for her debut karaoke performance. A huge crowd of her friends had gone to their local pub in Swords to celebrate the thirtieth birthday of one of the lads. Holly had been working overtime for two weeks. She really wasn't in the mood to go out partying. All she wanted was to have a nice long bath, put on the most unsexy pair of pyjamas she owned, eat lots of chocolate and snuggle up in front of the television with Gerry.

After standing on an overcrowded train all the way from Blackrock, Holly arrived at Sutton Station to see her local bus drive off and was forced to stand waiting for the next one in the freezing cold for half an hour. She arrived home to thumping music and crowds of people with cans of beer, some slumped on the couch she had intended to lie on. Gerry stood at the CD player acting DJ and trying to look cool. At that moment she had never seen him look so uncool.

'What is wrong with you?' he asked her after seeing her storming upstairs to the bedroom.

'Gerry, I am tired, I am pissed off, and you didn't even ask me if it was all right to invite all these people over. And, by the way, *who are they?*' she yelled.

'They're friends of Conor's and, by the way, *this is my house too!*' he yelled back.

Holly began to gently massage her temples. 'Gerry,' she said, trying to stay calm, 'it would be fine if you had planned it in advance, *then* I wouldn't care, but today of all days, when I am so so tired,' her voice became weaker and weaker, 'I just wanted to relax in my own house.'

'Oh, every day's the same with you,' he snapped. 'You never want to do anything any more. You come home in your cranky moods and bitch about everything!'

Holly's jaw dropped. 'Excuse me! I have been working hard!'

'*It's Friday,*' he yelled. '*It's the weekend!* Let your hair down for a change and stop acting like a *granny!*' And he stormed out of the bedroom and slammed the door.

After spending a long time in the bedroom hating Gerry and dreaming of a divorce, she managed to think about what he had said. And he was right. OK, he wasn't right in the way he had phrased it, but she *had* been cranky and she knew it.

Holly was the type of person who finished work at 5 p.m. and was running for her train by 5.01. She never took work home and she phoned in sick as many Monday mornings as possible. But owing to a momentary lapse of concentration when looking for new employment, she had found herself accepting an office job that forced her to work late. She hadn't gone out for weeks and she fell asleep the minute her head hit the pillow every night. Come to think of it, that was probably Gerry's main problem.

But tonight would be different. She intended to show her neglected friends and husband that she was still the fun and frivolous Holly who could drink them all under the table. This show of antics began by preparing homemade cocktails. These worked their magic and at eleven o'clock they were all dancing down the road to the pub where a karaoke was taking place. Holly demanded to be first up and heckled the host until she got her way. The pub was packed that night and there was a rowdy crowd who were out on a stag night.

The DJ gave Holly a huge build-up after believing her lies of being a professional singer. Gerry lost all power of speech and sight from laughing so hard, but Holly was determined to show him that she could still let her hair down. She decided to sing 'Like a Virgin' and dedicated it to the man who was getting married the next day. As soon as she started singing, Holly had never heard so many boos in her whole life, but she was so drunk she didn't care. Eventually, when people began to throw things at the stage, she handed back the microphone, tripped down the steps in her stilettos and fell flat on her face.

Gerry lost his voice from laughing so loudly and Denise and Sharon took photographs of the scene of the crime.

Holly vowed *never* to do karaoke again.

'**H**olly Kennedy? Are you here?' the karaoke host's voice boomed. The applause died down as everyone looked round in search of Holly. Well, they would be a long time looking, she thought as she lowered the toilet seat and sat down to wait for the excitement to settle so they could move on to their next victim. She closed her eyes and prayed for this moment to pass.

Outside the cubicle the toilet door open and slammed.

'Holly?' It was Sharon. 'Holly, I know you're in there, so listen, OK?'

Holly sniffed back the tears that were beginning to well.

'I know that this is an absolute nightmare for you but you need to relax, OK?' Sharon paused.

The DJ's voice said into the microphone, 'Ladies and gentlemen, it appears that our singer is currently in the toilets.' The entire room erupted in laughter.

'Oh, Sharon!' Holly's voice trembled in fear.

'Holly, you don't have to do this. Nobody is forcing you . . .'

'Ladies and gentlemen, let's let Holly know that she's up next!' yelled the DJ. 'Come on!' Everybody began to chant her name.

'OK, well, at least nobody who cares about you is forcing you to do this. But if you don't do this, I know you'll never forgive yourself. Gerry wanted you to do this for a reason.'

'*Holly! Holly! Holly!*'

'Oh, Sharon!' Holly repeated again, panicking. Suddenly the walls of the cubicle felt like they were closing in on her; beads of sweat formed on her forehead. She burst through the door, her eyes red and puffy.

'Don't mind them, Holly,' Sharon said coolly, 'they can't make you do anything you don't want to do.'

Holly's lower lip began to tremble.

'Don't!' Sharon said. 'Don't even think about it!'

'I can't sing, Sharon,' Holly whispered.

'I know that! Screw them! You're never gonna see their ugly mugs *ever again!* Who cares what they think? I don't, do you?'

Holly thought about it for a minute. 'No,' she whispered.

'What? I didn't hear you. Do you care what they think?'

'No,' she said, a little stronger.

'Louder!' Sharon shook her by the shoulders.

'No!' she yelled.

'Louder!'

'NOOOOOOOOO! I DON'T CARE WHAT THEY THINK!' Holly screamed. The two of them began to giggle.

'Just let this be another silly Holly day so we can laugh about it a few months from now,' Sharon pleaded.

Holly took a deep breath and charged towards the door like a woman on a mission. She came face to face with her adoring fans, who were all chanting her name. She took an extremely theatrical bow and, to the sounds of claps and laughter, headed towards the stage.

Holly had everybody's attention now, whether she liked it or not. The music started and her whole table held their thumbs up. It was corny but strangely comforting. Holding the microphone tightly, with an extremely shaky and timid voice she sang: '"What would you do if I sang out of tune? Would you stand up and walk out on me?"' ·

Denise and Sharon howled with laughter at the choice of song and gave a big cheer. Holly struggled on, singing dreadfully. Just when she felt she was about to hear boos her family and friends joined in. '"Ooh, I'll get by with a little help from my friends; yes, I'll get by with a little help from my friends."'

The crowd laughed and the atmosphere warmed a little more. Holly yelled at the top of her lungs, '"Do you *neeeed* anybody?"' A few people helped her out to sing, '"I need somebody to love."'

'"Do you *neeeed* anybody?"' she repeated and held the microphone out to the crowd and they all sang. Holly felt less nervous now and battled her way through the rest of the song. The people down the back resumed chatting, the bar staff carried on serving drinks. When she had finally finished singing, a few polite tables up the front and her own table were the only people to acknowledge her. The DJ took the microphone and managed to say between laughs, 'Please give it up for the incredibly brave Holly Kennedy!'

Her family and friends cheered. Denise and Sharon approached her with cheeks wet from tears of laughter.

'I'm so proud of you!' Sharon said, throwing her arms round Holly's neck. 'It was awful!'

'Thanks for helping me, Sharon,' she said as she hugged her friend.

Abbey cheered and Jack shouted, 'Terrible! Absolutely terrible!' Holly's mother smiled and Holly's father could barely look her in the eye he was laughing so much.

All Ciara could manage was to repeat over and over again, 'I never knew anyone could be so bad.'

Declan waved at her with a camera in his hand and gave her the thumbs-down. Holly hid in the corner at the table. She couldn't remember the last time she had felt so proud.

John shuffled over and leaned against the wall beside her. He said, 'Gerry's probably here, you know,' and looked at her with watery eyes.

Poor John, he missed his best friend too. She gave him an encouraging smile. He was right. Holly *could* feel Gerry's presence. She could feel him wrapping his arms round her and giving her one of the hugs she missed so much.

After an hour the singers had finally finished, and Daniel and the DJ headed off to tot up the voting slips. It was obvious Holly wasn't going to win, but on the off chance that she did, she shuddered at the thought of having to return to repeat the experience in two weeks' time. The DJ played a CD of a drumroll as Daniel took to the stage in his black leather jacket and slacks and was greeted by wolf whistles and screams from the girls. Richard looked excited and crossed his fingers at Holly.

'OK, so the two people that will be going through to the final are'— Daniel paused for dramatic effect—'Keith and Samantha!'

Holly jumped up and danced around in a huddle with Denise and Sharon. Richard looked on confused, and the rest of Holly's family congratulated her on her victorious loss.

Holly sat back down and sipped her drink thoughtfully. Sharon and John seemed engrossed in a heated discussion, Abbey and Jack were like love-struck teenagers as usual, Ciara was intent on getting to know Daniel better, and Denise was . . . Where was Denise?

Holly looked around the club and spotted her sitting on the stage striking a very provocative pose for the karaoke host. Holly's parents had gone, which left . . . Richard. Richard sat squashed between Ciara and Daniel, taking a sip from his drink every few seconds.

Holly moved over and sat opposite him. 'You enjoying yourself?'

He looked up. 'Yes, thank you, I'm having fun, Holly.'

'I'm surprised you came, I didn't think this would be your scene.'

'Oh, you know . . . you have to support the family.'

'So where's Meredith tonight?'

'Emily and Timothy,' he said, as if that explained it all.

'You working tomorrow?'

'Yes,' he said suddenly, knocking back his drink, 'so I best be off. You were a great sport tonight, Holly.' He looked round awkwardly at his family, debating whether to interrupt them and say goodbye, but eventually deciding against it. He nodded to Holly and off he went, manoeuvring his way through the crowd.

Holly was once again alone. As much as she wanted to grab her bag and run home, she knew she should sit this one out. There would be plenty of times when she would be the only singleton in the company of couples, and she needed to adapt. Holly wondered whether this had been Gerry's intention. She had stood on a stage and sung to hundreds of people, and now she was stuck in a situation where she was surrounded by couples. Whatever his plan was, she was being forced to become braver without him.

Holly smiled as she watched her sister nattering away to Daniel. Ciara was so carefree and confident. For as long as Holly could remember, Ciara had never managed to hold down a job or a boyfriend, she was always lost in a dream of visiting another far-off country. She turned her attention to Jack, still lost in a world with Abbey. She wished she could be more like him, the cool English teacher all the teenagers respected. Holly sighed loudly and drained her drink.

Daniel looked over. 'Holly, can I get you another drink?'

'Ah, no, thanks, Daniel, I'm heading home soon anyway.'

'Oh, Hol!' protested Ciara. 'It's so early! No, you're staying. Get her a vodka and Coke,' she ordered Daniel, 'and I'll have the same again.'

'Ciara!' Holly exclaimed.

'No, it's OK! I asked.' Daniel headed off to the bar.

'Ciara, that was so rude,' Holly gave out to her sister.

'What? It's not like he has to pay for it, he owns the bloody place,' she said defensively. 'Where's Richard?'

'Gone home.'

'No! How long ago?' She jumped down from her seat.

'I dunno, about five or ten minutes. Why?'

'He's supposed to be driving me home!' She threw everyone's coats into a pile while she rooted around for her bag.

'Ciara, you'll never catch him, he's been gone far too long.'

'No, I will. He's parked ages away and he'll have to drive back down this road to get home. I'll get him while he's passing.' She found her bag and legged it out of the door yelling, 'Bye, Holly!'

Daniel placed the drinks on the table and sat down again. 'Where's Ciara gone?'

'Oh, she's really sorry but she had to chase my brother for a lift.' Holly bit her lip. 'Sorry for being so rude to you earlier.' She started laughing. 'You must think we're the rudest family in the world. Ciara doesn't mean what she says half the time.'

'And you did?' he smiled.

'At the time, yes.' She laughed again.

'Hey, it's fine, just means there's more drink for you.' He slid the glass across the table towards her, then stared past her shoulder with amusement. 'Well, it looks like your friend is having a good night.'

Holly turned and saw Denise and the DJ wrapped round each other. Her provocative poses had obviously worked.

'Oh, no, not the horrible DJ who forced me to come out of the toilet,' Holly groaned.

'That's my friend Tom O'Connor from Dublin FM. He's working here tonight because the karaoke went out live on the radio,' Daniel said.

'*What?*'

His face broke into a smile. 'Only joking; just wanted to see the look on your face.'

'Don't do that to me,' Holly put her hand on her heart. 'Having the people in here hear me was bad enough, never mind the entire city.'

'If you hate it so much, why did you enter?' Daniel asked.

'Oh, my hilarious husband thought it would be funny to enter his tone-deaf wife into a singing competition.'

Daniel laughed. 'You weren't *that* bad! Is your husband here?' he asked, looking round.

Holly smiled. 'Yeah, he's definitely here . . . somewhere.'

Five

HOLLY SECURED her bedsheet onto the washing line with a peg and thought about how she had bumbled around for the remainder of May trying to get her life into some sort of order. Days went by when she felt so confident that her life would be OK, and then just as quickly the feeling would disappear and she would feel her sadness setting in once more. She had tried to find a routine she could happily fall into, instead of wandering around like a zombie. Unfortunately, the routine hadn't turned out exactly as she had hoped. She found herself immobile for hours in the living room, reliving every argument they had had, wishing she could take back every horrible word she had ever said to him. She chastised herself for walking away from him when she should have hugged him; when she held grudges for days instead of forgiving him; when she went straight to sleep some nights instead of making love to him. The bad times had all been such a waste of time.

There were her happy days, when she would walk around in a day-dream with nothing but a smile on her face, catching herself giggling when a joke of theirs would suddenly pop into her head. She would fall into days of deep, dark depression; then finally build up the strength to snap out of it for another few days. But the tiniest thing would trigger off her tears again. That was her routine. It was a tiring process, and most of the time she couldn't be bothered battling with her mind. It was far stronger than her body.

She reread Gerry's original letter over and over, analysing each word and each sentence, and each day she came up with a new meaning. But the fact was that she would never *really* know *exactly* what he meant because she would never speak to him *ever again*. It was this thought that she had the most difficulty trying to come to terms with.

June brought another envelope from Gerry.

Holly sat out in the sun, revelling in the new brightness of life, and read the fourth message. She loved the bumps of Gerry's handwriting under her finger as it ran over the dried ink. Inside, he had listed the items in the house that belonged to him and explained what he wanted Holly to do with them. At the bottom it read:

> *PS, I love you, Holly, and I <u>know</u> you love me. You don't need my belongings to remember me by, you don't need to keep them as proof that I existed or still exist in your mind. You don't need to wear my sweater to feel me around you; I'm <u>always</u> wrapping my arms around you.*

Holly almost wished he would ask her to do karaoke again. She would have jumped from an aeroplane for him; run a thousand miles; *anything* except empty out his wardrobes and rid herself of his presence. But he was right and she knew it. The physical Gerry was gone.

It was an emotionally draining experience. It took her days to complete. She relived a million memories with every garment and piece of paper she bagged. Every time an item left her fingers it was like saying goodbye to a part of Gerry all over again. It was difficult; so difficult.

Despite her wishes to do this alone, Jack had called round to offer some brotherly support, and she had appreciated it. Every item had a history and they would talk and laugh about the memories. He was there for her when she cried and he was there when she finally clapped her hands together, ridding her skin of the dust that remained.

She laughed as she bagged the dusty cassettes of his favourite rock band from his schooldays. He would blast the heavy-metal music from every speaker in the house to torment Holly with its screeching guitars and badly produced sound quality. She always told him she couldn't wait to see the end of those tapes, but now the relief didn't wash over her as once she hoped it would.

Her eyes rested upon a crumpled ball lying in the back corner of the wardrobe—Gerry's lucky football jersey. It was still covered in grass and mud stains from its last victorious day on the pitch. She held it close to her and inhaled deeply; the smell of beer and sweat was faint, but still there. She put it aside to be washed and passed on to John.

So many objects, so many memories. Objects that were once so full of life and importance but that now lay limp on the floor. Without him they were just *things*. Gerry's wedding tuxedo, his suits, shirts and ties that he would moan about having to wear every morning before going to work. The fashions of the years gone by, shiny suits and shell track suits bundled away. A snorkel from their first time scuba diving, a shell that he had picked up off the ocean floor ten years ago, his collection of beer mats. Letters and birthday cards from friends and family sent to him over the years. Valentine's Day cards from Holly. Childhood teddies put aside to be sent back to his parents. Records of bills, his golf clubs for John, books for Sharon, memories, tears and laughter for Holly.

His entire life bundled into twenty refuse sacks.

His and her memories bundled away into Holly's mind.

Each item unearthed dust, tears, laughter and memories. She bagged the items, cleared the dust, wiped her eyes and filed away the memories.

Holly's mobile began to ring, disrupting her thoughts, and she dropped the laundry basket onto the grass and ran through the patio doors to the kitchen to answer it. 'Hello?'

'*I'm gonna make you a star!*' Declan's voice screeched hysterically and he broke into uncontrollable laughter.

Holly searched her brain to figure out what he could be talking about. 'Declan, are you drunk?'

'Maybe jus a li'l bit, but that's completely irrelevant,' he hiccuped.

'Declan, it's ten o'clock in the morning!' Holly laughed. 'Have you been to bed yet?'

'Nope,' he hiccuped again. 'I'm on the train home now. I'm in Galway. The 'wards were on last night,' he said, as if she should know.

'Oh, sorry for my ignorance, but what awards were you at?'

'The student media 'wards and I won!' he yelled, and Holly heard what sounded like the entire carriage celebrating with him. She was delighted.

'And the prize is that my film is gonna be aired on Channel 4 next week! Can you believe it?' There were more cheers this time and Holly could barely make out what he was saying. 'You're gonna be famous, sis!' was the last thing she heard before the line went dead.

She rang round her family to share the good news, but they had all received similar phone calls. Ciara chattered on like an excited school-girl about how Daniel had offered Club Diva so they could watch the documentary next Wednesday on the big wall screen at Hogan's.

Holly sat at the kitchen table wondering what she should wear next week; she wanted to look sexy and gorgeous for a change. Maybe Denise had something in her shop. She picked up the phone and called her at work.

'Hello, Casuals,' answered a very polite Denise.

'Hello, Casuals, Holly here. I know I'm not supposed to call you at work but Declan's documentary won some student award thingy and it's gonna be aired on Wednesday night.'

'Oh, that's so cool, Holly! Are we gonna be in it?'

'Yeah, I think so. We're all meeting up at Hogan's to watch it. You up for that?'

'Oooh, of course! I can bring my new boyfriend.' She giggled.

'What new boyfriend?'

'Tom!'

'The karaoke guy?' Holly asked in shock.

'Yeah, of course! Oh, Holly, I'm so in love.' She giggled again.

'In love? But you only met him a few weeks ago!'

'I don't care; it only takes a minute . . . as the saying goes.'

'Wow, Denise . . . I don't know what to say! I mean . . . it's great news.'

'Oh, try not to sound too enthusiastic, Holly,' Denise said sarcastically. 'Anyway, I can't wait for you to meet him, you'll really *really* like him.' She rambled on about how great he was.

'Denise, aren't you forgetting that I've met him?' Holly interrupted in the middle of a story about how Tom had saved a child from drowning.

'Yeah, I know, but I'd rather you meet him when you're not acting like a demented woman hiding in toilets.'

Holly rolled her eyes. 'Look forward to it then . . .'

Holly arrived at Hogan's and pushed through the pub crowd to make her way upstairs to Club Diva. The traditional band was in full swing and the crowd was joining in on all their favourite Irish songs. It was only seven thirty, so Club Diva wasn't officially open yet. She was the first to arrive and settled herself at a table right in front of the big screen.

A glass smashing over by the bar made her jump and she looked up to see Daniel's head emerging from behind the bar, a dustpan and brush in his hand.

'Oh, hiya, Holly. I didn't realise anyone had come in.'

'I came early for a change.' She walked over to greet him.

'Well, you're really early,' he said, looking at his watch. 'The others probably won't be here for another hour or so.'

Holly looked confused. 'But the show starts at eight, doesn't it?'

'I was told nine, but I could be wrong.' Daniel reached for that day's paper and looked at the TV page. 'Yep, nine o'clock, Channel Four.'

'Oh, no, I'm sorry. I'll go and wander round town for a bit.'

'Don't be silly, the shops are all closed by now. You can keep me company—that's if you don't mind . . .'

'Well, I don't mind if you don't mind.'

'I don't mind,' he said, smiling. He leaned his hands against the taps in a typical barman's pose. 'So, now, what can I get you?'

'Well, this is great. I'll have a sparkling water, please.'

'Nothing stronger?' He raised his eyebrows.

'Better not or I'll be drunk by the time everyone gets here.'

'Good thinking.' He reached behind him to the fridge. He was wearing faded blue jeans and a light blue shirt that made his blue eyes twinkle. He slid the glass towards her.

'Can I get you anything?' she asked him.

'No, thanks, I'll take care of this one.'

'Please. You've bought me plenty of drinks. It's my turn.'

'OK, I'll have a Budweiser then, thanks.' He leaned against the bar.

'What? Do you want me to get it?' Holly laughed, jumping off her stool and walking round the bar. 'I always wanted to work behind a bar when I was a kid,' she said, grabbing a pint glass.

'Well, there's a spare job if you're looking for one,' Daniel said, watching her pulling down on the tap.

'No, thanks. I think I do a better job on the other side.' She took out her purse and handed him money. 'Keep the change,' she laughed.

'Thanks.' He turned to the cash register, then walked round the bar to join her. 'Has your husband deserted you again tonight?' he teased.

Holly bit her lip. She didn't want the poor man to ask her every time he saw her. 'Daniel, I don't mean to make you uncomfortable, but my husband passed away.'

Daniel blushed slightly. 'Oh, Holly, I'm sorry, I didn't know.'

'I know you didn't.' She smiled to show him it was all right.

'Well, I didn't meet him the other night, but if someone had told me, I would have gone to the funeral to pay my respects.' He sat beside her at the bar.

'No, Gerry died in February, Daniel. He wasn't here the other night.'

'But I thought you told me he was here . . .' He trailed off, thinking he had misheard her.

'Oh, yeah.' Holly looked down at her feet with embarrassment. 'Well, he wasn't here,' she said, looking around the club, 'but he was here,' she put her hand on her heart.

'Ah, I see.' He finally understood. 'Well, then, you were even braver the other night than I thought,' he said gently.

Holly was surprised by how at ease he seemed. Usually people either wandered off or changed the subject. She felt she could talk openly without fear of crying. She briefly explained the story of The List.

'So that's why I ran off during Declan's gig that time.'

'It wasn't because they were so terrible by any chance?' Daniel joked, then he looked lost in thought. 'Ah, yes, that was the 30th of April.'

'Yeah, I couldn't wait any longer to open it,' Holly explained.

'I have arrived!' announced Denise to the empty room as she swanned in, dolled up to the nines. Tom strolled in behind her, unable to take his eyes off her.

'God, *you're* dressed up,' Holly remarked. In the end she had decided to wear just a pair of jeans, black boots and a very simple black top.

'Well, it's not every day I get to go to my own premiere, is it?'

Tom and Daniel greeted each other with hugs. 'Baby, this is my friend Daniel,' Tom said, introducing Denise to Daniel.

'Hi, Tom.' Holly shook Tom's hand after Denise had introduced her. 'I'm sorry about the last time I met you, I wasn't feeling very sane that night.' Holly blushed at the memory of the karaoki.

'Oh, that's no problem.' Tom smiled kindly. 'If you hadn't entered then I wouldn't have met Denise, so I'm glad you did.'

After a while Holly discovered that she was enjoying herself; she wasn't just pretending to laugh, she was genuinely happy.

Minutes later the rest of the Kennedy family arrived, along with Sharon and John, and Holly ran down to greet them.

'Meredith not with you tonight?' she asked Richard boldly.

'No, she's not,' he snapped rudely, and headed over to the bar.

'Why does he bother coming at all?' she moaned to Jack while he held her head to his chest, playfully consoling her.

'OK, everyone!' Declan was standing on a stool to address the gathering. 'Because Ciara couldn't decide what to wear tonight, we're all late and *my* documentary is about to start any minute. So if you can just all shut up and sit down that would be great.'

'Oh, Declan.' Holly's mother admonished him for his rudeness.

Holly spotted Ciara glued to Daniel's side at the bar. She laughed to herself and settled down to watch the documentary. As soon as the announcer introduced it, everybody cheered.

The title *Girls and the City* appeared over a beautiful night-time shot of Dublin, followed by footage of Sharon, Denise, Abbey and Ciara all squashed in the back of a taxi.

Sharon was speaking. 'Hello! I'm Sharon and this is Abbey, Denise and Ciara.' Each of the girls posed for her close-up as she was introduced. 'And we're heading to our best friend Holly's house because it's her birthday today . . .'

The scene changed to the girls surprising Holly with shouts of 'Happy birthday' at her door. It returned to Sharon in the taxi.

'Tonight it's gonna be just us girls and *no* men . . .'

The scene switched to Holly holding the presents up to the camera. Then it returned to Sharon in the taxi. 'We are gonna do lots and *lots* of drinking . . .'

Now Holly was popping open the champagne, then the girls were knocking back shots in Boudoir, and eventually it showed Holly with the crooked tiara drinking out of a champagne bottle with a straw.

'We are gonna go clubbing . . .'

There was then a shot of the girls in Boudoir doing some embarrassing moves on the dance floor. Sharon was shown next, speaking sincerely. 'But nothing too mad! We're gonna be good girls tonight!'

The next scene showed the girls protesting wildly as they were escorted out of the club by three bouncers.

Holly stared in shock over at Sharon, who was equally surprised. The men laughed their hearts out and slapped Declan on the back. Holly, Sharon, Denise, Abbey and even Ciara slithered down in their seats with humiliation. What on earth had Declan done?

Holly held her breath. How drunk must they all have been to completely forget the events of that night? The truth terrified her.

Once again a new title took over the screen: 'Journey to the City'. It showed the girls scrambling over one another to get into the seven-seater taxi. Holly had actually thought she was quite sober at that stage. 'Oh, Nick,' she moaned drunkenly to the taxi driver from the passenger seat, 'I'm thirty today, can you believe it?'

Nick—who couldn't give a flying flute what age she was—glanced over at her and laughed, 'Sure you're only a young one still, Holly.' The camera zoomed in on Holly's face and she cringed at the sight of herself. She looked so drunk, so *sad*.

'But what am I gonna do, Jim?' she whinged. 'I have no job, no husband, no children and I'm thirty! Did I tell you that?'

'Ah, Holly, worry about all that shite tomorrow, love.'

The camera stayed with Holly as she leaned her head against the window, lost in thought for the rest of the journey. Holly couldn't get over how lonely she looked. She didn't like it. She looked round the room in embarrassment and turned back in time to see herself screaming to the girls on O'Connell Street.

'OK, girls. We are going to Boudoir and *no one* is going to stop us, *especially* any *silly bouncers* who *think* they own the place,' and she marched off in what she thought at the time was a straight line. All the girls cheered and followed after her.

The scene immediately jumped to the two bouncers outside Boudoir shaking their heads. 'Not tonight, girls, sorry.'

'But,' Denise said calmly, 'do you not know who we are?'

'No.' They both stared over their heads, ignoring them.

'Huh!' Denise put her hands on her hips. 'But this is the very, very famous . . . em . . . Princess Holly from the royal family of . . . Finland.'

On camera Holly frowned at Denise.

Her family howled with laughter. 'You couldn't write a script better than this,' Declan laughed.

'Oh, she's royalty, is she?' the bouncer with a moustache smirked. 'Finland got a royal family, Paul?'

'Don't think so, boss.'

Holly gave them both a royal wave. 'You see?' Denise said. 'You'll be very embarrassed if you don't let her in.'

'Supposing we let her in, then you'll have to stay outside.' Moustache Man motioned for the people behind them to pass.

'Oh, no, no,' Denise laughed. 'I'm her lady in waiting.'

'One *must* have a drink,' Holly said. 'One is *dreadfully* thirsty.'

Paul and Moustache Man snorted and tried to keep a straight face. 'No, honestly, girls, you need to be a member.'

'But I am a member, of the royal family!' Holly said.

Denise pleaded. 'The princess and I will be no trouble at all.'

Moustache Man raised his eyes to the sky. 'All right then, go on in,' he said, stepping aside.

'God bless you,' Holly said as she passed.

'She's out of her mind,' laughed Moustache Man, regaining his composure as Ciara's entourage approached.

'Is it OK if my film crew follow me in?' Ciara said confidently in a brilliant Australian accent.

'Hold on while I check.' Paul turned his back and spoke into the walkie-talkie. 'Yeah, that's no problem, go ahead.'

'That's that Australian singer, isn't it?' Moustache Man said.

'Yeah, good song that.'

'Tell the boys inside to keep an eye on the princess and her lady. We don't want them bothering that singer with the pink hair.'

As Holly watched the inside of Boudoir on the screen she remembered being disappointed by the club. There had always been a mystery as to what Boudoir looked like. The girls had read in a magazine that there was a water feature Madonna had apparently jumped into one night. Holly had imagined a huge champagne waterfall cascading down the wall of the club that continued to flow in little bubbling streams while the glamorous people sat round it and occasionally dipped their glasses into it. But instead of her waterfall, what Holly got was an over-sized fish bowl in the centre of the circular bar. The room wasn't as big as she thought it would be, and it was decorated in rich reds and gold. On the far side was a huge gold curtain acting as a partition, which was blocked by another menacing-looking bouncer.

At the top of the room was the main attraction, a massive king-size bed, which was tilted on a platform towards the rest of the club. On top of the gold silk sheets were two skinny models dressed in gold body paint and gold thongs. It was all a bit too tacky.

'Look at the size of those thongs!' gasped Denise. 'I have a plaster on my baby finger bigger than those.'

Beside her in Club Diva, Tom began to nibble on Denise's baby finger. Holly returned her gaze to the screen.

'Good evening and welcome to the twelve o'clock news, I'm Sharon McCarthy.' Sharon stood with a bottle in her hand serving as a micro-phone. Declan had angled the camera so that he could get Ireland's famous newsreaders in the shot.

'Today, on the thirtieth birthday of Princess Holly of Finland, her royal self and her lady in waiting succeeded in being granted access to the famous celebrity hangout Boudoir. Also present is Australian rock chick Ciara . . . and it appears that Ireland's favourite newsreader Tony Walsh was seen smiling just moments ago. Here I have a witness to the fact. Welcome, Denise.'

'Well, I was just over there beside his table when I saw it happening.' Denise sucked in her cheekbones.

'Can you explain to us what happened?'

'Well, I was standing there minding my own business when Mr Walsh took a sip of his drink and smiled.'

'Gosh, Denise, and are you sure it was a smile?'

'Well, it could have been trapped wind causing him to make a face, but others around me thought it was a smile.'

'So there were others who witnessed this?'

'Yes, Princess Holly here saw the whole thing.'

The camera panned across to Holly where she stood drinking from a champagne bottle with a straw. 'So, Holly, can you tell us, was it wind or a smile?'

Holly looked confused, then rolled her eyes. 'Oh, wind. Sorry, I think it's this champagne that's doing it to me.'

Club Diva erupted in laughter and Holly hid her face in shame.

'OK, then,' Sharon said, 'so you heard it here first. The night when Ireland's grimmest presenter was seen smiling. Back to you at the studio.' As she looked up and saw Tony Walsh standing beside her, Sharon gulped and said, 'Good evening,' and the camera was switched off. Everyone in the club was laughing at this stage, including the girls. The whole thing was just so ridiculous.

The camera was switched back on and focused on the mirror in the Ladies. Declan was filming through a slit in the doorway and Denise and Sharon's reflections were visible.

'Where's Holly?' Sharon asked.

'Last time I saw her she was doing a few funky moves on the dance floor,' said Denise. The two of them laughed.

'Ah . . . our poor little disco diva. I hope she finds someone gorgeous out there and snogs the face off him.'

'Yeah,' agreed Denise. 'Come on, let's find her a man.'

Just after the girls left, a cubicle door opened and out stepped Holly. Through the crack in the door you could see her eyes were red from crying. She blew her nose and stared miserably at herself in the mirror.

The scene changed and the words 'Operation Gold Curtain' came up. Denise screamed, 'Declan, you bastard!' and rushed off to the toilet. Declan lit himself a cigarette.

'Time for Operation Gold Curtain,' Denise was announcing.

'Huh?' Sharon and Holly had collapsed in a drunken stupor.

'Operation Gold Curtain. Time to infiltrate the VIP bar!'

'You mean this isn't it?' Sharon said sarcastically.

'No! That's where the real celebs go!' Denise said excitedly, pointing at the gold curtain.

'I don't really care where the celebs are,' piped up Holly.

Denise groaned and rolled her eyes. 'Girls! Abbey and Ciara are in there, why aren't we?'

Jack looked curiously at Abbey, who shrugged her shoulders weakly. None of this was jogging anybody's memory except of course Denise's, and she had fled the room.

Once Sharon and Holly had heard that Abbey and Ciara were in the VIP bar, they sat up attentively and listened to Denise. 'OK, girlies, here's what we're gonna do!'

The camera followed the three girls as they very suspiciously approached the gold curtain and loitered around. Sharon finally built up the courage to tap the bouncer on the shoulder, causing him to turn round and provide Denise with enough time to escape under the curtain. She got down on her hands and knees and stuck her head through to the VIP bar. Holly kicked her in the bum to hurry her along.

'I can see them!' Denise hissed loudly. 'Oh my God! They're speaking to that Hollywood actor guy!' She took her head back out and looked at Holly, just as the giant bouncer turned his head towards them.

'No, no, no!' Denise said. 'This is Princess Holly of Finland. I am bowing to her. Join me!'

Sharon quickly got on her knees and the two of them began to worship Holly's feet. Holly looked around awkwardly as everyone in the club began to stare, and she once again gave the royal wave.

'Oh, Holly!' her mother said, trying to catch her breath after laughing so hard.

The big burly bouncer spoke into his walkie-talkie. 'Boys, got a situation with the princess and the lady.'

Denise looked at both girls in panic and mouthed, 'Hide!' The girls jumped to their feet and fled. The camera searched through the crowds but couldn't find them.

From her seat in Club Diva, Holly groaned loudly as it finally clicked with her what was about to happen.

Paul and Moustache Man rushed upstairs to the club and met a very big man at the gold curtain. 'What's going on?' Moustache Man asked.

'Those girls you told us to keep an eye on tried to crawl through to the other side,' the big man said. You could tell his previous job involved killing people.

'Where are they?' Moustache Man asked.

The big man looked away. 'They're hiding, boss.'

Moustache Man rolled his eyes. 'Well, start looking then.'

The camera secretly followed the three bouncers as they patrolled the club looking under tables and behind curtains. There was a bit of commotion at the top of the club and they headed towards the noise to sort it out. The two skinny dancers in gold body paint had stopped dancing and were staring with horrified expressions at the bed. The camera panned across. Underneath the gold silk sheets Sharon, Denise and Holly were rolling around, trying to make themselves as flat as possible so they wouldn't be noticed. A crowd gathered and soon the music was shut down. The three big lumps froze.

The bouncers counted to three and pulled the covers off the bed. Three startled-looking girls appearing like deer caught in headlights.

'*One* just had to get forty winks before *one* left,' Holly said.

Everyone watching the screen howled with laughter.

The scene changed to 'The Long Journey Home'. The girls were in the taxi. Abbey sat with her head hanging out of the window by order of the taxi driver: 'You are not throwing up in my cab.' Sharon and

Denise had fallen asleep, with their heads resting on each other.

The camera turned to focus on Holly, who was sitting in the passenger seat once again. This time she wasn't talking the ear off the driver; she rested her head on the seat back and stared straight into the night. Holly knew what she was thinking as she watched herself. Time to go home to that empty house alone again.

'Happy birthday, Holly,' Abbey's voice trembled.

Holly turned to smile at her and came face to face with the camera. 'Are you *still* filming with that thing? Turn it off!' and she knocked the camera out of Declan's hand. The end.

As Daniel went to turn the lights up in the club, Holly slipped quickly away through the nearest door. She needed to collect her thoughts before everyone started talking. She found herself in a tiny storeroom surrounded by empty crates. She sat down on one and thought about what she had just seen. She was in shock. She felt confused and angry with Declan; he had told her that he was making a documentary about club life. And he had literally made a show of her and her friends.

But the last thing she wanted to do right now was to scream at Declan in front of everyone. If it had been anyone else but her on the TV, Holly would have thought it very deserving of the award. But it *was* her . . . She didn't mind so much the bits of her and her friends being so silly, it was more the sneaky shots of her unhappiness that bothered her.

Thick salty tears trickled down her face. She had seen on television how she truly felt, lost and alone. She cried for Gerry, she cried for herself with big, heaving sobs that hurt her ribs whenever she tried to catch her breath. She didn't want to be alone any more, and she didn't want her family seeing the loneliness she tried so hard to hide. She just wanted Gerry back and didn't care about anything else. She just wanted him. She heard the door open behind her and felt big strong arms wrapping themselves round her frail body. She cried as if months of built-up anguish were all tumbling out at once.

'What's wrong? Didn't she like it?' Declan ask worriedly.

'Just leave her be,' her mum said softly, and the door closed. Daniel stroked her hair and rocked her softly.

After crying what felt like all the tears in the world, she let go of Daniel. 'Sorry,' she sniffed, drying her face with her sleeves.

'There's no need to be sorry,' he said gently.

She sat in silence while trying to compose herself.

'If you're upset about the documentary, there's no need,' he said, sitting down on a crate opposite her.

'Yeah, right,' she said sarcastically, wiping her tears again.

'No, really.' He smiled. 'I thought it was very funny. You all looked like you were having a great time. Nobody but you noticed whatever it is that's upsetting you.'

Holly felt mildly better. 'Are you sure?'

'I'm sure I'm sure,' he said, smiling. 'Now, you really have to stop hiding in all the rooms in my club, or I might take it personally.'

'Are the girls OK?' There was loud laughter from outside.

'They're fine, as you can hear,' he said. 'Ciara's delighted everyone will think she's a star, Denise has finally come out of the toilet and Sharon just can't stop laughing. Although Jack's giving Abbey a hard time about throwing up on the way home.'

Holly giggled. 'Thanks, Daniel.' She smiled at him.

'You ready to go and face your public?'

'Think so.' Holly stepped outside to find everyone sitting round the table happily sharing jokes and stories. Holly sat beside her mum. Elizabeth gave her daughter a kiss on the cheek.

'So is it OK?' Declan asked Holly, afraid he had upset his sister.

Holly threw him a look.

'I thought you would like it, Hol,' he said worriedly.

'I hate surprises,' she said, rubbing her stinging eyes.

'Let that be a lesson,' Frank warned his son. 'You shouldn't film people without them knowing. It's illegal.'

'I bet they didn't know that when they chose him for the award,' Elizabeth agreed.

'You're not gonna tell them, Holly?' Declan asked worriedly.

'Not if you're nice to me for the next few months.'

Declan made a face; he was stuck and he knew it. 'Whatever,' he said.

Holly was standing over the sink with her sleeves rolled up, when she heard the familiar voice.

'Hi, honey.'

He stood at the open patio doors. 'Hello, you,' she smiled.

'Miss me?'

'Of course.'

'Have you found that new husband yet?'

'Of course I have, he's upstairs asleep,' she laughed.

Gerry tutted. 'Shall I go up and suffocate him for sleeping in our bed?'

'Ah, give him another hour or so. He needs his rest.'

He looked happy, she thought, fresh-faced and still as beautiful as she remembered. He was wearing her favourite blue top, which she had bought him one Christmas. He stared at her from under his long eyelashes with his big brown puppy eyes.

'Are you coming in?' she asked, smiling.

'No, I just popped by to see how you are. Everything OK?' He leaned against the doorjamb, hands in his pockets.

'So-so,' she said. 'Could be better.'

'I hear you're a TV star now,' he grinned.

'A very reluctant one,' she laughed. 'I miss you, Gerry.'

'I haven't gone far,' he said softly.

'You leaving me again?'

'For the time being.'

She smiled. 'See you soon.'

Holly woke up with a smile on her face and felt like she'd slept for days. 'Good morning, Gerry,' she said, happily staring up at the ceiling.

The phone rang beside her. 'Hello?'

'Oh my God, Holly, just take a look at the weekend papers,' Sharon said in a panic.

Six

HOLLY LEAPT OUT OF BED, threw on a track suit and drove to her nearest newsagent. She parked the car, walked into the shop and found the newsstand, where she began to leaf through the pages of a newspaper. The man behind the counter coughed loudly and Holly looked up at him. 'This is not a library, young lady, you'll have to buy that,' he said.

'I know that,' she said, irritated. Honestly, how on earth was anyone supposed to know which paper to buy if they didn't even know which paper contained what they were looking for? She ended up picking up every single newspaper and slammed them down on the counter, smiling sweetly at him.

The man started to scan them into the register one by one.

She stared longingly at the chocolate display in front of her and then grabbed two king-size bars from the bottom of the pile. One by one the rest of the chocolate bars began to slide onto the floor. Holly bent down with a red face to pick them up. So many had fallen she had to make several trips up and down. The shop was silent, apart from a few coughs from the queue forming behind her. Then she remembered she needed milk, so she rushed to retrieve a pint from the fridge.

She made her way back to the top of the queue and added the milk to her pile. The newsagent stopped scanning. 'Mark,' he yelled.

A spotty young teenager appeared from the aisles, a pricing gun in his hand. 'Yeah?' he said grumpily.

'Open the other till, will ya, son.' He glared at her.

Holly made a face at him.

Mark dragged his body over to the second till, and the queue rushed across to it. Holly grabbed a few packets of crisps from below the counter and added them to her purchases.

'Anything else?' the newsagent asked sarcastically.

'No, thank you, that will be all.' She paid her money and fumbled with her purse, trying to put the change back in.

'Next,' the newsagent nodded to the customer behind her.

'Excuse me,' Holly said. 'May I have a bag, please.'

'That'll be twenty cents.'

Holly found her money again, slammed the coin on the counter and began to fill the bag with her items.

'Next,' he said. Holly began stuffing the bag full in panic.

'I'll wait till the lady is ready,' the customer said politely.

Holly smiled at him appreciatively. As she turned to leave the shop, Mark, the boy behind the counter, startled her by yelling, 'Hey, I know you! You're the girl from the telly!'

Holly swirled round in surprise and the plastic handle of the carrier bag broke from the weight of all the newspapers. Her shopping went rolling in all directions.

The friendly customer got down on his knees to help her while the rest of the shop watched in amusement.

'It is you, isn't it?' the boy laughed.

Holly smiled up weakly at him from the floor.

'I knew it!' He clapped his hands together. 'You're cool!'

Holly's face went red. 'Em . . . could I have another bag, please?'

'Yeah, that'll be—'

'There you go,' the friendly customer placed a twenty-cent coin on the counter. 'I'm Rob,' he said, and held out his hand.

'I'm Holly.' She took his hand, a little embarrassed by his overfriend-liness. 'Thanks for the help,' she said gratefully, getting to her feet.

'No problem.' He held the door open for her. He was good-looking, she thought, a few years older than her, and had the oddest coloured eyes, a kind of a grey-green colour.

He cleared his throat.

She blushed, suddenly realising she had been staring at him like a fool. She walked out to her car and placed the bulging bag on the back seat. Rob followed her over. Her heart did a little flip.

'Hi, again,' he said. 'Em . . . I was wondering if you would like to go for a drink?' Then he laughed, glancing at his watch. 'Actually, it's a bit too early for that. How about a coffee?'

He rested himself coolly against the car, his hands in the pockets of his jeans, acting as if asking a stranger out for coffee was the most natural thing in the world. Was this what people did these days?

'Em . . .' Holly thought about it. What harm could it do to go for a coffee with a man who had been so polite to her? The fact that he was absolutely gorgeous also helped. But, regardless of his beauty, Holly really craved some company and he seemed like a nice, decent man to talk to.

She was just about to say yes when he glanced down at her hand and his smile faded. 'Oh, sorry, I didn't realise . . .' He backed away from her awkwardly. 'I have to rush off anyway.' He smiled quickly at her and took off down the road.

Holly stared after him, confused. Had she said something wrong? She looked down at her hand and saw her wedding ring sparkle back at her. She sighed loudly and rubbed her face tiredly. She wasn't in the mood to go home, she was sick of staring at the walls all day and talking to herself. It was only ten o'clock and it was beautifully sunny and warm. Across the road her local café, the Greasy Spoon, was setting up tables and chairs outside. Her stomach grumbled. She took her newspapers from the car with both hands, slammed the door and wandered across to the café.

A plump lady was cleaning the tables. 'Want to sit here, love?'

'Yes. I'll have the Irish breakfast.'

'No problem, love.' She waddled into the café.

Holly flicked through the pages of one of the tabloids and came to a small article in the review section that caught her eye.

GIRLS AND THE CITY A HIT IN THE RATINGS
by Tricia Coleman

For any of you unfortunate people who missed out on the outrageously funny *Girls and the City* last Wednesday night, do not despair. It will be back soon.

The hilarious fly-on-the-wall TV documentary, directed by Irishman Declan Kennedy, follows five Dublin girls out for a night on the town. They lift the lid on the mysterious world of celebrity life in trendy club Boudoir and provide us with thirty minutes of stomach-aching laughter.

Last Wednesday, the latest ratings reveal, four million people tuned in. The show is to be repeated on Sunday at 11 p.m. on Channel 4. This is must-see TV, so don't miss it!

Holly tried to keep her cool. This was obviously great news for Declan but disastrous for her. Having that documentary aired once was bad enough. She had let him off lightly the other night because he had been so excited, but she really needed to have a serious talk with him.

She flicked through the rest of the papers and saw what it was Sharon was ranting about. Every single tabloid had an article about the documentary and one had even printed a photograph of Denise, Sharon and Holly from a few years ago. How they had got their hands on it she did not know. And she wasn't too happy with the use of the words 'mad girls', 'drunken girls', and how they were 'well up for it'. What did that even mean?

Holly's food finally arrived and she stared at it in shock. The plate was piled high with sausages, bacon, eggs, hash browns, black and white pudding, baked beans, fried potatoes, mushrooms, tomatoes and five slices of toast. Holly looked around her with embarrassment, hoping no one would think she was a complete pig. She hadn't had much of an appetite lately, but she finally felt ready to eat.

When she reached her parents' house it was almost two o'clock. Holly rang the doorbell for the fourth time and still no one answered. She crossed the grass and pressed her face against the living-room window to see if there was any sign of life, and heard the screaming match.

'Ciara, get the damn door!'

'No, I said! I . . . am . . . busy.'

'Well, so am I!'

Holly rang the doorbell again just to add fuel to the fire.

'*Declan!*' Ouch, that was a bloodcurdling scream.

'Get it yourself, you lazy cow!'

Holly took out her mobile phone and rang the house.

'*Ciara, answer the phone!*'

'*No!*'

'Oh, for God's sake,' Holly snapped loudly and hung up. She dialled Declan's mobile number.

'Yeah?'

'Declan, open the door now or I'll kick it in,' Holly growled.

'Oh, sorry, I thought Ciara had answered it,' he lied.

He opened the door in his boxer shorts and Holly stormed in.

'Mum and Dad are out,' he said lazily and headed upstairs.

'Hey, where are you going?'

'Back to bed.'

'No you are not,' Holly said calmly. 'You are going to sit here with me'—she patted the couch—'and we're gonna have a long chat about *Girls and the City.*'

'No,' Declan moaned. 'Do we have to do this now? I'm really, really tired.' He rubbed his eyes with his fists.

'Declan, it's two o'clock in the afternoon. Sit!' she said.

He dragged his weary body over to the couch, where he stretched out along the entire thing, leaving no room for Holly. She rolled her eyes and dragged her dad's armchair close.

'I feel like I'm with a shrink,' he laughed, crossing his arms behind his head and staring up at her from the couch.

'Good, because I'm really going to pick your brains.'

'Oh, Holly, we talked about this the other night,' Declan whinged.

'Did you honestly think that was all I was going to say? "Oh, I'm sorry, Declan, but I didn't like the way you publicly humiliated me and my friends. See you next week"?'

'Obviously not.'

'Come on, Declan,' she said, softening her tone. 'I just want to understand why you thought it would be such a great idea not to tell me you were filming us.'

'You *knew* I was filming,' he said defensively.

'For a documentary about *club life!*'

'And it *was* about club life,' Declan laughed.

'Oh, you think you're so bloody clever.' She counted to ten to prevent herself from attacking him. 'Come on,' she said. 'Don't you think I'm going through enough right now?'

Declan sat up. 'I know you've been through hell, Holly, but I thought this would cheer you up. I wasn't lying when I said I was going to film the club, but when I brought it back to college to begin the edit, everyone thought it was so funny that I couldn't *not* show it to people.'

'Yeah, but you put it on TV, Declan.'

'I didn't know that was the prize, honestly,' he said. 'Nobody knew, not even my lecturers. How could I say no to it when I won?'

Holly gave up and ran her fingers through her hair.

'I honestly thought you would like it,' he said. 'I checked with Ciara and *even she* said you'd like it. I'm sorry if I upset you.'

Holly froze. What had he just said? 'Ciara knew about the tape?'

Declan desperately tried to think of a way to back out of it. Coming up with nothing, he threw himself back on the couch and covered his head with a cushion, knowing he had just started World War III.

'Oh, Holly, don't say anything, she'll kill me!' came his muffled reply.

Holly bounded out of her seat and stormed upstairs, thumping her feet and yelling threats. She pounded on Ciara's door.

'Don't come in!' yelled Ciara from inside.

'You are in so much trouble, Ciara!' Holly screamed. She opened the door and burst her way in, putting on her most terrifying face.

'I told you not to come in!' wailed Ciara. She was sitting on the floor with a photo album on her lap and tears were streaming down her face.

'**O**h, Ciara, what's wrong?' Holly said soothingly to her younger sister. She couldn't remember the last time she'd seen her cry, in fact, she didn't know Ciara even knew *how* to cry.

'Nothing's wrong,' Ciara said, snapping the album shut and sliding it under her bed. She wiped her face roughly.

'Something *is* wrong,' Holly said, crossing the room to join her sister on the floor. She wasn't sure how to deal with Ciara like this.

'I'm fine,' Ciara snapped.

'OK,' Holly said. 'But if there's something upsetting you, you know you can talk to me about it, don't you?'

Ciara refused to look at her and just nodded her head. Holly began to stand up to leave her in peace when all of a sudden Ciara burst into tears again. Holly quickly sat back down and wrapped her arms protectively round her younger sister, stroking her silky pink hair.

'Do you want to tell me what's wrong?' she asked softly.

Ciara gurgled some sort of reply and slid the photo album back out. She opened it with trembling hands and flicked a few pages.

'Him,' she said sadly, pointing to a photograph of her and some guy Holly didn't recognise. Holly barely recognised her sister. The photograph was taken on a boat in Sydney Harbour. Ciara was sitting happily on the man's knee with her arms round his neck. She had blonde hair and her features looked much softer.

'Is that your boyfriend?' Holly asked carefully.

'Was,' Ciara sniffed, and a tear landed on the page.

'Is that why you came home?'

Ciara gasped for breath. 'We had a fight.'

'Did he . . . He didn't hurt you or anything, did he?'

'No,' Ciara spluttered. 'It was just over something really stupid and I said I was leaving and he said he was glad . . .' She started sobbing again. Holly held her in her arms and waited. 'He didn't even come to the airport to say goodbye to me.'

Holly rubbed Ciara's back. 'Has he called you since?'

'No, and I've been home for two months, Holly,' she wailed, looking up with such sad eyes that Holly felt like crying too.

'Then maybe he's not the right kind of person for you.'

'But I love Mathew, Holly. I only booked the flight because I was angry, I didn't think he would let me go . . .' She stared for a long time at the photograph.

Ciara's bedroom windows were wide open and Holly listened to the familiar sound of the waves on the beach. She had shared this room with Ciara while they were growing up, and a weird sense of comfort embraced her.

Ciara began to calm down beside her. 'Sorry, Hol.'

'Hey, you don't need to be sorry at all. You should have told me all this instead of keeping it inside.'

'This is minor compared to what happened to you. I feel stupid crying about it.' She wiped her tears, angry with herself.

'Ciara, losing someone you love is always hard, no matter if they're alive or . . .' She couldn't finish the sentence.

'It's just that you've been so brave, Holly, I don't know how you do it. And here I am crying over a stupid boyfriend I only went out with for a few months.'

'Me? Brave?' Holly laughed. 'I wish.'

'Yes, you are,' Ciara insisted. 'Everyone says so. If I were you, I'd be lying in a ditch somewhere.'

'Don't go giving me ideas, Ciara.' Holly smiled at her.

'You're OK, though, aren't you?' Ciara said worriedly.

Holly slid her wedding ring up and down her finger. She thought about that question for a while.

'I'm lots of things, Ciara. I'm lonely, I'm tired, I'm sad, I'm happy, I'm lucky, I'm unlucky; I'm a million things every day, but I suppose OK is one of them.'

'And you're brave,' Ciara assured her. 'And in control.'

'No, you were always the brave one. As for being in control, I don't know what I'm doing from one day to the next.'

Ciara's forehead creased. 'I am far from being brave, Holly.'

'Yes, you are. All those things that you do, like jumping out of aeroplanes and snowboarding off cliffs . . .'

'Oh, no, that's not brave, that's foolish. Anybody can bungee jump off a bridge. You could do it *if you had to.*'

'Yes, and if your husband died you would cope *if you had to*. There's nothing brave about it. There's no choice involved.'

Ciara and Holly stared at each other, aware of the other's battle.

Ciara was the first to speak. 'Well, I guess you and I are more alike than we thought.' She smiled at her big sister and Holly hugged her tightly. 'So, was there something you were going to scream at me about earlier on?'

'No, forget about it, it was nothing,' Holly replied.

It was eight o'clock when Holly finally drove up her driveway, and it was still bright. The world never felt quite so depressing when it was bright. She had spent hours chatting with Ciara, who had changed her mind at least twenty times about whether or not she should call Mathew in Australia. By the time Holly left, Ciara was adamant she would never speak to him again, which probably meant she had already called him by now.

She walked up the path to the front door and stared at the garden curiously. Was it her imagination or did it look a little tidier? Something about it looked different.

The sound of a lawnmower started and Holly spun round to see her neighbour, who was out working in his garden. She waved over to thank him, presuming it was he who had helped her, and he held his hand up in response.

It had always been Gerry's job to do the garden. He wasn't necessarily a keen gardener, it was just that Holly was an incredibly unkeen gardener, so somebody had to do the dirty work. Their patch of grass surrounded by a few shrubs and flowers now looked little more than an overgrown field. When Gerry died, the garden had died along with him.

Which reminded her of the orchid in the house. She rushed inside, filled a jug with water and poured it over the extremely thirsty-looking plant. She threw a chicken curry into the microwave and thought back over her day. She looked down at her wedding ring. When that man Rob had walked away from her, Holly had felt so awful. He had given her that look as if she were about to initiate an affair. She felt guilty for even *considering* his invitation for coffee. She still *felt* married, and going for a coffee would have seemed like she was betraying her husband. Gerry had been gone almost five months now, but her heart and soul still belonged to him.

Holly twisted her ring round her finger. At what point should she take it off? Where was the rule book for widows that explained when exactly the ring should be taken off? And when it finally did come off, where would she put it, where *should* she put it? In the bin? Beside her bed so she could be reminded of him every single day? She wasn't ready to give up her Gerry yet; as far as she was concerned, he was still living.

The microwave beeped. She took the dish out and threw it straight in the bin. She had suddenly lost her appetite.

Later that night Denise rang her in a tizzy. 'Switch Dublin FM on quick!' Holly raced to the radio and flicked the switch. 'I'm Tom O'Connor and you're listening to Dublin FM. If you've just joined us, we are talking about bouncers. In light of the amount of persuasion it took the *Girls and the City* girls to blag their way into the club Boudoir, we wanna know what your thoughts on bouncers are. Do you like them? Do you understand why they are the way they are? Or are they too strict? The number to call is . . .'

Holly picked the phone back up.

'Well?' Denise said.

'What the hell have we started, Denise?'

'Oh, I know,' she giggled. 'Did you see the papers today?'

'Yeah, it's all a bit silly, really.'

They remained quiet while they listened to the radio. Some guy was giving out about bouncers and Tom was trying to calm him down.

'Oh, listen to my baby,' Denise said. 'Doesn't he sound sexy?'

'Em . . . yeah. I take it you two are still together?'

'Of course.' Denise sounded insulted. 'Why wouldn't we be?'

'Well, it's been quite a while now, Denise, that's all.' Holly quickly tried to explain so she wouldn't hurt her friend's feelings. 'And you always said you couldn't be with a man for over a month!'

'Yes, well, I said I *couldn't* but I never said I *wouldn't*. Tom is different, Holly,' Denise said breathily.

Holly was surprised. 'Oh, so what's so different with Tom then?' She rested the phone between her ear and shoulder and settled down in a chair to examine her nails.

'Oh, there's just this *connection*. It's like he's my soul mate. He's so thoughtful, he makes me laugh *all the time*, and I haven't got sick of him like all the other guys. *Plus* he's good-looking.'

Holly stifled a yawn. Denise tended to say this after the first week of going out with all her new boyfriends and then she would quickly change her mind. But then again, perhaps she meant what she said this time; after all, Denise and Tom had been together for several weeks now.

'I'm very happy for you,' she said.

The next day Holly dragged herself out of bed to go for a stroll in the park. She needed to start doing some exercise and she also needed to start thinking about job-hunting. She had definitely ruled out clothes stores (the possibility of having a boss like Denise had talked her out of that one), restaurants, hotels and pubs, and she didn't want another nine-to-five office job, which left . . . nothing.

She sat down on a park bench opposite the playground and listened to the children's screams of delight. Why did people have to grow up? She wanted to be irresponsible, she wanted to be looked after. And then she could grow up all over again and meet Gerry all over again and force him to go to the doctor months earlier and then she would be sitting beside Gerry here on the bench watching their children play-ing. What if, what if, what if . . .

She thought about the stinging remark Richard had made about never having to bother with that children nonsense. She wished so much she could have a little Gerry running around the playground while she shouted at him to be careful. She and Gerry had just started talking about having children a few months before he was diagnosed. They had been so excited about it, and used to lie in bed for hours trying to decide names and create scenarios in their heads of what it would be like to be parents.

Well, think of the devil, Holly thought to herself, seeing Richard leaving the playground with Emily and Timmy. He looked so relaxed, and she watched in surprise as he chased the children round the park. They looked like they were having fun, not a very familiar sight. She zipped up her layer of extra-thick skin in preparation for their conversation.

'Hello, Holly!' Richard said happily, spotting her and walking across the grass to her.

'Hello,' Holly said, greeting the kids as they ran over to her and gave her a big hug. It made a nice change. 'You're far from home,' she said to Richard. 'What brings you all the way here?'

'I brought the children to see Grandma and Granddad, didn't I?' he said, ruffling Timmy's head.

'*And* we had McDonald's,' Timmy said excitedly, and Emily cheered.

'Oh, you lucky things!' Holly said. 'Isn't your daddy the best?'

Richard looked pleased.

'Junk food?' Holly questioned her brother.

'Ah.' He waved his hand dismissively and sat down beside her. 'Everything in moderation, isn't that right, Emily?'

Five-year-old Emily nodded her head.

'One McDonald's meal isn't going to kill them,' Holly agreed.

Timmy grabbed at his throat and pretended to choke. His face went red as he made gagging noises and he collapsed on the grass and lay still. Richard and Holly laughed. Emily looked like she was going to cry.

'Oh dear,' Richard joked. 'Looks like we were wrong, Holly, the McDonald's did kill Timmy.'

Holly looked at her brother in shock for calling his son Timmy. Richard got up and threw him over his shoulder. 'Well, we better go and bury him now.' Timmy giggled as he dangled upside-down.

'Oh, he's alive!' Richard laughed.

'No, I'm not,' giggled Timmy.

'OK, we best be off,' grinned Richard. 'Bye, Holly.'

'Bye, Holly,' the children cheered, and Richard walked off with Timmy slung over his shoulder as little Emily skipped and danced beside her father, gripping his hand.

Holly stared in amusement at the stranger walking off with two children. Who was this man who claimed to be her brother?

Seven

BARBARA FINISHED SERVING her customers, and as soon as they left the building she ran into the staff room and lit up a cigarette. Melissa, her colleague, had called in sick that morning, so she was stuck all by herself today. And of course it was the busiest day they'd had in ages. As soon as November came, with those horrible depressing dark nights and sheets of rain, everyone came running in the door booking holidays to hot sunny countries.

Her boss had gone out to run errands and Barbara was really looking forward to her cigarette break. Then, just her luck, the bell over the door sounded. Barbara cursed, puffing on the cigarette furiously and spraying perfume all around so her boss wouldn't notice the smoke. She left the staff room expecting to see the customer sitting behind the counter, but instead the old man was still making his way towards it.

'Hello, sir, how can I help you?' she said, surprised to see how young the man actually was. His body was hunched and the walking stick in his hand seemed to be the only thing preventing him from collapsing. His skin was very white and pasty, but he had big brown puppy eyes that seemed to smile at her. She couldn't help but smile back.

'I was hoping to book a holiday,' he said, 'but I was wondering if you could help me choose a place.'

Usually Barbara would have silently screamed at the customer for making her do this unbelievably impossible task. Most of her customers were so fussy that she could be sitting there for hours. But she surprised herself. 'No problem, sir. My name is Barbara. Why don't you take a seat and we'll search through the brochures.' She pointed to a chair and looked away so she didn't have to watch him struggle. 'Now,' she said, full of smiles, 'is there any country in particular you would like to go to?'

'Em . . . the Canary Islands. Lanzarote, I think. A summer holiday.'

They worked their way through the brochures and finally the man found a place he liked. Barbara was happy he took her advice into account, unlike other customers who just ignored her knowledge.

'OK, any month in particular?' she said.

'August?' he asked, and those big brown eyes looked so deep into Barbara's soul she just wanted to give him a big hug.

'August is a good month. Would you like a sea view or a pool view? The sea view is an extra thirty euros.'

He stared into space with a smile on his face. 'A sea view, please.'

'Good choice. Can I take your name and address, please?'

'Oh . . . this isn't actually for me.' Those brown eyes looked sad. 'It's a surprise for my wife and her friends.'

'Well, that's very thoughtful of you, sir.' She finished taking his details and he settled the bill. She began to print the arrangements from the computer to give to him.

'Oh, do you mind if I leave the details here with you? I want to surprise my wife and I would be afraid of leaving papers around the house in case she finds them.'

'That's no problem, sir. Usually the flight times aren't confirmed till a few weeks before. I'll give instructions not to call the house until then.'

'Thank you for your help, Barbara,' he said, smiling.

'It's been a pleasure, Mr—'

'It's Gerry.'

'It's been a pleasure, Gerry. Your wife will have a wonderful time. My friend went there and she loved it.' Barbara felt the need to reassure him his wife would be fine.

'Well, I'd better head back home. I'm not even supposed to be out of bed, you know.' He shrugged sheepishly.

Barbara jumped to her feet and ran round the other side of the counter to hold the door open for him. He smiled appreciatively as he walked past her and she watched as he slowly climbed into the taxi that had been waiting outside for him.

It was July 1st and Barbara sat grumpily behind the counter of Swords Travel Agents. It was the hottest day of the year, all her customers kept on bragging as they strolled in in their shorts and skimpy tops, filling the room with the smell of suncream. Barbara squirmed in her uncomfortable uniform and banged on the fan as it stalled.

'Oh, leave it, Barbara,' Melissa moaned. 'That'll only make it worse.'

'As if that could be possible,' Barbara grumbled.

'What is it with you today?' Melissa laughed.

'Oh, nothing much. It's just the hottest day of the year and we're stuck in this *crappy* job in this *stuffy* room.'

'Look, why don't you go outside to get some air and I'll deal with this next customer.' Melissa nodded to the woman making her way in.

'Thanks, Mel,' said Barbara, grabbing her cigarettes.

'Hello, can I help you?' Melissa smiled at the woman.

'Yes, I was wondering if Barbara still works here?'

Barbara froze just as she was reaching the door. She groaned and headed back to her seat. She looked at the woman behind the counter.

'Yes, 'I'm Barbara.'

'Oh, good.' The lady looked relieved and dived onto the stool in front of her. 'I was afraid you might not work here any more.'

'She wishes,' Melissa muttered under her breath.

'Can I help you?'

'Oh God, I really hope you can,' the lady said a bit hysterically, and rooted through her bag. 'I received this today from my husband and I was wondering if you could explain it to me.'

Barbara frowned at the crumpled piece of paper on the counter. A page had been torn out of a holiday brochure and written on it were the words: *Swords Travel Agents. Attn: Barbara.* 'My friend went there on holiday, but other than that it means nothing to me. Can't you ask your husband for more information?'

'No, he's not here any more,' the lady said sadly.

'OK, maybe your name will come up on the computer.'

'It's Holly Kennedy.' Her voice shook.

'Holly Kennedy, Holly Kennedy,' Melissa was listening in on their conversation. 'That name rings a bell. Oh, hold on, I was about to call you this week! I was under strict instructions from Barbara not to ring you until July for some reason—'

'Oh!' Barbara interrupted. 'You're Gerry's wife?'

'Yes!' Holly threw her hands to her face in shock. 'He was in here?'

'Yes, he was.' Barbara smiled. 'He was a lovely man.' She reached out to Holly's hand on the counter. Her heart went out to the lady. She was so young and it must be so hard for her right now. 'Melissa, can you get some tissues, please, while I explain to Holly exactly why her husband was here? She let go of Holly's hand to tap away at the computer and Melissa returned with a box of tissues.

'OK, Holly,' she said softly. 'Gerry has arranged a holiday for you and a Sharon McCarthy and a Denise Hennessey to go to Lanzarote for one week, arriving on the 30th July, to return home on the 5th August, He was adamant that he find the perfect place for you.' She tapped the crumpled page in front of her. 'You'll have a fab time, believe me. There are loads of restaurants and bars and . . .' She trailed off, realising Holly probably didn't give a damn whether she had a good time or not.

'When did he come in?' Tears poured from Holly's eyes.

'Let me see . . .' Barbara tapped away. 'The booking was made on the 28th of November.'

'November?' Holly gasped. 'What time of day was this?'

'I really can't remember. It was a long time ago—'

'Yes, of course, I'm sorry,' Holly interrupted.

Barbara told her as much as she could remember until Holly could think of no more questions to ask.

'Oh, thank you, Barbara, thank you so much.' Holly reached over the counter and gave her a big hug.

'No problem at all.' Barbara hugged her back. 'Let us know how you get on.' She smiled. 'Here are your details.' She handed her a thick envelope and watched her walk out.

Holly eventually arrived at her house and waved to Sharon and Denise, who were sitting on her garden wall sunbathing. They jumped up and rushed over to greet her.

'Well, you both got here quickly,' she said, trying to inject energy into her voice. She felt utterly drained.

'Sharon left work as soon as you called and she collected me from town,' Denise explained, studying Holly's face.

'Oh, you didn't have to do that,' Holly said lifelessly as she put the key in the door.

'Hey, have you been working in your garden?' Sharon asked.

'No, my neighbour's been doing it, I think.' Holly pulled the key from the door and searched through the bunch for the correct one.

'You think?' Denise tried to keep the conversation going while Holly battled with yet another key in the lock.

'Well, it's either my neighbour or a little leprechaun lives down the end of my garden,' Holly snapped, getting frustrated with the keys. Denise and Sharon motioned to each other to stay quiet, as Holly was obviously stressed.

'Oh, sod it!' Holly yelled and threw her keys on the ground.

Sharon picked them up. 'Hey, hon, don't worry about it. I swear the bloody things jump around on the keyring just to piss us off.' She worked her way through the keys, the door opened and Holly rushed in to turn the alarm off.

'OK, why don't you two make yourselves comfortable in the living room and I'll join you in a minute.' Holly headed into the bathroom to splash cold water on her face. She needed to be as excited about this holiday as Gerry had intended. When she felt a little more alive she joined the girls in the living room and sat opposite them.

'OK. I opened the envelope for July today and this is what it said.' She handed them the small card:

Have a good Holly day!
PS, I love you . . .

'Is that it?' Denise wrinkled up her nose, unimpressed.

'Well, Holly, I think it's a lovely note,' Sharon lied. 'It's so thoughtful and it's . . . a lovely play on words.'

Holly had to giggle. 'No, you fool!' she said, hitting her over the head with a cushion. 'Sharon, you are so supportive you make me sick! This was inside.' Holly handed them the crumpled page.

She watched with amusement as the girls tried to figure out Gerry's writing. 'Oh my God!' Denise gasped.

'What what what?' Sharon demanded. 'Did Gerry buy you a holiday?'

'Girls,' Holly said with a smile beginning to spread across her face, 'he bought *us* a holiday!'

The girls both squealed with excitement.

'Oh, this is incredible,' Denise said after the news had sunk in. 'Gerry's such a sweetie.'

Holly nodded, feeling proud of her husband, who had once again managed to surprise them all.

'So you went down to see this Barbara person?' Sharon asked.

'Yes, and she was the sweetest girl.' Holly smiled. 'She sat with me for ages, telling me about their conversation.'

'That was nice.' Denise sipped her wine. 'When was it, by the way?'

'He went in at the end of November.'

'November?' Sharon echoed. 'That was after the second operation.'

They all nodded silently.

'Well, it looks like we're all off to Lanzarote!' Denise cheered and she held her glass up. 'To Gerry!'

'To Gerry!' Holly and Sharon joined in.

'Are you sure Tom and John won't mind?' Holly asked.

'Of course John won't mind!' Sharon laughed.

'And me and Tom can go away for a week another time. That way we're not stuck together for two weeks on our first holiday.'

'You practically live together anyway,' Sharon said.

Denise gave a quick smile but didn't answer and the two of them dropped the subject. That annoyed Holly, because her friends were always doing that. She wanted to hear how they were getting on in their relationships, but nobody seemed to tell her any of the juicy gossip.

They seemed to be afraid to tell her about how happy they were or about the good news in their lives. Then again they also refused to moan about the bad things. So instead of being informed of what was really going on, she was stuck with this mediocre chitchat about . . . nothing.

'I have to say that leprechaun is doing a great job, Holly.' Denise cut into her thoughts as she looked out of the window.

'Oh, I know. I suppose I should go next door and thank him properly.'

After Denise and Sharon had headed off home, Holly grabbed a bottle of wine from the stash under the stairs and carried it next door to her neighbour. She rang the bell and waited.

'Hi, Holly,' he said, opening the door. 'Come in.'

Holly looked past him and saw the family sitting round the kitchen table eating supper. 'No, I won't disturb you, I just came to give you this'—she handed him the wine—'as a token of my thanks.'

'Well, Holly, this is really thoughtful of you, but thanks for what, if you don't mind me asking?'

'Oh, for tidying up my garden,' she said, blushing.

'But I haven't been tidying it, I'm sorry to say.'

'Oh. I thought you had been.' She laughed. 'You can keep that anyway.' She ran off with her face burning with embarrassment. What kind of fool wouldn't know who was tidying her own garden?

She knocked on a few more doors and nobody seemed to know what she was talking about. Everyone seemed to have jobs and lives, and remarkably enough they didn't spend their days monitoring her garden. As she walked in through her door the phone was ringing and she ran to answer it.

'Hello?' she panted.

'What were you doing, running a marathon?'

'No, I was chasing leprechauns.'

'Oh, cool.' Ciara didn't even question her. 'It's my birthday in two weeks.'

Holly had completely forgotten. 'Yeah, I know, Ciara.'

'Well, Mum and Dad want us all to invite friends to a barbecue. So will you tell Sharon and John, Denise and her DJ bloke, and that Daniel guy too?' She laughed hysterically. 'He's yummy!'

'Ciara, I hardly know the man. Ask Declan to ask him.'

'No, because I want you to subtly tell him that I love him and want to have his babies.'

Holly groaned.

'Stop it!' Ciara gave out. 'He's *my* birthday treat!'

'OK, I'll call the others and . . .'

Ciara had already hung up.

Holly decided to get the most awkward phone call out of the way first and she dialled the number for Hogan's.

'Hi, can I speak to Daniel Connelly, please?'

'Yeah, hold on.' 'Greensleeves' belted out into her ear.

'Hello?'

'Hi, Daniel? It's Holly Kennedy.'

'Who?' he yelled.

'It's Holly Kennedy? Declan's sister?'

'Oh, Holly, hiya. Hold on a second while I go somewhere quieter.'

Holly was stuck listening to 'Greensleeves' again, and she danced round her bedroom and started singing along.

'Sorry, Holly.' Daniel laughed. 'You like "Greensleeves"?'

'Em, no, not really.' Her face went scarlet. 'I was just ringing to invite you to a barbecue.'

'Oh, great, yeah, I would love to come.'

'It's Ciara's birthday on Friday week—you know my sister, Ciara?'

'Er, yes, the one with the pink hair.'

Holly laughed. 'Yeah, well, she wanted me to invite you and to subtly tell you that she wants to marry you and have your babies.'

Daniel started laughing. 'Yes . . . that was very subtle all right.'

'Em, well, Denise and your friend Tom are coming, and Declan will be there, of course, so you'll know a few people.'

'Are you going?'

'Of course!'

'Good. I'll know even more people then, won't I?' He chuckled.

'Oh . . . great. Ciara'll be delighted you're coming.' She was just about to hang up when a thought popped into her head. 'Oh, one more thing. Is that position behind the bar still available?'

Thank God it was a beautiful day, Holly thought, as she walked round to the back of her parents' house. It had rained and rained this week. Ciara was in hysterics about what would become of her barbecue and she'd been hell to be with all week. Luckily for everyone's sake the weather had returned to its former splendour.

Holly followed the sounds of laughter and was glad to see that the garden was full with family and friends. Denise had already arrived with Tom and Daniel, and they had all flaked out on the grass. Sharon had arrived without John and she was sitting chatting to Holly's mum, no doubt discussing Holly's progress in life.

Holly frowned as she noted that Jack was once again not present. Ever since he had helped her to carry out the task of clearing out

Gerry's things, he had been unusually distant. Even when they were children Jack had always been great at understanding Holly's needs and feelings without her having to point them out to him, but when she had told him that she needed space after Gerry's death, she didn't mean she wanted to be *completely* ignored and isolated. It was out of character for him not to be in contact for so long. Nerves fluttered through Holly's stomach and she prayed that he was all right.

Ciara was in the middle of the garden, loving being the centre of attention. She was dressed in a pink bikini top and blue denim cut-offs.

Holly approached with her present, which was immediately grabbed and ripped open. 'Oh, Holly, I love it!'

'I thought you would,' Holly said, glad she had chosen the right thing. It was a butterfly bellybutton ring, which had a little pink crystal in each wing. She had chosen it so it would coordinate with Ciara's new butterfly tattoo and her pink hair, of course.

'I'm gonna wear it now, actually,' Ciara said, ripping out her current bellybutton ring and piercing the butterfly through her skin.

'Ugh,' Holly shuddered. 'I could have lived without seeing that, thank you very much.'

There was a beautiful smell of barbecued food in the air and Holly's mouth began to water. She wasn't surprised to see all the men huddled round the barbecue. Spotting Richard, she marched over and charged right in. 'Richard, did you tidy my garden?'

Richard looked confused. 'Excuse me, did I what?'

'Did you tidy my garden?' she repeated. She didn't know why she was acting angry, just a force of habit probably, because if he had tidied it he had done her a huge favour.

'When?' Richard looked around frantically, as though he had been accused of murder.

'I don't know when,' she snapped. 'During the past few weeks.'

'No, Holly, some of us have to work,' he snapped back.

Holly glared at him and went to join Denise, Tom and Daniel.

'Hi, Daniel.' She greeted him with a kiss on the cheek.

'Hi, Holly. Long time no see.' He handed her a beer.

'You still haven't found that leprechaun?' Denise laughed.

'No,' Holly said. She explained the story to Tom and Daniel.

'Do you think maybe your husband organised it?' Tom blurted out.

'No.' Holly scowled at Denise for telling Tom her business.

Denise just held her hands up helplessly and shrugged.

Holly turned to Daniel, ignoring the other two. 'Thanks for coming, Daniel.'

'No problem at all. I was glad to come.'

It was weird seeing him out of his usual wintery clothes; he was dressed in a navy vest and combat shorts.

'You're very brown,' she commented.

'I was in Miami for a while last month.'

'Ooh, lucky you. Did you enjoy it?'

'Had a great time.' He nodded. 'Have you ever been?'

She shook her head. 'But at least us girls are heading off to Lanzarote shortly. Can't wait.'

'Yes, I heard that. I'd say that was a nice surprise for you.' He gave her a smile, his eyes crinkling at the corners.

They chatted for a while about his holiday. 'I hope you didn't go with another woman or poor Ciara will be devastated,' she joked, and then kicked herself for being so nosy.

'No, I didn't,' he said. 'Laura and I broke up a few months ago.'

'Oh, I'm sorry to hear that. Were you together long?'

'Seven years.' He looked away and she changed the subject.

'By the way, Daniel, I just wanted to thank you for looking out for me after the documentary. Most men run away when they see a girl cry.'

'No problem at all, Holly. I don't like to see you upset.'

'You're a good friend,' Holly said, thinking aloud. 'Maybe I can get to know as much about you as you know about me.' She laughed.

'Yeah, I'd like that,' Daniel agreed.

'Oh, did you give Ciara that birthday present?'

'No.' He laughed. 'She's been kind of . . . busy.'

Holly turned and spotted her sister flirting with one of Declan's friends. So much for wanting Daniel's babies. 'I'll call her over, will I?'

'Go on,' Daniel said.

'Ciara!' Holly called. 'Got another pressie for you!'

'Ooh! What is it?' Ciara collapsed on the grass beside them.

Holly nodded over at Daniel. 'It's from him.'

Ciara turned excitedly to face him.

'I was wondering if you would like a job working behind the bar at Club Diva?'

Ciara's hands flew to her mouth. 'Oh, Daniel, that would be brill!' she squealed and threw her arms round him.

Any excuse, Holly thought. 'OK, OK, that's enough, Ciara. You don't want to kill your new boss.'

Suddenly the garden became very quiet and Holly's parents appeared with a large birthday cake singing 'Happy Birthday'. Someone followed behind them with a huge bouquet of flowers. Her parents placed the cake on the table in front of Ciara and the stranger behind them slowly removed the bouquet from his face.

'Mathew!' Ciara gasped. Her face went white.

'I'm sorry for being such a fool, Ciara.' Mathew's Australian accent echoed round the garden. He actually looked like he was acting out a scene from an Australian soap, but then drama always seemed to work for Ciara. 'I love you! Please take me back!' he announced. Everyone turned to stare at Ciara to see what she would say.

Her lower lip started to tremble. She ran to Mathew and jumped on him, wrapping her legs round his waist and her arms round his neck.

Holly was overcome with emotion and tears welled in her eyes at the sight of her sister being reunited with the man she loved. Declan grabbed his camera and began filming.

Daniel put his arm round Holly's shoulders. 'I'm sorry, Daniel,' Holly said, wiping her eyes. 'I think you've just been dumped.'

'Not to worry,' he laughed. 'I shouldn't mix business with pleasure, anyway.' He seemed relieved.

Holly smiled at the jazz band as she passed and looked around for Denise. They had arranged to meet up in the girls' favourite bar, Juicy, favoured for its extensive cocktail menu and relaxing music. Holly had no intentions of getting drunk tonight, as she wanted to be able to enjoy her holiday as much as she could, starting the next day. She intended to be bright-eyed and bushy-tailed for her week of relaxation from Gerry. She spotted Denise snuggling up to Tom on a comfortable large black leather couch in the conservatory area that overlooked the River Liffey. Dublin was lit up for the night and all its colours were reflected in the water. Daniel sat opposite Denise and Tom, sucking fiercely on a strawberry daiquiri, eyes surveying the room. Nice to see Tom and Denise were ostracising everyone again.

'Sorry I'm late,' Holly apologised, approaching her friends. 'I just wanted to finish packing before I came out.'

'You're not forgiven,' Daniel said quietly into her ear as he gave her a welcoming hug and kiss.

Denise looked up at Holly and smiled, Tom waved slightly and they returned their attention to each other.

'I don't know why they even bother inviting other people out. They just sit there staring into each other's eyes, ignoring everyone else. They don't even talk to each other! And then they make you feel like you've interrupted them if you strike up a conversation. I think they've got some weird telepathic conversation going on there,' Daniel said, sitting down again and taking another sip from his glass. He made a face at the sweet taste. 'And I really need a beer.'

Holly laughed. 'It sounds like you've been having a fantastic night.'

'Sorry,' Daniel apologised. 'It's just been so long since I've spoken to another human being, I've forgotten my manners.'

Holly grinned. 'Well, I've come to rescue you.' She picked up the menu and surveyed the choice of drinks before her. She chose a drink with the lowest alcohol content and snuggled down in the cosy chair. 'I could fall asleep here,' she remarked, snuggling further down.

Daniel raised his eyebrows. 'Then I would *really* take it personally.'

'Don't worry, I won't,' she assured him. 'So, Mr Connelly, since you know absolutely *everything* about me, tonight I am on a mission to find out all about you. So be prepared for my interrogation.'

Daniel smiled. 'OK, I'm ready.'

Holly thought about her first question. 'Where are you from?'

'Born and reared in Dublin.' He took a sip of the red cocktail and winced again. 'And if any of the people I grew up with saw me drinking this stuff and listening to jazz, I'd be in trouble.'

Holly giggled.

'After I finished school I joined the army,' he continued.

Holly raised her eyes, impressed. 'Why did you decide to do that?'

He didn't even think about it. 'Because I hadn't a clue what I wanted to do with my life, and the money was good.'

'So much for saving innocent lives.'

'I only stayed with the army for a few years.'

'Why did you leave?' Holly sipped on her lime-flavoured drink.

'Because I realised I had urges to drink cocktails and listen to jazz music and they wouldn't permit it in the army barracks,' he explained.

'Really, Daniel.' Holly laughed.

He smiled. 'Sorry, it just wasn't for me. My parents had moved down to Galway to run a pub and the idea of that appealed to me. So I moved down to Galway to work there. Eventually my parents retired and I took over the pub, but I decided a few years ago that I wanted to own one of my own. I worked really hard, saved my money, took out the biggest mortgage ever and moved back to Dublin and bought Hogan's. And here I am, talking to you.'

Holly smiled. 'Well, that's a wonderful life story, Daniel.'

'Nothing special, but a life all the same.' He returned her smile.

'So where does the ex come into all this?' Holly asked.

'She's right in between running the pub in Galway and leaving to come to Dublin.'

'Ah . . . I see,' Holly nodded, understanding. She drained her glass and picked up the menu again. 'I think I'll have Sex on the Beach.'

'When? On your holidays?' Daniel teased.

Holly thumped him playfully on the arm. Not in a million years.

Eight

'WE'RE ALL GOING on our summer Holly days!' the girls sang in the car all the way to the airport. John had offered to drive them but he was fast regretting it. Holly felt like she was back at school and off on an excursion. Her bag was packed with sweets and magazines, and they couldn't stop singing cheesy songs. Their flight wasn't until 9 p.m., so they wouldn't arrive until the early hours of the morning.

They reached the airport and piled out of the car. John lifted their suitcases from the boot, they all gave him a hug and then dragged their luggage across the departure lounge to the long check-in queue.

'I told you we should have come earlier,' Sharon moaned.

'We'd just wait at the boarding gate,' reasoned Holly.

'Yeah, but at least there's a bar there,' Denise pointed out.

After thirty minutes of queuing they finally checked in.

'Why is that girl staring at me?' Denise said through gritted teeth, eyeing up the girl at the end of the bar.

'Probably because you're staring at her.' Sharon checked her watch. 'Only fifteen more minutes.'

'No, honestly, girls. I'm not being paranoid here.'

'Well, why don't you ask her, then?' Sharon sniggered.

'Oh, here she comes,' Denise sang and turned her back.

Holly looked up and saw a skinny, blonde-haired girl heading towards them. 'Hi, there!' the girl squeaked. 'I didn't mean to be rude by staring, but I just had to see if it was really you!'

'It's us all right,' Sharon said sarcastically, 'in the flesh.'

'Oh, I just *knew* it!' the girl squealed. 'My friends kept telling me I was wrong but I *knew* it was you! That's them over there.' She pointed to the end of the bar and the other four girls twinkled their fingers back. 'My name's Cindy and I just love that show you're all in. And you play Princess Holly, don't you?' She pointed a manicured nail in Holly's face.

Holly opened her mouth to speak but Cindy kept on talking. 'When are you making the next one?'

'Oh, we're in discussions right now,' Denise lied.

'Fantastic!' Cindy clapped her hands. 'What's it about?'

'Well, we can't really say, but we have to go to Hollywood.'

Cindy looked like she was going to have a heart attack. 'Oh my God! Wow!' She looked down at Denise's boarding pass on the table. 'Wow, you girls are going to Lanzarote?'

Denise grabbed her pass and shoved it in her bag.

'I'm going there too. We're staying in a place called Costa Palma Palace. Where are you guys staying?'

Holly's heart sank. 'Oh, I can't remember, girls, can you?'

Sharon and Denise shook their heads vigorously.

'Oh, well, not to worry. I'll see you when we land anyway.' Cindy gave them each a big hug and tottered back to her friends.

Four hours later the plane glided over the sea and landed at Lanzarote Airport. The girls made their way to the luggage reclaim and stood for almost an hour waiting for their bags while the majority of the crowd headed out to their coaches. At last they went to meet their holiday rep.

'Kennedy, McCarthy and Hennessey?' the young woman dressed in a red uniform said in a thick London accent.

The girls nodded.

'Hi, I'm Victoria and I'll show you to the coach.' She led them outside.

It was two o'clock in the morning, and yet a warm breeze greeted them. Holly smiled to the girls, who felt it too; now they were really on holiday. They stepped onto the coach.

'Woo-hoo,' Cindy waved at them. 'I kept you all a seat back here!'

The girls trudged down to the back seat of the bus.

Forty-five minutes later they reached Costa Palma Palace and the excitement once again returned to Holly's stomach. Tall palm trees lined the centre of the drive and a large fountain was lit up with blue lights outside the main entrance. The girls were booked into a studio apartment containing one bedroom with twin beds, a kitchen and living area with a sofa bed, a bathroom and a balcony. Holly stepped onto the balcony and looked out to sea. Although it was too dark to see anything, she could hear the water gently lapping up against the sand.

'Hol, do you mind if I sleep on the sofa bed?' Denise called. 'That way I can keep the door open and smoke . . .'

'Only if you *do* keep the door open, Denise,' Sharon yelled back.

At nine o'clock that morning Sharon woke Holly. 'I've been down to the pool and the Germans have nicked all the sunbeds,' she said grumpily. 'I'll be down on the beach if you want me.'

Holly mumbled a response and went back to sleep again.

At ten o'clock Denise jumped on her in bed and they decided to get up and join Sharon.

The sand was hot and they had to keep moving so as not to burn the soles of their feet. They spotted Sharon sitting under an umbrella.

'Oh, this is so beautiful, isn't it?' Denise looked around.

Sharon looked up from her book and smiled. 'Heaven.'

Holly looked around to see if Gerry had come to the same heaven. Nope, no sign of him. All around her there were couples: couples massaging suncream onto each other's bodies, couples walking hand in hand along the beach. Holly didn't have any time to be depressed, as Denise had stepped out of her sundress and was hopping around on the hot sand in nothing but a skimpy leopardskin thong.

'Will one of you put suncream on me?'

Sharon put her book down. 'I'll do it.'

Denise sat at the end of Sharon's sunbed. 'You know what, Sharon? You'll get an awful tan line if you keep that sarong on.'

Sharon looked down at herself. 'What tan? I never get a tan. I've nice Irish skin, Denise. Besides, I look like such a blob these days I wouldn't want to scare everyone off.'

Holly looked at Sharon, annoyed at her for calling herself a blob. She'd put a little weight on but was by no means fat.

'Why don't you go up to the swimming pool then and scare all those Germans away?' Denise joked.

'Yeah, girls, we really need to get up earlier tomorrow to get a place by the pool,' Holly suggested. 'The beach gets boring after a while.'

The girls relaxed on the beach for the rest of the day, occasionally dipping themselves into the sea to cool down. They ate lunch at the beach bar and that night they enjoyed dinner in one of the many restaurants not far from the complex.

'I can't believe it's ten o'clock and we're heading back to the apartment already,' said Denise, staring longingly at the huge choice of bar.

People overflowed from the bars onto the streets, music vibrating from every building. Holly could almost feel the ground pulsing beneath her. There was loud laughter, clinking glasses and singing. Tanned young bodies hung out in big groups around outdoor tables.

Looking at the average age of the clientele, Holly felt old. 'Well, we can go to a bar if you want,' she said uncertainly.

Denise stopped walking and assessed the bars.

'All right, beautiful.' A very attractive man flashed his pearly whites at Denise. He had an English accent. 'Are you coming with me?'

Denise stared at the young man for a while, lost in thought. Sharon and Holly smirked at each other, knowing that Denise wouldn't be going to bed early after all.

Finally Denise snapped out of her trance. 'No, thank you, I have a boyfriend and I love him,' she announced. 'Come on, girls,' she said to

Holly and Sharon, and walked off in the direction of the apartment.

The two girls remained on the street, mouths open in shock. They had to run to catch up with her.

'Who are you?' Sharon said. 'And what have you done with my man-eating friend?'

'OK.' Denise held her hands up in the air and grinned. 'Maybe being single isn't all it's cracked up to be.'

Holly lowered her eyes and kicked a stone along the path as they made their way back to their resort. It sure wasn't.

A silence fell between them as the music faded away slowly.

'That street made me feel so old,' Sharon said suddenly.

'Me too!' Denise's eyes widened. 'Since when did people start going out so young?'

Sharon began to laugh. 'Denise, we are getting older.'

'Well, it's not like we're old old. I mean, we could stay out all night if we wanted to, we just . . . are tired. We've had a long day . . .'

Sharon was watching Holly. 'Holly, are you OK? You haven't said a word for ages.'

'Yeah, I was just thinking about Gerry.'

'Let's go down to the beach,' Denise suggested, and they slipped out of their shoes and allowed their feet to sink into the cool sand.

The sky was clear black and a million little stars twinkled; it was as if someone had thrown glitter up into a massive black net. The full moon rested low over the horizon where the sea met the sky. The girls sat in its path, the water gently lapping before them. The air was warm but a slight breeze brushed past Holly. She closed her eyes and filled her lungs with fresh air.

'That's why he brought you here, you know,' Sharon said, watching her friend relaxing.

Holly's eyes remained closed and she smiled.

'You don't talk about him much, Holly,' Denise said.

Holly's eyes opened. 'I know.'

Denise drew circles in the sand. 'Why not?'

Holly thought for a while. 'I don't know whether to be sad or happy when I talk about him. It's like, if I'm happy, certain people judge and expect me to be crying my eyes out. When I'm upset it makes people feel uncomfortable.' She stared out to the sparkling sea. 'I can't tease about him in conversation like I used to because it feels wrong. I can't talk about things he told me in confidence because they're his secrets.'

The three girls sat crosslegged on the soft sand.

'John and I talk about Gerry all the time.' Sharon looked at Holly with glittering eyes. 'We talk about the times he made us laugh, which was *a lot*. We even talk about the things he did that *really* annoyed us.'

Holly raised her eyebrows.

Sharon continued, 'Because to us, that's just how Gerry was. He wasn't all nice. We remember *all* of him.'

There was a long silence.

Denise was first to speak. 'I wish my Tom had known Gerry.'

Holly looked at her in surprise. A tear ran down her cheek.

'Gerry was my friend too,' Denise said, tears pricking in her eyes. 'So I try to tell Tom things about him just so he knows that one of the nicest men on this earth was *my* friend. But I can't believe that someone I now love so much doesn't know a friend I loved for ten years.'

Holly reached out to hug her friend. 'Well, then, we'll just have to keep telling Tom about him, won't we, Denise?'

They didn't bother meeting up with their holiday rep the next morning, as they had no intention of going on any tours or taking part in any silly sports tournaments. Instead, they headed over to the beach again.

'Do you ever hear from Gerry's parents, Holly?' Sharon asked as she and Holly lounged on their Lilos in the sea.

'Yeah, they send me postcards every few weeks.'

'So they're still on that cruise? Do you miss them?'

'To be honest, I don't think they feel we have any connection any more. Their son's gone and they have no grandchildren.'

'That's bull, Holly. You're their daughter-in-law.'

'Oh, well, I don't know.' Holly sighed.

'They're a bit backward, aren't they?'

'Yeah, *very*. They hated me and Gerry "living in sin", as they said. Couldn't wait for us to get married. And *then* they couldn't understand why I wouldn't change my name.'

'Yeah, I remember that,' Sharon said.

'Hello, girls.' Denise floated out to meet them.

'Hey, where have you been?' Holly asked.

'Oh, chatting to some bloke from Miami. Nice guy.'

'Miami? That's where Daniel went on holiday,' Holly said.

'Hmm,' Sharon mused, 'nice guy, Daniel, isn't he?'

'Really nice,' Holly agreed. 'Very easy to talk to.'

'Tom was telling me he's been through the wars recently,' Denise said, turning to lie on her back.

Sharon's ears pricked up at the sound of gossip, 'Why's that?'

'Oh, he was engaged to some chick called Laura, and it turned out she was sleeping with someone else. That's why he moved to Dublin and bought the pub, to get away from her.'

'Where did he live before?' Sharon asked.

'Galway. He used to run a pub there,' Holly explained.

'Oh,' Sharon said. 'He doesn't have a Galway accent.'

'Well, he grew up in Dublin and joined the army, then he left and moved to Galway to work in his parents' pub. When his father retired, he took over the pub. He met Laura and they were together for seven years. When they broke up he moved back to Dublin and bought Hogan's.' Holly caught her breath.

'Don't know much about him, do you?' Denise teased.

'Well, if you and Tom had paid the slightest bit more attention to us the other night in Juicy's, maybe I wouldn't know so much about him,' Holly replied playfully.

Denise sighed loudly. 'God, I really miss Tom,' she said sadly.

'Did you tell the guy from Miami that?' Sharon laughed.

'No, I was just chatting to him,' Denise said defensively. 'To be honest, nobody else interests me. It's really weird.'

Sharon smiled at her. 'I think they call it love, Denise.'

They lay in silence for a while, all lost in their own thoughts, allowing the gentle motion of the waves to soothe them.

'Bloody hell!' Denise yelled. 'Look how far out we are!'

Holly sat up immediately. They were out so far from shore everybody on the beach looked like ants.

'Oh God!' panicked Sharon, and as soon as Sharon panicked Holly knew they were in trouble.

'Start swimming, quick!' Denise yelled, and they all lay on their stomachs and started splashing. After just a few minutes they gave up, out of breath. It was no use, the tide was moving out too quickly, and the waves were just too strong.

'Help!' Denise screamed at the top of her lungs and waved her arms around wildly.

'I don't think they can hear us,' Holly said.

'Oh, could we be any more stupid?' Sharon gave out and ranted on about the dangers of Lilos in the sea.

'Oh, forget about that, Sharon,' Denise snapped. 'We're here now so let's all scream together.'

They all sat up on their Lilos. 'OK, one, two, three . . . HELP!' They all waved their arms frantically.

Eventually they stopped screaming and stared at the dots on the beach.

'Tell me there aren't sharks out here,' Denise whimpered.

'Oh, please, Denise,' Sharon snapped viciously, 'that is the last thing we need to be reminded of right now.'

Holly gulped and stared down into the sea. The once-clear blue water had darkened. Denise continued her bloodcurdling screams.

'Jesus, Denise,' Sharon snapped, 'the only thing that's gonna respond to that is a dolphin.'

Holly wasn't sure whether to laugh or cry. 'At least one good thing came out of this,' she said.

'There's a good thing?' Sharon said.

'Well, the three of us always talked about going to Africa,' she giggled. 'And by the looks of things, we're halfway there.'

The girls looked out to sea, to their future destination.

'It's a cheaper mode of transport too,' Sharon joined in.

Denise stared at them as if they were mad, and just one look at her, lying in the middle of the ocean naked but for a leopardskin thong, was enough to set the girls off laughing.

'What?' Denise looked at them wide-eyed.

'I'd say we're in deep, deep trouble here,' Sharon giggled.

'Yeah,' Holly agreed, 'we're in way over our heads.'

They lay there laughing and crying for a few minutes more till the sound of a speedboat caused Denise to start waving frantically again.

'It's just like a regular night out with the girls,' Sharon giggled, watching Denise being dragged to the boat by a muscular lifeguard.

'I think they're in shock,' one lifeguard said to the other as they pulled the remaining hysterical girls onto the boat.

'Quick, save the Lilos!' Holly managed to blurt out.

'Lilo overboard!' Sharon screamed.

The lifeguards looked at each other worriedly, as they wrapped warm blankets round the girls and sped back to shore.

As they approached the beach, a large crowd was gathering. The girls looked at one another and laughed even harder. When they were lifted off the boat there was huge applause.

'They clap now, but where were they when we needed them?' Sharon grumbled.

'There they are!' Cindy and the Barbie Brigade pushed their way through the crowd. 'Oh my God!' she squeaked. 'I saw the whole thing through my binoculars and called the lifeguards. Are you OK?'

'Oh, we're fine,' Sharon said. 'We were the lucky ones. The poor Lilos never even had a chance.' They all cracked up laughing and were ushered away to be looked at by a doctor.

That night the girls realised the seriousness of what had happened and their mood drastically changed. They sat in silence throughout dinner, all thinking about how lucky they were to have been rescued and kicking themselves for being so careless. Holly had reacted unusually out there on the water, and it bothered her to think about why she had. After the initial panic of thinking she was going to die, she had become feverishly giddy as she realised that if she did die she knew she would be with Gerry. It bothered her to think that she didn't care whether she lived or died. She needed to change her perspective on life.

The next morning Holly woke to the sound of Sharon throwing up in the toilet. She followed her in and gently held her hair back.

'You OK?' she asked worriedly after Sharon had stopped.

'Yeah, it's just those bloody dreams I had all night. I dreamt I was on a boat and on a Lilo. I think it was just seasickness.'

'I had those dreams too. It was scary yesterday, wasn't it?'

Sharon smiled weakly. 'I'm never going on a Lilo again.'

When the three of them arrived down at the swimming pool, Denise and Sharon joined the Barbie Brigade. Well, it was the least they could do, seeing as they were the ones who had called for help. But before Holly was dragged into any conversation she signalled to Sharon that she was leaving, and Sharon gave her an encouraging wink, knowing why she was disappearing.

Holly wrapped her sarong round her hips and carried her small beach bag down to the shore. She couldn't believe that she'd fallen asleep before midnight the previous night. She had planned to get up quietly, without waking the others, sneak out onto the balcony and open Gerry's sixth message. Now she found a quiet corner, away from all the excited shouts of children playing and stereos blaring out the latest chart songs, and made herself comfortable on her beach towel. It was still early and already the sun was hot.

Holly carefully pulled Gerry's sixth envelope out of her bag as if it were the most delicate thing in the world, and she ran her fingers along the neatly written word 'August', and gently tore open the seal.

> Hi, Holly,
>
> I hope you're having a wonderful holiday. You're looking beautiful in that bikini! I hope I picked the right place. It's the place you and I almost went for our honeymoon, remember? I'm glad you finally got to see it.
>
> Apparently, if you stand at the very end of the beach near the rocks and look round to the left, you'll see a lighthouse. I'm told that's where the dolphins gather. I know you love dolphins . . . tell them I said hi.
>
> PS, I love you, Holly . . .

With shaking hands, Holly put the card back into the envelope and secured it safely in a pocket of her bag. She felt Gerry's eyes on her as she stood up and rolled up the beach towel. She ran to the end of the beach, which suddenly stopped because of a cliff. She put her trainers on and began to climb the rocks.

And there it was.

Exactly where Gerry had described it, the lighthouse sat high on the cliff, bright white as though it were some sort of torch to heaven. Holly climbed over the rocks and made her way round the little cove. She was on her own now. It was completely private. And then she heard the noises. The squeaks of dolphins playing near the shore away from all the tourists on the beaches. Holly collapsed on the sand to listen.

Gerry sat beside her.

He may even have held her hand.

Holly felt happy enough to head back to Dublin, relaxed, de-stressed and brown. Just what the doctor ordered. That didn't stop her from groaning when the plane landed in Dublin Airport to heavy rain.

'Well, it looks like the leprechaun didn't do any work while you were away,' Denise said, looking at the garden as John reached Holly's home.

Holly gave her friends a hug and a kiss. There was a horrible musty smell inside her quiet, empty house and she went to open the patio doors to let the fresh air circulate.

She froze just as she was turning the key in the door.

Her entire back garden had been transformed.

The grass was cut. The weeds were gone. The garden furniture had been polished and varnished. A fresh coat of paint gleamed from her garden walls. Flowers had been planted and underneath the great oak sat a wooden bench. Holly looked round in shock; who was doing all this?

Nine

IN THE DAYS FOLLOWING her return from Lanzarote, Holly kept a low profile. It wasn't something she, Denise and Sharon talked about, but after living in each other's ears for a week, Holly was sure they all agreed it was healthy to spend some time apart.

Ciara was impossible to get hold of, as she was either working at Daniel's club or spending time with Mathew. Jack was down in Cork and Declan was . . . well, who knew where Declan was.

Now she was back, Holly wasn't exactly bored with her life, but she wasn't exactly overjoyed either. It just seemed so . . . nothing and so pointless. She'd had the holiday to look forward to, but now felt she had no real reason to get out of bed in the morning. And as she was taking time out from her friends, she really had nobody else to talk to. There was only so much conversation she could have with her parents. Compared to last week's sweltering heat in Lanzarote, Dublin was wet and ugly, which meant she couldn't even work at maintaining her tan or appreciate her new back garden.

Some days she never even got out of bed, she just watched television and waited . . . waited for next month's message from Gerry, wondering what journey he would take her on next. When he was alive she'd lived for him, and now that he was gone she lived for his messages. Everything was about him.

Something that she did feel she should do was to catch the leprechaun. After further interrogation of her neighbours she still knew nothing more of her mystery gardener, and she was beginning to think the whole thing had just been an awful mistake. Eventually she had herself convinced that a gardener was working on the wrong garden, so she checked the post every day for a bill that she was going to refuse to pay. But no bill arrived, of that variety anyway. Plenty of others arrived: electricity bills, phone bills, insurance bills. Everything that came through her door seemed to be a bill, and she hadn't a clue how she was going to continue paying them all. But she had become numb to all those irrelevant problems in life. She just dreamed the impossible dreams.

One day Denise called. 'Hiya, how are you?' she asked.

'Oh, full of the joys of life,' Holly said.

'Oh, me too!' she giggled in response.

'So what's happening?'

'I'm calling to invite you out for dinner tomorrow night. It's short notice, so if you're busy . . . cancel whatever you've planned.'

'Hold on and let me check my diary,' Holly said sarcastically.

'No problem,' Denise said seriously, and was silent while she waited.

Holly rolled her eyes. 'Oh, whaddaya know? I appear to be free tomorrow night.'

'Oh, goody,' Denise said happily. 'We're meeting at Chang's at eight.'

'Who's we?'

'Sharon and John and some of Tom's friends. We haven't been out together for ages, so it'll be fun.'

'OK then, see you tomorrow.' Holly hung up feeling angry. Had it completely slipped Denise's mind that Holly was still a grieving widow and that life just wasn't fun any more? She stormed upstairs and opened her wardrobe. Now what piece of old and disgusting clothing would she wear tomorrow night, and how on earth was she going to afford an expensive meal? She could barely afford to keep her car on the road. She grabbed all her clothes from her wardrobe and flung them across the room, screaming her head off until she finally felt sane again.

Holly arrived at the restaurant at eight twenty, as she had spent hours trying on different outfits. Eventually she settled with the one she had been instructed to wear by Gerry for the karaoke, just so she could feel closer to him.

As she was walking towards the table her heart sank.

Couples R Us.

She paused halfway there and quickly sidestepped behind a wall. She wasn't sure she could go through with this. She hadn't the strength to keep battling with her emotions. She looked around to find the easiest escape route; the fire escape beside the kitchen door. The moment she stepped out into the cool fresh air she felt free again. She walked across the car park, trying to formulate an excuse to tell Denise.

'Hi, Holly.'

She froze and slowly turned round. She spotted Daniel leaning against his car, smoking a cigarette.

'Hiya, Daniel. I didn't know you smoked.'

'Only when I'm stressed.'

'You're stressed?' They greeted each other with a hug.

'I was figuring out whether to join the Happy Couples.' He nodded towards the restaurant.

Holly smiled. 'You too?'

He laughed. 'Well, I won't tell them I saw you if that's what you want.'

'So you're going in?'

'Have to face the music some time,' he said, grimly stubbing out his cigarette with his foot.

Holly thought about what he'd said. 'I suppose you're right.'

'You don't have to go in if you don't want to. I don't want to be the cause of you having a miserable night.'

'On the contrary, it would be nice to have another loner in my company. There are so very few in existence.'

Daniel laughed and held out his arm. 'Shall we?'

Holly linked her arm in his and they made their way towards the restaurant. It was comforting to know she wasn't alone in feeling alone.

'By the way, I'm getting out of here as soon as we finish the main course,' he laughed.

'Traitor,' she answered, thumping him on the arm. 'Well, I have to leave early anyway, to catch the last bus home.' She hadn't had the money to fill the tank in the car for the past few days.

'Well, then, we have the perfect excuse. I'll say I'm driving you home and you have to be home by . . .?'

'Half eleven?' At midnight she was planning to open the September envelope.

'Perfect time.' He smiled, and they made their way into the restaurant, feeling slightly reinforced by each other's company.

'Here they are!' Denise announced as they reached the table.

Holly sat beside Daniel. 'Sorry we're late.'

'Holly, this is Catherine and Mick, Peter and Sue, Joanne and Conal, Tina and Bryan, John and Sharon you know, Geoffrey and Samantha, and last but not least, this is Des and Simon.'

Holly smiled and nodded at all of them.

'Hi, we're Daniel and Holly,' Daniel said smartly.

'We had to order already,' Denise explained. 'But we ordered loads of dishes so we can all share them.'

Holly and Daniel nodded.

Everyone fell into conversation and Daniel turned to Holly. 'Did you enjoy your holiday?'

'Oh, I had a fabulous time,' she answered. 'We took it easy and relaxed, didn't do anything wild and weird.'

'Just what you needed,' he smiled. 'I heard about your near-death experience, though.'

Holly rolled her eyes. 'I bet Denise gave you the exaggerated version.'

'Well, she just told me about how you were surrounded by sharks and had to be airlifted by a helicopter.'

'She didn't!'

'No, not really,' he laughed.

'OK, everyone,' Denise called. 'You're probably wondering why Tom and I invited you all here tonight. Well, we have an announcement to make.' She grinned.

Holly's eyes widened.

'Myself and Tom are getting married!'

Holly's hands flew up to her mouth in shock. 'Oh, Denise!' she gasped, and walked round the table to hug them. 'That's wonderful news! Congratulations!'

She looked at Daniel's face; it had gone white.

They popped open a bottle of champagne and everyone raised their glasses for a toast. 'Hold on! Hold on!' Denise stopped them. 'Sharon, did you get a glass?'

Everyone looked at Sharon. Tom poured her a glass.

'No, no, no! Not for me, thanks,' she said.

'Why not?' Denise huffed.

Sharon looked at John. 'Well, I didn't want to say anything . . .'

Everyone urged her to speak.

'Well . . . John and I are going to have a baby!'

Holly just froze in shock. Tears filled her eyes as she went over to congratulate Sharon and John. Then she sat down and took deep breaths. This was all too much.

'So let's make a toast to Tom and Denise's engagement and Sharon and John's baby!'

Everyone clinked glasses and Holly ate dinner in silence, not really tasting anything.

'You want to make that time eleven o'clock?' Daniel asked quietly, and she nodded in agreement.

After dinner they made their excuses to leave and nobody really tried to persuade them to stay. Holly left her last thirty euros towards the bill.

For a while, they sat in the car in silence. Holly wanted to feel happy for her friends, but she couldn't shake off the feeling of being left behind. Everyone else's lives were moving on except hers.

'That was some night, wasn't it?' Daniel said at last.

Holly shook her head with disbelief. 'Daniel, I have known those girls all of my life, and I did *not* see any of that coming. Although Sharon wasn't drinking when we were away, and she did throw up a few mornings, but she said it was seasickness . . .' Her brain went into overdrive as things started to add up.

'Seasickness?' Daniel asked, confused.

'After our near-death experience,' she explained.

'Oh, right.' This time neither of them laughed.

'It's funny,' he said, 'the lads always said that myself and Laura would be the first to get married. I didn't think Laura would marry before me.'

'She's getting married?' Holly asked.

'He used to be a friend of mine, too.' He laughed bitterly.

'Obviously he's not any more.'

'Nope.' He pulled up outside her house. 'Ah, well, we all get our fair share of bad luck. You know that better than anyone.'

'Huh, fair share,' she repeated.

'I know, there's nothing fair about it, but don't worry, we'll have our good luck, too.'

They sat in silence for another while, then Holly glanced at her watch.

Daniel read her mind. 'So how're the messages from above going?'

Holly sat forward. 'Well, I've another one to open tonight, actually. So . . .' She turned to look at him.

'Oh, right,' he said. 'I'd better let you go, then.'

Holly bit her lip. 'Thanks a million for the lift, Daniel.'

'No problem at all.' They gave each other a quick hug.

'See you soon,' she said. She waved him off, then headed for the house and let herself in. 'Right, Gerry,' she said, walking into the kitchen. 'What have you got in store for me this month?'

Holly held the tiny envelope tightly and glanced up at the kitchen clock. It was twelve fifteen. Usually Sharon and Denise would have called her by now, all excited to hear about what was inside the envelope. But it seemed news of an engagement and a pregnancy beat the news of a message from Gerry these days. Holly scorned herself for being so bitter. She wanted to be back in the restaurant right now celebrating with her friends like the old Holly would have done. But she couldn't bring herself even to smile for them.

She was jealous of them and their good fortune. She was angry with them for moving on. Even in the company of friends she felt alone; in a room of a thousand people she would feel alone. But it was when she roamed the rooms of her quiet house that she felt most alone.

She couldn't remember the last time she'd felt truly happy. She missed going to bed at night with absolutely nothing on her mind. She hated the butterflies in her tummy every time she remembered Gerry. She missed the feeling of being loved, of knowing Gerry was watching her as she watched television or ate her dinner. She missed sensing his eyes on her as she entered a room; she missed his touches, his hugs, his words of advice, his words of love.

She hated counting down the days till she could read another one of his messages because they were all she had left of him, and after this one there would be only three more. And she hated to think of what her life might be like when there would be no more Gerry.

She slowly opened her seventh envelope.

Shoot for the moon, and if you miss you'll still be among the stars.
Promise me you will find a job you love this time!
PS, I love you . . .

Holly read and reread the message, trying to discover how it made her feel. She had been dreading going back to work for such a long time, had believed that she wasn't ready. But now she knew she had no choice. If Gerry said it was to be, it would be. Holly's face broke into a smile. 'I promise, Gerry,' she said happily. She studied his writing for a long time as she always did, and when she was satisfied she had analysed every word, she rushed over to the kitchen drawer, took out a notepad and pen and began to write her own list of possible jobs.

1. FBI agent?—Am not American. Do not want to live in America.
   Have no police experience.
2. Lawyer—Hated school. Hated studying. .
3. Doctor—Ugghh.
4. Nurse—Unflattering uniforms.
5. Waitress—Would eat all the food.
6. Beautician—Bite my nails and wax as rarely as possible. Do not
   want to see areas of other people's bodies.
7. Secretary—NEVER AGAIN.
8. Actress—Could not possibly outdo my wonderful performance
   in the critically acclaimed *Girls and the City*.
9. Hotshot businesswoman in control of life—Hmm . . . Must do
   research tomorrow . . .

Holly finally collapsed onto her bed and dreamed of being a big hotshot advertising woman making a huge presentation on the top floor of a skyscraper overlooking Grafton Street. Well, he did say aim for the moon . . . She woke up early and walked to her local library to look up jobs on the Internet.

The librarian directed her to the row of computers on the far side of the room. 'It's five euros for every twenty minutes online.'

Holly handed over ten euros. It was all she had managed to take out of her bank account that morning. She couldn't believe that was all she had left.

'No, no,' the librarian said, handing back her money, 'you can pay when you finish.'

Holly reached the computers and realised that there were none free. She stood drumming her fingers on her handbag and looking around. Her eyes nearly popped out of her head as she spotted Richard tapping away. She tiptoed over and touched him on the shoulder. He jumped with fright and swirled round in his chair.

'Hiya,' she whispered.

'Oh, hello, Holly. What are you doing here?' he said uneasily, as if she had caught him doing something naughty.

'I'm just waiting for a computer,' she explained. 'I'm finally looking for a job,' she said proudly.

'Oh, right.' He shut down his screen. 'You can use this one.'

'Oh, no, you don't have to rush for me!' she said quickly.

'Not at all. I was just doing some research for work.'

'All the way over here?' she said, surprised. 'Don't they have computers in Blackrock?' She wasn't quite sure what it was that Richard did for a living, and it would seem rude to ask him after he'd worked there more than ten years. She knew it involved wearing a white coat, wandering round a lab and dropping colourful substances into test tubes.

'My work brings me everywhere,' Richard joked awkwardly. He said a quick goodbye and made his way over to pay at the desk.

Holly sat down at the computer and quickly became engrossed in her job-hunting.

Forty minutes later she made her way to the desk. The librarian tapped away on the computer. 'That's fifteen euros, please.'

Holly gulped. 'I thought you said five for twenty minutes.'

'Yes, that's right.' She smiled at her.

'But I was only online for forty minutes.'

'Actually, you were on for forty-four minutes, which cuts into the extra twenty minutes.'

Holly lowered her voice. 'Look, this is really embarrassing, but I actually only have the ten on me now. Is there any way I can come back with the rest later on today?'

The librarian shook her head. 'I'm sorry, but we can't allow that. You need to pay the entire amount.'

'But I *don't have* the entire amount,' Holly protested.

The woman stared back blankly.

'Fine,' Holly huffed, taking out her mobile.

'Sorry, but you can't use that in here.' The librarian pointed to the NO MOBILE PHONES sign on the counter.

Holly looked up slowly at her and counted to five in her head. 'If you won't let me use my phone, I can't phone somebody for help. If I can't phone somebody, then they can't come here with the money and I can't pay you. So may I go outside to use the phone?'

'As long as you stand in front of the entrance where I can see you.' The woman shuffled papers and pretended to go back to work.

Holly stood outside the door and thought about who to call. She didn't want Denise and Sharon to know about her failures in life now that they were both so blissfully happy. She couldn't call Ciara because she was on a day shift at Hogan's pub. Jack was back teaching at the school, Declan was at college and Richard wasn't even an option.

Tears rolled down her face as she scrolled down the list of names in her phone book. The majority hadn't even called her since Gerry had died. She turned her back on the librarian so she wouldn't see that she was upset, and dialled the first number that came into her head.

'Hi, this is Gerry, please leave a message after the beep and I'll get back to you as soon as I can.'

Holly's mum's car pulled up outside the library. Watching her mother's happy face as she parked in the car park brought back memories. Her mum used to collect her from school every day when she was little, and she was always so relieved to see that familiar car come to rescue her after her hellish day. Holly had always hated school—well, she had until she met Gerry. Then she would look forward to going there each day so they could sit together.

Holly's eyes filled with tears again as Elizabeth rushed over to her and wrapped her arms round her. 'Oh, my poor, poor Holly. OK, love, why don't you wait in the car and I'll go in and deal with the librarian?'

Holly did as she was told and sat in the car.

'Silly woman,' her mother grumbled as she climbed back into the car. She glanced over at her daughter, who looked so lost. 'Why don't we go home and we can relax?'

Holly smiled gratefully and a tear trickled down her face. Home. She liked the sound of that. Her mother started up the car.

In the living room at Portmarnock, Holly snuggled up on the couch with her mother.

'I rang you last night at home, were you out?' her mum said. She took a sip of her tea.

Oh, the wonders of the magical tea. The answer to all of life's little problems. You have a gossip and you make a cup of tea, you get fired from your job and you have a cup of tea, your husband tells you he has a brain tumour and you have a cup of tea . . .

'Yeah, I went out to dinner with the girls and about a hundred other people.' Holly rubbed her eyes tiredly.

'How are the girls?' Elizabeth said fondly. She had always got on well with Holly's friends.

'Sharon's pregnant and Denise got engaged,' Holly said.

'Oh,' Elizabeth squeaked, not sure how to react in front of her obviously distressed daughter. 'How do you feel about that?'

Holly stared down at her hands and tried to compose herself. She wasn't successful and her shoulders began to tremble and she tried to hide her face behind her hair.

'Oh, Holly,' Elizabeth said sadly, putting her cup down and moving closer to her daughter. 'It's perfectly normal to feel like this.'

Holly couldn't manage to get any words out of her mouth.

The front door banged. 'We're hoooome!' Ciara announced.

'Great,' Holly sniffed, resting her head on her mum's chest.

'*Where is everyone?*' Ciara shouted.

'Just a minute, love,' Elizabeth called out.

'*I have news!*' Ciara's voice got louder. Mathew burst open the door carrying her in his arms. 'Me and Mathew are moving back to Australia!' she yelled happily into the room. She froze as she saw her sister in her mum's arms, quickly jumped down and led Mathew out.

'Now Ciara's going too, Mum.' Holly cried even harder, and Elizabeth cried softly for her daughter.

Holly stayed in the guest bedroom that night and woke up to a madhouse the following morning. She smiled at the familiar sound of her brother and sister running around the house screaming about how they were late for college and late for work. The world went on, simple as that, and there was no bubble big enough to protect her.

At lunchtime Holly's dad dropped her home and squeezed a cheque for five thousand euros into her hand.

'Dad, I can't accept this,' Holly said, overcome with emotion.

'Take it,' he said, gently. 'Let us help you, love.'

'I'll pay back every cent,' she said, hugging him tightly.

Holly stood at the door and waved her father off down the road. She looked at the cheque in her hand and immediately a weight was lifted from her shoulders. She could think of twenty things she could do with this cheque, and for once buying clothes wasn't one of them.

On the table in the hall she noticed the red light flashing on the answering machine. She sat on the stairs and hit the button.

She had five new messages.

One was from Sharon ringing to see if she was OK because she hadn't heard from her all day. The second was from Denise ringing to see if she was OK because she hadn't heard from her all day. The two girls had obviously been talking to each other. The third was from Sharon, the fourth was from Denise and the fifth was just someone hanging up. Holly pressed delete and ran upstairs to change. She wasn't ready to talk to Sharon and Denise yet. She needed to get her life in order first so she could be more supportive to them.

She sat in the spare room in front of her computer and began to type up a CV. It took her two hours to finally print out something half decent, but reading back over it she decided that she had somehow managed to make herself look intelligent and even she would hire herself. She dressed smartly and drove down to the recruitment office in the car, which she had finally managed to fill with petrol. There was to be no more time-wasting. She was going to find a job.

A few days later Holly sat out on her newly renovated garden furniture in her back garden, sipping on a glass of red wine. She looked around at the neat, landscaped lines and decided that whoever was working on her garden had to be a professional. She breathed in and allowed the sweet scent of the flowers to fill her nostrils. It was eight o'clock and already it was beginning to get dark. The bright light evenings were gone, and everybody was once again preparing for hibernation in the winter months.

She thought about the message she had received on her answering machine that day. It had been from the recruitment agency and she had been shocked to receive a reply from them so quickly. The woman on the phone said that there had been a great response to her CV, and already Holly had a job interview lined up. Butterflies fluttered around her stomach at the thought of it. It was for a job selling advertising space for a magazine that circulated throughout Dublin. It was something she had no experience in, but Gerry had told her to shoot for the moon . . .

Holly also thought about the phone call she had just received from Denise. Denise had been so excited on the phone she didn't seem to be at all bothered by the fact that Holly hadn't talked to her since they'd all met up for dinner. She had been all talk about her wedding, planned for New Year's Eve, and all Holly had to do was make a few noises to let her know she was still listening . . . although she wasn't.

Sharon hadn't called since the day after she had announced her pregnancy, and Holly knew she would have to call her soon, but she just couldn't bring herself to do it. She was still trying to get her head round the fact that Sharon and John were managing to achieve everything that everyone had always assumed Holly and Gerry would do first. Sharon had always said she hated kids, Holly thought angrily. She would call Sharon when she was good and ready.

It began to get chilly and Holly took her glass of wine inside. All she could do was wait for her job interview and pray for success. She went into the living room, put her and Gerry's favourite album of love songs on the CD player and snuggled up on the couch, where she closed her eyes and pictured them dancing round the room together.

The following day she was woken by the sound of a car in her driveway. She got out of bed and threw on Gerry's dressing gown. She peeped out of the curtains and jumped back as she saw Richard stepping out of his car. She really wasn't in the mood for one of his visits. She paced her bedroom floor, feeling guilty as she ignored the doorbell ringing. She knew she was being horrible, but she just couldn't bear sitting down with him for another awkward conversation.

She breathed a sigh of relief as she heard his car door bang shut. She stepped into the shower and allowed the warm water to run over her face and she was once again lost in a world of her own. Twenty minutes later she padded downstairs in her disco diva slippers. A scraping noise from outside made her prick her ears up and listen closely. There it was again. A scraping noise and a rustling . . . Holly's eyes widened as she realised that her leprechaun was outside.

She crept into the living room and got down on her knees. Peering above the windowsill she gasped as she saw Richard's car still sitting in the driveway. Even more surprising was the sight of Richard on his hands and knees with a small gardening implement, planting new flowers. She crawled away from the window and sat on the carpet in shock.

A few minutes later she stood up and brushed the dust off her clothes. She peeked out from behind the curtain again and saw Richard packing up his gardening equipment. Holly kicked off her slippers and shoved her feet into her trainers. As soon as Richard drove down the road she ran outside and hopped into her car. She was going to chase her leprechaun.

She managed to stay three cars behind him just like they did in the movies, and she slowed down as she saw him pulling over. He parked his car and went into the newsagent, returned with a newspaper and crossed the road to the Greasy Spoon.

She backed into a free space, crossed the road and looked inside the café. Richard was sitting with his back to her, hunched over his paper and drinking a cup of tea. She marched over with a smile on her face.

'God, Richard, do you ever go to work?' she joked loudly, causing him to jump. She was about to say more but stopped herself as he looked up with tears in his eyes and his shoulders began to shake.

Ten

HOLLY PULLED OUT A CHAIR and sat down beside Richard. She looked at him in shock, not knowing what to do or what to say. Tears rolled down his face and he tried with all his might to stop them.

'Richard, what's wrong?' She awkwardly patted his arm.

The plump lady made her way round the counter and placed a box of tissues on the table beside Holly.

'Here you go,' Holly said, handing Richard a tissue. He wiped his eyes and blew his nose loudly.

'I'm sorry for crying,' he said, embarrassed.

'Hey, it's my new hobby these days, so don't knock it.'

He smiled sadly. 'Everything just seems to be falling apart.'

'Like what?' she asked, concerned at her brother's transformation into somebody she didn't know at all. Come to think of it, she had seen so many sides to him over the past few months he had her slightly baffled.

Richard took a deep breath and gulped back his tea.

'Richard, I've recently learned that talking about things helps,' Holly said gently. 'And coming from me that's a huge tip, because I used to think I was superwoman, able to keep all my feelings inside. Why don't you tell me about it?'

He looked doubtful.

'I won't laugh, I won't say anything if you don't want me to. I won't tell a soul what you tell me,' she assured him.

He focused on the salt and pepper shakers at the centre of the table and spoke quietly. 'I lost my job.'

Holly remained silent and waited for him to say more. After a while, Richard looked up to face her.

'Richard, I know you loved your job, but you can find another one.'

'I lost my job in April, Holly.' He spoke angrily. 'It is now September. There's nothing for me, not in my line of work.'

'Oh.' Holly didn't know quite what to say. 'But Meredith is working, so you still have a regular income. Just take the time you need to find the right job—'

'Meredith left last month.' This time his voice was weaker.

Holly's hands flew to her mouth. 'The kids?'

'They're living with her,' he said, and his voice cracked.

'Oh, Richard, I'm so sorry,' she said, fidgeting with her hands. Should she hug him or leave him alone?

'I'm sorry too,' he said miserably.

'It wasn't your fault, so don't tell yourself it was.'

'Wasn't it?' he said, his voice beginning to shake. 'She told me I was a pathetic man who couldn't even look after his own family.' He broke down again.

'Oh, never mind that silly bitch. You are an excellent father and a loyal husband,' she said, and realised she meant every word of it. 'Timmy and Emily love you because you're fantastic with them, so don't mind what that demented woman says.' She wrapped her arms round him and hugged him while he cried.

Richard's tears finally subsided and he pulled away from her and grabbed another tissue. Holly's heart went out to him; he had always tried so hard to do the right thing and to create a perfect life and family.

'Where are you staying?' she asked.

'In a b. and b. down the road,' he said, pouring another cup of tea.

'You can't stay there. Why didn't you tell any of us?'

'Because I thought we could work it out, but we can't . . . She's made up her mind.'

'What about Mum and Dad?' she asked.

Richard shook his head. 'No, I wouldn't want to dump myself on them. I'm a grown man now.'

'Oh, Richard, don't be silly.' She made a face. 'There is absolutely nothing wrong with returning to the house you grew up in now and again. It's good for the soul.'

He looked uncertain. 'I don't think that's such a good idea.'

'Ciara's heading back to Australia in a few weeks.'

His face relaxed a little.

Holly smiled. 'So, what do you think?'

Richard smiled too, but it quickly faded. 'I couldn't ask Mother and Father, Holly, I wouldn't know what to say.'

'I'll go with you, and I'll talk to them for you. Honestly, Richard, they'll be delighted. You're their son and they love you. We all do,' she added, placing her hand over his.

'OK,' he finally agreed, and she linked her arm in his as they headed out to their cars.

'Oh, by the way, Richard, thank you for my garden.'

'You know?' he asked, surprised.

She nodded. 'You have a huge talent.'

Her brother's face relaxed into a shy smile.

Two days later Holly looked at herself in the toilet mirror of the office building where her interview was taking place. She had lost so much weight that she had had to go out and purchase a new suit. The jacket was long and went to just above her knees and it was fastened tightly by one button at the waist. The trousers were just the right fit and fell perfectly over her boots. The outfit was black with light blue lines going through, and she matched it with a light blue top underneath. She felt like a hotshot advertising businesswoman in control of her life, and all she needed to do now was to sound like one.

She took her seat again and looked around the office while she waited. The colours were warm, and light poured in from the large Georgian windows. The ceilings were high and there was a lovely feeling of space. Holly could sit there all day thinking. Her heart didn't even jump as her name was called.

Shoot for the moon, she whispered to herself, shoot for the moon.

Holly knocked lightly on the door and a deep gruff voice told her to enter. Her heart did a little flip at the sound of it, feeling as if she had been summoned to the principal's office at school. She wiped her clammy hands on her suit and entered the room

'Hello,' she said more confidently than she felt. She walked across the room and held out her hand to the man who had stood up from his chair. He greeted her with a big smile and a warm handshake. He looked to be in his late fifties, with a big physique and silver hair.

'Holly Kennedy, isn't it?' he said, taking his seat and glancing down at her CV. She sat opposite him.

'That's right,' she said, placing her handbag on the floor and resting her sweaty hands on her lap.

He put his glasses on the end of his nose and flicked through her CV in silence. Holly glanced round his desk and her eyes fell upon a silver photo frame with three pretty girls close to her age, all smiling happily at the camera. When she looked up she realised he had put the CV down and was watching her.

'Before we start talking about you, I'll explain who I am and what the job entails. I'm Chris Feeney, founder and editor of the magazine. As you know, the running of any media organisation is hugely reliant on the advertising we receive. Unfortunately, our last man had to leave in a hurry, so I'm looking for somebody who could begin work almost immediately.'

Holly nodded. 'That would be no problem at all. In fact I'm eager to begin work as soon as possible.'

'I see you've been out of the work force for over a year now, am I correct in saying that?' He stared at her over the rim of his glasses.

'Yes, that's right. Unfortunately my husband was ill, and I had to take time off work to be with him.'

'I see. Well, I hope he's fully recovered now.'

Holly wasn't sure, did he want to hear about her personal life? He continued to look at her and she realised he was waiting for an answer.

'Well, no, actually, Mr Feeney. Unfortunately he passed away in February. He had a brain tumour.'

'I'm very sorry,' Chris said. 'It must be hard for you being so young and all.' He looked down at his desk. 'My wife lost her life to breast cancer just last year, so I understand how you may be feeling.'

'I'm sorry to hear that,' Holly said sadly, looking at the kind man across the desk.

'They say it gets easier.' He smiled.

'So they say,' Holly said grimly. 'Apparently gallons of tea does the trick.'

He started to laugh, a big guffaw of a laugh. 'Yes! I've been told that one too, and my daughters inform me that fresh air is also a healer.'

Holly smiled. 'Are they your daughters?' She indicated the photograph on the desk.

'Indeed they are,' he said proudly. 'My three little doctors who try to keep me alive,' he laughed. 'Unfortunately the garden no longer looks like that, though,' he said, referring to the background.

'Wow, is that your garden?' Holly said, wide-eyed. 'It's beautiful. I presumed it was the Botanic Gardens, or somewhere like that.'

'It was Maureen's speciality. You can't get me out of the office long enough to sort through that mess.'

'Oh, don't talk to me about gardens,' Holly said, rolling her eyes. 'I'm not exactly Ms Greenfingers myself. My place looks like a jungle.' Well, it did look like a jungle, she thought to herself.

They looked at each other and smiled.

'Anyway, getting back to the interview,' Chris Feeney said. 'Have you experience working with the media at all?'

Holly didn't like the way he said 'at all'.

'Yes, I have, actually.' She returned to business mode. 'I worked in an estate agent's advertising new properties, so I was on the other end of what this job requires.'

'But you have never actually worked on a magazine?'

Holly racked her brains. 'I was responsible for printing up a weekly newsletter for a company I worked for . . .' She rambled on and on, grasping at every little straw she could as she went through every job she'd ever worked at. Eventually she grew bored with the sound of her own voice. She was underqualified for this job and she knew it, but she also knew that she could do it if he would just give her the chance.

Chris took off his glasses. 'I see. Well, Holly, you have a great deal of experience in the workplace, but I notice you haven't stayed in any job for longer than nine months.'

'I was searching for the right job for me,' Holly said.

'So how do I know you won't desert me?'

'Because this *is* the right job,' Holly said seriously. She took a deep breath as she felt her chances slipping away from her. 'Mr Feeney, I'm a very hard worker. When I love something I give it one hundred per cent. What I don't know I am more than willing to learn so that I can do my best for myself and for the company. If you put your trust in me, I won't let you down.' She stopped herself just short of getting down on her knees and begging for the damn job. Her face blushed as she realised what she had just done.

'Well, then, I think that's a good note to finish on,' Mr Feeney said, smiling at her. He stood up and held his hand out. 'Thank you for taking the time to come down here. We'll be in touch.'

Holly decided to drop in on Ciara at work, where she could have a bite to eat. She rounded the corner and entered Hogan's pub. It was packed with smartly dressed people on their lunch breaks, some even having a few sneaky pints before heading back to the office. Holly found a small table in the corner.

'Excuse me,' she called out loudly, and clicked her fingers in the air, 'can I get some service here, please?'

The people around her threw her looks for being so rude to the staff. Ciara swirled round with a scowl, but it broke into a smile when she spotted her sister grinning at her. 'I was about to smack the head off you,' she laughed, approaching the table.

'I hope you don't speak to all your customers like that,' Holly teased.

'Not *all* of them. You having lunch here today?'

Holly nodded. 'Mum told me you were working lunches, but I thought you were working in the club upstairs?'

'That man has got me working all the hours under the sun. He's treating me like a slave,' Ciara moaned.

Daniel walked up. 'Did I hear someone mention me?'

Ciara's face froze. 'No, no, I was just talking about Mathew. He has me up all hours of the night, I'm like his sex slave . . .' She wandered over to the bar to get a notepad and pen.

'Sorry I asked,' Daniel said, staring at Ciara. 'Mind if I join you?' he asked Holly.

Holly pulled out a stool for him. 'OK, what's good to eat here?' she asked, looking through the menu.

Ciara mouthed 'Nothing' behind Daniel's back.

'The toasted special is my favourite,' Daniel suggested, and Ciara shook her head wildly at Holly.

'What are you shaking your head at?' Daniel said, catching Ciara in the act again.

'Oh, it's just that . . . Holly is allergic to onions.'

Holly nodded her head. 'Yes . . . they, eh, make my head bloat.' She blew her cheeks out. 'Terrible things, onions. Fatal in fact.' Ciara rolled her eyes at her sister.

'OK, leave the onions out,' Daniel suggested, and Holly agreed. Ciara stuck her fingers in her mouth and pretended to gag as she walked away.

Daniel studied Holly's outfit. 'You're looking very smart today.'

'Yes, well, I was just at a job interview.' Holly winced at the thought of it. 'Let's just say I won't expect a call anytime soon.'

'Oh, well, not to worry,' Daniel said, smiling. 'Still have that job upstairs if you're interested.'

'I thought you gave that job to Ciara.'

'Holly, you know your sister; we had a bit of a *situation*.'

Holly laughed. 'What did she do this time?'

'Some guy at the bar said something she didn't quite like so she served him his pint over his head.'

'Oh, no!' Holly gasped. 'I'm surprised you didn't fire her.'

'Couldn't do that to a Kennedy family member, could I?'

Ciara arrived with Holly's food, slammed the plate down on the table and turned on her heel.

'Hey!' Daniel frowned, taking Holly's plate away. 'There are onions in it. Ciara must have given the wrong order again.'

'No, no, she didn't.' Holly grabbed the plate back. 'I'm only allergic to red onions,' she blurted out.

'How odd. I didn't think there was a huge difference.'

'Oh, there is. They may be part of the same family but the red onion contains deadly toxins . . .'

'Toxins?' Daniel said disbelievingly.

'Well, they're toxic to me, aren't they?' she mumbled, and bit into the sandwich to shut herself up.

'Have you spoken to Denise or Sharon lately?'

'Just Denise,' she said, looking away. 'You?'

'Tom has my head done in with all this talk of weddings. Wants me to be his best man.'

'How do you feel about it?'

'Ah,' Daniel sighed. 'Happy for him, in a selfish and bitter kind of way.' He laughed.

'Know how you feel.' Holly nodded. 'You haven't spoken to your ex lately or anything?'

'Who, Laura?' he said, surprised. 'Never want to see the woman again.'

'Is she a friend of Tom's?'

'Not as friendly as they used to be, thank God.'

'So she won't be invited to the wedding then?'

Daniel's eyes widened. 'You know, I never even considered that.' There was a silence as Daniel contemplated the thought. 'I think I'm meeting up with Tom and Denise tomorrow night to discuss the wedding plans, if you feel like coming out.'

Holly rolled her eyes. 'Gee, thanks, well, that just sounds like the best fun ever, Daniel.'

Daniel started laughing. 'I know, that's why I don't want to go on my own. Call me later, if you decide to come.'

Holly nodded.

'Right, here's the bill,' Ciara said, dropping a piece of paper on the table and sauntering off. Daniel watched after her and shook his head.

Holly's heart began to pound as she spotted Sharon's car outside her house. It had been a long time since Holly had spoken to her. She should have been the one to visit Sharon first and she knew it. She pulled up and got out, then walked towards Sharon's car. She was surprised to see John stepping out. There was no Sharon to be seen. Her throat became dry; she hoped Sharon was OK.

'Hi, Holly,' John said grimly, banging the car door behind him.

'John! Where's Sharon?' she asked.

'I just came from the hospital.'

Holly's hands flew to her face. 'Oh my God! Is she OK?'

John looked confused. 'Yeah, she's just having a checkup. I'm going back to collect her after I leave here.'

Holly's hands dropped to her sides. 'Oh,' she said, feeling stupid.

'You know, if you're that concerned about her then you should call her.' John's icy blue eyes stared straight into hers.

Holly bit her lip, feeling guilty. 'Yeah, I know. Why don't you come inside and I'll make us a cup of tea.'

She flicked the switch on the kettle and busied herself while John made himself comfortable at the table.

'Sharon misses you, you know.'

Holly carried the mugs over to the table. 'I miss her too.'

'It's been a while now, Holly, and you know the two of you used to speak to each other every day.' John took the mug from her hand and placed it in front of him.

'Things used to be very different, John,' Holly said angrily.

'Look, we all know what you've been through—'

'I know you all *know* what I've been through, John, but you don't seem to understand I'm *still* going through it.'

There was a silence.

'I can't just move on with my life like you're all doing and pretend nothing's happened.'

'Do you think that that's what we're doing?'

'Well, let's look at the evidence, shall we?' she said sarcastically. 'Sharon's having a baby. Denise is getting married—'

'Holly, that's called living. You seem to have forgotten how to do that. I miss Gerry too. He was my best mate. We went to school together, we played on the same football team. I was his best man at his wedding and he was at mine. Whenever I had a problem I went to Gerry, whenever I wanted to have a bit of fun I went to Gerry. I told him some things that I would never have told Sharon and he told me things he wouldn't have told you. Just because I wasn't married to him doesn't mean that I don't feel like you do.'

Holly sat stunned. John took a deep breath.

'Yes, it's difficult. Yes, it's horrible. Yes, it's the worst thing that has ever happened to me in my whole life. But I can't just stop going to the pub because there's two blokes laughing and joking on the stools Gerry and I used to sit on. I can't stop going to football matches just because it's somewhere we used to go together all the time.'

Tears welled in Holly's eyes and John continued talking.

'Sharon knows you're hurting but you have to understand that this is a hugely important time in her life, too, and she needs her best friend to help her through it. She needs your help just like you need hers.'

Holly sobbed hot tears. 'I'm trying, John.'

'I know you are.' He grabbed her hands. 'But Sharon needs you. Avoiding the situation isn't going to help anyone.'

'But I went for a job interview today,' she sobbed childishly.

John tried to hide his smile. 'That's great news, Holly. And how did it go?'

'Shite,' she sniffed, and John started laughing. He allowed a silence to fall between them before he spoke again.

'She's almost five months pregnant, you know.'

'What?' Holly looked up in surprise. 'She didn't tell me she was pregnant when we were in Lanzarote.'

'She was afraid to,' he said gently. 'She thought you might get mad at her and never want to speak to her again.'

Holly wiped her eyes aggressively. She looked away. 'I meant to call her, I really did. I picked up the phone every day but I just couldn't do it. Then I'd say that I'd call the next day, and the next day I would be busy . . . Oh, I'm sorry, John. I'm truly happy for the both of you.'

'Thank you, but it's not me that needs to hear this.'

'But I've been so awful! She'll never forgive me now!'

'Oh, don't be stupid, Holly. It's Sharon we're talking about here. It will all be forgotten about by tomorrow.'

Holly raised her eyebrows at him hopefully.

'Well, maybe not *tomorrow*. Next year perhaps . . . but she'll forgive you eventually.' His icy eyes warmed and twinkled at her.

'Stop it!' Holly giggled. 'Can I come with you to see her?'

Butterflies fluttered around in Holly's stomach as they pulled up outside the hospital. Sharon stood alone outside, waiting to be collected. She looked so cute Holly had to smile at the sight of her friend. As Holly looked at Sharon dressed in a polo neck and jeans, she could see the swelling of a bump. Holly stepped out of the car and Sharon's face froze.

Oh, no, Sharon was going to scream at her. She was going to tell her she hated her and that she never wanted to see her again and that she was a crappy friend and that . . .

Sharon's face broke into a smile and she held her arms out. 'Come here to me, you fool,' she said softly.

Holly ran into her arms. There, with her best friend hugging her tight, she felt the tears begin again. 'Oh, Sharon, I'm so sorry, I'm a horrible person. I'm so so so so so so sorry, please forgive me. I never meant to—'

'Oh, shut up, you whiner, and hug me.' Sharon cried too, and they squeezed each other for a long time as John looked on.

'Ahem.' John cleared his throat loudly.

'Oh, come here you.' Holly smiled and dragged him into their huddle.

'I presume this was your idea.' Sharon looked at her husband.

'No, not at all,' John said, winking at Holly. 'I just passed Holly in the street and told her I'd give her a lift . . .'

'Yeah, right,' Sharon said sarcastically, as the three of them walked towards the car and got inside.

'So what did they say?' Holly asked Sharon from the back. 'Is it a boy or a girl?'

'It's an "it" for now,' Sharon said. 'They're not too sure yet.'

'Would you want to know if they could tell you?'

Sharon scrunched her nose up. 'I don't know, I haven't figured that out yet.' She looked across at John again, and the two of them shared a secret smile.

A familiar pang of jealousy hit Holly and she sat quietly while the three of them headed back to Holly's house in John's car. Later, sitting round her kitchen table, they made up for lost time.

'Sharon, Holly went for a job interview today,' John said when he managed to get a word in edgeways.

'Oooh, really? I didn't know you were job-hunting already!'

'Gerry's new mission for me,' Holly smiled.

'Oh, was that what it was this month? I was just dying to know! So how did it go?'

Holly grimaced and held her head in her hands. 'Oh, it was awful, Sharon. I made a total fool of myself.'

'Really?' Sharon giggled. 'What was the job?'

'Selling advertising space for that magazine, X.'

'Ooh, that's cool, I read that at work all the time.'

'What kind of magazine is it?' asked John.

'Oh, it has fashion, sports, culture, food, reviews . . .'

'And adverts,' Holly joked.

'What was so wrong with the interview? You can't have been that bad.' Sharon looked intrigued.

'Oh, I think it's bad when the interviewer asks if you have any experience and you tell him you once printed up a newsletter.' Holly banged her head playfully off the kitchen table.

Sharon burst out laughing. 'I hope you weren't referring to that crappy little leaflet you printed up on the computer.'

John and Sharon howled with laughter.

'Ah well, it was *advertising* the company . . .' Holly giggled.

'Remember, you made us all go out and post them round people's houses? It took us days to do!'

'Hey, I remember that,' John laughed. 'Remember, you sent me and Gerry out to post hundreds of them one night?'

'Yeah?' Holly was afraid to hear what came next.

'Well, we shoved them in the skip at the back of Bob's pub and went in for a few pints.'

Holly's mouth dropped open. 'You sly little bastards! Because of you two the company went bust and I lost my job!'

'Oh, I'd say it went bust the minute people took a look at those leaflets, Holly,' John teased.

'Shut up, you,' Holly laughed. 'Hey, what else did you and Gerry get up to that I don't know about?'

John's eyes danced. 'Ah, a true friend never reveals secrets.'

But something had been unlocked. And for the first time since Gerry had died, the three of them laughed and laughed, and Holly learned how to talk about her husband again. It used to be that the four of them gathered together: Holly, Gerry, Sharon and John. This time three gathered to remember the one they had lost. Soon they would be four again, with the arrival of Sharon and John's baby.

Life went on.

That Sunday, Richard called by to visit Holly with the kids. She had told him he was welcome to bring them whenever it was his day with them. They played outside in the garden while Richard and Holly finished off their lunch and watched them through the patio doors.

'They seem really happy, Richard,' Holly said.

'Yes, they do, don't they?' He smiled as he watched them chasing each other around. 'I want things to be as normal for them as possible. They don't quite understand what's going on.'

'What have you told them?'

'Oh, that Mummy and Daddy don't love each other any more and that I moved away so that we can be happier.'

'And they're OK with that?'

'Timothy is OK but Emily is worried that we might stop loving her and that she will have to move away.' His eyes were sad.

Poor Emily, Holly thought, watching her dancing around with her scary-looking doll. She couldn't believe that she was having this conversation with Richard. He seemed like a different person these days. But then again, they now had something in common. They both understood what it was like to feel lonely and unsure of themselves.

'How's everything going at Mum and Dad's house?'

Richard swallowed a forkful of potato and nodded. 'Good. They're being extremely generous.'

'Ciara bothering you at all?'

'Ciara is . . . Ciara,' he smiled. 'We don't see eye to eye on a lot of things.'

'Well, I wouldn't worry about that,' Holly said. 'The majority of the world wouldn't see eye to eye with her.' She sat back in her seat, trying to decide how to phrase what she was going to say. 'We're all different, Richard. Ciara is eccentric, Declan is a dreamer, Jack is a joker, I'm . . . well, I don't know what I am. But you were always very controlled. It's not necessarily a bad thing.'

'I've always thought you were very thoughtful,' Richard said, after a long silence.

'When?' Holly asked incredulously.

'Well, I wouldn't be sitting here eating lunch with the kids running around having fun outside if you weren't thoughtful now, but I was referring to when we were children.'

'Jack and I were always so awful to you,' she said softly.

'You weren't *always* awful, Holly.' He gave her an amused smile. 'Besides, that's what brothers and sisters are for, to make each other's lives as difficult as possible. It forms a great basis for life, toughens you up. Anyway, I was the bossy older brother.'

'So how does that make me thoughtful?' Holly asked.

'You idolised Jack. You used to follow him around and you would do exactly what he told you to do.' He started laughing. 'I used to hear him telling you to say things to me and you would run into my room terrified and blurt them out and run away again.'

Holly looked at her plate, feeling embarrassed.

'But you always came back,' Richard continued. 'You would always creep back into my room silently and watch me working at my desk, and I knew that was your way of saying sorry.' He smiled. 'None of our siblings had a conscience in that house. Not even me. You were the only one, always the sensitive one.'

He continued eating and Holly sat in silence. She didn't remember idolising Jack, but she supposed Richard was right. Jack had always been her favourite brother; Gerry had always got along with Jack the best. However, she realised she had been making excuses for him every time he didn't call round or phone her when he said he would. In fact, she had been making excuses for him ever since Gerry died.

The next day, Holly jumped around the house ecstatically as she replayed the message on the answering machine for the third time.

'Hi, Holly,' came the gruff voice. 'This is Chris Feeney here from magazine X. I'm just calling to say that I was very impressed with your interview. Em . . .' He stalled a bit. 'Well, no doubt you'll be delighted to know that I've decided to welcome you as a new member of the team. I would love you to start as soon as possible, so call and we'll discuss it.'

Holly rolled around her bed in terrified delight and pressed the PLAY button again. She had aimed for the moon, and she'd landed!

Eleven

HOLLY STARED UP at the tall Georgian building and her body tingled with excitement. It was her first day of work and she felt that good times were ahead of her in this building. It was situated in the centre of town, and the busy offices of magazine X were on the first floor above a small café. Holly had got very little sleep the night before owing to nerves and excitement; however, she didn't feel the same dread that she usually felt before starting a new job. She had phoned Mr Feeney back immediately and then shared the news with her family and friends. They had been ecstatic, and just before she left the house that morning she had received a beautiful bouquet of flowers from her parents, wishing her luck on her first day.

But although she had felt excited when she sat down to eat her breakfast, she had also felt sad. Sad that Gerry wasn't there to share her new start. They had performed a little ritual every time Holly started a new job. Gerry would wake Holly up with breakfast in bed and then he would pack her bag with ham and cheese sandwiches, an apple, a packet of crisps and a bar of chocolate. Mind you, they only ever did that on her first day, every other day they would tumble out of bed late as usual, race each other to the shower and then wander around the kitchen half asleep, grumbling at each other while they grabbed a quick cup of coffee. They would give one another a kiss goodbye and go their separate ways, then start all over again the next day. If Holly had known that their time was so precious . . .

This morning, she had woken to an empty house in an empty bed to no breakfast. She had allowed herself to imagine that when she woke up Gerry would miraculously be there to greet her, but with death there were no exceptions. Gone meant gone.

Now, poised at the entrance, Holly checked herself to see that she looked presentable and made her way up the wooden staircase. She entered the waiting-room area and the secretary she recognised from the interview came from behind the desk to greet her.

'Hi, Holly,' she said happily, shaking her hand. 'Welcome to our humble abode.' She looked about the same age as Holly and had long blonde hair. 'I'm Alice, by the way, and I work out here in Reception, as you know. Well, the boss man's waiting for you.'

'I'm not late, am I?' Holly asked, worriedly glancing at her watch.

'No, not at all,' Alice said, leading her down to Mr Feeney's office. 'Don't mind Chris and all the other lot, they're all workaholics. I think Chris actually lives in his office. The man isn't normal,' she said, tapping on his door lightly and leading her in.

'Who's not normal?' Chris asked gruffly, standing up from his chair.

'You.' Alice smiled, and closed the door behind her.

'See how my staff treat me?' Chris's handshake was once again warm and welcoming, and Holly felt immediately at ease.

'Thank you for hiring me, Mr Feeney,' she said genuinely.

'You can call me Chris, and there's no need to thank me. Right, why don't you follow me and I'll show you round the place.' He started leading her down the hall. The walls were hung with framed covers of every *X* magazine published for the last twenty years.

'In here is our office of little ants.' He pushed open the door and Holly looked into the huge office. There were about ten desks in all, with people all sitting in front of their computers and talking on the phone. They looked up and waved politely. Holly smiled at them. 'These are the wonderful journalists who help pay my bills,' Chris explained. 'That's John-Paul, the fashion editor; Mary, our food woman; and Brian, Sean, Gordon, Aishling and Tracey. Everyone, this is Holly!' They smiled and waved again and continued talking on the phone.

Chris led her to the room next door. 'This is where all our computer nerds hide. That's Dermot and Wayne, and they're in charge of layout and design, so you'll be keeping them informed about what advertisements are going where. Lads, this is Holly.'

'Hi, Holly.' They both stood up and shook her hand and then continued working on their computers.

'I have them well trained,' Chris chuckled, and headed back down the way they had come. Holly glanced at the walls feeling excited. This was like nothing she had ever experienced before.

'In here is your office,' Chris said, pushing the door open

Holly couldn't stop herself from smiling as she looked around at the small room. She had never had her own office before. It was just big enough to fit a desk and filing cabinet. There was a computer sitting on the desk with piles and piles of folders. Opposite the desk was a bookcase crammed with stacks of old magazines. A huge Georgian window practically covered the entire wall behind her desk, and the room had a bright and airy feel to it.

She placed her new briefcase on the desk. 'It's perfect,' she said.

'**R**ight, Ciara, are you sure you've got your passport?' Holly's mum asked for the third time since leaving the house.

'Yes, Mum,' Ciara groaned. 'I told you a billion times, it's right here.'

'Show me.' Elizabeth twisted round in the passenger seat.

'No! I'm not showing it to you. You should just take my word for it. I'm not a baby any more, you know.'

Declan snorted and Ciara elbowed him. 'Shut up, you.'

'Ciara, just show Mum the passport so you can put her mind at rest,' Holly said tiredly.

'Fine,' she huffed, lifting her bag onto her lap. 'It's in here, look . . . no, hold on, it's in here . . . no, actually maybe I put it in . . . Oh, fuck!'

'Bloody hell, Ciara,' Holly's dad growled, slamming on the brakes and turning the car round.

'What?' she said defensively. 'I put it in here, Dad. Someone must have taken it out,' she grumbled, emptying the contents of her bag in the car.

'Oh, Ciara,' Holly moaned as a pair of knickers went flying over her face.

'Ah, shut up,' Ciara grumbled again. 'You won't have to put up with me for much longer.'

Everyone in the car went silent as they realised that was true. Ciara would be in Australia for God only knew how long, and they would all miss her, loud and irritating though she was.

Holly sat squashed in the back seat with Declan and Ciara. Richard was driving Mathew and Jack, and they were probably at the airport already. This was the second time they had returned to the house, as Ciara had forgotten her lucky nose ring and demanded that her dad turn the car round earlier. An hour after setting off, they reached the airport in what should have been only a twenty-minute drive.

'Pet, keep in touch with us a lot more this time, won't you?' Elizabeth cried as she hugged her daughter.

'Of course I will. Oh, please, don't cry, Mum, or you'll get me started.'

A lump formed in Holly's throat as she stood on the tips of her toes to hug the enormous Mathew. 'Take care of my sister.'

'Don't worry, she's in good hands,' he smiled.

'Look after her now, won't you?' Frank smacked him on the back. Mathew was intelligent enough to know it was more of a warning than a question and gave a very persuasive answer.

'Bye, Richard,' Ciara said. 'Stay away from that Meredith bitch now. You're far too good for her.' She gave him a big hug and Declan too. 'You can come over any time you like, Dec, maybe make a movie or something about me. And, Jack, look after my big sis,' she said, squeezing Holly tightly. 'Ooh, I'm gonna miss you,' she said sadly.

'Me too,' Holly's voice shook.

'OK, I'm going now before all you depressing people make me cry,' she said, trying to sound happy.

Holly stood in silence with her family and they all watched as Ciara and Mathew walked away, hand in hand. Even Declan had a tear in his eye, but pretended he was about to sneeze.

'Just look at the lights, Declan.' Jack threw his arm round his baby brother. 'They say that helps you sneeze.'

Declan stared up at the lights and avoided watching his favourite sister walking away. Frank held his wife close as she waved at her daughter, while tears rolled down her cheeks.

Holly stared out of the window. She was flying through her work this week. She didn't know it was possible to actually *enjoy* work so much. She had stayed in happily through lunch breaks and had even worked late. But it was only her third week, after all; give her time. The office had developed a light-hearted banter and she loved feeling that she was a part of the team; as though she were actually doing something that made an impact on the finished product. Every time she made a deal she thanked Gerry for pushing her all the way to the top.

She heard the radio go on in Chris's office next door. On the hour without fail, he turned on the news, and all the news seeped into Holly's brain. She had never felt so intelligent.

She glanced back down at her work again; a freelancer had written an article on how he travelled around Ireland trying to find the cheapest pint. It was very amusing, but there was a huge gap at the bottom of the page and it was up to Holly to fill it. She flicked through her book of contacts and an idea came to her immediately. She picked up the phone and dialled.

'Hogan's.'

'Hi, Daniel Connelly, please.'

'One moment.'

Bloody 'Greensleeves' again. She danced around the room to the music while she waited.

'Hello?'

'Daniel? Hiya, it's Holly.'

'How are you doin', Holly?'

'I'm grand, thanks, you?'

'Couldn't be better. How's that snazzy job of yours?'

'Well, actually, that's why I'm calling.' Holly sounded guilty.

He laughed. 'So what's up?'

'Do I remember you saying you needed to advertise Club Diva more?' Well, he had actually thought he was saying it to Sharon, but she knew he wouldn't remember that minor detail.

'I do recall saying that, yes.'

'How would you like to advertise it in *X*?'

'Is that the name of the magazine you work on?'

'No, I just thought it would be an interesting question, that's all,' she joked. 'Of course it's where I work!'

'Oh, *of course*, I'd forgotten. That's the magazine that has offices just round the corner from me!' he said sarcastically. 'The one that causes you to walk by my front door every day, and yet you still don't call in. Why don't I see you at lunchtime?' he teased. 'Isn't my pub good enough for you?'

'Oh, everyone here eats their lunch at their desks,' she explained. 'So what do you think?'

'I think that's very boring of you all.'

'No, I mean what do you think about the ad?'

'Yeah, sure, that's a good idea.'

'OK, well, I'll put it in the November issue. Would you like it placed monthly?'

'Would you like to tell me how much that would set me back?'

Holly totted up the figures and told him.

'Hmm,' he said. 'I'll have to think about that, but I'll definitely go for the November edition.'

'OK, that's great. You'll be a millionaire after this goes to print.'

'I'd better be,' he laughed. 'By the way, there's a launch party for some new drink coming up next week. Can I put your name down?'

'Yeah, that would be good. What new drink is it?'

'Blue Rock, a new alco-pop drink that's apparently going to be huge. Tastes like shite but it's free all night.'

'Wow, you're such a good advertisement for it,' she laughed. 'When is it on?' She took out her diary and made a note of it. 'That's perfect, I can come straight after work.'

'Well, make sure you bring your bikini to work in that case. The party has a beach theme.'

'But it's almost winter, you nutter.'

'Hey, it wasn't my idea. The slogan is "Blue Rock, the hot new drink for winter".'

'Ugghh, how tacky,' she groaned. 'OK, thanks, Daniel. Have a think about what you want your ad to say and get back to me.'

'Will do. What time do you finish work?'

'Six.'

'OK, why don't you come round here at six, and I'll take you somewhere to have a bite?'

'Great.' She hung up the phone and then froze. Had she just agreed to go on a date with Daniel? She sat quietly as she went over the conversation in her head. Finally she stood up and went next door to Chris's office, a new thought occurring to her.

'You finished dancing in there?' he chuckled.

'Yeah, I just made up a routine. Came in to show you,' she joked. 'No, actually, it's just an idea.'

'Take a seat.' He nodded to the chair in front of him. 'What's the idea?'

'Well, you know Hogan's round the corner?'

Chris nodded.

'I was just on to the owner to place an ad and he was telling me that they're having a launch party for a new alco-pop drink. It has a beach theme, all the staff will be in bikinis and that kind of thing.'

'In the middle of autumn?' He raised his eyebrows.

'It's apparently the hot new drink for winter.'

He rolled his eyes. 'Tacky.'

Holly smiled. 'That's what I said. Anyway, I just thought it might be worth covering.'

'That's great, Holly. I'll get one of the lads onto it.'

Holly smiled happily. 'By the way, did you get your garden sorted yet?'

Chris frowned. 'I've had about ten people come down to look at it. They tell me it'll cost six grand.'

'Wow, six grand! That's a lot of money.'

'Well, it's a big garden, so they have a point.'

'What was the cheapest quote?'

'Five and a half grand, why?'

'Because my brother will do it for five,' she blurted out.

'Five?' His eyes nearly popped out of his head. 'Is he good?'

'Remember I told you my garden was a jungle?'

He nodded.

'Well, it's a jungle no longer. He did a great job on it, but he works alone, so it takes him longer.'

'For that price I don't care. Have you his business card?'

'Yeah, hold on and I'll get it.' She stole some impressive-looking card stock from Alice's desk, typed up Richard's name and mobile number in fancy writing, and printed it out. She cut it into a small rectangular shape, making it look like a business card.

'That's great,' Chris said, reading it. 'I think I'll give him a call now.'

'No, no,' Holly said quickly. 'He's up to his eyeballs today. You'll get him easier tomorrow.'

Holly couldn't concentrate during the last hour of work; she kept on watching the clock, willing the time to go more slowly. Why didn't it go this fast when she was waiting to open her messages from Gerry? She opened her bag for the millionth time that day to double-check that Gerry's eighth message was still tucked safely in the inside pocket. As it was the last day of the month she had decided to bring the October envelope with her to work. She wasn't sure why, but she couldn't face leaving it sitting on the kitchen table. She was only hours away from being that much closer to Gerry again, but she was also dreading her dinner with Daniel.

At six o'clock on the dot she heard Alice switch off her computer and clatter down the wooden stairs. She prayed that Chris would dump another load on her desk just so she would have to stay late and cancel dinner. She and Daniel had been out together before, so why was she worrying now? Something was niggling at the back of her mind. There was something in his voice that worried her, and something happened to her stomach when his voice came on the phone that made her feel uneasy about meeting up with him.

She slowly shut down her computer and packed her briefcase with meticulous care, then finally headed outside. Her heart beat wildly as she spotted Daniel walking down the road to meet her. The cool autumn months had arrived, so he was back to wearing his black leather jacket with blue jeans. His black hair was messy and stubble lined his chin. He had that just-out-of-bed look. Holly's stomach lurched again and she looked away.

'I'm so sorry, Daniel,' she apologised. 'I should have come to Hogan's, but I got tied up and I couldn't call,' she lied.

'Don't worry about it, I'm sure it was important.' He smiled at her and she felt instantly guilty. This was Daniel, her friend. What on earth was wrong with her?

'So where would you like to go?' he asked.

'How about in there?' Holly said, looking at the small café on the ground floor of her office building. She wanted to go to the least intimate and most casual place possible.

Daniel scrunched up his nose. 'I'm a bit hungrier than that, if you don't mind. I haven't eaten all day.'

They walked along together and eventually he settled on an Italian restaurant. Inside it was quiet, with just a few candlelit tables occupied by couples.

'They make you sick, don't they?' Daniel laughed, following Holly's gaze to a couple on the far side of the room who were kissing across the table.

'Actually no,' Holly said quietly. 'They make me sad.'

Daniel hadn't heard her, as he was busy reading through the menu. 'What are you having?'

'A Caesar salad. I just don't have a very big appetite.'

Holly tried to control the conversation, steering it into safe territory, and they spent the evening talking about the ad, what angle to take and what information to give. She left the restaurant feeling a little panicked about why she had been so uncomfortable with a man that she was certain only wanted to be her friend.

She stepped outside for a breath of fresh air while Daniel kindly paid the bill. He was extremely generous, there was no denying that, and she was glad of his friendship. It just didn't feel quite right to be eating in an intimate restaurant with anyone other than Gerry. She should be back at home sitting at her kitchen table waiting until midnight.

She froze as she spotted a couple walking towards her. 'Holly, is that you?' she heard the familiar voice.

'Hello, there!' She tried to sound surprised.

'How are you?' the woman asked, giving her a feeble hug. 'What are you doing standing out here in the cold?'

'Oh, you know . . . I was just having a bite to eat,' Holly smiled pointing at the restaurant.

'Well, good for you.' The man patted her on the back. 'It's good to get out and do things on your own.'

She glanced at the door. 'Yes, it's nice to do that . . .'

'There you are!' Daniel laughed, stepping outside. 'I thought you had run off on me.' He wrapped his arm loosely round her shoulders.

Holly smiled at him weakly and turned to face the couple.

'Oh, sorry, I didn't see you there.' Daniel smiled.

The couple stared back at him stonily.

'Daniel, this is Judith and Harold. They're Gerry's parents.'

Holly cursed at the driver in front of her. She was fuming. She was mad at herself for feeling that she had been caught in a bad situation last night, when really there was nothing to it. She had a headache and the traffic was driving her insane. Poor Daniel, she thought. Gerry's parents had been so rude to him, ending their conversation abruptly and walking away. Oh, why did they have to see her the one time she was happy? They could have come round to the house any other day and found her living the life of the perfect grieving widow. Well, screw them, she thought angrily.

She decided Ciara would cheer her up, but just as she pulled up outside her parents' house, she remembered that Ciara wasn't there.

She rang the doorbell and Declan answered. 'What's wrong with you?'

'Nothing,' she said, feeling sorry for herself. 'Where's Mum?'

'In the kitchen with Dad and Richard. I'd leave them alone for a bit.'

'Oh, OK.' She felt lost. 'What are you up to?'

'I'm just watching what I filmed today. It's for a documentary on homelessness. Do you wanna watch it?'

'Yeah.' She smiled gratefully and settled herself down on the couch. A few minutes into the video and Holly was in tears, but for once they weren't for herself. Declan had done an incisive, heart-rending interview with a remarkable man who was living on the streets of Dublin. The fact that Gerry's parents had bumped into her and Daniel now seemed such a stupid thing to worry about.

'Oh, Declan, that was excellent,' she said, drying her eyes when it had finished. 'Are you happy with it?'

'It's hard to be happy about the fact that what he has to say is *so* bad that it's making a great documentary.' Declan shrugged. 'Anyway I'm off to bed, I'm knackered.' He kissed her on the top of the head as he passed, which really touched Holly. Her baby brother was growing up.

Holly glanced at the clock on the mantelpiece and noticed it was almost midnight. She reached for her bag and took out the October envelope from Gerry. She was even more intrigued by this one, as the envelope was larger than the others. She ran her fingers over the writing once again and tore the seal open. Holly slid the card out and a dried sunflower fell onto her lap, along with a small pouch of seeds. Her hands shook as she touched the delicate petals. His message read:

A sunflower for my sunflower. To brighten the dark October days you hate so much. Plant some more, and be safe in the knowledge a warm and bright summer awaits.
PS, I love you . . .
PPS, Could you please pass this card on to John?

Holly lifted the second card that had fallen onto her lap and read the words through her tears and laughter.

To John,
Happy 32nd birthday! You're getting old, my friend, but I hope you have many, many more birthdays. Enjoy life and take care of my wife and Sharon. You're the man now!
Lots of love, your friend Gerry

Holly read and reread every single word Gerry had written. She stood up from the couch and walked to the kitchen. She felt a new bounce in her step and she couldn't wipe the grin off her face. She tapped lightly on the kitchen door.

'Come in,' Elizabeth called.

Holly stepped in and looked round at her parents and Richard sitting at the table with cups of tea in their hands.

'Oh, hello, love,' her mum said, happily getting up to give her a hug and a kiss. 'I didn't hear you come in.'

'I was just watching Declan's documentary.' Holly beamed at her family and felt like giving them all a hug.

'It's great, isn't it?' Frank stood up to hug her.

Holly joined them at the table. 'Have you found a job yet?' she asked Richard.

He shook his head sadly as if he were going to cry.

'Well, I did.'

He looked at her, disgusted that she could say such a thing. 'Well, I know *you* did.'

'No, Richard.' She grinned. 'I mean I got *you* a job.'

'You what?'

'You heard me. My boss will be calling you tomorrow.'

His face fell. 'Oh, Holly, that's very nice of you indeed, but I have no interest in advertising. My interest is in science.'

'And gardening.'

'Yes, I like gardening.' He looked confused.

'That's why my boss will be calling you. To ask you to work on his garden. I told him you'll do it for five thousand; I hope that's OK.' She smiled at him as his mouth dropped open.

He was completely speechless so Holly kept on talking. 'And here are your business cards.' She handed him a pile of cards.

Richard and her parents picked up the cards and read them in silence. Suddenly Richard started laughing, jumped out of his chair pulling Holly with him, and danced her around the kitchen while her parents looked on and cheered.

Twelve

'OK, THIS IS THE LAST ONE, I promise, girls!' Denise called as her bra was sent flying over the changing-room door.

Sharon and Holly groaned and collapsed onto their chairs again. 'You said that an hour ago,' Sharon complained, kicking off her shoes and massaging her swollen ankles.

'Yeah, but I mean it this time. I have a really good feeling about this dress,' Denise said, full of excitement.

'You said *that* an hour ago too,' Holly grumbled, resting her head back on the chair and closing her eyes.

They had been dragged to every single wedding-gown boutique in the city and Sharon and Holly were exhausted and extremely fed up. Whatever excitement they had felt for Denise and her wedding had been drained from their systems. And if Holly heard Denise's irritating squeals one more time . . .

'Oooh, I love it!' Denise shrieked.

'OK, here's the plan,' Sharon whispered to Holly. 'If she walks out of there looking like a meringue that has sat on a bicycle pump we are going to tell her she looks beautiful.'

Holly giggled. 'Oh, Sharon, we can't do that!'

'Oooh, wait till you see!' Denise shrieked again.

'On second thoughts . . .' Holly looked at Sharon miserably.

'Ta-da!' Denise stepped out of the dressing room and Holly's eyes widened. She looked at Sharon uncertainly and tried not to laugh at the look on her face.

'Do you like it?' Denise squealed, and Holly winced.

'Yes,' Sharon said unenthusiastically.

'Are you sure?'

'Yes.'

'Do you think Tom will be happy when he looks down the aisle and sees me walking towards him?'

'Yes,' Sharon repeated.

'Do you think it's worth the money?'

'Yes.'

'It'll be nicer with a tan, won't it?'

'Yes.'

'Oh, but does it make my bum look enormous?'

'Yes.'

Holly looked at Sharon, startled, and realised that she wasn't even listening to the questions any more.

Denise carried on, obviously not even listening to the answers. 'So will I get it?'

'No!' Holly interrupted before Sharon said yes again.

'No?' Denise asked.

'No,' Holly confirmed.

'Oh.' Denise turned to face Sharon. 'Do you agree with Holly?'

'Yes.'

'All right, then, I trust you two,' Denise said, sadly. 'To be honest I wasn't really that keen on it myself.'

Sharon put her shoes back on. 'OK, Denise, let's go and get something to eat before I drop dead.'

The three of them trudged into Bewley's Café and managed to grab their usual spot overlooking Grafton Street.

'Oh, I hate shopping on Saturdays,' Holly moaned, watching people bump and crush one another on the busy street below.

'Gone are the days of shopping midweek, now you're no longer a lady of leisure,' Sharon teased, as she picked up her club sandwich.

'I know, and I'm *so* tired, but I feel like I've earned the tiredness this time,' Holly said happily.

'Tell us about the little episode with Gerry's parents,' Sharon said with a mouthful of food.

Holly rolled her eyes. 'They were just so rude to Daniel.'

'They can't tell you who to see and who not to see,' Sharon gave out.

'Sharon, I'm not seeing him.' Holly tried to set the record straight. 'I have no intentions of seeing anyone for at least twenty years. We were just having a business dinner.'

'Oooh, a *business* dinner!' Sharon and Denise giggled.

'Well, that's what it was, but it was also nice to have a bit of company,' Holly admitted. 'When everyone else is busy it's nice to have someone else to chat to. Especially male company.'

'Yeah, I understand,' Sharon nodded. 'It's good for you to get out and meet new people anyway.'

Denise giggled. 'Well, Holly, I'm glad you get along with him, because you're going to have to dance with him at the wedding.'

'Why?' Holly looked at Denise confused.

'Because it's tradition for the best man to dance with the maid of honour.' Her eyes sparkled.

Holly gasped. 'You want me to be your maid of honour?'

Denise nodded, full of excitement. 'Don't worry, I already asked Sharon and she doesn't mind.'

'Oh, I would love to,' Holly said. 'But, Sharon, are you sure?'

'I'm happy just being a blown-up bridesmaid. I'll need to borrow Denise's marquee to wear as a dress!'

'I hope you don't go into labour at the wedding.' Denise's eyes widened.

'Don't worry, Denise, I'm not due till the end of January. Oh, by the way, I forgot to show you the photograph of the baby.' Sharon rooted through her bag and pulled out a small photograph.

'Where is it?' Denise moved the scan closer.

'There.' Sharon pointed out the area.

'Whoa! That's one big boy,' Denise exclaimed.

Sharon rolled her eyes. 'Denise, that's a leg, you fool, we still don't know the sex yet.'

'Oh.' Denise blushed. 'Well, congratulations, Sharon, it looks like you're having a little alien.'

'Oh, stop it, Denise,' Holly laughed. 'I think it's beautiful.'

'Good.' Sharon looked at Denise and Denise nodded. 'Because I wanted to ask you something. John and I would love it if you would be our baby's godmother.'

Holly gasped with shock for the second time that day, and tears filled her eyes.

'You didn't cry when I asked you to be maid of honour,' Denise huffed.

'Oh, Sharon, I would be honoured.' Holly gave her friend a big hug.

Holly pushed through the crowds in Hogan's pub and made her way upstairs to Club Diva. Her jaw dropped as she approached the door. A group of young muscular males dressed in swimwear were banging out Hawaiian drumbeats. Skinny female models in skimpy bikinis greeted all the guests by wrapping beautiful multicoloured garlands of flowers round their necks. Holly could barely recognise the club; it had been completely transformed. A water feature came into view as they entered. Aqua-blue water cascaded down from rocks.

Holly looked around for Denise and Tom and saw her friend being photographed as she held her hand up to the camera to show off her sparkly engagement ring. Holly laughed at the big celebrity couple.

The bar staff were also dressed in bikinis and swimwear and they lined the entrance with trays of blue drinks in their hands. Holly lifted a drink from a tray and took a sip, trying not to make a face from its overly sweet taste. The floors were scattered with sand; each table was sheltered by a huge bamboo umbrella; the bar stools were all big kettle drums; and there was a wonderful smell of barbecue in the air. Holly darted to the nearest table, helped herself to a kebab and found herself facing Daniel.

'Em, hello. The place looks great,' she said.

'Yeah, it worked well.' He looked pleased. Daniel wore faded blue jeans and a blue Hawaiian shirt with big pink and yellow flowers. He still hadn't shaved and Holly wondered how painful it would be to kiss him with that sharp stubble . . . Why was she even wondering about it?

'Daniel,' she said, 'once again I'm really sorry about the other night.'

'Oh, there's no need to apologise again, Holly. I just felt uncomfortable for you.' He smiled and placed his hands on her shoulders as though he were going to say something more, but someone called him over to the bar.

Holly hoped that Daniel didn't think there was more to the dinner than there really had been. He had called her almost every day since that episode, and she realised she looked forward to his calls. There was that niggling thing at the back of her mind again. She wandered over to Denise and joined her on the sunbed, where she was sipping on the blue concoction.

'So what do you think of the hot new drink for winter?' Holly indicated the bottle.

Denise rolled her eyes. 'Tacky. I've only had a few and my head is spinning already.'

Denise banged the till closed with her hip and handed over the receipt. 'Thanks.' Her smile faded as soon as the customer turned away from the counter. She sighed loudly, staring at the long queue in front of the cash register, grumpily grabbed the item of clothing from the next customer, de-tagged it, scanned it and wrapped it.

'Excuse me, are you Denise Hennessey?' she heard a deep voice ask, and she looked up to see where the sexy voice had come from. She frowned as she saw a police officer before her and tried to think if she had done anything illegal in the past few days. When she was satisfied she was crime-free she smiled. 'Yes, I am.'

'I'm Officer Ryan and I was wondering if you would accompany me to the station, please.'

It was more of a statement than a question, and Denise's mouth dropped open in shock. He was no longer the sexy officer. He was the lock-you-up-for-ever-in-a-cell-type officer. She gulped. 'What for?'

'Everything will be explained to you down at the station.' He walked round the counter and Denise looked at the long line of customers helplessly. Everybody just stared back at her.

'Check his ID, love,' one of the customers shouted.

Her voice shook as she demanded to see his ID, which was a completely useless operation, as she had never seen a police ID before nor did she know what a real one would look like. Her hand trembled as she studied it closely, but she didn't read a thing. She was too self-conscious of the customers and staff that had gathered, who must all be thinking the same thing: she was a criminal.

'I refuse to go until you tell me what this is about.'

'Ms Hennessey, if you just work with me here, then there will be no need to use these.' He took out a pair of handcuffs from his trouser pocket. 'There's no need to make a scene.'

'But I didn't do anything!' she protested, starting to panic.

'Well, we can discuss that down at the station, can't we?' He began to get irate.

Denise crossed her arms across her chest. 'I said I will *not* go with you until you tell me what this is about.'

'OK then,' he shrugged. 'If you insist.' He opened his mouth to speak and she yelled as she felt the cold silver handcuffs being slapped round her wrists. She was in so much shock she couldn't speak as he led her out of the shop.

'Good luck, love,' the customer shouted again.

Images of sharing a cell with a psycho murderer jumped into Denise's mind. Maybe she would find a little bird with a broken wing and nurse it and teach it to fly to pass the years inside, like in the movie . . .

Her face reddened as they stepped out into Grafton Street, and the crowds immediately scattered. Denise kept her eyes down to the ground, hoping nobody she knew would spot her. Her heart beat wildly and she briefly thought of escape, but she was already being led towards a blue minibus with blacked-out windows. Denise sat in the front row of seats behind the driver and, although she could sense people behind her, she sat rigidly in her seat, too terrified to turn round.

'Where are we going?' she asked as they drove past the police station.

The female police officer driving the bus and Officer Ryan ignored her.

'Hey! I thought you were taking me to the station!'

No answer.

'*I haven't done anything wrong!*'

Still no answer.

'Dammit! I'm innocent, I tell you!'

Denise started kicking the seat to get their attention. Her blood started to boil when the female officer pushed a cassette in the player. Denise's eyes widened at the choice of song.

Officer Ryan stood up, a big grin on his face. 'Denise, you have been very naughty.' He stood up and made his way in front of her. She gulped as he started to gyrate his hips to the song 'Hot Stuff'.

She was about to give him a great big kick between his legs when she heard whooping and laughing. She twisted herself round and spotted her sisters, Holly, Sharon and about five other friends. She finally figured out what was really happening when her sisters placed a veil on her head screaming, 'Happy hen party!'

'Oh, you bitches!' Denise spat at them, using every curse word invented, and even making up a few of her own.

The girls continued to hold their stomachs, doubled up with laughter.

'Oh, you are so lucky I didn't kick you in the balls!' Denise screamed at the gyrating policeman.

'Denise, this is Ken,' her sister Fiona giggled, 'and he's your stripper for the day.'

Denise narrowed her eyes. 'I almost had a heart attack, I hope you know! What will my customers think? And my staff! Oh my God, my staff think I'm a criminal.'

Sharon giggled. 'They were all just playing along.'

'When I go back to work I'm going to fire the lot of them.'

'Don't worry,' her sister said. 'We told your staff to inform the customers after you left the shop.'

Denise rolled her eyes. 'Well, knowing *them* they deliberately won't, and I will be *so* fired.'

'Denise! Stop *worrying!*' Fiona said. 'Your boss thought it was *funny*, now relax and enjoy the weekend.'

'Weekend? Where are we going for the weekend?' Denise looked round at her friends, startled.

'We're going to Galway, and that's all you need to know,' Sharon said.

The room was still spinning. Having closed her eyes, Holly was now unable to sleep. It was five o'clock in the morning, which meant that she had been drinking for almost twelve hours. Her stomach became queasy and she sat up on the bed and tried to keep her eyes open so she could avoid the feeling of seasickness.

She turned to face Denise on the bed so that they could talk, but the sound of her friend's snores ended all thought of communication between them. Holly sighed and felt her way across the bedcovers in the dark for the remote control. She watched as the television demonstrated a new knife to slice oranges without spraying yourself in the face with the juice. Eventually she rushed to the toilet and hung her head over the toilet seat, prepared for whatever might come. She wished she hadn't drunk so much, but with all the talk of husbands and happiness she had dreaded to think what the next two days would be like. Denise's friends were twice as bad as Denise. They were loud and hyper and acted exactly the way girls should on a hen weekend, but Holly just didn't have the energy to keep up with them.

It felt like only yesterday that Holly had had her own hen party, but in fact it was more than seven years ago. Back then she had been so excited and the future had looked so bright. She was to marry the man of her dreams and they would live the rest of their lives together. Now, life had become a nightmare for her.

Yes, she had finally managed to drag herself out of bed every morning. Yes, she had succeeded in finding a new job. But these were just formalities, something else to check off on the 'things that normal people do' list. It was as if her body had become one great jigsaw, just like the green fields with their pretty grey stone walls connecting the whole of Ireland. She had started working on the corners and the edges of her jigsaw because they were the easy bits, and now she needed to do all the bits in between, the hard parts. Nothing she had done so far had managed to fill that hole in her heart.

Holly pretended to have a coughing fit just so the girls would wake up. She needed to talk, she needed to cry, she needed to vent all her frustrations and disappointments. But what more advice could they give her? She repeated the same old worries over and over. Sometimes her friends would succeed in getting through to her and she would feel positive and confident, only to find herself thrown back into despair.

Tired of staring at the four walls, she threw on a track suit and made her way downstairs to the hotel bar.

Charlie groaned with frustration as the table down the back began to roar with laughter again. He wiped down the bar counter and glanced at his watch. Five thirty and he was still here working. He had thought he was so lucky when the girls from the hen party had gone to bed earlier than expected, and he was about to go home when this overbearing crowd arrived from a nightclub in Galway city. And they were still here. They weren't even residents of the Galway Inn, but the group included the daughter of the owner, who had brought them. Her and her arrogant boyfriend, and he couldn't stand them.

'Don't tell me you're back for more!' he laughed as one of the women from the hen party walked in. She bumped into the wall as she tried to make her way to the high stool.

'I just came down for a glass of water,' she hiccuped.

'There you go.' Charlie placed a glass of water on a beer mat.

She squinted at his name tag. 'Thanks. Charlie?'

'Did you girls have fun tonight?'

Holly sighed. 'I suppose.'

'Are you OK?' Charlie watched her. He had a horrible feeling she was going to cry, but he was used to it.

'I miss my husband,' she whispered. Her shoulders trembled.

'How long are you here for?' he asked.

'The weekend,' she told him.

'Have you never gone the weekend without him?'

'Only once. And that was at my own hen party seven years ago.' A tear spilled down the woman's face.

Charlie shook his head. 'Seven years lucky, isn't that what they say? Don't worry, your husband's probably miserable without you.'

'Oh God, I hope not.' Holly's eyes widened.

'That's the spirit.' Charlie smiled, then jumped as he saw his boss's daughter coming towards the bar with one of those looks on her face.

'Hey, Charlie,' she yelled. 'Maybe if you stopped chatting and did a bit of work, me and my friends wouldn't be so thirsty.'

Holly's mouth dropped open. That woman had a nerve. And her perfume was so strong it made Holly start to cough.

'I'm sorry, do you have a problem?' The woman demanded, looking Holly up and down.

'Yes, actually,' Holly slurred, taking a sip of her water. 'Your perfume is disgusting and it's making me want to throw up.'

Charlie started laughing and dropped to his knees behind the counter, pretending to look for a lemon to slice, and tried to block out the sounds of the two women snapping at each other.

'What's the delay here?' a deep voice enquired. Charlie shot to his feet at the sound of the woman's fiancé's voice. He was even worse. 'Why don't you sit down, honey, and I'll bring the drinks over,' said the man.

'Fine, at least *someone* is polite around here,' she snapped, looking Holly up and down once more before storming back to her table. Holly watched her hips go boom-boom-boom as they went from side to side. She must be a model or something, she decided. That would explain the tantrums.

'So how are you?' the man beside Holly asked.

'I'm fine,' Holly replied, staring straight ahead.

'I'm Stevie,' he said, holding out his hand to her.

'I'm Holly,' she mumbled and took his hand lightly.

'Holly, that's a lovely name.' He held her hand for much too long and Holly was forced to look up into his eyes.

'Eh . . . thanks,' she said, and her face flushed.

'Can I buy you a drink, Holly?' Stevie asked smoothly.

'No, thanks, I have one here.' She sipped on her water again.

'OK, well, I'm just going to bring these drinks down to my table and then I'll be back to buy the lovely Holly a drink.' He walked away.

'Who the hell is that idiot?' Holly asked, looking bewildered, and Charlie laughed, delighted that she was a lady with sense.

He lowered his voice. 'That's Stevie, boyfriend of Laura, that blonde bitch who was here a minute ago. Her dad owns this hotel.'

Holly stared at the beautiful Laura, thinking nasty thoughts. 'Well, anyway, good night, Charlie.'

'You off to bed?'

'It's about time; it's after six. I hope you get home soon.' She smiled.

'I wouldn't bet on it,' he replied, and watched her leave the bar. Stevie followed after her and Charlie made his way closer to the door just to make sure she was OK. Laura, noticing her fiancé's sudden departure, left her table at the same time. They both stared down the corridor in the direction Holly and Stevie had headed.

Laura gasped and her hand flew to her mouth.

'Hey!' Charlie called out angrily as he witnessed a distressed Holly pushing a drunken Stevie away from her.

Holly angrily wiped her mouth, disgusted at Steve's attempts to kiss her. She backed away from him. 'I think you've got the wrong idea here, Stevie. Go back to the bar to your *fiancée*.'

Stevie wobbled on his feet and slowly turned to face Laura and an angry Charlie who was charging towards them.

'Stevie!' Laura shrieked. 'How could you?' Tears streaming down her face, she ran from the hotel, closely followed by a protesting Stevie.

The next day Holly and Sharon went for a walk on the beach just outside Galway city. Although it was October, the air had warmth in it and Holly didn't need her coat. She stood and listened to the water lapping.

'Are you OK?' Sharon wrapped her arm round Holly's shoulders.

Holly sighed. 'Every time someone asks me that question, Sharon, I say, "I'm fine, thank you," but to be honest, I'm not. Do people *really* want to know how you feel?' Holly smiled. 'The next time I'm going to say, "Well, actually, I'm not very well at all, thank you. I'm feeling a bit depressed and lonely." Then say how it pisses me off when everyone says time is a healer when at the same time they also say absence makes the heart grow fonder, which really confuses me, because that means that the longer he's gone the more I want him. Nothing is healing at all and every morning I wake up in my empty bed it feels like salt is being rubbed into those unhealing wounds. And then I'll say how much I miss my husband and how I feel like I'm just waiting for my world to end so that I can join him.' Holly took a deep breath. 'What do you think?'

'Oooh!' Sharon jumped and her arm flew away from Holly's shoulders.

'Oooh? I say all that and all you can say is "Oooh"?'

Sharon placed her hand over her bump and laughed. 'No, you silly, the baby kicked! Feel it!'

Holly placed her hand over Sharon's swollen belly and felt the tiny little kick. 'Oh, Sharon, if only every minute of my life were filled with perfect little moments like this I would never moan again.'

'I think this little boy is going to be a footballer like his daddy!' Sharon laughed.

'Boy?' Holly gasped. 'You're having a boy?'

Sharon nodded happily. 'Holly, meet baby Gerry. Gerry, meet your godmother Holly.'

Holly smiled as she flicked through the November magazine's pages. It would be out in the shops tomorrow, November 1st, and she felt so excited. Her first magazine would be on the shelves and she could also open Gerry's November letter. Tomorrow would be a good day.

Although she had only sold the ad space, she felt great pride in being a member of a team that managed to produce something so professional. And she felt that she had really proved herself. She had taken her job by the reins and guided it through to success.

Time to get working on the December edition. But before she started work, first she had to call Denise.

'Hello? Ridiculously expensive clothes shop. Pissed-off manager speaking, how can I help you?'

'Denise! You can't answer the phone like that!'

Denise giggled. 'Oh, don't worry, I have caller ID so I knew it was you.'

'Hmm.' Holly was suspicious; she didn't think Denise had caller ID on her work phone. 'I got a message you called.'

'Oh, yeah, I was just ringing you to confirm that you are coming to the Christmas Ball. Tom is going to buy a table this year. It's on the 30th of November.'

'Oh, the 30th . . .' Holly paused and pretended to flick through some pages on her desk very loudly. 'No, Denise, I can't. Sorry. I have a deadline. I'll be far too busy . . .' Well, she did have a deadline, but the magazine would be out in the shops on December 1st. She didn't really need to be in work on the 30th at all.

'Well, that makes a change,' Denise muttered under her breath.

'What did you say?' Holly asked, getting slightly angry.

'Nothing,' Denise said shortly.

'I heard you. You said "that makes a change", didn't you? Well, it just so happens that I take my work seriously, Denise, and I have no plans to lose my job because of a stupid ball. And you might not understand this, Denise, but funnily enough I would find it *a bit difficult*, to say the least, to go to a place that Gerry and I had been going to together for the past ten years.' She slammed the phone down and burst into tears.

Her weeping eventually died down into little sobs as she realised that everyone must have heard everything she'd said. She felt so embarrassed she was afraid to go to the toilets for a tissue. She wiped her eyes on the end of her shirt, then sat up to attention as she heard a light rapping sound on her door.

'Come in.' Her voice shook.

Chris entered her office with two cups of tea in his hands.

'Tea?' he offered, raising his eyebrows at her. She smiled weakly, remembering the joke they had shared on the day of her interview. He placed the mug down in front of her and relaxed in the chair opposite.

'Having a bad day?' he asked as gently as his gruff voice allowed.

She nodded as tears rolled down her face. 'I'm sorry, Chris.' She swallowed hard as she tried to compose herself. 'This won't affect my work.'

He waved his hand dismissively. 'Holly, I'm not worried about that. You're a great worker.'

She smiled, grateful for the compliment. At least she was doing something right.

'Would you like to go home early?'

'No, thanks. Work will keep my mind off things.'

He shook his head sadly. 'That's not the way to go about it, Holly. I should know. I've buried myself inside these walls and it doesn't help things. Not in the long run, anyway.' He handed her a tissue. 'You need to love more than just your job. I know I'm not the greatest example, but I'm learning too.' He placed his hand on the desk and started to brush away imaginary crumbs while he thought about what to say next. 'I heard you don't want to go to this ball.'

Holly cringed at the fact he had heard her phone conversation.

Chris continued. 'There were a million places I refused to go to when Maureen died. We used to go for walks in the Botanic Gardens every Sunday, and I just couldn't go there any more after I lost her. There were a million little memories contained in every flower and tree that grew in there. The bench we used to sit on, her favourite rose garden, just everything about it reminded me of her.'

'Did you go back?' Holly asked, sipping the hot tea.

'A few months ago,' he said sadly. 'It was a difficult thing to do, but I did it and now I go every Sunday again. You have to confront things, Holly, and think of things positively.' He leaned forward in his chair and stared directly into her eyes. 'Some people go through life searching and never find their soul mates. They *never* do. You and I did, we just happened to have them for a shorter period of time. It's sad, but it's life. So you go to this ball, Holly, and you embrace the fact that you had someone whom you loved and who loved you back.'

Tears trickled down Holly's face as she realised he was right. She needed to remember Gerry and be happy about the love they shared. She thought of the line he had written in his last letter: *Remember our wonderful memories, but please don't be afraid to make some more.*

She wanted to hang on to every single shred of memory of the two of them together. It was scaring her that she was forgetting his face. When she dreamed about him now he was always somebody she made up in her mind. She still rang his mobile phone, paying the mobile company every month just to hear his voice on his answering machine. His smell had faded from the house; his clothes were long gone. He was fading from her mind, but she couldn't let go because he was all she had.

'I'm so sorry, Denise,' Holly apologised to her friend. They were sitting in the staff room at Denise's workplace. 'I didn't mean to lose my temper on the phone. Just because I'm feeling extra-sensitive these days, it doesn't give me the right to take it out on you.'

'No, I've been so excited by this wedding that I didn't stop to think about how you might be feeling.' Her eyes rested on her friend, whose face looked so pale against her dark jacket.

'But you were right to be excited,' Holly insisted.

'And you're right to be upset,' Denise said firmly. 'I didn't think. I just didn't think.' She held her hands to her cheeks as she shook her head. 'Don't come to the ball if you don't feel comfortable, Holly. We'll all understand.' She reached out to hold her friend's hands.

Holly felt confused. Chris had succeeded in convincing her to go to the ball, but now one of her best friends was saying it was OK not to go. She got up and hugged Denise goodbye, promising to call her later to give her a decision.

Just before reaching the office, Holly poked her head into Hogan's. She was feeling much more at ease with Daniel. Since that evening in the restaurant, where she had felt so uncomfortable, she had realised that she was being ridiculous. She understood now why she had felt that way. Before, the only close friendship she'd had with a man was with Gerry, and that was a romantic relationship. The idea of becoming so close to Daniel seemed strange and unusual. Holly had since convinced herself that there didn't need to be a romantic link for her to share a friendship with an unattached man. Even if he was good-looking.

And the ease she now felt had become a feeling of companionship. They could talk for hours, discussing her feelings, her life, his feelings, his life, and she knew that they had a common enemy: loneliness. She knew that he was suffering from a different kind of grief but they were helping each other through the difficult days when all they needed was a caring ear or someone to make them laugh.

'Well?' he said, walking round from behind the bar. 'Will Cinderella go to the ball?'

Holly smiled and scrunched up her nose, about to tell him that she wouldn't be going, when she stopped herself. 'Are you going?'

He smiled and scrunched up his nose and she laughed. 'Well, it's going to be another case of Couples R Us,' he said. He pulled out a high stool for her at the bar and she sat down.

Holly giggled. 'We could just be terribly rude and ignore them.'

'Then what would be the point of going?' Daniel sat beside her and rested his leather boot on the footrest of her stool. 'You don't expect me to talk to you all night, do you? Maybe I'm bored with you.'

'Fine then!' Holly pretended to be insulted. 'I was planning on ignoring you anyway.'

'Phew!' Daniel wiped his brow and pretended to look relieved. 'I'm definitely going then.'

Holly became serious. 'I think I really need to be there.'

Daniel stopped laughing. 'Well, then, we shall go.'

Holly smiled at him. 'I think it would be good for you too, Daniel.'

His foot dropped from the footrest and he turned his head away to survey the lounge. 'Holly, I'm fine,' he said unconvincingly.

Holly hopped off her stool and kissed him roughly on the forehead. 'Daniel Connelly, stop trying to be all macho and strong. It doesn't wash with me.'

They hugged each other goodbye and Holly marched back to her office, determined not to change her mind again.

Thirteen

'OH, HOLLY, you look fabulous!' Sharon said excitedly.

'I look like crap,' Holly grumbled.

'Oh, stop saying that,' Sharon said angrily. 'I look like a blimp and do you hear me complaining? Accept the fact that you're a babe!' She smiled at her in the mirror. 'You'll be fine.'

'I just want to stay home tonight, Sharon. I have to open Gerry's last message.' Holly couldn't believe the time had come to open the last one. She wanted to stay in and savour the last special moment.

'I know, but that can wait a few hours, can't it?'

Holly was just about to say no when John shouted up the stairs. 'Come on, girls! The taxi's waiting! We have to collect Tom and Denise!'

Before Holly followed Sharon downstairs she slid open the drawer of her dressing table and took out the November letter from Gerry that she had opened weeks ago. She needed his words of encouragement to help her out now. She slid the card from the envelope and read:

Cinderella must go to the ball this month. And she will look glamorous and beautiful and have the time of her life just like always . . . But no white dresses this year . . .
PS, I love you . . .

Holly took a deep breath and followed Sharon downstairs.

'Wow,' Daniel said, 'you look fabulous, Holly.'

'I look like—' Holly started to grumble, and Sharon shot her a look. 'But thanks,' she quickly added. Denise had helped her choose a simple black halter-neck dress.

They all piled into the seven-seater taxi, and after picking up Tom and Denise, they made it to the hotel in record time.

They stepped up to the table just inside the function room. The woman sitting behind it smiled at them. 'Hello, Sharon; hello, John; hi, Denise . . . Oh, gosh! Hello, Holly. It's really good of you to come considering . . .' She flicked through the guest list to tick off their names.

'Let's go to the bar,' Denise said, linking Holly's arm.

As they walked across the room, a woman Holly hadn't seen for years approached. 'Holly, I was sorry to hear about Gerry. He was a lovely man.'

'Thank you.' Holly smiled and was led away again by Denise. They finally reached the bar.

'Hi there, Holly,' a familiar voice behind her said.

'Oh, hello, Patrick,' she said, turning to face the man who sponsored the charity. He was large and overweight with a bright red face, probably due to the stress of running one of Ireland's most successful businesses.

'You're looking as lovely as always.' He gave her a kiss on the cheek. 'Can I get you a drink?'

'Oh, no, thanks,' she smiled.

'Ah, let me.' He held his hand up to attract the barman's attention. 'What'll you have?'

Holly gave in. 'A white wine then, please, if you insist.'

'I might as well get a drink for that miserable husband of yours,' he laughed, searching the room for Gerry. 'What's he having?'

'Oh, he's not here,' Holly said, feeling uncomfortable.

'Ah, why not? What's he up to?' Patrick asked loudly.

'Em, he passed away early in the year, Patrick,' Holly said gently, hoping not to embarrass him.

'Oh,' Patrick reddened even more. 'I'm very sorry to hear that.'

'Thank you,' Holly said, counting the seconds in her head till he left the conversation. He escaped after three seconds, saying he had to take his wife her drink. Denise had made her way back to the group with their drinks, so Holly picked up her glass of wine and headed over.

'Hi, Holly.'

She turned to see who had called her name.

'Oh, hello, Jennifer.' She was faced with another woman she knew only from attending the ball. She was dressed in an over-the-top ball gown and dripping in expensive jewellery.

'How are you? You look fab.' She sipped her champagne and looked Holly up and down. 'Gerry not with you tonight?'

'No, he passed away in February,' she said.

'Oh, gosh, I'm so sorry to hear that. I had no idea. He was so *young*.' She placed a hand on Holly's arm. 'You must feel miserable. How on earth did you come here tonight? With all these couples around?'

'Yes, it is hard, but I'm dealing with it. Trying to be positive, you know? You just have to learn to move on.' Holly smiled. 'Anyway, speaking of moving on, I'd better go and join my friends,' she said, politely. She made her way over to the table and took her seat.

'Are you OK?' Daniel asked quietly from beside her.

'Yes, I'm fine, thank you,' she replied, taking a sip of wine. She glanced over at Jennifer, who was in a huddle with her female friends talking and staring over at Holly and Daniel.

'You don't have to give me that answer, Holly. It's me.'

Holly smiled and groaned. 'I feel like I'm back at Gerry's funeral again. Having to pretend to be all strong and superwoman-like even though all some of them want is for me to be devastated because it's so *awful*.' She mimicked Jennifer and rolled her eyes.

He nodded. 'When Laura and I broke up, for months everywhere I went I was telling people.'

'Any word on Laura?' Holly asked.

Daniel's eyes lit up. 'Yes, actually. I do have a bit of gossip on her. A friend who works as a barman in Laura's dad's hotel told me her boyfriend tried to come on to some other woman and Laura caught him, so they split up.' He laughed evilly, with a twinkle in his eye.

Holly froze. 'Eh . . . Daniel, what hotel does her father own?'

'Oh, the Galway Inn. It's brilliant, isn't it? I can tell you, if I ever met the woman who split them up I would buy her the most expensive bottle of champagne I could find.'

Holly smiled weakly. 'Would you now . . .?' He'd better start saving his money then. Holly stared at his face curiously. She would have bet all her money against those two ever being together; Laura didn't seem his type, whatever his 'type' was.

'Em, Daniel, I was just wondering . . . Laura seems to sound like a bit of a bitch, to be honest.' She bit her lip and studied his face to see if she had insulted him. 'Well, my question is really, whatever did you see in her? You're so different, well, at least you *sound* like you're so different.'

His lips broke into a sad smile. 'Laura isn't really a bitch, Holly. Well, for leaving me for my best friend she is . . . but when we were together, never. Dramatic, yes.' He smiled. 'You see, I loved the drama of our relationship. I found it exciting; she *enthralled* me.' His face became animated. 'I loved waking up in the morning and wondering what kind of mood she would be in that day, I loved the passion of our fights and I loved how we would make love after them. She would make a song and dance about most things, but I suppose that's what I found attractive about her. Our temperaments contrasted, but we made a good team . . .' He looked into the face of his new friend and saw her concern. 'She didn't treat me badly, Holly, she was just . . .'

'Dramatic,' Holly finished for him. He nodded.

Holly watched his face as he got lost in another memory.

'You miss her,' she said gently, putting her hand on his arm.

Daniel snapped out of his daydream and stared deeply into Holly's eyes. A shiver went down her spine. 'Wrong again, Holly Kennedy.' He nodded his head and frowned, as though she had said the most bizarre thing ever. 'Completely and *utterly* wrong.'

After dinner, Daniel took Holly by the hand and led her to the dance floor. As soon as they reached it the song ended and Eric Clapton's 'Wonderful Tonight' began. The floor began to empty out and Holly was left facing Daniel. She gulped. She hadn't planned on this. She had only ever danced with Gerry to this song.

Daniel placed one hand lightly on her waist and gently took her hand and they began to circle round. Holly was stiff. Dancing with another man felt wrong. She shuddered. Daniel must have thought she was cold because he pulled her closer as if to keep her warm. She was led round the floor in a trance until the song ended and she made the excuse of having to go to the toilet. She locked herself in a cubicle and leaned against the door, taking deep breaths. She had been doing so well. Even with everyone asking her about Gerry she had remained calm. But the dance had shaken her. Perhaps it was time to go home, while the going was good.

Holly made her way back to the table and started to say goodbye to everyone. Daniel stood up to go with her. 'You're not leaving me here on my own,' he laughed. 'We can share a cab.'

Holly was slightly irritated when Daniel hopped out of the taxi and followed her to her house, as she was looking forward to opening the envelope from Gerry. It was a quarter to twelve, which gave her fifteen minutes. With luck he would have drunk his tea and gone by then. She had also called another taxi to arrive at her house in half an hour.

'Ah, so this is the famous envelope,' Daniel said, picking it up from the kitchen table.

Holly's eyes widened; she felt protective of that envelope, and she wasn't happy with him touching it, removing Gerry's trace from it.

'December,' he said, reading the outside and running his fingers along the lettering. Eventually he placed it back on the table and Holly breathed a sigh of relief and continued to fill the kettle.

'How many more envelopes are left?' Daniel asked, taking his overcoat off and walking over to join her at the counter.

'That's the last one.' Holly's voice was husky.

'So what are you going to do after that?'

'What do you mean?' she asked, feeling confused.

'Well, as far as I can see, that list is like the Ten Commandments. What the list says goes, as far as your life is concerned. So what will you do when there aren't any more?' His blue eyes twinkled.

'I'll just live my life,' she replied, turning her back and flicking the switch on the kettle.

'Will you be able to do that?' He walked closer to her. 'You'll have to make your own decisions then,' he said softly.

Holly rubbed her face tiredly. 'Daniel, what's this about?'

'I'm asking you this because I'm going to say something to you now, and you are going to have to make your own decision.' He looked her straight in the eye and her heart beat wildly. 'There will be no list, you'll have to follow your own heart.'

Holly backed away a little. A feeling of dread pulled at her heart. 'Daniel, I don't think that this is the right time to talk about—'

'This is a perfect time,' he said. 'You already know what I'm going to say to you, Holly, and I *know* you already know how I feel about you.'

Holly's mouth dropped open and she glanced at the clock.

It was midnight.

Gerry touched Holly's nose and smiled to himself as she wrinkled up her nose in her sleep. He loved watching her sleep; she looked like a princess, so beautiful and peaceful.

He tickled her nose again and smiled as her eyes slowly opened. 'Good morning, sleepyhead.'

'Good morning, beautiful.' She cuddled closer to him and rested her head on his chest. 'How are you feeling today?'

'Like I could run the London marathon,' he joked.

'Now that's what I call a quick recovery.' She lifted her head and kissed him on the lips. 'What do you want for breakfast?'

'You,' he said, biting her nose.

'Not on the menu today unfortunately. How about a fry?'

'No,' he frowned. 'That's too heavy for me,' and his heart melted as he saw Holly's face fall. He tried to perk himself up. 'But I would love a big, huge bowl of vanilla ice cream!'

'Ice cream!' She laughed. 'For breakfast?'

'Yes.' He grinned. 'I always wanted that for breakfast when I was a kid but my darling mother wouldn't allow me to have it. Now I don't care any more.' He smiled bravely.

'Then ice cream you shall have,' Holly said happily, hopping out of bed. 'OK, I'll be back in a minute.' He heard her racing downstairs and clattering around in the kitchen.

Lately he had noticed her racing around every time she left his side. It was as if she were afraid to leave him for too long on his own, and he knew what that meant. Bad news for him. He had finished his radiation therapy, which they had prayed would target the residual tumour. It had failed, and now all he could do was lie around all day, as he felt too weak to get up most of the time. It just seemed so pointless to him because it wasn't even as if he were waiting to recover. His heart beat wildly at the thought. He was afraid; afraid of where he was going, afraid of what was happening to him and afraid for Holly. She was so strong; she was his rock and he couldn't imagine his life without her, but he needn't worry about that scenario, because it was she who would be without him. He felt angry, sad, jealous and scared for her. He wanted to stay with her and carry out every wish and promise they had ever made to each other, but he knew he was fighting a losing battle. After two operations the tumour had returned, and it was growing rapidly inside him.

He and Holly had become even closer over the past few months, which was something he knew was a bad idea, for Holly's sake, but he couldn't bear to distance himself from her. He was enjoying the chats till the early hours of the morning, and giggling just like when they were teenagers. But that was on their good days.

They had their bad days, too.

He wouldn't think about that now. And his new little project was keeping him busy. As he mapped out his plan to remain with Holly even when he was gone, he was also fulfilling a promise.

He heard Holly thudding up the stairs; his plan was working.

'Babe, there's no more ice cream left,' she said sadly. 'Is there anything else you would enjoy?'

'Nope,' he shook his head. 'Just the ice cream, please.'

'Oh, but I have to go to the shop to get it,' she complained.

'Don't worry, hon, I'll be fine for a few minutes.' He lifted his mobile off the bedside table and placed it on his chest.

'OK.' Holly bit her lip. 'I'll only be down the road.'

She threw on a track suit, gave him a long kiss and raced downstairs.

As soon as Gerry knew it was safe, he pulled back the covers. He sat on the edge of the mattress waiting for the dizziness to pass, then he made his way to the wardrobe. He took out an old shoe box from the top shelf that contained nine full envelopes. He took out the tenth, empty envelope and wrote 'December' on the front. Today was December 1st, and he moved forward one year, knowing he wouldn't be around. He imagined Holly to be a karaoke genius, relaxed from her holiday in Spain, and hopefully happy in a new job she loved.

He imagined her on this very day in one year's time and he thought hard about what to write. Tears filled his eyes as he placed the full stop beside the sentence; he kissed the page, sealed it in the envelope and hid it back in the shoe box.

He wiped the tears from his eyes and slowly made his way back to his bed, where the phone was ringing.

'Hello?' he said, trying to control his voice, and he smiled when he heard the sweetest voice on the other end. 'I love you too, Holly . . .'

'No, Daniel, this isn't right,' Holly said, upset, and pulled her hand away from his grip.

'But why isn't it right?' he pleaded.

'It's too soon,' she said, feeling so confused.

'Too soon because that's what people have been telling you, or because that's what your heart's telling you?'

'Oh, Daniel, I don't know,' she said, pacing the kitchen floor. '*Please* stop asking me so many questions.'

Her heart beat wildly and her head was spinning. This felt wrong— It all felt so wrong. 'I can't, Daniel. I'm married! I love Gerry!' she said in a panic.

'Gerry?' he asked, his eyes widening as he went over to the table and grabbed the envelope. 'This is Gerry! This is what I'm competing with! It's a *list*, Holly. A list you have allowed to run your life. Now you have to think for yourself. Gerry's gone,' he said gently, walking back over to her. 'Gerry's gone and I'm here. I'm not saying I could ever take his place, but at least give us a chance.'

She took the envelope from his hand and hugged it close. 'Gerry's not gone,' she sobbed. 'He's here, every time I open these.'

There was a silence as Daniel watched her crying. She looked so lost and helpless, he just wanted to hold her.

'It's a piece of paper,' he said softly, stepping closer to her again.

'Gerry is *not* a piece of paper,' she said angrily through her tears. 'He was a living, breathing human being I loved. Gerry is a million billion happy memories.'

'So what am I?' Daniel asked.

'You'—she took a deep breath—'are a kind, and incredibly thoughtful friend who I respect and appreciate—'

'How do you feel about me?' His voice shook slightly.

She stared at the ground. 'I feel strongly about you, Daniel, but I need time.' She paused. 'Lots of time.'

He smiled sadly. 'Then I will wait.'

The doorbell rang and Holly silently breathed a sigh of relief. 'That's your taxi.' Holly's voice shook.

'I'll call you tomorrow.' He kissed her on the top of the head and made his way to the front door. Holly stood in the middle of the kitchen, going over and over the scene that had just occurred.

Still in shock, she eventually made her way slowly upstairs. She slipped out of her dress and wrapped herself in Gerry's dressing gown. She climbed into bed like a child and flicked on the bedside lamp. She stared at the envelope, thinking about what Daniel had said.

She took the phone off the hook and switched the power off her mobile. She needed to savour this special and final moment, to say goodbye to Gerry's contact with her.

She slowly tore open the envelope, trying not to rip the paper.

Don't be afraid to fall in love again. Open your heart and follow where it leads you . . . and remember, shoot for the moon . . .
PS, I will always love you . . .

'Oh, Gerry,' she sobbed, and her shoulders shook as her body heaved from the pain of her tears.

She got very little sleep that night and the times she did nod off, her dreams were obscure images of Daniel's and Gerry's faces and bodies mingled together. She woke in a sweat at 6 a.m. and decided to get up and go for a walk to clear her jumbled thoughts. Her heart felt heavy as she walked along the path of her local park. She had bundled herself up well to protect herself from the stinging cold, yet her head felt hot. Hot from the tears, from her brain working overtime.

How on earth had she found herself in this situation? Just as soon as she was getting round to picking up the pieces of her shattered life, she dropped them all again. She wasn't looking to become entangled in some ridiculous love triangle. The third person wasn't even around. And, anyway, if she were in love with Daniel, wouldn't she be the first person to realise it? If she didn't love him, then she should come right out and say it . . . but she was thinking about it . . .

And why was Gerry urging her to find a new love? What had he been *thinking* when he wrote that message? Had he already let go of her before he died? Had it been *so* easy for him to resign himself to the fact that she would meet someone else?

After hours of tormenting herself, she headed back to her house. 'OK, Gerry,' she announced as she stepped inside. 'I've been for a walk and I've thought deeply about what you said. And I've come to the conclusion that you had lost your mind when you wrote that message.'

She had three weeks left at work until she could take her Christmas holidays, which meant she would have to avoid Daniel for fifteen working days. That seemed possible. She hoped that by the time of Denise's wedding she would have made a decision. But first she had to get through her first Christmas alone and she was dreading it.

'OK, where do you want me to put it?' Richard panted, dragging the Christmas tree into her living room. A trail of pine needles led all the way out of the living-room door, down the hall and out to her car. Holly sighed, she would have to vacuum the house again.

'Holly!' Richard repeated, and she jumped from her thoughts.

'You look like a talking tree, Richard.' She giggled. All she could see were his brown shoes sticking out.

'Holly,' he grunted, losing his balance slightly under the weight.

'Oh, sorry,' she said quickly. 'Just by the window.'

She winced as he set lamps and photo frames crashing around him as he made his way over to the window. 'There now,' he said, wiping his hands and stepping back to look at his work.

Holly frowned. 'It looks a little bit bare, don't you think?'

'Well, you will have to decorate it, of course.'

'I know that, Richard. I was referring to the fact that it only has about five branches left. It's got bald patches,' she moaned.

'Well, I told you to buy a tree earlier, Holly, not to leave it until Christmas Eve. I sold the best ones weeks ago.'

Holly frowned. She really didn't want a Christmas tree this year. Richard had insisted, though, and Holly felt that she had to help him out with his new Christmas tree-selling venture in addition to his flourishing landscaping business.

She couldn't believe it was Christmas Eve already. She'd spent the past few weeks working overtime trying to get the January issue of the magazine ready. She had ignored all Daniel's calls and had ordered Alice to tell him she was in a meeting if and when he phoned the office.

Richard's voice snapped her back to reality.

'Sorry, what?'

'I said would you like me to help you decorate it?'

Holly's heart fell. No, that was her and Gerry's job, nobody else's. 'It's OK. I'm sure you've better things to be doing.'

'Well, actually I would quite like to do it,' he said. 'Usually myself, Meredith and the children do it together, but this year . . .' he trailed off.

'Oh.' Holly hadn't even thought about Richard's Christmas as being difficult. 'OK, then, why not?' she smiled.

Richard beamed and he looked like such a child.

'Oh, but the only thing is I'm not too sure where the decorations are. Gerry stored them in the attic somewhere . . .'

'No problem,' he smiled encouragingly. 'That used to be my job too.' He bounded up the stairs to the attic.

Holly opened a bottle of red wine and pressed PLAY on the CD player; Bing Crosby's 'White Christmas' began to play softly in the background. Richard returned with a black sack slung over his shoulder and a dusty Santa hat on. 'Ho-ho-ho!'

Holly giggled and handed him his glass of wine.

'No, no,' he waved his hand, 'I'm driving.'

'You can have one glass at least, Richard,' she said, feeling disappointed.

'No, no,' he repeated, 'I don't drink and drive.'

Holly threw her eyes up to heaven and knocked back his glass of wine, before beginning on her own. By the time Richard left she had finished the bottle and was opening another. She noticed the red light flashing on the answering machine. Hoping it wasn't a message from who she thought it was from, she hit the PLAY button.

'Hi, Sharon, it's Daniel Connelly here. Sorry to bother you, but I had your phone number from when you called the club months ago . . . I was hoping you could pass on a message for me. Denise has been so busy I couldn't rely on her to remember.' He laughed. 'Anyway, I was wondering if you could just tell Holly that I'm going down to my family in Galway for Christmas. I haven't been able to get through to her on her mobile, and I don't have her home number . . . so if you could just tell her that I'll have my mobile with me if she wants to reach me.' He paused. 'Anyway, I'll see you all at the wedding next week. OK, thanks.'

The second message was from Denise telling her that Daniel was looking for her, the third message was from Declan also telling her that Daniel was looking for her and the fourth message was from Daniel again. 'Hi, Holly, it's Daniel here. Declan gave me your number. I can't believe you never gave me your home number, yet I've a sneaking suspicion I've had it all along without realising . . .' There was a silence as he exhaled. 'Anyway, I really need to talk to you, Holly. I think it should be before we see each other at the wedding. Please, please take my calls.' Another deep breath and exhalation. 'OK, well, that's all. Bye.'

Holly pressed PLAY again, lost in thought.

She sat staring at the tree and listening to Christmas songs. And she cried. She cried for her Gerry and for her balding Christmas tree.

Fourteen

'HAPPY CHRISTMAS, LOVE!' Frank opened the door to a shivering Holly standing on the doorstep.

'Happy Christmas, Dad.' She smiled, and gave him a big bear hug. The beautiful smell of pine mixed with wine and Christmas dinner cooking in the kitchen filled her nostrils, and she was hit with a pang of loneliness. Christmas was Gerry. It was their special time together when they would hide from the stresses of work and just relax and entertain their friends and family and enjoy their time alone. She missed him so much it gave her a sick feeling in the pit of her stomach.

She had visited the graveyard that morning to wish him a happy Christmas. It was the first time she had been there since the funeral. Gerry had wanted to be cremated, which meant that she had to stand in front of a wall that had his name engraved on it. She told him about her year and what her plans were for the day; she told him Sharon and John were expecting a baby boy and they were calling him Gerry; she told him that she was to be his godmother; that she was to be maid of honour at Denise's wedding. She explained what Tom was like, because Gerry had never met him, and she talked about her new job. She wanted to get some deep spiritual feeling that Gerry was there with her, but she really just felt like she was talking to a drab grey wall.

All in all, it hadn't been a good morning.

'Oh, happy Christmas, dear!' Elizabeth announced, walking out of the kitchen with open arms. Holly started to cry. Elizabeth's face was flushed from the heat of the kitchen and the warmth of her body warmed Holly's heart.

'I'm sorry.' She wiped her face. 'I didn't want to do that.'

'Hush,' Elizabeth said, hugging her even tighter.

Holly had called round to visit her mother the previous week in a panic about what to do about the Daniel situation.

'So how do you feel about him?' Elizabeth had asked.

'I like him, Mum, I really do, but I don't know if I'll *ever* feel ready for another relationship. He's not Gerry, but I'm not expecting him to be. What I feel now is a different kind of feeling; but a nice one, too.'

'It's important not to rush into things, Holly, but whether it's with Daniel, the man on the moon, or alone, I just want you happy.'

As comforting as her mother had been to her that day, Holly was no closer to making her decision. First, she had to get through Christmas.

The rest of Holly's family joined them in the living room and greeted her with hugs. They gathered round the tree and exchanged gifts and Holly allowed the tears to flow throughout. She hadn't the energy to hide them; she hadn't the energy to care. But the tears were a strange mixture of happiness and sadness. A peculiar sensation of feeling alone yet loved.

She sneaked away from the family so she could have a moment to herself; her head was a jumble of thoughts that needed to be sorted and filed. She found herself in her old bedroom, staring out of the window into the dark, blustery day. The sea was fierce and threatening and Holly shuddered at its power.

'So this is where you're hiding.'

Holly turned to see Jack watching her from the bedroom door. She smiled weakly and turned round to face the sea again, uninterested in her brother and his recent lack of support. She listened to the waves and watched the black water swallow the sleet that had begun to fall. She heard Jack sigh loudly and felt his arm round her shoulder.

'Sorry,' he said softly.

Holly raised her eyebrows, unimpressed, and continued to stare ahead.

He nodded to himself slowly. 'You're right to treat me like this, Holly, I've been acting like a complete idiot lately. And I'm so sorry.'

Holly turned to face him, her eyes glistening. 'You let me down, Jack.'

He closed his eyes slowly as though the very thought of that pained him. 'I know. I just didn't handle the whole situation well, Holly. I found it so hard to deal with Gerry . . . you know . . .'

'Dying,' Holly finished for him.

'Yeah.' He clenched and unclenched his jaw and looked like he had finally accepted it.

'It wasn't exactly easy for me, you know, Jack.' A silence fell between them. 'But you helped me pack away all his things. You went through his belongings with me and made the whole thing so much easier,' Holly said, feeling confused. 'You were there with me for that, why did you just suddenly disappear?'

'God, that was so tough to do.' He shook his head sadly. 'You were so strong, Holly . . . you *are* strong,' he corrected himself. 'Getting rid of his things just tore me up, being in the house and him not being there just . . . *got* to me. And then I noticed you were getting closer to Richard, so I just figured it would be OK for me to take a step back because you had him . . .' He shrugged his shoulders and blushed at the ridiculousness of finally explaining his feelings.

'You fool, Jack,' Holly said, thumping him playfully in the stomach. 'As if Richard could ever take your place.'

He smiled. 'Oh, I don't know, you two seem very pally these days.'

Holly became serious again. 'Richard has been very supportive over the past year, and, believe me, people haven't failed to surprise me during this whole experience,' she added pointedly. 'Give him a chance, Jack.'

He stared out to the sea and nodded slowly, digesting this.

Holly wrapped her arms round him and felt the familiar comforting hug of her brother. Hugging her even tighter, Jack said, 'I'm here for you now. I'm going to stop being so selfish and take care of my little sister.'

'Hey, your little sister is doing just fine on her own, thank you very much,' she said sadly as she watched the sea crash violently against the rocks, its spray kissing the moon.

They sat down for their meal and everyone oohed and aahed at the spread of food before them.

'I got an email from Ciara today,' Declan announced. 'She sent this picture.' He passed round the photograph he had printed off.

Holly smiled at the sight of her sister lying on the beach eating barbecued Christmas lunch with Mathew. Her hair was blonde and her skin was tanned, and they both looked so happy. After travelling round the world searching and searching, Ciara, she reckoned, had finally found contentment. She passed the photo on to Jack.

'They're saying it might snow today,' Holly announced.

'No, it won't snow,' Richard said. 'It's too cold for that.'

Holly frowned. 'Richard, how could it be too cold to snow?'

He wiped his fingers on the napkin that was tucked into his black woolly jumper with a Christmas tree emblazoned across the front. 'It needs to get milder before it can snow.'

Holly giggled. 'Richard, it's about minus a million in the Antarctic and it snows there. That's hardly mild.'

'That's the way it works,' he said matter-of-factly.

'Whatever you say.' Holly rolled her eyes.

'He's right, actually,' Jack added after a while, and everyone stopped chewing to stare at him. That was not a phrase they often heard. Jack went on to explain how snow worked and Richard helped him out on the scientific parts. Abbey raised her eyebrows at Holly and they shared a secret look of shock.

'You want some vegetables with your gravy, Dad?' Declan asked seriously, offering him a bowl of broccoli.

Everyone looked at Frank's plate and laughed.

'Ha-ha,' Frank said, taking the bowl from his son. 'Anyway, we live too close to the sea to get any.'

'To get what? Gravy?' Holly teased and they laughed again.

'Snow, silly,' he said, grabbing her nose like he used to when she was a child.

'Well, I bet you all a million quid that it snows today,' Declan said, eagerly glancing around.

'Then you'd better start saving, Declan, because if your brainiac brothers say it ain't so, it ain't so!' Holly joked.

'Better pay up then, boys.' Declan nodded towards the window.

'Oh my God!' Holly exclaimed. 'It's snowing!'

'So much for that theory, then,' Jack said to Richard, and they laughed.

Everyone deserted the dinner table and threw on their coats to run outside like excited children. Elizabeth wrapped her arms round her daughter's shoulders. 'Well, it looks like Denise will have a white Christmas for her white wedding,' she smiled.

Holly's heart beat wildly at the thought of Denise's wedding. In just a few days she would have to confront Daniel. As if her mother had been reading her mind she asked quietly, 'Have you thought about what to say to Daniel yet?'

Holly glanced up at the snowflakes glistening down from the black, star-filled sky in the moonlight. The moment felt so magical; right there and then she made her final decision.

'Yes, I have.' She smiled and took a deep breath.

'Good.' Elizabeth kissed her on the cheek. 'And remember, God leads you to it and takes you through it.'

'He'd better. I'm going to need Him a lot over the next while.'

'**S**haron, don't carry that case, it's too heavy!' John yelled at his wife, and Sharon dropped the bag angrily.

'John, I am not an invalid. I am *pregnant!*'

'I know that, but the doctor said not to lift heavy things.' He walked to her side of the car and grabbed the bag.

'Well, screw the doctor, he's never been bloody pregnant,' Sharon yelled, watching John storm off.

Holly banged down the boot of the car loudly. She had had enough of John and Sharon's tantrums; she had been stuck listening to them bicker all the way down to Wicklow in the car. Now all she wanted was to go and relax in the hotel.

She grabbed her bag and glanced up at the building. It was more like a castle. As the venue for their New Year's Eve wedding, Tom and Denise couldn't have picked a more beautiful place. The house was covered in dark green ivy climbing up its ageing walls and a huge fountain adorned the front courtyard. Acres and acres of beautifully kept lush green gardens surrounded the hotel. Denise didn't get her white Christmas wedding, after all; the snow had melted minutes after it had arrived.

Still, it had been a beautiful moment for Holly to share with her family on Christmas Day, and it had succeeded in lifting her spirits for a short time. Now all she wanted to do was find her room and pamper herself. She dragged her bag behind her over the cobble-stones and was suddenly jerked forward and sent flying as someone tripped over her luggage.

'Sorry,' she heard a singsong voice say and she watched the tall blonde's hips go boom-boom towards the hotel. Holly frowned. She knew that walk from somewhere, but . . .

Laura.

Oh, no! she thought, panicking. Tom and Denise had invited Laura after all! She had to find Daniel quickly so that she could warn him. And then if the moment was right she would finish off that chat with him. She rushed towards the reception area, which was crowded with angry people and luggage. Denise's voice was instantly recognisable above all the noise.

'Look, I don't *care* if you've made a mistake! *Fix it!*' Denise held her hand up in a very startled receptionist's face. 'I don't want to hear any more excuses! Just get ten more rooms for my guests!'

Holly spotted Tom and headed over to him, beating her way through the crowd.

'Hi, Holly,' he said, looking very distracted.

'What room is Daniel in?' she asked quickly.

'Daniel?' he asked, looking confused.

'Yes, Daniel! Your best man.'

'I really don't know; ask Denise.'

Holly gulped. Denise looked possessed, and she had no intention of asking her in that mood. She queued in line behind the other guests and twenty minutes later she reached the front.

'Could you tell me what room Daniel Connelly is in, please?'

The receptionist shook his head. 'I'm sorry, we can't give out guests' room numbers.'

'Look, I'm a friend of his,' Holly smiled sweetly.

The man smiled politely. 'I'm sorry, it's against policy—'

'Listen!' she yelled and even Denise shut up screaming beside her. 'It's very important you tell me!'

'Holly.' Denise placed her hand on her arm. 'What's wrong?'

'I need to know what room Daniel's in!' Holly yelled.

Denise looked startled. 'It's room three forty-two.'

'Thank you!' Holly yelled angrily, not knowing why she was still shouting, and stormed off in the direction of the elevators.

Upstairs, she rushed down the corridor dragging her bag behind her and checking the door numbers. When she reached his room she knocked furiously on the door. As she heard footsteps approaching the door she realised she hadn't even thought about what she was going to say. She took a deep breath as the door was pulled open.

She stopped breathing.

It was Laura.

'Honey, who is it?' Daniel walked out of the bathroom, a towel wrapped round his body.

'You!' Laura screeched.

Holly glanced from Laura to Daniel and back to Laura again. She gathered from their semi-nakedness that Daniel had already known Laura was coming to the wedding. He hung on to his towel tightly, his face a picture of shock. Nobody spoke for a while. Then eventually someone spoke and Holly wished it hadn't been that particular person.

'What are *you* doing here?' Laura hissed.

Holly's mouth opened and closed like a goldfish's. Daniel's forehead wrinkled in confusion as he stared from one woman to the other. 'Do you two . . . do you two know each other?'

'Ha!' Laura's face twisted in contempt. 'I caught this little bitch kissing my boyfriend!'

'Your *boyfriend*?' Daniel yelled, crossing the room to join them at the door.

'Sorry . . . ex-boyfriend,' Laura mumbled, staring at the floor.

Holly crossed her arms over her chest. 'Yeah, Stevie, wasn't it? A good friend of Daniel's, if I remember correctly.'

Daniel's face reddened as he looked at them both. 'You kissed Stevie?' he said, slowly getting the gist of the story.

'No, I did *not* kiss Stevie.' Holly looked at Laura and laughed. 'I take it you're back with Daniel, so what does it matter anyway?' She then turned to Daniel. 'We were down in Galway for Denise's hen weekend and Stevie was drunk and tried to kiss me in the hotel.'

'Oh, you're such a liar,' Laura said. 'I saw what happened.'

'And so did Charlie, the barman,' Holly told Daniel. 'So you can go there and ask him, if you don't believe me. But I really don't care. I came to have that chat with you but you're obviously busy.' She marched off down the corridor to the elevator, dragging her suitcase behind her.

She pressed the button and breathed a sigh of relief. When the doors opened, she stepped in and closed her tired eyes. She didn't even feel angry with Daniel; in fact, in a really childish way, she was glad he had done something to stop them from having their little chat. So she had been dumped and not the other way round. But Daniel couldn't have been that much in love with her, she reasoned, if he was able to go back to Laura so quickly. Ah well, at least she didn't hurt his feelings . . . But she did think he was a complete fool for taking Laura back.

Denise looked at Holly excitedly as someone rapped a spoon against their glass and the speeches began. Holly fumbled nervously with her hands in her lap, going over and over her speech in her head. She should have written it down because now she couldn't remember the start of it.

Her heart beat wildly as Daniel sat down and everyone applauded. She was next. Sharon grabbed her hand and Holly smiled back at her shakily. Denise's father announced that Holly was going to speak and the room turned to face her. All she could see was a sea of faces. She stood up and glanced down the room and spotted John sitting at a table with his and Gerry's friends. John gave her the thumbs up and Holly's speech went out of the window as a new one formed in her head.

'Please forgive me if I get a little emotional while I speak, but I am just so happy for Denise today. She is my best friend . . .' she paused and glanced down at Sharon. 'Well, one of them.'

The room laughed.

'Finding someone you love is a wonderful feeling. But finding a true soul mate is an even *better* feeling. A soul mate understands you like no other, loves you like no other, will be there for you *for ever*, no matter what. I know a thing or two about that, and I know that Denise has found a soul mate in Tom.' A lump formed in Holly's throat and she took a moment to compose herself. 'I am honoured to have been asked to share this beautiful day with Denise and Tom, and here's to them having many more beautiful days like this together.'

Everyone cheered and reached for their glasses.

'However!' Holly held her hand up. The noise died down and once again all eyes were on her.

'However, some here today will be aware of the list a marvellous man thought up.' John's table cheered. 'And one of its rules was to *never, ever* wear a 'spensive white dress.'

John's table went wild and Denise broke down in hysterics.

'So, on behalf of Gerry,' Holly said, 'I will forgive Denise for breaking that rule only because she looks so amazing. And I will ask you all to join me in a toast to Tom and Denise and her very, very 'spensive white dress. I should know, because I was dragged round every bridal shop in Ireland!'

The guests all held up their glasses. 'To Tom and Denise and her very, very 'spensive white dress!'

Holly's face beamed as John's table held their glasses up to her and cheered. And then the party began.

Tears formed in Holly's eyes as she watched Tom and Denise dancing together for the first time as husband and wife, and she remembered that feeling. That feeling of excitement, of hope, of pure happiness and pride, a feeling of not knowing what the future held but being so ready to face it all. And that thought made her happy; she wouldn't cry about it, she would embrace it. She had enjoyed every second of her life with

Gerry, but now it was time to move on. Sure it would be difficult, but it didn't feel as difficult as it had a few months ago.

She had been given a wonderful gift: life. Sometimes, cruelly, it was taken away too soon, but it was what you did with it that counted.

'May I have this dance?' She looked up to see Daniel smiling at her.

'Sure.' She smiled back and took his hand.

'May I say that you're looking very beautiful tonight?'

'You may,' Holly smiled again. She was happy with how she looked. Denise had chosen a beautiful lilac-coloured dress for her with a corset top, and there was a large slit up the side.

'That was a lovely speech,' he told her. 'I realise that what I said to you was selfish of me. You said you weren't ready and I didn't listen.'

'That's OK, Daniel; I don't think I'll be ready for a long, long time. But thank you for getting over me so fast.' She nodded over at Laura, sitting moodily on her own at the table.

Daniel bit his lip. 'I know it must seem crazy fast to you, but when you didn't return any of my calls, even I got the hint you weren't ready for a relationship. And when I went home for the holidays and met up with Laura, that old flame just sparked again. You were right, I never got over her. Believe me, if I hadn't known with all my heart that you weren't in love with me, I never would have brought her to the wedding.'

Holly smiled at Daniel. 'Sorry for avoiding you all month. I was having a bit of "me" time. But I still think you're a fool.' She shook her head as she watched Laura scowl back at her.

Daniel sighed. 'I know she and I have a lot to discuss over the next while and we're really going to take things slowly, but like you said, for some people love just lives on.'

Holly threw her eyes up to heaven. 'Oh, don't start quoting me on that one,' she said, laughing. 'Ah well, as long as you're happy, I suppose. Although I don't see how you ever will be.' She sighed dramatically and Daniel laughed too.

'I am happy, Holly. I guess I just can't live without the drama.' He glanced over at Laura, and his eyes softened. 'I need someone who is passionate about me, and for better or for worse, Laura is passionate. What about you? Are you happy?' He studied Holly's face.

Holly thought about it. 'Tonight I'm happy. I'll worry about tomorrow when tomorrow comes. But I'm getting there . . .'

Holly gathered in a huddle with Sharon, John, Denise and Tom and awaited the countdown.

'Five . . . four . . . three . . . two . . . one! HAPPY NEW YEAR!' Balloons of all colours of the rainbow fell from the ceiling.

Holly hugged her friends happily with tears in her eyes.

'Happy New Year.' Sharon kissed her on the cheek.

Holly placed her hand over Sharon's bump and held Denise's hand tightly. 'Happy *New* Year for all of us!'

Epilogue

HOLLY FLICKED through the newspapers to see which one contained a photo of Denise and Tom on their wedding day. It wasn't every day that Ireland's top radio DJ and a girl from *Girls and the City* got married. That's what Denise liked to think anyway.

'Hey!' the grumpy newsagent yelled at her. 'This is not a library. You either buy it or put it down.'

Holly sighed and began to gather every newspaper from the news-stand once again. She had to take two trips to the counter due to the weight of the papers. Once again a queue had formed behind the till. Holly smiled to herself and took her time. She made her way with the last of the papers and began to add chocolate and packets of sweets to the pile.

'Oh, and may I have a bag too, please.' She batted her eyelashes and smiled sweetly.

The old man stared at her as though she were a naughty schoolgirl. 'Mark!' he yelled angrily.

The spotty teenager appeared from the shopping aisles.

'Open the other till, son,' he was ordered. Half the queue behind Holly moved over to the other side.

'Thank you.' Holly smiled and made her way to the door. Just as she was about to pull it open it was pushed from the other side, causing her purchases to spill out all over the floor.

'I'm so sorry,' the man said, bending down to help her.

'Oh, it's OK,' Holly replied politely.

'Ah, it's you! The chocoholic!' Holly looked up startled.

It was the friendly customer with the grey-green eyes who had helped her before.

Holly giggled. 'We meet again,' she said.

'Holly, isn't it?' he asked, handing her the chocolate bars.

'That's right. Rob, isn't it?' she replied.

'You've a good memory,' he laughed.

'As do you,' she grinned. She piled everything back into her bag, and got back onto her feet.

'Well, I'm sure I'll bump into you again soon.' Rob smiled and made his way over to the queue.

Holly stared after him in a daze. Finally she walked over. 'Rob, is there any chance you'd like to go for that coffee today? If you can't, that's fine . . .' She bit her lip.

He smiled and glanced down nervously at the ring on her finger.

'Oh, don't worry about that,' she held her hand out. 'It only represents a lifetime of happy memories these days.'

He nodded his head. 'Well, in that case I would love to.'

They crossed the road and headed to the Greasy Spoon.

Holly smiled to herself as she sat at the table waiting for him to bring back the drinks. He seemed nice. She relaxed back in her chair and gazed out of the window into the cold January day that caused the trees to dance wildly in the wind. She thought about what she had learned. She was a woman who had taken advice from a man she loved and she had tried her hardest to help to heal herself. She now felt confidence within herself to reach for what she wanted.

She was a woman who made mistakes, who sometimes cried on a Monday morning or at night alone in bed. She was a woman who often became bored with her life and found it hard to get up in the morning. She was a woman who sometimes questioned what reason she had to live on this planet and who sometimes just got things wrong.

On the other hand, she was a woman with a million happy memories, who knew what it was like to experience true love and who was ready to experience more life, more love, and make new memories. Whether it happened in ten months or ten years, Holly would obey Gerry's final message. Whatever lay ahead, she knew she would open her heart and follow where it led her.

In the meantime, she would just live.

Cecelia Ahern

When Cecelia Ahern sold her first novel, *PS, I Love You,* for a seven-figure sum, no one was more surprised than the author herself. 'It was amazing. Even now I can hardly believe it happened.'

Having completed a degree in journalism and media communications at Dublin's Griffith College, she was about to start a Masters in film production when the idea for the novel 'just popped into my head one day when I was daydreaming'. She decided that she had to stop everything and write it down. 'I just knew that I had something special, and as I wrote I passed on the pages to my mum. She read them, and laughed and cried in all the right places, and she was so encouraging that I continued. Then one day we were watching Irish author Cathy Kelly on the television and my mum said that she played golf with Cathy's publicist.' The publicist gave Cecelia the name of an agent in Ireland and she sent off four chapters of her novel. 'Then she asked for another chapter, then another. After ten chapters she said she would represent me—I was shocked because I was just looking for advice really. She is a wonderful agent and she worked passionately hard for months and months to get me the right publishing deal. I was in a shop changing-room when she called me to say she had been successful. I don't remember getting dressed afterwards. When I got home I had to check that I hadn't accidentally walked off in stolen gear!'

Cecelia wrote *PS, I Love You* mainly at night. 'I would start writing at around ten and write until six or seven in the morning. I'm a night-time person—my mind comes alive at night.'

Holly Kennedy, the main character in *PS, I Love You*, is certainly not Cecelia Ahern in disguise—'in fact I went out of my way to make her very different from me'—but when writing about Holly, Cecelia took on many of her heroine's moods. 'If Holly was upset then I was upset, if she was drunk then I felt a little wobbly—and I don't even drink alcohol!'

PS, I Love You became one of the biggest-selling debut novels of the last decade and was selected for the 2004 Richard and Judy Summer Read campaign. It was also made into a major motion picture starring Hilary Swank, Lisa Kudrow, Kathy Bates, Gerard Butler and Harry Connick, Jr.

Despite the overnight success, the blonde and strikingly pretty Cecelia did not allow fame to go to her head. Then again, as the daughter of former Irish prime minister Bertie Ahern, and the sister-in-law of Nicky Byrne of the Irish band Westlife, she was well used to the spotlight, although she is at heart a very private person. Just recently Cecelia and her childhood sweetheart, Irish hurdler-turned-actor David Keoghan, surprised guests when they tied the knot at St Nicholas of Myra church in Kinsealy, north Dublin, having told everyone that the event was their daughter Robin's christening.

To date, Cecelia has written a further six best-selling novels and is now enjoying taking a year out to look after Robin. She admits, though, that she misses the excitement of writing, publishing and promoting her books and can't wait to get back to work in the New Year.

Also from Cecelia Ahern:

Fiction:
PS, I Love You, Where Rainbows End, If You Could See Me Now, A Place Called Here, Thanks for the Memories, The Gift, The Book of Tomorrow.

Short Stories:
The Every Year Collection, Short and Sweet, Moments, Ladies Night (Girls Night in 4) Irish Girls are Back in Town, The Things That I Remember, Girls Night In, Mrs Whippy, Mallard and May, Table for Two.

Television:
Samantha Who?

Movies:
PS, I Love You.

Theatre:
Mrs Whippy.